A Descent into Egypt and Others

ALGERNON BLACKWOOD

A Descent into Egypt and Others

Collected Short Fiction
Volume 4: 1913–1917

Edited by S. T. Joshi

Hippocampus Press

New York

Published by Hippocampus Press
P.O. Box 641, New York, NY 10156.
www.hippocampuspress.com

Hippocampus Press logo designed by Anastasia Damianakos.

First edition
1 3 5 7 9 8 6 4 2

ISBN 978-1-61498-432-0 six-volume set
ISBN 978-1-61498-468-9 volume 4
ISBN 978-1-61498-495-5 ebook

Contents

Introduction 7
Wayfarers 9
The Sacrifice 29
Her Birthday 52
Violence 55
Jimbo's Longest Day 62
Who Was She? 67
A Barmecide Feast 87
The Kiss of a Psychologist 92
H. S. H. 99
The Story Hour 112
The Tradition 117
Transition 122
A Desert Episode 128
What Nobody Understands 142
Maria 147
By Water 152
A Bit of Wood 159
The Night-Wind 163
The Falling Glass 172
Breakfast Honey 179
The Philosopher 185
The Daisy World 189
The Wings of Horus 203
The Regeneration of Lord Ernie 223
The Damned 286

A Descent into Egypt 362
Non-Human 428
An Egyptian Hornet 434
The God 440
The Soldier's Visitor 445
The Paper Man 450
The Other Wing 454
Cain's Atonement 472
The Celestial Motor-'bus 479
The Snake 483
Initiation 487
Proportion 510
Camping Out 516
The Tryst 523
The Touch of Pan 534
The Laughter of Courage 554
Appendix 557
    Egypt: An Impression 559
Bibliography 569

Introduction

Algernon Blackwood's tales of 1913–17 present a fascinating variety of setting, motif, and philosophical import. The core stories in the volume—"Wayfarers," "The Regeneration of Lord Ernie," "The Damned," "The Sacrifice," and "A Descent into Egypt"—were gathered in *Incredible Adventures* (1914), one of the cornerstone volumes in the entire history of weird fiction. In these stories, set in England, Switzerland, and Egypt, Blackwood's use of symbolism—whereby the weird phenomena are manipulated to convey the complexities of human character—is at its height. It takes a sympathetic mind and imagination to appreciate such stories. H. P. Lovecraft, when he first read the volume in 1920, reacted negatively; but in later years he reversed that judgment. "A weird story," he wrote in a 1935 letter to R. H. Barlow, "to be a serious aesthetic effort, must form primarily a *picture of a mood*—& such a picture certainly does not call for any clever jack-in-the-box fillip. There are weird stories which more or less conform to this description . . . especially in Blackwood's 'Incredible Adventures'."

These stories were written when Blackwood was living in Switzerland; but he was obliged to return to England upon the outbreak of World War I in August 1914. Several stories in this volume deal with the war; some were frankly written as war propaganda. But other themes come to the fore as well. "Wayfarers" once again exhibits the reincarnation theme, a dominant one in Blackwood's writing at this time, as seen in "A Desert Episode," "Cain's Atonement," and others. The power of Nature is underscored in such narratives as "Initiation" and "The Touch of Pan." Aside from "A Descent into Egypt" and "A Desert Episode," Egypt remains a powerful trigger for Blackwood's imagination in such stories as "By Water," "An Egyptian Hornet," and "The Wings of Horus." His essay "Egypt: An Impression" (1913) conveys his sentiments on the region in terms strikingly similar to that of "A Descent into Egypt."

Several tales were conceived as additions to or extracts from novels that Blackwood was writing at this time. "Jimbo's Longest Day," resurrecting the character from *Jimbo: A Fantasy* (1909), was apparently designed to be inserted into the fantasy *The Extra Day* (1915). "What Nobody Understands" was in fact incorporated into that novel, as were "The Night-Wind" and "The Daisy World." "Who Was She?" is an early version of Chapters 3, 4, and 5 of another fantasy, *The Promise of Air* (1918). Otherwise, the stories in this volume were mostly gathered in *Ten Minute Stories* (1914) and *Day and Night Stories* (1917); but an unusual number were uncollected.

Blackwood continued publishing in the *Westminster Gazette,* the *Morning Post,* and the *New Witness* (the successor to the *Eye-Witness*); he also began appearing in the *Quest,* a theosophical magazine edited by G. R. S. Mead, and *Country Life,* the well-known (and still running) journal of English rural life. His work also began appearing in American periodicals such as *Century Magazine.* "Camping Out" appeared in *Blackie's Children's Annual,* heralding Blackwood's extensive later work for such periodicals for juvenile readers.

—S. T. JOSHI

Wayfarers

I

I missed the train at Evain, and, after infinite trouble, discovered a motor that would take me, ice-axe and all, to Geneva. By hurrying, the connection might be just possible. I telegraphed to Haddon to meet me at the station, and lay back comfortably, dreaming of the precipices of Haute Savoie. We made good time; the roads were excellent, traffic of the slightest, when—crash! There was an instant's excruciating pain, the sun went out like a snuffed candle, and I fell into something as soft as a bed of flowers and as yielding to my weight as warm water. . . .

It was *very* warm. There was a perfume of flowers. My eyes opened, focussed vividly upon a detailed picture for a moment, then closed again. There was no context—at least, none that I could recall—for the scene, though familiar as home, brought nothing that I definitely remembered. Broken away from any sequence, unattached to any past, unaware even of my own identity, I simply saw this picture as a camera snaps it off from the world, a scene apart, with meaning only for those who knew the context:

The warm, soft thing I lay in was a bed—big, deep, comfortable; and the perfume came from flowers that stood beside it on a little table. It was in a stately, ancient chamber, with lofty ceiling and immense open fireplace of stone; old-fashioned pictures—familiar portraits and engravings I knew intimately—hung upon the walls; the floor was bare, with dignified, carved furniture of oak and mahogany, huge chairs and massive cupboards. And there were latticed windows set within deep embrasures of grey stone, where clambering roses patterned the sunshine that cast their moving shadows on the polished boards. With the perfume of the flowers there mingled, too, that delicate, elusive odour of age—of wood, of musty tapestries in spacious halls and corridors, and of chambers long unopened to the sun and air.

By the door that stood ajar far away at the end of the room—very far away it seemed—an old lady, wearing a little cap of silk embroidery, was whispering to a man of stern, uncompromising figure, who, as he listened, bent down to her with a grave and even solemn face. A wide stone corridor was just visible through the crack of the open door behind her.

The picture flashed, and vanished. The numerous details I took in because they were well known to me already. That I could not supply the context was merely a trick of the mind, the kind of trick that dreams play. Darkness swamped vision again. I sank back into the warm, soft, comfortable bed of delicious oblivion. There was not the slightest desire to know; sleep and soft forgetfulness were all I craved.

But a little later—or was it a very great deal later?—when I opened my eyes again, there was a thin trail of memory. I remembered my name and age. I remembered vaguely, as though from some unpleasant dream, that I was on the way to meet a climbing friend in the Alps of Haute Savoie, and that there was need to hurry and be very active. Something had gone wrong, it seemed. There had been a stupid, violent disaster, pain in it somewhere, an accident. Where were my belongings? Where, for instance, was my precious ice-axe—tried old instrument on which my life and safety depended? A rush of jumbled questions poured across my mind. The effort to sort them hurt atrociously. . . .

A figure stood beside my bed. It was the same old lady I had seen a moment ago—or was it a month ago, even last year perhaps? And this time she was alone. Yet, though familiar to me as my own right hand, I could not for the life of me attract her name. Searching for it brought the pain again. Instead, I asked an easier question; it seemed the most important somehow, though a feeling of shame came with it, as though I knew I was talking nonsense:

"My ice-axe—is it safe? It should have stood any ordinary strain. It's ash. . . ." My voice failed absurdly, caught away by a whisper halfway down my throat. What *was* I talking about? There was vile confusion somewhere.

She smiled tenderly, sweetly, as she placed her small, cool hand upon my forehead. Her touch calmed me as it always did, and the pain retreated a little.

"All your things are safe," she answered, in a voice so soft beneath the distant ceiling it was like a bird's note singing in the sky. "And *you* are also safe. There is no danger now. The bullet has been taken out and all is going well. Only you must be patient, and lie very still, and rest." And then she added the morsel of delicious comfort she knew quite well I waited for: "Marion is near you all day long, and most of the night besides. She rarely leaves you. She is in and out all day."

I stared, thirsting for more. Memory put certain pieces in their place again. I heard them click together as they joined. But they only tried to join. There were several pieces missing. They must have been lost in the disaster. The pattern was too ridiculous.

"I ought to tel—telegraph—" I began, seizing at a fragment that poked its end up, then plunged out of sight again before I could read more of it. The pieces fell apart; they would not hold together without these missing fragments. Anger flamed up in me.

"They're badly made," I said, with a petulance I was secretly ashamed of; "you have chosen the wrong pieces! I'm not a child—to be treated—" A shock of heat tore through me, led by a point of iron, with blasting pain.

"Sleep, my poor dear Félix, sleep," she murmured soothingly, while her tiny hand stroked my forehead, just in time to prevent that pointed, hot thing entering my heart. "Sleep again now, and a little later you shall tell me their names, and I will send on horseback quickly—"

"Telegraph—" I tried to say, but the word went lost before I could pronounce it. It was a nonsense word, caught up from dreams. Thought fluttered and went out.

"I will send," she whispered, "in the quickest possible way. You shall explain to Marion. Sleep first a little longer; promise me to lie quite still and sleep. When you wake again, she will come to you at once."

She sat down gently on the edge of the enormous bed, so that I saw her outline against the window where the roses clambered to come in. She bent over me—or was it a rose that bent in the wind across the stone embrasure? I saw her clear blue eyes—or was it two raindrops upon a withered roseleaf that mirrored the summer sky?

"Thank you," my voice murmured with intense relief, as everything sank away and the old-world garden seemed to enter by the latticed windows. For there was a power in her way that made obedience sweet, and her little hand, besides, cushioned the attack of that cruel iron point so that I hardly felt its entrance. Before the fierce heat could reach me, darkness again put out the world. . . .

Then, after a prodigious interval, my eyes once more opened to the stately, old-world chamber that I knew so well; and this time I found myself alone. In my brain was a stinging, splitting sensation, as though Memory shook her pieces together with angry violence, pieces, moreover, made of clashing metal. A degrading nausea almost vanquished me. Against my feet was a heated metal body, too heavy for me to move, and bandages were tight round my neck and the back of my head. Dimly, it came back to me that hands had been about me hours ago, soft, ministering hands that I loved. Their perfume lingered still. Faces and names fled in swift procession past me, yet without my making any attempt to bid them stay. I asked myself no questions. Effort of any sort was utterly beyond me. I lay and watched and waited, helpless and strangely weak.

One or two things alone were clear. They came, too, without the effort to think them:

There had been a disaster; they had carried me into the nearest house; and—the mountain heights, so keenly longed for, were suddenly denied me. I was being cared for by kind people somewhere far from the world's high routes. They were familiar people, yet for the moment I had lost the name. But it was the bitterness of losing my holiday climbing that chiefly savaged me, so that strong desire returned upon itself unfulfilled. And, knowing the danger of frustrated yearnings, and the curious states of mind they may engender, my trembling brain registered a decision automatically:

"Keep careful watch upon yourself," it whispered.

For I saw the peaks that towered above the world, and felt the wind rise from the hidden valleys. The perfume of lonely ridges came to me, and I saw the snow against the blue-black sky. Yet I could not reach them. I lay, instead, broken and useless upon my back, in a soft, deep, comfortable bed. And I loathed the thought. A dull and evil fury rose within me. Where was Haddon? He would get me out of it if any one could. And where was my dear, old trusted ice-axe? Above all, who were these gentle, old-world people who cared for me? . . . And, with this last thought, came some fairy touch of sweetness so delicious that I was conscious of sudden resignation—more, even of delight and joy.

This joy and anger ran races for possession of my mind, and I knew not which to follow: both seemed real, and both seemed true. The cruel confusion was an added torture. Two sets of places and people seemed to mingle.

"Keep a careful watch upon yourself," repeated the automatic caution.

Then, with returning, blissful darkness, came another thing—a tiny point of wonder, where light entered in. I thought of a woman. . . . It was a vehement, commanding thought; and though at first it was very close and real—as much of To-day as Haddon and my precious ice-axe—the next second it was leagues away in another world somewhere. Yet, before the confusion twisted it all askew, I knew her; I remembered clearly even where she lived; that I knew her husband, too—had stayed with them in—in Scotland—yes, in Scotland. Yet no word in this life had ever crossed my lips, for she was not free to come. Neither of us, with eyes or lips or gesture, had ever betrayed a hint to the other of our deeply hidden secret. And, although for me she was *the* woman, my great yearning—long, long ago it was, in early youth—had been sternly put aside and buried with all the vigour nature gave me. Her husband was my friend as well.

Only, now, the shock had somehow strained the prison bars, and the yearning escaped for a moment full-edged, and vehement with passion long denied. The inhibition was destroyed. The knowledge swept deliciously upon me that we had the right to be together, because we always *were* together. I had the right to ask for her.

My mind was certainly a mere field of confused, ungoverned images. No thinking was possible, for it hurt too vilely. But this one memory stood out with violence. I distinctly remember that I called to her to come, and that she had the right to come because my need was so peremptory. To the one most loved of all this life had brought me, yet to whom I had never spoken because she was in another's keeping, I called for help, and called, I verily believe, aloud:

"Please come!" Then, close upon its heels, the automatic warning again: "Keep close watch upon yourself . . . !"

It was as though one great yearning had loosed the other that was even greater, and had set it free.

Disappearing consciousness then followed the cry for an incalculable distance. Down into subterraneans within myself that were positively frightening it plunged away. But the cry was real; the yearning appeal held authority in it as of command. Love gave the right, supplied the power as well. For it seemed to me a tiny answer came, but from so far away that it was scarcely audible. And names were nowhere in it, either in answer or appeal.

"I am always here. I have never, never left you!"

The unconsciousness that followed was not complete, apparently. There was a memory of effort in it, of struggle, and, as it were, of searching. Some one was trying to get at me. I tossed in a troubled sea upon a piece of wreckage that another swimmer also fought to reach. Huge waves of transparent green now brought this figure nearer, now concealed it, but it came steadily on, holding out a rope. My exhaustion was too great for me to respond, yet this swimmer swept up nearer, brought by enormous rollers that threatened to engulf us both. The rope was for my safety, too. I saw hands outstretched. In the deep water I saw the outline of the body, and once I even saw the face. But for a second, merely. The wave that bore it crashed with a horrible roar that smothered us both and swept me from my piece of wreckage. In the violent flood of water the rope whipped against my feeble hands. I grasped it. A sense of divine security at once came over me—an intolerable sweetness of utter bliss and comfort, then blackness and suffocation as of the grave. The white-hot point of iron struck me. It beat audibly against my heart. I heard the knocking. The pain brought me up to the surface, and the knocking of my dreams was in reality a knocking on the door. Some one was gently tapping.

Such was the confusion of images in my pain-wracked mind, that I expected to see the old lady enter, bringing ropes and ice-axes, and followed by Haddon, my mountaineering friend; for I thought that I had fallen down a deep crevasse and had waited hours for help in the cold, blue darkness of the ice. I was too weak to answer, and the knocking for that matter was not repeated. I did not even hear the opening of the door, so softly did she move into the room. I only knew that before I actually saw her, this wave of intolerable sweetness drenched me once again with bliss and peace and comfort, my pain retreated, and I closed my eyes, knowing I should feel that cool and soothing hand upon my forehead.

The same minute I did feel it. There was a perfume of old gardens in the air. I opened my eyes to look the gratitude I could not utter, and saw, close against me—not the old lady, but the young and lovely face my worship had long made familiar. With lips that smiled their yearning and eyes of brown that held tears of sympathy, she sat down beside me on the bed. The warmth and fragrance of her atmosphere enveloped me. I sank away into a garden where spring melts magically into summer. Her arms were round my neck. Her face dropped down, so that I felt her hair upon my cheek and eyes. And then, whispering my name twice over, she kissed me on the lips.

"Marion," I murmured.

"Hush! Mother sends you this," she answered softly. "You are to take it all; she made it with her own hands. But *I* bring it to you. You must be quite obedient, please."

She tried to rise, but I held her against my breast.

"Kiss me again and I'll promise obedience always," I strove to say. But my voice refused so long a sentence, and anyhow her lips were on my own before I could have finished it. Slowly, very carefully, she disentangled herself, and my arms sank back upon the coverlet. I sighed in happiness. A moment longer she stood beside my bed, gazing down with love and deep anxiety into my face.

"And when all is eaten, all, mind, *all*," she smiled, "you are to sleep until the doctor comes this afternoon. You are much better. Soon you shall get up. Only, remember," shaking her finger with a sweet pretence of looking stern, "I shall exact complete obedience. You must yield your will utterly to mine. You are in my heart, and my heart must be kept very warm and happy."

Her eyes were tender as her mother's, and I loved the authority and strength that were so real in her. I remembered how it was this strength that had sealed the contract her beauty first drew up for me to sign. She bent down once more to arrange my pillows.

"What happened to—to the motor?" I asked hesitatingly, for my thoughts *would* not regulate themselves. The mind presented such incongruous fragments.

"The—what?" she asked, evidently puzzled. The word seemed strange to her. "What is that?" she repeated, anxiety in her eyes.

I made an effort to tell her, but I could not. Explanation was suddenly impossible. The whole idea dived away out of sight. It utterly evaded me. I had again invented a word that was without meaning. I was talking nonsense. In its place my dream came up. I tried to tell her how I had dreamed of climbing dangerous heights with a stranger, and had spoken another language with him than my own—English, was it?—at any rate, not my native French.

"Darling," she whispered close into my ear, "the bad dreams will not come back. You are safe here, quite safe." She put her little hand like a flower on my forehead and drew it softly down the cheek. "Your wound is already healing. They took the bullet out four days ago. I have got it," she added with a touch of shy embarrassment, and kissed me tenderly upon my eyes.

"How long have you been away from me?" I asked, feeling exhaustion coming back.

"Never once for more than ten minutes," was the reply. "I watched with you all night. Only this morning, while mother took my place, I slept a little. But, hush!" she said, with dear authority again; "you are not to talk so much. You must eat what I have brought, then sleep again. You must rest and sleep. Good-bye, good-bye, my love. I shall come back in an hour, and I shall always be within reach of your dear voice."

Her tall, slim figure, dressed in the grey I loved, crossed silently to the door. She gave me one more look—there was all the tenderness of passionate love in it—and then was gone.

I followed instructions meekly, and when a delicious sleep stole over me soon afterwards, I had forgotten utterly the ugly dream that I was climbing dangerous heights with another man, forgotten as well everything else, except that it seemed so many days since my love had come to me, and that my bullet wound would after all be healed in time for our wedding on the day so long, so eagerly waited for.

And when, several hours later, her mother came in with the doctor—his face less grave and solemn this time—the news that I might get up next day and lie a little in the garden, did more to heal me than a thousand bandages or twice that quantity of medical instructions.

I watched them as they stood a moment by the open door. They went out very slowly together, speaking in whispers. But the only thing I caught was the mother's voice, talking brokenly of the great wars. Napoleon, the doctor was saying in a low, hushed tone, was in full retreat from Moscow, though the news had only just come through. They passed into the corridor then, and there was a sound of weeping as the old lady murmured something about her son and the cruelty of heaven. "Both will be taken from me," she was sobbing softly, while he stooped to comfort her; "one in marriage, and the other in death." They closed the door then, and I heard no more.

II

Convalescence seemed to follow very quickly then, for I was utterly obedient as I had promised, and never spoke of what could excite me to my own detriment—the wars and my own unfortunate part in them. We talked instead of our love, our already too-long engagement, and of the sweet dream of happiness that life held waiting for us in the future. And, indeed, I was sufficiently weary of the world to prefer repose to much activity, for my body was almost incessantly in pain, and this old garden where we lay between high walls of stone, aloof from the busy world and very peaceful, was far more to my taste just then than wars and fighting.

The orchards were in blossom, and the winds of spring showered their rain of petals upon the long, new grass. We lay, half in sunshine, half in shade, beneath the poplars that lined the avenue towards the lake, and behind us rose the ancient grey-stone towers where the jackdaws nested in the ivy and the pigeons cooed and fluttered from the woods beyond.

There was loveliness everywhere, but there was sadness too, for though we both knew that the wars had taken her brother whence there is no return, and that only her aged, failing mother's life stood between ourselves and the stately property, there hid a sadness yet deeper than either of these thoughts in both our hearts. And it was, I think, the sadness that comes with spring. For spring, with her lavish, short-lived promises of eternal beauty, is ever a symbol of passing human happiness, incomplete and always unfulfilled. Promises made on earth are playthings, after all, for children. Even while we make them so solemnly, we seem to know they are not meant to hold. They are made, as spring is made, with a glory of soft, radiant blossoms that pass away before there is time to realise them. And yet they come again with the return of spring, as unashamed and glorious as if Time had utterly forgotten.

And this sadness was in her too. I mean it was part of her and she was part of it. Not that our love could change to pass or die, but that its sweet, so long-desired accomplishment must hold sway, and, like the spring, must melt and vanish before it had been fully known. I did not speak of it. I well understood that the depression of a broken body can influence the spirit with its poisonous melancholy, but it must have betrayed itself in my words and gestures, even in my manner too. At any rate, she was aware of it. I think, if truth be told, she felt it too. It seemed so painfully inevitable.

My recovery, meanwhile, was rapid, and from spending an hour or two in the garden, I soon came to spend the entire day. For the spring came on with a rush, and the warmth increased deliciously. While the cuckoos called to one another in the great beech-woods behind the château, we sat and talked and sometimes had our simple meals or coffee there together, and I particularly recall the occasion when solid food was first permitted me and she gave me a delicate young *bondelle,* fresh caught that very morning in the lake. There were leaves of sweet, crisp lettuce with it, and she picked the bones out for me with her own white hands.

The day was radiant, with a sky of cloudless blue, soft airs stirred the poplar crests; the little waves fell on the pebbly beach not fifty metres away, and the orchard floor was carpeted with flowers that seemed to have caught from heaven's stars the patterns of their yellow blossoms. The bees droned peacefully among the fruit trees; the air was full of musical deep hummings. My former vigour stirred delightfully in my blood, and I knew no pain, beyond occasional dull twinges in the head that came with a rush of temporary darkness over my mind. The scar was healed, however, and the hair had grown over it again. This temporary darkness alarmed her more than it alarmed me. There were grave complications, apparently, that I did not know of.

But the deep-lying sadness in me seemed independent of the glorious weather, due to causes so intangible, so far off, that I never could dispel them by arguing them away. For I could not discover what they actually were. There was a vague, distressing sense of restlessness that I ought to have been elsewhere and otherwise, that we were together for a few days only, and that these few days I had snatched unlawfully from stern, imperative duties. These duties were immediate, but neglected. In a sense, I had no right to this spring-tide of bliss her presence brought me. I was playing truant somehow, somewhere. It was *not* my absence from the regiment; that I know. It was infinitely deeper, set to some enormous scale that vaguely frightened me, while it deepened the sweetness of the stolen joy.

Like a child, I sought to pin the sunny hours against the sky and make them stay. They passed with such a mocking swiftness, snatched momentarily from some big oblivion. The twilights swallowed our days together before they had been properly tasted, and on looking back, each afternoon of happiness seemed to have been a mere moment in a flying dream. And I must have somehow betrayed the aching mood, for Marion turned of a sudden and gazed into my face with yearning and anxiety in the sweet brown eyes.

"What is it, dearest?" I asked, "and why do your eyes bring questions?"

"You sighed," she, answered, smiling a little sadly; "and sighed so deeply. You are in pain again. The darkness, perhaps, is over you?" And her hand stole out to meet my own. "You are in pain?"

"Not physical pain," I said, "and not *the* darkness either. I see *you* clearly," and would have told her more, as I carried her soft fingers to my lips, had I not divined from the expression in her eyes that she read my heart and knew all my strange, mysterious forebodings in herself.

"I know," she whispered before I could find speech, "for I feel it too. It is the shadow of separation that oppresses you—yet of no common, measurable separation you can understand. Is it not that?"

Leaning over then, I took her close into my arms, since words in that moment were mere foolishness. I held her so that she could not get away; but even while I did so it was like trying to hold the spring, or fasten the flying hour with a fierce desire. All slipped from me, and my arms caught at the sunshine and the wind.

"We have both felt it all these weeks," she said bravely, as soon as I had released her, "and we both have struggled to conceal it. But now"—she hesitated for a second, and with so exquisite a tenderness that I would have caught her to me again but for my anxiety to hear her further words—"now that you are well, we may speak plainly to each other, and so lessen our pain by sharing it." And then she added, still more softly: "You feel there is 'something' that shall take you from me—yet what it is you cannot discover nor divine. Tell me, Félix—all your thought, that I in turn may tell you mine."

Her voice floated about me in the sunny air. I stared at her, striving to focus the dear face more clearly for my sight. A shower of apple blossoms fell about us, and her words seemed floating past me like those passing petals of white. They drifted away. I followed them with difficulty and confusion. With the wind, I fancied, a veil of indefinable change slipped across her face and eyes.

"Yet nothing that could alter feeling," I answered; for she had expressed my own thought completely. "Nor anything that either of us can control. Only—perhaps, that everything must fade and pass away, just as this glory of the spring must fade and pass away—"

"Yet leaving its sweetness in us," she caught me up passionately, "and to come again, my beloved, to come again in every subsequent life, each time with an added sweetness in it too!" Her little face showed suddenly the courage of a lion in its eyes. Her heart was ever braver than my own, a vigorous, fighting soul. She spoke of lives, I prattled of days and hours merely.

A touch of shame stole over me. But that delicate, swift change in her spread too. With a thrill of ominous warning I noticed how it rose and grew about her. From within, outwards, it seemed to pass—like a shadow of great blue distance. Shadow was somewhere in it, so that she dimmed a little before my very eyes. The dreadful yearning searched and shook me, for I could not understand it, try as I would. She seemed going from me—drifting like her words and like the apple blossoms.

"But when we shall no longer be here to know it," I made answer quickly, yet as calmly as I could, "and when we shall have passed to some other place—to other conditions—where we shall not recognise the joy and wonder. When barriers of mist shall have rolled between us—our love and passion so made-over that we shall not know each other"—the words rushed out feverishly, half beyond control—"and perhaps shall not even dare to speak to each other of our deep desire—"

I broke off abruptly, conscious that I was speaking out of some unfamiliar place where I floundered, helpless among strange conditions. I was saying things I hardly understood myself. Her bigger, deeper mood spoke through me, perhaps.

Her darling face came back again; she moved close within reach once more.

"Hush, hush!" she whispered, terror and love both battling in her eyes. "It is the truth, perhaps, but you must not say such things. To speak them brings them closer. A chain is about our hearts, a chain of fashioning lives without number, but do not seek to draw upon it with anxiety or fear. To do so can only cause the pain of wrong entanglement, and interrupt the natural running of the iron links." And she placed her hand swiftly upon my mouth, as though divining that the bleak attack of anguish was again upon me with its throbbing rush of darkness.

But for once I was disobedient and resisted. The physical pain, I realised vividly, was linked closely with this spiritual torture. One caused the other somehow. The disordered brain received, though brokenly, some hints of darker and unusual knowledge. It had stammered forth in me, but through her it flowed easily and clear. I saw the change move more swiftly then across her face. Some ancient look passed into both her eyes.

And it was inevitable; I must speak out, regardless of mere bodily well-being.

"We shall have to face them some day," I cried, although the effort hurt abominably, "then why not now?" And I drew her hand down and kissed it passionately over and over again. "We are not children, to hide our faces among shadows and pretend we are invisible. At least we have the Present—the Moment that is here and now. We stand side by side in the heart of this deep spring day. This sunshine and these flowers, this wind across the lake, this sky of blue and this singing of the birds—all, all are ours *now*. Let us use the moment that Time gives, and so strengthen the chain you speak of that shall bring us again together times without number. We shall then, perhaps, remember. Oh, my heart, think what that would mean—to remember!"

Exhaustion caught me, and I sank back among my cushions. But Marion rose up suddenly and stood beside me. And as she did so, another Sky dropped softly down upon us both, and I smelt again the incense of old, old gardens that brought long-forgotten perfumes, incredibly sweet, but with it an ache of far-off, passionate remembrance that was pain. This great ache of distance swept over me like a wave.

I know not what grand change then was wrought upon her beauty, so that I saw her defiant and erect, commanding Fate because she understood it. She towered over me, but it was her soul that towered. The rush of internal darkness in me blotted out all else. The familiar, present sky grew dim, the sunshine faded, the lake and flowers and poplars dipped away. Conditions a thousand times more vivid took their place. She stood out, clear and shining in the glory of an undressed soul, brave and confident with an eternal love that separation strengthened but could never, never change. The deep sadness, I abruptly realised, was very little removed from joy—because, somehow, it was the condition of joy. I could not explain it more than that.

And her voice, when she spoke, was firm with a note of steel in it; intense, yet devoid of the wasting anger that passion brings. She was determined beyond Death itself, upon a foundation sure and lasting as the stars. The heart in her was calm, because she *knew*. She was magnificent.

"We are together—always," she said, her voice rich with the knowledge of some unfathomable experience, "for separation is temporary merely, forging new links in the ancient chain of lives that binds our hearts eternally together." She looked like one who has conquered the adversity Time brings, by accepting it. "You speak of the Present as though our souls were already fitted now to bid it stay, needing no further fashioning. Looking only to the Future, you forget our ample Past that has made us what we are. Yet our Past is here and now, beside us at this very moment. Into the hollow cups of weeks and months, of years and centuries, Time pours its flood beneath our eyes. Time is our schoolroom. . . . Are you so soon afraid? Does not separation achieve that which companionship never could accomplish? And how shall we dare eternity together if we cannot be strong in separation first?"

I listened while a flood of memories broke up through film upon film and layer upon layer that had long covered them.

"This Present that we seem to hold between our hands," she went on in that earnest, distant voice, "*is* our moment of sweet remembrance that you speak of, of renewal, perhaps, too, of reconciliation—a fleeting instant when we may kiss again and say good-bye, but with strengthened hope and courage revived. But we may not stay together finally—we *cannot*—until long discipline and pain shall have perfected sympathy and schooled our love by searching, difficult tests, that it may last for ever."

I stretched my arms out dumbly to take her in. Her face shone down upon me, bathed in an older, fiercer sunlight. The change in her seemed in an instant then complete. Some big, soft wind blew both of us ten thousand miles away. The centuries gathered us back together.

"Look, rather, to the Past," she whispered grandly, "where first we knew the sweet opening of our love. Remember, if you can, how the pain and separation have made it so worth while to continue. And be braver thence."

She turned her eyes more fully upon my own, so that their light persuaded me utterly away with her. An immense new happiness broke over me. I listened, and with the stirrings of an ampler courage. It seemed I followed her down an interminable vista of remembrance till I was happy with her among the flowers and fields of our earliest pre-existence.

Her voice came to me with the singing of birds and the hum of summer insects.

"Have you so soon forgotten," she sighed, "when we knew together the perfume of the hanging Babylonian Gardens, or when the Hesperides were so soft to us in the dawn of the world? And do you not remember," with a little rise of passion in her voice, "the sweet plantations of Chaldea, and how we tasted the odour of many a drooping flower in the gardens of Alcinous and Adonis, when the bees of olden time picked out the honey for our eating? It is the fragrance of those first hours we knew together that still lies in our hearts to-day, sweetening our love to this apparent suddenness. Hence comes the full, deep happiness we gather so easily To-day. . . . The breast of every ancient forest is torn with storms and lightning . . . that's why it is so soft and full of little gardens. You have forgotten too easily the glades of Lebanon, where we whispered our earliest secrets while the big winds drove their chariots down those earlier skies . . ."

There rose an indescribable tempest of remembrance in my heart as I strove to bring the pictures into focus; but words failed me, and the hand I eagerly stretched out to touch her own, met only sunshine and the rain of apple blossoms.

"The myrrh and frankincense," she continued in a sighing voice that seemed to come with the wind from invisible caverns in the sky, "the grapes and pomegranates—have they all passed from you, with the train of apes and peacocks, the tigers and the ibis, and the hordes of dark-faced slaves? And this little sun that plays so lightly here upon our woods of beech and pine—does it bring back nothing of the old-time scorching when the olive slopes, the figs and ripening cornfields heard our vows and watched our love mature? . . . Our spread encampment in the Desert—do not these sands upon our little beach revive its lonely majesty for you, and have you forgotten the gleaming towers of Semiramis . . . or, in Sardis, those strange lilies that first tempted our souls to their divine disclosure . . . ?"

Conscious of a violent struggle between pain and joy, both too deep for me to understand, I rose to seize her in my arms. But the effort dimmed the flying pictures. The wind that bore her voice down the stupendous vista fled back into the caverns whence it came. And the pain caught me in a vice of agony so searching that I could not move a muscle. My tongue lay dry against my lips. I could not frame a word of any sentence. . . .

Her voice presently came back to me, but fainter, like a whisper from the stars. The light dimmed everywhere; I saw no more the vivid, shining scenery she had summoned. A mournful dusk instead crept down upon the world she had momentarily revived.

". . . we may not stay together," I heard her little whisper, "until long discipline shall have perfected sympathy, and schooled our love to last. For this love of ours *is* for ever, and the pain that tries it is the furnace that fashions precious stones. . . ."

Again I stretched my arms out. Her face shone a moment longer in that forgotten fiercer sunlight, then faded very swiftly. The change, like a veil, passed over it. From the place of prodigious distance where she had been, she swept down towards me with such dizzy speed. As she was To-day I saw her again, more and more.

"Pain and separation, then, are welcome," I tried to stammer, "and we will desire them"—but my thought got no further into expression than the first two words. Aching blotted out coherent utterance.

She bent down very close against my face. Her fragrance was about my lips. But her voice ran off like a faint thrill of music, far, far away. I caught the final words, dying away as wind dies in high branches of a wood. And they reached me this time through the droning of bees and of waves that murmured close at hand upon the shore.

". . . for our love is of the soul, and our souls are moulded in Eternity. It is not yet, it is not now, our perfect consummation. Nor shall our next time of meeting know it. We shall not even speak. . . . For I shall not be free . . ." was what I heard. She paused.

"You mean we shall not know each other?" I cried, in an anguish of spirit that mastered the lesser physical pain.

I barely caught her answer:

"My discipline then will be in another's keeping—yet only that I may come back to you . . . more perfect . . . in the end. . . ."

The bees and waves then cushioned her whisper with their humming. The trail of a deeper silence led them far away. The rush of temporary darkness passed and lifted. I opened my eyes. My love sat close beside me in the shadow of the poplars. One hand held both my own, while with the other she arranged my pillows and stroked my aching head. The world dropped back into a tiny scale once more.

"You have had the pain again," Marion murmured anxiously, "but it is better now. It is passing." She kissed my cheek. "You must come in. . . ."

But I would not let her go. I held her to me with all the strength that was in me. "I had it, but it's gone again. An awful darkness came with it," I whispered in the little ear that was so close against my mouth. "I've been dreaming," I told her, as memory dipped away, "dreaming of you and me—together somewhere—in old gardens, or forests—where the sun was—"

But she would not let me finish. I think, in any case, I could not have said more, for thought evaded me, and any language of coherent description was in the same instant beyond my power. Exhaustion came upon me, that vile, compelling nausea with it.

"The sun here is too strong for you, dear love," I heard her saying, "and you must rest more. We have been doing too much these last few days. You must have more repose." She rose to help me move indoors.

"I have been unconscious, then?" I asked, in the feeble whisper that was all I could manage.

"For a little while. You slept, while I watched over you."

"But I was away from you! Oh, how could you let me sleep, when our time together is so short?"

She soothed me instantly in the way she knew we both loved so. I clung to her until she released herself again.

"Not away from me," she smiled, "for I was with you in your dreaming."

"Of course, of course you were"; but already I knew not exactly why I said it, nor caught the deep meaning that struggled up into my words from such unfathomable distance.

"Come," she added, with her sweet authority again, "we must go in now. Give me your arm, and I will send out for the cushions. Lean on me. I am going to put you back to bed."

"But I shall sleep again," I said petulantly, "and we shall be separated."

"We shall dream together," she replied, as she helped me slowly and painfully towards the old grey walls of the château.

III

Half an hour later I slept deeply, peacefully, upon my bed in the big stately chamber where the roses watched beside the latticed windows.

And to say I dreamed again is not correct, for it can only be expressed by saying that I saw and knew. The figures round the bed were actual, and in life. Nothing could be more real than the whisper of the doctor's voice—that solemn, grave-faced man who was so tall—as he said, sternly yet brokenly, to some one: "You must say good-bye; and you had better say it *now*." Nor could anything be more definite and sure, more charged with the actuality of living, than the figure of Marion, as she stooped over me to obey the terrible command. For I saw her face float down towards me like a star, and a shower of pale spring blossoms rained upon me with her hair. The perfume of old, old gardens rose about me as she slipped to her knees beside the bed and kissed my lips—so softly it was like the breath of wind from lake and orchard, and so lingeringly it was as though the blossoms lay upon my mouth and grew into flowers that she planted there.

"Good-bye, my love; be brave. It is only separation."

"It is death," I tried to say, but could only feebly stir my lips against her own.

I drew her breath of flowers into my mouth . . . and there came then the darkness which is final.

The voices grew louder. I heard a man struggling with an unfamiliar language. Turning restlessly, I opened my eyes—upon a little, stuffy room, with white walls whereon no pictures hung. It was very hot. A woman was standing beside the bed, and the bed was very short. I stretched, and my feet kicked against the boarding at the end.

"Yes, he *is* awake," the woman said in French. "Will you come in? The doctor said you might see him when he woke. I think he'll know you." She spoke in French. I just knew enough to understand.

And of course I knew him. It was Haddon. I heard him thanking her for all her kindness, as he blundered in. His French, if anything, was worse than my own. I felt inclined to laugh. I did laugh.

"By Jove! old man, this is bad luck, isn't it? You've had a narrow shave. This good lady telegraphed—"

"Have you got my ice-axe? Is it all right?" I asked. I remembered clearly the motor accident, everything.

"The ice-axe is right enough," he laughed, looking cheerfully at the woman, "but what about yourself? Feel bad still? Any pain, I mean?"

"Oh, I feel all right," I answered, searching for the pain of broken bones, but finding none. "What happened? I was stunned, I suppose?"

"Bit stunned, yes," said Haddon. "You got a nasty knock on the head, it seems. The point of the axe ran into you, or something."

"Was that all?"

He nodded. "But I'm afraid it's knocked our climbing on the head. Shocking bad luck, isn't it?"

"I telegraphed last night," the kind woman was explaining.

"But I couldn't get here till this morning," Haddon said. "The telegram didn't find me till midnight, you see." And he turned to thank the woman in his voluble, dreadful French. She kept a little pension on the shores of the lake. It was the nearest house, and they had carried me in there and got the doctor to me all within the hour. It proved slight enough, apart from the shock. It was not even concussion. I had merely been stunned. Sleep had cured me, as it seemed.

"Jolly little place," said Haddon, as he moved me that afternoon to Geneva, whence, after a few days' rest, we went on into the Alps of Haute Savoie, "and lucky the old body was so kind and quick. Odd, wasn't it?" He glanced at me.

Something in his voice betrayed he hid another thought. I saw nothing "odd" in it at all, only very tiresome. "What's its name?" I asked, taking a shot at a venture.

He hesitated a second. Haddon, the climber, was not skilled in the delicacies of tact.

"Don't know its present name," he answered, looking away from me across the lake, "but it stands on the site of an old château—destroyed a hundred years ago—the Château de Bellerive."

And then I understood my old friend's absurd confusion. For Bellerive chanced also to be the name of a married woman I knew in Scotland—at least, it was her maiden name, and she was of French extraction.

The Sacrifice

I

Limasson was a religious man, though of what depth and quality were unknown, since no trial of ultimate severity had yet tested him. An adherent of no particular creed, he yet had his gods; and his self-discipline was probably more rigorous than his friends conjectured. He was so reserved. Few guessed, perhaps, the desires conquered, the passions regulated, the inner tendencies trained and schooled—not by denying their expression, but by transmuting them alchemically into nobler channels. He had in him the makings of an enthusiastic devotee, and might have become such but for two limitations that prevented. He loved his wealth, labouring to increase it to the neglect of other interests; and, secondly, instead of following up one steady line of search, he scattered himself upon many picturesque theories, like an actor who wants to play all parts rather than concentrate on one. And the more picturesque the part, the more he was attracted. Thus, though he did his duty unshrinkingly and with a touch of love, he accused himself sometimes of merely gratifying a sensuous taste in spiritual sensations. There was this unbalance in him that argued want of depth.

As for his gods—in the end he discovered their reality by first doubting, then denying their existence.

It was this denial and doubt that restored them to their thrones, converting his dilettante skirmishes into genuine, deep belief; and the proof came to him one summer in early June when he was making ready to leave town for his annual month among the mountains.

With Limasson mountains, in some inexplicable sense, were a passion almost, and climbing so deep a pleasure that the ordinary scrambler hardly understood it. Grave as a kind of worship it was to him; the preparations for an ascent, the ascent itself in particular, involved a concentration that seemed symbolical as of a ritual. He not only loved the heights, the massive grandeur, the splendour of vast proportions blocked in space, but loved them with a respect that held a touch of awe. The emotion mountains stirred in him, one might say, was of that profound, incalculable kind that held kinship with his religious feelings, half realised though these were. His gods had their invisible thrones somewhere among the grim, forbidding heights. He prepared himself for this annual mountaineering with the same earnestness that a holy man might approach a solemn festival of his church.

And the impetus of his mind was running with big momentum in this direction, when there fell upon him, almost on the eve of starting, a swift series of disasters that shook his being to its last foundations, and left him stunned among the ruins. To describe these is unnecessary. People said, "One thing after another like that! What appalling luck! Poor wretch!" then wondered, with the curiosity of children, how in the world he would take it. Due to no apparent fault of his own, these disasters were so sudden that life seemed in a moment shattered, and his interest in existence almost ceased. People shook their heads and thought of the emergency exit. But Limasson was too vital a man to dream of annihilation. Upon him it had a different effect—he turned and questioned what he called his gods. They did not answer or explain. For the first time in his life he doubted. A hair's breadth beyond lay definite denial.

The ruin in which he sat, however, was not material; no man of his age, possessed of courage and a working scheme of life, would permit disaster of a material order to overwhelm him. It was collapse of a mental, spiritual kind, an assault upon the roots of character and temperament. Moral duties laid suddenly upon him threatened to crush. His *personal* existence was assailed, and apparently must end. He must spend the remainder of his life caring for others who were nothing to him. No outlet showed, no way of escape, so diabolically complete was the combination of events that rushed his inner trenches. His faith was shaken. A man can but endure so much, and remain human. For him the saturation point seemed reached. He experienced the spiritual equivalent of that physical numbness which supervenes when pain has touched the limit of endurance. He laughed, grew callous, then mocked his silent gods.

It is said that upon this state of blank negation there follows sometimes a condition of lucidity which mirrors with crystal clearness the forces driving behind life at a given moment, a kind of clairvoyance that brings explanation and therefore peace. Limasson looked for this in vain. There was the doubt that questioned, there was the sneer that mocked the silence into which his questions fell; but there was neither answer nor explanation, and certainly not peace. There was no relief. In this tumult of revolt he did none of the things his friends suggested or expected. He merely followed the line of least resistance. He yielded to the impetus that was upon him when the catastrophe came. To their indignant amazement he went out to his mountains.

All marvelled that at such a time he could adopt so trivial a line of action, neglecting duties that seemed paramount; they disapproved. Yet in reality he was taking no definite action at all, but merely drifting with the momentum that had been acquired just before. He was bewildered with so much pain, confused with suffering, stunned with the crash that flung him helpless amid undeserved calamity. He turned to the mountains as a child to its mother, instinctively. Mountains had never failed to bring him consolation, comfort, peace. Their grandeur restored proportion whenever disorder threatened life. No calculation, properly speaking, was in his move at all; but a blind desire for a violent physical reaction such as climbing brings. And the instinct was more wholesome than he knew.

In the high upland valley among lonely peaks whither Limasson then went, he found in some measure the proportion he had lost. He studiously avoided thinking; he lived in his muscles recklessly. The region with its little Inn was familiar to him; peak after peak he attacked, sometimes with, but more often without a guide, until his reputation as a sane climber, a laurelled member of all the foreign Alpine Clubs, was seriously in danger. That he overdid it physically is beyond question, but that the mountains breathed into him some portion of their enormous calm and deep endurance is also true. His gods, meanwhile, he neglected utterly for the first time in his life. If he thought of them at all, it was as tinsel figures imagination had created, figures upon a stage that merely decorated life for those whom pretty pictures pleased. Only—he had left the theatre and their make-believe no longer hypnotised his mind. He realised their impotence and disowned them. This attitude, however, was subconscious; he lent to it no substance, either of thought or speech. He ignored rather than challenged their existence.

And it was somewhat in this frame of mind—thinking little, feeling even less—that he came out into the hotel vestibule after dinner one evening, and took mechanically the bundle of letters the porter handed to him. They had no possible interest for him; in a corner where the big steam-heater mitigated the chilliness of the hall, he idly sorted them. The score or so of other guests, chiefly expert climbing men, were trailing out in twos and threes from the dining-room; but he felt as little interest in them as in his letters: no conversation could alter facts, no written phrases change his circumstances. At random, then, he opened a business letter with a typewritten address—it would probably be impersonal, less of a mockery, therefore, than the others with their tiresome sham condolences. And, in a sense, it was impersonal; sympathy from a solicitor's office is mere formula, a few extra ticks upon the universal keyboard of a Remington. But as he read it, Limasson made a discovery that startled him into acute and bitter sensation. He had imagined the limit of bearable suffering and disaster already reached. Now, in a few dozen words, his error was proved convincingly. The fresh blow was dislocating.

This culminating news of additional catastrophe disclosed within him entirely new reaches of pain, of biting, resentful fury. Limasson experienced a momentary stopping of the heart as he took it in, a dizziness, a violent sensation of revolt whose impotence induced almost physical nausea. He felt like—death.

"Must I suffer all things?" flashed through his arrested intelligence in letters of fire.

There was a sullen rage in him, a dazed bewilderment, but no positive suffering as yet. His emotion was too sickening to include the smaller pains of disappointment; it was primitive, blind anger that he knew. He read the letter calmly, even to the neat paragraph of machine-made sympathy at the last, then placed it in his inner pocket. No outward sign of disturbance was upon him; his breath came slowly; he reached over to the table for a match, holding it at arm's length lest the sulphur fumes should sting his nostrils.

And in that moment he made his second discovery. The fact that further suffering was still possible included also the fact that some touch of resignation had been left in him, and therefore some vestige of belief as well. Now, as he felt the crackling sheet of stiff paper in his pocket, watched the sulphur die, and saw the wood ignite, this remnant faded utterly away. Like the blackened end of the match, it shrivelled and dropped off. It vanished. Savagely, yet with an external calmness that enabled him to light his pipe with untrembling hand, he addressed his futile deities. And once more in fiery letters there flashed across the darkness of his passionate thought:

"Even this you demand of me—this cruel, ultimate sacrifice?"

And he rejected them, bag and baggage; for they were a mockery and a lie. With contempt he repudiated them for ever. The stage of doubt had passed. He denied his gods. Yet, with a smile upon his lips; for what were they after all but the puppets his religious fancy had imagined? They never had existed. Was it, then, merely the picturesque, sensational aspect of his devotional temperament that had created them? That side of his nature, in any case, was dead now, killed by a single devastating blow. The gods went with it.

Surveying what remained of his life, it seemed to him like a city that an earthquake has reduced to ruins. The inhabitants think no worse thing could happen. Then comes the fire.

Two lines of thought, it seems, then developed parallel in him and simultaneously, for while underneath he stormed against this culminating blow, his upper mind dealt calmly with the project of a great expedition he would make at dawn. He had engaged no guide. As an experienced mountaineer, he knew the district well; his name was tolerably familiar, and in half an hour he could have settled all details, and retired to bed with instructions to be called at two. But, instead, he sat there waiting, unable to stir, a human volcano that any moment might break forth into violence. He smoked his pipe as quietly as though nothing had happened, while through the blazing depths of him ran ever this one self-repeating statement: "Even this you demand of me, this cruel, ultimate sacrifice! . . ." His self-control, dynamically estimated, just then must have been very great and, thus repressed, the store of potential energy accumulated enormously.

With thought concentrated largely upon this final blow, Limasson had not noticed the people who streamed out of the *salle à manger* and scattered themselves in groups about the hall. Some individual, now and again, approached his chair with the idea of conversation, then, seeing his absorption, turned away. Even when a climber whom he slightly knew reached across him with a word of apology for the matches, Limasson made no response, for he did not see him. He noticed nothing. In particular he did not notice two men who, from an opposite corner, had for some time been observing him. He now looked up—by chance?—and was vaguely aware that they were discussing him. He met their eyes across the hall, and started.

For at first he thought he knew them. Possibly he had seen them about in the hotel—they seemed familiar—yet he certainly had never spoken with them. Aware of his mistake, he turned his glance elsewhere, though still vividly conscious of their attention. One was a clergyman or a priest; his face wore an air of gravity touched by sadness, a sternness about the lips counteracted by a kindling beauty in the eyes that betrayed enthusiasm nobly regulated. There was a suggestion of stateliness in the man that made the impression very sharp. His clothing emphasised it. He wore a dark tweed suit that was strict in its simplicity. There was austerity in him somewhere.

His companion, perhaps by contrast, seemed inconsiderable in his conventional evening dress. A good deal younger than his friend, his hair, always a tell-tale detail, was a trifle long; the thin fingers that flourished a cigarette wore rings; the face, though picturesque, was flippant, and his entire attitude conveyed a certain insignificance. Gesture, that faultless language which challenges counterfeit, betrayed unbalance somewhere. The impression he produced, however, was shadowy compared to the sharpness of the other. "Theatrical" was the word in Limasson's mind, as he turned his glance elsewhere. But as he looked away he fidgeted. The interior darkness caused by the dreadful letter rose about him. It engulfed him. Dizziness came with it. . . .

Far away the blackness was fringed with light, and through this light, stepping with speed and carelessness as from gigantic distance, the two men, suddenly grown large, came at him. Limasson, in self-protection, turned to meet them. Conversation he did not desire. Somehow he had expected this attack.

Yet the instant they began to speak—it was the priest who opened fire—it was all so natural and easy that he almost welcomed the diversion.

A phrase by way of introduction—and he was speaking of the summits. Something in Limasson's mind turned over. The man was a serious climber, one of his own species. The sufferer felt a certain relief as he heard the invitation, and realised, though dully, the compliment involved.

"If you felt inclined to join us—if you would honour us with your company," the man was saying quietly, adding something then about "your great experience" and "invaluable advice and judgment."

Limasson looked up, trying hard to concentrate and understand.

"The Tour du Néant?" he repeated, mentioning the peak proposed. Rarely attempted, never conquered, and with an ominous record of disaster, it happened to be the very summit he had meant to attack himself next day.

"You have engaged guides?" He knew the question foolish.

"No guide will try it," the priest answered, smiling, while his companion added with a flourish, "but we—we need no guide—if *you* will come."

"You are unattached, I believe? You are alone?" the priest enquired, moving a little in front of his friend, as though to keep him in the background.

"Yes," replied Limasson. "I am quite alone."

He was listening attentively, but with only part of his mind. He realised the flattery of the invitation. Yet it was like flattery addressed to some one else. He felt himself so indifferent, so—dead. These men wanted his skilful body, his experienced mind; and it was his body and mind that talked with them, and finally agreed to go. Many a time expeditions had been planned in just this way, but to-night he felt there was a difference. Mind and body signed the agreement, but his soul, listening elsewhere and looking on, was silent. With his rejected gods it had left him, though hovering close still. It did not interfere; it did not warn; it even approved; it sang to him from great distance that this expedition cloaked another. He was bewildered by the clashing of his higher and his lower mind.

"At one in the morning, then, if that will suit you . . ." the older man concluded.

"I'll see to the provisions," exclaimed the younger enthusiastically, "and I shall take my telephoto for the summit. The porters can come as far as the Great Tower. We're over six thousand feet here already, you see, so . . ." and his voice died away in the distance as his companion led him off.

Limasson saw him go with relief. But for the other man he would have declined the invitation. At heart he was indifferent enough. What decided him really was the coincidence that the Tour du Néant was the very peak he had intended to attack himself *alone,* and the curious feeling that this expedition cloaked another somehow—almost that these men had a hidden motive. But he dismissed the idea—it was not worth thinking about. A moment later he followed them to bed. So careless was he of the affairs of the world, so dead to mundane interests, that he tore up his other letters and tossed them into a corner of the room—unread.

II

Once in his chilly bedroom he realised that his upper mind had permitted him to do a foolish thing; he had drifted like a schoolboy into an unwise situation. He had pledged himself to an expedition with two strangers, an expedition for which normally he would have chosen his companions with the utmost caution. Moreover, he was guide; they looked to him for safety, while yet it was they who had arranged and planned it. But who were these men with whom he proposed to run grave bodily risks? He knew them as little as they knew him. Whence came, he wondered, the curious idea that this climb was really planned by another who was no one of them?

The thought slipped idly across his mind; going out by one door, it came back, however, quickly by another. He did not think about it more than to note its passage through the disorder that passed with him just then for thinking. Indeed, there was nothing in the whole world for which he cared a single brass farthing. As he undressed for bed, he said to himself: "I shall be called at one . . . but why am I going with these two on this wild plan? . . . And who made the plan?" . . .

It seemed to have settled itself. It came about so naturally and easily, so quickly. He probed no deeper. He didn't care. And for the first time he omitted the little ritual, half prayer, half adoration, it had always been his custom to offer to his deities upon retiring to rest. He no longer recognised them.

How utterly broken his life was! How blank and terrible and lonely! He felt cold, and piled his overcoats upon the bed, as though his mental isolation involved a physical effect as well. Switching off the light by the door, he was in the act of crossing the floor in the darkness when a sound beneath the window caught his ear. Outside there were voices talking. The roar of falling water made them indistinct, yet he was sure they were voices, and that one of them he knew. He stopped still to listen. He heard his own name uttered—"John Limasson." They ceased. He stood a moment shivering on the boards, then crawled into bed beneath the heavy clothing. But in the act of settling down, they began again. He raised himself again hurriedly to listen. What little wind there was passed in that moment down the valley, carrying off the roar of falling water; and into the moment's space of silence dropped fragments of definite sentences:

"They are close, you say—close down upon the world?" It was the voice of the priest surely.

"For days they have been passing," was the answer—a rough, deep tone that might have been a peasant's, and a kind of fear in it, "for all my flocks are scattered."

"The signs are sure? You know them?"

"Tumult," was the answer in much lower tones. "There has been tumult in the mountains . . ."

There was a break then as though the voices sank too low to be heard. Two broken fragments came next end of a question—beginning of an answer.

". . . the opportunity of a life-time?"

". . . if he goes of his own free will, success is sure. For acceptance is . . ."

And the wind, returning, bore back the sound of the falling water, so that Limasson heard no more. . . .

An indefinable emotion stirred in him as he turned over to sleep. He stuffed his ears lest he should hear more. He was aware of a sinking of the heart that was inexplicable. What in the world were they talking about, these two? What was the meaning of these disjointed phrases? There lay behind them a grave significance almost solemn. That "tumult in the mountains" was somehow ominous, its suggestion terrible and mighty. He felt disturbed, uncomfortable, the first emotion that had stirred in him for days. The numbness melted before its faint awakening. Conscience was in it—he felt vague prickings—but it was deeper far than conscience. Somewhere out of sight, in a region life had as yet not plumbed, the words sank down and vibrated like pedal notes. They rumbled away into the night of undecipherable things. And, though explanation failed him, he felt they had reference somehow to the morrow's expedition: how, what, wherefore, he knew not; his name had been spoken—then these curious sentences; that was all. Yet to-morrow's expedition, what was it but an expedition of impersonal kind, not even planned by himself? Merely his own plan taken and altered by others—made over? His personal business, his personal life, were not really in it at all.

The thought startled him a moment. He had no personal life . . . !

Struggling with sleep, his brain played the endless game of disentanglement without winning a single point, while the under-mind in him looked on and smiled—because it *knew*. Then, suddenly, a great peace fell over him. Exhaustion brought it perhaps. He fell asleep; and next moment, it seemed, he was aware of a thundering at the door and an unwelcome growling voice, *"'s ist bald ein Uhr, Herr! Aufstehen!"*

Rising at such an hour, unless the heart be in it, is a sordid and depressing business; Limasson dressed without enthusiasm, conscious that thought and feeling were exactly where he had left them on going to sleep. The same confusion and bewilderment were in him; also the same deep solemn emotion stirred by the whispering voices. Only long habit enabled him to attend to detail, and ensured that nothing was forgotten. He felt heavy and oppressed, a kind of anxiety about him; the routine of preparation he followed gravely, utterly untouched by the customary joy; it was mechanical. Yet through it ran the old familiar sense of ritual, due to the practice of so many years, that cleansing of mind and body for a big Ascent—like initiatory rites that once had been as important to him as those of some priest who approached the worship of his deity in the temples of ancient time. He performed the ceremony with the same care as though no ghost of vanished faith still watched him, beckoning from the air as formerly. . . . His knapsack carefully packed, he took his ice-axe from beside the bed, turned out the light, and went down the creaking wooden stairs in stockinged feet, lest his heavy boots should waken the other sleepers. And in his head still rang the phrase he had fallen asleep on—as though just uttered:

"The signs are sure; for days they have been passing—close down upon the world. The flocks are scattered. There has been tumult—tumult in the mountains." The other fragments he had forgotten. But who were "they"? And why did the word bring a chill of awe into his blood?

And as the words rolled through him Limasson felt tumult in his thoughts and feelings too. There had been tumult in his life, and all his joys were scattered—joys that hitherto had fed his days. The signs were sure. Something was close down upon his little world—passing—sweeping. He felt a touch of terror.

Outside in the fresh darkness of very early morning the strangers stood waiting for him. Rather, they seemed to arrive in the same instant as himself, equally punctual. The clock in the church tower sounded one. They exchanged low greetings, remarked that the weather promised to hold good, and started off in single file over soaking meadows towards the first belt of forest. The porter—mere peasant, unfamiliar of face and not connected with the hotel—led the way with a hurricane lantern. The air was marvellously sweet and fragrant. In the sky overhead the stars shone in their thousands. Only the noise of falling water from the heights, and the regular thud of their heavy boots broke the stillness. And, black against the sky, towered the enormous pyramid of the Tour du Néant they meant to conquer.

Perhaps the most delightful portion of a big ascent is the beginning in the scented darkness while the thrill of possible conquest lies still far off. The hours stretch themselves queerly; last night's sunset might be days ago; sunrise and the brilliance coming seem in another week, part of dim futurity like children's holidays. It is difficult to realise that this biting cold before the dawn, and the blazing heat to come, both belong to the same to-day.

There were no sounds as they toiled slowly up the zigzag path through the first fifteen hundred feet of pinewoods; no one spoke; the clink of nails and ice-axe points against the stones was all they heard. For the roar of water was felt rather than heard; it beat against the ears and the skin of the whole body at once. The deeper notes were below them now in the sleeping valley; the shriller ones sounded far above, where streams just born out of ponderous snow-beds tinkled sharply. . . .

The change came delicately. The stars turned a shade less brilliant, a softness in them as of human eyes that say farewell. Between the highest branches the sky grew visible. A sighing air smoothed all their crests one way; moss, earth, and open spaces brought keen perfumes; and the little human procession, leaving the forest, stepped out into the vastness of the world above the tree-line. They paused while the porter stooped to put his lantern out. In the eastern sky was colour. The peaks and crags rushed closer.

Was it the Dawn? Limasson turned his eyes from the height of sky where the summits pierced a path for the coming day, to the faces of his companions, pale and wan in the early twilight. How small, how insignificant they seemed amid this hungry emptiness of desolation. The stupendous cliffs fled past them, led by headstrong peaks crowned with eternal snows. Thin lines of cloud, trailing half-way up precipice and ridge, seemed like the swish of movement—as though he caught the earth turning as she raced through space. The four of them, timid riders on the gigantic saddle, clung for their lives against her titan ribs, while currents of some majestic life swept up at them from every side. He drew deep draughts of the rarefied air into his lungs. It was very cold. Avoiding the pallid, insignificant faces of his companions, he pretended interest in the porter's operations; he stared fixedly on the ground. It seemed twenty minutes before the flame was extinguished, and the lantern fastened to the pack behind. This Dawn was unlike any he had seen before.

For, in reality, all the while, Limasson was trying to bring order out of the extraordinary thoughts and feelings that had possessed him during the slow forest ascent, and the task was not crowned with much success. The Plan, made by others, had taken charge of him, he felt; and he had thrown the reins of personal will and interest loosely upon its steady gait. He had abandoned himself carelessly to what might come. Knowing that he was leader of the expedition, he yet had suffered the porter to go first, taking his own place as it was appointed to him, behind the younger man, but before the priest. In this order, they had plodded, as only experienced climbers plod, for hours without a rest, until half-way up a change had taken place. He had wished it, and instantly it was effected. The priest moved past him, while his companion dropped to the rear—the companion who for ever stumbled in his speed, whereas the older man climbed surely, confidently. And thereafter Limasson walked more easily—as though the relative positions of the three were of importance somehow. The steep ascent of smothering darkness through the woods became less arduous. He was glad to have the younger man behind him.

For the impression had strengthened as they climbed in silence that this ascent pertained to some significant Ceremony, and the idea had grown insistently, almost stealthily, upon him. The movements of himself and his companions, especially the positions each occupied relatively to the other, established some kind of intimacy that resembled speech, suggesting even question and answer. And the entire performance, while occupying hours by his watch, it seemed to him more than once, had been in reality briefer than the flash of a passing thought, so that he saw it within himself—pictorially. He thought of a picture worked in colours upon a strip of elastic. Some one pulled the strip, and the picture stretched. Or some one released it again, and the picture flew back, reduced to a mere stationary speck. All happened in a single speck of time.

And the little change of position, apparently so trivial, gave point to this singular notion working in his under-mind—that this ascent was a ritual and a ceremony as in older days, its significance approaching revelation, however, for the first time—now. Without language, this stole over him; no words could quite describe it. For it came to him that these three formed a unit, himself being in some fashion yet the acknowledged principal, the leader. The labouring porter had no place in it, for this first toiling through the darkness was a preparation, and when the actual climb began, he would disappear, while Limasson himself went first. This idea that they took part together in a Ceremony established itself firmly in him, with the added wonder that, though so often done, he performed it now for the first time with full comprehension, knowledge, truth. Empty of personal desire, indifferent to an ascent that formerly would have thrilled his heart with ambition and delight, he understood that climbing had ever been a ritual for his soul and of his soul, and that power must result from its sincere accomplishment. It was a symbolical ascent.

In words this did not come to him. He felt it, never criticising. That is, he neither rejected nor accepted. It stole most sweetly, grandly, over him. It floated into him while he climbed, yet so convincingly that he had felt his relative position must be changed. The younger man held too prominent a post, or at least a wrong one—in advance. Then, after the change, effected mysteriously as though all recognised it, this line of certainty increased, and there came upon him the big, strange knowledge that all of life is a Ceremony on a giant scale, and that by performing the movements accurately, with sincere fidelity, there may come—knowledge. There was gravity in him from that moment.

This ran in his mind with certainty. Though his thought assumed no form of little phrases, his brain yet furnished detailed statements that clinched the marvellous thing with simile and incident which daily life might apprehend: that knowledge arises from action; that to do the thing invites the teaching and explains it. Action, moreover, is symbolical; a group of men, a family, an entire nation, engaged in those daily movements which are the working out of their destiny, perform a Ceremony which is in direct relation somewhere to the pattern of greater happenings which are the teachings of the Gods. Let the body imitate, reproduce—in a bedroom, in a wood—anywhere—the movements of the stars, and the meaning of those stars shall sink down into the heart. The movements constitute a script, a language. To mimic the gestures of a stranger is to understand his mood, his point of view—to establish a grave and solemn intimacy. Temples are everywhere, for the entire earth is a temple, and the body, House of Royalty, is the biggest temple of them all. To ascertain the pattern its movements trace in daily life, *could* be to determine the relation of that particular ceremony to the Cosmos, and so learn power. The entire system of Pythagoras, he realised, could be taught without a single word—by movements; and in everyday life even the commonest act and vulgarest movement are part of some big Ceremony—a message from the Gods. Ceremony, in a word, is three-dimensional language, and action, therefore, is the language of the Gods. The Gods he had denied were speaking to him . . . passing with tumult close across his broken life. . . . Their passage it was, indeed, that had caused the breaking!

In this cryptic, condensed fashion the great fact came over him—that he and these other two, here and now, took part in some great Ceremony of whose ultimate object as yet he was in ignorance. The impact with which it dropped upon his mind was tremendous. He realised it most fully when he stepped from the darkness of the forest and entered the expanse of glimmering, early light; up till this moment his mind was being prepared only, whereas now he knew. The innate desire to worship which all along had been his, the momentum his religious temperament had acquired during forty years, the yearning to have proof, in a word, that the Gods he once acknowledged were really true, swept back upon him with that violent reaction which denial had aroused.

He wavered where he stood. . . .

Looking about him, then, while the others rearranged burdens the returning porter now discarded, he perceived the astonishing beauty of the time and place, feeling it soak into him as by the very pores of his skin. From all sides this beauty rushed upon him. Some radiant, wingéd sense of wonder sped past him through the silent air. A thrill of ecstasy ran down every nerve. The hair of his head stood up. It was far from unfamiliar to him, this sight of the upper mountain world awakening from its sleep of the summer night, but never before had he stood shuddering thus at its exquisite cold glory, nor felt its significance as now, so mysteriously *within himself*. Some transcendent power that held sublimity was passing across this huge desolate plateau, far more majestic than the mere sunrise among mountains he had so often witnessed. There was Movement. He understood why he had seen his companions insignificant. Again he shivered and looked about him, touched by a solemnity that held deep awe.

Personal life, indeed, was wrecked, destroyed, but something greater was on the way. His fragile alliance with a spiritual world was strengthened. He realised his own past insolence. He became afraid.

III

The treeless plateau, littered with enormous boulders, stretched for miles to right and left, grey in the dusk of very early morning. Behind him dropped thick guardian pine-woods into the sleeping valley that still detained the darkness of the night. Here and there lay patches of deep snow, gleaming faintly through thin rising mist; singing streams of icy water spread everywhere among the stones, soaking the coarse rough grass that was the only sign of vegetation.

No life was visible; nothing stirred; nor anywhere was movement, but of the quiet trailing mist and of his own breath that drifted past his face like smoke. Yet through the splendid stillness there *was* movement; that sense of absolute movement which results in stillness—it was owing to the stillness that he became aware of it—so vast, indeed, that only immobility could express it. Thus, on the calmest day in summer, may the headlong rushing of the earth through space seem more real than when the tempest shakes the trees and water on its surface; or great machinery turn with such vertiginous velocity that it appears steady to the deceived function of the eye. For it was not through the eye that this solemn Movement made itself known, but rather through a massive sensation that owned his entire body as its organ. Within the league-long amphitheatre of enormous peaks and precipices that enclosed the plateau, piling themselves upon the horizon, Limasson felt the outline of a Ceremony extended. The pulses of its grandeur poured into him where he stood. Its vast design was knowable because they themselves had traced—were even then tracing—its earthly counterpart in little. And the awe in him increased.

"This light is false. We have an hour yet before the true dawn," he heard the younger man say lightly. "The summits still are ghostly. Let us enjoy the sensation, and see what we can make of it."

And Limasson, looking up startled from his reverie, saw that the far-away heights and towers indeed were heavy with shadow, faint still with the light of stars. It seemed to him they bowed their awful heads and that their stupendous shoulders lowered. They drew together, shutting out the world.

"True," said his companion, "and the upper snows still wear the spectral shine of night. But let us now move faster, for we travel very light. The sensations you propose will but delay and weaken us."

He handed a share of the burdens to his companion and to Limasson. Slowly they all moved forward, and the mountains shut them in.

And two things Limasson noted then, as he shouldered his heavier pack and led the way: first, that he suddenly knew their destination though its purpose still lay hidden; and, secondly, that the porter's leaving before the ascent proper began signified finally that ordinary climbing was not their real objective. Also—the dawn was a lifting of inner veils from off his mind, rather than a brightening of the visible earth due to the nearing sun. Thick darkness, indeed, draped this enormous, lonely amphitheatre where they moved.

"You lead us well," said the priest, a few feet behind him, as he picked his way unfalteringly among the boulders and the streams.

"Strange that I do so," replied Limasson, in a low tone, "for the way is new to me, and the darkness grows instead of lessening." The language seemed hardly of his choosing. He spoke and walked as in a dream.

Far in the rear the voice of the younger man called plaintively after them:

"You go so fast, I can't keep up with you," and again he stumbled and dropped his ice-axe among the rocks. He seemed for ever stooping to drink the icy water, or clambering off the trail to test the patches of snow as to quality and depth. "You're missing all the excitement," he cried repeatedly. "There are a hundred pleasures and sensations by the way."

They paused a moment for him to overtake them; he came up panting and exhausted, making remarks about the fading stars, the wind upon the heights, new routes he longed to try up dangerous couloirs, about everything, it seemed, except the work in hand. There was eagerness in him, the kind of excitement that saps energy and wastes the nervous force, threatening a probable collapse before the arduous object is attained.

"Keep to the thing in hand," replied the priest sternly. "We are not really going fast; it is you who are scattering yourself to no purpose. It wears us all. We must husband our resources," and he pointed significantly to the pyramid of the Tour du Néant that gleamed above them at an incredible altitude.

"We are here to amuse ourselves; life is a pleasure, a sensation, or it is nothing," grumbled his companion; but there was a gravity in the tone of the older man that discouraged argument and made resistance difficult. The other arranged his pack for the tenth time, twisting his axe through an ingenious scheme of straps and string, and fell silently into line behind his leaders. Limasson moved on again . . . and the darkness at length began to lift. Far overhead, at first, the snowy summits shone with a hue less spectral; a delicate pink spread softly from the east; there was a freshening of the chilly wind; then suddenly the highest peak that topped the others by a thousand feet of soaring rock, stepped sharply into sight, half golden and half rose. At the same instant, the vast Movement of the entire scene slowed down; there came one or two terrific gusts of wind in quick succession; a roar like an avalanche of falling stones boomed distantly—and Limasson stopped dead and held his breath.

For something blocked the way before him, something he knew he could not pass. Gigantic and unformed, it seemed part of the architecture of the desolate waste about him, while yet it bulked there, enormous in the trembling dawn, as belonging neither to plain nor mountain. Suddenly it was there, where a moment before had been mere emptiness of air. Its massive outline shifted into visibility as though it had risen from the ground. He stood stock still. A cold that was not of this world turned him rigid in his tracks. A few yards behind him the priest had halted too. Further in the rear they heard the stumbling tread of the younger man, and the faint calling of his voice—a feeble, broken sound as of a man whom sudden fear distressed to helplessness.

"We're off the track, and I've lost my way," the words came on the still air. "My axe is gone . . . let us put on the rope! . . . Hark! Do you hear that roar?" And then a sound as though he came slowly groping on his hands and knees.

"You have exhausted yourself too soon," the priest answered sternly. "Stay where you are and rest, for we go no further. This is the place we sought."

There was in his tone a kind of ultimate solemnity that for a moment turned Limasson's attention from the great obstacle that blocked his further way. The darkness lifted veil by veil, not gradually, but by a series of leaps as when some one inexpertly turns a wick. He perceived then that not a single Grandeur loomed in front, but that others of similar kind, some huger than the first, stood all about him, forming an enclosing circle that hemmed him in.

Then, with a start, he recovered himself. Equilibrium and common sense returned. The trick that sight had played upon him, assisted by the rarefied atmosphere of the heights and by the witchery of dawn, was no uncommon one, after all. The long straining of the eyes to pick the way in an uncertain light so easily deceives perspective. Delusion ever follows abrupt change of focus. These shadowy encircling forms were but the rampart of still distant precipices whose giant walls framed the tremendous amphitheatre to the sky.

Their closeness was a mere gesture of the dusk and distance.

The shock of the discovery produced an instant's unsteadiness in him that brought bewilderment. He straightened up, raised his head, and looked about him. The cliffs, it seemed to him, shifted back instantly to their accustomed places; as though after all they *had* been close; there was a reeling among the topmost crags; they balanced fearfully, then stood still against a sky already faintly crimson. The roar he heard, that might well have seemed the tumult of their hurrying speed, was in reality but the wind of dawn that rushed against their ribs, beating the echoes out with angry wings. And the lines of trailing mist, streaking the air like proofs of rapid motion, merely coiled and floated in the empty spaces.

He turned to the priest, who had moved up beside him.

"How strange," he said, "is this beginning of new light! My sight went all astray for a passing moment. I thought the mountains stood right across my path. And when I looked up just now it seemed they all ran back." His voice was small and lost in the great listening air.

The man looked fixedly at him. He had removed his slouch hat, hot with the long ascent, and as he answered, a long thin shadow flitted across his features. A breadth of darkness dropped about them. It was as though a mask were forming. The face that now was covered had been—naked. He was so long in answering that Limasson heard his mind sharpening the sentence like a pencil.

He spoke very slowly: "*They* move perhaps even as Their powers move, and Their minutes are our years. Their passage ever is in tumult. There is disorder then among the affairs of men; there is confusion in their minds. There may be ruin and disaster, but out of the wreckage shall issue strong, fresh growth. For like a sea, They pass."

There was in his mien a grandeur that seemed borrowed marvellously from the mountains. His voice was grave and deep; he made no sign or gesture; and in his manner was a curious steadiness that breathed through the language a kind of sacred prophecy.

Long, thundering gusts of wind passed distantly across the precipices as he spoke. The same moment, expecting apparently no rejoinder to his strange utterance, he stooped and began to unpack his knapsack. The change from the sacerdotal language to this commonplace and practical detail was singularly bewildering.

"It is the time to rest," he added, "and the time to eat. Let us prepare." And he drew out several small packets and laid them in a row upon the ground. Awe deepened over Limasson as he watched, and with it a great wonder too. For the words seemed ominous, as though this man, upon the floor of some vast Temple, said: "Let us prepare a sacrifice . . . !" There flashed into him, out of depths that had hitherto concealed it, a lightning clue that hinted at explanation of the entire strange proceeding—of the abrupt meeting with the strangers, the impulsive acceptance of their project for the great ascent, their grave behaviour as though it were a Ceremonial of immense design, his change of position, the bewildering tricks of sight, and the solemn language, finally, of the older man that corroborated what he himself had deemed at first illusion. In a flying second of time this all swept through him—and with it the sharp desire to turn aside, retreat, to run away.

Noting the movement, or perhaps divining the emotion prompting it, the priest looked up quickly. In his tone was a coldness that seemed as though this scene of wintry desolation uttered words:

"You have come too far to think of turning back. It is not possible. You stand now at the gates of birth—and death. All that might hinder, you have so bravely cast aside. Be brave now to the end."

And, as Limasson heard the words, there dropped suddenly into him a new and awful insight into humanity, a power that unerringly discovered the spiritual necessities of others, and therefore of himself. With a shock he realised that the younger man who had accompanied them with increasing difficulty as they climbed higher and higher—was but a shadow of reality. Like the porter, he was but an encumbrance who impeded progress. And he turned his eyes to search the desolate landscape.

"You will not find him," said his companion, "for he is gone. Never, unless you weakly call, shall you see him again, nor desire to hear his voice." And Limasson realised that in his heart he had all the while disapproved of the man, disliked him for his theatrical fondness of sensation and effect, more, that he had even hated and despised him. Starvation might crawl upon him where he had fallen and eat his life away before he would stir a finger to save him. It was with the older man he now had dreadful business in hand.

"I am glad," he answered, "for in the end he must have proved my death—our death!"

And they drew closer round the little circle of food the priest had laid upon the rocky ground, an intimate understanding linking them together in a sympathy that completed Limasson's bewilderment. There was bread, he saw, and there was salt; there was also a little flask of deep red wine. In the centre of the circle was a miniature fire of sticks the priest had collected from the bushes of wild rhododendron. The smoke rose upwards in a thin blue line. It did not even quiver, so profound was the surrounding stillness of the mountain air, but far away among the precipices ran the boom of falling water, and behind it again, the muffled roar as of peaks and snow-fields that swept with a rolling thunder through the heavens.

"They are passing," the priest said in a low voice, "and They know that you are here. You have now the opportunity of a lifetime; for, if you yield acceptance of your own free will, success is sure. You stand before the gates of birth and death. They offer you life."

"Yet . . . I denied Them!" He murmured it below his breath.

"Denial is evocation. You called to them, and They have come. The sacrifice of your little personal life is all They ask. Be brave—and yield it."

He took the bread as he spoke, and, breaking it in three pieces, he placed one before Limasson, one before himself, and the third he laid upon the flame which first blackened and then consumed it.

"Eat it and understand," he said, "for it is the nourishment that shall revive your fading life."

Next, with the salt, he did the same. Then, raising the flask of wine, he put it to his lips, offering it afterwards to his companion. When both had drunk there still remained the greater part of the contents. He lifted the vessel with both hands reverently towards the sky. He stood upright.

"The blood of your personal life I offer to Them in your name. By the renunciation which seems to you as death shall you pass through the gates of birth to the life of freedom beyond. For the ultimate sacrifice that They ask of you is—this."

And bending low before the distant heights, he poured the wine upon the rocky ground.

For a period of time Limasson found no means of measuring, so terrible were the emotions in his heart, the priest remained in this attitude of worship and obeisance. The tumult in the mountains ceased. An absolute hush dropped down upon the world. There seemed a pause in the inner history of the universe itself. All waited—till he rose again. And, when he did so, the mask that had for hours now been spreading across his features, was accomplished. The eyes gazed sternly down into his own. Limasson looked—and recognised. He stood face to face with the man whom he knew best of all others in the world . . . himself.

There had been death. There had also been that recovery of splendour which is birth and resurrection.

And the sun that moment, with the sudden surprise that mountains only know, rushed clear above the heights, bathing the landscape and the standing figure with a stainless glory. Into the vast Temple where he knelt, as into that greater inner Temple which is mankind's true House of Royalty, there poured the completing Presence which is—Light.

"For in this way, and in this way only, shall you pass from death to life," sang a chanting voice he recognised also now for the first time as indubitably his own.

It was marvellous. But the birth of light is ever marvellous. It was anguish; but the pangs of resurrection since time began have been accomplished by the sweetness of fierce pain. For the majority still lie in the pre-natal stage, unborn, unconscious of a definite spiritual existence. In the womb they grope and stifle, depending ever upon another. Denial is ever the call to life, a protest against continued darkness for deliverance. Yet birth is the ruin of all that has hitherto been depended on. There comes then that standing alone which at first seems desolate isolation. The tumult of destruction precedes release.

Limasson rose to his feet, stood with difficulty upright, looked about him from the figure so close now at his side to the snowy summit of that Tour du Néant he would never climb. The roar and thunder of *Their* passage was resumed. It seemed the mountains reeled.

"They are passing," sang the voice that was beside him and within him too, "but They have known you, and your offering is accepted. When They come close upon the world there is ever wreckage and disaster in the affairs of men. They bring disorder and confusion into the mind, a confusion that seems final, a disorder that seems to threaten death. For there is tumult in Their Presence, and apparent chaos that seems the abandonment of order. Out of this vast ruin, then, there issues life in new design. The dislocation is its entrance, the dishevelment its strength. There has been birth. . . ."

The sunlight dazzled his eyes. That distant roar, like a wind, came close and swept his face. An icy air, as from a passing star, breathed over him.

"Are you prepared?" he heard.

He knelt again. Without a sign of hesitation or reluctance, he bared his chest to the sun and wind. The flash came swiftly, instantly, descending into his heart with unerring aim. He saw the gleam in the air, he felt the fiery impact of the blow, he even saw the stream gush forth and sink into the rocky ground, far redder than the wine. . . .

He gasped for breath a moment, staggered, reeled, collapsed . . . and within the moment, so quickly did all happen, he was aware of hands that supported him and helped him to his feet. But he was too weak to stand. They carried him up to bed. The porter, and the man who had reached across him for the matches five minutes before, intending conversation, stood, one at his feet and the other at his head. As he passed through the vestibule of the hotel, he saw the people staring, and in his hand he crumpled up the unopened letters he had received so short a time ago.

"I really think—I can manage alone," he thanked them. "If you will set me down, I can walk. I felt dizzy for a moment."

"The heat in the hall—" the gentleman began in a quiet, sympathetic voice.

They left him standing on the stairs, watching a moment to see that he had quite recovered. Limasson walked up the two flights to his room without faltering. The momentary dizziness had passed. He felt quite himself again, strong, confident, able to stand alone, able to move forward, able to *climb.*

Her Birthday

It was her birthday on the morrow, and I set forth to find a suitable and worthy present. My means, judged by the standards of the big merchants, seemed trivial; yet, could I but discover the right gift, no matter how insignificant, I felt sure that it would please her, and so make me doubly happy. And the kind of gift I already knew, for I had a specimen of it in my humble lodgings; only of so poor a type that I was ashamed to offer it. I must find somewhere a much, much better one, if possible, perfect and without a single flaw. I went, therefore, into the great shops and saw a thousand wonderful and lovely things. . . .

So particular was I, however, and so difficult to suit, that I wearied the salesfolk, and began to feel despondent. All that they showed me was so wrong—so cheap. In the matter of actual expense there was no disagreement, for I mentioned plainly beforehand the price that I would pay, or, rather, that I was prepared to pay. But in the nature and quality of the goods there was no satisfying me at all. Everything that they spread before my eyes seemed ordinary, trifling, even spurious. Marvellously fashioned, and of the most costly description, they yet seemed somewhere counterfeit. The goods were sham. Already she possessed far better. There was nowhere—and I went to the very best emporiums where the rich and favoured of the world bought their offerings—there was nowhere the little genuine thing I sought. The finest that was set before me seemed unworthy. I compared one and all with the specimen, broken yet authentic, that I had at home. And even the cleverest of the salesfolk was unable to deceive me, because I *knew.*

"And this, for instance?" I asked at length, far from content, yet thinking it might just do perhaps in place of anything better I could find. "How much is this magnificent, jewelled thing, with its ingenious little surprise for each day in the entire year? You mentioned—?"

"Ten million pounds, sir," said the man obsequiously, while he eyed me with a close and questioning glance.

"Ten million only!" And I laughed in his face.

"That was the price you named, sir," he murmured.

I drew myself up, looking disdainfully, pityingly at him. And, though he met my eye, he hesitated. Over his tired features there stole a soft and marvellous expression. Something more tender than starlight shone in his little eyes. And, as he answered in a gentle voice that was almost a whisper, I saw him smile as a man may smile when he understands a divine, unutterable thing. Glory touched him for an instant with high radiance, and a hint of delicious awe hid shyly in his voice. I barely caught the words, so low he murmured them:

"I fear, sir, that what you want is not to be had at all—in our establishment. You will hardly find it. It is not in the market." He seemed to bow his head in reverence a moment. "It is not—for sale."

And so I went back to my dingy lodgings, having made no single purchase. I looked fondly at my own little specimen, trying to imagine it had somehow gained in value, in beauty, almost in splendour. At least, I said to myself, it is not spurious. It is real. . . .

And, sitting down to my table, I dipped my broken pen into a penny bottle of inferior ink, and began my birthday letter:—

"This is your birthday, dear, and I send you *all my love*—" Being young, I underlined the words describing my little present, thinking to increase its value thus.

But I did not complete the sentence, for there was another thing that I must find to send her, or she would be disappointed. And a birthday comes but once a year. But, again, though I already possessed a tiny specimen of this other thing I sought, it did not seem to me nearly good enough to offer. Though genuine, it was worn by frequent use. Its lustre had dimmed a little, for I touched it daily. It seemed too ordinary and common for a special present. I was ashamed to send it.

So I set out again and searched . . . and searched . . . in every likely and unlikely place, even groping in the dark about the altars of the churches where I found by chance the doors ajar, and penetrating to those secret shrines where those who seek truth, it is said, go in to pray. For I knew that there was this other little present from me that she would look for—because she had need of it. . . .

And my search was wonderful and full of high adventure, yet so long that the moon had drawn the hood over the door of her silver tent, and the stars were fading in the east behind the towers of the night, before I returned home, footsore, aching, empty-handed, and very humble in my heart. For nowhere had I been able to find this other little thing she would be pleased to have from me. To my amazement, yet to my secret joy, I found nothing better than what I had at home—nothing, that is, indubitably genuine. In quantity it was not anywhere for sale. It was more rare than I had guessed—and I felt delicious triumph in me.

I sat down, humble, reverent, but incommunicably proud and happy, to my unfinished letter. Unless I posted it immediately she would not get it when she woke upon her birthday morning. I finished it. I posted it just as it was—brief, the writing a little shaky, the paper cheap, blot, smudge, and all:

". . . and my worship."

And then, like a scrap of paper that enclosed the other gifts, yet need not be noticed unless she wished it, I added (above the little foolish name she knew me by) another tiny present—all that I had brought into the world or could take out with me again when I left it:

I wrote: "Yours ever faith-fully."

Violence

But what seems so odd to me, so horribly pathetic, is that such people don't resist," said Leidall, suddenly entering the conversation. The intensity of his tone startled everybody; it was so passionate, yet with a beseeching touch that made the women feel uncomfortable a little. "As a rule, I'm told, they submit willingly, almost as though—"

He hesitated, grew confused, and dropped his glance to the floor; and a smartly dressed woman eager to be heard, seized the opening. "Oh, come now," she laughed; "one always hears of a man being *put* into a strait waistcoat. I'm sure he doesn't slip it on as if he were going to a dance!" And she looked flippantly at Leidall, whose casual manners she resented. "People are *put* under restraint. It's not in human nature to accept it—healthy human nature, that is?" But for some reason no one took her question up. "That is so, I believe, yes," a polite voice murmured, while the group at tea in the Dover Street Club turned with one accord to Leidall as to one whose interesting sentence still remained unfinished. He had hardly spoken before, and a silent man is ever credited with wisdom.

"As though—you were just saying, Mr. Leidall?" a quiet little man in a dark corner helped him.

"As though, I meant, a man in that condition of mind is not insane—all through," Leidall continued stammeringly; "but that some wise portion of him watches the proceeding with gratitude, and welcomes the protection against himself. It seems awfully pathetic. Still," again hesitating and fumbling in his speech—"er—it seems queer to me that he should yield quietly to enforced restraint—the waistcoat, handcuffs, and the rest." He looked round hurriedly, half suspiciously, at the faces in the circle, then dropped his eyes again to the floor. He sighed, leaning back in his chair. "I cannot understand it," he added, as no one spoke, but in a very low voice, and almost to himself. "One would expect them to struggle furiously."

Some one had mentioned that remarkable book, *The Mind that Found Itself,* and the conversation had slipped into this serious vein. The women did not like it. What kept it alive was the fact that the silent Leidall, with his handsome, melancholy face, had suddenly wakened into speech, and that the little man opposite to him, half invisible in his dark corner, was assistant to one of London's great hypnotic doctors, who could, an' he would, tell interesting and terrible things. No one cared to ask the direct question, but all hoped for revelations, possibly about people they actually knew. It was a very ordinary tea-party indeed. And this little man now spoke, though hardly in the desired vein. He addressed his remarks to Leidall across the disappointed lady.

"I think, probably, your explanation *is* the true one," he said gently, "for madness in its commoner forms is merely want of proportion; the mind gets out of right and proper relations with its environment. The majority of madmen are mad on one thing only, while the rest of them is as sane as myself—or you."

The words fell into the silence. Leidall bowed his agreement, saying no actual word. The ladies fidgeted. Some one made a jocular remark to the effect that most of the world was mad anyhow, and the conversation shifted with relief into a lighter vein—the scandal in the family of a politician. Everybody talked at once. Cigarettes were lit. The corner soon became excited and even uproarious. The tea-party was a great success, and the offended lady, no longer ignored, led all the skirmishes—towards herself. She was in her element. Only Leidall and the little invisible man in the corner took small part in it; and presently, seizing the opportunity when some new arrivals joined the group, Leidall rose to say his adieux, and slipped away, his departure scarcely noticed. Dr. Hancock followed him a minute later. The two men met in the hall; Leidall already had his hat and coat on. "I'm going West, Mr. Leidall. If that's your way too, and you feel inclined for the walk we might go together." Leidall turned with a start. His glance took in the other with avidity—a keenly-searching, hungry glance. He hesitated for an imperceptible moment, then made a movement towards him, half inviting, while a curious shadow dropped across his face and vanished. It was both pathetic and terrible. The lips trembled. He seemed to say, "God bless you; *do* come with me!" But no words were audible.

"It's a pleasant evening for a walk," added Dr. Hancock gently; "clean and dry under foot for a change. I'll get my hat and join you in a second." And there was a hint, the merest flavour of authority in his voice.

That touch of authority was his mistake. Instantly Leidall's hesitation passed. "I'm sorry," he said abruptly, "but I'm afraid I must take a taxi. I have an appointment at the Club and I'm late already." "Oh, I see," the other replied, with a kindly smile; "then I mustn't keep you. But if you ever have a free evening, won't you look me up, or come and dine? You'll find my telephone number in the book. I should like to talk with you about—those things we mentioned at tea." Leidall thanked him politely and went out. The memory of the little man's kindly sympathy and understanding eyes went with him.

"Who was that man?" some one asked, the moment Leidall had left the tea-table. "Surely he's not the Leidall who wrote that awful book some years ago?"

"Yes—the *Gulf of Darkness*. Did you read it?"

They discussed it and its author for five minutes, deciding by a large majority that it was the book of a madman. Silent, rude men like that always had a screw loose somewhere, they agreed. Silence was invariably morbid.

"And did you notice Dr. Hancock? He never took his eyes off him. That's why he followed him out like that. I wonder if *he* thought anything!"

"I know Hancock well," said the lady of the wounded vanity. "I'll ask him and find out." They chattered on, somebody mentioned a *risqué* play, the talk switched into other fields, and in due course the tea-party came to an end.

And Leidall, meanwhile, made his way towards the Park on foot, for he had not taken a taxi after all. The suggestion of the other man, perhaps, had worked upon him. He was very open to suggestion. With hands deep in his overcoat pockets, and head sunk forward between his shoulders, he walked briskly, entering the Park at one of the smaller gates. He made his way across the wet turf, avoiding the paths and people. The February sky was shining in the west; beautiful clouds floated over the houses; they looked like the shore-line of some radiant strand his childhood once had known. He sighed; thought dived and searched within; self-analysis, that old, implacable demon, lifted its voice; introspection took the reins again as usual. There seemed a strain upon the mind he could not dispel. Thought circled poignantly. He knew it was unhealthy, morbid, a sign of these many years of difficulty and stress that had marked him so deeply, but for the life of him he could not escape from the hideous spell that held him. The same old thoughts bored their way into his mind like burning wires, tracing the same unanswerable questions. From this torture, waking or sleeping, there was no escape. Had a companion been with him it might have been different. If, for instance, Dr. Hancock—

He was angry with himself for having refused—furious; it was that vile, false pride his long loneliness had fostered. The man was sympathetic to him, friendly, marvellously understanding; he could have talked freely with him, and found relief. His intuition had picked out the little doctor as a man in ten thousand. Why had he so curtly declined his gentle invitation? Dr. Hancock *knew;* he guessed his awful secret. But how? In what had he betrayed himself?

The weary self-questioning began again, till he sighed and groaned from sheer exhaustion. He *must* find people, companionship, some one to talk to. The Club—it crossed his tortured mind for a second—was impossible; there was a conspiracy among the members against him. He had left his usual haunts everywhere for the same reason—his restaurants, where he had his lonely meals; his music hall, where he tried sometimes to forget himself; his favourite walks, where the very policemen knew and eyed him. And, coming to the bridge across the Serpentine just then, he paused and leaned over the edge, watching a bubble rise to the surface.

"I suppose there *are* fish in the Serpentine?" he said to a man a few feet away.

They talked a moment—the other was evidently a clerk on his way home—and then the stranger edged off and continued his walk, looking back once or twice at the sad-faced man who had addressed him. "It's ridiculous, that with all our science we can't live under water as the fish do," reflected Leidall, and moved on round the other bank of the water, where he watched a flight of duck whirl down from the darkening air and settle with a long, mournful splash beside the bushy island. "Or that, for all our pride of mechanism in a mechanical age, we cannot really fly." But these attempts to escape from self were never very successful. Another part of him looked on and mocked. He returned ever to the endless introspection and self-analysis, and in the deepest moment of it—ran into a big, motionless figure that blocked his way. It was the Park policeman, the one who always eyed him. He sheered off suddenly towards the trees, while the man, recognising him, touched his cap respectfully. "It's a pleasant evening, sir; turned quite mild again." Leidall mumbled some reply or other, and hurried on to hide himself among the shadows of the trees. The policeman stood and watched him, till the darkness swallowed him. "He knows too!" groaned the wretched man. And every bench was occupied; every face turned to watch him; there were even figures behind the trees. He dared not go into the street, for the very taxi-drivers were against him. If he gave an address, he would not be driven to it; the man would *know,* and take him elsewhere. And something in his heart, sick with anguish, weary with the endless battle, suddenly yielded.

"There *are* fish in the Serpentine," he remembered the stranger had said. "And," he added to himself, with a wave of delicious comfort, "they lead secret, hidden lives that no one can disturb." His mind cleared surprisingly. In the water he could find peace and rest and healing. Good Lord! How easy it all was! Yet he had never thought of it before. He turned sharply to retrace his steps, but in that very second the clouds descended upon his thought again, his mind darkened, he hesitated. Could he get out again when he had had enough? Would he rise to the surface? A battle began over these questions. He ran quickly, then stood still again to think the matter out. Darkness shrouded him. He heard the wind rush laughing through the trees. The picture of the whirring duck flashed back a moment, and he decided that the best way was by air, and not by water. He would *fly* into the place of rest, not sink or merely float; and he remembered the view from his bedroom window, high over old smoky London town, with a drop of eighty feet on to the pavements. Yes, that was the best way. He waited a moment, trying to think it all out clearly, but one moment the fish had it, and the next the birds. It was really impossible to decide. Was there no one who could help him, no one in all this enormous town who was sufficiently on his side to advise him on the point? Some clear-headed, experienced, kindly man?

And the face of Dr. Hancock flashed before his vision. He saw the gentle eyes and sympathetic smile, remembered the soothing voice and the offer of companionship he had refused. Of course, there was one serious drawback: Hancock *knew*. But he was far too tactful, too sweet and good a man to let that influence his judgment, or to betray in any way at all that he did know.

Leidall found it in him to decide. Facing the entire hostile world, he hailed a taxi from the nearest gate upon the street, looked up the address in a chemist's telephone-book, and reached the door in a condition of delight and relief. Yes, Dr. Hancock was at home. Leidall sent his name in. A few minutes later the two men were chatting pleasantly together, almost like old friends, so keen was the little man's intuitive sympathy and tact. Only Hancock, patient listener though he proved himself to be, was uncommonly full of words. Leidall explained the matter very clearly. "Now, what is your decision, Dr. Hancock? Is it to be the way of the fish or the way of the duck?" And, while Hancock began his answer with slow, well-chosen words, a new idea, better than either, leaped with a flash into his listener's mind. It was an inspiration. For where could he find a better hiding-place from all his troubles than—inside Hancock himself? The man was kindly; he surely would not object. Leidall this time did not hesitate a second. He was tall and broad; Hancock was small; yet he was sure there would be room. He sprang upon him like a wild animal. He felt the warm, thin throat yield and bend between his great hands . . . then darkness, peace and rest, a nothingness that surely was the oblivion he had so long prayed for. He had accomplished his desire. He had secreted himself for ever from persecution—inside the kindliest little man he had ever met—inside Hancock. . . .

He opened his eyes and looked about him into a room he did not know. The walls were soft and dimly coloured. It was very silent. Cushions were everywhere. Peaceful it was, and out of the world. Overhead was a skylight, and one window, opposite the door, was heavily barred. Delicious! No one could get in. He was sitting in a deep and comfortable chair. He felt rested and happy. There was a click, and he saw a tiny window in the door drop down, as though worked by a sliding panel. Then the door opened noiselessly, and in came a little man with smiling face and soft brown eyes—Dr. Hancock.

Leidall's first feeling was amazement. "Then I didn't get into him properly after all! Or I've slipped out again, perhaps! The dear, good fellow!" And he rose to greet him. He put his hand out, and found that the other came with it in some inexplicable fashion. Movement was cramped. "Ah, then I've had a stroke," he thought, as Hancock pressed him, ever so gently, back into the big chair. "Do not get up," he said soothingly but with authority; "sit where you are and rest. You must take it very easy for a bit; like all clever men who have overworked—"

"I'll get in the moment he turns," thought Leidall. "I did it badly before. It must be through the back of his head, of course, where the spine runs up into the brain," and he waited till Hancock should turn. But Hancock never turned. He kept his face towards him all the time, while he chatted, moving gradually nearer to the door. On Leidall's face was the smile of an innocent child, but there lay a hideous cunning behind that smile, and the eyes were terrible.

"Are those bars firm and strong," asked Leidall, "so that no one can get in?" He pointed craftily, and the doctor, caught for a second unawares, turned his head. That instant Leidall was upon him with a roar, then sank back powerless into the chair, unable to move his arms more than a few inches in any direction. Hancock stepped up quietly and made him comfortable again with cushions.

And something in Leidall's soul turned round and looked another way. His mind became clear as daylight for a moment. The effort perhaps had caused the sudden change from darkness to great light. A memory rushed over him. "Good God!" he cried. "I am violent. I was going to do you an injury—you, who are so sweet and good to me!" He trembled dreadfully, and burst into tears. "For the sake of heaven," he implored, looking up, ashamed and keenly penitent, "put me under restraint. Fasten my hands before I try it again." He held both hands out willingly, beseechingly, then looked down, following the direction of the other's kind brown eyes. His wrists, he saw, already wore steel handcuffs, and a strait waistcoat was across his chest and arms and shoulders.

Jimbo's Longest Day

The Longest Day has in it for children a strange, incommunicable thrill. It begins so early in the morning, for one thing, that half of it—the first half—belongs to the mystery of night. It steals upon the world as though from Fairyland, a thing apart from the rush and scurry of ordinary days; it is so long that nothing happens quickly in it; there is a delicious leisure throughout its shining hours that makes it possible to carry out a hundred schemes unhurried. No voice can call "Time's up!"; no one can urge "Be quick!"; it passes, true, yet passes like a dream that flows in a circle, having neither proper beginning nor definite end. Christmas Day and Easter Day seem short and sharp by comparison. They are measurable. The Longest Day brims with a happy, endless wonder from dawn to sunset. Exceptional happenings are its prerogative.

All this, and something more no elder can quite grasp, lay stealthily in Jimbo's question: "Uncle, to-morrow's the Longest Day. What shall we do?" He glanced across the room at his mother, prepared for a prohibitive remark of some sort. But mother, deep in a stolen book, paid no attention. He looked back at me. "It's all right; she's not listening; but we can go outside to discuss it, if you prefer," his expression said. I beckoned him over to me, however, for safety's sake. My position was fairly strong, I knew, because the stolen book was mine, and had been taken from my work-table. Jimbo's mother has this way with books, her passion almost unmoral. If a book comes to me for review, if a friend makes me a present of a book, if I buy or borrow one—the instant it comes into the house she knows it. "I just looked in to see if your room had been dusted," she says; "I'm sorry to disturb you," and is gone again. But she has seen the new book. Her instinct is curious. I used to think she bribed the postman. She smells a new arrival, and goes straight for it. "Were you looking for *this?*" she will ask innocently an hour later when I catch her with it, household account-books neglected by her side. "I'm so sorry. I was just peeping into it." And she is incorrigible, as unashamed. No book is ever lost, at any rate. "Mother's got it," indicates its hiding-place infallibly.

So I felt safe enough discussing plans for the Longest Day with Jimbo, and talked openly with him, while I watched her turn the pages.

"It's the *very* beginning I like," he said. "I want to see it start. The sun rises at 3.44, you see. That's a quarter to four—three hours and a quarter before I usually get up. How shall we manage it, d'you think?" He had worked it all out.

"There's hardly any night either," I said, "for the sun sets at 8.18, and that leaves very little time for darkness. It's light at two, remember."

He stared into my face. "Maria has an alarum clock. She wakes with that. It's by her bed in the attic room, you know."

Mother turned a page noisily, but did not look up. There was no cause for alarm, though we instinctively lowered our voices at once. I cannot say how it was so swiftly, so deftly arranged between us that *I* was to steal the clock, set it accurately for two in the morning, rise, dress, and come to fetch Jimbo. But the result was clear beyond equivocation, and I had accepted the duty as a man should. Generously he left this exciting thing to me. "And suppose it doesn't go off and wake you," he enquired anxiously, "will you be sure to get up and *make* it go off? Because we might miss the beginning of the day unless you do." I explained something about the mechanism of the mind and the mechanism of an alarum clock that seemed to satisfy him, and then he asked another vital question: "What *is* exactly the Longest Day, uncle? I thought all days were about the same—like that," and he stretched an imaginary line in the air with one hand, so that Mac, the terrier, thought he wanted to play a moment. I explained that too, to his satisfaction, whereupon he nestled much closer to me, glancing first over his shoulder at his mother, and enquired whether "everything knew it was the Longest Day—birds, cows, and out-of-door things all over the world—rabbits, I mean—like that? They know, I suppose?"

"They certainly must find it longer than other days, ordinary days, just common days," I said. "I'm sure of that." And then I cleared my throat so loudly that mother looked up from her book with an unmistakable start. "Oh, I'm *so* sorry," she exclaimed, with unblushing mendacity, "but d'you want your book? Were you looking for it? I just took a peep—" And when I turned to leave the room with it beneath my arm Jimbo had vanished, leaving no trace behind him.

That night he went to bed without a murmur at half-past eight. He trusted me implicitly. There were no questions: "Have you got the clock?" or "How did you get it?" or anything of the kind—just his absolute confidence that I *had* got it and that I *would* wake him. At the stairs, however, he turned and made a sign. Leading me through the back door of the Sussex cottage, we found ourselves a moment in the orchard together. And then, saying no word, he pointed. He pointed everywhere; he stared about him, listening; he looked up into my face, and then at the orchard, and then back into my face again. His whole little person stood on tiptoe, observing, watching, listening. And at first I was disappointed, for I noticed nothing unusual anywhere. "Well, what is it?" my manner probably expressed. But neither of us said a word. The saffron sky shone between the trunks of the apple trees; swallows darted to and fro; a blackbird whistled out of sight; and over the hedge a big cow thrust her head towards us, her body concealed. In the foreground were beehives. The air was very still and scented. My pipe smoke hung almost motionless. I moved from one foot to the other.

"Aha!" I said mysteriously below my breath, "aha!"

And that was sufficient for him. He knew I had seen and understood. He came a step nearer to me, his face solemn and expectant.

"It's begun already, you see. Isn't it wonderful? Everything knows."

"And is getting ready," I added, "for its coming."

"The Longest Day," he whispered, looking about him with suppressed excitement and ready, if necessary, to believe the earth would presently stop turning. He gave one curious look at the sky, shuddered an instant with intense delight, gave my hand a secret squeeze, and disappeared like a goblin into the cottage. But behind him lingered something his little presence had evoked. Wonder and expectation are true words of power, and anticipation constructs the mould along which Imagination later shall lead her fairy band. I realised what he had seen. The orchard, the cow, the beehives *did* look different. They were inviting, as though something was on the way. The very sky, as the summer dusk spread down it, wore colouring no ordinary June evening knew. Midsummer Eve set free the fairies, and Jimbo knew it. The roses seemed to flutter everywhere on wings. . . . The very lilac blooms had eyes. . . . I heard a rustle as of skirts high up among the peeping stars. . . .

How it came about is more than I can say, for I went to bed with a whirr of wings and flowers in my head. The stillness of the night was magical, four short hours of transparent darkness that seemed to gleam and glimmer without hiding anything. Maria's alarum clock was *not* beside my bed, for the simple reason that I had not asked for it. Jimbo and the Longest Day between them had cast a glamour over me that had nothing to do with hours, minutes, seconds. It was delicious and inexplicable. Yet at other times I am an ordinary person, who knows that time is money and money is difficult to come by without uncommon effort. All this came for nothing. Jimbo did it.

And what did I do for Jimbo? I cannot say. His is the grand old magical secret. He believed and wondered; he waited and asked no futile questions; time and space obeyed his imperious little will; waking or sleeping he dreamed, creating the world anew. I shut no eye that night. I watched the wheeling constellations rise and pass. The whole, clear summer night was rich with the silence of the gods. I dreamed, perhaps, beside my open window, where the roses and the clematis climbed, shining like lamps of starry beauty above the tiny lawn. . . . And at half-past one, when the east began to whisper stealthily that Some one was on the way, I left my chair and stole quietly down the narrow passage-way to Jimbo's room. . . . I was clever in my wickedness. I knew that if I waked him, whispering that the Longest Day was about to break, he would open half an eye, turn over in his thick childhood sleep, and murmur, as in dream, "Then let it come." And so, a little weary, if the truth be told, I did all this, and—to my intense surprise—discovered Jimbo perched, wide awake and staring, at the casement window. He had never closed an eye, nor half an eye. He was watchful and alert, but undeniably tired out, as I was.

"Jimbo," I whispered, stealing in upon him, "the Longest Day is very near. It's so close you can hear it coming down the sky. It's softer than any dream you ever dreamed in your life. Come out—if you will—we'll see it from the orchard."

He turned towards me in his little nightshirt like a goblin. His eyes were very big, but the eyelids held open with an effort.

"Uncle," he said in a tiny voice, "do you think it's really come at last? It's been terribly slow, but I suppose that's because it's such an awful length. Wasn't it *wonderful?*"

And I tucked him up. Before the sheet was round his shoulder he was asleep, . . . and next morning when we met at breakfast, he just asked me slyly, "Do you think mother guessed or saw anything of what *we* saw?" We glanced across the table, full of secret signs, together. Mother's letters were piled beside her plate, a book beneath them. It was my stolen book. She had clearly sat up half the night devouring it.

"No," I whispered, "I don't think mother guesses anything at all. Besides," I added, "to-day is the Longest Day, so in any case she'd be a very long time finding out." And, as he seemed satisfied, I felt my conscience clear, and said no more about it.

Who Was She?

I

There were times in the life of Arthur Minns when he didn't know whether he was standing on his head or his feet. "Everything looks different suddenly," as he expressed it. He saw things upside down, or inside out, or backwards forwards. And the condition first betrayed itself one afternoon when he returned unexpectedly from work—he was traveller to a publishing house—and found his wife talking over the teacups with a caller. He burst into the room before he knew that any one was there and did not know how to escape without appearing rude. They were talking of many things, the sins of their neighbours in Maida Vale, chiefly, and after the pause and interruption caused by his unwelcome entrance, the caller, searching for a suitable subject, asked:

"You've heard about Captain Fox, I suppose?"

Mrs. Minns opened her eyes as though to read the other's thoughts. Evidently she had not heard.

"What's the latest about *him?*" she enquired cautiously.

"He's going to marry her," was the reply. "I know it for a fact. But don't say anything about it yet, because I heard it from Lady Spears who . . ." She dragged a good deal of Burke into the complicated explanation, making it as impressive as she could. Captain Fox was a gay young spark, no better than he should be, who paid rather frequent visits upon the young widow of the ground-floor flat, who should have been better than she was. The widow made her living by literature—phrase used by the other occupants of the building, but not by the neighbourhood—and "the Captain" was well connected, very. Hence the malicious interest in their doings. To find that honest courtship explained the friendship was a violent disappointment. Mrs. Marks, the caller, being chiefly responsible for the darker interpretation, wished to be the first to announce the innocent one, to claim authorship, indeed.

"Who'd ever have guessed *that?*" exclaimed Mrs. Minns, off her guard a moment. "You always told me—"

The face of her caller betrayed a passing flush.

"One always hoped," she began primly, when the other interrupted her with a firm, clear question. It was this question that first started the odd condition enjoyed subsequently by Minns, and referred to in the opening sentence. Mrs. Minns asked it, and Mrs. Minns was a good, clean, honest soul, while Arthur Minns was even simpler—a hard-working, gentle, saving, and generous little man who knew the selling value of an author as well as he knew the title of every book his firm had published in the past twenty years. Just at this moment his wholesome little mind was wondering sweetly whether Captain and Mrs. Fox would be happy in their married life. *He* had been uncommonly happy himself; he longed for others to be the same. His natural thought ran spontaneously upon the chances of the new couple—on lines domestic, financial, love-in-a-cottage, children, and the rest. Yet vaguely only: there was nothing he could have *said.*

"Who *was* she, I wonder. Do you know?" came the amazing question.

And, hearing it, Arthur felt his world turn upside down a moment. He realised, that is, that his excellent, dear little wife saw it upside down.

Which came to the same thing. For his wife was a good, true woman, no modern complexity in her. Her present gossip was merely tact—adopting her caller's mood from sheer politeness. And for his wife to ask such a question was as if he had asked it himself. His world turned inside out. He rose abruptly, finding the energy to invent a true escaping-sentence.

"You ask who she *was,*" he said, not with intentional rudeness, yet firmly and with clear decision, "when what you ought to ask should be—"

Both ladies stared at him with surprise, waiting for him to finish. He was picking up the cup his sudden gesture had overturned.

"Who and what she *is,*" concluded Mr. Minns with the astonishment of positive rebuke in his tone. "What does—what *can* it matter who she was? It's what she *is* that's of importance. The Captain's got to live with *that.* 'Who she was' is like thinking backwards and seeing things upside down." And the escaping-sentence: "If you'll excuse me, Mrs. Marks, I have to go upstairs to see a book"—he hesitated, stammered, and ended in confusion—"about a book." And off he went, making a formal little bow at the door. He went into the dining-room down the passage, vaguely aware that he had not behaved very nicely. "But, of course, I'm not a gentleman exactly," he said to himself, "what's called a gentleman, that is. Father was a chemist at Guildford."

He stood still a moment, then dropped into a chair beside the table with the red and black check cloth. His mind was working on all by itself, as it were.

"What I said was true, anyhow. People always ask, 'Who WAS she?' What the devil does that matter? It's what you ARE that counts. Father was a chemist, but I—I—"

He got up and walked over to the clock, because the clock stood on the mantelpiece with a mirror behind it. He wanted to see his own face. He stared at himself a moment without speaking, thinking, or feeling anything. He put his tie straight and picked a bit of cotton from his shoulder.

"I am Arthur Minns, not a gentleman quite, not of much account anywhere perhaps, but a true workman, earning £250 a year, knowing all about the outside, but nothing about the inside, of books, thirty-seven years old, with a boy at the Grammar School, and a girl of sixteen in the house, and married to—to—" He paused, turned from the mirror, and sat down. Who *was* she, now? It cost him an effort to remember—"To Mary Lumley, daughter of a corn-chandler in Norfolk, who might die any moment and leave us enough to live on," he went on, in a more comfortable position, passing his hand across his forehead, "and my life is insured, and I've put a bit by, and Alfred's to be a solicitor's clerk, and everything's going smoothly, except that taxes—"

The sound of an opening door disturbed him. He felt all confused in his mind. He heard Mrs. Marks saying loudly, "And please say good-bye for me to your 'usband," —it was suspiciously like a dropped h—as though intending he should hear and understand she bore him no ill will for his bad manners, and, as the steps went downstairs, the two questions came back upon him like pistol shots:

"Who *was* she? Who *am* I?"

He realised he had been wandering from the point.

"I'm a centre of life, independent and unafraid," thought flashed an answer. "I'm what I make myself, what I think myself. I'm *not* seeing things upside down; I'm beginning to think for myself, and that's what it is. No one, nor nothing, nor anything anywhere in the world," he went on, mixed in speech, but clear in mind, "can prevent me from being anything I feel myself, will myself, say I am. I've never read nor thought nor bothered my head about things before. By heavens! I'll begin. I *have* begun . . . !"

"What's the matter, Artie? Have you got a headache, or is it the books bothering you, dear?" His wife had stolen in upon him.

She put her hand upon his forehead, and he got up from his chair and faced her.

"I've made a discovery," he said with exhilaration in his manner, "a great discovery." He looked triumphantly at her. "I am."

"*What* are you?" she asked, thinking he was joking, and his sentence left unfinished on purpose.

"I am," he repeated with emphasis. "I have discovered that I am, that I exist. Your question to that woman made me suddenly see it."

His wife looked flustered, but said nothing. Arthur continued:

"As yet, I don't know exactly what I am, but I mean to find out. Up till now I've been automatic, just doing things because other people do 'em. But I've discovered that's not necessary. I'm going to do things in future because I want to. But first I must find out *why* I am what I am. Then the explanation'll come—of everything. Do you see what I mean? It's a case of 'Enquire within upon everything.'"

"Do you mean you're going to start in the publishing line, Artie?" It had always been her secret ambition.

"That may come later," he told her, "when I've something to say. For it's big, you know, it's really big, this discovery of mine. Most people never find it out at all. She"—indicating with his thumb the direction Mrs. Marks had taken—"hasn't, for instance. She simply isn't aware that she exists. She isn't."

"Isn't what, dear?"

"She *is not,* I mean because she doesn't know she is," he said loudly.

"Oh, that way. I see." Mrs. Minns looked a wee bit frightened.

"There are strange, big things about these days, I know," she said after a pause, thinking of the books with queer titles his employers published. "You have been reading too much, thinking and—"

"Mary," he interrupted, in a tone that convinced her his head was momentarily turned, "that's the whole trouble. I've never thought in my life."

"But why should you, dear?" she soothed him, wondering if fits began this way, or if people who lost their memory and wandered off had symptoms like this first. "You always do your work splendidly. Don't think, is what I say. It always leads to trouble—"

"Hardly ever—till this moment," he was saying in the grave, emphatic way that so alarmed her. "Not even when I asked you to marry me, when Alfred was born, or Joan, or when we took this flat, or anything."

"You've made a great success of your life without it anyhow, Joe, dear. And no woman could ask more than that. D'you feel unwell? Joan can fetch Dr. Monson in a moment."

"I feel better and bigger and stronger," he replied, "than ever in my life before. I have never been really alive till this moment. I *am*—and for the first time I know it. I'm experiencing." He stopped short, as Joan went down the passage, pausing a moment to look in, then tactfully going on her way again. "Mary," he said, as their heads turned back from the door together, "do you know what 'experiencing' is? D'you realise what the word means?"

She sat down, resting her arms upon the table. She looked quietly into his eyes, as one who is about to speak out of greater knowledge.

"Joe, dear, I *have* had experiences of my own, you know."

"Yes, yes, I know, you good old soul. I know, I know. But what I mean is—do you get the meaning, the real meaning of the word?"

She sighed audibly. "Not *your* meaning, perhaps," she meant. But she did not say it. She was a precious woman, words few in her.

"It means," he said, delighted with her exquisite silence, "it means—er—" He thought hard a moment. "Experience," he went on, "is that 'something' which changes potatoes into nourishment, and so into emotion. That's it. Until you eat potatoes, you don't exist. Until you have experiences, you don't exist. When you have experiences, and know that you have them, you—*per*sist."

She gasped aloud. She took his hand—very quietly, hoping he

would mistake it for a caress, while surreptitiously she felt his pulse.

"Joe, dear," she said, softly as in their courtship days—she loved him very dearly—"such ideas don't come into your head from nowhere. Has some one been talking to you? Have you been reading these books?"

For his pulse was very quiet.

"Have you been reading the firm's books, dear?"

She asked it gently, forgivingly, as a mother might ask her boy—"Have you been tasting father's whisky?" The books were meant to sell to booksellers, to the public, to people who needed that particular kind of excitement. Her husband was to be trusted. He was not supposed to know what they contained. His "line" of trade was chiefly medical, psychological, religious, philosophical. Fiction was another "line"—for the apprentice. Joe was an expert "traveller." He was expected to talk about his wares, but not as one who read them. Merely their selling value was his strong point.

By the expression of his face she knew the answer.

He leaned back in his chair, just as he did sometimes when he asked what there was for dinner—the same real interest in his eyes—and he answered very calmly:—

"My dear, I have. *Cogito ergo sum.* For the first time I understood, in theory, that I existed. My reading taught me that. But I never knew it in practice until just now, when I heard you ask that question about the future Mrs. Fox: 'Who was she?' And then I knew also that you—"

"You what?" enquired Mrs. Minns, bridling.

"Were unaware that you existed," he replied point blank.

"Aren't you a little beside yourself, Joe,—sort of excited, or something?" she asked, proud of her tact and self-control. "What else could I have said? How could I have put it different?"

"Mary," he answered gently, "you should have said, 'What *is* she?' For that would have meant you thought for yourself. It would have meant that you knew you *were,* and that you knew she *was.*"

"Original," said Mrs. Minns slowly, catching her husband's meaning.

"True," he answered, "just as when, years ago you were looking at the prehistoric things in the Crystal Palace grounds, and the band was playing a waltz, and the sun was lovely, and you said, 'Yes.' Do you remember?"

Somehow or other she had got upon his knee, and their faces were close together. She understood his meaning—in a way. She looked into his glorious eyes. He *was* the exceptional man she had always believed him to be. Something big, caught from his proximity, stirred strangely in her. She said, at random, something bigger than she knew:

"Then you mean, that until a person thinks for himself upon the common little everyday things of life, he's not really alive—independent, true, *real,* as it were? Is that it, Joe, darling?"

He smiled indulgently. He kissed her paternally. He realised what a long way he had travelled.

"That's part of it," he replied, kissing her. "To ask who she *was,* is to accept the judgment of the common mass. To ask what she *is* means that you think for yourself—and want the truth. If a man asked me who *you* were—I'd—" Mr. Minns made a violent movement that half shook her from his knee.

"What dear?" she murmured adoringly.

"Knock him down," said Mr. Minns with grandeur.

Then Joan came in noisily, singing down the corridor as she came. But, before she could ask whether it was to be cold lamb or curry for supper, her father was on his feet.

"I'm going to take you both out to-night," he said. "We'll dine at a restaurant in the West End." And they did.

II

Now, Joan was no ordinary girl; some called her backward, some considered her deficient, but the majority described her as a natural idiot. Tall, slim, and dark, with plenty of hair and the eyes of a wild animal, she was out of the common in an unattractive sort of way. Tom, her brother, with the mind of a solicitor's clerk, looked down upon her; her mother, fond, conventional, socially ambitious, despaired of her; her father alone held the opinion "There's something in that girl. She's always herself. But town-life over-weights and hides her; and in the end will suffocate. It'll snuff her out. She's meant for country." He was aware of something unusually real in her. They were great friends. "I want more air," she said once. "In a field or garden I'd grow enormous like a bean plant. In these streets I'm just a stone squashed down by crowds. I'm in a hole, and can't breathe. I prefer a fewity." Even her words were her own like this, "I'd like room to dance in. Life is a dance. I'd learn it in a field. I'd be a bird girl."

It was her father's secret ambition too: a cottage, a garden with things that grew silently into beauty, flowers, vegetables, plants; sweet laughing winds; the rush of living rain at midnight; water to drink from a deep, cool well instead of from metal pipes; a large, inviting horizon in which a man might lose himself; and—above all—birds, birds, birds. Both he and Joan loved birds.

"After a month in real private country—loose country, talking, dancing, running country—" She paused.

"Liquid, fluid, as it were," he put in, delighted.

"Yes, but deep and clear as a river when it avoids cities," she went on, "in country like that, do you know what'd happen to me, father, after a few months of waiting?"

"I know, but I can't quite say," he answered. "Tell me, child, for I'd love to hear your own description."

"I'd fly," was her answer. "Everything in me would fly about like a bird, picking up things, and all over the place without a plan—a fixed, heavy plan like a street or square in London here—and yet getting on all the time—getting further."

"And how would you learn, dear?"

"Birds," she laughed. "There's bird-teaching, I'm sure." She flitted across to another chair as she said it. She came closer to her father, who was listening with both ears, watching, drinking in something he didn't understand yet knew was true—somewhere.

"You're rather like one, d'you know," he smiled. "Like a bird, I mean."

She was perched on his knee before he knew it. Her small voice twittered on into his ear. Something about her sparkled, flashed, and vanished, and it reminded him of sunshine on swift-fluttering wings through the speckled shade of an orchard. She darted, whirred, and came to rest. He stroked her.

"Father, you know everything before I say it," she went on, her face shining with happiness that made her almost beautiful. "If I could only live like a bird, I could *live*. Here it's all a big, dirty cage." She flitted to the window, pointing to roofs and walls and chimney pots, black with grime. The same instant she was back again upon his knees. "To live like a bird is to be alive, I'm sure, I'm sure. I know it. It's all routing here."

Whether she meant rotten, routine, or living in a rut, he did not ask. He felt her meaning. He stroked her.

"There's a nest in a garden waiting for us somewhere," he said, living the dream with her in his heart. "And it's got an orchard, high deep grass, wild flowers, hills in the distance, with a tremendous sky where the winds go tearing about like the rush of an enormous bird, and real country people who drop in of an evening and say real things. All alive, I mean, and always moving. They say the country's stagnation. It isn't. It's a perfect rush—"

"Like a bird, of course," she put in, chirruping with pleasure. "Oh, father, think hard about that place, and we'll attract it nearer and nearer, till in the end we drop into it and grow like—"

"Beans," he laughed.

"Birds," she rippled, and hopped from his knee across the room, and was down the passage and out of sight before he could draw another breath.

There was something alert as lightning in the girl. She woke a similar thing in him, too. It had nothing to do with brain as intellect, or with reason, or with knowledge in the ordinary sense the world gives to these words. But it had to do, he dimly felt, with another bigger thing. What that bigger thing might be perplexed him. He was aware that it drove hugely past, alertness in such a massive thing conveying the impression of magnificent power. There was unspeakable grandeur in it somewhere, glory, dignity, beauty; yet this subtle alertness too, and this swift, protean sparkle. It was towering as a night of stars, alluring as a peeping wild flower, but prodigious also as though all the oceans flowed suddenly between narrow banks in a flood of clearest water, very rapid, terrifyingly deep. For a robe it wore the lustrous colouring of untold age. His imagery, when he tried to visualise, grew mixed. He called it Experience. But sometimes he told himself he knew its Christian name—its familiar, little, intimate nickname, which was Wisdom.

And so he was rather glad that Joan, like himself, was but half educated; that she was backward, and that he knew only the outsides of books. For facts, he vaguely felt, might come between them and this august yet precious thing they knew together. Birds could teach it, but Ornithology hid it.

Lately, however, as his wife divined, he *had* been dipping in between the covers of the goods he travelled in. Caught by the bait of several drugging titles, he had nibbled—in the train, in waiting-rooms, in the "parlours" of commercial hotels where he put up for the night. He had found names and descriptions of various things, but they were the names and descriptions given by others to their own sensations. The ordered classification merely developed snap-shots. He recognised photographs of dead things that *he* had always known alive. The names made stationary what for him had danced with incessant movement. Only he did not realise this until he saw the photographs. The alleged accuracy of a photograph was a shouting, insolent falsehood, pretending that what was alive was dead, that what rushed was stationary. Dogs and savages cannot recognise the photographs of their masters. The resemblance has to be taught. Everything flows, his shilling Heraclitus told him. He had always known it. Joan lived it. Birds taught it. To classify is to photograph—a prevarication. To publish a snap-shot of a jumping horse is to teach what is not true. To boast about it is to glory shamelessly in ignorance. The sole value of names, of classification, of photographing lay in stopping life for an instant so that its flow might be realised—as a momentary stage in an incessant process. And he looked at a group of acquaintances his wife had "Kodaked" ten days ago, and realised with delight how they all had rushed away, torn on ahead, lived, since she had told that lie in black and white about them.

Joan, catching him in the act of destroying it, had said, "I know why you're doing that, father."

"Why?" he asked, half ashamed and half surprised.

"Because you don't want to stop them," was her answer, "and because it wasn't fair of mother to catch them in the act like that."

And, as he stared at her curious peeping face, she came quickly up to him, saying passionately, imploringly:

"Oh, *do* let's get into the country soon, and live along with it, and grow and know things. I feel so stuck still here, and always caught-in-the-act like that photo. It's so dead. The streets are all nailed down on to the ground. In the country they run about—"

He interrupted her on purpose.

"But in a city life is supposed to be much richer than in the country," he said. "You know that?"

"It goes round and round like a circle, though; it doesn't go *on.* I'm living other people's lives here. I want to live my own. Everybody here lives the same thing over and over again till they get so hot they get ill. I want to be cool and naked like a fern. Here I'm being photographed all day long. Oh, father, I'm so tired of it. Do let's go soon and live hoppily like the birds."

"You mean happily?" he asked, laughing with her.

"It's the same thing," she laughed back, "it's like wings or running water.

> Flow, fly, flow,
> Wherever I am, I *go;*
> Live on the run,
> Like a bird—it's fun,
> Flow, fly, flow!"

and was dancing to and fro over the carpet, when the door opened and in came her brother Tom.

He looked surprised, ashamed, then vexed. It was Saturday afternoon. He had been six months now in the office.

"I've brought Mr. Halliday with me," he said, "to have tea. We've just been to a matinée at the Coliseum. Joan, this is Mr. Halliday, our junior clerk. My sister, Harold."

Joan instantly looked gauche and ugly. She shook hands with a speckled youth, whose shy want of manners did not prevent his eyeing her all over. He sat down beside his friend, talking of the singing, dancing, juggling, and so on they had witnessed. All the time he talked *at* something else in her. But she hid it away as cleverly as a bird hides its nest. The callow youth, without realising it, was hunting for a nest. In the country he might have found it. He would have been sunburned, for one thing, instead of speckled. The wind, the rain, the starlight would have guided him. His natural instinct would have flowed out in a dance of spontaneous running movement. Here, however, it seemed rigid, ugly, diseased. He was living the life of others.

"You were dancing just as we came in," said Mr. Halliday. "Does that line of things attract you? You are going on the stage, perhaps?"

Joan looked past him out of the window, and saw the swallows flashing about the sky.

"I can dance," she replied, "quite wonderfully, but not on a stage."

"But you'd be a great success, I think, from what I saw," opined the callow junior clerk. And somehow he said it falsely,—unpleasantly.

She didn't flush, she didn't stammer, at first she didn't answer even. She watched the swallows a moment, as though she had not heard him.

"You stare, you don't watch and enjoy," she said suddenly, turning upon him, "and an audience like that . . . !" She stopped, got up from her chair, put her head out of the open window, and spat into the street. When she turned back, she saw that her mother had come into the room and was leading the others into the dining-room for tea. Her father's face wore a singular expression—it seemed, of exultation. Tom, black as a thunder-cloud, waited for her.

"You're nothing but a little barbarian," he said angrily. The life of others he led had been sorely wounded. "I can never bring Mr. Halliday here again. You're simply not a lady."

"I'm a bird," she laughed in his face. "And you men can never understand that, because no man has a bird in him, but only a creepy, crawly animal. We go on two legs, you on four."

"I'm ashamed of you, Joan. You're nothing but a savage." He snapped at her. He could have struck her. His face was flushed, but his neck thin, scraggy, white. "In the City we—" he began with a clown's dignity. "Live like rats in a drain," she interrupted quickly, perched a moment in front of his face. "You don't breathe or dance. Tom," she added with a gesture of her arms like flapping wings, "if you were alive, you'd be—a mole. But you're not. You're a lot of other people. You're a herd—always enclosed and always feeding."

She danced down the corridor and into her room, locked the door, slipped out of some tight clothing, and began to sing her bird-song of incessant movement:

"Flow! Fly! Flow!
Wherever I *am* I *go;*
I live on the run
Like the birds—it's fun
Flow, fly, flow . . ."

She sang it to a tiny, uneven, twittering melody that was made up of half notes. It went on and on, repeating itself without end. It seemed to have no real end at all.

III

"Oh, she's all in the air," people said. And it was truer than they knew. She had an affinity with all that flew. This bird-idea was in her heart and blood. Whatever flew, whatever rose above the ground, whatever passed swiftly, suddenly from place to place, without deliberation, without calculation, without weighing risk and profit—this appealed to her. Yet there must be steadiness in it somewhere, too. It must get somewhere. A swallow or a butterfly she approved, but not a bat. The latter, for all its darting swiftness, was a sham; it was an earth-crawler really, frightened into ridiculous movement by finding itself aloft like a blown leaf; like a flying fish, it was wrong and out of place. But the former were perfect. They were ideal. They were almost spirits.

And when her father said he was glad she was half educated, he only meant glad that she had left school and teachers before her butterfly mind had become a rigid, accurate, mechanical thing. She might play with books as he himself did, fluttering over the covers, smelling their perfume, glancing at sentences and chapter headings, at indices even, but she must not build nests in them. A book, like a photograph, was an evillish thing that nailed a flowing thing into a fixed pattern. In the author's mind an idea was true, but when he had put it down in black and white he had put down only a snap-shot of it, the idea was already far away; when printed it was merely the pattern of its coffin that the reader saw.

"Not poetry-books," Joan qualified this, "because poetry runs clean off the page. It's alive and wingy. It sings my bird-song—

> Flow, fly, flow,
> Wherever I *am*—I *go*."

She had this unerring instinct for the bird in everything, the quality that flashes, darts, is gone before it can be killed by capture. A bird is everywhere and nowhere. It's all over the place at once. Look at it, and it's no longer there. Listen to it, and it's gone. Touch it, and you catch a sunbeam that warms the hand but loses half its beauty. Catch it—and it's dead. But no one ever caught a swallow or a butterfly naturally on the wing. Even the eye, the mind, the following thought grows dizzy in the effort.

For the cow in the field she had no song. "Wherever I am, I stay," was without a tune of its own. A cow couldn't leave the ground. She wanted something with incessant movement that could touch the earth, yet leave it at will. Wings and water could. Birds and rain both flew. Half the time a river (the only real water for her) flowed over the earth, without stopping on it, and half the time it was a cloud in the sky, yet never lived there. "Flow, fly, flow; wherever I am, I go,"—this was the little song of life and change and movement that came out of her curious heart and. mind. "Live on the run, like a bird, that's fun!"

She applied her principle unconsciously to people, too. Few men had the bird in them except her father. Mother was a badger, half the time out of sight below the earth. She felt respect, but no genuine love, for mother.

"A whale or a badger, I really don't know which," she said. "That's mother."

"Joan, I cannot allow you to speak in that way of your parent and my wife." The sentence was unreal. He chose it deliberately, as it seemed, from some book or other. It was sparklingly true, what she said, only it could not be said. "You were born out of mother, and so must think her holy."

"I only meant that she is not birdy," was the answer, "and that she likes fat, salt water, or sticky earth. I mean that I never see her on the surface much, and never for an instant *above* it. A fish is all right, but not a half-and-half thing."

"She built your nest for you. She taught you how to fly. Remember that." He lit his pipe to hide the laughter that would bubble up.

"But she never flew with me, Father—as you do," Joan replied triumphantly. "Besides, you know, I *like* whales and badgers. I only say they're not birds."

She paused, stared hard at him a moment, and then, with anxiety in her tone, she added: "And you said that as if some one had taught it you, Father. Some one's put bird-lime near you—some book, I suspect."

"Grammar's all right enough in its way," he told her hurriedly (meaning that there were correct and incorrect ways of saying a thing), and so the little matter was nicely settled up, and they flew on to other things as their way invariably was. But, after that, whenever mother was in the room, they thought of something under ground or under water that emerged for a brief moment to stare at them and wonder (heavens!) how they lived. They wondered how (on earth!) she lived. They were in different worlds.

For a long time now, Arthur Minns, "travelling" in tabloid knowledge, had been absorbing what is called the Spirit of the Age. On the paper wrappers of his books—chiefly Knowledge Primers—were printed neat and striking epitomes of the contents. Written by expert minds, these epitomes were admirable brief statements. There was no room for argument. They merely gave the entire book in a few short sentences that hit the mind—and stayed in it. They left the impression that the problem was proved, though actually it was merely stated. Hundreds of those statements he had read, until they flowed like a single sentence through his consciousness, each *résumé* a word, as it were, in the phrase describing the knowledge—or at least the tendencies—of the day. Minns was thus a concise phrase-book, who taught the grammar of the twentieth century. For his Firm, alert and enterprising, had the gift of scenting a given tendency before it was understood by the mass—while still "in the air," that is—yet while the mass still wanted to know about it; then, of choosing the writer who could crystallise it in simple language that made the man in the street feel at home and up to date. The What's in the Air To-day Publishing Co. was well named; it had the bird quality. These Picturesque Knowledge Primers sold like wildfire. They purveyed knowledge in tabloid form and advertised the hungry public into nourishment. The latest thing in politics or in diseases, in painting or in flying, in feminism or call-of-the-wild, in music, scouting, cubism, futurism, feeding, dancing, clothing, ancient philosophy re-dressed, or modern pulpit pretending to be neo—everything that thrills the public to-day, from pageantry and Dalcroze to higher-thought and psychics, they touched with clever condensing accuracy of aim, and grew fat upon the proceeds. The stream of little books flowed forth, written by birds, distributed in flocks, scattered broadcast like seed in a wind, each picked up eagerly and discarded for the next—winged knowledge in sparrow doses. The Managing Director, Fox

Martin, senior (*né* Max Levi), was a genius in his way, sure as a hawk, clairvoyant as a raven. His Bergson sold as well as his Exercises for the Bedroom—because he chose the writer. He hovered, swooped, struck—and the primer was caught and issued in its thousands. His advertising was consummate, for it convinced the ordinary man he *ought* to know that particular thing-in-the-air-to-day just as he ought to wear a high collar with his evening clothes or a slit in his coat behind with flannels. He aimed at the men, just as the machine-made novel aims at the women.

Minns, *the* traveller *facile princeps,* for this kind of goods, knew, therefore, everything that was "in-the-air-to-day," without knowing in the least why it was to be believed, or what the arguments were. And yet he knew that he was right. He knew things as a bird does, gathering them on every wind, and shaping his inner life swiftly, unburdened by reasoning calculation built on facts. Thus, useless in debate; he was amazing in short conversation. He was a walking Index.

And the feeling in him that everything flowed and nothing was stationary was strong. He dealt in shooting ideas, not in dead, photographic detail. He flashed from one subject to another; flowed through all categories, ancient and modern; skimmed the cream off modern tendencies and swept above the knowledge of the day with a bird's-eye view, unburdened by fact or argument.

Of late, moreover, he had enjoyed these curious upside-down and inside-out experiences, because he had filled himself to the saturation point, and become, as it were, stationary. He could hold no more without—a change. He stopped. He took a snap-shot photograph of himself, realised that he existed as a separate, vital entity, and thenceforward watched himself expectantly to see what the change was going to be. Hitherto he had been mechanical, whereas now he was an engine capable of self-direction—an engine stoked to the brim. When the air is at the saturation point, the tiniest additional percentage of moisture causes rain to fall. It's the final straw that makes the camel sit down and consider the next step. So with Arthur Minns. He was ready to discharge. And it was this chance remark of his under-ground wife, asking who the widow *was* instead of what she is, that took the photograph and made him say "I am." All he had read was included in the affirmation. The epitomes had become part of his consciousness. Like the weary camel, like the moisture tired of balancing in the air, he wanted to sit down now and consider. His daughter's longing for the country was his, too.

At dinner that night in a West End restaurant near Piccadilly Circus he broached the subject and listened patiently to his wife's objections.

"What's the good, even if we had the means, Artie? Burying ourselves like that."

Joan hopped, as it were. She recognised her mother's instinctive dread that she would go under ground or under water and never come up again.

"None of the nice people, the county families, would call. There'd only be the vicar, and the local doctor, or p'raps a gentleman farmer or two. We know much better class in town, and there's always chances of getting to know better still. Besides, who'd there be for Joan? The girl wouldn't have a look in, simply. And the winters are so sloppy in a country cottage. Think of the Sundays. And the chickens and pigs I really couldn't ever abide, and howling winds at night, and owls in the eaves, and rats in the attics. You see, we'd have no standing at all."

"But just a week-end cottage, mother," Joan put in, "just a place of flowers and orchards and a little stream to flit down to over-night, so to say—*that,* now, you'd like, wouldn't you?"

"Oh, that's different," she said more brightly, "only that's not what father means. He means a place to live in altogether. The week-end idea is right enough. That's what everybody does who can afford to. Lady Spears has a bungalow on the Thames. But that means more money than we shall ever see, and even for that you want to keep a motor or a horse and dog-cart, or a little steam launch to get about in. Then the handy places are very expensive, and we couldn't go very far because of Tom. Tom could come down and bring his friends if it was near enough."

"Grandfather might give us a little nest cheap," suggested Joan. She didn't "see" Tom in the cottage.

But mother turned up her nose as she sipped her glass of Asti Spumante that accompanied the west end dinner by way of champagne. She didn't approve of Essex.

"Nobody lives there," she said. "There's no society. Your grandfather only stays there because his father did before him, and there's the business to keep going. If we ever did such a thing as to move to the country, it'd have to be the Surrey pinewoods or the Thames."

She looked across the table questioningly at her husband. The music played rag-time. The waiters bustled. There was movement and excitement in the air about them. Arthur looked quite distinguished in his evening dress, and she felt proud and distinguished herself. She only wished he were a publisher. Still, no one need feel ashamed of being interested in the book line. Literature was not a trade.

"Some place, yes, where the country's really alive," he agreed. "I don't want to vegetate any more than you do, dear, I can assure you."

"Nor I, mother," laughed Joan. "I simply want to fly about all the time."

"Johanna," was the reply, half reproachfully, "you always talk as if we kept you in a cage at home. The more you fly the better we like it; I only say choose places worth flying to—"

Her husband interrupted abruptly.

"It was nothing but a little dream of my own, really," he said lightly. "A castle in the air, an airy adventure, a flash of country in the brain." He laughed and called the waiter.

"Black, white or Turkish?" he asked his wife. "And what liqueur, dear?"

"Turkish and Grand Marnier," was the prompt reply, and she would have said "fine champagne," only felt uncertain how "fine" should be pronounced. They sipped their coffee and talked of other things. It was no good, this speculative talk, it was too much in the air. The key of mother's mind was always: Who *was* she? She lived underground, using the worn old narrow routes. Joan and her father made their own pathways in the trackless medium of the air. During the remainder of the evening they kept to the earth beside mother.

That night in the pokey flat, after the girl had gone to bed, Mrs. Minns observed to her husband:

"Do you know, Artie, I think a little change would do her a lot of good. She's getting restless here, and seems to take to nobody. Why not take her with you sometimes on your literary trips?"

This was her name for his journeys to provincial booksellers when soliciting orders for his employer's wares, or when occasionally he was sent to interview one of the Primer writers upon some detail of length, material, or date of completion.

"If we could afford it," he replied.

"Father might help," she said, showing that she had considered the matter already. "It would be good for her—educational, I mean."

Her husband agreed, and they fell asleep on that agreement.

A few days later a reply was received from Mrs. Minns' father, the corn-chandler in Essex, enclosing a cheque for £20 "as a starter." The parents were delighted. Joan preened her wings and began at once her short flying journeys about the country with her father. He avoided the Commercial Traveller Hotels and took her to little Inns, where they were very cosy together. They went from Northumberland to Cornwall, and from Norfolk to the edge of Wales. She acquired a bird's-eye knowledge of the map of England. These short trips gave her somehow the general "feel" of the various counties, each with its different "note," in much the same way as the Primers gave her father his surface impression of England's mental condition. She noticed and remembered the living arteries which are rivers, he the streams of thought and theory which are tendencies. The two maps were shown and explained, and each was wonderfully alert in understanding the other's meaning. The girl drank in her father's knowledge, while he in his turn "felt" the country as a dancing sheet beneath them, flowing, liquid, alive. A new language grew into existence between them, a kind of shorthand, almost a symbol language—they realised it first when talking of their journeys at the dinner table, and Mrs. Minns looked puzzled. Her face betrayed an odd anxiety; she asked perplexed questions, looking *up* at them as a badger might look up at wheeling pigeons from the opening of its hole.

Mentally she turned tail and dived out of sight below ground, where, with her feet on solid earth, her back and sides touching material that did not yield, she felt more at home, the darkness comforting and safe.

Joan and her husband flew too near the sun. It dazzled her. They could have talked for hours without her catching the drift, only they were far too fond of her to do so. They resented going underground with her, but they came down and settled on earth, folded their wings, used words instead of unintelligible chirrupings, and chatted with her through the opening of the hole.

One afternoon, then, in Chester, they received a telegram that, for a moment, stopped the flow of things, though immediately afterwards the rush went on with greater impetus than ever.

"Father passed away return at once funeral to-morrow Epping."

And the family found itself with a solid little income of its own, free to fly and settle where it would. The London nest became impossible.

A Barmecide Feast

He realised that he was asleep—sure sign that he was just about to wake; and something whispered that it was very early, and that it would be far better if he could prevent waking. For a long time he made a half-hearted effort, craving a continuation of the delicious state of unconsciousness. But it lay beyond his powers. He moved; he turned over in bed, yet still keeping his eyes tightly shut. "I'm waking," he whispered to himself. "What a bore!" The springs in his eyelids were released. The room, he saw, was tinged with that thin, clear light which means very early morning, and he gave up the struggle. "Hang this early waking! I shall be tired all day now!" And he noticed with disgust the candle and pillow-book, left hours ago in the comforting darkness. He lay back, staring angrily at the white ceiling. But nothing banishes sleep so effectively as anger. Jones, disgruntled and annoyed, sat up in bed at two o'clock in the morning, in the little Sussex cottage where he was spending the weekend with a married cousin of slight acquaintance, and remembered next that even in his sleep there was something that had bothered him. His dreams, now forgotten, had been anxious, troubled, searching. What was it? His mind sent scurrying messengers. Memory became active. He was painfully wide awake now. Ah! He had found it. The night before—it seemed so long ago, so far away—a plan had been arranged: a bicycling trip across the Downs, himself as leader; the children had been sent early to bed on purpose, and he had fallen asleep, thinking hard about the route, yet uncertain of it. He dared not fail, for the children thought him marvellous. And the search had been continued in his dreams, endlessly, in vain. He had failed utterly; the children would never believe in him again. There was still a sinking sensation at his heart, a kind of gnawing that craved for satisfaction. . . . And then, suddenly, he realised the truth: that he was hungry! Accustomed to late dinners in London, the light country supper in the cottage at seven o'clock had damaged interior routine, and his interior had wakened him at 2 A.M. to inform him of the fact. Jones felt very empty indeed.

The next minute he stood in the middle of the room, his mind holding but a single thought—Larder. His interior and the cottage larder were two points in space, and he sought the straight line between them. Behind this flickered lighter pictures, which explained themselves without effort on his part, as he remembered the wife's apology that the butcher in this isolated region often failed them, that F.H.B. (family hold back) had been mentioned at the table, and that his two helpings of bread-and-butter pudding, so stuffing at the moment, could not possibly be expected to satisfy for long. But it was the geographical situation of the larder, what he might find there, and how awkward it would be if he were discovered on the prowl—it was this that occupied his thought as, in slippers and pyjamas, he cautiously opened his door and peered forth into the silent emptiness of the outside world. His one terror was that he might see, or be seen by, his cousin's wife—his hostess. Why, exactly, he could not explain quite; but it would reflect on her housekeeping, for one thing; she would be so full of apologies, for another; and, for a third, she would load him with more than he wanted. She might even watch him eat, or catch him disappearing into his room with a plateful of assorted nourishment stolen from her larder. He felt guilty and ashamed the moment he opened his bedroom door and stole softly on tiptoe down the narrow corridor, that creaked beneath his tread as though each separate board was loose. He felt so light and empty that this surprised him; his weight, though small, seemed centred in his feet. The thick matting on the stairs was a great relief, and he crept safely past his hostess' door, astonished at the extraordinary silence everywhere. Husband and wife, both of heavy build, were born snorers, he would have said, yet no faintest sound was audible, and he pictured them now, sitting up in bed, disturbed by the creaking that he made—and listening. Distributing his weight carefully with one hand on the banisters and another on the wall, he next got past the maid's room, and the room where the children slept with the diminutive watch-dog, and successfully reached the ground floor, where the bricks of the hall struck chill through his thin Egyptian slippers. Those pointed yellow slippers, from a Cairo bazaar, looked painfully ludicrous, he realised, and the colour of his pyjamas was in shouting contrast. The whole house watched him with a grin. Everywhere was a silence of tombs and catacombs. Only a rustling of early wind against the black front door was audible. The dining-room and drawing-room stared suspiciously at his back; but already a certain carelessness was in him, for no one slept on this floor, and he could move with greater freedom. Would the larder door be locked? What would he find there? Should he take the food upstairs with him or—horrors! Was that whispering? The long, dark passage gaped before him, and at the further end, behind a door it seemed, came a faint sound of voices, subdued and cautious. There was a stealthy step. A latch rattled. He shrank against the wall, standing stock still. In the semi-gloom he might have been hidden but for those glaring yellow slippers, a size too large for him, and for the striped pyjamas, looking like a convict's. He waited, breathing only through his nose—trying, indeed, not to breathe at all.

Yes; the steps and voices were unmistakable. No thought of ghosts or burglars had yet entered his mind, and a voice, if any, should have come from overhead: "Who's there?" or "I'll fire unless you come out and show yourself"; but whispers and steps so close to him were an unexpected shock. For a moment he hardly knew what was best to do. He forgot his hunger altogether, and braced himself for action. It was quite plain that strangers had broken into the cottage, attracted by its extreme loneliness, and were at this very moment in larder or kitchen at the end of the passage, arranging their booty, perhaps just making ready to depart. And he remembered then that he had smelt flowers and grass and earth as he came down the staircase—sign that a door or window had been opened below—and that the air in the hall was uncommonly fresh and sweet. "There are two of them," Jones reflected, in this awkward moment of greatness which had been thrust upon him, "and I have no weapon, not even a poker!"

A door half-way down the passage opened softly, so close that the gush of warmer air reached his nostrils, and he knew it was the kitchen; while a voice, whispering to his companion, was just audible: "There's no one. It's all right. We might go upstairs now if you're—" The stealthy closing of the door smothered the rest of the sentence, but not before he had caught another sentence spoken simultaneously by the companion. Jones heard both. And the other was a man's voice, gruff and short and cautious: "What did you do with the knife? You had it last . . ." And, hearing it, Jones, in his unsheltering pyjamas, felt so helpless that his modicum of courage failed him. Hungry, cold, and weaponless, taken utterly by surprise, he felt in no condition to meet two desperate tramps at close quarters, one of them with a knife. He hurriedly, wildly, reviewed a dozen possibilities. It was a moment for clear, quick thinking and decisive action. Shouting was useless; there were no passers-by or policemen in the lonely country lane outside. Had there been a single burglar only he might have faced him, rousing the household at the same time by cries for help. But against two he could do nothing. And cold steel always filled him with peculiar terror. His mind flashed the only possible course—to dart upstairs and waken his cousin. His cousin was sure to have a pistol in his bedroom. And Jones was in the very act of turning to put his plan in execution when the door of the kitchen opened wide again. He had been too slow, too long reflecting. He was fairly caught. Two figures, he saw, were already in passage. They moved quickly and on tiptoe. They were within three feet of him. He knew a sharp moment of hysterical terror first before his courage—at heart he was no coward—came to help him.

"Arthur!" he yelled, at the top of his voice. "Arthur! There are burglars in the house. Quick! With the pistol—!" and flung himself at the same moment with violence against the still advancing figures. And to protect his body from the point of entering steel, he caught at the first thing handy he could find—the thick door-mat on which he stood. Holding it before him like a shield, still shouting far help as he charged, Jones hurled himself with reckless onslaught against—his hostess and her husband.

All three collapsed against the wall with a crash, then sprawled through the open door into the kitchen. The disentanglement was at first in silence, for the shock of bewildered astonishment was too great for speech. The breathless chorus of explanation, apology, unanswered questions, and questionable answers came next, pell-mell.

"I thought—I was sure—I heard a noise," prevaricated Jones, "and came down to see." The elucidation, all three, clothed not for daylight, standing upon the kitchen floor, lasted some time, for Jones stuck to his story so manfully that the burden of explanation was transferred to his host and hostess. It was resourceful, but not strictly honest, on his part. For the life of him, however, he could not find it in his heart to admit the truth.

Only a portion of the truth he told. "Of course, I thought you were burglars," he repeated. "I heard steps and voices, and something about a knife when you opened the door first to go upstairs—"

He looked his cousin straight in the eye, as a brave man should. It was left to his hostess to confess her soul, and her husband's, too, They looked so sheepish, standing there in the morning light without an adequate reason for being out of their bedroom together at such an hour. Jones had managed the situation admirably—for himself—in one way.

"The fact is, Mr. Jones," she said, then paused a moment: "we both woke up—"

"Yes," he helped her. She said it so awkwardly, almost guiltily, that he wondered what was coming.

"Feeling hungry," she concluded, with a little, shame-faced laugh, "dreadfully hungry—"

"And stole down to get something to eat," put in her husband, boldly filling in the pause.

"I'm frightfully sorry—so ashamed—we disturbed your sleep like this," she added, and then went softly upstairs again to see if the children had slept safely through the noise of battle.

Jones waited a little longer while his cousin, laughing over the adventure, put away the delicious eatables. But, somehow or other, he had not the courage to ask a single crumb. There was loaf and butter on the kitchen table, cake as well, but he did not touch them.

He put away the saw-toothed bread knife in the drawer his cousin opened, then followed him upstairs to bed again. But not to sleep. He ate nothing till nine o'clock, when he came down to breakfast, weary and unrefreshed, obliged to tell his story all over again with convincing detail for the children's benefit, joining in the laugh against himself, while he devoured the biggest breakfast of his life.

The Kiss of a Psychologist

There is a peculiar sense of exasperation in being accused of something you have not done when yet the look of the thing is hopelessly against you. That is to say, you have done it, only not in the way you stand accused of. A basis of hard fact is there, of course: you have been seen, heard, caught, but the rest is stupid misunderstanding, the stupider the more dangerous. Your heart knows its innocence, because in some way that a K.C. would ridicule or a police-sergeant ignore, you—your Self—had no part in it. *You* were elsewhere at the time. But the spiritual alibi is unconvincing, and the more you explain the deeper you stand committed. The wisest course is to own up and ask forgiveness. For a fact is a fact, and subtle explanation proves you not merely a villain, but a clever, obstinate, unrepentant villain into the bargain.

At first Jim Hardy was uncertain whether his wife had actually seen or not. He wondered, at least, how much she had seen. She was so deadly quiet. He felt awkward, foolish, yet innocent and wholly unashamed. She smiled brightly and continued to show the effusive joy of her home-coming. Yet, all the time, she *had* seen everything; only she kept the card with triumph up her sleeve, aware of the instinct to produce it later with overwhelming effect. Also, she was too proud and sweet and childish to admit at once, and the collapse of her happiness was too radical for her to realise it completely in that awful moment. She abhorred and despised jealousy, and was determined to feel none, above all not to betray that she felt it. Moreover, she held him in her power so utterly (alas!) that she could afford to wait: he was not the rock she had believed him to be, but common clay like other men. It was a devastating shock. But, contrariwise somehow, there was a fierce sweetness in the pain she felt, for their coming together again would be marvellous, the making-up scene delicious and adorable. "Later he'll tell me of his own accord—all, all, all—and beg forgiveness. The wretch!" And so she remained strong, magnanimous, and brave. She was very contained. But it was rather ghastly for them both. He advanced with the impetuous happiness of a boy to take her in his arms; and it was then, suddenly, that the assumed role of silent heroine deserted her in a flash, and her self-control all melted. Pain, anger, and bitter disappointment flamed in her young cheeks. "James," she said, freezingly, "I saw everything." And she drew herself up into an accusing statue of unrelenting marble. "Mabel," she added, glancing round, "has left the room. She is probably waiting for you in the hall." The trembling in her voice was stupid, but she could not prevent it. The stone statue attitude she managed admirably. She moved no single inch to meet him. "You had better go to her at once. I interrupted you—both." She gulped the tears down, but the blood rushed to her head and burned her eyes.

For a moment he knew something of what Dreyfus felt upon his Devil's Island. The fact that Mabel was a niece, and that he knew his wife was secretly jealous of her, tied his tongue. His foolish, impetuous mistake was obvious, but the pettiness of the truth dismayed him hopelessly. Then and there he could have strangled Mabel with a bootlace—gladly. For Mabel was less to him than the maid who did his room, whom he had hardly seen, and whose name he did not even know. Mabel had popped into the flat to greet the returning Mrs. Hardy, whom she loved. Jim found her in the drawing-room, ran up with joy and excitement in his heart, crying: "Isn't it splendid? Minnie will be back in half an hour! I've had a wire"—and the stupid thing had somehow happened. Mabel herself, bursting with great news of her own, looked radiant with happiness and adorably pretty—which made it worse. His heart, his thought, his body, none of him at all, in fact, was really in that boyish, impetuous embrace. He hugged her as he might have hugged a child, a dog, a kitten. His Self—only he could never prove it—was elsewhere: with his wife. He could have danced about the room, for his fortnight's loneliness was over, and Minnie was coming back "in half an hour." Instead, she came back that very minute, saw the embrace, heard the words (as she thought) "we've half an hour"—and experienced the first shock of shattering disillusion her young life had ever known. Mabel discreetly—neither of them actually saw her go—had slipped out of the room until the explanations were safely over.

He stopped, unable to find words at first, but still holding his arms out wide. Mrs. Hardy gazed at him speechlessly, tears rising behind the ice that glittered in her eyes. He saw them. He made a plunge to seize her bodily.

"You may keep your embraces for Mabel," she said, icily. "You know perfectly well, Jim—"

That "Jim," uttered inadvertently, was too much for her. Her voice failed her badly. She drew back from his arrested advance as though he were a leper, turning towards the window with a gulp of agony and anger. The traffic went by as if nothing had happened. She saw it with amazement. By rights all London should have looked different. The world was dark. The sun had set, yet London rolled on just the same as usual. The indifference, the cruelty of life appalled her.

He straightened himself and took a long, deep breath—a very audible breath indeed. "Minnie," he said, in a flat, dull voice, yet a shade of defiance in it somewhere, "I admit it. I did kiss Mabel. But it was really you I kissed. I was simply mad with joy at your return. I couldn't contain myself."

She made a curious movement with her hand by the window, but she did not turn. He paused, trying wildly to interpret the gesture, to guess what its significance might be.

"Can't you *understand?"* he continued, moving cautiously six inches nearer. Then, as she still said nothing and made no movement, he plunged recklessly among the sentences that filled his mind, the more confidently because he was telling the simple, though curious, truth. "It was pure excitement. I could have kissed anything in sight—the cook, the postman, the boy who brought your telegram. My emotion *had* to find some outlet. Ask any psychologist, and he'll tell you. That kiss was really an enormous compliment to you. It was simply a—"

"James," Mrs. Hardy stopped him coldly—the cold horribly assumed to hide the fiery pain within—"you kissed her on the lips. I saw it. And you expected me by a later train"—here she turned slowly round—"for I heard you say so. It was"—she gulped dreadfully over the abominable word she hardly understood—"an assignation."

"Minnie!" he gasped, hopelessly. "But Minnie—!"

"And I, in my blind, big love, came home early on purpose to surprise you. I—did—surprise—you!" They stared at each other in silence for ten seconds. "On the lips," Mrs. Hardy repeated, in a lifeless voice.

"Because her beastly lips came first," he cried, "and she stuck 'em up into my face. I wasn't looking for them. I'd just as soon have kissed her knuckles or—the coffee-pot—or the poker—or any old thing that happened to be about—"

He stopped dead as he saw the expression in her face. She simply did not believe him. There was sweetness, patience, forgiveness, and—contempt, but utter disbelief. It was awful. They had been married six months. This meant the destruction of two young, happy lives. His head began to spin. He was very much of a boy. "God bless you, sweetheart," he cried, passionately, flinging out his arms towards her in despair, "I tell you before heaven it was merely the boy in me that kissed her. It was my high spirits for you. I was so wild with joy—*for you.* And, besides, she came in really to announce—" And again he stuck, realising his grave predicament from the look in his wife's gleaming eyes. She would simply never believe him again if he went on with these explanations, and yet he must go on because they were the truth. He understood that resigned expression in her suffering face, and his mind dashed, headlong for another chance of safety. "And, do remember one thing, Minnie: Mabel is nothing but a niece—"

"*My* niece," was the frigid rejoinder, like a steel trap closing on his heart. "Mabel is no relation to you at all. And, what's more, James, you know perfectly well that the wretched girl's in love with you into the bargain. So there!" And she stamped her foot as she produced this final proof with an air of triumph that she hated. "The pair of you! Bah!" she added, amid signs of general collapse. "And to think that I can't go away for a week without—without—" The sentence died away among ominous sounds.

"Minnie," he asked, gravely, sadly, finally, as it were, "have you no trust in me at all? Mabel came here, I tell you, to—"

"Until now I had," she interrupted, tears swimming in her eyes and her lips trembling. "You can hardly expect me to doubt my own senses. And I don't want to hear what Mabel came here for. It's all the same to me. She came to see you, and you can never explain away *that!*"

That he sought to justify himself was utterly fatal in her eyes. He passed his hand wearily across his forehead, true anguish in his heart. He turned towards the door, thinking it best perhaps to leave her for a little to think it over. But his love prevented that. Besides, Mabel was in the hall. He scorned, too, the smallest prevarication. Unworldly-wise, not clever, boyish to the end, he stuck to the simple truth. He did not realise sufficiently that he was dealing with a jealous woman. Making no attempt this time to come nearer to her, he sank into a chair and heaved a long, big sigh.

"Minnie, sit down a moment and listen to me," he said, solemnly, so solemnly, indeed, that she obeyed him. She also sighed. The full confession was now to come, she thought, with a pang of deadly hopelessness.

"You're no psychologist, bless your little precious heart," he began, steadily, "or you would understand at once what it is I'm saying, and would just laugh and forgive. I can only tell you, darling, there's nothing, *nothing* really to forgive at all. A man only acts—a man is only guilty, where his consciousness acts. And his consciousness may be miles away from a given act at a given moment. In a moment's anger against some one who has injured me I might seize the kitten and squeeze it till it died, and my real sin would be against my enemy, and not against the innocent kitten. I was an ass—a hopeless, idiotic ass—to let—I mean, to kiss the girl—"

"Sly, deceitful minx!"

"But, upon my soul, if it had been the charwoman, I'd have—well, I'd have *felt* like hugging her just the same. My thoughts, my feelings, my consciousness, don't you see, were all for you, and for you alone." And he rose, half impulsively, to go across to her, perhaps to take her in his arms. He did not do so, however. There was still something in her face that stopped him. She was melting a little, but had not melted yet to the point where she could touch him. Her pride was still desperately wounded. Once that was healed, touch could bring the final cure, but not before. "It was an unconscious, a purely vicarious kiss," he continued, firmly. "I tell you there was nothing in it. My arms were hungry for you and for you only. It's the first time, Minnie, the very first time during the whole fortnight you've left me lonely that I've set eyes on the creature."

Mrs. Hardy visibly softened. That was a provable statement. She loved his saying "creature." "Then, what brought her here at all?" she asked, in a low voice, not raising her eyes from the ground. "How did she know I was coming back to-day? Who told her?"

"That's just what I've been trying to make you listen to all this time," he replied, with another sigh. "Mabel telephoned—"

"Indeed!"

"—to the cook. I was out. I went to get stalls for to-night—your favourite opera—and to order lilies of the valley round the corner—your favourite flower. I was simply intoxicated into this extravagance by the idea of your return. I came back, full of happiness, and found Mabel in the room. I fairly bubbled over. My consciousness was no more in that kiss than—than in the drunken man who embraces a policeman in the street." He fumbled in his grammar, snatching at the first available simile. Also, in his confidence, sure of his own innocence, he made the mistake of over-statement.

"But the drunken man *does* like the policeman—at the moment," said his wife, coldly, betraying pathetically her desire to believe and understand.

"Well, then," he answered, desperately but very calmly, "no more than in a child who excitedly hugs a dog because it's been allowed to sit up half an hour longer than usual."

"The child does love the dog. It wouldn't hug the poker, would it?"

"It would," he said, with decision, "if there was nothing else handy about. It'd hug a poker or a cushion or anything that was close enough." He felt obliged to stick to his simile. They stared hard into each other's eyes for nearly half a minute. "Minnie," he went on, with the gravity of ultimate truth in voice and eyes and manner, "this one thing you shall and must believe of me: that, since we married, I have neither kissed nor wanted to kiss a single living thing but you. And that's the truth."

He paused to note the effect of this. Surely an intuitive woman, he felt, must recognise truth when she hears it. A sign of wavering in her severe and uncompromising expression encouraged him. The look of injury passed a little. "And, as I said before," he continued, with authority, "if you were a psychologist, darling, just the least little bit of a psychologist—"

"But what I don't understand, Jim," she interrupted him, with a sudden return of distrust and agony in her face again, "is why Mabel came to the flat at all. Why did she come at all? Can you tell me that?"

"I've been trying to for ever so long, but you wouldn't let me," he cried. "Mabel came in to announce her engagement to Frank. They're to be married in six weeks. She was wild with joy and excitement, simply bubbling over, and she came in to tell you—"

"And to kiss anything in sight—anything that was close enough to reach, I suppose—"

How much longer the explanation might have lasted it is impossible to say, for sentences and words are bound to flow until the emotion producing them has subsided. Jim Hardy, however, could really think of nothing more to say. He simply got up and went over to her. She, too, got up. She tried to leave the room. She would gladly have spun out the scene a little longer—though not much longer. But she never reached the door. She made no real resistance, and as he felt her sink into his arms it seemed to him he was ready to confess anything in the world if she wanted it.

"God bless you for one thing," he said, softly.

"And that is?" she asked, looking up into his face above her.

"That you didn't say you were sorry you ever married me," he laughed.

"You see, Jim, I'm no psychologist," she whispered, "but just a woman who loves. But next time I go away I'll fill your room with pokers and cushions and little dogs, unless you'd rather have a policeman or a kitten!"

"Better not go away at all," he smiled, as they went out into the hall and saw the opera tickets and the flowers on the table. "It's cheaper, as well as safer."

H. S. H.

In the mountain Club Hut, to which he had escaped after weeks of gaiety in the capital, Delane, young travelling Englishman, sat alone, and listened to the wind that beat the pines with violence. The firelight danced over the bare stone floor and raftered ceiling, giving the room an air of movement, and though the solid walls held steady against the wild spring hurricane, the cannonading of the wind seemed to threaten the foundations. For the mountain shook, the forest roared, and the shadows had a way of running everywhere as though the little building trembled. Delane watched and listened. He piled the logs on. From time to time he glanced nervously over his shoulder, restless, half uneasy, as a burst of spray from the branches dashed against the window, or a gust of unusual vehemence shook the door. Over-wearied with his long day's climb among impossible conditions, he now realised, in this mountain refuge, his utter loneliness; for his mind gave birth to that unwelcome symptom of true loneliness—that he was not, after all, alone. Continually he heard steps and voices in the storm. Another wanderer, another climber out of season like himself, would presently arrive, and sleep was out of the question until first he heard that knocking on the door. Almost—he expected some one.

He went for the tenth time to the little window. He peered forth into the thick darkness of the dropping night, shading his eyes against the streaming pane to screen the firelight in an attempt to see if another climber—perhaps a climber in distress—were visible. The surroundings were desolate and savage, well named the Devil's Saddle. Black-faced precipices, streaked with melting snow, rose towering to the north, where the heights were hidden in seas of vapour; waterfalls poured into abysses on two sides; a wall of impenetrable forest pressed up from the south; and the dangerous ridge he had climbed all day slid off wickedly into a sky of surging cloud. But no human figure was, of course, distinguishable, for both the lateness of the hour and the elemental fury of the night rendered it most unlikely. He turned away with a start, as the tempest delivered a blow with massive impact against his very face. Then, clearing the remnants of his frugal supper from the table, he hung his soaking clothes at a new angle before the fire, made sure the door was fastened on the inside, climbed into the bunk where white pillows and thick Austrian blankets looked so inviting, and prepared finally for sleep.

"I must be over-tired," he sighed, after half an hour's weary tossing, and went back to make up the sinking fire. Wood is plentiful in these climbers' huts; he heaped it on. But this time he lit the little oil lamp as well, realising—though unwilling to acknowledge it—that it was not over-fatigue that banished sleep, but this unwelcome sense of expecting some one, of being not quite alone. For the feeling persisted and increased. He drew the wooden bench close up to the fire, turned the lamp as high as it would go, and wished unaccountably for the morning. Light was a very pleasant thing; and darkness now, for the first time since childhood, troubled him. It was outside; but it might so easily come in and swamp, obliterate, extinguish. The darkness seemed a positive thing. Already, somehow, it was established in his mind—this sense of enormous, aggressive darkness that veiled an undesirable hint of personality. Some shadow from the peaks or from the forest, immense and threatening, pervaded all his thought. "This can't be entirely nerves," he whispered to himself. "I'm not so tired as all that!" And he made the fire roar. He shivered and drew closer to the blaze. "I'm out of condition; that's part of it," he realised, and remembered with loathing the weeks of luxurious indulgence just behind him.

For Delane had rather wasted his year of educational travel. Straight from Oxford, and well supplied with money, he had first saturated his mind in the latest Continental thought—the science of France, the metaphysics and philosophy of Germany—and had then been caught aside by the gaiety of capitals where the lights are not turned out at midnight by a Sunday School police. He had been surfeited, physically, emotionally, and intellectually, till his mind and body longed hungrily for simple living again and simple teaching—above all, the latter. The Road of Excess leads to the Palace of Wisdom—for certain temperaments (as Blake forgot to add), of which Delane was one. For there was stuff in the youth, and the reaction had set in with violent abruptness. His system rebelled. He cut loose energetically from all soft delights, and craved for severity, pure air, solitude, and hardship. Clean and simple conditions he must have without delay, and the tonic of physical battling. It was too early in the year to climb seriously, for the snow was still dangerous and the weather wild, but he had chosen this most isolated of all the mountain huts in order to make sure of solitude, and had come, without guide or companion, for a week's strenuous life in wild surroundings, and to take stock of himself with a view to full recovery.

And all day long as he climbed the desolate, unsafe ridge, his mind—good, wholesome, natural symptom—had reverted to his childhood days, to the solid worldly wisdom of his church-going father, and to the early teaching (oh, how sweet and refreshing in its literal spirit!) at his mother's knee. Now, as he watched the blazing logs, it came back to him again with redoubled force; the simple, precious, old-world stories of heaven and hell, of a paternal Deity, and of a daring, subtle, personal devil—

The interruption to his thoughts came with startling suddenness, as the roaring night descended against the windows with a thundering violence that shook the walls and sucked the flame half-way up the wide stone chimney. The oil lamp flickered and went out. Darkness invaded the room for a second, and Delane sprang from his bench, thinking the wet snow had loosened far above and was about to sweep the hut into the depths. And he was still standing, trembling and uncertain, in the middle of the room, when a deep and sighing hush followed sharp upon the elemental outburst, and in the hush, like a whisper after thunder, he heard a curious steady sound that, at first, he thought must be a footstep by the door. It was then instantly repeated. But it was not a step. It was some one knocking on the heavy oaken panels—a firm, authoritative sound, as though the new arrival had the right to enter and was already impatient at the delay.

The Englishman recovered himself instantly, realising with keen relief the new arrival—at last.

"Another climber like myself, of course," he said, "or perhaps the man who comes to prepare the hut for others. The season has begun." And he went over quickly, without a further qualm, to unbolt the door.

"Forgive!" he exclaimed in German, as he threw it wide, "I was half asleep before the fire. It is a terrible night. Come in to food and shelter, for both are here, and you shall share such supper as I possess."

And a tall, cloaked figure passed him swiftly with a gust of angry wind from the impenetrable blackness of the world beyond. On the threshold, for a second, his outline stood full in the blaze of firelight with the sheet of darkness behind it, stately, erect, commanding, his cloak torn fiercely by the wind, but the face hidden by a low-brimmed hat; and an instant later the door shut with resounding clamour upon the hurricane, and the two men turned to confront one another in the little room.

Delane then realised two things sharply, both of them fleeting impressions, but acutely vivid: First, that the outside darkness seemed to have entered and established itself between him and the new arrival; and, secondly, that the stranger's face was difficult to focus for clear sight, although the covering hat was now removed. There was a blur upon it somewhere. And this the Englishman ascribed partly to the flickering effect of firelight, and partly to the lightning glare of the man's masterful and terrific eyes, which made his own sight waver in some curious fashion as he gazed upon him. These impressions, however, were but momentary and passing, due doubtless to the condition of his nerves and to the semi-shock of the dramatic, even theatrical entrance. Delane's senses, in this wild setting, were guilty of exaggeration. For now, while helping the man remove his cloak, speaking naturally of shelter, food, and the savage weather, he lost this first distortion and his mind recovered sane proportion. The stranger, after all, though striking, was not of appearance so uncommon as to cause alarm; the light and the low doorway had touched his stature with illusion. He dwindled. And the great eyes, upon calmer subsequent inspection, lost their original fierce lightning. The entering darkness, moreover, was but an effect of the upheaving night behind him as he strode across the threshold. The closed door proved it.

And yet, as Delane continued his quieter examination, there remained, he saw, the startling quality which had caused that first magnifying in his mind. His senses, while reporting accurately, insisted upon this arresting and uncommon touch: there was, about this late wanderer of the night, some evasive, lofty strangeness that set him utterly apart from ordinary men.

The Englishman examined him searchingly, surreptitiously, but with a touch of passionate curiosity he could not in the least account for nor explain. There were contradictions of perplexing character about him. For the first presentment had been of splendid youth, while on the face, though vigorous and gloriously handsome, he now discerned the stamp of tremendous age. It was worn and tired. While radiant with strength and health and power, it wore as well this certain signature of deep exhaustion that great experience rather than physical experience brings. Moreover, he discovered in it, in some way he could not hope to describe, man, woman, and child. There was a big, sad earnestness about it, yet a touch of humour too; patience, tenderness, and sweetness held the mouth; and behind the high pale forehead intellect sat enthroned and watchful. In it were both love and hatred, longing and despair; an expression of being ever on the defensive, yet hugely mutinous; an air both hunted and beseeching; great knowledge and great woe.

Delane gave up the search, aware that something unalterably splendid stood before him. Solemnity and beauty swept him too. His was never the grotesque assumption that man must be the highest being in the universe, nor that a thing is a miracle merely because it has never happened before. He groped, while explanation and analysis both halted. "A great teacher," thought fluttered through him, "or a mighty rebel! A distinguished personality beyond all question! Who can he be?" There was something regal that put respect upon his imagination instantly. And he remembered the legend of the countryside that Ludwig of Bavaria was said to be about when nights were very wild. He wondered. Into his speech and manner crept unawares an attitude of deference that was almost reverence, and with it—whence came this other quality?—a searching pity.

"You must be wearied out," he said respectfully, busying himself about the room, "as well as cold and wet. This fire will dry you, sir, and meanwhile I will prepare quickly such food as there is, if you will eat it." For the other carried no knapsack, nor was he clothed for the severity of mountain travel.

"I have already eaten," said the stranger courteously, "and, with my thanks to you, I am neither wet nor tired. The afflictions that I bear are of another kind, though ones that you shall more easily, I am sure, relieve."

He spoke as a man whose words set troops in action, and Delane glanced at him, deeply moved by the surprising phrase, yet hardly marvelling that it should be so. He found no ready answer. But there was evidently question in his look, for the other continued, and this time with a smile that betrayed sheer winning beauty as of a tender woman:

"I saw the light and came to it. It is unusual—at this time."

His voice was resonant, yet not deep. There was a ringing quality about it that the bare room emphasised. It charmed the young Englishman inexplicably. Also, it woke in him a sense of infinite pathos.

"You are a climber, sir, like myself," Delane resumed, lifting his eyes a moment uneasily from the coffee he brewed over a corner of the fire. "You know this neighbourhood, perhaps? Better, at any rate, than I can know it?" His German halted rather. He chose his words with difficulty. There was uncommon trouble in his mind.

"I know all wild and desolate places," replied the other, in perfect English, but with a wintry mournfulness in his voice and eyes, "for I feel at home in them, and their stern companionship my nature craves as solace. But, unlike yourself, I am no climber."

"The heights have no attraction for you?" asked Delane, as he mingled steaming milk and coffee in the wooden bowl, marvelling what brought him then so high above the valleys. "It is their difficulty and danger that fascinate me always. I find the loneliness of the summits intoxicating in a sense."

And, regardless of refusal, he set the bread and meat before him, the apple and the tiny packet of salt, then turned away to place the coffee pot beside the fire again. But as he did so a singular gesture of the other caught his eyes. Before touching bowl or plate, the stranger took the fruit and brushed his lips with it. He kissed it, then set it on the ground and crushed it into pulp beneath his heel. And, seeing this, the young Englishman knew something dreadfully arrested in his mind, for, as he looked away, pretending the act was unobserved, a thing of ice and darkness moved past him through the room, so that the pot trembled in his hand, rattling sharply against the hearthstone where he stooped. He could only interpret it as an act of madness, and the myth of the sad, drowned monarch wandering through this enchanted region, pressed into him again unsought and urgent. It was a full minute before he had control of his heart and hand again.

The bowl was half emptied, and the man was smiling—this time the smile of a child who implores the comfort of enveloping and understanding arms.

"I am a wanderer rather than a climber," he was saying, as though there had been no interval, "for, though the lonely summits suit me well, I now find in them only—terror. My feet lose their sureness, and my head its steady balance. I prefer the hidden gorges of these mountains, and the shadows of the covering forests. My days"—his voice drew the loneliness of uttermost space into its piteous accents—"are passed in darkness. I can never climb again."

He spoke this time, indeed, as a man whose nerve was gone for ever. It was pitiable almost to tears. And Delane, unable to explain the amazing contradictions, felt recklessly, furiously drawn to this trapped wanderer with the mien of a king yet the air and speech sometimes of a woman and sometimes of an outcast child.

"Ah, then you have known accidents," Delane replied with outer calmness, as he lit his pipe, trying in vain to keep his hand as steady as his voice. "You have been in one perhaps. The effect, I have been told, is—"

The power and sweetness in that resonant voice took his breath away as he heard it break in upon his own uncertain accents:

"I have—fallen," the stranger replied impressively, as the rain and wind wailed past the building mournfully, "yet a fall that was no part of any accident. For it was no common fall," the man added with a magnificent gesture of disdain, "while yet it broke my heart in two." He stooped a little as he uttered the next words with a crying pathos that an outcast woman might have used. "I am," he said, "engulfed in intolerable loneliness. I can never climb again."

With a shiver impossible to control, half of terror, half of pity, Delane moved a step nearer to the marvellous stranger. The spirit of Ludwig, exiled and distraught, had gripped his soul with a weakening terror; but now sheer beauty lifted him above all personal shrinking. There seemed some echo of lost divinity, worn, wild yet grandiose, through which this significant language strained towards a personal message—for himself.

"In loneliness?" he faltered, sympathy rising in a flood.

"For my Kingdom that is lost to me for ever," met him in deep, throbbing tones that set the air on fire. "For my imperial ancient heights that jealousy took from me—"

The stranger paused, with an indescribable air of broken dignity and pain.

Outside the tempest paused a moment before the awful elemental crash that followed. A bellowing of many winds descended like artillery upon the world. A burst of smoke rushed from the fireplace about them both, shrouding the stranger momentarily in a flying veil. And Delane stood up, uncomfortable in his very bones. "What can it be?" he asked himself sharply. "Who is this being that he should use such language?" He watched alarm chase pity, aware that the conversation held something beyond experience. But the pity returned in greater and ever greater flood. And love surged through him too. It was significant, he remembered afterwards, that he felt it incumbent upon himself to stand. Curious, too, how the thought of that mad, drowned monarch haunted memory with such persistence. Some vast emotion that he could not name drove out his subsequent words. The smoke had cleared, and a strange, high stillness held the world. The rain streamed down in torrents, isolating these two somehow from the haunts of men. And the Englishman stared then into a countenance grown mighty with woe and loneliness. There stood darkly in it this incommunicable magnificence of pain that mingled awe with the pity he had felt. The kingly eyes looked clear into his own, completing his subjugation out of time. "I would follow you," ran his thought upon its knees, "follow you with obedience for ever and ever, even into a last damnation. For you are sublime. You shall come again into your Kingdom, if my own small worship—"

Then blackness sponged the reckless thought away. He spoke in its place a more guarded, careful thing:

"I am aware," he faltered, yet conscious that he bowed, "of standing before a Great One of some world unknown to me. Who he may be I have but the privilege of wondering. He has spoken darkly of a Kingdom that is lost. Yet he is still, I see, a Monarch." And he lowered his head and shoulders involuntarily.

For an instant, then, as he said it, the eyes before him flashed their original terrific lightnings. The darkness of the common world faded before the entrance of an Outer Darkness. From gulfs of terror at his feet rose shadows out of the night of time, and a passionate anguish as of sudden madness seized his heart and shook it.

He listened breathlessly for the words that followed. It seemed some wind of unutterable despair passed in the breath from those non-human lips:

"I am still a Monarch, yes; but my Kingdom is taken from me, for I have no single subject. Lost in a loneliness that lies out of space and time, I am become a throneless Ruler, and my hopelessness is more than I can bear." The beseeching pathos of the voice tore him in two. The Deity himself, it seemed, stood there accused of jealousy, of sin and cruelty. The stranger rose. The power about him brought the picture of a planet, throned in mid-heaven and poised beyond assault. "Not otherwise," boomed the startling words as though an avalanche found syllables, "could I now show myself to—you."

Delane was trembling horribly. He felt the next words slip off his tongue unconsciously. The shattering truth had dawned upon his soul at last.

"Then the light you saw, and came to—?" he whispered.

"Was the light in your heart that guided me," came the answer, sweet, beguiling as the music in a woman's tones, "the light of your instant, brief desire that held love in it." He made an opening movement with his arms as he continued, smiling like stars in summer. "For you summoned me; summoned me by your dear and precious belief: how dear, how precious, none can know but I who stand before you."

His figure drew up with an imperial air of proud dominion. His feet were set among the constellations. The opening movement of his arms continued slowly. And the music in his tones seemed merged in distant thunder.

"For your single, brief belief," he smiled with the grandeur of a condescending Emperor, "shall give my vanished Kingdom back to me."

And with an air of native majesty he held his hand out—to be kissed.

The black hurricane of night, the terror of frozen peaks, the yawning horror of the great abyss outside—all three crowded into the Englishman's mind with a slashing impact that blocked delivery of any word or action. It was not that he refused, it was not that he withdrew, but that Life stood paralysed and rigid. The flow stopped dead for the first time since he had left his mother's womb. The God in him was turned to stone and rendered ineffective. For an appalling instant God was *not.*

He realised the stupendous moment. Before him, drinking his little soul out merely by his Presence, stood one whose habit of mind, not alone his external accidents, was imperial with black prerogative before the first man drew the breath of life. August procedure was native to his inner process of existence. The stars and confines of the universe owned his sway before he fell, to trifle away the dreary little centuries by haunting the minds of feeble men and women, by hiding himself in nursery cupboards, and by grinning with stained gargoyles from the roofs of city churches. . . .

And the lad's life stammered, flickered, threatened to go out before the enveloping terror of the revelation.

"I called to you . . . but called to you in play," thought whispered somewhere deep below the level of any speech, yet not so low that the audacious sound of it did not crash above the elements outside; "for . . . till now . . . you have been to me but a . . . coated bogy . . . that my brain disowned with laughter . . . and my heart thought picturesque. If you are here . . . *alive!* May God forgive me for my . . ."

It seemed as though tears—the tears of love and profound commiseration—drowned the very seed of thought itself.

A sound stopped him that was like a collapse in heaven. Some crashing, as of a ruined world, passed splintering through his little timid heart. He did not yield, but he understood—with an understanding which seemed the delicate first sign of yielding—the seductiveness of evil, the sweet delight of surrendering the Will with utter recklessness to those swelling forces which disintegrate the heroic soul in man. He remembered. It was true. In the reaction from excess he *had* definitely called upon his childhood's teaching with a passing moment of genuine belief. And now that yearning of a fraction of a second bore its awful fruit. The luscious Capitals where he had rioted passed in a coloured stream before his eyes; the Wine, the Woman, and the Song stood there before him, clothed in that Power which lies insinuatingly disguised behind their little passing show of innocence. Their glamour donned this domino of regal and virile grandeur. He felt entangled beyond recovery. The idea of God seemed sterile and without reality. The one real thing, the one desirable thing, the one possible, strong. and beautiful thing—was to bend his head and kiss those imperial fingers. He moved noiselessly towards the Hand. He raised his own to take it and lift it towards his mouth—

When there rose in his mind with startling vividness a small, soft picture of a child's nursery, a picture of a little boy, kneeling in scanty night-gown with pink upturned soles, and asking ridiculous, audacious things of a shining Figure seated on a summer cloud above the kitchen-garden walnut tree.

The tiny symbol flashed and went its way, yet not before it had lit the entire world with glory. For there came an absolutely routing power with it. In that half-forgotten instant's craving for the simple teaching of his childhood days, Belief had conjured with two immense traditions. This was the second of them. The appearance of the one had inevitably produced the passage of its opposite. . . .

And the Hand that floated in the air before him to be kissed sank slowly down below the possible level of his lips. He shrank away. Though laughter tempted something in his brain, there still clung about his heart the first aching, pitying terror. But size retreated, dwindling somehow as it went. The wind and rain obliterated every other sound; yet in that bare, unfurnished room of a climber's mountain hut, there was a silence, above the roar, that drank in everything and broke the back of speech. In opposition to this masquerading splendour Delane had set up a personal, paternal Deity.

"I thought of you, perhaps," cried the voice of self-defence, "but I did not call to you with real belief. And, by the name of God, I did not summon you. For your sweetness, as your power, sickens me; and your hand is black with the curses of all the mothers in the world, whose prayers and tears—"

He stopped dead, overwhelmed by the cruelty of his reckless utterance.

And the Other moved towards him slowly. It was like the summit of some peaked and terrible height that moved. He spoke. He changed appallingly.

"But *I* claim," he roared, "your heart. I claim you by that instant of belief you felt. For by that alone you shall restore to me my vanished Kingdom. You shall worship me."

In the countenance was a sudden awful power; but behind the stupefying roar there was weakness in the voice as of an imploring and beseeching child. Again, deep love and searching pity seared the Englishman's heart as he replied in the gentlest accents he could find to master:

"And I claim *you,*" he said, "by my understanding sympathy, and by my sorrow for your God-forsaken loneliness, and by my love. For no Kingdom built on hate can stand against the love you would deny—"

Words failed him then, as he saw the majesty fade slowly from the face, grown small and shadowy. One last expression of desperate energy in the eyes struck lightnings from the smoky air, as with an abandoned movement of the entire figure, he drew back, it seemed, towards the door behind him.

Delane moved slowly after him, opening his arms. Tenderness and big compassion flung wide the gates of love within him. He found strange language, too, although actual, spoken words did not produce them further than his entrails where they had their birth:

"Toys in the world are plentiful, Sire, and you may have them for your masterpiece of play. But you must seek them where they still survive; in the churches, and in isolated lands where thought lies unawakened. For they are the children's blocks of make-believe whose palaces, like your once tremendous kingdom, have no true existence for the thinking mind."

And he stretched his hands towards him with the gesture of one who sought to help and save, then paused as he realised that his arms enclosed sheer blackness, with the emptiness of wind and driving rain.

For the door of the hut stood open, and Delane balanced on the threshold, facing the sheet of night above the abyss. He heard the waterfalls in the valley far below. The forest flapped and tossed its myriad branches. Cold draughts swept down from spectral fields of melting snow above; and the blackness turned momentarily into the semblance of towers and bastions of thick beaten gloom. Above one soaring turret, then, a space of sky appeared, swept naked by a violent, lost wind—an opening of purple into limitless distance. For one second, amid the vapours, it was visible, empty and untenanted. The next, there sailed across its small diameter a falling Star. With an air of slow and endless leisure, yet at the same time with terrific speed, it dived behind the ragged curtain of the clouds, and the space closed up again. Blackness returned upon the heavens.

And through this blackness, plunging into that abyss of woe whence he had momentarily risen, the figure of the marvellous stranger melted utterly away. Delane, for a fleeting second, was aware of the earnestness in the sad, imploring countenance; of its sweetness and its power so strangely mingled; of its mysterious grandeur; and of its pathetic childishness. But, already, it was sunk into interminable distance. A star that would be baleful, yet was merely glorious, passed on its endless wandering among the teeming systems of the universe. Behind the fixed and steady stars, secure in their appointed places, it set. It vanished into the pit of unknown emptiness. It was gone.

"God help you!" sighed across the sea of wailing branches, echoing down the dark abyss below. "God give you rest at last!"

For he saw a princely, nay, an imperial Being, homeless for ever, and for ever wandering, hunted as by keen remorseless winds about a universe that held no corner for his feet, his majesty unworshipped, his reign a mockery, his Court unfurnished, and his courtiers mere shadows of deep space. . . .

And a thin, grey dawn, stealing up behind clearing summits in the east, crept then against the windows of the mountain hut. It brought with it a treacherous, sharp air that made the sleeper draw another blanket near to shelter him from the sudden cold. For the fire had died out, and an icy draught sucked steadily beneath the doorway.

The Story Hour

"Daddy, please tell us a story. There's just time. There's half an hour. It's nice and dark—"

"Yes, please do. An awful story. Ugh!"

"Something fearful—terribly fearful—"

"But not fearful enough to come upstairs into bed with us," added the timid one.

There was a general scuffle for seats, with bitter complaints that he only had two knees. There was also criticism of life—that he had "no lap, no proper lap," that it was too dark to see his face, that everybody in turn had "got the best place," and that "there was very little time." At length peace and quiet were established. The big arm-chair resembled a group of bees upon a honeycomb. The fire burned dully, and the ceiling was thick with monstrous, fluttering shadows.

"Do begin now at once, please."

"Or you'll never, never finish in time."

"We're all ready—ages and ages ago."

A deep hush was over the room, nothing but confused breathing audible.

"Once, very long ago—" he began.

"How long?"

"Oh, ever so long, longer than anything."

"But that's not really long."

"So long ago," he continued, adapting Time for their benefit, "that the chalk cliffs of England still lay beneath the sea—"

"Was Grannie alive then?"

"Or the Head Gardener?"

"Oh, much, much longer ago than that," he comforted them, "so long, in fact, that neither Grannie nor the Head Gardener was even thought of—there lived a man who—"

"Where did he live? What country, I mean, please?"

"There lived a man in England—"

"But England was beneath the sea with the chalk cliffs, you said."

"There lived a man in a queer little island called Ingland, spelt 'I n g,' not 'E n g,' who—"

"Oh, I see. It wasn't our England, then?"

"On a queer little tiny island called Ingland, who was very lonely because he was the only person on it, and—"

"Were there animals and things, too?"

"And the only animals who lived on it with him were a squirrel who lived in the only tree, a rabbit who lived in the only hole, and a small grey mouse who made its nest in the pocket of his other coat."

"Friendly? Did he love them?"

"So friendly that he loved them better than himself, and went to tea with the rabbit in its hole, and climbed up the tree to share a nut breakfast with the squirrel, and—and—"

"He doesn't know what to do with the mouse," a voice broke in upon the fatal hesitation. "It's all make-up."

"And went out for walks with the mouse when the ground was too wet and the mouse complained of chilly feet," he continued, triumphantly. "In the pocket of his coat, all snug and warm, it stood on its hind legs and peered out upon the world with its nose just over the edge of the pocket-flap—as you do in the motor sometimes."

"He liked the mouse best, then?"

"What sort of coat was it? An overcoat or just an ordinary one? Was that the only pocket in it?"

"It was made of the best leaves from the squirrel's tree, and from the rabbit's last year's fur, and the mouse fastened the edges together with long hairs picked from the best place on its back. And so they walked about the tiny island and enjoyed the view, till one day the mouse declared the ground was *always* wet, and was getting wetter and wetter. And the man got frightened."

"Ugh! It's going to get awful in a minute!" And the children nestled closer.

"And why, please, was it getting wetter and wetter?"

"For a long time," continued the man, who earned his living daily at a London desk, and at night justified his existence by offering the raw material of epics unto little children, "no one could discover. That was the extraordinary part of it. No one could make out why it got wetter and wetter and wetter—"

"Perhaps it just rained like here."

"For it never rained, and the sky was always blue, while the ground got finally so wet that the very floor of the man's hut turned spongey till it splashed each time he went to answer the bell—er—I mean to look at the weather. And in the end he got so frightened that he simply stayed indoors, put on both his coats, and told stories to the mouse about a far country that was always dry—"

"But didn't the rabbit know anything?"

"For all this time the rabbit was simply too terrified to come out of its hole at all. It declared the island was nothing but a stupid swamp and sulked in bed—"

"I like rabbits, though."

"Till one day the squirrel came to call, and, without waiting for the man to answer the door, it bustled into the room, hopping and jerking its head, swept the water away with its bushy tail, and, climbing up on to the man's shoulder, it whispered something frightfully important and secret into his left ear."

"But why into his left ear?"

"Because it was the right one, and the other was stone deaf?"

"What did it tell him?"

In the hush that followed a coal was heard falling softly into the grate. A fainter sound was also audible. It was far away in the upper reaches of the house. But it was coming nearer. It was footsteps—the most awful sound that childhood knows.

"Oh, quick! Quick! What did it tell him in his good ear?"

"Two words," continued the story-teller in a lower voice. "It said: '*The Sea.*'"

Everybody sat up and looked at everybody else. No word was uttered. The steps outside had reached the second floor.

"From its perch on the top of the only tree the squirrel had seen what was happening. The sea was rising. The island had already grown much smaller. In a little time the rising water would cover it and everybody would be drowned."

"Couldn't none of them swim at all?" enquired some one.

"What in the world did they do? Who thought of it first?"

He chose the question last but one. "The rabbit, just at that very minute, came out of its hole and told them how to escape. 'I'll dig a hole,' it said, 'and empty the sea into it.'"

The teller fixed his eyes upon each listener in turn, challenging disapproval. He met, however, only silence and breathless admiration in the place of criticism. He heard the approaching steps outside the door. He made swift and desperate calculations. It was just possible, he decided.

"So they dug and dug and dug. The man took off both his coats, the rabbit scraped with all four paws, the mouse made numerous little channels with its pointed toes to guide the water in, and the squirrel brushed it faster with its mop-like tail. The rising sea poured down the deepening hole. And, as it poured, the level of the ocean got lower and lower and lower. The shores of the little island stretched further and further and further. As the level sank there appeared great white fields of chalk that were miles and miles in length, and one morning the squirrel, scampering down from the top of the tree where it had gone to report upon the actual state of affairs, squeaked in its chattering voice of pleasure, 'We are saved. We can run across dry land and this island is an island no longer.' For an island, of course, is a portion of land entirely surrounded by water—"

"We know that."

"And the sea had sunk so low that France and Spain and Holland touched England. They had emptied it all down the rabbit's hole."

"What happened then?"

"The squirrel picked up its tail, the rabbit went on tiptoe, the mouse turned its whiskers up, and, all dry as a bone, they skipped across without even wetting their feet. And when they got there—" There was a knock at the door, but no one answered.

"They told all the squirrels, rabbits, and mice they met that—"

The knock was repeated louder than before, but no one answered.

"They came from a lovely land called Ingland, where it was nice and dry, and—well, and that they had better all come over and live there happily ever after and enjoy themselves—"

He broke off in the middle and said "Come in." But no single head was turned. The entry was ignored.

"And that's why England to-day is full of rabbits, mice, and squirrels, and why everybody pretends it's dry and comfortable and cosy, and why people only leave it when they go away for holidays that cannot be avoided, and why—"

"I beg your pardon, sir, but it's gone half past seven," said an awful voice.

"And why— Why, I do declare, it's time for bed."

The Tradition

The noises outside the little flat at first were very disconcerting after living in the country. They made sleep difficult. At the cottage in Sussex where the family had lived, night brought deep, comfortable silence, unless the wind was high, when the pine trees round the duck-pond made a sound like surf, or if the gale was from the south-west, the orchard roared a bit unpleasantly.

But in London it was very different; sleep was easier in the daytime than at night. For after nightfall the rumble of the traffic became spasmodic instead of continuous; the motor-horns startled like warnings of alarm; after comparative silence the furious rushing of a taxicab touched the nerves. From dinner till eleven o'clock the streets subsided gradually; then came the army from theatres, parties, and late dinners, hurrying home to bed. The motor-horns during this hour were lively and incessant, like bugles of a regiment moving into battle. The parents rarely retired until this attack was over. If quick about it, sleep was possible then before the flying of the night-birds—an uncertain squadron—screamed half the street awake again. But, these finally disposed of, a delightful hush settled down upon the neighbourhood, profounder far than any peace of the countryside. The deep rumble of the produce wagons, coming in to the big London markets from the farms—generally about three A.M.—held no disturbing quality.

But sometimes in the stillness of very early morning, when streets were empty and pavements all deserted, there was a sound of another kind that was startling and unwelcome. For it was ominous. It came with a clattering violence that made nerves quiver and forced the heart to pause and listen. A strange resonance was in it, a volume of sound, moreover, that was hardly justified by its cause. For it was hoofs. A horse swept hurrying up the deserted street, and was close upon the building in a moment. It was audible suddenly, no gradual approach from a distance, but as though it turned a corner from soft ground that muffled the hoofs, on to the echoing, hard paving that emphasised the dreadful clatter. Nor did it die away again when once the house was reached. It ceased as abruptly as it came. The hoofs did not go away.

It was the mother who heard them first, and drew her husband's attention to their disagreeable quality.

"It is the mail-vans, dear," he answered. "They go at four A.M. to catch the early trains into the country."

She looked up sharply, as though something in his tone surprised her.

"But there's no sound of wheels," she said. And then, as he did not reply, she added gravely, "You have heard it too, John. I can tell."

"I have," he said. "I have heard it—twice."

And they looked at one another searchingly, each trying to read the other's mind. She did not question him; he did not propose writing to complain in a newspaper; both understood something that neither of them understood.

"I heard it first," she then said softly, "the night before Jack got the fever. And as I listened, I heard him crying. But when I went in to see he was asleep. The noise stopped just outside the building." There was a shadow in her eyes as she said this, and a hush crept in between her words. "I did not hear it *go.*" She said this almost beneath her breath.

He looked a moment at the ground; then, coming towards her, he took her in his arms and kissed her. And she clung very tightly to him.

"Sometimes," he said in a quiet voice, "a mounted policeman passes down the street, I think."

"It is a horse," she answered. But whether it was a question or mere corroboration he did not ask, for at that moment the doctor arrived, and the question of little Jack's health became the paramount matter of immediate interest. The great man's verdict was uncommonly disquieting.

All that night they sat up in the sick room. It was strangely still, as though by one accord the traffic avoided the house where a little boy hung between life and death. The motor-horns even had a muffled sound, and heavy drays and wagons used the wide streets; there were fewer taxicabs about, or else they flew by noiselessly. Yet no straw was down; the expense prohibited that. And towards morning, very early, the mother decided to watch alone. She had been a trained nurse before her marriage, accustomed when she was younger to long vigils. "You go down, dear, and get a little sleep," she urged in a whisper. "He's quiet now. At five o'clock I'll come for you to take my place."

"You'll fetch me at once," he whispered, "if—" then hesitated as though breath failed him. A moment he stood there staring from her face to the bed. "If you hear anything," he finished. She nodded, and he went downstairs to his study, not to his bedroom. He left the door ajar. He sat in darkness, listening. Mother, he knew, was listening, too, beside the bed. His heart was very full, for he did not believe the boy could live till morning. The picture of the room was all the time before his eyes—the shaded lamp, the table with the medicines, the little wasted figure beneath the blankets, and mother close beside it, listening. He sat alert, ready to fly upstairs at the smallest cry.

But no sound broke the stillness; the entire neighbourhood was silent; all London slept He heard the clock strike three in the dining-room at the end of the corridor. It was still enough for that. There was not even the heavy rumble of a single produce wagon, though usually they passed about this time on their way to Smithfield and Covent Garden markets. He waited, far too anxious to close his eyes. . . . At four o'clock he would go up and relieve her vigil. Four, he knew, was the time when life sinks to its lowest ebb. . . . Then, in the middle of his reflections, thought stopped dead, and it seemed his heart stopped too.

Far away, but coming nearer with extraordinary rapidity, a sharp, clear sound broke out of the surrounding stillness—a horse's hoofs. At first it was so distant that it might have been almost on the high roads of the country, but the amazing speed with which it came closer, and the sudden increase of the beating sound, was such, that by the time he turned his head it seemed to have entered the street outside. It was within a hundred yards of the building. The next second it was before the very door. And something in him blenched. He knew a moment's complete paralysis. The abrupt cessation of the heavy clatter was strangest of all. It came like lightning, it struck, it paused. It did not go away again. Yet the sound of it was still beating in his ears as he dashed upstairs three steps at a time. It seemed in the house as well, on the stairs behind him, in the little passage-way, *inside the very bedroom.* It was an appalling sound. Yet he entered a room that was quiet, orderly, and calm. It was silent. Beside the bed his wife sat, holding Jack's hand and stroking it. She was soothing him; her face was very peaceful. No sound but her gentle whisper was audible.

He controlled himself by a tremendous effort, but his face betrayed his consternation and distress. "Hush," she said beneath her breath; "he's sleeping much more calmly now. The crisis, bless God, is over, I do believe. I dared not leave him."

He saw in a moment that she was right, and an untellable relief passed over him. He sat down beside her, very cold, yet perspiring with heat.

"You heard—?" he asked after a pause.

"Nothing," she replied quickly, "except his pitiful, wild words when the delirium was on him. It's passed. It lasted but a moment, or I'd have called you."

He stared closely into her tired eyes. "And his words?" he asked in a whisper. Whereupon she told him quietly that the little chap had sat up with wide-opened eyes and talked excitedly about a "great, great horse" he heard, but that was not "coming for him." "He laughed and said he would not go with it because he 'was not ready yet.' Some scrap of talk he had overheard from us," she added, "when we discussed the traffic once. . . ."

"But you heard nothing?" he repeated almost impatiently.

No, she had heard nothing. After all, then, he *had* dozed a moment in his chair. . . .

Four weeks later Jack, entirely convalescent, was playing a restricted game of hide-and-seek with his sister in the flat. It was really a forbidden joy, owing to noise and risk of breakages, but he had unusual privileges after his grave illness. It was dusk. The lamps in the street were being lit. "Quietly, remember; your mother's resting in her room," were the father's orders. She had just returned from a week by the sea, recuperating from the strain of nursing for so many nights. The traffic rolled and boomed along the streets below.

"Jack! Do come on and hide. It's your turn. I hid last."

But the boy was standing spellbound by the window, staring hard at something on the pavement. Sybil called and tugged in vain. Tears threatened. Jack would not budge. He declared he saw something.

"Oh, you're always seeing something. I wish you'd go and hide. It's only because you can't think of a good place, really."

"Look!" he cried in a voice of wonder. And as he said it his father rose quickly from his chair before the fire.

"Look!" the child repeated with delight and excitement. "It's a great big horse. And it's perfectly white all over." His sister joined him at the window. "Where? Where? I can't see it. Oh, *do* show me!"

Their father was standing close behind them now. "I heard it," he was whispering, but so low the children did not notice him. His face was the colour of chalk.

"Straight in front of our door, stupid! Can't you see it? Oh, I do wish it had come for me. It's *such* a beauty!" And he clapped his hands with pleasure and excitement. "Quick, quick! It's going away again!"

But while the children stood half-squabbling by the window, their father leaned over a sofa in the adjoining room above a figure whose heart in sleep had quietly stopped its beating. The great white horse had come. But this time he had not only heard its wonderful arrival. He had also heard it go. It seemed he heard the awful hoofs beat down the sky, far, far away, and very swiftly, dying into silence, finally up among the stars.

Transition

John Mudbury was on his way home from the shops, his arms full of Christmas presents. It was after six o'clock and the streets were very crowded. He was an ordinary man, lived in an ordinary suburban flat, with an ordinary wife and four ordinary children. *He* did not think them ordinary, but everybody else did. He had ordinary presents for each one, a cheap blotter for his wife, a cheap air-gun for the eldest boy, and so forth. He was over fifty, bald, in an office, decent in mind and habits, of uncertain opinions, uncertain politics, and uncertain religion. Yet he considered himself a decided, positive gentleman, quite unaware that the morning newspaper determined his opinions for the day. He just lived—from day to day. Physically, he was fit enough, except for a weak heart (which never troubled him); and his summer holiday was bad golf, while the children bathed and his wife read "Garvice" on the sands. Like the majority of men, he dreamed idly of the past, muddled away the present, and guessed vaguely—after imaginative reading on occasions—at the future.

"I'd like to survive all right," he said, "provided it's better than this," surveying his wife and children, and thinking of his daily toil. "Otherwise—!" and he shrugged his shoulders as a brave man should.

He went to church regularly. But nothing in church *convinced* him that he did survive, just as nothing in church enticed him into hoping that he would. On the other hand, nothing in life persuaded him that he didn't, wouldn't, couldn't. "I'm an Evolutionist," he loved to say to thoughtful cronies (over a glass), having never heard that Darwinism had been questioned. . . .

And so he came home gaily, happily, with his bunch of Christmas presents "for the wife and little ones," stroking himself upon their keen enjoyment and excitement. The night before he had taken "the wife" to see *Magic* at a select London theatre where the Intellectuals went—and had been extraordinarily stirred. He had gone questioningly, yet expecting something out of the common. "It's *not* musical," he warned her, "nor farce, nor comedy, so to speak"; and in answer to her question as to what the Critics had said, he had wriggled, sighed, and put his gaudy necktie straight four times in quick succession. For no "Man in the Street," with any claim to self-respect, could be expected to understand what the Critics had said, even if he understood the Play. And John had answered truthfully: "Oh, they just said things. But the theatre's always full—and that's the only test."

And just now, as he crossed the crowded Circus to catch his 'bus, it chanced that his mind (having glimpsed an advertisement) was full of this particular Play, or, rather, of the effect it had produced upon him at the time. For it had *thrilled* him—inexplicably: with its marvellous speculative hint, its big audacity, its alert and spiritual beauty. . . . Thought plunged to find something—plunged after this bizarre suggestion of a bigger universe, after this quasi-jocular suggestion that man is not the only—then dashed full-tilt against a sentence that memory thrust beneath his nose: "Science does *not* exhaust the Universe"—and at the same time dashed full-tilt against destruction of another kind as well . . . !

How it happened, he never exactly knew. He saw a Monster glaring at him with eyes of blazing fire. It was horrible! It rushed upon him. He dodged. . . . Another Monster met him round the corner. Both came at him simultaneously. . . . He dodged again—a leap that might have cleared a hurdle easily, but was too late. Between the pair of them—his heart literally in his gullet—he was mercilessly caught. . . . Bones crunched. . . . There was a soft sensation, icy cold and hot as fire. Horns and voices roared. Battering-rams he saw, and a carapace of iron. . . . Then dazzling light. . . . "Always *face* the traffic!" he remembered with a frantic yell—and, by some extraordinary luck, escaped miraculously on to the opposite pavement. . . .

There was no doubt about it. By the skin of his teeth he had dodged a rather ugly death. First . . . he felt for his presents—all were safe. And then, instead of congratulating himself and taking breath, he hurried homewards—*on foot,* which proved that his mind had lost control a bit!—thinking only how disappointed the wife and children would have been if—if anything had happened. . . . Another thing he realised, oddly enough, was that he no longer really *loved* his wife, but had only great affection for her. What made him think of that, heaven only knows, but he *did* think of it. He was an honest man without pretence. This came as a discovery somehow. He turned a moment, and saw the crowd gathered about the entangled taxicabs, policemen's helmets gleaming in the lights of the shop windows . . . then hurried on again, his thoughts full of the joy his presents would give . . . of the scampering children . . . and of his wife—bless her silly heart!—eyeing the mysterious parcels. . . .

And, though he never could explain *how,* he presently stood at the door of the jail-like building that contained his flat, having walked the whole three miles! His thoughts had been so busy and absorbed that he had hardly noticed the length of weary trudge. . . . "Besides," he reflected, thinking of the narrow escape, "I've had a nasty shock. It was a d——d near thing, now I come to think of it. . . ." He did feel a bit shaky and bewildered. . . . Yet, at the same time, he felt extraordinarily jolly and light-hearted. . . .

He counted his Christmas parcels . . . hugged himself in anticipatory joy . . . and let himself in swiftly with his latchkey. "I'm late," he realised, "but when she sees the brown-paper parcels, she'll forget to say a word. God bless the old faithful soul." And he softly used the key a second time and entered his flat on tiptoe. . . . In his mind was the master impulse of that afternoon—the pleasure these Christmas presents would give his wife and children. . . .

He heard a noise. He hung up hat and coat in the pokey vestibule (they never called it "hall") and moved softly towards the parlour door, holding the packages behind him. Only of them he thought, not of himself—of his family, that is, not of the packages. Pushing the door cunningly ajar, he peeped in slyly. To his amazement, the room was full of people! He withdrew quickly, wondering what it meant. A party? And without his knowing about it! Extraordinary! . . . Keen disappointment came over him. But, as he stepped back, the vestibule, he saw, was full of people too.

He was uncommonly surprised, yet somehow not surprised at all People were congratulating him. There was a perfect mob of them. Moreover, he knew them all—vaguely remembered them, at least. And they all knew him.

"Isn't it a game?" laughed some one, patting him on the back. "*They* haven't the least idea . . . !"

And the speaker—it was old John Palmer, the bookkeeper at the office—emphasised the "they."

"Not the least idea," he answered with a smile, saying something he didn't understand, yet knew was right.

His face, apparently, showed the utter bewilderment he felt. The shock of the collision had been greater than he realised evidently. His mind was wandering. . . . Possibly! Only the odd thing was—he had never felt so clear-headed in his life. Ten thousand things grew simple suddenly. But, how thickly these people pressed about him, and how—familiarly!

"My parcels," he said, joyously pushing his way across the throng. "These are Christmas presents I've bought for them." He nodded toward the room. "I've saved for weeks—stopped cigars and billiards and—and several other good things—to buy them."

"Good man!" said Palmer with a happy laugh. "It's the heart that counts."

Mudbury looked at him. Palmer had said an amazing truth, only—people would hardly understand and believe him. . . . Would they?

"Eh?" he asked, feeling stuffed and stupid, muddled somewhere between two meanings, one of which was gorgeous and the other stupid beyond belief.

"If you *please,* Mr. Mudbury, step inside. They are expecting you," said a kindly, pompous voice. And, turning sharply, he met the gentle, foolish eyes of Sir James Epiphany, a director of the Bank where he worked.

The effect of the voice was instantaneous from long habit.

"They are?" he smiled from his heart, and advanced as from the custom of many years. Oh, how happy and gay he felt! His affection for his wife was real. Romance, indeed, had gone, but he needed her—and she needed him. And the children—Milly, Bill, and Jean—he deeply loved them. Life *was* worth living indeed!

In the room was a crowd, but—an astounding silence. John Mudbury looked round him. He advanced towards his wife, who sat in the corner arm-chair with Milly on her knee. A lot of people talked and moved about. Momentarily the crowd increased. He stood in front of them—in front of Milly and his wife. And he spoke—holding out his packages. "It's Christmas Eve," he whispered shyly, "and I've—brought you something—something for everybody. Look!" He held the packages before their eyes.

"Of course, of course," said a voice behind him, "but you may hold them out like that for a century. They'll *never* see them!"

"Of course they won't. But I love to do the old, sweet thing," replied John Mudbury—then wondered with a gasp of stark amazement why he said it.

"*I* think——" whispered Milly, staring round her.

"Well, *what* do you think?" her mother asked sharply. "You're always thinking something queer."

"I think," the child continued dreamily, "that Daddy's already here." She paused, then added with a child's impossible conviction, "I'm sure he is. I *feel* him."

There was an extraordinary laugh. Sir James Epiphany laughed. The others—the whole crowd of them—also turned their heads and smiled. But the mother, thrusting the child away from her, rose up suddenly with a violent start. Her face had turned to chalk. She stretched her arms out—into the air before her. She gasped and shivered. There was an awful anguish in her eyes.

"Look!" repeated John, "these are the presents that I brought."

But his voice apparently was soundless. And, with a spasm of icy pain, he remembered that Palmer and Sir James—some years ago—had died.

"It's magic," he cried, "but—I love you, Jinny—I love you—and—and I have always been true to you—as true as steel. We need each other—oh, can't you see—we go on together—you and I—for ever and ever—"

"*Think,*" interrupted an exquisitely tender voice, "don't shout! *They* can't hear you—now." And, turning, John Mudbury met the eyes of Everard Minturn, their President of the year before. Minturn had gone down with the *Titanic.*

He dropped his parcels then. His heart gave an enormous leap of joy.

He saw her face—the face of his wife—look through him.

But the child gazed straight into his eyes. She *saw* him.

The next thing he knew was that he heard something tinkling . . .

far, far away. It sounded miles below him—inside him—he was sounding himself—all utterly bewildering—like a bell. It *was* a bell.

Milly stooped down and picked the parcels up. Her face shone with happiness and laughter. . . .

But a man came in soon after, a man with a ridiculous, solemn face, a pencil, and a note-book. He wore a dark blue helmet. Behind him came a string of other men. They carried something . . . something . . . he could not see exactly what it was. But when he pressed forward through the laughing throng to gaze upon it, he dimly made out two eyes, a nose, a chin, a deep red smear, and a pair of folded hands upon an overcoat. A woman's form fell down upon them then, and . . . he heard . . . soft sounds of children weeping strangely . . . and other sounds . . . sounds as of familiar voices . . . laughing . . . laughing gaily.

"They'll join us presently. It goes like a flash. . . ."

And, turning with great happiness in his heart, he saw that Sir James had said it, holding Palmer by the arm as with some natural yet unexpected love of sympathetic friendship.

"Come on," said Palmer, smiling like a man who accepts a gift in universal fellowship, "let's help 'em. They'll never understand. . . . Still, we can always try."

The entire throng moved up with laughter and amusement. It was a moment of hearty, genuine life at last. Delight and Joy and Peace were everywhere.

Then John Mudbury realised the truth—that he was *dead.*

A Desert Episode

I

Better put wraps on now. The sun's getting low," a girl said.

It was the end of a day's expedition in the Arabian Desert, and they were having tea. A few yards away the donkeys munched their *barsim;* beside them in the sand the boys lay finishing bread and jam. Immense, with gliding tread, the sun's rays slid from crest to crest of the limestone ridges that broke the huge expanse towards the Red Sea. By the time the tea-things were packed the sun hovered, a giant ball of red, above the Pyramids. It stood in the western sky a moment, looking out of its majestic hood across the sand. With a movement almost visible it leaped, paused, then leaped again. It seemed to bound towards. the horizon; then, suddenly, was gone.

"It *is* cold, yes," said the painter, Rivers. And all who heard looked up at him because of the way he said it. A hurried movement ran through the merry party, and the girls were on their donkeys quickly, not wishing to be left to bring up the rear. They clattered off. The boys cried; the thud of sticks was heard; hoofs shuffled through the sand and stones. In single file the picnickers headed for Helouan, some five miles distant. And the desert closed up behind them as they went, following in a shadowy wave that never broke, noiseless, foamless, unstreaked, driven by no wind, and of a volume undiscoverable. Against the orange sunset the Pyramids turned deep purple. The strip of silvery Nile among its palm trees looked like rising mist. In the incredible Egyptian afterglow the enormous horizons burned a little longer, then went out. The ball of the earth—a huge round globe that bulged—curved visibly as at sea. It was no longer a flat expanse; it turned. Its splendid curves were realised.

"Better put wraps on; it's cold and the sun is low"—and then the curious hurry to get back among the houses and the haunts of men. No more was said, perhaps, than this, yet, the time and place being what they were, the mind became suddenly aware of that quality which ever brings a certain shrinking with it—vastness; and more than vastness: that which is endless because it is also beginningless—eternity. A colossal splendour stole upon the heart, and the senses, unaccustomed to the unusual stretch, reeled a little, as though the wonder was more than could be faced with comfort. Not all, doubtless, realised it, though to two, at least, it came with a staggering impact there was no withstanding. For, while the luminous greys and purples crept round them from the sandy wastes, the hearts of these two became aware of certain common things whose simple majesty is usually dulled by mere familiarity. Neither the man nor the girl knew for certain that the other felt it, as they brought up the rear together; yet the fact that each *did* feel it set them side by side in the same strange circle—and made them silent. They realised the immensity of a moment: the dizzy stretch of time that led up to the casual pinning of a veil; to the tightening of a stirrup strap; to the little speech with a companion; the roar of the vanished centuries that have ground mountains into sand and spread them over the floor of Africa; above all, to the little truth that they themselves existed amid the whirl of stupendous systems all delicately balanced as a spider's web—that they were *alive.*

For a moment this vast scale of reality revealed itself, then hid swiftly again behind the débris of the obvious. The universe, containing their two tiny yet important selves, stood still for an instant before their eyes. They looked at it—realised that they belonged to it. Everything moved and had its being, *lived*—here in this silent, empty desert even more actively than in a city of crowded houses. The quiet Nile, sighing with age, passed down towards the sea; there loomed the menacing Pyramids across the twilight; beneath them, in monstrous dignity, crouched that Shadow from whose eyes of battered stone proceeds the nameless thing that contracts the heart, then opens it again to terror; and everywhere, from towering monoliths as from secret tombs, rose that strange, long whisper which, defying time and distance, laughs at death. The spell of Egypt, which is the spell of immortality, touched their hearts.

Already, as the group of picnickers rode homewards now, the first stars twinkled overhead, and the peerless Egyptian night was on the way. There was hurry in the passing of the dusk. And the cold sensibly increased.

"So you did no painting after all," said Rivers to the girl who rode a little in front of him, "for I never saw you touch your sketch-book once."

They were some distance now behind the others; the line straggled; and when no answer came he quickened his pace, drew up alongside, and saw that her eyes, in the reflection of the sunset, shone with moisture. But she turned her head a little, smiling into his face, so that the human and the non-human beauty came over him with an onset that was almost shock. Neither one nor other, he knew, were long for him, and the realisation fell upon him with a pang of actual physical pain. The acuteness, the hopelessness of the realisation, for a moment, were more than he could bear, stern of temper though he was, and he tried to pass in front of her, urging his donkey with resounding strokes. Her own animal, however, following the lead, at once came up with him.

"You felt it, perhaps, as I did," he said some moments later, his voice quite steady again. "The stupendous, everlasting thing—the—*life* behind it all." He hesitated a little in his speech, unable to find the substantive that could compass even a fragment of his thought. She paused, too, similarly inarticulate before the surge of incomprehensible feelings.

"It's—awful," she said, half laughing, yet the tone hushed and a little quaver in it somewhere. And her voice to his was like the first sound he had ever heard in the world, for the first sound a full-grown man heard in the world would be beyond all telling—magical. "I shall not try again," she continued, leaving out the laughter this time; "my sketch-book is a farce. For, to tell the truth"—and the next three words she said below her breath—"I dare not."

He turned and looked at her for a second. It seemed to him that the following wave had caught them up, and was about to break above her, too. But the big-brimmed hat and the streaming veil shrouded her features. He saw, instead, the Universe. He felt as though he and she had always, always been together, and always, always would be. Separation was inconceivable.

"It came so close," she whispered. "It—shook me!"

They were cut off from their companions, whose voices sounded far ahead. Her words might have been spoken by the darkness, or by some one who peered at them from within that following wave. Yet the fanciful phrase was better than any he could find. From the immeasurable space of time and distance men's hearts vainly seek to plumb, it drew into closer perspective a certain meaning that words may hardly compass, a formidable truth that belongs to that deep place where hope and doubt fight their incessant battle. The awe she spoke of was the awe of immortality, of belonging to something that is endless and beginningless.

And he understood that the tears and laughter were one—caused by that spell which takes a little human life and shakes it, as an animal shakes its prey that later shall feed its blood and increase its power of growth. His other thoughts—really but a single thought—he had not the right to utter. Pain this time easily routed hope as the wave came nearer. For it was the wave of death that would shortly break, he knew, over him, but not over her. Him it would sweep with its huge withdrawal into the desert whence it came: her it would leave high upon the shores of life—alone. And yet the separation would somehow not be real. They were together in eternity even now. They were endless as this desert, beginningless as this sky . . . immortal. The realisation overwhelmed. . . .

The lights of Helouan seemed to come no nearer as they rode on in silence for the rest of the way. Against the dark background of the Mokattam Hills these fairy lights twinkled brightly, hanging in mid-air, but after an hour they were no closer than before. It was like riding towards the stars. It would take centuries to reach them. There were centuries in which to do so. Hurry has no place in the desert; it is born in streets. The desert stands still; to go fast in it is to go backwards. Now, in particular, its enormous, uncanny leisure was everywhere—in keeping with that mighty scale the sunset had made visible. His thoughts, like the steps of the weary animal that bore him, had no progress in them. The serpent of eternity, holding its tail in its own mouth, rose from the sand, enclosing himself, the stars—and her. Behind him, in the hollows of that shadowy wave, the procession of dynasties and conquests, the great series of gorgeous civilisations the mind calls Past, stood still, crowded with shining eyes and beckoning faces, still waiting to arrive. There is no death in Egypt. His own death stood so close that he could touch it by stretching out his hand, yet it seemed as much behind as in front of him. What man called a beginning was a trick. There was no such thing. He was with this girl—*now,* when Death waited so close for him—yet he had never really begun. Their lives ran always parallel. The hand he stretched to clasp approaching death caught instead in this girl's shadowy hair, drawing her in with him to the centre where he breathed the eternity of the desert. Yet expression of any sort was as futile as it was unnecessary. To paint, to speak, to sing, even the slightest gesture of the soul, became a crude and foolish thing. Silence was here the truth. And they rode in silence towards the fairy lights.

Then suddenly the rocky ground rose up close before them; boulders stood out vividly with black shadows and shining heads; a flat-roofed house slid by; three palm trees rattled in the evening wind; beyond, a mosque and minaret sailed upwards, like the spars and rigging of some phantom craft; and the colonnades of the great modern hotel, standing upon its dome of limestone ridge, loomed over them. Helouan was about them before they knew it. The desert lay behind with its huge, arrested billow. Slowly, owing to its prodigious volume, yet with a speed that merged it instantly with the far horizon behind the night, this wave now withdrew a little. There was no hurry. It came, for the moment, no farther. Rivers knew. For he was in it to the throat. Only his head was above the surface. He still could breathe—and speak—and see. Deepening with every hour into an incalculable splendour, it waited.

II

In the street the foremost riders drew rein, and, two and two abreast, the long line clattered past the shops and cafés, the railway station and hotels, stared at by the natives from the busy pavements. The donkeys stumbled, blinded by the electric light. Girls in white dresses flitted here and there, arabîyehs rattled past with people hurrying home to dress for dinner, and the evening train, just in from Cairo, disgorged its stream of passengers. There were dances in several of the hotels that night. Voices rose on all sides. Questions and answers, engagements and appointments were made, little plans and plots and intrigues for seizing happiness on the wing—before the wave rolled in and caught the lot. They chattered gaily:

"You *are* going, aren't you? You promised—"

"Of course I am."

"Then I'll drive you over. May I call for you?"

"All right. Come at ten."

"We shan't have finished our bridge by then. Say ten-thirty."

And eyes exchanged their meaning signals. The group dismounted and dispersed. Arabs standing under the lebbekh trees, or squatting on the pavements before their dim-lit booths, watched them with faces of gleaming bronze. Rivers gave his bridle to a donkey-boy, and moved across stiffly after the long ride to help the girl dismount. "You feel tired?" he asked gently. "It's been a long day." For her face was white as chalk, though the eyes shone brilliantly.

"Tired, perhaps," she answered, "but exhilarated too. I should like to be there now. I should like to go back this minute—if some one would take me." And, though she said it lightly, there was a meaning in her voice he apparently chose to disregard. It was as if she knew his secret. "Will you take me—some day soon?"

The direct question, spoken by those determined little lips, was impossible to ignore. He looked close into her face as he helped her from the saddle with a spring that brought her a moment half into his arms. "Some day—soon. I will," he said with emphasis, "when you are—ready." The pallor in her face, and a certain expression in it he had not known before, startled him. "I think you have been overdoing it," he added, with a tone in which authority and love were oddly mingled, neither of them disguised.

"Like yourself," she smiled, shaking her skirts out and looking down at her dusty shoes. "I've only a few days more—before I sail. We're both in such a hurry, but you are the worst of the two."

"Because my time is even shorter," ran his horrified thought—for he said no word.

She raised her eyes suddenly to his, with an expression that for an instant almost convinced him she had guessed—and the soul in him stood rigidly at attention, urging back the rising fires. The hair had dropped loosely round the sun-burned neck. Her face was level with his shoulder. Even the glare of the street lights could not make her undesirable. But behind the gaze of the deep brown eyes another thing looked forth imperatively into his own. And he recognised it with a rush of terror, yet of singular exultation.

"It followed us all the way," she whispered. "It came after us from the desert—where it *lives.*"

"At the houses," he said equally low, "it stopped." He gladly adopted her syncopated speech, for it helped him in his struggle to subdue those rising fires.

For a second she hesitated. "You mean, if we had not left so soon—when it turned cold. If we had not hurried—if we had remained a little longer—"

He caught at her hand, unable to control himself, but dropped it again the same second, while she made as though she had not noticed, forgiving him with her eyes. "Or a great deal longer," she added slowly—"for ever?"

And then he was certain that she *had* guessed—not that he loved her above all else in the world, for that was so obvious that a child might know it, but that his silence was due to his other, lesser secret; that the great Executioner stood waiting to drop the hood about his eyes. He was already pinioned. Something in her gaze and in her manner persuaded him suddenly that she understood.

His exhilaration increased extraordinarily. "I mean," he said very quietly, "that the spell weakens here among the houses and among the—so-called living." There was masterfulness, triumph, in his voice. Very wonderfully he saw her smile change; she drew slightly closer to his side, as though unable to resist. "Mingled with lesser things we should not understand completely," he added softly.

"And that might be a mistake, you mean?" she asked quickly, her face grave again.

It was his turn to hesitate a moment. The breeze stirred the hair about her neck, bringing its faint perfume—perfume of young life—to his nostrils. He drew his breath in deeply, smothering back the torrent of rising words he knew were unpermissible. "Misunderstanding," he said briefly. "If the eye be single—" He broke off, shaken by a paroxysm of coughing. "You know my meaning," he continued, as soon as the attack had passed; "you feel the difference *here,*" pointing round him to the hotels, the shops, the busy stream of people; "the hurry, the excitement, the feverish, blinding child's play which pretends to be alive, but does not know it—" And again the coughing stopped him. This time she took his hand in her own, pressed it very slightly, then released it. He felt it as the touch of that desert wave upon his soul. "The reception must be in complete and utter resignation. Tainted by lesser things, the disharmony might be—" he began stammeringly.

Again there came interruption, as the rest of the party called impatiently to know if they were coming up to the hotel. He had not time to find the completing adjective. Perhaps he could not find it ever. Perhaps it does not exist in any modern language. Eternity is not realised to-day; men have no time to know they are alive for ever; they are too busy. . . .

They all moved in a clattering, merry group towards the big hotel. Rivers and the girl were separated.

III

There was a dance that evening, but neither of these took part in it. In the great dining-room their tables were far apart. He could not even see her across the sea of intervening heads and shoulders. The long meal over, he went to his room, feeling it imperative to be alone. He did not read, he did not write; but, leaving the light unlit, he wrapped himself up and leaned out upon the broad window-sill into the great Egyptian night. His deep-sunken thoughts, like to the crowding stars, stood still, yet for ever took new shapes. He tried to see behind them, as, when a boy, he had tried to see behind the constellations—out into space—where there is nothing.

Below him the lights of Helouan twinkled like the Pleiades reflected in a pool of water; a hum of queer soft noises rose to his ears; but just beyond the houses the desert stood at attention, the vastest thing he had ever known, very stern, yet very comforting, with its peace beyond all comprehension, its delicate, wild terror, and its awful message of immortality. And the attitude of his mind, though he did not know it, was one of prayer. . . . From time to time he went to lie on the bed with paroxysms of coughing. He had overtaxed his strength—his swiftly fading strength. The wave had risen to his lips.

Nearer forty than thirty-five, Paul Rivers had come out to Egypt, plainly understanding that with the greatest care he might last a few weeks longer than if he stayed in England. A few more times to see the sunset and the sunrise, to watch the stars, feel the soft airs of earth upon his cheeks; a few more days of intercourse with his kind, asking and answering questions, wearing the old familiar clothes he loved, reading his favourite pages, and then—out into the big spaces—where there is nothing.

Yet no one, from his stalwart, energetic figure, would have guessed—no one but the expert mind, not to be deceived, to whom in the first attack of overwhelming despair and desolation he went for final advice. He left that house, as many had left it before, knowing that soon he would need no earthly protection of roof and walls, and that his soul, if it existed, would be shelterless in the space behind all manifested life. He had looked forward to fame and position in this world; had, indeed, already achieved the first step towards this end; and now, with the vanity of all earthly aims so mercilessly clear before him, he had turned, in somewhat of a nervous, concentrated hurry, to make terms with the Infinite while still the brain was there. And had, of course, found nothing. For it takes a lifetime crowded with experiment and effort to learn even the alphabet of genuine faith; and what could come of a few weeks' wild questioning but confusion and bewilderment of mind? It was inevitable. He came out to Egypt wondering, thinking, questioning, but chiefly wondering. He had grown, that is, more childlike, abandoning the futile tool of Reason, which hitherto had seemed to him the perfect instrument. Its foolishness stood naked before him in the pitiless light of the specialist's decision. For—"Who can by searching find out God?"

To be exceedingly careful of over-exertion was the final warning he brought with him, and, within a few hours of his arrival, three weeks ago, he had met this girl and utterly disregarded it. He took it somewhat thus: "Instead of lingering I'll enjoy myself and go out—a little sooner. I'll *live.* The time is very short." His was not a nature, anyhow, that could heed a warning. He could not kneel. Upright and unflinching, he went to meet things as they came, reckless, unwise, but certainly not afraid. And this characteristic operated now. He ran to meet Death full tilt in the uncharted spaces that lay behind the stars. With love for a companion now, he raced, his speed increasing from day to day, she, as he thought, knowing merely that he sought her, but had not guessed his darker secret that was now his *lesser* secret.

And in the desert, this afternoon of the picnic, the great thing he sped to meet had shown itself with its familiar touch of appalling cold and shadow, familiar, because all minds know of and accept it; appalling because, until realised close, and with the mental power at the full, it remains but a name the heart refuses to believe in. And he had discovered that its name was—Life.

Rivers had seen the Wave that sweeps incessant, tireless, but as a rule invisible, round the great curve of the bulging earth, brushing the nations into the deeps behind. It had followed him home to the streets and houses of Helouan. He saw it *now,* as he leaned from his window, dim and immense, too huge to break. Its beauty was nameless, undecipherable. His coughing echoed back from the wall of its great sides. . . . And the music floated up at the same time from the ballroom in the opposite wing. The two sounds mingled. Life, which is love, and Death, which is their unchanging partner, held hands beneath the stars.

He leaned out farther to drink in the cool, sweet air. Soon, on this air, his body would be dust, driven, perhaps, against her very cheek, trodden on possibly by her little foot—until, in turn, she joined him too, blown by the same wind loose about the desert. True. Yet at the same time they would always be together, always somewhere side by side, continuing in the vast universe, *alive.* This new, absolute conviction was in him now. He remembered the curious, sweet perfume in the desert, as of flowers, where yet no flowers are. It was the perfume of life. But in the desert there is no life. Living things that grow and move and utter, are but a protest against death. In the desert they are unnecessary, because death there *is* not. Its overwhelming vitality needs no insolent, visible proof, no protest, no challenge, no little signs of life. The message of the desert is immortality. . . .

He went finally to bed, just before midnight. Hovering magnificently just outside his window, Death watched him while he slept. The wave crept to the level of his eyes. He called her name. . . .

And downstairs, meanwhile, the girl, knowing nothing, wondered where he was, wondered unhappily and restlessly; more—though this she did not understand—wondered motheringly. Until to-day, on the ride home, and from their singular conversation together, she had guessed nothing of his reason for being at Helouan, where so many come in order to find life. She only knew her own. And she was but twenty-five. . . .

Then, in the desert, when that touch of unearthly chill had stolen out of the sand towards sunset, she had realised clearly, astonished she had not seen it long ago, that this man loved her, yet that something prevented his obeying the great impulse. In the life of Paul Rivers, whose presence had profoundly stirred her heart the first time she saw him, there was some obstacle that held him back, a barrier his honour must respect. He could never tell her of his love. It could lead to nothing. Knowing that he was not married, her intuition failed her utterly at first. Then, in their silence on the homeward ride, the truth had somehow pressed up and touched her with its hand of ice. In that disjointed conversation at the end, which reads as it sounded, as though no coherent meaning lay behind the words, and as though both sought to conceal by speech what yet both burned to utter, she had divined his darker secret, and knew that it was the same as her own. She understood then it was Death that had tracked them from the desert, following with its gigantic shadow from the sandy wastes. The cold, the darkness, the silence which cannot answer, the stupendous mystery which is the spell of its inscrutable Presence, had risen about them in the dusk, and kept them company at a little distance, until the lights of Helouan had bade it halt. Life which may not, cannot end, had frightened her.

His time, perhaps, was even shorter than her own. None knew his secret, since he was alone in Egypt and was caring for himself. Similarly, since she bravely kept her terror to herself, her mother had no inkling of her own, aware merely that the disease was in her system and that her orders were to be extremely cautious. This couple, therefore, shared secretly together the two clearest glimpses of eternity life has to offer to the soul. Side by side they looked into the splendid eyes of Love and Death. Life, moreover, with its instinct for simple and terrific drama, had produced this majestic climax, breaking with pathos, at the very moment when it could not be developed—this side of the stars. They stood together upon the stage, a stage emptied of other human players; the audience had gone home and the lights were being lowered; no music sounded; the critics were a-bed. In this great game of Consequences it was known where he met her, what he said and what she answered, possibly what they did and even what the world thought. But "what the consequence was" would remain unknown, untold. That would happen in the big spaces of which the desert in its silence, its motionless serenity, its shelterless, intolerable vastness, is the perfect symbol. And the desert gives no answer. It sounds no challenge, for it is complete. Life in the desert makes no sign. It *is*.

IV

In the hotel that night there arrived by chance a famous International dancer, whose dahabîyeh lay anchored at San Giovanni, in the Nile below Helouan; and this woman, with her party, had come to dine and take part in the festivities. The news spread. After twelve the lights were lowered, and while the moonlight flooded the terraces, streaming past pillar and colonnade, she rendered in the shadowed halls the music of the Masters, interpreting with an instinctive genius messages which are eternal and divine.

Among the crowd of enthralled and delighted guests, the girl sat on the steps and watched her. The rhythmical interpretation held a power that seemed, in a sense, inspired; there lay in it a certain unconscious something that was pure, unearthly; something that the stars, wheeling in stately movements over the sea and desert know; something the great winds bring to mountains where they play together; something the forests capture and fix magically into their gathering of big and little branches. It was both passionate and spiritual, wild and tender, intensely human and seductively non-human. For it was original, taught of Nature, a revelation of naked, unhampered life. It comforted, as the desert comforts. It brought the desert awe into the stuffy corridors of the hotel, with the moonlight and the whispering of stars, yet behind it ever the silence of those grey, mysterious, interminable spaces which utter to themselves the wordless song of life. For it was the same dim thing, she felt, that had followed her from the desert several hours before, halting just outside the streets and houses as though blocked from further advance; the thing that had stopped her foolish painting, skilled though she was, because it hides behind colour and not in it; the thing that veiled the meaning in the cryptic sentences she and he had stammered out together; the thing, in a word, as near as she could approach it by any means of interior expression, that the realisation of death for the first time makes comprehensible—Immortality. It was unutterable, but it *was*. He and she were indissolubly together. Death was no separation. There was no death. . . . It was terrible. It was—she had already used the word—awful, full of awe.

"In the desert," thought whispered, as she watched spellbound, "it is impossible even to conceive of death. The idea is meaningless. It simply is not."

The music and the movement filled the air with life which, being there, must continue always, and continuing always can have never had a beginning. Death, therefore, was the great revealer of life. Without it none could realise that they are alive. Others had discovered this before her, but she did not know it. In the desert no one can realise death: it is hope and life that are the only certainty. The entire conception of the Egyptian system was based on this—the conviction, sure and glorious, of life's endless continuation. Their tombs and temples, their pyramids and sphinxes surviving after thousands of years, defy the passage of time and laugh at death; the very bodies of their priests and kings, of their animals even, their fish, their insects, stand to-day as symbols of their stalwart knowledge.

And this girl, as she listened to the music and watched the inspired dancing, remembered it. The message poured into her from many sides, though the desert brought it clearest. With death peering into her face a few short weeks ahead, she thought instead of—life. The desert, as it were, became for her a little fragment of eternity, focused into an intelligible point for her mind to rest upon with comfort and comprehension. Her steady, thoughtful nature stirred towards an objective far beyond the small enclosure of one narrow lifetime. The scale of the desert stretched her to the grandeur of its own imperial meaning, its divine repose, its unassailable and everlasting majesty. She looked beyond the wall.

Eternity! That which is endless; without pause, without beginning, without divisions or boundaries. The fluttering of her brave yet frightened spirit ceased, aware with awe of its own everlastingness. The swiftest motion produces the effect of immobility; excessive light is darkness; size, run loose into enormity, is the same as the minutely tiny. Similarly, in the desert, life, too overwhelming and terrific to know limit or confinement, lies undetailed and stupendous, still as deity, a revelation of nothingness because it is all. Turned golden beneath its spell that the music and the rhythm made even more comprehensible, the soul in her, already lying beneath the shadow of the great wave, sank into rest and peace, too certain of itself to fear. And panic fled away. "I am immortal . . . because I *am.* And what I love is not apart from me. It is myself. We are together endlessly because we *are.*"

Yet in reality, though the big desert brought this, it was Love, which, being of similar parentage, interpreted its vast meaning to her little heart—that sudden love which, without a word of preface or explanation, had come to her a short three weeks before. . . . She went up to her room soon after midnight, abruptly, unexpectedly stricken. Some one, it seemed, had called her name. She passed his door.

The lights had been turned up. The clamour of praise was loud round the figure of the weary dancer as she left in a carriage for her dahabîyeh on the Nile. A low wind whistled round the walls of the great hotel, blowing chill and bitter between the pillars of the colonnades. The girl heard the voices float up to her through the night, and once more, behind the confused sound of the many, she heard her own name called, but more faintly than before, and from very far away. It came through the spaces beyond her open window; it died away again; then—but for the sighing of that bitter wind—silence, the deep silence of the desert.

And these two, Paul Rivers and the girl, between them merely a floor of that stone that built the Pyramids, lay a few moments before the Wave of Sleep engulfed them. And, while they slept, two shadowy forms hovered above the roof of the quiet hotel, melting presently into one, as dreams stole down from the desert and the stars. Immortality whispered to them. On either side rose Life and Death, towering in splendour. Love, joining their spreading wings, fused the gigantic outlines into one. The figures grew smaller, comprehensible. They entered the little windows. Above the beds they paused a moment, watching, waiting, and then, like a wave that is just about to break, they stooped. . . .

And in the brilliant Egyptian sunlight of the morning, as she went downstairs, she passed his door again. She had awakened, but he slept on. He had preceded her. It was next day she learned his room was vacant. . . . Within the month she joined him, and within the year the cool north wind that sweetens Lower Egypt from the sea blew the dust across the desert as before. It is the dust of kings, of queens, of priests, princesses, lovers. It is the dust no earthly power can annihilate. It, too, lasts for ever. There was a little more of it . . . the desert's message slightly added to: Immortality.

What Nobody Understands

But sometimes Daddy was more successful. A vicarious success, it was true, yet one that redounded to his glory and honour.

"Oh, thank you, awfully, AWFULLY, *awfully*," Jimbo said. "That was twice as long as anything Daddy ever told. He said you could."

"But Uncle Henry's an author, and has to be long," explained Jinny, defending her father and praising her uncle at the same time.

For when Uncle Henry came to stay with them on visits of a month or so the father produced a set of sentences he kept slyly up his sleeve for the occasion. "Ask Uncle Henry; he's better at stories and things than I am. It's his business." This was the model. A variation ran: "Oh, don't bother me just now, children. I've got a lot of figures to digest." But the shortest version was simply: "Run and plague your uncle. I'm too busy."

"Try mother," was used when Uncle Henry was away. Only it had no result. Mother's mind was too confused to carry conviction. It was soaked in servants and things. In another sense it was too exact. The ingredients of her stories were like a cooking recipe. Besides, hers was the fatal gift of never forgetting the time. On the very stroke of the half-hour she said: "Now it's bed-time; you shall hear the rest tomorrow night." Daddy forgot, and Uncle Henry insisted upon "ten minutes more; I must get to the end before they go." Uncle Henry was the favourite, of course—in spite of his dreadful appearance.

For Uncle Henry was a very big man, and wore a beard that tickled. His voice was deep and gruff. "Like a dog's," according to Maria, the youngest. And his laugh was like a horse's neigh. He was rough, too, and "frightfully strong," for he could take a child under each arm and another on his back—and run! He never smiled while he told his stories, and though this made the stories seem extra real, it also alarmed—in the terrible places. Perched on his knees, they felt "like up the cedar," and when he stretched a leg or arm it was the great branch swaying in the wind.

His manner, too, was stern to severity, and his voice got so deep sometimes that they could "feel it rumbling inside," as though he had "swallowed the dinner gong." He was a very important man, besides. Daddy was just "inanoffiss," but Uncle Henry was an author, and the vagueness of his duties included awe. He wrote "storicalnovuls." His name was often in the newspapers. They connected him with the GOVERNMENT. It had to do somewhere with the Police. No one trifled with Uncle Henry.

Yet, strange to say, the children never could be properly afraid of him, although they tried very hard. Their audacity, their familiarity, their daring astonished everybody. The gardeners and coachman, to say nothing of the indoor servants, treated him as though he were some awful emperor. But the children simply pushed him about. He might have been a friendly Newfoundland dog that wore tail coats and walked on its hind legs for all they feared reprisals.

"No, children; it's impossible now. I'm busy over a scene of my storicalnovul. Ask your father." He growled it at them, frowning darkly.

The parental heels had just that instant vanished round the door.

"Father's got the figures, and says he can't."

"Or your mother—" he said, gruffly.

"Mother's doing servants in the housekeeper's room."

"Take your foot out of my waistcoat pocket this instant," he roared.

"Why ever should I?" enquired Maria. "How else can I climb up?"

He shook and swayed like the cedar branch, but he did not shake her off. "Because," he thundered, "there's money in it, and you've got holes in your stocking, and toes with you are worse than fingers."

And he strode across the floor, Jimbo clinging to one leg with both feet off the ground, and Jinny pushing him behind as though he were a heavy door that wouldn't open. He was very angry indeed. He told them plainly what he thought about them. He stormed and raved and lost all control of his manners and his tongue. He explained the philosophy of authors to them in brutal sentences. "Leave me alone, you little botherations!" he cried. "I'm in the middle of a scene in a storicalnovul." It was disgraceful that a man could lose his temper so. "Leave me alone or I'll—"

In the corner of the big nursery sofa there was sudden silence. Between the bars across the windows the wistaria leaves sifted the setting sunlight. The railway train stood motionless on its side upon the speckled carpet. A cat, so fat it couldn't unroll, lay in a ball of mystery against the high guard of wire netting before the fire. Outside the wind went moaning.

"—or I'll leave this house and never speak to you again," the sentence dropped into a whisper amid other sounds of general collapse among soft cushions.

It was one of those abrupt and sudden changes that bewilder the psychologists and make the evolutionists fear that, after all, Nature does make incalculable jumps.

"We're quite ready, thank you," whispered a voice.

And Time ran backwards, or else the clock stopped dead. Dusk slipped in between the window bars. The cedars on the lawn became gigantic. They heard the haystacks shuffling out of their tarpaulins. The whole house rose into the air and floated off. Mother, Daddy, nurses, beds dropped from the windows as it sailed away. All were left behind, forgotten, details of some stupid and uncomfortable life elsewhere.

"*Quite* ready," sighed the top of one cedar to the other.

"And waiting, too," an answer came from nowhere.

And then the Universe paused and settled with a fluttering sound of little wonder. The onceuponatime Moment entered the room. . . .

"There was a thing that nobody could understand," began the deep, gruff voice—

"Oh, I'm so glad. Daddy's once-upon-a-time is always a man or a little girl."

"And this thing that nobody could understand was something no one understood at all."

"That's twice they couldn't understand it," observed Jinny in the slight pause he made for effect. And Jimbo enquired fast upon her heels whether it was "alive or dead, or just a muddly thing that didn't matter?" Maria merely stared. She reserved her criticism for later on.

"It was alive," he went on, "and very beautiful, so beautiful, in fact, that people were astonished and felt rather ashamed because they couldn't understand it. Some declared it wasn't worth understanding at all; others said it might be worth understanding if they had the time to think about it; and the rest decided that it was nothing much, and promptly forgot that it existed. Their lives grew rather dull in consequence. A few, however, set to work to discover what it was. For the beauty of it set something in them burning."

"It was a firework, I think," remarked Maria, then felt she had said quite an awful thing. For Jimbo just looked at her. "It's alive, Uncle Henry told you," he stated. She was obliterated—for the moment.

"Yes," resumed the story-teller, "it was alive, and its beauty set the hearts of a few people on fire to know what it meant. It was difficult to find, however, and difficult to see properly when found. These people tried to copy it, and couldn't. Though it looked so simple, it was impossible to imitate. It went about so quickly that they couldn't catch hold of it and—"

"But have *you* seen it?" asked Maria, her head bobbing up into his face with eager curiosity.

It was a vital question. All waited anxiously for his reply.

"I have," he answered convincingly. "I saw it first when I was about your age, and I've never forgotten it since."

"But you've seen it since, hav'n't you? It's still in the world, isn't it?"

"I've seen it since; and it's still in the world. Only no one knows to this day why it's there. No one can explain it. No one can understand it. It's so beautiful that it makes you wonder, and it's so mysterious that it makes you—"

"What?" asked Jimbo for the others, while he paused a moment and stared into their gazing faces.

"—wonder still more," he added.

Another pause followed.

"Then is your heart still burning, Uncle Henry?" Jinny enquired, prodding him softly. "And does it matter much?"

"It matters a great deal, yes, because I want to find out, and cannot. And the burning goes on and on whenever I see the thing-that-nobody-can-understand, and even when I don't see it but just think about it—which is pretty often. Because, if I found out why it's there, I should know so much that I should give up writing storicalnovuls and become a sort of prophet instead."

They stared in great bewilderment. Their curiosity was immense. They were dying to know what the thing was, but it was against the

Rules to ask outright.

"But were their lives *very* dull—those people who forgot about it altogether?" Maria set this problem, suddenly recalling something at the beginning of the story.

She ran a nasty risk of being obliterated again. But Uncle Henry spoke before the others could interfere.

"Oh, very dull indeed. They had no sense of wonder."

"How awful for them!"

"Awful," he agreed, in a long-drawn whisper, shuddering.

And that shudder ran through every one. The children turned towards the darkening room. The gloomy cupboard was a blotch of shadow. The table frowned. The bookshelves listened. The white face of the cuckoo clock peered down upon them dimly from the opposite wall, and the chairs, it seemed, moved up a little closer. But through the windows the stars were beginning to peep, and they saw the crests of the friendly cedars waving in the wind against the fading sky.

He pointed. High above the cedars, where the first stars twinkled, the blue was deep and exquisitely shaded from the golden streak below it into a colour almost purple.

"The thing that nobody could understand was even more wonderful than that," he whispered. "But no one could tell why it was there; no one could guess; no one could find out. And still—no one can find out."

His voice grew lower and lower and lower still.

"To-morrow I'll show it to you. You see it for yourselves."

They hardly heard him now. The voice seemed far away.

"We'll go out and find one . . . by the stream . . . where the willows bend . . . and shake their pointed leaves. . . . We'll go to-morrow. . . ."

His voice died away inside his waistcoat. Not a sound was audible. The children were very close against him. In his big hands he took each face in turn and put his lips inside the rim of three small ears.

He told the secret then, while Wonder filled the room and hovered exquisitely above that crowded chair.

Awakened by the silence, presently, the ball of black unrolled itself beside the wire fender. It stretched its four black legs. And the children, hushed, happy, and with mysterious burning in their hearts, went off willingly to bed, to dream of Wonder all night long, and to ask themselves in sleep "Why has God put blue dust upon the body of a dragon-fly?"

Maria

Maria was a podgy child of marked individuality. It was said that she was seven years old, but *she* declared that eight was the figure, because some uncle or other had explained "you're in your eighth year." Wandering uncles are troublesome in this kind of way. Every time her age was mentioned she corrected the informant. She had a trick of moving her eyes without moving her head. Her podgy round face was difficult to turn, for it was a trifle heavy, and Maria was incorrigibly lazy; but her big blue eyes slipped round without the smallest trouble. The performance gave her the sly and knowing aspect of a goblin, but she had no objection to that, for it saved her trouble, and to save herself trouble was an object in itself. Nurses, governesses, and the like declared it was her sole object in existence.

"And this little person," one of those inquisitive, interfering visitors would ask, smiling fatuously, "how old is she, I wonder?"

"Seven," was the answer of the Authority in charge.

Maria's eyes rolled sideways, and a little upwards. She looked at the foolish questioner; the Authority who had answered was not worth a glance.

"No," she said flatly, with sublime defiance, "I'm much more than that. I'm in my eighth year, you see."

And the visitor, smiling that pleasant smile that makes children distrust, even dislike them, and probably venturing to pinch her cheek or pat her on the shoulder into the bargain, accepted the situation with another type of smile—the Smile-that-children-expect. As a matter of fact, children hate it. They see through its artificial humbug easily. They prefer a solemn and unsmiling face invariably. It's the latter that produces chocolates and sudden presents; it's the stern-faced sort that play hide-and-seek or stand on their heads. The Smilers are bored at heart. They mean to escape at the first opportunity. And the children never catch their sleeves or coat-tails to prevent them going.

"So you're in your eighth year, are you?" this Smiler chuckled with a foolish grin. He patted her cheek kindly. "Why, you're almost a grown-up person. You'll be going to dinner-parties soon." And he smiled again. Maria stood motionless and patient. Her eyes gazed straight before her. Her podgy face remained expressionless as dough.

"Answer the kind gentleman," said the Authority, reprovingly.

Maria did not budge. A finger and thumb, both dirty, rolled a portion of her pinafore into a pointed thing like string, distinctly black. She waited till the visitor withdrew. But this particular visitor did not withdraw.

"*I* know a little girl—" he began, with that condescending grin which meant that her rejection of his advances had offended him, "a little girl of about your age, who—"

But the remainder of the rebuke-concealed-in-a-story was heard only by the Authority. For Maria, relentless and unhumbugged, merely walked away. In the hall she discovered Jimbo, discreetly hiding.

"What's he come for?" the brother enquired promptly.

Maria's eyes just looked at him.

"To see Mother, I suppose," he answered himself, accustomed to his sister's goblin manners, "and talk about missions and subshkiptions and all that. Did he give you anything?"

"No, nothing."

"Did he call us bonny little ones?" His face mentioned that he could kill if necessary, or if his sister's honour required it.

"He didn't *say* it."

"Lucky for him," exclaimed Jimbo gallantly, rubbing his nose with the palm of his hand and snorting loudly. "What *did* he say then—the old Smiler?"

"He said," replied Maria, moving her head as well as her eyes, "that I wasn't really old, and that he knew another little girl who was nicer than me, and always told the truth, and—"

"Oh, come on," cried Jimbo, interrupting. "My trains are going in the schoolroom and I want a driver for an accident. We'll put the Smiler in the luggage van and he'll get smashed in the collision, and *all* the wheels will go over his head. Then he'll find out how old you really are. We'll fairly smash him!"

They disappeared. Jinny, who was reading a book on the Apocalypse, in a corner of the room, looked up a moment as they entered.

"What's up?" she asked, her mind a little dazed by the change of focus from stars, scarlet women, white horses, and mysterious "Voices," to dull, practical details of everyday existence. "What's on?" she repeated.

"Trains," replied Jimbo. "We're going to have an accident and kill a man dead."

"What's he done?" she enquired.

"Humbugged Maria with a lot of stuff—and gave her nothing—and didn't believe a single word she told him."

Jinny glanced without much interest at the railway laid out upon the floor, murmured, "Oh, I see," and resumed her reading of the wonderful book she had purloined from the top shelf of a neglected bookcase outside the gun-room. It absorbed her. She loved the tremendous words, the atmosphere of marvel and disaster, and especially the constant suggestion that the end of the world was near. Antichrist she simply adored. No other hero in any book she knew came near him.

"Come and help," urged Jimbo, picking up an engine that lay upon its side. "Come on!"

"No, thanks. I've got an Apocalypse. It's simply frightfully exciting."

"Shall we break *both* legs," asked Maria blandly, "or just his neck?"

"Neck will do," said Jimbo. "Only they must find the heart beneath the rubbish of the luggage van."

Jinny looked up in spite of herself. "Who is it?" she enquired, with an air of weighing conflicting interests.

"Mr. Jinks." It was Maria who supplied the information.

"But he's Daddy's offiss-partner man," Jinny objected, though without much vim or heat.

Maria did not answer. Her eyes were glued upon the other engine.

"All black and burnt and—full of the very horridest diseases," put in Jimbo, referring to the heart of the destroyed Mr. Jinks beneath the engine.

He glanced up enticingly at his elder sister, whom he longed to draw into the vindictive holocaust.

"He said things to Maria," he explained persuasively; "and it's not the first time either. Last Sunday he called me 'his little man,' and he's never given me a single thing since ever I can remember, years and years ago."

Then Jinny remembered that he invariably kissed her on both cheeks as though she was a silly little child.

"Oh, *that* man!" she exclaimed, realising fully now the enormities he had committed. She appeared to hesitate a minute. Then she flung down her Apocalypse suddenly. "Put him on a scarlet horse," she cried, "and pretend he's the Beast, and I'll come."

Maria's blue eyes wheeled half a circle towards Jimbo. She did not move her head. It signified agreement. Jimbo knew. Only her consent, as the insulted party, was necessary before he could approve.

"All right," he said to Jinny. "We'll put him in a special carriage with his horse, and I'll make out a label for the window so that everyone will know." He went over to the table and wrote "BEAST" in capital letters on a half sheet of paper. The cumbersome quill pen made two spongey blots.

"It's the End of the World *really* at the same time," decided Jinny, to a chorus of general approval, "not only the end of Mr. Jinks." She liked her horrors on a proper scale.

And the railway line was quickly laid across the room from the window to the wall. The lamps of oil on both engines were lit. The trains faced one another. Mr. Jinks and his scarlet horse thought themselves quite safe in their special carriage, unaware that it was labelled "Beast" with a label that overlapped the roof and hid all view of the landscape through the windows of one side. Apparently they slept in opposite corners, with full consciousness of complete security. Mr. Jinks was tucked up with woolly rugs and a newspaper lay across his knees. The scarlet horse had its head in a bag of oats, and its bridle was fastened to the luggage rack above. Both were supplied with iron footwarmers. There was a *fearful* fog; and the train was going at a *tremendous* pace.

So was the other train. They approached, they banged, they smashed to atoms. It was the most appalling collision that had ever been heard of, and the Guard and Engine Driver, as well as the Ticket

Collectors and Directors of the Company, were all executed by the Government the very next day from gallows that an angry London built in half an hour on the top of St. Paul's Cathedral dome.

It took place between the footstool and the fireplace in the thickest fog that England had ever known. And the horrid black heart of Mr. Jinks was discovered beneath the wreckage of a special carriage next the luggage van. It was simply black as coal and very nasty indeed. The little boy who found it was a porter's son, whose mother was so poor that she took in washing for members of Parliament, who paid their bills irregularly because they were very busy governing Ireland. He knew it was a cinder, but did not discover it was a heart until he showed it to his mother, and his mother said it was far too black to wash.

The accident to Mr. Jinks, therefore, was a complete success. The butler helped with the mending of the engine, and Maria informed at least one authority, "We do not know Mr. Jinks. We have other friends instead."

"But, remember," said Jinny, "we mustn't mention it to Daddy because Mr. Jinks is his partner-in-the-offiss."

"Was," said Jimbo.

The remains they decided to send to what they called the "Hospital for Parilysed Ineebrits with Incurable Afflictions of the Heart."

By Water

The night before young Larsen left to take up his new appointment in Egypt he went to the clairvoyante. He neither believed nor disbelieved. He felt no interest, for he already knew his past and did not wish to know his future. "Just to please me, Jim," the girl pleaded. "The woman is wonderful. Before I had been five minutes with her she told me your initials, so there *must* be something in it." "She read your thought," he smiled indulgently. "Even I can do that!" But the girl was in earnest. He yielded; and that night at his farewell dinner he came to give his report of the interview.

The result was meagre and unconvincing: money was coming to him, he was soon to make a voyage, and he would never marry. "So you see how silly it all is," he laughed, for they were to be married when his first promotion came. He gave the details, however, making a little story of it the way he knew she loved.

"But was that all, Jim?" The girl asked it, looking rather hard into his face. "Aren't you hiding something from me?" He hesitated a moment, then burst out laughing at her clever discernment. "There *was* a little more," he confessed, "but you take it all so seriously; I—"

He had to tell it then, of course. The woman had told him a lot of gibberish about friendly and unfriendly elements. "She said water was unfriendly to me; I was to be careful of water, or else I should come to harm by it. *Fresh* water only," he hastened to add, seeing that the idea of shipwreck was in her mind.

"Drowning?" the girl asked quickly.

"Yes," he admitted with reluctance, but still laughing; "she did say drowning, though drowning in no ordinary way."

The girl's face showed uneasiness a moment. "What does that mean—drowning in no ordinary way?" she asked, a catch in her breath.

But that he could not tell her, because he did not know himself. He gave, therefore, the exact words: "You will drown, but will not know you drown."

It was unwise of him. He wished afterwards he had invented a happier report, or had kept this detail back. "I'm safe in Egypt, anyhow," he laughed. "I shall be a clever man if I can find enough water in the desert to do me harm!" And all the way from Trieste to Alexandria he remembered the promise she had extracted—that he would never once go on the Nile unless duty made it imperative for him to do so. He kept that promise like the literal, faithful soul he was. His love was equal to the somewhat quixotic sacrifice it occasionally involved. Fresh water in Egypt there was practically none other, and in any case the natrum works where his duty lay had their headquarters some distance out into the desert. The river, with its banks of welcome, refreshing verdure, was not even visible.

Months passed quickly, and the time for leave came within measurable distance. In the long interval luck had played the cards kindly for him, vacancies had occurred, early promotion seemed likely, and his letters were full of plans to bring her out to share a little house of their own. His health, however, had not improved; the dryness did not suit him; even in this short period his blood had thinned, his nervous system deteriorated, and, contrary to the doctor's prophecy, the waterless air had told upon his sleep. A damp climate liked him best, and once the sun had touched him with its fiery finger.

His letters made no mention of this. He described the life to her, the work, the sport, the pleasant people, and his chances of increased pay and early marriage. And a week before he sailed he rode out upon a final act of duty to inspect the latest diggings his company were making. His course lay some twenty miles into the desert behind El-Chobak and towards the limestone hills of Guebel Haidi, and he went alone, carrying lunch and tea, for it was the weekly holiday of Friday, and the men were not at work.

The accident was ordinary enough. On his way back in the heat of early afternoon his pony stumbled against a boulder on the treacherous desert film, threw him heavily, broke the girth, bolted before he could seize the reins again, and left him stranded some ten or twelve miles from home. There was a pain in his knee that made walking difficult, a buzzing in his head that troubled sight and made the landscape swim, while, worse than either, his provisions, fastened to the saddle, had vanished with the frightened pony into those blazing leagues of sand. He was alone in the Desert, beneath the pitiless afternoon sun, twelve miles of utterly exhausting country between him and safety.

Under normal conditions he could have covered the distance in four hours, reaching home by dark; but his knee pained him so that a mile an hour proved the best he could possibly do. He reflected a few minutes. The wisest course was to sit down and wait till the pony told its obvious story to the stable, and help should come. And this was what he did, for the scorching heat and glare were dangerous; they were terrible; he was shaken and bewildered by his fall, hungry and weak into the bargain; and an hour's painful scrambling over the baked and burning little gorges must have speedily caused complete prostration. He sat down and rubbed his aching knee. It was quite a little adventure. Yet, though he knew the Desert might not be lightly trifled with, he felt at the moment nothing more than this—and the amusing description of it he would give in his letter, or—intoxicating thought—by word of mouth. In the heat of the sun he began to feel drowsy. A soft torpor crept over him. He dozed. He fell asleep.

It was a long, a dreamless sleep . . . for when he woke at length the sun had just gone down, the dusk lay awfully upon the enormous desert, and the air was chilly. The cold had waked him. Quickly, as though on purpose, the red glow faded from the sky; the first stars shone; it was dark; the heavens were deep violet. He looked round and realised that his sense of direction had gone entirely. Great hunger was in him. The cold already was bitter as the wind rose, but the pain in his knee having eased, he got up and walked a little—and in a moment lost sight of the spot where he had been lying. The shadowy desert swallowed it. "Ah," he realised, "this is not an English field or moor. I'm in the Desert!" The safe thing to do was to remain exactly where he was; only thus could the rescuers find him; once he wandered he was done for. It was strange the search-party had not yet arrived. To keep warm, however, he was compelled to move, so he made a little pile of stones to mark the place, and walked round and round it in a circle of some dozen yards' diameter. He limped badly, and the hunger gnawed dreadfully; but, after all, the adventure was not so terrible. The amusing side of it kept uppermost still. Though fragile in body, his spirit was not unduly timid or imaginative; he *could* last out the night, or, if the worst came to the worst, the next day as well. But when he watched the little group of stones, he saw that there were dozens of them, scores, hundreds, thousands of these little groups of stones. The desert's face, of course, is thickly strewn with them. The original one was lost in the first five minutes. So he sat down again. But the biting cold, and the wind that licked his very skin beneath the light clothing, soon forced him up again. It was ominous; and the night huge and shelterless. The shaft of green zodiacal light that hung so strangely in the western sky for hours had faded away; the stars were out in their bright thousands; no guide was anywhere; the wind moaned and puffed among the sandy mounds; the vast sheet of desert stretched appallingly upon the world; he heard the jackals cry. . . .

And with the jackals' cry came suddenly the unwelcome realisation that no play was in this adventure any more, but that a bleak reality stared at him through the surrounding darkness. He faced it—at bay. He was genuinely lost. Thought blocked in him. "I must be calm and think," he said aloud. His voice woke no echo; it was small and dead; something gigantic ate it instantly. He got up and walked again. Why did no one come? Hours had passed. The pony had long ago found its stable, or—had it run madly in another direction altogether? He worked out possibilities, tightening his belt. The cold was searching; he never had been, never could be warm again; the hot sunshine of a few hours ago seemed the merest dream. Unfamiliar with hardship, he knew not what to do, but he took his coat and shirt off, vigorously rubbed his skin where the dried perspiration of the afternoon still caused clammy shivers, swung his arms furiously like a London cab-man, and quickly dressed again. Though the wind upon his bare back was fearful, he felt warmer a little. He lay down exhausted, sheltered by an overhanging limestone crag, and took snatches of fitful dog's-sleep, while the wind drove overhead and the dry sand pricked his skin. One face continually was near him; one pair of tender eyes; two dear hands smoothed him; he smelt the perfume of light brown hair. It was all natural enough. His whole thought, in his misery, ran to her in England—England where there were soft fresh grass, big sheltering trees, hemlock and honeysuckle in the hedges—while the hard black Desert guarded him, and consciousness dipped away at little intervals under this dry and pitiless Egyptian sky. . . .

It was perhaps five in the morning when a voice spoke and he started up with a horrid jerk—the voice of that clairvoyante woman. The sentence died away into the darkness, but one word remained: *Water!* At first he wondered, but at once explanation came. Cause and effect were obvious. The clue was physical. His body needed water, and so the thought came up into his mind. He was thirsty.

This was the moment when fear first really touched him. Hunger was manageable, more or less—for a day or two, certainly. But thirst! Thirst and the Desert were an evil pair that, by cumulative suggestion gathering since childhood days, brought terror in. Once in the mind it could not be dislodged. In spite of his best efforts, the ghastly thing grew passionately—because his thirst grew too. He had smoked much; had eaten spiced things at lunch; had breathed in alkali with the dry, scorched air. He searched for a cool flint pebble to put into his burning mouth, but found only angular scraps of dusty limestone. There were no pebbles here. The cold helped a little to counteract, but already he knew in himself subconsciously the dread of something that was coming. What was it? He tried to hide the thought and bury it out of sight. The utter futility of his tiny strength against the power of the universe appalled him. And then he knew. The merciless sun was on the way, already rising. Its return was like the presage of execution to him. . . .

It came. With true horror he watched the marvellous swift dawn break over the sandy sea. The eastern sky glowed hurriedly as from crimson fires. Ridges, not noticeable in the starlight, turned black in endless series, like flat-topped billows of a frozen ocean. Wide streaks of blue and yellow followed, as the sky dropped sheets of faint light upon the wind-eaten cliffs and showed their under sides. They did not advance; they waited till the sun was up—and then they moved; they rose and sank; they shifted as the sunshine lifted them and the shadows crept away. But in an hour there would be no shadows any more. There would be no shade! . . .

The little groups of stones began to dance. It was horrible. The unbroken, huge expanse lay round him, warming up, twelve hours of blazing hell to come. Already the monstrous Desert glared, each bit familiar, since each bit was a repetition of the bit before, behind, on either side. It laughed at guidance and direction. He rose and walked; for miles he walked, though how many, north, south, or west, he knew not. The frantic thing was in him now, the fury of the Desert; he took its pace, its endless, tireless stride, the stride of the burning, murderous Desert that is—waterless. He felt it alive—a blindly heaving desire in it to reduce him to its conditionless, awful dryness. He felt—yet knowing this was feverish and *not* to be believed—that his own small life lay on its mighty surface, a mere dot in space, a mere heap of little stones. His emotions, his fears, his hopes, his ambition, his love—mere bundled group of little unimportant stones that danced with apparent activity for a moment, then were merged in the undifferentiated surface underneath. He was included in a purpose greater than his own.

The will made a plucky effort then. "A night and a day," he laughed, while his lips cracked smartingly with the stretching of the skin, "what is it? Many a chap has lasted days and days . . . !" Yes, only he was not of that rare company. He was ordinary, unaccustomed to privation, weak, untrained of spirit, unacquainted with stern resistance. He knew not how to spare himself. The Desert struck him where it pleased—all over. It played with him. His tongue was swollen; the parched throat could not swallow. He sank. . . . An hour he lay there, just wit enough in him to choose the top of a mound where he could be most easily seen. He lay two hours, three, four hours. . . . The heat blazed down upon him like a furnace. . . . The sky, when he opened his eyes once, was empty . . . then a speck became visible in the blue expanse; and presently another speck. They came from nowhere. They hovered very high, almost out of sight. They appeared, they disappeared, they—reappeared. Nearer and nearer they swung down, in sweeping stealthy circles . . . little dancing groups of them, miles away but ever drawing closer—the vultures. . . .

He had strained his ears so long for sounds of feet and voices that it seemed he could no longer hear at all. Hearing had ceased within him. Then came the water-dreams, with their agonising torture. He heard *that* . . . heard it running in silvery streams and rivulets across green English meadows. It rippled with silvery music. He heard it splash. He dipped hands and feet and head in it—in deep, clear pools of generous depth. He drank; with his skin he drank, not with mouth and throat alone. Ice clinked in effervescent, sparkling water against a glass. He swam and plunged. Water gushed freely over back and shoulders, gallons and gallons of it, bathfuls and to spare, a flood of gushing, crystal, cool, life-giving liquid. . . . And then he stood in a beech wood and felt the streaming deluge of delicious summer rain upon his face; heard it drip luxuriantly upon a million thirsty leaves. The wet trunks shone, the damp moss spread its perfume, ferns waved heavily in the moist atmosphere. He was soaked to the skin in it. A mountain torrent, fresh from fields of snow, foamed boiling past, and the spray fell in a shower upon his cheeks and hair. He dived head foremost. . . . Ah, he was up to the neck . . . and *she* was with him; they were under water together; he saw her eyes gleaming into his own beneath the copious flood.

The voice, however, was not hers. . . . "You will drown, yet you will not know you drown . . . !" His swollen tongue called out a name. But no sound was audible. He closed his eyes. There came sweet unconsciousness. . . .

A sound in that instant *was* audible, though. It was a voice—voices—and the thud of animal hoofs upon the sand. The specks had vanished from the sky as mysteriously as they came. And, as though in answer to the sound, he made a movement—an automatic, unconscious movement. He did not know he moved. And the body, uncontrolled, lost its precarious balance. He rolled; but he did not know he rolled. Slowly, over the edge of the sloping mound of sand, he turned sideways. Like a log of wood he slid gradually, turning over and over, nothing to stop him—to the bottom. A few feet only, and not even steep; just steep enough to keep rolling slowly. There was a—splash. But he did not know there was a splash.

They found him in a pool of water—one of these rare pools the Desert Bedouin mark preciously for their own. He had lain within three yards of it for hours. He was drowned . . . but he did not know he drowned. . . .

A Bit of Wood

He found himself in Meran with some cousins who had various slight ailments, but, being rich and imaginative, had gone to a sanatorium to be cured. But for its sanatoria, Meran might be a cheerful place; their ubiquity reminds a healthy man too often that the air is really good. Being well enough himself, except for a few mental worries, he went to a Gasthaus in the neighbourhood. In the sanatorium his cousins complained bitterly of the food, the ignorant "sisters," the inattentive doctors, and the idiotic regulations generally—which proves that people should not go to a sanatorium unless they are really ill. However, they paid heavily for being there, so felt that something was being accomplished, and were annoyed when he called each day for tea, and told them cheerfully how much better they looked—which proved, again, that their ailments were slight and quite curable by the local doctor at home. With one of the ailing cousins, a rich and pretty girl, he believed himself in love.

It was a three weeks' business, and he spent his mornings walking in the surrounding hills, his mind reflective, analytical, and ambitious, as with a man in love. He thought of thousands of things. He mooned. Once, for instance, he paused beside a rivulet to watch the buttercups dip, and asked himself, "Will she be like this when we're married—so anxious to be well that she thinks fearfully all the time of getting ill?" For if so, he felt he would be bored. He knew himself accurately enough to realise that he never could stand *that.* Yet money was a wonderful thing to have, and he, already thirty-five, had little enough! "Am I influenced by her money, then?" he asked himself . . . and so went on to ask and wonder about many things besides, for he was of a reflective temperament and his father had been a minor poet. And Doubt crept in. He felt a chill. He was not much of a man, perhaps, thin-blooded and unsuccessful, rather a dreamer, too, into the bargain. He had £100 a year of his own and a position in a Philanthropic Institution (due to influence) with a nominal salary attached. He meant to keep the latter after marriage. He would work just the same. Nobody should ever say *that* of him—!

And as he sat on the fallen tree beside the rivulet, idly knocking stones into the rushing water with his stick, he reflected upon those banal truisms that epitomise two-thirds of life. The way little unimportant things can change a person's whole existence was the one his thought just now had fastened on. His cousin's chill and headache, for instance, caught at a gloomy picnic on the Campagna three weeks before, had led to her going into a sanatorium and being advised that her heart was weak, that she had a tendency to asthma, that gout was in her system, and that a treatment of X-rays, radium, sunbaths and light baths, violet rays, no meat, complete rest, with big daily fees to experts with European reputations, were imperative. "From that chill, sitting a moment too long in the shadow of a forgotten Patrician's tomb," he reflected, "has come all this"—"all this" including his doubt as to whether it was herself or her money that he loved, whether he could stand living with her always, whether he need *really* keep his work on after marriage, in a word, his entire life and future, and her own as well—"all from that tiny chill three weeks ago!" And he knocked with his stick a little piece of sawn-off board that lay beside the rushing water.

Upon that bit of wood his mind, his mood, then fastened itself. It was triangular, a piece of sawn-off wood, brown with age and ragged. Once it had been part of a triumphant, hopeful sapling on the mountains; then, when thirty years of age, the men had cut it down; the rest of it stood somewhere now, at this very moment, in the walls of the house. This extra bit was cast away as useless; it served no purpose anywhere; it was slowly rotting in the sun. But each tap of the stick, he noticed, turned it sideways without sending it over the edge into the rushing water. It was obstinate. "It doesn't want to go in," he laughed, his father's little talent cropping out in him, "but, by Jove, it shall!" And he pushed it with his foot. But again it stopped, stuck end-ways against a stone. He then stooped, picked it up, and threw it in. It plopped and splashed, and went scurrying away downhill with the bubbling water. "Even that scrap of useless wood," he reflected, rising to continue his aimless walk, and still idly dreaming, "even that bit of rubbish may have a purpose, and may change the life of some one—

somewhere!"—and then went strolling through the fragrant pinewoods, crossing a dozen similar streams, and hitting scores of stones and scraps and fir cones as he went—till he finally reached his Gasthaus an hour later, and found a note from *her:* "We shall expect you about three o'clock. We thought of going for a drive. The others feel so much better."

It was a revealing touch—the way she put it on "the others." He made his mind up then and there—thus tiny things divide the course of life—that he could never be happy with such an "affected creature." He went for that drive, sat next to her consuming beauty, proposed to her passionately on the way back, was accepted before he could change his mind, and is now the father of several healthy children—and just as much afraid of getting ill, or of *their* getting ill, as she was fifteen years before. The female, of course, matures long, long before the male, he reflected, thinking the matter over in his study once. . . .

And that scrap of wood he idly set in motion out of impulse also went its destined way upon the hurrying water that never dared to stop. Proud of its new-found motion, it bobbed down merrily, spinning and turning for a mile or so, dancing gaily over sunny meadows, brushing the dipping buttercups as it passed, through vineyards, woods, and under dusty roads in neat, cool gutters, and tumbling headlong over little waterfalls, until it neared the plain. And so, finally, it came to a wooden trough that led off some of the precious water to a sawmill where bare-armed men did practical and necessary things. At the parting of the ways its angles delayed it for a moment, undecided which way to take. It wobbled. And upon that moment's wobbling hung tragic issues—issues of life and death.

Unknowing (yet assuredly not unknown), it chose the trough. It swung light-heartedly into the tearing sluice. It whirled with the gush of water towards the wheel, banged, spun, trembled, caught fast in the side where the cogs just chanced to be—and abruptly stopped the wheel. At any other spot the pressure of the water must have smashed it into pulp, and the wheel have continued as before; but it was caught in the *one* place where the various tensions held it fast immovably. It stopped the wheel, and so the machinery of the entire mill. It jammed like iron. The particular angle at which the double-handed saw, held by two weary and perspiring men, had cut it off a year before just enabled it to fit and wedge itself with irresistible exactitude. The pressure of the tearing water combined with the weight of the massive wheel to fix it tight and rigid. And in due course a workman—it was the foreman of the mill—came from his post inside to make investigations. He discovered the irritating item that caused the trouble. He put his weight in a certain way; he strained his hefty muscles; he swore—and the scrap of wood was easily dislodged. He fished the morsel out, and tossed it on the bank, and spat on it. The great wheel started with a mighty groan. But it started a fraction of a second before he expected it would start. He overbalanced, clutching the revolving framework with a frantic effort, shouted, swore, leaped at nothing, and fell into the pouring flood. In an instant he was turned upside down, sucked under, drowned. He was engaged to be married, and had put by a thousand *kronen* in the *Tiroler Sparbank*. He was a sober and hard-working man. . . .

There was a paragraph in the local paper two days later. The Englishman, asking the porter of his Gasthaus for something to wrap up a present he was taking to his cousin in the sanatorium, used that very issue. As he folded its crumpled and recalcitrant sheets with sentimental care about the precious object his eye fell carelessly upon the paragraph. Being of an idle and reflective temperament, he stopped to read it—it was headed "Unglücksfall," and his poetic eye, inherited from his foolish, rhyming father, caught the pretty expression "fliessandes Wasser." He read the first few lines. Some fellow, with a picturesque Tyrolese name, had been drowned beneath a mill-wheel; he was popular in the neighbourhood, it seemed; he had saved some money, and was just going to be married. It was very sad. "Our readers' sympathy" was with him. . . . And, being of a reflective temperament, the Englishman thought for a moment, while he went on wrapping up the parcel. He wondered if the man had really loved the girl, whether she, too, had money, and whether they would have had lots of children and been happy ever afterwards. And then he hurried out towards the sanatorium. "I shall be late," he reflected. "Such little, unimportant things delay one . . . !"

The Night-Wind

There were certain things that Uncle Henry, as a writer of "historical novels," had to explain, or else admit himself a disgraceful failure. For he sometimes read fancy bits aloud to the children, using the latter as a standard. These fancy bits were generally scenes of action: Escape; a Duke landing by night and dressed as a woman to avoid discovery; a dark man stealing "storical" documents from a tapestried chamber in a frightful castle where bats and cobwebs shared the draughty corridors. These and the like he read aloud, judging their success by the reception accorded to them. "Thank you very much, Uncle," meant failure; the imagination was left untouched. But questions were an indication of success; the scene was alive and real, the audience wanted more details. For he knew that it was the "child" in his readers that enjoyed such scenes, and if Jinny and Jimbo felt no interest, neither would Mr. and Mrs. William Smith of Peckham. To squeeze a question out of Maria, the youngest, however, raised hopes of at least a Second Edition!

These night-scenes, of course, were always windy; sometimes they were stormy. Either the wind rose at an unexpected and unwelcome moment, or else it dropped just when the cover of its roar was needed by the villain; at other times it merely misbehaved itself generally, as night-winds do. But as a rule it wailed, moaned, whistled, whispered, cried, sang, sighed, sobbed, or soughed. Keyholes and chimneys were its favourite places, and sometimes the rafters knew it, too. Thus, to the children, it became a known, expected thing with tastes and habits of its own. They looked for "Mr. Night-Wind," and recognised it when it came. "A night-wind story, please," was a classical form of attack between tea and bed-time. It had a personality and led a mysterious existence. It had qualities, privileges, prerogatives. It acquired a definite *locus standi* in the mythology of the country house. Owing to its various means of vocal expression—singing, moaning, and the rest—a face belonged to it with lips and mouth: teeth, too, since it whistled. It ran about the world, and so had feet; it flew, so wings pertained to it; it blew, and that meant cheeks of sorts. It was a large, swift, shadowy being whose ways were not the ordinary ways of daylight. It struck blows. It had gigantic hands. Moreover, it came out only after dark—an ominous and suspicious characteristic rather.

"Why isn't there a day-wind too?" enquired Jinny, thoughtfully.

"There is, but it's *quite* a different thing," Uncle Henry explained, calmly. "You might as well ask why midday and midnight aren't the same because they both come at twelve o'clock. They're simply different things, you see."

"Of course," Jimbo helped him unexpectedly; "and a man can't be a woman, can it?"

Mr. Night-Wind's nature, accordingly, remained a mystery rather, and its sex, in spite of the deceptive "Mr.," was also undetermined. Whether it saw with eyes, or just felt its way about like a blind thing, wandering, was another secret matter undetermined. Each child visualised it differently. Its hiding-place in the daytime was equally unknown. Owls, bats, and burglars guessed its habits best, and that it came out of a hole in the sky was, perhaps, the only detail all unanimously agreed upon. It was a pathetic being, rather.

This Night-Wind used to come crying round the bedroom windows sometimes, and the children liked it, although they did not understand all its melancholy beauty. They heard the different voices in it, although they did not catch the meaning of the words it sang. They heard its footsteps, too. Its way of moving awed them. Moreover, it was forever trying to get in.

"It's wings," said Jinny, "big, dark wings, very soft and feathery."

"It's a woman with sad black eyes," thought Jimbo. "That's how I like it."

"It's some one," declared Maria, who was asleep before it came, so rarely heard it at all. And they turned to Uncle Henry, who knew all that sort of thing, or, at any rate, could describe it. He found the words. They lay hidden in his thick back hair apparently—there was none on the top!—for he always scratched his head a good deal when they asked him questions about such difficult matters. "What is it *real-*

ly—the Mr. Night-Wind?" they asked gravely; "and why does it sound so *very* different from the wind in the morning or the afternoon?"

"There *is* a difference," he replied carefully, realising it for the first time now that they asked. "It's a quick, dark, rushing thing, and it moves like—like anything."

"We know *that,*" they told him contemptuously, yet with considerate patience.

"And it has long hair," he added hurriedly, looking into Jimbo's staring eyes. "That's what makes it swish. The swishing, rushing, hushing sound it makes—that's its hair against the walls and tiles, you see."

"It *is* a woman, then?" said Jimbo, proudly.

All looked up, wondering. An extraordinary thing was in the air. A mystery that had puzzled them for ages was about to be explained. They drew closer round the sofa, and Maria blundered against the table, knocking some books off with a resounding noise.

"Hush! Hush!" said Uncle Henry, holding up a finger and glancing over his shoulder into the darkened room. "It may be coming now . . . Listen!"

"Yes; but it is a woman, isn't it?" insisted Jimbo in a hurried whisper. He had to justify himself before his sisters. Uncle Henry must see to that first.

The big man opened his eyes very wide. He shuddered. "It's a—Thing," was the answer, given in a whisper that increased the excitement of anticipation. "It certainly is a—Thing! Now hush! Listen! It's coming!"

They listened then intently. And a sound was heard. Out of the starry summer night it came, quite softly, and from very far away—upon discovery bent, upon adventure. Reconnoitering, as from deep ambush in the shrubberies where the blackbirds hid and whistled, it flew down against the house, stared in at the nursery windows, fluttered up and down the glass with a marvellous, sweet humming—and was gone again.

"Listen!" the man's voice whispered; "it will come back presently. It saw us. It's awfully shy—"

"Why is it awfully shy?" asked Jinny in an undertone.

"Because people make it mean so much more than it means to mean," he replied, darkly. "It never gets a chance to be just itself and play its own lonely game—"

"*We've* called it things too," objected Maria.

"But we haven't written books about it and put it into poetry," Uncle Henry corrected her with an audacity that silenced them. "We play our game; it plays its."

"It plays its," repeated Jimbo, amused by the sound of the words.

"And that's why it's shy," the man held them to the main point, "and dislikes showing itself—"

"But why is its game lonely?" some one asked, and there was a general feeling that Uncle Henry had been caught this time without an answer. For what explanation could there possibly be of that? Their faces were half triumphant, half disappointed already.

He smiled quietly. He knew everything—everything in the world. "It's unhappy as well as shy," he sighed, "because nothing will play with it. Everything is asleep at night. It comes out just when other things go in. Trees answer it, but they answer in their sleep. Birds, tucked away in nests and hiding-places, don't even answer at all. The butterflies are gone, the insects lost. Leaves and twigs don't care about being blown when there's no one there to see them. They hide too. If there are clouds, they're dark and sulky, keeping their jolly sides towards the stars and moon. Nothing will play with Mr. Night-Wind. So it either plays with the tiles on the roof and the telegraph wires—dead things that make a lot of noise, but never leave their places for a proper game—or else it just—plays with itself. Since the beginning of the world the Night-Wind has been shy and lonely and unhappy."

It was unanswerable. They understood. Their sense of pity was gently touched, their love as well.

"Do pigs really see the wind, as Daddy says?" enquired Maria abruptly, feeling the conversation beyond her. She merely obeyed the laws of her practical, matter-of-fact nature. But no one answered her; no one even heard the question. Another sound absorbed their interest and attention. There was a low, faint tapping on the window-pane. A hush, like church, fell over everybody.

And Uncle Henry stood up to his full height suddenly, and opened his arms wide. He drew a long, deep breath.

"Come in," he said, splendidly.

The tapping, however, grew fainter and fainter, till it finally ceased.

Everybody waited expectantly, but it was not repeated. Nothing happened. Nobody came in. The tapper had retreated.

"It was a twig," whispered Jinny after a pause. "The Virgin Creeper—"

"But it was the wind that shook it," exclaimed Uncle Henry, still standing and waiting as though he expected something. "The Night-Wind—"

A roaring sound over the roof drowned his words; it rose and fell like laughter, then like crying. It dropped closer, rushed headlong past the window, rattled and shook the sash, then dived away into the darkness. Its violence startled them. A deep lull followed instantly, and the little tapping of the twig was heard again. Odd! Just when the Night-Wind seemed furthest off it was all the time quite near. It had not really gone at all; it was hiding against the outside walls. It was watching them, trying to get in. The tapping continued for half a minute or more—a series of hurried, gentle little knocks, as from a child's smallest finger tip.

"It wants to come in. It's trying," whispered some one.

"It's awfully shy."

"It's lonely and frightfully unhappy."

"It likes us and wants to play."

There was another pause and silence. No one knew quite what to do.

"There's too much light. Let's put the lamp out!" said a genius, using the voice of Jinny.

As though by way of answer there followed instantly a sudden burst of wind. The torrent of it drove against the house; it boomed down the chimney, puffing an odour of soot into the room; it shook the door into the passage; it lifted an edge of carpet, flapping it. It shouted, whistled, sang, using a dozen different voices all at once. The roar fell into syllables. It was amazing. A great throat uttered words. They could scarcely believe their ears. The wind was shouting with a joyful, boisterous shout: "Open the window! *I'll* put out the light!"

All heard the wonderful thing. Yet it seemed quite natural in a way. Uncle Henry, still standing and waiting as though he knew not exactly what was going to happen, moved forward at once and boldly opened the window's lower sash. In swept the mighty visitor, the stranger from the air. The lamp gave one quick flicker and went out. Deep stillness followed. There was a silence like the moon. The shy Night-Wind had come into the room.

Ah, there was awe and wonder then! The silence was so unexpected. The whole wind, not merely part of it, was in. It had come so gently, softly, delicately too! In the darkness the outline of the window-frame was visible; Uncle Henry's big figure blocked against the stars. Jinny's head could be seen in silhouette against the other window, but Jimbo and Maria, being smaller, were merged in the pool of shadow below the level of the sill. A large, spread thing passed fluttering up and down the room a moment, then came to rest. It settled over everything at once. A rustle was audible as of trailing, floating hair.

"It's hiding in the corners and behind the furniture," whispered Uncle Henry. "Keep quiet. If you frighten it—whew!"—he whistled softly—"it'll be off above the tree-tops in a second!"

A low, soft whistle answered to his own; somewhere in the room it sounded; there was no mistaking it, though the exact direction was difficult to tell, for while Jimbo said it was through the keyhole, Jinny declared positively it came from the door of the big, broken cupboard opposite. Maria stated flatly, "Chimney."

"Hush! It's talking." It was Uncle Henry's voice breathing very low. "It likes us. It feels we're friendly."

A murmur as of leaves was audible, or as of a pine bough sighing in a tiny breeze. Yet there were words as well—actual spoken words:

"Don't look for me, please," they heard. "I do not want to be seen. But you may touch me. I like that." The children spread their hands out in the darkness, groping, searching, feeling. "Ah, your touch!" the sighing voice continued. "It's like my softest lawn. Your hair feels as my grass feels on the hilltops, and the skin of your cheeks is cool and smooth as the water-surface of my lily ponds at midnight. I know you"—it raised its tone to singing. "You are children! I kiss you all!"

"I feel you," Jinny said, in her clear, quiet voice. "But you are cold."

"Not really," was the answer that seemed all over the room at once. "That's only the touch of space. I've come from very high up to-night. There's been a change. The lower wind was called away suddenly to the sea, and I dropped down with hardly a moment's warning to take its place. The sun has been very tiresome all day—overheating the currents."

"Uncle, *you* ask it everything," whispered Jimbo, "simply everything!"

"Say how we love it, please," sighed Jinny. "I feel it closing both my eyes."

"It's over all my face," put in Maria, drawing her breath in loudly.

"But my hair's lifting!" Jinny exclaimed. "Oh, it's lovely, lovely!"

Uncle Henry straightened himself up in the darkness. They could hear him breathing with the effort. "Please tell us what you do," he said. "We all can feel you touching us. Play with us as you play with trees and clouds and sleeping flowers underneath the hedgerows."

A singing, whistling sound passed softly round the room: there was a whirr and flutter as when a flight of bees or little birds goes down the sky, and a voice, a plaintive yet happy voice, like the plover who call to each other on the moors, was audible:

I run about the world at night,
Yet cannot see;
My hair has grown so thick these million years,
It covers me.
So, like a big, blind thing,
I run about,
And know all things by touching them
I touch them with my wings;
I know each one of you
By touching you;
I touch your hearts!

"I feel you!" cried Jinny. "I feel you touching me!"

"And I, and I!" the others cried. "It's simply wonderful!"

An enormous sigh of happiness went through that darkened room.

"Then play with me!" they heard. "Oh, children, play with me!"

The wild, high sweetness in the windy voice was irresistible. The children rose with one accord. It was too dark to see, but they flew about the room without a fault or slip. There was no stumbling; they seemed guided, lifted, swept. The sound of happy, laughing voices filled the air. They caught the Wind and let it go again; they chased it round the table and the sofa; they held it in their arms until it panted with delight, half smothered into silence, then marvellously escaping from them on the elastic, flying feet that tread on forests, clouds, and mountain tops. It rushed and darted, drove them, struck them lightly, pushed them suddenly from behind, then met their faces with a puff and shout of glee. It caught their feet: it blew their eyelids down. Just when they cried, "It's caught! I've got it in my hands!" it shot laughing up against the ceiling, boomed down the chimney, or whistled shrilly as it escaped beneath the crack of the door into the passage. The keyhole was its easiest escape. It grew boisterous, singing with delight, yet was never for a moment rough. It cushioned all its blows with feathers.

"Where are you now? I felt your hair all over me. You've gone again!" It was Jinny's voice as she tore across the floor.

"You're whacking me on the head!" cried Jimbo. "Quick, quick! I've got you in my hands!" He flew headlong over the sofa where Maria sat clutching the bolster to prevent being blown on to the carpet.

They felt its soft, gigantic hands all over them; its silky coils of hair entangled every movement; they heard its wings, its rushing, sighing voice, its velvet feet. The room was in a whirr and uproar.

"Uncle Henry! Can't *you* help? You're the biggest!"

"But it's blown me inside out," he answered, in a curiously muffled voice.

"My fingers are blown off. It's taken all my breath away."

The pictures rattled on the wall; loose bits of paper fluttered everywhere; the curtains flapped out horizontally into the air.

"Catch it! Hold it! Stop it!" cried the breathless voices.

"Join hands," he gasped. "We'll try." And, holding hands, they raced across the floor. They managed to encircle something with their spread arms and legs. Into the corner by the door they forced a great, loose, flowing thing against the wall. Wedged tight together like a fence, they stooped. They pounced upon it.

"We've caught it!" shouted Jimbo. "We've got you!"

There was a laughing whistle in the keyhole just behind them. It was gone!

The window shook. They heard the wild, high laughter. It was out of the room. The next minute it passed shouting above the cedar tops and up into the open sky. And their own laughter went out to follow it across the night.

* * *

The room became suddenly very still again. Some one had closed the window. The twig no longer tapped. The game was over. Uncle Henry collected them, an exhausted crew, upon the sofa by his side.

"It was very wonderful," he whispered. "We've done what no one has ever done before: We've played with the Night-Wind, and the Night-Wind's played with us. It feels happier now. It will always be our friend."

"It was awfully strong," said Jimbo, in a tone of awe. "It fairly banged me."

"And awfully gentle though," sighed Jinny. "It kissed me hundreds of times."

"I felt it stroking me all down the back," announced Maria.

"It's only a child really," Uncle Henry explained, half to himself, "a great wild child that plays with itself in space—"

He went on murmuring for several minutes, but the children hardly heard the words he used. They had their own sensations. For the wind had touched their hearts and made them think. They heard it singing now above the cedars as they had never heard it sing before. It was alive and lovely; it meant a new thing to them. For they had their little aching sorrows too; it had taken them all away; they had their little passionate yearnings and desires: it had prophesied fulfilment. The dreamy melancholy of childhood, the long, long days, the haunted nights, the everlasting afternoons—all these were in its wild, great, windy voice, the sighing, the mystery, the laughter too. The joy of strange fulfilment woke in their wind-kissed hearts. The Night-Wind was their friend; they had played with it. Now everything could come true.

And next day Maria, lost to the authorities for over an hour, was at length discovered by the forbidden pigsties in a fearful state of mess, but very pleased and happy about something. She was watching the pigs with eyes brimful of questioning wonder and excitement. She was listening intently too. She wanted to find out for certain whether pigs really—really and truly—saw—anything unusual!

The Falling Glass

The preparations were so interesting and suggestive that they almost compensated for the temporary loss of our expedition. For three the calm and cloudless sky pretended that bad weather had left the world for ever. This sunny peace, this heaven without a stain, surely must always be. Our peak ran sharp and still into the spotless blue, looking as though it never could be otherwise. Its serene majesty seemed unassailable by any troubling thing, by weather least of all. Then, just when our security was greatest and we had resolved to start next day at dawn, my companion came in to supper, with the ominous remark: "The glass has begun to fall a bit." This, for us, was the beginning of the change, the first *we* knew of it; in reality, of course, the actual beginning lay leagues away—many leagues and many hours—in Siberia or Norway, far out on the Atlantic or between the Sahara and the Mediterranean. The glass falling in our little mountain valley was in reply to changes *there*. And this first hint of trouble communicated itself instantly to ourselves; it might be nothing or it might be grave. There was menace in it, and our sense of security was shaken, for the hearts of climbing men lie close enough to Nature; we were aware of resistance, even of possible attack. That tremor of the sensitive mercury was a presage of something coming; at any rate, of something trying to come. In spite of the depression, however, the warning brought a thrill of pleasure with it; the instinct of self-protection stirred; it woke that adorable element in life—resistance against a hostile power that could not be trifled with, certainly not ignored. Somewhere, somehow, was known that we had planned our great attack at dawn, and so a whisper travelled down from the enormous heights: "Beware! The enemy is on the move!" All this, and more, lay in the casual phrase: "The glass is falling."

Side by side with a natural annoyance there was this stimulus as well. For the beginnings of things are always very wonderful; alteration of what has been before, a new direction, purpose, and independence, all these are involved in every true beginning. There is anticipation and surprise, promise of novelty, too; something is going to happen; it may be something quite unprecedented. Beginnings, being in the nature of creation, are beyond language marvellous: the beginning of a day or of a night; of anger, when a rising temperature and the hasting run of blood betray in us the lurking savage who kills naturally; of illness, with its sharp reminder that life one day *must* stop; of love, when the sound of a voice changes the universe; or of spring, when a new softness in the air, nameless by any sense, proclaims the arrival of gigantic, flooding life. But the beginning of a storm is so wonderful that it can easily eat up disappointment. For the preparations are so long and gradual, so sure, so steadily matured, so cumulative; at first so negligible, yet with a hint of genuine grandeur coming, that the blood is stirred, and the heart, first warned, then awed. He is a fortunate man who, in these sophisticated days, can find it in him to acknowledge this trace of the primitive spirit of worship. That faint, mysterious tremor that runs through Nature everywhere is divine in its first gentle yet calculated insignificance.

The animal and vegetable world at once respond to it; birds and fishes know, the insects know as well; trees note it and keep very still; all take instantly their best precautions; and only men, not aware of it until it is too late, disregard the delicate warning at their peril. Few humans can feel that the pressure of the air has altered. They watch an instrument and whisper: "Ah, the glass is falling!" The change is born, of course, so very far away. How should they know? Culture has dulled their primitive awareness.

And that night the stars were ominously clear and brilliant. In the morning there were other signs as well. At three o'clock just when the east was blushing, my companion called me, or rather came into my room. "Up already!" he exclaimed; "I just came in to see. What do you think of it? That barometer was a fraud." We went out upon the wooden balcony and saw the distant ridges mercilessly outlined in the growing light; the summits were near enough to throw a rope across.

"Too close," I said, with misgivings born of long experience.

"But look!" he objected, "there's not a single cloud." He loathed my caution, deeming it proud imagination only. "It's simply brilliant," he added, his young eagerness unspoilt by knowledge. I shook my older head. Some inborn instinct made me firm for once. Ten years before I should have been overridden, and have started on our perilous two-days' climb with ample hope.

"It's a whole day to the hut," I reminded him, "and then—suppose we wake to mist and wind and possibly driving snow? Let's wait till we're certain and the glass is rising slowly. For instance, look at *that!*" And I pointed to a narrow straw of vapour that trailed clingingly across the first huge precipice, five hours away, good going. It was tinged with a faint, transparent pink—unduly luminous.

"That's nothing," he exclaimed contemptuously, "mere bit of early morning mist. Why, I've known—"

"But it's too low down," I interrupted. "On the top it would not matter, it has no business *there*. It means changed or changing temperature."

He shivered in his thin pyjamas, yet did not realise that *dry* cold would not have made him shiver. In the night a new thing had crept in upon the valley—dampness.

"And listen," I added, as the tops of the pines below the balcony stirred with a rustling sound that as quickly died away again.

"The morning wind," he cried, "that's all."

"But the sound of falling water with it. The north or east—good winds—would not move a single branch down here. Observe the lie of the land." He did so grumpily enough.

"It's from the south," I observed, "and it's blowing *up* the valley."

"There's hardly any wind at all, anyhow," he said impatiently.

"But what there is is southerly. The wind has changed. You feel its dampness? That damp is evil. Why, man, you can smell it!" For a strong odour of earth and grass and growing things lay behind the exquisite morning freshness of the dawn, and the fragrance, though so pleasant, was suspicious. It was moisture that brought it out.

"Oh, you know best, I suppose," he growled, "though it looks all right, and I should call it perfect." He glanced at me with a trifle more respect, however—that change of wind had shaken his confidence!—then shrugged his shoulders and moved off reluctantly to bed. "You tell the guides, then," he added, with resignation, and was gone before he caught my answer: "if they're fools enough to come!"

But the guides, of course, put in no appearance. They ought, by rights, to have ascertained the "Herr's" decision, but took it for granted his opinion would be their own. I admit there was this childish pride and pleasure in the disappointment, and to be right even in prophesying disaster holds a faint satisfaction. It was the "Herr's" pleasure, however, to sit up and watch this marvellous beginning of a storm. The preparations for its splendid climax were so indecipherably faint, yet so carefully planned, that though the brilliance of last night's stars had announced their coming, six hours had passed and brought them apparently no nearer. The storm was being massed for attack below the edges of the visible world. One thought of it as a living, monstrous thing that would presently come crowding and crashing down the heavens, alive for miles, and full of violent fury. It was too gigantic to move quickly; each separate detail must be trained and ready before the accumulated blow could fall; but hints of wind and moisture, like delicate antennæ, were stretched out in advance to warn the sensitive nerves of those who had them.

I brewed some chocolate, and, with rugs and blankets on the narrow balcony, I watched the paling stars. This slow beginning of terrific weather thrilled me. It was unbelievably slow, unnecessarily cautious; its growth, unhasting but unhindered, brooked no interference, however, and there was a hint of diabolical thoroughness in the steady way beginning crept towards fulfilment. All Nature was pressed into the service; the entire firmament laboured to one given end. The imagination became conscious almost of personal direction in this consummate marshalling of such huge forces in sympathetic combination. Yet once or twice, for all my pride of certainty—particularly at half-past five, for instance, when the advance seemed stayed—I confess I had misgivings, and was tempted to wake my friend again and scold the guides for their inexcusable delay. For the weather held so still and brilliant. "Look at the sky!" I would have cried to the men. "How could *you* have been deceived by those false, transient signs of change?" Some deity of luck preserved me from their inevitable answer: "We thought the 'Herr' could have told what's surely coming!"

It was of marvellous, though sinister, beauty, well worth the loss of hours of beauty sleep, even worth the loss of the expedition as well, to see the wonder of the dawn across the awful heights, falling on cliff and ridge, and stealing along the high, faint snowfields in the break between the periods. The colours may be guessed, but not described, with the aspect of veiled terror that they wore, of menace in the strange diffusion of the light, and in the apparent innocence of sun and shadow that masked their changed expression. For nowhere was expression quite the same as on an innocent morning. The rising of the valley out of sleep, the creeping light, the guileless freshness of the air that brought the tumbling water loud and close, the general stillness, peace, and calm—all these were different, but oh! so little different, to their normal aspect when the glass stood high. It was mere pretence, of course. The coming violence attempted to steal unnoticed and unawares upon the sky. Behind that treacherous calm it piled up forces that presently would shake the mountains and make the old woods howl. Yet at six o'clock the big peaks still looked friendly in the crystal atmosphere, and it was not till nearly nine that these first assurances of a perfect day began to fade. They passed, slipping away with an unnoticed skill that suggested cunning. No clouds were visible, and no wind to mention stirred, but there crawled into the air a certain dimness that lessened the first unearthly brilliance. Something waned, and the sting of the sharp, delicious heat was gone. Less than haze, it yet took the flash out of the sunshine, and while sound grew clearer, closer, the outlines of both trees and peaks stood blurred a little. Few would have noticed any definite change as yet, none, perhaps, but very keen observers with an interest at stake; but by half-past ten there lay an observable shadow over the entire heavens, cast by no cloud, but as though the tide of light rushed down, then halted and drew back. Before eleven it was a curious, faint veil, and an hour later it had dimmed the normal blaze of noon. There was a glare of unpleasant brilliance that hurt the eyes.

Then, from noon till perhaps after two o'clock, there came a pause when nothing happened, and only a great thick stillness settled over everything. And the pause was ominous, freighted with presentiment; the freshness of the upland world was gone entirely; it seemed a dull, exhausted, burnt-out day. The smell of grass and earth became more marked, and there were soft touches of moisture in the eyes and on the skin; the flies were "sticky," their tickling of the face and hands persistent, and that state of irritation known as "nerves on edge" required steady handling. But though outwardly all this time the signs had seemed minute, they had really been immense, and the entire heavens wrote the letters clear. For as the light had piled in waves upon the eastern sky, the west had given its too early answer, and the suspicious radiance that had brought so grand a dawn was of the same evil quality that had lit the stars too brilliantly the night before. By four o'clock, then, just as the shadows lengthened steeply in the nearer gorges, a delicate trail of fine-spun cloud came thinning down the sky from south to north at an incredible height above the tallest peaks. So tenuous as to be scarcely visible, it lined the atmosphere where no clouds were, and at five o'clock, when the afternoon was waning, there appeared as if by magic, in several spots at once, small patches of isolated mist that had darkness on their underside. Below the giddy ridge where our proposed night shelter perched—the hut—they gathered suddenly into a single line, and fifteen minutes later there was a barrier of dirty-looking cloud that was rising—rising in places at considerable speed. On the edges it leaped and coiled with a kind of hurrying impatience. Yet all this time—these twenty hours of interval—the entire heavens had conspired together to produce no more than this thickening cloud that was the first visible sign a townsman need have noticed with anxiety. The peaks, however, were close enough now to touch; a stifling, oven heat, airless as a concert hall, hung everywhere; there was a strange, deep stillness; and from the distant upper pastures the sound of cowbells came queerly down the village street. The birds had ceased their singing long before.

The wreaths and lines of vapour meanwhile spread and thickened, gaining ground, some rising, others sinking, new centres forming everywhere with a rapidity that argued admirable preparation. A coiling mist wrapped hurriedly about one summit after another, yet leaving the actual top in shining light. A ring was round the sun, immensely distant from it, with a diameter of many miles of sky. The heat in the valley, pressed down and running over, made breathing increasingly oppressive; the sunlight filtered badly and unevenly. The peasants looked skywards and said no word, but barn doors were shut and the cattle came to water early in the nearer pastures. In spots the air grew colder, and suddenly, with dramatic abruptness, solitary puffs of heated wind came rushing up our valley from the south. Heralded by clouds of dust they passed and went their way, first having tossed the waiting trees, not twice, but once, rattled the windows, closed the open doors—went their way upwards to bear word that all was ready for the main attack.

Long, ominous silences followed, but with the lurid sunset the change, so long maturing, now dropped swiftly. At dusk there was heavy roaring in the mountains as the winds let loose against the darkening cliffs. It was audible even on our balcony. And before the appointed time, there fell a sea of blackness on the world that blotted out in less than a dozen minutes the last vestiges of sunset or of gleaming distant snow. By 7.30 the true wind began to rise, or, properly speaking, began to reach us in our sunken hollow. Up the valley like a crying voice it swept, in no puffs now, but in a steady torrent. It wailed and moaned. None perhaps but a climber knows that desolate sound, that strange, wild whistling among rocks and trees, that shrill and angry calling to the earth. It is a threatening sound. He hears a host of javelins and lances flying, for he knows the sting and pierce of that sharp, wetted wind. There is grim foreboding in it, and presentiment in the hot and empty pauses that lie between the heavy gusts. And the upper wind came down to meet it. Again the deep roaring became audible, though where no man could tell, for it was everywhere and filled the inky sky. It descended with its battle howl from the iron fastnesses of scree and precipice and from the bitter snow-fields that had iced its fury. It was a wind that could blow a man from the securest foothold into space, mow down the older trees like matches, and even loosen rocks. It seemed the mountains stooped to heave their shoulders, driving it down with crushing power upon our village between the forests.

We had little sleep that night. The storm was, of course, the worst that had ever been known. It lasted with unabated fury and with torrential rain for forty hours. Its suddenness, the unenlightened said, was so extraordinary. It came, as it seemed, out of a clear and harmless sky. Only the few who watched as we had watched knew of its marvellous genesis and careful growth, its gradual and distant preparation, the birth of its small beginning hours and hours before it came.

Breakfast Honey

Every one who travels on the Continent knows that breakfast honey is not honey. It *may* be many things: treacle, glucose, glycerine, burnt sugar—only no bee has ever gathered it from flowers in the sunshine, nor has it ever known cool storage in cells of natural wax. In Switzerland, the land of its invention and discovery, it retains a honey-ish savour, but in some other countries even this is neglected. In Rome it is particularly—not honey. People there are perhaps too occupied labelling other kinds of excavated antiquities to trouble about so small a matter; they just swallow it, and pay. Jones, however, was exceedingly annoyed about it. He took it as a personal affront; or, rather, for once—he refused to take it.

Though constitutionally timid and uncomplaining, Jones came down to breakfast that morning in Rome feeling exactly like the worm that turned, or like the camel that objected to carrying the last, offensive straw—false honey. He was as the type of little traveller whom Head Waiters and gold-braided Porters overawed, who tipped beyond his means from sheer "suggestion" that it was expected of him, and behaved generally as if he were under an obligation to the hotel that took him in. The Head Waiter he called *It;* the Great Porter was *He* or *Him.* "There It is again!" he would sigh when tipping time came near; "I see Him waiting to catch me on the steps!" Considering himself very fortunate to be taken in by a big hotel at all, he was still more fortunate to be let out again; leaving was a kind of escape, sly or headlong as the case might be. Such folk were the prey of that numerous and predatory army called The Staff. Like many mild and timid persons he was, moreover, imaginative; he often pictured to himself with vivid satisfaction how splendidly he would act under repeated provocation, if he only—dared. Also, like most undaring folk, when he turned, he really turned. He went to lengths that were, of course, unreasonable. The accumulated grievances of years, meekly, even shamefully borne, discharged themselves in acts of intemperate relief.

And on this particular morning he came down to breakfast feeling unusually aggressive and resentful. It was Holy Week, and Rome was full to the lid. He was paying 20 francs a day for a cupboard of a room that had been forced upon him owing to his suggestionable appearance, and that gave upon a shaft at the back of the dingy building. "Très tranquille et donne sur la tour," was the persuasive description used when showing him upstairs. and he had taken it gladly enough at the moment, feeling himself lucky to be given any quarters at such a time. But the moment he was alone, free of the glamour of the obsequious yet intimidating Manager, judgment reasserted itself and he understood that he was being treated as usual. He saw dish-cloths drying on the glass roof just below the window; there were scraps of potato skin as well. And after a night in such a chamber, at 20 francs, it was natural that even Jones should come down to breakfast aware of the tradition of the Worm and Camel.

He ordered his tea with "Mind the water's really boiling, please," and began, like to Queen in the Parlour, eating bread and honey. Its treacly flavour offended him at once; his nature revolted; he prepared to strike. "And they can't give a fellow decent honey, even," he growled half audibly, "or tea made with boiling water!"—when the pot arrived and he tasted the stewed, insipid liquid.

Jones summoned a waiter and complained. "This water was *not* boiling," he said firmly. "I have asked particularly for boiling water. I must have tea made with boiling water." He was particular about his tea; at home he heated the cup as well.

"But, I assure you, sir—I saw it made myself—"

"Take it away," said Jones, sternly, "and bring me some fresh. And if it's not right I shall send it back again and complain." He felt boiling over, himself. But he knew quite well that the man would merely add a little hotter water, wait two minutes, and then bring back the vile concoction as before. He could complain again, but with a similar result. There was no real redress. And he was paying 20 francs a day for that! The waiter went off sulkily, grumbling beneath his breath. Jones decided to make an example then and there.

The breakfast-room was half full of other travellers, all suffering under similar oppression. He felt their sympathy was with him; they had overheard the dialogue; already they regarded him—their admiring glances proved it—as their champion. And his courage rose to the occasion. While fully aware that *It* was hovering grandly in the background, doing nothing useful, but looking very important with one eye on the rising storm, the sight only nerved him to decided action. That pompous and condescending individual, who would later rob him of a most substantial tip, was like a red rag to a bull. Jones rose; crossed the room in sight of everybody; entered the swing-doors into the kitchen—and caught the waiter in the very act.

Now, it was a plucky thing to do, and few would have taken so much trouble. The whole tourist world is afraid of a Head Waiter. Jones's life would be made miserable ever afterwards in the hotel; and, owing to the mysterious freemasonry among the craft, the boycott might even follow him to other hotels as well. But Jones did more. In the full sight and hearing of the room he called up *It*—the princely fellow with the black imperial and the bearing of a cardinal—and explained calmly in an audible voice what had happened. "I caught him adding more hot water," he concluded. "Now, please understand, that in future I *insist* upon proper attention to my orders, and having my tea made properly with *boiling* water. Otherwise—I shall complain to the Management—we shall *all*—complain!" And he glanced round at the other guests who watched him with intense approval. The ruler of the Imperial City bowed and smiled and murmured—he was considerably taken aback, it seemed—and Jones stalked off to his table amid the silent plaudits of the suffering, but less courageous onlookers. A trivial matter, perhaps, this detail of the tea; but the public had borne it meekly long enough; it was time that some one stopped the nuisance. The public paid.

And then, as the majestic being paused a moment by the table, Jones continued his campaign so well begun. He carried it a stage further. There was no holding him. "And will you bring me some honey, if you please?" he asked politely, yet with a splendid air of outraged rights. *It* indicated the round glass jar upon the table with a gesture of disdainful triumph. "It is here, sir—the honey," he observed coolly. "I asked for *honey*," repeated the determined Jones in a voice for all to hear, "not treacle and glucose mixed with glycerine. Please give me real, pure honey." With an expression that must have obliterated Jones at any other time, the Head Waiter repeated his omnipotent gesture. "This *is* honey, sir—the best quality and very pure indeed. All our oldest customers," he added, not meaning precisely what he said, "have always liked it."

For the first time in his life Jones looked *It* steadily in the eye. No sign of fear was in him. "You assure me this is real, pure honey?" he asked with deadly quiet. And the man, wincing perhaps the least bit in the world, gave the desired assurance languidly—to his own undoing and to the undoing of the hotel that supplied the abomination. Jones noted the hint of coming insolence, but he noted the wincing too. "As an employee of the Hotel," he said in a clear voice, one eye on the golden syrup at the same time, "you are responsible. *I* hold you responsible." "Yes, sir," he replied nonchalantly as he moved away, either not understanding quite what was meant or feeling that argument with such an extraordinary guest was beneath his serious notice. The delighted onlookers, however, had an inkling of what was going forward, for Jones went up to his room forthwith, and returned presently with a little bottle which he proceeded to fill with "honey," immensely cheered by the admiring smiles and whispers of some fifty people who watched the affair with encouraging amazement. For the whole room realised that it was being done for them as well as for himself. Thousands had been fed upon the nasty stuff for years, thousands had paid and suffered, and tens of thousands were too timid to complain effectively and resent the imposition. At last a Man had come to fight their battle for them. Jones stood before them as a Leader, a man prepared to have his rights and see that they had theirs, regardless of all personal risk and obloquy. He was their accredited representative, their hero. It was a moment—for a timid fellow like Jones—of some genuine distinction. The room, though silent, was lost in admiration of his courage.

He followed up the matter with sense and impetus. He went out into the hall, summoned a friend as witness, wrapped up the bottle in a hotel envelope, sealed, dated, and described it—"Breakfast Honey." That morning he took it to an analyst, and in return for ten francs received an exact account of the ingredients of which it was composed. And then he went to a lawyer. "I wish to sue the Hotel for damages," he explained, and asked under what law or city by-law he could be successful. "I intend," he said, "to make a test case of it, not for the money's sake, but for the sake of thousands of long-suffering travellers like myself, who are given this unwholesome stuff as 'honey.' Obtaining money by false pretences, or selling adulterated food—or whatever corresponds in Italy to our English 'Sale of Food and Drugs Act'—doesn't matter what it is, provided we can show up the Hotels that charge us such high prices and give us such cheap and nasty stuff to eat!" He was very enthusiastic and very determined. He felt he was acting on behalf of inarticulate millions who had been bullied into resigned acceptance for many years.

And, in due course, the case was actually tried, Jones coming over from England regardless of expense to attend the proceedings. The news had spread to half the cities of Europe; a test case indeed, and more—almost a *cause célèbre.* The Manager and Proprietor of the Hotel, the analyst, the waiter who served the stuff, and the manufacturer who made it, Jones's own friend who identified the sample, *It* and *He* as well—all being called as witnesses. It was proved that the contents of the bottle were taken from a jar of "matter" offered to customers in return for payment as "pure honey." Nothing could shake that careful evidence. An effort was made by the defendants' counsel to show that the bottle had been tampered with, but the seal and date, and the admirable witness, whose testimony Jones had been so prudent to ensure, proved too much for the best endeavours of the expensive talent arrayed against the plaintiff. The report of the chemist came as a shattering blow. The case lasted two entire days, fully reported in every journal, and Jones received a couple of threatening anonymous letters which were read aloud in Court, and only served to strengthen the popular feeling in his favour. But he also received a verdict, for five francs damages, while the Hotel had to pay the heavy costs of the trial and received an advertisement of a kind it by no means desired. All the newspapers published the chemist's damaging analysis. The travelling public, thenceforth, could insist upon its rights. It was an immense success. Jones was a hero, and the entire Tourist World was proud of him. . . .

"Tea all right, sir?" asked a waiter, interrupting the dream with which Jones consoled himself while he sipped a concoction *not* made with boiling water.

"Quite, thanks—yes," he replied meekly, helping himself to a jar of treacle and glucose on the table.

He was disgusted with the taste of both articles offered for his consumption, while he paid 20 francs a day for a cupboard of a room. But he was too timid to complain or make a fuss. For all this was merely the thing he would have liked to do. What he did—was what he always did. And when he left, he tipped *It* handsomely for doing nothing. He tipped *Him* too—for a similar reason.

The Philosopher

A very nice old lady stood with a very big dog on the edge of the pavement. It was in the outskirts of a country town; the sun was shining, the birds were singing, and may smothered the hedges like fresh-fallen snow. Dressed in shiny black, with objects in her bonnet that jerked and waggled, the old lady was a pleasant thing to see, for she expressed exactly what a typical old lady ought to look like. She was what is called "a perfect dear," and the dog, who seemed enormous beside her frailty, was what is called "a perfect beauty." She was vigorous, yet used a stick, a stick of gleaming ebony with a polished ivory handle. She was full of life, and obviously satisfied with life; had undoubtedly made her will—there was lots to leave as well!—and had no quarrel with existence on any score whatever. For life was kind to her, and illness had forgotten to interfere with her digestion. Peevishness was a stranger to her. She was happy. You could hear her in the drawing-room at home laughing with the best of them and teasing people far younger than herself in a deep and musical voice. You could hear her saying "People as young as I am, dear," before half the sentences she uttered; and she was going now on foot into the little town with her black stick, her neat black reticule, and her big, protective dog, upon good works intent. You could hear her laughing on the front-door steps as she came down into the garden while her son, or possibly her grandson, chided her: "It's absurd of you to walk, Grannie, when there are four motors and fourteen horses dying to pull you; but you are *so* obstinate in your young days—"

"I *am* young, Charles. You forget that I'm not yet seventy-eight!"

"Caesar will look after you, then, if you really won't let me come—"

"Better than you could," she smiled; then added slyly in her deep, teasing voice, "You have some one else to look after—a little younger than I am!"

It was the joke she had made first with his father thirty years before, probably with his grandfather as well a quarter of a century before *that.* She would surely live for ever. Death and illness had both forgotten her. The male figure on the steps watched her go until the shrubberies hid her, then turned and disappeared inside the ivy-covered old house that one day would be his own. She was a dear and wonderful old lady.

The day was glorious and very peaceful, with the calm beauty of a spring morning upon the entire countryside. The stillness seemed too deep for anything to break it, for anything to happen. Beside her fragile figure the dog looked more than large—he looked massive and gigantic, powerful as a pony, very steady, very sure of himself. The whip she carried with her reticule would hardly have disturbed a fly. But Caesar loved and followed her as though she were at least a lion-tamer. He obeyed with a slavish smile in his great brown eyes her slightest order. He keep brushing up against her to enquire what her wishes were. He protected her. He could have held the traffic up if necessary while she passed very slowly with him into safety.

And there she stood on the edge of the pavement, waiting to cross the road. Her stick was a foot in front of her as she leaned a little forward. She left the curb and stood a moment in the cobbled gutter. She looked steadily up the road, then down the road, then straight in front of her to choose her footsteps well. No tram, no car, no tradesman's cart was visible; the air was without dust; there was no sound but the piping of the birds. She glanced enquiringly at Caesar, and Caesar agreed, wagging his bushy tail with authority and confidence. Four of her little steps fitted into one leisurely stride of his great legs. His eyes said plainly: "Yes, you may cross with safety now, my dear. Keep close to me," as he sedately led the way. He never followed at such moments; he helped by guiding; and if he felt concern he did not show it. He invariably waited till the "old thing," as he called her to himself, was out of danger, and then he barked and bounded with tremendous energy just to inform the world at large the worst was over. But he *was* anxious all the same. He had known her "bundle about" most stupidly sometimes when sudden danger confused her and surprised the muscles into acting without an order from the brain. For, of course—and this was what he never could understand or realise—she had not got his absolute alertness and instinctive action. Where he could act instantaneously she had to think before the proper movement followed. She could neither leap nor bound nor save herself five times in thirty seconds before the horses' very hoofs.

And so in the middle of the road, when the reckless car came tearing round the unexpected corner at a wicked pace, and she pirouetted apparently on the point of her ebony stick, unable to execute the sudden leap of six inches that could have saved her—he merely barked at her to hurry up, with a helpful push of his great shoulder in the right direction. He wagged his beautiful tail and pranced. It was true he pushed her with his shaggy head, but he did not realise that she could be so clumsy, so dreadfully maladroit, as to let the stick catch right between her little feet. "If she had bounded sideways or even backwards! If she had dropped on all fours and leaped six inches after me . . . !" But she hadn't.

He observed the subsequent proceedings solemnly, ignoring the little dogs that came to whisper things about the pleasant weather; and he followed the car to the building in the town where his dog licence came from, and so eventually back to the house where he had his meals and kennel, wondering why they went so slowly and why she lay so still and made no sign to him. And on the steps he gambolled. He pranced and barked, thinking it strange that no one noticed him. And when his master spoke sadly to him, saying something about "Grannie was in *your* charge," he cocked his great head sideways and wagged his tail and gave a backwards leap in splendid spirits, and barked again, utterly puzzled why the whip came down and cut his glossy back. "Keep quiet, you brute, can't you?" explained nothing at all to him.

That is, it explained Fate to him as little as the skidding, hooting car had explained Fate to her. The car, the whip, his master, he himself as well, were symbols of some bigger Power that had to hurt things somehow for their own good—for everything in the happy, careless, lovely world was good, of course. He accepted things as they were, unable to understand very well. It all lay just beyond his powers of comprehension. It was all right somewhere, and some day he would know it all.

The occupants of the car, meanwhile, were acquitted of reckless driving, because Caesar was the only witness against them, and they silenced him by saying "the great brute" pushed the deceased inadvertently right under the wheels. But Caesar was not told of this. Nor did he understand quite why his master did not take the trouble to find the "old thing" and bring her out of the hiding place, but went about the house exactly as though she were not there, and as though he did not care a plate of dog-biscuit whether she was there or not. He had inherited, of course. Caesar noticed certain changes in the household. Life was a puzzle indeed. Then he forgot about it all, and just went on wagging his huge tail, and bounding and barking as before.

The Daisy World

Adventure means saying Yes, and being careless; children say Yes to everything and are very careless indeed: even their No is usually a Yes, inverted or deferred. "I won't play," parsed by a psychologist, means "I'll play when I'm ready." The adventurous spirit accepts what offers regardless of consequences; he who hesitates and thinks is a mere Policeman who prevents adventure. Now, everything offers itself to children, because they rightly think that everything belongs to them. Life is conditionless, if only people would let them accept it as it is. "Don't think; accept!" expresses the law of their swift and fluid being. They act on it. They take everything they can—get. But it is the Policeman who adds the 'get,' changing the whole significance of life with one ugly syllable.

Each of the children possessed and treasured an adventure of its very own: an adventure-in-chief, private and particular, that could not possibly have happened to anybody else in the world. Grown-ups have these too, of course, whether they be kings, or married men, or private detectives. The child in us persists until the last hair and tooth fall out.

Thus, Jinny, Jimbo, and Maria—three survivals in an age when education considers childhood a disease to be cured as hurriedly as possible—took their adventure the instant that it came, and each was proud with a complete assurance of superiority that his or her particular one was unique. To no one else in the world could such a thing have happened, least of all to the other two. Each took it characteristically, according to his or her individual nature—Jinny, with a sense of Romance called deathless; Jimbo, with a taste for Poetic Drama, a dash of the supernatural in it; and Maria, with a magnificent inactivity that ruled the world by waiting for things to happen, then claiming them as her own. Her masterly instinct for repose ran no risk of failure from misdirected energy. And to all three secrecy, of course, was essential: "Don't never tell the others, Uncle! Promise faithfully now!"

For, to every adventure Uncle Henry acted as audience, atmosphere, and chorus. He watched whatever happened—audience; believed in its reality—atmosphere; and explained without explaining away—chorus. He had the unusual faculty of being ten years young as well as forty years old, and a real adventure was not possible without him.

The secrecy, of course, was not preserved for long; sooner or later the glory must be shared so that 'the others' knew—and envied. For only then was the joy complete, the splendour properly fulfilled. And so the old tired world went round and life grew more and more wonderful each day. For children are an epitome of life—a self-creating universe.

That week was memorable for several reasons. Daddy, overworked in an office, went for a change by sea to Scotland, taking Mother with him; Aunt Emily, in her black silk dress that crackled with disapproval, went to Tunbridge Wells—an awful place in another century somewhere; and Uncle Henry was left behind to "take charge of 'em,'"—'em' being the children and himself. It was evidence of monumental trust and power, placing him in their imaginations even above the recognised Authorities. His sway was never for a moment questioned.

"No lessons, then!" he had insisted as a condition of acceptance, and after much confabulation the point was yielded with reluctance. Maria claimed the victory, of course, by merely sitting still and affirming that her state of health was not satisfactory. Anyhow, it was to be a ten days' holiday all round. They had the house and grounds entirely to themselves, and with the departure of the elders a sheet was pulled by some one off the world, a curtain rolled away, another drop-scene fell, the word No disappeared, they saw invisible things.

Another reason, however, made the week memorable—the daisies. It was extraordinary. The very day after the grown-ups left the daisies came. Like thousands of small white birds, with bright and steady eyes, they arrived and settled, thick and plentiful. They appeared in sheets and clouds upon the grass, all of their own accord and unexplained. In a night the lawns turned white. It seemed a pre-arranged invasion. Jinny, first awake that morning, looked out of her window to watch a squirrel playing, and noticed them. Then she told the others; and Maria, one eye above the blankets, ejaculated "Ah!" She claimed the daisies too.

Now, whereas a single daisy has no smell and seems a common, unimportant thing, a bunch of several hundred holds all the perfume of the spring. No flowers lie closer to the soil or bring the smell of earth more sweetly to the mind; upon the lips and cheeks they are softer than a kitten's fur, and lie against the skin like tired eyelids. They are, perhaps, the common people of the flower world, but they have in virtue of that fact the beauty and simplicity of the common people. They own a subdued and unostentatious strength, are humble and ignored, are walked upon, unnoticed, rarely thought about and never praised; they are cut off in early youth by mowing machines; yet their pain in fading is unreported, their little sufferings unsung. They cling to earth and never aspire to climb, but they hold the sweetest dew and nurse the tiniest little winds imaginable. Their patience is divine. They are proud to be the carpet for all walking, running things, and in their universal service is their strength. The rain stays longer with them than with grander flowers, and the best sunlight goes to sleep among them in great pools of fragrant and delicious heat. The daisies are a stalwart little people altogether.

But they have another quality as well—something elfin, wayward, mischievous. They peep and whisper. It is said they can cast spells. Certainly they can coax humans into their own lovely world and keep them there. There is a hint of impudence in their private conduct, half audacity, half wickedness, that shows itself a little in the way they stare unwinkingly all day at everything above them—at the stately things that tower proudly in the air—then just shut up at sunset without a word of explanation or apology. They see everything, but keep their opinions to themselves. Because people notice them so little, and even tread upon their tiny and enquiring faces, they are up to things all the time—undiscovered things. They know, it is said, the thoughts of Marble Whites and Clouded Brimstones, as well as the intentions of the disappearing golden flies; why wind keeps often close to the ground when the tree-tops are without a single breath; but, also, they know what is going on *below* the surface. They live, moreover, in every country of the globe, and their system of inter-communication is so perfect that even birds and flying things can learn from it. They prove their breeding by their perfect taste in dress, the well-bred being ever inconspicuous; and their simplicity conceals enormous, undecipherable wonder. One daisy out of doors is worth a hundred shelves of text books in the house. Their mischief, moreover, is not revenge, though some might think it so—but a natural desire to be recognised and thought about and talked about a little. Daisies, in a word, are—daisies.

And it was by way of the daisies that Jinny's great adventure came to her, the particular adventure that was her very own. For she had deep sympathy with flowers, a sympathy lacking in her brother and sister, and it was natural that her adventure in chief should come that way. She could play with flowers for long periods at a time; she knew their names and habits; she picked them gently, without cruelty, and never merely for the 'fun' of picking them; while the way she arranged them about the house proved that she understood their silent, inner natures, their likes and dislikes—in a word, their souls. As has been seen, she was the first to notice the arrival of the daisies. From the bedroom window she waved her arm to them, and showed plainly the pleasure that she felt. They arrived in troops and armies. Risen to the surface of the lawn like cream, she saw them staring wide-eyed with suspicious innocence at the sky. They stared at *her*.

"Just when the others have gone away!" was her instant thought, though unexpressed in words. There was meaning somewhere in this calculated arrival!

"They *are* alive," she asked that afternoon, "aren't they? But why do they all shut up at night? Who—" she changed the word—"what closes them?"

She was alone with Uncle Henry, and they had chosen with great difficulty a spot where they could lie down without crushing a single flower with their enormous bodies. With considerable difficulty they had found it. Having done a great many things since lunch—a feast involving several second helpings—they were feeling heavy and exhausted. So Jinny chose this moment for her simple question. The world required explanation.

"There's life in everything," he mumbled with his face against the grass, "everything that grows especially." And having said it he settled down comfortably again to doze. His pipe was out. He felt rather like a log.

"But stopping growing isn't dying," she informed him sharply.

"Oh, no," he agreed lazily. "You're alive for a long time after that."

"Because *you* stopped growing before I was born."

"And I'm not quite dead yet."

"Exactly," she said, "so daisies *are* alive."

It was absurd to think of dozing at such a time. He rolled round heavily and gazed at her through half closed eyelids. "A daisy breathes," he murmured, "and drinks and eats; sap circulates in its little body. Probably it feels as well. Delicate threads like nerves run through it everywhere. It knows when it is being picked or walked on. Oh yes; a daisy is alive all right enough." He sighed like a big dog that has just shaken a fly off its nose and lies waiting for the next attack. It came at once.

"But who knows it?" she asked. "I mean—there's no good being alive unless some one else knows it too!"

Then he sat up and stared at her. Jinny, he remembered, knew a lot of things she could tell to no one, not even to herself—and this seemed one of them. The question was a startling one.

"An intellectual mystic at thirteen!" he gasped. "How on earth did you manage it?"

"I'm not quite thirteen," she replied gravely, "and I'm not a mistylectual insect at all. But what's the good of being alive, even like a daisy, unless all the others know it—*us,* for instance?"

He still stared at her, sitting up stiffly, and propped by his hands upon the grass behind him. After prolonged reflection, during which he closed his eyes and opened them several times in succession, sighing laboriously while he did so, low mumbled words became audible:

"Forgive my apparent slowness," he said, "but I feel like a mowing machine this afternoon. I want oiling and pushing. The answer to your enquiry, however, is as follows: We could—*if* we took the trouble."

"Could know that daisies are alive?" she cried.

His great head nodded.

"If we thought about them very, very hard indeed," he replied, "and for a very, very long time, we could feel as they feel, and so understand them and know exactly *how* they are alive."

And the way he said it, the grave, thoughtful, solemn way, convinced her, who already was convinced beforehand.

"I do believe we could," she answered simply.

"I'm sure of it," he said.

"Let's try!" she whispered breathlessly.

For a minute and a half they stared into each other's eyes, knowing themselves upon the verge of an immense discovery. They balanced on the threshold of untold adventure. She did not doubt or question;

she did not jeer and tell him he was only humbugging. Her heart thrilled with the right conditions—expectation and delight. Her dark brown eyes were burning.

He murmured something then she did not properly understand.

"Expect and delight
Is the way to invite;
Delight and expect—
And you'll know things direct!"

"Let's try!" she repeated, and her face proved that she fulfilled his conditions without knowing it; she was delighted, and she expected everything.

He scratched his head, wrinkling his nose and pursing up his lips a moment. "There's a dodge about it," he explained, "a certain kind of dodge. To know a flower yourself you must feel like it. Its life, you see, is different to ours. It doesn't move and hurry, it just lives. It feels sun and wind and dew; it feels the insects' tread; it lifts its skin to meet the rain drops and the whispering butterflies. It doesn't run away. It has no fear of anything, because it has the whole green earth behind it, and it feels safe because millions of other daisies feel the same—"

"And smells because it's happy," put in Jinny. "Then what *is* a daisy? What is it really?"

She was 'expecting' vividly. Her mind was hungry for essentials. This mere description told her nothing real. She wanted to feel 'direct.'

What is a daisy? The little word already had a wonderful and living sound—soft, sweet, and beautiful. But to tell the truth about this ordinary masterpiece was no easy matter. An ostentatious lily, a blazing rose, a wayward hyacinth, a mass of showy wistaria—notorious, complicated flowers—presented fewer difficulties. A daisy seemed too simple to be told, its mystery and honour too humble for proud human minds to understand.

So he answered gently, while a Marble White sailed past between their very faces: "Let's think about it hard; perhaps we'll get it that way."

The butterfly sailed off across the lawn; another joined it, and then a third. They danced and flitted like winged marionettes on wires that the swallows pulled; and, as they vanished, a breath of scented air stole round the trunk of the big lime tree and stirred the daisies' heads. A thousand small white faces turned towards them; a thousand steady eyes observed them; a thousand slender necks were bent. There seemed a little wave of movement over the lawn as though the flowers pressed nearer, aware at last that they were being noticed. And both humans, the big one and the little one, felt a thrill of sudden happiness and beauty in their hearts. The rapture of the spring slipped into them. They concentrated all their thoughts on daisies. . . .

"I'm beginning to feel it already," whispered the Little Human, turning to gaze at him as though that breath of air impelled her to.

The wind blew her voice across his face like perfume; he looked, but could not see her clearly; she swayed a little; her eyes melted together into a single lovely circle, bright and steady within their fringe of feathery lashes. He tried to speak—"Delight and expect, and we'll know it direct"—but his voice spread across whole yards of lawn. It became a single word that rolled everywhere about him, rising and falling like a wave upon a sea of green: "Daisy, daisy, daisy." On all sides, beneath, above his head as well, it passed with the music of the wandering wind, and he kept repeating it—"Daisy, daisy!" *She* kept repeating it too, till the sound multiplied, yet never grew louder than a murmur as of air and grass and tiny leaves—"Daisy, daisy, daisy." It broke like a sea upon the coast-line of another world. It was everywhere.

But another sound lay underneath. As the crest of a breaking wave utters its separate note of foam above the general booming of the sea that bears it, so the flying wave of daisy-tones rose out of this deeper sound beneath. Both humans became aware that it was but a surface voice they imitated. They heard the foundation sound that bore it—deep, booming, thunderous, half lost and very far away. It was prodigious; yet there was safety and delight in it that brought no hint of fear. They swam, it seemed, upon the pulse of some enormous but very gentle life that rose about and through them in a swelling tide. They felt the heave of something that was strong enough to draw the moon, yet soft enough to close a daisy's eyes. They heard the deep, lost roar of it, rising and coming nearer. Ah, it was exquisite. They were in the Daisy world.

"The Earth!" he whispered. "And the spring is rising through it. Listen!"

"We're growing together," replied the Little Human. "We're rising with the spring!"

He tried to move and reach her, but found that he could not take a step in any direction, and that his feet were imbedded in the soft damp soil. The movement that he tried to make spread wide among a hundred others like himself. They rose on every side. All shared his movement as all had shared his voice. He heard his whole body murmuring, singing "Daisy, daisy, daisy . . ." And she leaned over, bending towards him a slim form in a graceful line of green that formed the segment of a circle. A little shining face came close for a moment against his own. It was rimmed with delicate spears of pink and white. It sang as it shone. The spring was in it. There were hundreds like it everywhere, yet he recognised it as one he knew. There were thousands, tens of thousands, yet this one he distinguished because he loved it.

Their faces touched like the fringes of two clouds, and then withdrew. They remained very close together, side by side among thousands like themselves, slowly rising on the same great tide. The Earth's round body was beneath them. They felt quite safe. But already they were different—they were otherwise than they had been.

"We're changing," he murmured, seizing some fragments of half-remembered speech. "We're marvellously changed!"

"We're daisies," he heard her vanishing reply, "two daisies on the lawn!"

And then their voices went. That was the end of speech, the end of thinking too. They only felt. . . .

Long periods passed above their heads and then the air about them turned gorgeous as a sunset sky. It was a Clouded Yellow that sailed lazily past their faces with spreading wings as large as clouds. They shared that saffron glory. The draught of cool air fanned them. The splendid butterfly left its beauty in them and sailed away. But that sunset sky had lasted for hours; that cool wind fanning them was a breeze that blew steadily from the hills making 'weather' for half an afternoon. Time and duration as humans measure them had passed away; there was existence without hurry; end and beginning had not been invented yet. They did not know things in the stupid sense of having names for them; all that there was they shared: that was enough. They knew by feeling.

For everything was plentiful and inexhaustible—the heavens emptied light and warmth upon them without stint or measure; space poured about them freely, for they had no wish to move; they felt themselves everywhere, for all they needed came to them without the painful effort of busy things that hunt and search outside themselves; both food and drink slipped into them unawares from an abundant source that equally supplied whole forests without a trace of lessening or loss. All life was theirs, full, free, and generous beyond conception. They owned the world, without even the trouble of knowing that they owned it. They lived, simply staring at the universe with eyes of exquisitely fashioned beauty. They knew joy and peace, and were content with that.

They did communicate; oh, yes, they shared each other's special happiness. There was, it is true, no sound of broken syllables, no speech which humans use to veil the very thing they would express; but there was that simpler language which all Nature knows, which cannot lie because it is unconscious, and by which constellations probably converse with buttercups or cedars with the flying drops of rain—there was gesture. For gesture and attitude can convey all the important and necessary things, while speech in the human sense is but an invention of some sprite who wanted people to wonder what he really meant. In sublimest moments it is never used even in the best circles of intelligence; it drops away quite naturally; souls know one another face to face in dumb yet eloquent gesture:

"The sun is out; I feel warm and happy; there is nothing in the world I need!"

"You are beside me," he replied. "I love you and we cannot go apart. I smell you even when no wind stirs. You are sweetest when the dew has gone and left you moist and shiny."

A little shiver of enjoyment quivered through her curving stem. His petals brushed her own. She answered:

"Wet or fine, we stand together, and never stop staring at each other until we close our faces—"

"In the long darkness; but even then we whisper while we grow—"

"And open our eyes exactly at the same moment when the light comes back—"

"And feel warm and soft, and smell more delicious than ever in the dawn."

These two brave daisies, growing on the lawn, had lives of concentrated, crammed enjoyment, asking no pity for their humble station in the universe. All treated them with unadulterated respect, and everything made love to them because they were so tender and so easily pleased. They knew, for instance, that their splendid Earth was turning with them, for they felt the swerve of her, sharing from their roots upwards her gigantic curve through space; they knew the sun was part of them, because they felt it drawing their sweet-flavoured food up all their dainty length till it glowed in health upon their small, flushed faces; also they knew that streams of water made a tumbling fuss and sent them messages of laughter, because they caught the little rumble of it through miles of trembling ground. And some among them—though these were prophets and poets but half believed, and looked upon as partly mad and partly wonderful—felt the sea itself far leagues away, bending their heads this way and that for hours at a stretch according to the thundering vibrations that the tide sent through the soil from distant shores.

But all, from the tallest spread-heads to the smallest button-faces—all knew the pleasure of the uncertain winds; all knew the game of holding flying things just a moment longer, by fascinating them, by drowsing them into sleepiness, by nipping their probosces, or by puffing perfume in their nostrils while they fastened their feet with the pressure of a hundred yellow rods. For they could regulate their perfume just as humans can regulate emotion. . . .

Enormous periods passed away. A cloud that for a man's 'ten minutes' hid the sun, wearied them with depression, so that they simply closed their eyes and went to sleep. Showers of rain they loved, because it washed and cooled them and they felt the huge satisfaction of the earth beneath them as it drank; the sweet sensation of wet soil that sponged their roots, the pleasant gush that sluiced their bodies and carried off the irritating dust. They also felt the heavier tumbling of the swollen streams in all directions. The drops from overhanging trees came down and played with them, bringing another set of perfumes altogether. A summer shower was, of course, 'a month' to them, a day of rain like weeks of holiday by the sea. But, most of all, they enjoyed the rough and tumble nonsense of the violent weather, when they were tied together by the ropes of running wind; for these were visiting days—all manner of strangers dropped in upon them from distant walks in life, and they never knew whether the next would be a fir-cone or one of those careless, irresponsible travellers, a bit of thistle-down. . . .

And for all their steadiness of life, they knew incessant change—the variety of a daisy's existence was proverbial. Nor was the surprise of being walked upon too alarming—it did not come to all—for they knew a way of bending beneath enormous pressure so that nothing broke, while sometimes it brought a queer delicious pleasure, as when the bare feet of some flying child passed lightly over them, leaving wild laughter upon a group of them. They knew, indeed, a thousand joys, proudest of all, however, that the big Earth loved them so that she carried millions of them everywhere she went.

And all, without exception, communicated their knowledge by movements, attitudes, and gestures they assumed; and, since each stood close to each, the enjoyment spread quickly till the entire lawn felt one undivided sensation by itself. Anything passing across it at such a moment, whether insect, bird, loose leaf, or even human being, would be aware of this—poets, it is said, have received their sweetest inspirations upon a daisied lawn in the flush of spring!—and thus, for a fleeting second, share another world. Nor is it always a sight of prey that makes the swallows dart so suddenly sidewards and away, but some chance message of joy or warning intercepted from the hosts of flowers in the soil.

And from this region of the flower-life comes, of course, the legend that fairies have emotions that last for ever, with eternal youth, and with loves that do not pass away to die. Because the measurement of existence is a mightier business than with overdeveloped humans-in-a-hurry. For knowledge comes chiefly through the eye, and the eye can perceive only about six times in a second—things that happen more quickly or more slowly than six times a second are invisible. No man can see the movement of a growing daisy, just as no man can distinguish the separate beats of a sparrow's wing: one is too slow and the other is too quick. But the daisy is practically all eye. It is aware of most delightful things. In its short life of months it lives through an eternity of unhurrying perceptions and of big sensations. Its youth, its loves, its pleasures are—to it—quite endless.

"I can see the old sun moving," she murmured, "but you will love me for ever, won't you?"

"Even till it sinks behind the hills," he answered; "I shall not change."

"So long we have been friends already," she went on. "Do you remember when we first met each other, and you looked into my opening eye?"

He sighed with joy, as he thought of the long stretch of time.

"That was in our first reckless youth," he answered, catching the gold of passionate remembrance from an amber fly that hovered for an instant and was gone. "I remember well. You were half hidden by a drop of hanging dew, but I discovered you! That lilac bud across the world was just beginning to open." And, helped by the wind, he bent his shining head, taller than hers by a sixtieth of an inch, towards the lilac trees beside the gravel path.

"So long ago," she murmured, happy with the exquisite belief in him, "so long ago as that! And you will never change or leave me—promise, oh, promise that!"

His stalk grew nearer to her own. He leaned protectively towards her face.

"Until that bud shall open fully to the light and smell its sweetest," he replied—the gesture of his petals told it plainly—"so long shall you and I enjoy our happy love."

It was an eternity to them.

"And longer still," she pleaded.

"And longer still," he whispered in the wind. "Even until the blossom falls."

Ah, it was good to be alive with such an age of happiness before them!

He felt the tears in her voice, however; he knew there was something that she longed to tell.

"What is your sadness?" he asked softly, "and why do you put such questions to me now? What is your little trouble?"

A moment's hesitation, a moment's hanging of the graceful head the width of a petal's top nearer to his shoulder—and then she told him.

"I was in darkness for a time," she faltered, "but it was a long, long time. It seemed that something came between us. I lost your face. I felt afraid."

And his laughter—for just then a puff of wind passed by and shook his sides for him—ran across many feet of lawn.

"It was a Bumble Bee," he comforted her. "It came between us for a bit, its shadow fell upon you, nothing more! Such things will happen;

we must be prepared for them. It was nothing in myself that dimmed the world."

"Another time I will be braver then," she told him, "and even in the darkness I shall know you close, ah, very close to me. . . ."

For a long, long stretch of time, then, they stood joyfully together and watched the lilac growing. They also saw the movement of the sun across the sky. An eternity passed over them. . . . The vast disc of the sun went slowly gliding. . . .

But all the enormous things that happened in their lives cannot be told. Lives crammed with a succession of such grand and palpitating adventures lie beyond the reach of clumsy words. The sweetness sometimes was intolerable, and then they shared it with the entire lawn and so obtained relief—in order to begin again. The humming of the rising spring continued with the thunderous droning of the turning Earth. Never uncared for, part of everything, full of the big, rich life that brims the world in May—ah, almost fuller than they could hold sometimes—they passed with existence along to their appointed end.

"We began so long ago, I simply can't remember it," she sighed.

Yet the sun they watched had not left a half degree behind him since they met.

"There was no beginning," he reproved her, smiling, "and there will never be any end."

And the wind spread their happiness like perfume everywhere until the whole white lawn of daisies lay singing their rapture to the sunshine. . . .

The minute under-world of grass and stalks seemed of a sudden to grow large. Yet till now they had not realised it as 'large'—but simply natural. A beetle, big and broad as a Newfoundland dog, went lumbering past them, brushing its polished back against their trembling necks. Yet, till now, they had not thought of it as 'big'—but simply normal. Its footsteps made a grating sound like the gardeners' nailed boots upon the gravel paths. It was strange and startling. Something was different, something was changing. They realised dimly that there was another world somewhere, a world they had left behind long, long ago, forgotten. Something was slipping from them, as sleep slips from the skin and eyes in the early morning when the bath comes 'pinging' upon the floor. What did it mean? Big and little, far and near, above, below, inside and outside—all were mixed together in a falling rush.

They themselves were changing.

They looked up. They saw an enormous thing rising behind them with vast caverns of square outline opening in its sides—a house. They saw huge, towering shapes whose tops were in the clouds—the familiar lime-trees. Big and tiny were mixed together.

And that was wrong. For either the forest of grass was as big as themselves—in which case they still were daisies; or else it was tiny and far below them—in which case they were hurrying humans again. There was this odd confusion . . . while consciousness swung home to its appointed centre and Adventure brought them back towards the old, dull starting place again.

There came an ominous and portentous sound that rushed towards them through the air and through the solid ground as well. They heard it and grew pale with terror. Across the entire lawn it rumbled nearer, growing in volume awfully. The very earth seemed breaking into bits about them. And then they knew.

It was the End of the World that their prophets had long foretold.

It crashed upon them before they had time to think. The roar was appalling. The whole lawn trembled. The daisies bowed their little faces in a crowd. They had no time even to close their innocent eyes. Before a quarter of their sweet and happy life was known, the End swept them from the world, unsung and unlamented. Two of them who had planned Eternity together fell side by side before one terrible stroke. . . .

"I do believe,—" said Jinny, brushing her tumbled hair out of her eyes.

"Not possible!" exclaimed Uncle Henry, sitting up and stretching himself just like a dog. "It's a thing I never do, *never,* NEVER!"

They stared at each other with suspiciously sleepy eyes.

"Promise," she whispered presently, "promise never to tell the others!"

"I promise faithfully," he answered. "But we'd better get up or we shall have our heads cut off like—all the other daisies."

He pulled her to her feet—out of the way of the heavy mowing machine which the gardener was pushing with a whirring, droning noise across the lawn.

The Wings of Horus

Binovitch had the bird in him somewhere: in his features, certainly, with his piercing eye and hawk-like nose; in his movements, with his quick way of flitting, hopping, darting; in the way he perched on the edge of a chair; in the manner he pecked at his food; in his twittering, high-pitched voice as well; and, above all, in his airy, flashing mind. He skimmed all subjects and picked their heart out neatly, as a bird skims lawn or air to snatch its prey. He had the bird's-eye view of everything. He loved birds and understood them instinctively; could imitate their whistling notes with astonishing accuracy. Their one quality he had not was poise and balance. He was a nervous little man; he was neurasthenic. And he was in Egypt by doctor's orders.

Such imaginative, unnecessary ideas he had! Such uncommon beliefs!

"The old Egyptians," he said laughingly, yet with a touch of solemn conviction in his manner, "were a great people. Their consciousness was different from ours. The bird idea, for instance, conveyed a sense of deity to them—of bird deity, that is: they had sacred birds—hawks, ibis, and so forth—and worshipped them." And he put his tongue out as though to say with challenge, "Ha, ha!"

"They also worshipped cats and crocodiles and cows," grinned Palazov. Binovitch seemed to dart across the table at his adversary. His eyes flashed; his nose pecked the air. Almost one could imagine the beating of his angry wings.

"Because everything alive," he half screamed, "was a symbol of some spiritual power to them. Your mind is as literal as a dictionary and as incoherent. Pages of ink without connected meaning! Verb always in the infinitive! If you were an old Egyptian, you—you"—he flashed and spluttered, his tongue shot out again, his keen eyes blazed—"you would take all those words and spin them into a great interpretation of life, a cosmic romance, as they did. Instead, you get the bitter, dead taste of ink in your mouth, and spit it over us—like that"—he made a quick movement of his whole body as a bird that shakes itself—"in empty phrases."

Khilkoff ordered another bottle of champagne, while Vera, his sister, said half nervously, "Let's go for a drive; it's moonlight." There was enthusiasm at once. Another of the party called the head waiter and told him to pack food and drink in baskets. It was only eleven o'clock. They would drive out into the desert, have a meal at two in the morning, tell stories, sing, and see the dawn.

It was in one of those cosmopolitan hotels in Egypt which attract the ordinary tourists as well as those who are doing a "cure," and all these Russians were ill with one thing or another. All were ordered out for their health, and all were the despair of their doctors. They were as unmanageable as a bazaar and as incoherent. Excess and bed were their routine. They lived, but none of them got better. Equally, none of them got angry. They talked in this strange personal way without a shred of malice or offence. The English, French, and Germans in the hotel watched them with remote amazement, referring to them as "that Russian lot." Their energy was elemental. They never stopped. They merely disappeared when the pace became too fast, then reappeared after a day or two, and resumed their "living" as before. Binovitch, despite his neurasthenia, was the life of the party. He was also a special patient of Dr. Plitzinger, the famous psychiatrist, who took a peculiar interest in his case. It was not surprising. Binovitch was a man of unusual ability and of genuine, deep culture. But there was something more about him that stimulated curiosity. There was this striking originality. He said and did surprising things.

"I could fly if I wanted to," he said once when the airmen came to astonish the natives with their biplanes over the desert, "but without all that machinery and noise. It's only a question of believing and understanding—"

"Show us!" they cried. "Let's see you fly!"

"He's got it! He's off again! One of his impossible, delightful moments!"

These occasions when Binovitch let himself go always proved wildly entertaining. He said monstrously incredible things as though he really believed them. They loved his madness, for it gave them new sensations.

"It's only levitation, after all, this flying," he exclaimed, shooting out his tongue between the words, as his habit was when excited; "and what is levitation but a power of the air? None of you can hang an orange in space for a second, with all your scientific knowledge; but the moon is always levitated perfectly. And the stars. D'you think they swing on wires? What raised the enormous stones of ancient Egypt? D'you really believe it was heaped-up sand and ropes and clumsy leverage and all our weary and laborious mechanical contrivances? Bah! It was levitation. It was the powers of the air. Believe in those powers, and gravity becomes a mere nursery trick—true where it is, but true nowhere else. To know the fourth dimension is to step out of a locked room and appear instantly on the roof or in another country altogether. To know the powers of the air, similarly, is to annihilate what you call weight—and fly."

"Show us, show us!" they cried, roaring with delighted laughter.

"It's a question of belief," he repeated, his tongue appearing and disappearing like a pointed shadow. "It's in the heart; the power of the air gets into your whole being. Why should I show you? Why should I ask my deity to persuade your scoffing little minds by any miracle? For it *is* deity, I tell you, and nothing else. I *know* it. Follow one idea like that, as I follow my bird idea—follow it with the impetus and undeviating concentration of a projectile—and you arrive at power. You know deity—the bird idea of deity, that is. *They* knew that. The old Egyptians knew it."

"Oh, show us, show us!" they shouted impatiently, wearied of his nonsense-talk. "Get up and fly! Levitate yourself, as they did! Become a star!"

Binovitch turned suddenly very pale, and an odd light shone in his keen brown eyes. He rose slowly from the edge of the chair where he was perched. Something about him changed. There was silence instantly.

"I *will* show you," he said calmly, to their intense amazement; "not to convince your disbelief, but to prove it to myself. For the powers of the air are with me here. I believe. And Horus, great falcon-headed symbol, is my patron god."

The suppressed energy in his voice and manner was indescribable. There was a sense of lifting, upheaving power about him. He raised his arms; his face turned upward; he inflated his lungs with a deep, long breath, and his voice broke into a kind of singing cry, half prayer, half chant:

> "O Horus,
> Bright-eyed deity of wind,
> *Feather my soul
> Though earth's thick air,
> To know thy awful swiftness—"

He broke off suddenly. He climbed lightly and swiftly upon the nearest table—it was in a deserted card-room, after a game in which he had lost more pounds than there are days in the year—and leaped into the air. He hovered a second, spread his arms and legs in space, appeared to float a moment, then buckled, rushed down and forward, and dropped in a heap upon the floor, while every one roared with laughter.

But the laughter died out quickly, for there was something in his wild performance that was peculiar and unusual. It was uncanny, not quite natural. His body had seemed, as with Mordkin and Nijinski, literally to hang upon the air a moment. For a second he gave the distressing impression of overcoming gravity. There was a touch in it of that faint horror which appals by its very vagueness. He picked himself up unhurt, and his face was as grave as a portrait in the Academy, but with a new expression in it that everybody noticed with this strange, half-shocked amazement. And it was this expression that extinguished the claps of laughter as wind takes away the sound of bells. Like many ugly men, he was an inimitable actor, and his facial repertory was endless and incredible. But this was neither acting nor clever manipulation of expressive features. There was something in his curious Russian physiognomy that made the heart beat slower. And that was why the laughter died away so suddenly.

"You ought to have flown farther," cried some one. It expressed what all had felt.

"Icarus didn't drink champagne," another replied, with a laugh; but nobody laughed with him.

"You went too near to Vera," said Palazov, "and passion melted the wax." But his face twitched oddly as he said it. There was some-

---

*The Russian is untranslatable. The phrase means, "Give my life wings."

thing he did not understand, and so heartily disliked.

The strange expression on the features deepened. It was arresting in a disagreeable, almost in a horrible, way. The talk stopped dead; all stared; there was a feeling of dismay in everybody's heart, yet unexplained. Some lowered their eyes, or else looked stupidly elsewhere; but the women of the party felt a kind of fascination. Vera, in particular, could not move her sight away. The joking reference to his passionate admiration for her passed unnoticed. There was a general and individual sense of shock. And a chorus of whispers rose instantly:

"Look at Binovitch! What's happened to his face?"

"He's changed—he's changing!"

"God! Why he looks like a—bird!"

But no one laughed. Instead, they chose the names of birds—hawk, eagle, even owl. The figure of a man leaning against the edge of the door, watching them closely, they did not notice. He had been passing down the corridor, had looked in unobserved, and then had paused. He had seen the whole performance. He watched Binovitch narrowly now with calm, discerning eyes. It was Dr. Plitzinger, the great psychiatrist.

For Binovitch had picked himself up from the floor in a way that was oddly self-possessed, and precluded the least possibility of the ludicrous. He looked neither foolish nor abashed. He looked surprised, but also he looked half angry and half frightened. As some one had said, he "ought to have flown farther." That was the incredible impression his acrobatics had produced—incredible, yet somehow actual. This uncanny idea prevailed, as at a séance where nothing genuine is expected to happen, and something genuine, after all, does happen. There was no pretence in this: Binovitch had flown.

And now he stood there, white in the face—with terror and with anger white. He looked extraordinary, this little, neurasthenic Russian, but he looked at the same time half terrific. Another thing, not commonly experienced by men, was in him, breaking out of him, affecting *directly* the minds of his companions. His mouth opened; blood and fury shone in his blazing eyes; his tongue shot out like an ant-eater's, though even in this the comic had no place. His arms were spread like flapping wings, and his voice rose dreadfully:

"He failed me, he failed me!" he tried to bellow. "Horus, my falcon-headed deity, my power of the air, deserted me! Hell take him! Hell burn his wings and blast his piercing sight! Hell scorch him into dust for his false prophecies! I curse him—I curse Horus!"

The voice that should have roared across the silent room emitted, instead, this high-pitched, bird-like scream. The added touch of sound, the reality it lent, was ghastly. Yet it was marvellously done and acted. The entire thing was a bit of instantaneous inspiration—his voice, his words, his gestures, his whole wild appearance. Only—here was the reality that caused the sense of shock—the expression on his altered features was genuine. *That* was not assumed. There was something new and alien in him, something cold and difficult to human life, something alert and swift and cruel, of another element than earth. A strange, rapacious grandeur had leaped upon the struggling features. The face looked hawk-like.

And he came forward suddenly and sharply towards Vera, whose fixed, staring eyes had never once ceased to watch him with a kind of anxious and devouring pain in them. She was both drawn and beaten back. Binovitch advanced on tiptoe. No doubt he still was acting, still pretending this mad nonsense that he worshipped Horus, the falcon-headed deity of forgotten days, and that Horus had failed him in his hour of need; but somehow there was just a hint of too much reality in the way he moved and looked. The girl, a little creature, with fluffy golden hair, opened her lips; her cigarette fell to the floor; she shrank back; she looked for a moment like some smaller, coloured bird trying to escape from a great pursuing hawk; she screamed. Binovitch, his arms wide, his bird-like face thrust forward, had swooped upon her. He leaped. Almost he caught her.

No one could say exactly what happened. Play, become suddenly and unexpectedly too real, confuses the emotions. The change of key was swift. From fun to terror is a dislocating jolt upon the mind. Some one—it was Khilkoff, the brother—upset a chair; everybody spoke at once, everybody stood up. An unaccountable feeling of disaster was in the air, as with those drinkers' quarrels that blaze out from nothing, and end in a pistol-shot and death, no one able to explain clearly how it came about. It was the silent, watching figure in the doorway who saved the situation. Before any one had noticed his approach, there he was among the group, laughing, talking, applauding—between Binovitch and Vera. He was vigorously patting his patient on the back, and his voice rose easily above the general clamour. He was a strong, quiet personality; even in his laughter there was authority. And his laughter now was the only sound in the room, as though by his mere presence peace and harmony were restored. Confidence came with him. The noise subsided; Vera was in her chair again. Khilkoff poured out a glass of wine for the great man.

"The Czar!" said Plitzinger, sipping his champagne, while all stood up, delighted with his compliment and tact. "And to your opening night with the Russian ballet," he added quickly a second toast, "or to your first performance at the Moscow Théâtre des Arts!" Smiling significantly, he glanced at Binovitch; he clinked glasses with him. Their arms were already linked, but it was Palazov who noticed that the doctor's fingers seemed rather tight upon the creased black coat. All drank, looking with laughter, yet with a touch of respect, towards Binovitch, who stood there dwarfed beside the stalwart Austrian, and suddenly as meek and subdued as any mole. Apparently the abrupt change of key had taken his mind successfully off something else.

"Of course—'The Fire-Bird,'" exclaimed the little man, mentioning the famous Russian ballet. "The very thing!" he exclaimed. "For *us,*" he added, looking with devouring eyes at Vera. He was greatly pleased. He began talking vociferously about dancing and the rationale of dancing. They told him he was an undiscovered master. He was delighted. He winked at Vera and touched her glass again with his. "We'll make our début together," he cried. "We'll begin at Covent Garden, in London. I'll design the dresses and the posters 'The Hawk and the Dove!' *Magnifique!* I in dark grey, and you in blue and gold! Ah, dancing, you know, is sacred. The little self is lost, absorbed. It is ecstasy, it is divine. And dancing in air—the passion of the birds and stars—ah! they are the movements of the gods. You know deity that way—by living it."

He went on and on. His entire being had shifted with a leap upon this new subject. The idea of realising divinity by dancing it absorbed him. The party discussed it with him as though nothing else existed in the world, all sitting now and talking eagerly together. Vera took the cigarette he offered her, lighting it from his own; their fingers touched; he was as harmless and normal as a retired diplomat in a drawing room. But it was Plitzinger whose subtle manœuvring had accomplished the change so cleverly, and it was Plitzinger who presently suggested a game of billiards, and led him off, full now of a fresh enthusiasm for cannons, balls, and pockets, into another room. They departed arm in arm, laughing and talking together.

Their departure, it seemed, made no great difference at first. Vera's eyes watched him out of sight, then turned to listen to Baron Minski, who was describing with gusto how he caught wolves alive for coursing purposes. The speed and power of the wolf, he said, was impossible to realise; the force of their awful leap, the strength of their teeth, which could bite through metal stirrup-fastenings. He showed a scar on his arm and another on his lip. He was telling truth, and everybody listened with deep interest. The narrative lasted perhaps ten minutes or more, when Minski abruptly stopped. He had come to an end; he looked about him; he saw his glass, and emptied it. There was a general pause. Another subject did not at once present itself. Sighs were heard; several fidgeted; fresh cigarettes were lighted. But there was no sign of boredom, for where one or two Russians are gathered together there is always life. They produce gaiety and enthusiasm as wind produces waves. Like great children, they plunge whole-heartedly into whatever interest presents itself at the moment. There is a kind of uncouth gambolling in their way of taking life. It seems as if they are always fighting that deep, underlying, national sadness which creeps into their very blood.

"Midnight!" then exclaimed Palazov, abruptly, looking at his watch; and the others fell instantly to talking about that watch, admiring it and asking questions. For the moment that very ordinary timepiece became the centre of observation. Palazov mentioned the price. "It never stops," he said proudly, "not even under water." He looked up at everybody, challenging admiration. And he told how, at a country house, he made a bet that he would swim to a certain island in the lake, and won the bet. He and a girl were the winners, but as it was a horse they had bet, he got nothing out of it for himself, giving the horse to her. It was a genuine grievance in him. One felt he could have cried as he spoke of it. "But the watch went all the time," he said delightedly, holding the gun-metal object in his hand to show, "and I was twelve minutes in the water with my clothes on."

Yet this fragmentary talk was nothing but pretence. The sound of clicking billiard-balls was audible from the room at the end of the corridor. There was another pause. The pause, however, was intentional. It was not vacuity of mind or absence of ideas that caused it. There was another subject, an unfinished subject that each member of the group was still considering. Only no one cared to begin about it till at last, unable to resist the strain any longer, Palazov turned to Khilkoff, who was saying he would take a "whisky-soda," as the champagne was too sweet, and whispered something beneath his breath; whereupon Khilkoff, forgetting his drink, glanced at his sister, shrugged his shoulders, and made a curious grimace. "He's all right now"—his reply was just audible—"he's with Plitzinger." He cocked his head sidewise to indicate that the clicking of the billiard-balls still was going on.

The subject was out: all turned their heads; voices hummed and buzzed; questions were asked and answered or half answered; eyebrows were raised, shoulders shrugged, hands spread out expressively. There came into the atmosphere a feeling of presentiment, of mystery, of things half understood; primitive, buried instinct stirred a little, the kind of racial dread of vague emotions that might gain the upper hand if encouraged. They shrank from looking something in the face, while yet this unwelcome influence drew closer round them all. They discussed Binovitch and his astonishing performance. Pretty little Vera listened with large and troubled eyes, though saying nothing. The Arab waiter had put out the lights in the corridor, and only a solitary cluster burned now above their heads, leaving their faces in shadow. In the distance the clicking of the billiard-balls still continued.

"It was not play; it was real," exclaimed Minski vehemently. "I can catch wolves," he blurted; "but birds—ugh!—and human birds!" He was half inarticulate. He had witnessed something he could not understand, and it had touched instinctive terror in him. "It was the way he leaped that put the wolf first into my mind, only it was not a wolf at all." The others agreed and disagreed. "It was play at first, but it was reality at the end," another whispered; "and it was no animal he mimicked, but a bird, and a bird of prey at that!"

Vera thrilled. In the Russian woman hides that touch of savagery which loves to be caught, mastered, swept helplessly away, captured utterly and deliciously by the one strong enough to do it thoroughly. She left her chair and sat down beside an older woman in the party, who took her arm quietly at once. Her little face wore a perplexed expression, mournful, yet somehow wild. It was clear that Binovitch was not indifferent to her.

"It's become an *idée fixe* with him," this older woman said. "The bird idea lives in his mind. He lives it in his imagination. Ever since that time at Edfu, when he pretended to worship the great stone falcons outside the temple—the Horus figures—he's been full of it." She stopped. The way Binovitch had behaved at Edfu was better left unmentioned at the moment, perhaps. A slight shiver ran round the listening group, each one waiting for some one else to focus their emotion, and so explain it by saying the convincing thing. Only no one ventured. Then Vera abruptly gave a little jump.

"Hark!" she exclaimed, in a staccato whisper, speaking for the first time. She sat bolt upright. She was listening. "Hark!" she repeated. "There it is again, but nearer than before. It's coming closer. I hear it." She trembled. Her voice, her manner, above all her great staring eyes, startled everybody. No one spoke for several seconds; all listened. The halls and corridors lay in darkness, and gloom was over the big hotel. Everybody was in bed.

"Hear what?" asked the older woman soothingly, yet with a perceptible quaver in her voice, too. She was aware that the girl's hand tightened upon her arm.

"Do you not hear it, too?" the girl whispered.

All listened without speaking. All watched her paling face. Something wonderful, yet half terrible, seemed in the air about them. There was a dull murmur, audible, faint, remote, its direction hard to tell. It had come suddenly from nowhere. They shivered. That strange racial thrill again passed into the group, unwelcome, unexplained. It was aboriginal; it belonged to the unconscious primitive mind, half childish, half terrifying.

"*What* do you hear?" her brother asked angrily—the irritable anger of nervous fear.

"When he came at me," she answered very low, "I heard it first. I hear it now again. Listen! He's coming."

And at that minute, out of the dark mouth of the corridor, emerged two human figures, Plitzinger and Binovitch. Their game was over; they were going up to bed. They passed the open door of the card-room. But Binovitch was being half dragged, half restrained, for he was apparently attempting to run down the passage with flying, dancing leaps. He bounded. It was like a huge bird trying to rise for flight, while his companion kept him down by force upon the earth. As they entered the strip of light, Plitzinger changed his own position, placing himself swiftly between his companion and the group in the dark corner of the room. He hurried Binovitch along as though he sheltered him from view. They passed into the shadows down the passage. They disappeared. And every one looked significantly, questioningly, at his neighbour, though at first saying no word. It seemed that a curious disturbance of the air had followed them audibly.

Vera was the first to open her lips. "You heard it *then,*" she said breathlessly, her face whiter than the ceiling.

"Damn!" exclaimed her brother furiously. "It was wind against the outside walls—wind in the desert. The sand is driving."

Vera looked at him. She shrank closer against the side of the older woman, whose arm was tight about her.

"It was *not* wind," she whispered simply. She paused. All waited uneasily for the completion of her sentence. They stared into her face like peasants who expected a miracle.

"Wings," she whispered. "It was the sound of wings."

And at four o'clock in the morning, when they all returned exhausted from their excursion into the desert, little Binovitch was sleeping soundly and peacefully in his bed. They passed his door on tiptoe. But he did not hear them. He was dreaming. His spirit was at Edfu, experiencing with that ancient deity who was master of all flying life those strange enjoyments upon which his own troubled human heart was passionately set. Safe with that mighty falcon whose powers his lips had scorned a few hours before, his soul, released in vivid dream, went sweetly flying. It was amazing, it was gorgeous. He skimmed the Nile at lightning speed. Dashing down headlong from the height of the great Pyramid, he chased with faultless accuracy a little dove that sought vainly to hide from his terrific pursuit beneath the palm trees. For what he loved must worship where he worshipped, and the majesty of those tremendous effigies had fired his imagination to the creative point where expression was imperative.

Then suddenly, at the very moment of delicious capture, the dream turned horrible, becoming awful with the nightmare touch. The sky lost all its blue and sunshine. Far, far below him the little dove enticed him into nameless depths, so that he flew faster and faster, yet never fast enough to overtake it. Behind him came a great thing down the air, black, hovering, with gigantic wings outstretched. It had terrific eyes, and the beating of its feathers stole his wind away. It followed him, crowding space. He was aware of a colossal beak, curved like a scimitar and pointed wickedly like a tooth of steel. He dropped. He faltered. He tried to scream.

Through empty space he fell, caught by the neck. The huge spectral falcon was upon him. The talons were in his heart. And in sleep he remembered then that he had cursed. He recalled his reckless language. The curse of the ignorant is meaningless; that of the worshipper is real. This attack was on his soul. He had invoked it. He realised next, with a shock of ghastly horror, that the dove he chased was, after all, the bait that had lured him purposely to destruction, and awoke with a suffocating terror upon him, and his entire body bathed in icy perspiration. Outside the open window he heard a sound of wings retreating with powerful strokes into the surrounding darkness of the sky.

The nightmare made its impression upon Binovitch's impressionable and dramatic temperament. It aggravated his tendencies. He related it next day to Mme. de Drühn, the friend of Vera, telling it with that somewhat boisterous laughter some minds use to disguise less kind emotions. But he received no encouragement. The mood of the previous night was not recoverable; it was already ancient history. Russians never make the banal mistake of repeating a sensation till it is exhausted; they hurry on to novelties. Life flashes and rushes with them, never standing still for exposure before the cameras of their minds. Mme. de Drühn, however, took the trouble to mention the matter to Plitzinger, for Plitzinger, like Freud of Vienna, held that dreams revealed subconscious tendencies which sooner or later must betray themselves in action.

"Thank you for telling me," he smiled politely, "but I have already heard it from him." He watched her eyes a moment, really examining her soul. "Binovitch, you see," he continued, apparently satisfied with what he saw, "I regard as that rare phenomenon—a genius without an outlet. His spirit, intensely creative, finds no adequate expression. His power of production is enormous and prolific; yet he accomplishes nothing." He paused an instant. "Binovitch, therefore, is in danger of poisoning—himself." He looked steadily into her face, as a man who weighs how much he may confide. "Now," he continued, "*if* we can find an outlet for him, a field wherein his bursting imaginative genius can produce results—above all, *visible* results"—he shrugged his shoulders—"the man is saved. Otherwise"—he looked extraordinarily impressive—"there is bound to be sooner or later—"

"Madness?" she asked very quietly.

"An explosion, let us say," he replied gravely. "For instance, take this Horus obsession of his, quite wrong archæologically though it is. *Au fond* it is megalomania of a most unusual kind. His passionate interest, his love, his worship of birds, wholesome enough in themselves, find no satisfying outlet. A man who *really* loves birds neither keeps them in cages nor shoots nor stuffs them. What, then, can he do? The commonplace bird-lover observes them through glasses, studies their habits, then writes a book about them. But a man like Binovitch, overflowing with this intense creative power of mind and imagination, is not content with that. He wants to know them from within. He wants to feel what they feel, to live their life. He wants to *become* them. You follow me? Not quite. Well, he seeks to be identified with the object of his sacred, passionate adoration. All genius seeks to know the thing itself from its own point of view. It desires union. That tendency, unrecognised by himself, perhaps, and therefore subconscious, hides in his very soul." He paused a moment. "And the sudden sight of those majestic figures at Edfu—that crystallisation of his *idée fixe* in granite—took hold of this excess in him, so to speak—and is now focussing it towards some definite act. Binovitch sometimes—feels himself a bird! You noticed what occurred last night?"

She nodded; a slight shiver passed over her.

"A most curious performance," she murmured; "an exhibition I never want to see again."

"The most curious part," replied the doctor coolly, "was its truth."

"Its truth!" she exclaimed beneath her breath. She was frightened by something in his voice and by the uncommon gravity in his eyes. It seemed to arrest her intelligence. She felt upon the edge of things beyond her. "You mean that Binovitch did for a moment—hang—in the air?" The other verb, the right one, she could not bring herself to use.

The great man's face was enigmatical. He talked to her sympathy, perhaps, rather than to her mind,

"Real genius," he said smilingly, "is as rare as talent, even great talent, is common. It means that the personality, if only for one second, becomes everything; becomes the universe; becomes the soul of the world. It gets the flash. It is identified with the universal life. Being everything and everywhere, all is possible to it—in that second of vivid realisation. It can brood with the crystal, grow with the plant, leap with the animal, fly with the bird: genius unifies all three. That is the meaning of 'creative.' It is faith. Knowing it, you can pass through fire and not be burned, walk on water and not sink, move a mountain, fly. Because you *are* fire, water, earth, air. Genius, you see, is madness in the magnificent sense of being superhuman. Binovitch has it."

He broke off abruptly, seeing he was not understood. Some great enthusiasm in him he deliberately suppressed.

"The point is," he resumed, speaking more carefully, "that we must try to lead this passionately constructive genius of the man into some human channel that will absorb it, and therefore render it harmless."

"He loves Vera," the woman said, bewildered, yet seizing this point correctly.

"But would he marry her?" asked Plitzinger at once.

"He is already married."

The doctor looked steadily at her a moment, hesitating whether he should utter all his thought.

"In that case," he said slowly after a pause, "it is better he or she should leave."

His tone and manner were exceedingly impressive.

"You mean there's danger?" she asked.

"I mean, rather," he replied earnestly, "that this great creative flood in him, so curiously focussed now upon his Horus-falcon-bird idea, may result in some act of violence—"

"Which would be madness," she said, looking hard at him.

"Which would be disastrous," he corrected her. And then he added slowly: "Because in the mental moment of creation he might overlook material laws."

* * *

The costume ball two nights later was a great success. Palazov was a Bedouin, and Khilkoff an Apache; Mme. de Drühn wore a national head-dress; Minski looked almost natural as Don Quixote; and the entire Russian "set" was cleverly, if somewhat extravagantly, dressed. But Binovitch and Vera were the most successful of all the two hundred dancers who took part. Another figure, a big man dressed as a Pierrot, also claimed exceptional attention, for though the costume was commonplace enough, there was something of dignity in his appearance that drew the eyes of all upon him. But he wore a mask, and his identity was not discoverable.

It was Binovitch and Vera, however, who must have won the prize, if prize there had been, for they not only looked their parts, but acted them as well. The former in his dark grey feather tunic, and his falcon mask, complete even to the brown hooked beak and tufted talons, looked fierce and splendid. The disguise was so admirable, yet so entirely natural, that it was uncommonly seductive. Vera, in blue and gold, a charming head-dress of a dove upon her loosened hair, and a pair of little dove-pale wings fluttering from her shoulders, her tiny twinkling feet and slender ankles well visible, too, was equally successful and admired. Her large and timid eyes, her flitting movements, her light and dainty way of dancing—all added touches that made the picture perfect.

How Binovitch contrived his dress remained a mystery, for the layers of wings upon his back were real; the large black kites that haunt the Nile, soaring in their hundreds over Cairo and the bleak Mokattam Hills, had furnished them. He had procured them none knew how. They measured five feet across from tip to tip; they swished and rustled as he swept along; they were true falcons' wings. He danced with Nautch-girls and Egyptian princesses and Rumanian Gipsies; he danced well, with beauty, grace, and lightness. But with Vera he did not dance at all; with her he simply flew. A kind of passionate abandon was in him as he skimmed the floor with her in a way that made everybody turn to watch them. They seemed to leave the ground together. It was delightful, an amazing sight; but it was peculiar. The strangeness of it was on many lips. Somehow its queer extravagance communicated itself to the entire ball-room. They became the centre of observation. There were whispers.

"There's that extraordinary bird-man! Look! He goes by like a hawk. And he's always after that dove-girl. How marvellously he does it! It's rather awful. Who is he? I don't envy *her*."

People stood aside when he rushed past. They got out of his way. He seemed for ever pursuing Vera, even when dancing with another partner. Word passed from mouth to mouth. A kind of telepathic interest was established everywhere. It was a shade too real sometimes, something unduly earnest in the chasing wildness, something unpleasant. There was even alarm.

"It's rowdy; I'd rather not see it; it's quite disgraceful," was heard. "*I* think it's horrible; you can see she's terrified."

And once there was a little scene, trivial enough, yet betraying this reality that many noticed and disliked. Binovitch came up to claim a dance, programme clutched in his great tufted claws, and at the same moment the big Pierrot appeared abruptly round the corner with a similar claim. Those who saw it assert he had been waiting, and came on purpose, and that there was something protective and authoritative in his bearing. The misunderstanding was ordinary enough—both men had written her name against the dance—but "No. 13, Tango" also included the supper interval, and neither Hawk nor Pierrot would give way. They were very obstinate. Both men wanted her. It was awkward.

"The Dove shall decide between us," smiled the Hawk politely, yet his taloned fingers working nervously. Pierrot, however, more experienced in the ways of dealing with women, or more bold, said suavely:

"I am ready to abide by her decision"—his voice poorly cloaked this aggravating authority, as though he had the right to her—"only I engaged this dance before His Majesty Horus appeared upon the scene at all, and therefore it is clear that Pierrot has the right of way."

At once, with a masterful air, he took her off. There was no withstanding him. He meant to have her and he got her. She yielded meekly. They vanished among the maze of coloured dancers, leaving the Hawk, disconsolate and vanquished, amid the titters of the onlookers. His swiftness, as against this steady power, was of no avail.

It was then that the singular phenomenon was witnessed first. Those who saw it affirm that he changed absolutely into the part he played. It was dreadful; it was wicked. A frightened whisper ran about the rooms and corridors:

"An extraordinary thing is in the air!"

Some shrank away, while others flocked to see. There were those who swore that a curious, rushing sound was audible, the atmosphere visibly disturbed and shaken; that a shadow fell upon the spot the couple had vacated; that a cry was heard, a high, wild, searching cry: "Horus! bright deity of wind," it began, then died away. One man was positive that the windows had been opened and that something had flown in. It was the obvious explanation. The thing spread rapidly. As in a fire-panic, there was consternation and excitement. Confusion caught the feet of all the dancers. The music fumbled and lost time. The leading pair of tango dancers halted and looked round. It seemed that everybody pressed back, hiding, shuffling, eager to see, yet more eager not to be seen, as though something unusual, dangerous, hostile, terrible, had broken loose. In rows against the wall they stood. For a great space had made itself in the middle of the ball-room, and into this empty space reappeared suddenly the Pierrot and the Dove.

It was like a challenge. A sound of applause, half voices, half clapping of gloved hands, was heard. The couple danced exquisitely into the arena. All stared. There was an impression that a set piece had been prepared, and that this was its beginning. The music again took heart. Pierrot was strong and dignified, no whit nonplussed by this abrupt publicity. The Dove, though faltering, seemed deliciously obedient. They danced together like a single outline. She was captured utterly. And to the man who needed her the sight was naturally agonising—the protective way the Pierrot held her, the right and strength of it, the mastery, the complete possession.

"He's still got her!" some one breathed too loud, uttering the thought of all. "Good thing it's not the Hawk!"

And, to the absolute amazement of the throng, this sight was then apparent. A figure dropped through space. That high, shrill cry again was heard:

"Feather my soul . . . to know thy awful swiftness!"

Its singing loveliness touched the heart, its appealing, passionate sweetness was marvellous, as from an upper gallery this figure of a man, dressed as a strong, dark bird, shot down with splendid grace and ease. The feathers swept; the wings spread out as sails that take the wind. Like a hawk that darts with unerring power and aim upon its prey, this thing of mighty wings rushed down into the empty space where the two danced. Observed by all, he entered, swooping beautifully, stretching his wings like any eagle. He dropped. He fixed his point of landing with consummate skill close beside the astonished dancers. He landed.

It happened with such swiftness that it brought the dazzle and blindness as when lightning strikes. People in different parts of the room saw different details; a few saw nothing at all after the first startling shock, closing their eyes, or holding their arms before their faces as in self-protection. The touch of panic fear caught the entire room. The nameless thing that all the evening had been vaguely felt was come. It had suddenly materialised.

For this incredible thing occurred in the full blaze of light upon the open floor. Binovitch, grown in some sense formidable, opened his dark, big wings about the girl. The long grey feathers moved, causing powerful draughts of wind that made a rushing sound. An aspect of the terrible was about him, like an emanation. The great beaked head was poised to strike, the tufted claws were raised like fingers that shut and opened, and the whole presentment of his amazing figure focussed in an attitude of attack that was magnificent and terrible. No one who saw it doubted. Yet there were those who swore that it was not Binovitch at all, but that another outline, monstrous and shadowy, towered above him, draping his lesser proportions with two colossal wings of darkness. That some touch of strange divinity lay in it may be claimed, however confused the wild descriptions afterward. For many lowered their heads and bowed their shoulders. There was terror. There was also awe. The onlookers swayed as though some power passed over them across the air.

A sound of wings was certainly in the room.

Then some one screamed; a shriek broke high and clear; and emotion, ordinary human emotion, unaccustomed to terrific things, swept loose. The Hawk and Vera flew. Beaten back against the wall as by a stroke of whirlwind, the Pierrot staggered. He watched them go. Out of the lighted room they flew, out of the crowded human atmosphere, out of the heat and artificial light, the walled-in, airless halls that were a cage. All this they left behind. They seemed things of wind and air, made free happily of another element. Earth held them not. Towards the open night they raced with this extraordinary lightness as of birds, down the long corridor and on to the southern terrace, where great coloured curtains were hung suspended from the columns. A moment they were visible. Then the fringe of one huge curtain, lifted by the wind, showed their dark outline for a second against the starry sky. There was a cry, a leap. The curtain flapped again and closed. They vanished. And into the ball-room swept the cold draught of night air from the desert.

But three figures instantly were close upon their heels. The throng of half-dazed, half-stupefied onlookers, it seemed, projected them as though by some explosive force. The general mass held back, but, like projectiles, these three flung themselves after the fugitives down the corridor at high speed—the Apache, Don Quixote, and, last of them, the Pierrot. For Khilkoff, the brother, and Baron Minski, the man who caught wolves alive, had been for some time keenly on the watch, while Dr. Plitzinger, reading the symptoms clearly, never far away, had been faithfully observant of every movement. His mask tossed aside, the great psychiatrist was now recognised by all. They reached the parapet just as the curtain flapped back heavily into place; the next second all three were out of sight behind it. Khilkoff was first, however, urged forward at frantic speed by the warning words the doctor had whispered as they ran. Some thirty yards beyond the terrace was the brink of the crumbling cliff on which the great hotel was built, and there was a drop of sixty feet to the desert floor below. Only a low stone wall marked the edge.

Accounts varied. Khilkoff, it seems, arrived in time—in the nick of time—to seize his sister, virtually hovering on the brink. He heard the loose stones strike the sand below. There was no struggle, though it appears she did not thank him for his interference at first. In a sense she was beside—outside—herself. And he did a characteristic thing: he not only brought her back into the ball-room, but he *danced* her back. It was admirable. Nothing could have calmed the general excitement better. The pair of them danced in together as though nothing was amiss. Accustomed to the strenuous practice of his Cossack regiment, this young cavalry officer's muscles were equal to the semi-dead weight in his arms. At most the onlookers thought her tired, perhaps. Confidence was restored—such is the psychology of a crowd—and in the middle of a thrilling Viennese waltz he easily smuggled her out of the room, administered brandy, and got her up to bed. The absence of the Hawk, meanwhile, was hardly noticed; comments were made and then forgotten; it was Vera in whom the strange, anxious sympathy had centred. And, with her obvious safety, the moment of primitive, childish panic passed away. Don Quixote, too, was presently seen dancing gaily as though nothing untoward had happened; supper intervened; the incident was over; it had melted into the general wildness of the evening's irresponsibility. The fact that Pierrot did not appear again was noticed by no single person.

But Dr. Plitzinger was otherwise engaged, his heart and mind and soul all deeply exercised. A death-certificate is not always made out quite so simply as the public thinks. That Binovitch had died of suffocation in his swift descent through merely sixty feet of air was not conceivable; yet that his body lay so neatly placed upon the desert after such a fall was stranger still. It was not crumpled, it was not torn; no single bone was broken, no muscle wrenched; there was no bruise. There was no indenture in the sand. The figure lay sidewise as though in sleep, no sign of violence visible anywhere, the dark wings folded as a great bird folds them when it creeps away to die in loneliness. Beneath the Horus mask the face was smiling. It seemed he had floated into death upon the element he loved. And only Vera had seen the enormous wings that, hovering invitingly above the dark abyss, bore him so softly into another world. Plitzinger, that is, saw them, too, but he said firmly that they belonged to the big black falcons that haunt the Mokattam Hills and roost upon these ridges, close beside the hotel, at night. Both he and Vera, however, agreed on one thing: the high, sharp cry in the air above them, wild and plaintive, was certainly the black kite's cry—the note of the falcon that passionately seeks its mate. It was the pause of a second, when she stood to listen, that made her rescue possible. A moment later and she, too, would have flown to death with Binovitch.

The Regeneration of Lord Ernie

I

John Hendricks was bear-leading at the time. He had originally studied for Holy Orders, but had abandoned the Church later for private reasons connected with his faith, and had taken to teaching and tutoring instead. He was an honest, upstanding fellow of five-and-thirty, incorruptible, intelligent in a simple, straightforward way. He played games with his head, more than most Englishmen do, but he went through life without much calculation. He had qualities that made boys like and respect him; he won their confidence. Poor, proud, ambitious, he realised that fate offered him a chance when the Secretary of State for Scotland asked him if he would give up his other pupils for a year and take his son, Lord Ernie, round the world upon an educational trip that might make a man of him. For Lord Ernie was the only son, and the Marquess's influence was naturally great. To have deposited a regenerated Lord Ernie at the castle gates might have guaranteed Hendricks' future. After leaving Eton prematurely the lad had come under Hendricks' charge for a time, and with such excellent results—"I'd simply swear by that chap, you know," the boy used to say—that his father, considerably impressed, and rather as a last resort, had made this proposition. And Hendricks, without much calculation, had accepted it. He liked "Bindy" for himself. It was in his heart to "make a man of him," if possible. They had now been round the world together and had come up from Brindisi to the Italian Lakes, and so into Switzerland. It was middle October. With a week or two to spare they were making leisurely for the ancestral halls in Aberdeenshire.

The nine months' travel, Hendricks realised with keen disappointment, had accomplished, however, very little. The job had been exhausting, and he had conscientiously done his best. Lord Ernie liked him thoroughly, admiring his vigour with a smile of tolerant good-nature through his ceaseless cigarette smoke. They were almost like two boys together. "You *are* a chap and a half, Mr. Hendricks. You really ought to be in the Cabinet with my father." Hendricks would deliver up his useless parcel at the castle gates, pocket the thanks and the hard-earned fee, and go back to his arduous life of teaching and writing in dingy lodgings. It was a pity, even on the lowest grounds. The tutor, truth to tell, felt undeniably depressed. Hopeful by nature, optimistic, too, as men of action usually are, he cast about him, even at the last hour, for something that might stir the boy to life, wake him up, put zest and energy into him. But there was only Paris now between them and the end; and Paris certainly could not be relied upon for help. Bindy's desire for Paris even was not strong enough to count. No desire in him was ever strong. There lay the crux of the problem in a word—Lord Ernie was without desire which is life.

Tall, well-built, handsome, he was yet such a feeble creature, without the energy to be either wild or vicious. Languid, yet certainly not decadent, life ran slowly, flabbily in him. He took to nothing. The first impression he made was fine—then nothing. His only tastes, if tastes they could be called, were out-of-door tastes: he was vaguely interested in flying, yet not enough to master the mechanism of it; he liked motoring at high speed, being driven, not driving himself; and he loved to wander about in woods, making fires like a Red Indian, provided they lit easily, yet even this, not for the poetry of the thing nor for any love of adventure, but just "because." "I like fire, you know; like to watch it burn." Heat seemed to give him curious satisfaction, perhaps because the heat of life, he realised, was deficient in his six-foot body. It was significant, this love of fire in him, though no one could discover why. As a child he had a dangerous delight in fireworks—anything to do with fire. He would watch a candle flame as though he were a fire-worshipper, but had never been known to make a single remark of interest about it. In a wood, as mentioned, the first thing he did was to gather sticks—though the resulting fire was never part of any purpose. He had no purpose. There was no wind or fire of life in the lad at all. The fine body was inert.

Hendricks did wrong, of course, in going where he did—to this little desolate village in the Jura Mountains—though it was the first time all these trying months he had allowed himself a personal desire. But from Domo Dossola the Simplon Express would pass Lausanne, and from Lausanne to the Jura was but a step—all on the way home, moreover. And what prompted him was merely a sentimental desire to revisit the place where ten years before he had fallen violently in love with the pretty daughter of the Pasteur, M. Leysin, in whose house he lodged. He had gone there to learn French. The very slight detour seemed pardonable.

His spiritless charge was easily persuaded.

"We might go home by Pontarlier instead of Bâle, and get a glimpse of the Jura," he suggested. "The line slides along its frontiers a bit, and then goes bang across it. We might even stop off a night on the way—if you cared about it. I know a curious old village—Villaret—where I went at your age to pick up French."

"Top-hole," replied Lord Ernie listlessly. "All on the way to Paris, ain't it?"

"Of course. You see there's a fortnight before we need get home."

"So there is, yes. Let's go." He felt it was almost his own idea and that he decided it.

"If you'd *really* like it."

"Oh, yes! Why not? I'm sick of cities." He flicked some dust off his coat sleeve with an immaculate silk handkerchief, then lit a cigarette. "Just as you like," he added, with a drawl and a smile. "I'm ready for anything." There was no keenness, no personal desire, no choice in reality at all; flabby good-nature merely.

A suggestion was invariably enough, as though the boy had no will of his own, his opposition rarely more than negative sulking that soon flattened out because it was forgotten. Indeed, no sign of positive life lay in him anywhere—no vitality, aggression, coherence of desire and will; vacuous rather than imbecile; unable to go forward upon any definite line of his own, as though all wheels had slipped their cogs; a pasty soul that took good enough impressions, yet never mastered them for permanent use. Nothing stuck. He would never make a politician, much less a statesman. The family title would be borne by a nincompoop. Yet all the machinery was there, one felt—if only it could be driven, made to go. It was sad. Lord Ernie was heir to great estates, with a name and position that might influence thousands.

And Hendricks had been a good selection, with his virility and gentle, understanding firmness. He understood the problem. "You'll do what no one else could," the anxious father told him, "for he worships you, and you can sting without hurting him. You'll put life and interest into him if anybody in this world can. I have great hopes of this tour. I shall always be in your debt, Mr. Hendricks." And Hendricks had accepted the onerous duty in his big, high-minded way. He was conscientious to the backbone. This little side-trip was his sole deflection, if such it can be called even. "Life, light and cheerful influences," had been his instructions; "nothing dull or melancholy; an occasional fling, if he wants it—I'd welcome a fling as a good sign—and as much intercourse with decent people, and stimulating sightseeing as you can manage—or can stand," the Earl added with a smile. "Only you won't over-tax the lad, will you? Above all, let him think *he* chooses and decides, when possible."

Villaret, however, hardly complied with these conditions; there was melancholy in it; Hendricks' mind—whose reflexes the spongy nature of the empty lad absorbed too easily—would be in a minor key. Yet a night could work no harm. Whence came, he wondered, the fleeting notion that it might do good? Was it, perhaps, that Leysin, the vigorous old Pasteur, might contribute something? Leysin had been a considerable force in his own development, he remembered; they had corresponded a little since; Leysin was out of the common, certainly, restless energy in him as of the sea. Hendricks found difficulty in sorting out his thoughts and motives but Leysin was in them somewhere—this idea that his energetic personality might help. His vitalising effect, at least, would counteract the melancholy.

For Villaret lay huddled upon unstimulating slopes, the robe of gloomy pinewoods sweeping down towards its poverty from bleak heights and desolate gorges. The peasants were morose, ill-living folk. It was a dark untaught corner in a range of otherwise fairy mountains, a backwater the sun had neglected to clean out. Superstitions, Hendricks remembered, of incredible kind still lingered there; a touch of the sinister hovered about the composite mind of its inhabitants. The Pasteur fought strenuously this blackness in their lives and thoughts; in the village itself with more or less success—though even there the drinking and habits of living were utterly unsweetened—but on the heights, among the somewhat arid pastures, the mountain men remained untamed, turbulent, even menacing. Hendricks knew this of old, though he had never understood too well. But he remembered how the English boys at *la cure* were forbidden to climb in certain directions, because the life in these scattered châlets was somehow loose and violent. There was danger there, the danger, however, never definitely stated. Those lonely ridges lay cursed beneath dark skies. He remembered, too, the savage dogs, the difficulty of approach, the aggressive attitude towards the plucky Pasteur's visits to these remote upland *pâturages*. They did not lie in his parish: Leysin made his occasional visits as man and missionary; for extraordinary rumours, Hendricks recalled, were rife, of some queer worship of their own these lawless peasants kept alive in their distant, windy territory, planted there first, the story had it, by some renegade priest whose name was now forgotten.

Hendricks himself had no personal experiences. He had been too deeply in love to trouble about outside things, however strange. But Marston's case had never quite left his memory—Marston, who climbed up by unlawful ways, stayed away two whole days and nights, and came back suddenly with his air of being broken, shattered, appallingly used up, his face so lined and strained it seemed aged by twenty years, and yet with a singular new life in him, so vehement, loud, and reckless, it was like a kind of sober intoxication. He was packed off to England before he could relate anything. But he had suffered shocks. His white, passionate face, his boisterous new vigour, the way M. Leysin screened his view of the heights as he put him personally into the Paris train—almost as though he feared the boy would see the hills and make another dash for them!—made up an unforgettable picture in the mind.

Moreover, between the sodden village and that string of evil châlets that lay in their dark line upon the heights there had been links. Exactly of what nature he never knew, for love made all else uninteresting; only, he remembered swarthy, dark-faced messengers descending into the sleepy hamlet from time to time, big, mountain-limbed fellows with wind in their hair and fire in their eyes; that their visits produced commotion and excitement of difficult kinds; that wild orgies invariably followed in their wake; and that, when the messengers went back, they did not go alone. There was life up there, whereas the village was moribund. And none who went ever cared to return. Cudrefin, the young giant *vigneron,* taken in this way, from the very side of his sweetheart too, came back two years later as a messenger himself. He did not even ask for the girl, who had meanwhile married another. "There's life up there with us," he told the drunken loafers in the "Guillaume Tell," "wind and fire to make you spin to the devil—or to heaven!" He was enthusiasm personified. In the village he had been merely drinking himself stupidly to death. Vaguely, too, Hendricks remembered visits of police from the neighbouring towns, some of them on horseback, all armed, and that once even soldiers accompanied them, and on another occasion a bishop, or whatever the church dignitary was called, had arrived suddenly and promised radical assistance of a spiritual kind that had never materialised—oh, and many other details that now trooped back with suggestions time had certainly not made smaller. For the love had passed along its way and gone, and he was free now to the invasion of other memories, dwarfed at the time by that dominating, sweet passion.

Yet all the tutor wanted now, this chance week in late October, was to see again the corner of the mossy forest where he had known that marvellous thing, first love; renew his link with Leysin who had taught him much; and see if, perchance, this man's stalwart, virile energy might possibly overflow with benefit into his listless charge. The expenses he meant to pay out of his own pocket. Those wild pagans on the heights—even if they still existed—there was no need to mention. Lord Ernie knew little French, and certainly no word of patois. For one night, or even two, the risk was negligible.

Was there, indeed, risk at all of any sort? Was not this vague uneasiness he felt merely conscience faintly pricking? He could not feel that he was doing wrong. At worst, the youth might feel depression for a few hours—speedily curable by taking the train.

Something, nevertheless, did gnaw at him in subconscious fashion, producing a sense of apprehension; and he came to the conclusion that this memory of the mountain tribe was the cause of it—a revival of forgotten boyhood's awe. He glanced across at the figure of Bindy lounging upon the hotel lawn in an easy-chair, full in the sunshine, a newspaper at his feet. Reclining there, he looked so big and strong and handsome, yet in reality was but a painted lath without resistance, much less attack, in all his many inches. And suddenly the tutor recalled another thing, the link, however, undiscoverable, and it was this: that the boy's mother, a Canadian, had suffered once severely from a winter in Quebec, where the Marquess had first made her acquaintance. Frost had robbed her, if he remembered rightly, of a foot—with the result, at any rate, that she had a wholesome terror of the cold. She sought heat and sun instinctively—fire. Also, that asthma had been her sore affliction—sheer inability to take a full, deep breath. This deficiency of heat and air, therefore, were in her mind. And he knew that Bindy's birth had been an anxious time, the anxiety justified, moreover, since she had yielded up her life for him.

And so the singular thought flashed through him suddenly as he watched the reclining, languid boy, Cudrefin's descriptive phrase oddly singing in his head—

"Heat and fire, fire and wind—why, it's the very thing he lacks! And he's always after them. I wonder—!"

II

The lumbering yellow *diligence* brought them up from the Lake shore, a long two hours, deposited them at the opening of the village street, and went its grinding, toiling way towards the frontier. They arrived in a blur of rain. It was evening. Lowering clouds drew night before her time upon the world, obscuring the distant summits of the Oberland, but lights twinkled here and there in the nearer landscape, mapping the gloom with signals. The village was very still. Above and below it, however, two big winds were at work, with curious results. For a lower wind from the east in gusty draughts drove the body of the lake into quick white horses which shone like wings against the deep *basses Alpes,* while a westerly current swept the heights immediately above the village. There was this odd division of two weathers, presaging a change. A narrow line of clear bright sky showed up the Jura outline finely towards the north, stars peeping sharply through the pale moist spaces. Hurrying vapours, driven by the upper westerly wind, concealed them thinly. They flashed and vanished. The entire ridge, five thousand feet in the air, had an appearance of moving through the sky. Between these opposing winds at different levels the village itself lay motionless, while the world slid past, as it were, in two directions.

"The earth seems turning round," remarked Lord Ernie. He had been reading a novel all day in train and steamer, and smoking endless cigarettes in the *diligence,* his companion and himself its only occupants. He seemed suddenly to have waked up. "What is it?" he asked with interest.

Hendricks explained the queer effect of the two contrary winds. Columns of peat smoke rose in thin straight lines from the blur of houses, untouched by the careering currents above and below. The winds whirled round them.

Lord Ernie listened attentively to the explanation.

"I feel as if I were spinning with it—like a top," he observed, putting his hand to his head a moment. "And what are those lights up there?"

He pointed to the distant ridge, where fires were blazing as though stars had fallen and set fire to the trees. Several were visible, at regular intervals. The sharp summits of the limestone mountains cut hard into the clear spaces of northern sky thousands of feet above.

"Oh, the peasants burning wood and stuff, I suppose," the tutor told him.

The youth turned an instant, standing still to examine them with a shading hand.

"People live up there?" he asked. There was surprise in his voice, and his body stiffened oddly as he spoke.

"In mountain châlets, yes," replied the other a trifle impatiently, noticing his attitude. "Come along now," he added, "let's get to our rooms in the carpenter's house before the rain comes down. You can see the windows twinkling over there," and he pointed to a building near the church. "The storm will catch us." They moved quickly down the deserted street together in the deepening gloom, passing little gardens, doors of open barns, straggling manure heaps, and courtyards of cobbled stones where the occasional figure of a man was seen. But Lord Ernie lingered behind, half loitering. Once or twice, to the other's increasing annoyance, he paused, standing still to watch the heights through openings between the tumble-down old houses. Half a dozen big drops of rain splashed heavily on the road.

"Hurry up!" cried Hendricks, looking back, "or we shall be caught. It's the mountain wind—the *coup de joran*. You can hear it coming!" For the lad was peering across a low wall in an attitude of fixed attention. He made a gesture with one hand, as though he signalled towards the ridges where the fires blazed. Hendricks called pretty sharply to him then. It was possible, of course, that he misinterpreted the movement; it *may* merely have been that he passed his fingers through his hair, across his eyes, or used the palm to focus sight, for his hat was off and the light was quite uncertain. Only Hendricks did not like the lingering or the gesture. He put authority into his tone at once. "Come along, will you; come along, Bindy!" he called.

The answer filled him with amazement.

"All right, all right. I'll follow in a moment. I like this."

The tutor went back a few steps towards him. The tone startled him.

"Like what?" he asked.

And Lord Ernie turned towards him with another face. There was fighting in it. There was resolution.

"This, of course," the boy answered steadily, but with excitement shut down behind, as he waved one arm towards the mountains. "I've dreamed this sort of thing; I've known it somewhere. We've seen nothing like it all our stupid trip." The flash in his brown eyes passed then, as he added more quietly, but with firmness: "Don't wait for me; I'll follow."

Hendricks stood still in his tracks. There was a decision in the voice and manner that arrested him. The confidence, the positive statement, the eager desire, the hint of energy—all this was new. He had never encouraged the boy's habit of vivid dreaming, deeming the narration unwise. It flashed across him suddenly now that the "deficiency" might be only on the surface. Energy and life hid, perhaps, subconsciously in him. Did the dreams betray an activity he knew not how to carry through and correlate with his everyday, external world? And were these dreams evidence of deep, hidden desire—a clue, possibly, to the energy he sought and needed, the exact kind of energy that might set the inert machinery in motion and drive it?

He hesitated an instant, waiting in the road. He was on the verge of understanding something that yet just evaded him. Bindy's childish, instinctive love of fire, his passion for air, for rushing wind, for oceans of limitless—

There came at that moment a deep roaring in the mountains. Far away, but rapidly approaching, the ominous booming of it filled the air. The westerly wind descended by the deep gorges, shaking the forests, shouting as it came. Clouds of white dust spiralled into the sky off the upper roads, spread into sheets like snow, and swept downwards with incredible velocity. The air turned suddenly cooler. More big drops of rain splashed and thudded on the roofs and road. There was a feeling of something violent and instantaneous about to happen, a sense almost of attack. The *joran* tore headlong down into the valley.

"Come on, man," he cried at the top of his voice. "That's the *joran!* I know it of old! It's terrific. Run!" And he caught the lad, still lingering, by the arm.

But Lord Ernie shook himself free with an excitement almost violent.

"I've been up there with those great fires," he shouted. "I know the whole blessed thing. But where was it? Where?" His face was white, eyes shining, manner strangely agitated. "Big, naked fellows who dance like wind, and rushing women of fire, and—"

Two things happened then, interrupting the boy's wild language. The *joran* reached the village and struck it; the houses shook, the trees bent double, and the cloud of limestone dust, painting the darkness white, swept on between Hendricks and the boy with extraordinary force, even separating them. There was a clatter of falling tiles, of banging doors and windows, and then a burst of icy rain that fell like iron shot on everything, raising actual spray. The air was in an instant thick. Everything drove past, roared, trembled. And, secondly—just in that brief instant when man and boy were separated—there shot between them with shadowy swiftness the figure of a man, hatless, with flying hair, who vanished with running strides into the darkness of the village street beyond—all so rapidly that sight could focus neither the manner of his coming nor of his going. Hendricks caught a glimpse of a swarthy, elemental type of face, the swing of great shoulders, the leap of big loose limbs—something rushing and elastic in the whole appearance—but nothing he could claim for definite detail. The figure swept through the dust and wind like an animal—and was gone. It was, indeed, only the contrast of Lord Ernie's whitened skin, of his graceful, half-elegant outline, that enabled him to recall the details that he did. The weather-beaten visage seemed to storm away. Bindy's delicate aristocratic face shone so pale and eager. But that a real man had passed was indubitable, for the boy made a flurried movement as though to follow. Hendricks caught his arm with a determined grip and pulled him back.

"Who was that? Who was it?" Lord Ernie cried breathlessly, resisting with all his strength, but vainly.

"Some mountain fellow, of course. Nothing to do with us." And he dragged the boy after him down the road. For a second both seemed to have lost their heads. Hendricks certainly felt a gust of something strike him into momentary consternation that was half alarm.

"From up there, where the fires are?" asked the boy, shouting above the wind and rain.

"Yes, yes, I suppose so. Come along. We shall be soused. Are you mad?" For Bindy still held back with all his weight, trying to turn round and see. Hendricks used more force. There was almost a scuffle in the road.

"All right, I'm coming. I only wanted to look a second. You needn't drag my arm out." He ceased resistance, and they lurched forward together. "But what a chap he was! He went like the wind. Did you see the light streaming out of him—like fire?"

"Like what?" shouted Hendricks, as they dashed now through the driving tempest.

"Fire!" bawled the boy. "It lit me up as he passed—fire that lights but does not burn, and wind that blows the world along—"

"Button your coat and run!" interrupted the other, hurrying his pace, and pulling the lad forcibly after him.

"Don't twist! You're hurting! I can run as well as you!" came back, with an energy Bindy had never shown before in his life. He was breathless, panting, charged with excitement still. "It touched me as he passed—fire that lights but doesn't burn, and wind that blows the heart to flame—let me go, will you? Let go my hand."

He dashed free and away. The torrential rain came down in sheets now from a windless sky, for the *joran* was already miles beyond them, tearing across the angry lake. They reached the carpenter's house, where their lodging was, soaked to the skin. They dried themselves, and ate the light supper of soup and omelette prepared for them—ate it in their dressing-gowns. Lord Ernie went to bed with a hot-water bottle of rough stone. He declared with decision that he felt no chill. His excitement had somewhat passed.

"But I say, Mr. Hendricks," he remarked, as he settled down with his novel and a cigarette, calmed and normal again, "this *is* a place and a half, isn't it? It stirs me all up. I suppose it's the storm. What do *you* think?"

"Electrical state of the air, yes," replied the tutor briefly.

Soon afterwards he closed the shutters on the weather side, said good-night, and went into his own room to unpack. The singular phrase Bindy had used kept singing through his head: "Fire that lights but doesn't burn, and wind that blows the heart to flame"—the first time he had said "blows the world along." Where on earth had the boy got hold of such queer words? He still saw the figure of that wild mountain fellow who had passed between them with the dust and wind and rain. There was confusion in the picture, or rather in his memory of it, perhaps. But it seemed to him, looking back now, that the man in passing had paused a second—the briefest second merely—and had spoken, or, at any rate, had stared closely a moment into Bindy's face, and that some communication had been between them in that moment of elemental violence.

III

Pasteur Leysin Hendricks remembered very well. Even now in his old age he was a vigorous personality, but in his youth he had been almost revolutionary; wild enough, too, it was rumoured, until he had turned to God of his own accord as offering a larger field for his strenuous vitality. The little man was possessed of tireless life, a born leader of forlorn hopes, attack his métier, and heavy odds the conditions that he loved. Before settling down in this isolated spot—*pasteur de l'église indépendente* in a protestant Canton—he had been a missionary in remote pagan lands. His horizon was a big one, he had seen strange things. An uncouth being, with a large head upon a thin and wiry body supported by steely bowed legs, he had that courage which makes itself known in advance of any proof. Hendricks slipped over to *la cure* about nine o'clock and found him in his study. Lord Ernie was asleep; at least his light was out, no sound or movement audible from his room. The *joran* had swept the heavens of clouds. Stars shone brilliantly. The fires still blazed faintly upon the heights.

The visit was not unexpected, for Hendricks had already sent a message to announce himself, and the moment he sat down, met the Pasteur's eye, heard his voice, and observed his slight imperious gestures, he passed under the influence of a personality stronger than his own. Something in Leysin's atmosphere stretched him, lifting his horizon. He had come chiefly—he now realised it—to borrow help and explanation with regard to Lord Ernie; the events of two hours before had impressed him more than he quite cared to own, and he wished to talk about it. But, somehow, he found it difficult to state his case; no opening presented itself; or, rather, the Pasteur's mind, intent upon something of his own, was too preoccupied. In reply to a question presently, the tutor gave a brief outline of his present duties, but omitted the scene of excitement in the village street, for as he watched the furrowed face in the light of the study lamp, he realised both anxiety and spiritual high pressure at work below the surface there. He hesitated to intrude his own affairs at first. They discussed, nevertheless, the psychology of the boy, and the unfavourable chances of regeneration, while the old man's face lit up and flashed from time to time, until at length the truth came out, and Hendricks understood his friend's preoccupation.

"What you're attempting with an individual," Leysin exclaimed with ardour, "is precisely what I'm attempting with a crowd. And it's difficult. For poor sinners make poor saints, and the lukewarm I will spue out of my mouth." He made an abrupt, resentful gesture to signify his disgust and weariness, perhaps his contempt as well. "Cut it down! Why cumbereth it the ground?"

"A hard, uncharitable doctrine," began the tutor, realising that he must discuss the Parish before he could introduce Bindy's case effectively. "You mean, of course, that there's no material to work on?"

"No energy to direct," was the emphatic reply. "My sheep here are—real sheep; mere negative, drink-sodden loafers without desire. Hospital cases! I could work with tigers and wild beasts, but who ever trained a slug?"

"Your proper place is on the heights," suggested Hendricks, interrupting at a venture. "There's scope enough up there, or used to be. Have they died out, those wild men of the mountains?" And hit by chance the target in the bull's-eye.

The old man's face turned younger as he answered quickly.

"Men like that," he exclaimed, "do not die off. They breed and multiply." He leaned forward across the table, his manner eager, fervent, almost impetuous with suppressed desire for action. "There's evil thinking up there," he said suggestively, "but, by heaven, it's alive; it's positive, ambitious, constructive. With violent feeling and strong desire to work on, there's hope of some result. Upon vehement impulses like that, pagan or anything else, a man can work with a will. Those are the tigers; down here I have the slugs!"

He shrugged his shoulders and leaned back into his chair. Hendricks watched him, thinking of the stories told about his missionary days among savage and barbarian tribes.

"Born of the vital landscape, I suppose?" he asked. "Wind and frost and blazing sun. Their wild energy, I mean, is due to—"

A gesture from the old man stopped him. "You know who started them upon their wild performances," he said gravely in a lower voice; "you know how that ambitious renegade priest from the Valais chose them for his nucleus, then died before he could lead them out, trained and competent, upon his strange campaign? You heard the story when you were with me as a boy—?"

"I remember Marston," put in the other, uncommonly interested, "Marston—the boy who—" He stopped because he hardly knew how to continue. There was a minute's silence. But it was not an empty silence, though no word broke it. Leysin's face was a study.

"Ah, Marston, yes," he said slowly, without looking up; "you remember him. But that is at my door, too, I suppose. His father was ignorant and obstinate; I might have saved him otherwise." He seemed talking to himself rather than to his listener. Pain showed in the lines about the rugged mouth. "There was no one, you see, who knew how to direct the great life that woke in the lad. He took it back with him, and turned it loose into all manner of useless enterprises, and the doctors mistook his abrupt and fierce ambitions for—for the hysteria which they called the vestibule of lunacy. . . . Yet small characters may have big ideas. . . . They didn't understand, of course. . . . It was sad, sad, sad." He hid his face in his hands a moment.

"Marston went wrong, then, in the end?" for the other's manner suggested disaster of some kind. Hendricks asked it in a whisper. Leysin uncovered his face, looped his neck with one finger, and pointed to the ceiling.

"Hanged himself!" murmured Hendricks, shocked.

The Pasteur nodded, but there was impatience, half anger in his tone.

"They checked it, kept it in. Of course, it tore him!"

The two men looked into each other's eyes for a moment, and something in the younger of them shrank. This was all beyond his ken a little. An odd hint of bleak and cruel reality was in the air, making him shiver along nerves that were normally inactive. The uneasiness he felt about Lord Ernie became alarm. His conscience pricked him.

"More than he could assimilate," continued Leysin. "It broke him. Yet, had outlets been provided, had he been taught how to use it, this elemental energy drawn direct from Nature—" He broke off abruptly, struck perhaps by the expression in his listener's eyes. "It seems incredible, doesn't it, in the twentieth century? I know."

"Evil?" asked Hendricks, stammering rather.

"Why evil?" was the impatient reply. "How can any force be evil? That's merely a question of direction."

"And the priest who discovered these forces and taught their use, then—?"

"Was genuinely spiritual and followed the truth in his own way. He was not necessarily evil." The little Pasteur spoke with vehemence. "You talk like the religion-primers in the kindergarten," he went on. "Listen. This man, sick and weary of his lukewarm flock, sought vital, stalwart systems who might be clean enough to use the elemental powers he had discovered how to attract. Only the bias of the users could make it 'evil' by wrong use. His idea was big and even holy—to train a corps that might regenerate the world. And he chose unreasoning, unintellectual types with a purpose—primitive, giant men who could assimilate the force without risk of being shattered. Under his direction he intended they should prove as effective as the twelve disciples of old who were fisher-folk. And, had he gone on—"

"He, too, failed then?" asked the other, whose tangled thoughts struggled with incredulity and belief as he heard this strange new thing. "He died, you mean?"

"Maison de santé," was the laconic reply, "straight waistcoats, padded cells, and the rest; but still alive, I'm told. It was more than he could manage."

It was a startling story, even in this brief outline, deep suggestion in it. The tutor's sense of being out of his depth increased. After nine months with a lifeless, devitalised human being, this was—well, he seemed to have fallen in his sleep from a comfortable bed into a raging mountain torrent. Strong currents rushed through and over him. The lonely, peaceful village outside, sleeping beneath the stars, heightened the contrast.

"Suppressed or misdirected energy again, I suppose," he said in a low tone, respecting his companion's emotion. "And these mountain men," he asked abruptly, "do they still keep up their—practices?"

"Their ceremonies, yes," corrected the other, master of himself again. "Turbulent moments of nature, storms and the like, stir them to clumsy rehearsals of once vital rituals—not entirely ineffective, even in their incompleteness, but dangerous for that very reason. This *joran,* for instance, invariably communicates something of its atmospherical energy to themselves. They light their fires as of old. They blunder through what they remember of *his* ceremonies. With the glasses you may see them in their dozens, men and women, leaping and dancing. It's an amazing sight, great beauty in it, impossible to witness even from a distance without feeling the desire to take part in it. Even my people feel it—the only time they ever get alive,"—he jerked his big head contemptuously towards the street—"or feel desire to act. And some one from the heights—a messenger perhaps—will be down later, this very evening probably, on the hunt—"

"On the hunt?" Hendricks asked it half below his breath. He felt a touch of awe as he heard this experienced, genuinely religious man speak with conviction of such curious things. "On the hunt?" he repeated more eagerly.

"Messengers do come down," was the reply. "A living belief always seeks to increase, to grow, to add to itself. Where there's conviction there's always propaganda."

"Ah, converts—?"

Leysin shrugged his big black shoulders. "Desire to add to their number—desire to *save,*" he said. "The energy they absorb overflows, that's all."

The Englishman debated several questions vaguely in his mind; only his mind, being disturbed, could not hold the balance exactly true. Leysin's influence, as of old, was upon him. A possibility, remote, seductive, dangerous, began to beckon to him, but from somewhere just outside his reasoning mind.

"And they always know when one of their kind is near," the voice slipped in between his tumbling thoughts, "as though they get it instinctively from these universal elements they worship. They select their recruits with marvellous judgment and precision. No messenger ever goes back alone; nor has a recruit ever been known to return to the lazy squalor of the conditions whence he escaped."

The younger man sat upright in his chair, suddenly alert, and the gesture that he made unconsciously might have been read by a keen psychiatrist as evidence of mental self-defence. He felt the forbidden impulse in him gathering force, and tried to call a halt. At any rate, he called upon the other man to be explicit. He enquired point-blank what this religion of the heights might be. What were these elements these people worshipped? In what did their wild ceremonies consist?

And Leysin, breaking bounds, let his speech burst forth in a stream of explanation, learned of actual knowledge, as he claimed, and uttered with a vehement conviction that produced an undeniable effect upon his astonished listener. Told by no dreamer, but by a righteous man who lived, not merely preached his certain faith, Hendricks, before the half was heard, forgot what age and land he dwelt in. Whole blocks of conventional belief crumbled and fell away. Brick walls erected by routine to mark narrow paths of proper conduct—safe, moral, advisable conduct—thawed and vanished. Through the ruins, scrambling at him from huge horizons never recognised before, came all manner of marvellous possibilities. The little confinement of modern thought appalled him suddenly. Leysin spoke slowly, said little, was not even speculative. It was no mere magic of words that made the dim-lit study swim these deep waters beyond the ripple of pert creeds, but rather the overwhelming sense of sure conviction driving behind the statements. The little man had witnessed curious things, yes, in his missionary days, and that he had found truth in them in place of ignorant nonsense was remarkable enough. That silly superstitions prevalent among older nations could be signs really of their former greatness, linked mightily close to natural forces, was a startling notion, but it paved the way in Hendricks' receptive mind just then for the belief that certain so-called elements might be worshipped—known intimately, that is—to the uplifting advantage of the worshippers. And what elements more suitable for adoring imitation than wind and fire? For in a human body the first signs of what men term life are heat which is combustion, and breath which is a measure of wind. Life means fire, drawn first from the sun, and breathing, borrowed from the omnipresent air; there might credibly be ways of assaulting these elements and taking heaven by storm; of seizing from their inexhaustible stores an abnormal measure, of straining this huge raw supply into effective energy for human use—vitality. Living with fire and wind in their most active moments; closely imitating their movements, following in their footsteps, understanding their "laws of being," going *identically* with them—there lay a hint of the method. It was once, when men were primitively close to Nature, instinctual knowledge. The ceremony was the teaching. The Powers of fire, the Principalities of air, existed; and humanity *could* know their qualities by the ritual of imitation, could actually absorb the fierce enthusiasm of flame and the tireless energy of wind. Such transference was conceivable.

Leysin, at any rate, somehow made it so. His description of what he had personally witnessed, both in wilder lands and here in this little mountain range of middle Europe, had a reality in it that was upsetting to the last degree. "There is nothing more difficult to believe," he said, "yet more certainly true, than the effect of these singular elemental rites." He laughed a short dry laugh. "The mediæval superstition that a witch could raise a storm is but a remnant of a once completely efficacious system," he concluded, "though how that strange being, the Valais priest, re-discovered the process and introduced it here, I have never been able to ascertain. That he did so results have proved. At any rate, it lets in life, life moreover in astonishing abundance; though, whether for destruction or regeneration, depends, obviously, upon the use the recipient puts it to. That's where direction comes in."

The beckoning impulse in the tutor's bewildered thoughts drew closer. The moment for communicating it had come at last. Without more ado he took the opening. He told his companion the incident in the village street, the boy's abrupt excitement, his new-found energy, the curious words he used, the independence and vitality of his attitude. He told also of his parentage, of his mother's disabilities, his craving for rushing air in abundance, his love of fire for its own sake, of his magnificent physical machinery, yet of his uselessness.

And Leysin, as he listened, seemed built on wires. Searching questions shot forth like blows into the other's mind. The Pasteur's sudden increase of enthusiasm was infectious. He leaped intuitively to the thing in Hendricks' thought. He understood the beckoning.

The tutor answered the questions as best he could, aware of the end in view with trepidation and a kind of mental breathlessness. Yes, unquestionably, Bindy *had* exchanged communication of some sort with the man, though his excitement had been evident even sooner.

"And you saw this man yourself?" Leysin pressed him.

"Indubitably—a tall and hurrying figure in the dusk."

"He brought energy with him? The boy felt it and responded?"

Hendricks nodded. "Became quite unmanageable for some minutes," he replied.

"He assimilated it though? There was no distress exactly?" Leysin asked sharply.

"None—that I could see. Pleasurable excitement, something aggressive, a rather wild enthusiasm. His will began to act. He used that curious phrase about wind and fire. He turned alive. He wanted to follow the man—"

"And the face—how would you describe it? Did it bring terror, I mean, or confidence?"

"Dark and splendid," answered the other as truthfully as he could. "In a certain sense, rushing, tempestuous, yet stern rather."

"A face like the heights," suggested Leysin impatiently, "a windy, fiery aspect in it, eh?"

"The man swept past like the spirit of a storm in imaginative poetry—" began the tutor, hunting through his thoughts for adequate description, then stopped as he saw that his companion had risen from his chair and begun to pace the floor.

The Pasteur paused a moment beside him, hands thrust deep into his pockets, head bent down, and shoulders forward. For twenty seconds he stared into his visitor's face intently, as though he would force into him the thought in his own mind. His features seemed working visibly, yet behind a mask of strong control.

"Don't you see what it is? Don't you see?" he said in a lower, deeper tone. "*They knew.* Even from a distance they were aware of his coming. He is one of themselves." And he straightened up again. "He belongs to them."

"One of them? One of the wind-and-fire lot?" the tutor stammered.

The restless little man returned to his chair opposite, full of suppressed and vigorous movement, as though he were strung on springs.

"He's *of* them," he continued, "but in a peculiar and particular sense. More than merely a possible recruit, his empty organism would provide the very link they need, the perfect conduit." He watched his companion's face with careful keenness. "In the country where I first experienced this marvellous thing," he added significantly, "he would have been set apart as the offering, the sacrifice, as they call it there. The tribe would have chosen him with honour. He would have been the special bait to attract."

"Death?" whispered the other.

But Leysin shook his head. "In the end, perhaps," he replied darkly, "for the vessel might be torn and shattered. But at first charged to the brim and crammed with energy—with transformed vitality they could draw into themselves through him. A monster, if you will, but to them a deity; and superhuman, in our little sense, most certainly."

Then Hendricks faltered inwardly and turned away. No words came to him at the moment. In silence the minds of the two men, one a religious, the other a secular teacher, and each with a burden of responsibility to the race, kept pace together without speech. The religious, however, outstripped the pedagogue. What he next said seemed a little disconnected with what had preceded it, although Hendricks caught the drift easily enough—and shuddered.

"An organism needing heat," observed Leysin calmly, "can absorb without danger what would destroy a normal person. Alcohol, again, neither injures nor intoxicates—up to a given point—the system that really requires it."

The tutor, perplexed and sorely tempted, felt that he drifted with a tide he found it difficult to stem.

"Up to a point," he repeated. "That's true, of course."

"Up to a given point," echoed the other, with significance that made his voice sound solemn. "Then rescue—in the nick of time."

He waited two full minutes and more for an answer; then, as none was audible, he said another thing. His eyes were so intent upon the tutor's that this latter raised his own unwillingly, and understood thus all that lay behind the pregnant little sentence.

"With a number it would not be possible, but with an individual it could be done. Brim the empty vessel first. Then rescue—in the nick of time! Regeneration!"

IV

In the Englishman's mind there came a crash, as though something fell. There was dust, confusion, noise. Moral platitudes shouted at conventional admonitions. Warnings laughed and copy-book maxims shrivelled up. Above the lot, rising with a touch of grandeur, stood the pulpit figure of the little Pasteur, his big face shining clear through all the turmoil, strength and vision in the flaming eyes—a commanding outline with spiritual audacity in his heart. And Hendricks saw then that the man himself was standing erect in the centre of the room, one finger raised to command attention—listening. Some considerable interval must have passed while he struggled with his inner confusion.

Leysin stood, intently listening, his big head throwing a grotesque shadow on wall and ceiling.

"Hark!" he exclaimed, half whispering. "Do you hear that? Listen."

A deep sound, confused and roaring, passed across the night, far away, and slightly booming. It entered the little room so that the air seemed to tremble a moment. To Hendricks it held something ominous.

"The wind," he whispered, as the noise died off into the distance; "yet a moment ago the night was still enough. The stars were shining." There was tense excitement in the room just then. It showed in Leysin's face, which had gone white as a cloth. Hendricks himself felt extraordinarily stirred.

"Not wind, but human voices," the older man said quickly. "It's shouting. Listen!" and his eyes ran round the room, coming to rest finally in a corner where his hat and cloak hung from a nail. A gesture accompanied the look. He wanted to be out. The tutor half rose to take his leave. "You have duties to-night elsewhere," he stammered. "I'm forgetting." His own instinct was to get away himself with Bindy by the first early *diligence*. He was afraid of yielding.

"Hush!" whispered Leysin peremptorily. "Listen!"

He opened the window at the top, and through the crack, where the stars peeped brightly, there came, louder than before, the uproar of human voices floating through the night from far away. The air of the great pine forests came in with it. Hendricks listened intently a moment. He positively jumped to feel a hand upon his arm. Leysin's big head was thrust close up into his face.

"That's the commotion in the village," he whispered. "A messenger has come and gone; some one has gone back with him. To-night I shall be needed—down here, but to-morrow night when the great ritual takes place—up there—!"

Hendricks tried to push him away so as not to hear the words; but the little man seemed immovable as a rock. The impulse remained probably in the mind without making the muscles work. For the tutor, sorely tempted, longed to dare, yet faltered in his will.

"—if you felt like taking the risk," the words continued seductively, "we might place the empty vessel near enough to let it fill, then rescue it, charged with energy, in the nick of time." And the Pasteur's eyes were aglow with enthusiasm, his voice even trembling at the thought of high adventure to save another's soul.

"Watch merely?" Hendricks heard his own voice whisper, hardly aware that he was saying it, "without taking part?" He said it thickly, stupidly, a man wavering and unsure of himself. "It would be an experience," he stammered. "I've never—"

"Merely watch, yes; look on; let him see," interrupted the other with eagerness. "We must be very careful. It's worth trying—a last resort."

They still stood close together. Hendricks felt the little man's breath on his face as he peered up at him.

"I admit the chance," he began weakly.

"There is no chance," was the vigorous reply, "there is only Providence. You have been guided."

"But as to risk and failure, what of them? What's involved?" he asked, recklessness increasing in him.

"New wine in old bottles," was the answer. "But here, you tell me, the vessel is not damaged, but merely empty. The machinery is all right. If he merely watches, as from a little distance—"

"Yes, yes, the machinery *is* there, I agree. The boy has breeding, health, and all the physical qualities—good blood and nerves and muscles. It's only that life refuses to stay and drive them." His heart beat with violence even as he said it; he felt the energy and zeal from the older man pour into him. He was realising in himself on a smaller scale what might take place with the boy in large. But still he shrank. Leysin for the moment said no more. His spiritual discernment was equal to his boldness. Having planted the seed, he left it to grow or die. The decision was not for him.

In the light of the single lamp the two men sat facing each other, listening, waiting, while Leysin talked occasionally, but in the main kept silence. Some time passed, though how long the tutor could not say. In his mind was wild confusion. How could he justify such a mad proposal? Yet how could he refuse the opening, preposterous though it seemed? The enticement was very great; temptation rushed upon him. Striving to recall his normal world, he found it difficult. The face of the old Marquess seemed a mere lifeless picture on a wall—it watched but could not interfere. Here was an opportunity to take or leave. He fought the battle in terms of naked souls, while the ordinary four-cornered morality hid its face awhile. He heard himself explaining, delaying, hedging, half-toying with the problem. But the redemption of a soul was at stake, and he tried to forget the environment and conditions of modern thought and belief. Sentences flashed at him out of the battle: "I must take him back worse than when I started, or—what? A violent being like Marston, or a redeemed, converted system with new energy? It's a chance, and my last." Moreover, odd, half-comic detail—there was the support of the Church, of a protestant clergyman whose fundamental beliefs were similar to the evangelical persuasions of the boy's family. Conversion, as demoniacal possession, were both traditions of the blood. After all, the old Marquess might understand and approve. "You took the opening God set in your way in his wisdom. You showed faith and courage. Far be it from me to condemn you." The picture on the wall looked down at him and spoke the words.

The wild hypothesis of the intrepid little missionary-pasteur swept him with an effect like hypnotism. Then, suddenly, something in him seemed to decide finally for itself. He flung himself, morality and all, upon this vigorous other personality. He leaned across the table, his face close to the lamp. His voice shook as he spoke.

"Would *you?"* he asked—then knew the question foolish, and that such a man would shrink from nothing where the redemption of a soul was at stake; knew also that the question was proof that his own decision was already made.

There was something grotesque almost in the torrent of colloquial French Leysin proceeded to pour forth, while the other sat listening in amazement, half ashamed and half exhilarated. He looked at the stalwart figure, the wiry bowed legs as he paced the floor, the shortness of the coat-sleeves and the absence of shirt-cuffs round the powerful lean wrists. It was a great fighting man he watched, a man afraid of nothing in heaven or earth, prepared to lead a forlorn hope into a hostile unknown land. And the sight, combined with what he heard, set the seal upon his half-hearted decision. He would take the risk and go.

"Pfui!" exclaimed the little Pasteur as though it might have been an oath, his loud whisper breaking through into a guttural sound, "pfui! Bah! Would that *my* people had machinery like that so that I could use it! I've no material to work on, no force to direct, nothing but heavy, sodden clay. Jelly!" he cried, "negative, useless, lukewarm stuff at best." He lowered his voice suddenly, so as to listen at the same time. "I might as well be a baker kneading dough," he continued. "They drink and yield and drink again; they never attack and drive; they're not worth labouring to save." He struck the wooden table with his fist, making the lamp rattle, while his listener started and drew back. "What good can weak souls, though spotless, be to God? The best have long ago gone up to them," and he jerked his leonine old head towards the mountains. "Where there's *life* there's hope," he stamped his foot as he said it, "but the lukewarm—pfui!—I will spue them out of my mouth!"

He paused by the window a moment, listened attentively, then resumed his pacing to and fro. Clearly, he longed for action. Indifference, half-heartedness had no place in his composition. And Hendricks felt his own slower blood take fire as he listened.

"Ah!" cried Leysin louder, "what a battle I could fight up there for God, could I but live among them, stem the flow of their dark strong vitality, then twist it round and up, up, up!" And he jerked his finger skywards. "It's the great sinners we want, not the meek-faced saints. There's energy enough among those devils to bring a whole Canton to the great Footstool, could I but direct it." He paused a moment, standing over his astonished visitor. "Bring the boy up with you, and let him drink his fill. And pray, pray, I say, that he become a violent sinner first in order that later there shall be something worth offering to God. Over one *sinner* that repenteth—"

A rapid, nervous knocking interrupted the flow of words, and the figure of a woman stood upon the threshold. With the opening of the door came also again the roaring from the night outside. Hendricks saw the tall, somewhat dishevelled outline of the wife—he remembered her vaguely, though she could hardly see him now in his darker corner—and recalled the fact that she had been sent out to Leysin in his missionary days, a worthy, illiterate, but adoring woman. She wore a shawl, her hair was untidy, her eyes fixed and staring. Her husband's sturdy little figure, as he rose, stood level with her chin.

"You hear it, Jules?" she whispered thickly. "The *joran* has brought them down. You'll be needed in the village." She said it anxiously, though Hendricks understood the *patois* with difficulty. They talked excitedly together a moment in the doorway, their outlines blocked against the corridor where a single oil lamp flickered. She warned, urging something; he expostulated. Fragments reached Hendricks in his corner. Clearly the woman worshipped her husband like a king, yet feared for his safety. He, for his part, comforted her, scolded a little, argued, told her to "believe in God and go back to bed."

"They'll take you too, and you'll never return. It's not your parish anyhow . . ." a touch of anguish in her tone.

But Leysin was impatient to be off. He led her down the passage. "My parish is wherever I can help. I belong to God. Nothing can harm me but to leave undone the work He gives me." The steps went farther away as he guided her to the stairs. Outside the roar of voices rose and fell. Wind brought the drifting sound, wind carried it away. It was like the thunder of the sea.

And the Englishman, using the little scene as a flashlight upon his own attitude, saw it for an instant as God might have seen it. Leysin's point of view was high, scanning a very wide horizon. His eye being single, the whole body was full of light. The risk, it suddenly seemed, was—nothing; to shirk it, indeed, the merest cowardice.

He went up and seized the Pasteur's hand.

"To-morrow," he said, a trifle shakily perhaps, yet looking straight into his eyes. "If we stay over—I'll bring the lad with me—provided he comes willingly."

"You will stay over," interrupted the other with decision. "Come to supper at seven. Come in mountain boots. Use persuasion, but not force. He shall see it from a distance—without taking part."

"From a distance—yes," the tutor repeated, "but without taking part."

"I know the signs," the Pasteur broke in significantly. "We can rescue him in the nick of time—charged with energy and life, yet before the danger gets—"

A sudden clangour of bells drowned the whispering voice, cutting the sentence in the middle. It was like an alarm of fire. Leysin sprang sharply round.

"The signal!" he cried; "the signal from the church. Some one's been taken. I must go at once—I shall be needed." He had his hat and cloak on in a moment, was through the passage and into the street, Hendricks following at his heels. The whole place seemed alive. Yet the roadway was deserted, and no lights showed at the windows of the houses. Only from the farther end of the village, where stood the cabaret, came a roar of voices, shouting, crying, singing. The impression was that the population was centred there. Far in the starry sky a line of fires blazed upon the heights, throwing a lurid reflection above the deep black valley. Excitement filled the night.

"But how extraordinary!" exclaimed Hendricks, hurrying to overtake his alert companion; "what life there is about! Everything's on the rush." They went faster, almost running. "I feel the waves of it beating even here." He followed breathlessly.

"A messenger has come—and gone," replied Leysin in a sharp, decided voice. "What you feel here is but the overflow. This is the aftermath. I must work down here with my people—"

"I'll work with you," began the other. But Leysin stopped him.

"Keep yourself for to-morrow night—up there," he said with grave authority, pointing to the fiery line upon the heights, and at the same time quickening his pace along the street. "At the moment," he cried, looking back, "your place is yonder." He jerked his head towards the carpenter's house among the vineyards. The next minute he was gone.

V

And Hendricks, accredited tutor to a sprig of nobility in the twentieth century, asked himself suddenly how such things could possibly be. The adventure took on abruptly a touch of nightmare. Only the light in the sky above the cabaret windows, and the roar of voices where men drank and sang, brought home the reality of it all. With a shudder of apprehension he glanced at the lurid glare upon the mountains. He was committed now; not because he had merely promised, but because he had definitely made up his mind.

Lighting a match, he saw by his watch that the visit had lasted over two hours. It was after eleven. He hurried, letting himself in with the big house-key, and going on tiptoe up the granite stairs. In his mind rose a picture of the boy as he had known him all these weary, sight-seeing months—the mild brown eyes, the facile indolence, the pliant, watery emotions of the listless creature, but behind him now, like storm clouds, the hopes, desires, fears the Pasteur's talk had conjured up. The yearning to save stirred strongly in his heart, and more and more of the little man's reckless spiritual audacity came with it. His own affection for the lad was genuine, but impatience and adventure pushed eagerly through the tenderness. If only, oh, if only he could put life into that great six-foot, big-boned frame! Some energy as of fire and wind into that inert machinery of mind and body! The idea was utterly incredible, but surely no harm could come of trying the experiment. There *were* the huge and elemental forces, of course, in Nature, and if . . . A sound in the bedroom, as he crept softly past the door, caught his attention, and he paused a moment to listen. Lord Ernie was not asleep, then, after all. He wondered why the sound got somehow at his heart. There was shuffling behind the door; there was a voice, too—or was it voices? He knocked.

"Who is it?" came at once, in a tone he hardly recognised. And, as he answered, "It's I, Mr. Hendricks; let me in," there followed a renewal of the shuffling, but without the sound of voices, and the door flew open—it was not even locked. Lord Ernie stood before him, dressed to go out. In the faint starlight the tall ungainly figure filled the doorway, erect and huge, the shoulders squared, the trunk no longer drooping. The listlessness was gone. He stood upright, limbs straight and alert; the sagging limp had vanished from the knees. He looked, in this semi-darkness, like another person, almost monstrous. And the tutor drew back instinctively, catching an instant at his breath.

"But, my dear boy! why aren't you asleep?" he stammered. He glanced half nervously about him. "I heard you talking, surely?" He fumbled for a match; but, before he found it, the other had turned on the electric switch. The light flared out. There was no one else in the room. "Is anything wrong with you? What's the matter?"

But the boy answered quietly, though in a deeper voice than Hendricks had ever known in him before: "I'm all right; only I couldn't sleep. I've been watching those fires on the mountains. I—I wanted to go out and see."

He still held the field-glasses in his hand, swinging them vigorously by the strap. The room was littered with clothes, just unpacked, the heavy shooting boots in the middle of the floor; and Hendricks, noticing these signs, felt a wave of excitement sweep through him, caught somehow from the presence of the boy. There was a sense of vitality in the room—as though a rush of active movement had just passed through it. Both windows stood wide open, and the roar of voices was clearly audible. Lord Ernie turned his head to listen.

"That's only the village people drinking and shouting," said Hendricks, closely watching each movement that he made. "It's perfectly natural, Bindy, that you feel too excited to sleep. We're in the mountains. The air stimulates tremendously—it makes the heart beat faster." He decided not to press the lad with questions.

"But I never felt like this in the Rockies or the Himalayas," came the swift rejoinder, as he moved to the window and looked out. "There was nothing in India or Japan like *that!*" He swept his hand towards the wooded heights that towered above the village so close. He talked volubly. "All those things we saw out there were sham—done on purpose for tourists. Up there it's real. I've been watching through the glasses till—I felt I simply must go out and join it. You can see men dancing round the fires, and big, rushing women. Oh, Mr. Hendricks, isn't it all glorious—all too glorious and ripping for words!" And his brown eyes shone like lamps.

"You mean that it's spontaneous, natural?" the other guided him, welcoming the new enthusiasm, yet still bewildered by the startling change. It was not mere nerves he saw. There was nothing morbid in it.

"They're doing it, I mean, because they have to," came the decided answer, "and because they feel it. They're not just copying the world." He put his hand upon the other's arm. There was dry heat in it that Hendricks felt even through his clothes. "And that's what *I* want," the boy went on, raising his voice, "what I've always wanted without knowing it—real things that can make me alive. I've often had it in my dreams, you know, but now I've found it."

"But I didn't know. You never told me of those dreams."

The boy's cheeks flushed, so that the colour and the fire in his eyes made him positively splendid. He answered slowly, as out of some part he had hitherto kept deliberately concealed.

"Because I never could get hold of it in words. It sounded so silly even to myself, and I thought Father would train it all away and laugh at it. It's awfully far down in me, but it's so real I knew it must come out one day, and that I should find it. Oh, I say, Mr. Hendricks," and he lowered his voice, leaning out across the window-sill suddenly, "*that* fills me up and feeds me"—he pointed to the heights—"and gives me life. The life I've seen till now was only a kind of show. It starved me. I want to go up there and feel it pouring through my blood." He filled his lungs with the strong mountain air, and paused while he exhaled it slowly, as though tasting it with delight and understanding. Then he burst out again, "I vote we go. Will you come with me? What d'you say. Eh?"

They stared at each other hard a moment. Something as primitive and irresistible as love passed through the air between them. With a great effort the older man kept the balance true.

"Not to-night, not now," he said firmly. "It's too late. To-morrow, if you like—with pleasure."

"But to-morrow *night,*" cried the boy with a rush, "when the fires are blazing and the wind is loose. Not in the stupid daylight."

"All right. To-morrow night. And my old friend, Monsieur Leysin, shall be our guide. He knows the way, and he knows the people too."

Lord Ernie seized his hands with enthusiasm. His vigour was so disconcerting that it seemed to affect his physical appearance. The body grew almost visibly; his very clothes hung on him differently; he was no longer a nonentity yawning beneath an ancient pedigree and title; he was an aggressive personality. The boy in him rushed into manhood, as it were, while still retaining boyish speech and gesture. It was uncanny. "We'll go more than once, I vote; go again and again. This *is* a place and a half. It's *my* place with a vengeance—!"

"Not exactly the kind of place your father would wish you to linger in," his tutor interrupted. "But we might stay a day or two—especially as you like it so."

"It's far better than the towns and the rotten embassies; better than fifty Simlas and Bombays and filthy Cairos," cried the other eagerly. "It's just the thing I need, and when I get home I'll show 'em something. I'll prove it. Why, they simply won't know me!" He laughed, and his face shone with a kind of vivid radiance in the glare of the electric light. The transformation was more than curious. Waiting a moment to see if more would follow, Hendricks moved slowly then towards the door, with the remark that it was advisable now to go to bed since they would be up late the following night—when he noticed for the first time that the pillow and sheets were crumpled and that the bed had already been lain in. The first suspicion flashed back upon him with new certainty.

Lord Ernie was already taking off his heavy coat, preparatory to undressing. He looked up quickly at the altered tone of voice.

"Bindy," the tutor said with a touch of gravity, "you *were* alone just now—weren't you—of course?"

The other sat up from stooping over his boots. With his hands resting on the bed behind him, he looked straight into his companion's eyes. Lying was not among his faults. He answered slowly after a decided interval.

"I—I was asleep," he whispered, evidently trying to be accurate, yet hesitating how to describe the thing he had to say, "and had a dream—one of my real, vivid dreams when something happens. Only, this time, it was more real than ever before. It was"—he paused, searching for words, then added—"sweet and awful."

And Hendricks repeated the surprising sentence. "Sweet and awful, Bindy! What in the world do you mean, boy?"

Lord Ernie seemed puzzled himself by the choice of words he used.

"I don't know exactly," he went on honestly, "only I mean that it was awfully real and splendid, a bit of my own life somewhere—somewhere else—where it lies hidden away behind a lot of days and months that choke it up. I can never get at it except in woods and places, quite alone, hearing the wind or making fires, or—in sleep." He hid his face in his hands a moment, then looked up with a hint of censure in his eyes. "Why didn't you tell me that such things *were* done? You never told me," he repeated.

"I didn't know it myself until this evening. Leysin—"

"I thought you knew everything," Lord Ernie broke in in that same half-chiding tone.

"Monsieur Leysin told me to-night for the first time," said Hendricks firmly, "that such people and such practices existed. Till now I had never dreamed that such superstitions survived anywhere in the world at all." He resented the reproach. But he was also aware that the boy resented his authority. For the first time his ascendency seemed in question; his voice, his eye, his manner did not quell as formerly. "So you mean, when you say 'sweet and awful,' that it was very real to you?" he asked. He insisted now with purpose. "Is that it, Bindy?"

The other replied eagerly enough. "Yes, that's it, I think—partly. This time it was more than dreaming. It was real. I got there. I remembered. That's what I meant. And after I woke up the thing still went on. The man seemed still in the room beside the bed, calling me to get up and go with him—"

"Man! What man?" The tutor leant upon the back of a chair to steady himself. The wind just then went past the open windows with a singing rush.

"The dark man who passed us in the village, and who pointed to the fires on the heights. He came with the wind, you remember. He pulled my coat."

The boy stood up as he said it. He came across the naked boarding, his step light and dancing. "Fire that heats but does not burn, and wind that blows the heart alight, or something—I forget now exactly. *You* heard it too." He whispered the words with excitement, raising his arms and knees as in the opening movements of a dance.

Hendricks kept his own excitement down, but with a distinctly conscious effort.

"I heard nothing of the kind," he said calmly. "I was only thinking of getting home dry. You say," he asked with decision, "that you *heard* those words?"

Lord Ernie stood back a little. It was not that he wished to conceal, but that he felt uncertain how to express himself. "In the street," he said, "I heard nothing; the words rose up in my own head, as it were. But in the dream, and afterwards too, when I was wide awake, I heard them out loud, clearly: Fire that heats but does not burn, and wind that blows the heart to flame—that's how it was."

"In French, Bindy? You heard it in French?"

"Oh, it was no language at all. The eyes said it—both times." He spoke as naturally as though it was the Durbah he described again. Only this new aggressive certainty was in his voice and manner. "Mr. Hendricks," he went on eagerly, "*you* understand what I mean, don't you? When certain people look at one, words start up in the mind as though one heard them spoken. I heard the words in my head, I suppose; only they seemed so familiar, as though I'd known them before—always—"

"Of course, Bindy, I understand. But this man—tell me—did he stay on after you woke up? And how did he go?" He looked round at the barely furnished room for hiding-places. "It was really the dream you carried on after waking, wasn't it?"

Then Bindy laughed, but inwardly, as to himself. There was the faintest possible hint of derision in his voice. "No doubt," he said; "only it was one of my big, real dreams. And how he went I can't explain at all, for I didn't see. You knocked at the door; I turned, and found myself standing in the room, dressed to go out. There was a rush of wind outside the window—and when I looked he was no longer there. The same minute you came in. It was all as quick as that. I suppose I dressed—in my sleep."

They stood for several minutes, staring at each other without speaking. The tutor hesitated between several courses of action, unable, for the life of him, to decide upon any particular one. His instinct on the whole was to stop nothing, but to encourage all possible expression, while keeping rigorous watch and guard. Repression, it seemed to him just then, was the least desirable line to take. Somewhere there was truth in the affair. He felt out of his depth, his authority impaired, and under these temporary disadvantages he might so easily make a grave mistake, injuring instead of helping. While Lord Ernie finished his undressing he leaned out of the window, taking great draughts of the keen night air, watching the blazing fires and listening to the roar of voices, now dying down into the distance.

And the voice of his thinking whispered to him, "Let it all come out. Repress nothing. Let him have the entire adventure. If it's nonsense it can't injure, and if it's true it's inevitable." He drew his head in and moved towards the door. "Then it's settled," he said quietly, as though nothing unusual had happened; "we'll go up there to-morrow night—with Monsieur Leysin to show us the way. And you'll go to sleep now, won't you? For to-morrow we may be up very late. Promise me, Bindy."

"I'm dead tired," came the answer from the sheets. "I certainly shan't dream any more, if that's what you mean. I promise."

Hendricks turned the light out and went softly from the room. He could always trust the boy.

"Good-night, Bindy," he said.

"Good-night," came the drowsy reply.

Upstairs he lingered a long time over his own undressing, listening, waiting, watching for the least sound below. But nothing happened. Once, for his own peace of mind, he stole stealthily downstairs to the boy's door; then, reassured by the heavy breathing that was distinctly audible, he went up finally and got into bed himself. The night was very still now. It was cool, and the stars were brilliant over lake and forest and mountain. No voices broke the silence. He only heard the tinkle of the little streams beyond the vineyards. And by midnight he was sound asleep.

VI

And next day broke as soft and brilliant as though October had stolen it from June; the Alps gleamed through an almost summery haze across the lake; the air held no hint of coming winter; and the Jura mountains wore the true blue of memory in Hendricks' mind. Patches of red and yellow splashed the great pinewoods here and there where beech and ash put autumn in the vast dark carpet.

The tutor woke clear-headed and refreshed. All that had happened the night before seemed out of proportion and unreasonable. There had been exaggerated emotion in it: in himself, because he returned to a place still charged with potent memories of youth; and in Lord Ernie, because the lad was overwrought by the electrical disturbance of the atmosphere. The nearness of the ancestral halls, which they both disliked, had emphasised it; the ominous, wild weather had favoured it; and the coincidence of these pagan rites of superstitious peasants had focussed it all into a melodramatic form with an added touch of the supernatural that was highly picturesque and—dangerously suggestive. Hendricks recovered his common sense; judgment asserted itself again.

Yet, for all that, certain things remained authentic. The effect upon the boy was not illusion, nor his words about fire and wind mere meaningless invention. There hid some undivined and significant correspondence between the gaps in his deficient nature and these two turbulent elements. The talk of Leysin, as the conduct of his wife, remained authentic; those facts were too steady to be dismissed, the Pasteur too genuinely in earnest to be catalogued in dream. Neither daylight nor common sense could dissipate their actuality. Truth lay somewhere in it all.

Thus the day, for the tutor, was a battle that shifted with varying fortune between doubt and certainty. In the morning his mind was decided: the wild experiment was unjustifiable; in the afternoon, as the sunshine grew faint and melancholy, it became "interesting, for what harm could come of it?" but towards evening, when shadows lengthened across the purple forests and the trees stood motionless in the calm and windless air, the adventure seemed, as it had seemed the night before, not only justifiable, but right and necessary. It only became inevitable, however, when, after tea together on the balcony, Lord Ernie, mentioning the subject for the first time that day, asked pointedly what time the Pasteur expected them to supper; then, noticing the flush of hesitancy in his companion's eyes, added in his strange deep voice, "You promised we should go." Withdrawal after that was out of the question. To retract would have meant, for one thing, final loss of the boy's confidence—a possibility not to be contemplated for a moment.

Until this moment no word of the preceding night had passed the lips of either. Lord Ernie had been quiet and preoccupied, silent rather, but never listless. He was peaceful, perhaps subdued a little, yet with a suppressed energy in his bearing that Hendricks watched with secret satisfaction. The tutor, closely observant, detected nothing out of gear; life stirred strongly in him; there was purpose, interest, will; there was desire; but there was nothing to cause alarm.

Availing himself then of the lad's absorption in his own affairs, he wandered forth alone upon his sentimental tour of inspection. No ghost of emotion rose to stalk beside him. That early tragedy, he now saw clearly, had been no more than youthful explosion of mere physical passion, wholesome and natural, but due chiefly to propinquity. His thoughts ran idly on; and he was even congratulating himself upon escape and freedom when, abruptly, he remembered a phrase Bindy had used the night before, and stumbled suddenly upon a clue when least expecting it.

He came to a sudden halt. The significance of it crashed through his mind and startled him. "There are big rushing women . . ." It was the first reference to the other sex, as evidence of their attraction for him, Hendricks had ever known to pass his lips. Hitherto, though twenty years of age, the lad had never spoken of women as though he was aware of their terrible magic. He had not discovered them as females, necessary to every healthy male. It was not purity, of course, but ignorance: he had felt nothing. Something had now awakened sex in him, so that he knew himself a man, and naked. And it had revolutionised the world for him. This new life came from the roots, transforming listless indifference into positive desire; the will woke out of sleep, and all the currents of his system took aggressive form. For all energy, intellectual, emotional, or spiritual, is fundamentally one: it is primarily sexual.

Hendricks paused in his sentimental walk, marvelling that he had not realised sooner this simple truth. It brought a certain logical meaning even into the pagan rites upon the mountains, these ancient rites which symbolised the marriage of the two tremendous elements of wind and fire, heat and air. And the lad's quiet, busy mood that morning confirmed his simple discovery. It involved restraint and purpose. Lord Ernie was alive. Hendricks would take home with him to those ancestral halls a vessel bursting with energy—creative energy. It was admirable that he should witness—from a safe distance—this primitive ceremony of crude pagan origin. It was the very thing. And the tutor hurried back to the house among the vineyards, aware that his responsibility had increased, but persuaded more than ever that his course was justified.

The sky held calm and cloudless through the day, the forests brooding beneath the hazy autumn sunshine. Indications that the second hurricane lay brewing among the heights were not wanting, however, to experienced eyes. Almost a preternatural silence reigned; there was a warm heaviness in the placid atmosphere; the surface of the lake was patched and streaky; the extreme clarity of the air an ominous omen. Distant objects were too close. Towards sunset, moreover, the streaks and patches vanished as though sucked below, while thin strips of tenuous cloud appeared from nowhere above the northern cliffs. They moved with great rapidity at an enormous height, touched with a lurid brilliance as the sun sank out of sight; and when Hendricks strolled over with Lord Ernie to *la cure* for supper there came a sudden rush of heated wind that set the branches sharply rattling, then died away as abruptly as it rose.

They seemed reflected, too, these disturbances, in the human atmospheres about the supper table—there was suppression of various emotions, emotions presaging violence. Lord Ernie was exhilarated, Hendricks uneasy and preoccupied, the Pasteur grave and thoughtful. In Hendricks was another feeling as well—that he had lightly summoned a storm which might carry him off his feet. The boy's excitement increased it, as wind-puffs fan a starting fire. His own judgment had somewhere played him false, betraying him into this incredible adventure. And yet he could not stop it. The Pasteur's influence was over him perhaps. He was ashamed to turn back. He was committed. The unusual circumstances found the weakness in his character.

For somewhere in the preposterous superstition there lay a big forgotten truth. He could not believe it, and yet he did believe it. The world had forgotten how to live truly close to Nature.

A desultory conversation was carried on, chiefly between the two men, while the boy ate hungrily, and Mme. Leysin watched her husband with anxiety as she served the simple meal.

"So you are coming with us, and you like to come?" the Pasteur observed quietly, Hendricks translating.

Lord Ernie replied with a gesture of unmistakable enthusiasm.

"A wild lot of men and women," Leysin went on, keeping his eye hard upon him, "with an interesting worship of their own copied from very ancient times. They live on the heights, and mix little with us valley folk. You shall see their ceremonies to-night."

"They get the wind and fire into themselves, don't they?" asked the boy keenly, and somewhat to the distress of the translator who rendered it, "They get into wind and fire."

"They worship wind and fire," Leysin replied, "and they do it by means of a wonderful dance that somehow imitates the leap of flame and the headlong rush of wind. If you copy the movements and gestures of a person you discover the emotion that causes them. You share it. Their idea is, apparently, that by imitating the movements they invite or attract the force—draw these elemental powers into their systems, so that in the end—"

He stopped suddenly, catching the tutor's eye. Lord Ernie seemed to understand without translation; he had laid down his knife and fork and was leaning forward across the table, listening with deep absorption. His expression was alert with a new intelligence that was almost cunning. An acute sensibility seemed to have awakened in him.

"As with laughing, I suppose?" he said in an undertone to Hendricks quickly. "If you imitate a laughter, you laugh yourself in the end and feel all the jolly excitement of laughter. Is that what he means?"

The tutor nodded with assumed indifference. "Imitation is always infectious," he said lightly; "but, of course, you will not imitate these wild people yourself, Bindy. We'll just look on from a distance."

"From a distance!" repeated the boy, obviously disappointed. "What's the good of that?' A look of obstinacy passed across his altered face.

Hendricks met his eyes squarely. "At a circus," he said firmly, "you just watch. You don't imitate the clown, do you?"

"If you look on long enough, you do," was the rather dogged reply.

"Well, take the Russian dancers we saw in Moscow," the other insisted patiently, "you felt the power and beauty without jumping up and whirling in your stall?"

Bindy half glared at him. There was almost contempt in his quiet answer: "But your mind whirled with them. And later your body would too; otherwise it's given you nothing." He paused a second. "I can only get the fun of riding by being on a horse's back and doing his movements exactly with him—not by watching him."

Hendricks smiled and shrugged his shoulders. He did not wish to discourage the enthusiasm lying behind this analysis. The uneasiness in him grew apace. He said something rapidly in French, using an undertone and laughter to confuse the actual words.

"Of course we must not interfere with their ceremonies," put in the Pasteur with decision. "It's sacred to them. We can hide among the trees and watch. You would not leave your seat in church to imitate the priest, would you?" He glanced smilingly at the eager youth before him.

"If he did something real, I would." It was said with a bright flash in the eyes. "Anything real I'd copy like a shot. Only, I never find it."

The reply was disconcerting rather: and Hendricks, as he hurriedly translated, made a clatter with his knife and fork, for something in him rose to meet the truth behind the curious words. From that moment, as though catching a little of the boy's exhilaration, he passed under a kind of spell perhaps. It was, in spite of the exaggeration, oddly stimulating. This dull little meal at the village *cure* masked an accumulating vehemence, eager to break loose. He heard the old father's voice: "Well done, Hendricks! You have accomplished wonders!" He would take back the boy—alive. . . .

Yet all the time there were streaks and patches on his soul as upon the surface of the lake that afternoon. There were signs of terror. He felt himself letting go, an increasing recklessness, a yielding up more and more of his own authority to that of this triumphant boy. Bindy understood the meaning of it all and felt secure; Hendricks faltered, hesitated, stood on the defensive. Yet, ever less and less. Already he accepted the other's guidance. Already Lord Ernie's leadership was in the ascendant. Conviction invariably holds dominion over doubt.

They ate little. It was near the end of the meal when the wind, falling from a clear and starlit sky, struck its first violent blow, dropping with the force of an explosion that shook the wooden house, and passing with a roar towards the distant lake. The oil lamp, suspended from the ceiling, trembled; the Pasteur looked apprehensively at the shuttered windows; and Lord Ernie, with startling abruptness, stood up. His eyes were shining. His voice was brisk, alert, and deep.

"The wind, the wind!" he cried. "Think what it'll be up there! We shall feel it on our bodies!" His enthusiasm was like a rush of air across the table. "And the fire!" he went on. "The flames will lick all over, and tear about the sky. I feel wild and full of them already! How splendid!" And the flame of the little lamp leaped higher in the chimney as he said it.

"The violence of the *coup de joran* is extraordinary," explained Leysin as he got up to turn down the wick, "and the second outburst—" The rest of his sentence was drowned by the noise of Hendricks' voice telling the boy to sit down and finish his supper. And at the same moment the Pasteur's wife came in as though a stroke of wind drove behind her down the passage. The door slammed in the draught. There was a momentary confusion in the room above which her voice rose shrill and frightened.

"The fires are alight, Jules," she whispered in her half intelligible *patois,* "the forest is burning all along the upper ridge." Her face was pale and her speech came stumbling. She lowered her lips to her husband's ear. "They'll be looking out for recruits to-night. Is it necessary, is it right for you to go?" She glanced uneasily at the English visitors. "You know the danger—"

He stopped her with a gesture. "Those who look on at life accomplish nothing," he answered impatiently. "One must act, always act. Chances are sent to be taken, not stared at." He rose, pushing past her into the passage, and as he did so she gave him one swift comprehensive look of tenderness and admiration, then hurried after him to find his hat and cloak. Willingly she would have kept him at home that night, yet gladly, in another sense, she saw him go. She fumbled in her movements, ready to laugh or cry or pray. Hendricks saw her pain and understood. It was singular how the woman's attitude intensified his own misgivings; her behaviour, the mere expression of her face alone, made the adventure so absolutely real.

Three minutes later they were in the village street. Hendricks and Lord Ernie, the latter impatient in the road beyond, saw her tall figure stoop to embrace him. "I shall pray all night: I shall watch from my window for your return. God, who speaks from the whirlwind, and whose pathway is the fire, will go with you. Remember the younger men; it is ever the younger men that they seek to take . . . !" Her words were half hysterical. The kiss was given and taken; the open doorway framed her outline a moment; then the buttress of the church blotted her out, and they were off.

VII

And at once the curious confusion of strong wind was upon them. Gusts howled about the corners of the shuttered houses and tore noisily across the open yards. Dust whirled with the rapidity as of some spectral white machinery. A tile came clattering down about their feet, while overhead the roofs had an air of shifting, toppling, bending. The entire village seemed scooped up and shaken, then dropped upon the earth again in tottering fashion.

"This way," gasped the little Pasteur, blown sideways like a sail, "follow me closely." Almost arm-in-arm at first they hurried down the deserted street, past lampless windows and tight-fastened doors, and soon were beyond the cabaret in that open stretch between the village and the forest where the wind had unobstructed way. Far above them ran the fiery mountain ridge. They saw the glare reflected in the sky as the tempest first swept them all three together, then separated them in the same moment. They seemed to spin or whirl. "It's far worse than I expected," shouted their guide; "here! Give me your hand!" then found, once disentangled from his flapping cloak, that no one stood beside him. For each of them it was a single fight to reach the shelter of the woods, where the actual ascent began. An instant the Pasteur seemed to hesitate. He glanced back at the lighted window of *la cure* across the fields, at the line of fire in the sky, at the figure disappearing in the blackness immediately ahead. "Where's the boy?" he shouted. "Don't let him get too far in front. Keep close. Wait till I come!" They staggered back against each other. "Look how easily he's slipped ahead already!"

"This howling wind—" Hendricks shouted, as they advanced side by side, pushing their shoulders against the storm.

The rest of the sentence vanished into space. Leysin shoved him forward, pointing to where, some twenty yards in front, the figure of Lord Ernie, head down, was battling eagerly with the hurricane. Already he stood near to the shelter of the trees waving his arms with energy towards the summits where the fire blazed. He was calling something at the top of his voice, urging them to hurry. His voice rushed down upon them with a pelt of wind.

"Don't let him get away from us," bawled Leysin, holding his hands cup-wise to his mouth. "Keep him in reach. He may see, but must not take part . . ." A blow full in the face that smote him like the flat of a great sword clapped the sentence short. "That's *your* part. He won't obey me!" Hendricks heard it as they plunged across the wind-swept reach, panting, struggling, forcing their bodies sideways like two-legged crabs against the terrific force of the descending *joran.* They reached the protection of the forest wall without further attempt at speech. Here there was sudden peace and silence, for the tall, dense trees received the tempest's impact like a cushion, stopping it. They paused a moment to recover breath.

But although the first exhaustion speedily passed, that original confusion of strong wind remained—in Hendricks' mind at least,—for wind violent enough to be battled with has a scattering effect on thought and blows the very blood about. Something in him snapped its cables and blew out to sea. His breath drew in an impetuous quality from the tempest each time he filled his lungs. There was agitation in him that caused an odd exaggeration of the emotions. The boy, as they came up, leaped down from a boulder he had climbed. He opened his arms, making of his cloak a kind of sail that filled and flapped.

"At last!" he cried, impatient, almost vexed. "I thought you were never coming. The wind blew me along. We shall be late—"

The tutor caught his arm with vigour. "You keep by us, Ernest; d'you hear now? No rushing ahead like that. Leysin's the guide, not you." He even shook him. But as he did so he was aware that he himself resisted something that he did not really want to resist, something that urged him forcibly; a little more and he would yield to it with pleasure, with abandon, finally with recklessness. A reaction of panic fear ran over him.

"It was the wind, I tell you," cried the boy, flinging himself free with a hint of insolence in his voice, "for it's alive. I mean to see everything. The wind's our leader and the fire's our guide." He made a movement to start on again.

"You'll obey me," thundered Hendricks, "or else you'll go home. D'you understand?"

With exasperation, yet with uneasy delight, he noted the words Bindy made use of. It was in him that he might almost have uttered them himself. He stepped already into an entirely new world. Exhilaration caught him even now. Putting the brake on was mere pretence. He seized the lad by both shoulders and pushed him to the rear, then placed himself next, so that Leysin moved in front and led the way. The procession started, diving into the comparative shelter of the forest. "Don't let him pass you," he heard in rapid French; "guide him, that's all. The power's already in his blood. Keep yourself in hand as well, and follow me closely." The roar of the storm above them carried the words clean off the world.

Here in the forest they moved, it seemed, along the floor of an ocean whose surface raged with dreadful violence; any moment one or other of them might be caught up to that surface and whirled off to destruction. For the procession was not one with itself. The darkness, the difficulty of hearing what each said, the feeling, too, that each climbed for himself, made everything seem at sixes and sevens. And the tutor, this secret exultation growing in his heart, denied the anxiety that kept it pace, and battled with his turbulent emotions, a divided personality. His power over the boy, he realised, had gravely weakened. A little time ago they had seemed somehow equal. Now, however, a complete reversal of their relative positions had taken place. The boy was sure of himself. While Leysin led at a steady mountaineer's pace on his wiry, short, bowed legs, Hendricks, a yard or two behind him, stumbled a good deal in the darkness, Lord Ernie for ever on his heels, eager to push past. But Bindy never stumbled. There was no flagging in his muscles. He moved so lightly and with so sure a tread that he almost seemed to dance, and often he stopped aside to leap a boulder or to run along a fallen trunk. Path there was none. Occasional gusts of wind rushed gustily down into these depths of forest where they moved, and now, from time to time, as they rose nearer to the line of fire on the ridge, an increasing glare lit up the knuckled roots or glimmered on the bramble thickets and heavy beds of moss. It was astonishing how the little Pasteur never missed his way. Periods of thick silence alternated with moments when the storm swept down through gullies among the trees, reverberating like thunder in the hollows.

Slowly they advanced, buffeted, driven, pushed, the wildness of some Walpürgis night growing upon all three. In the tutor's mind was this strange lift of increasing recklessness, the old proportion gone, the spiritual aspect of it troubling him to the point of sheer distress. He followed Leysin as blindly with his body as he followed this new Bindy eagerly with his mind. For this languid boy, now dancing to the tune of flooding life at his very heels, seemed magical in the true sense: energy created as by a wizard out of nothing. From lips that ordinarily sighed in listless boredom poured now a ceaseless stream of questions and ejaculations, ringing with enthusiasm. How long would it take to reach the fiery ridge? Why did they go so slowly? Would they arrive too late? Would their intrusion be welcomed or understood? Already one great change was effected—accepted by Hendricks, too—that the rôle of mere spectator was impossible. The answers Hendricks gave, indeed, grew more and more encouraging and sympathetic. He, too, was impatient with their leader's crawling pace. Some elemental spell of wind and fire urged him towards the open ridge. The pull became irresistible. He despised the Pasteur's caution, denied his wisdom, wholly rejected now the spirit of compromise and prudence. And once, as the hurricane brought down a flying burst of voices, he caught himself leaping upon a big grey boulder in their path. He leaped at the very moment that the boy behind him leaped, yet hardly realised that he did so; his feet danced without a conscious order from his brain. They met together on the rounded top, stumbled, clutched one another frantically, then slid with waving arms and flying cloaks down the slippery surface of damp moss—laughing wildly.

"Fool!" cried Hendricks, saving himself. "What in the world—?"

"*You* called," laughed Bindy, picking himself up and dropping back to his place in the rear again. "It's the wind, not me; it's in our feet. Half the time you're shouting and jumping yourself!"

And it was a few minutes after this that Lord Ernie suddenly forged ahead. He slipped in front as silently as a shadow before a moving candle in a room. Passing the tutor at a moment when his feet were entangled among roots and stones, he easily overtook the Pasteur and found himself in the lead. He never stumbled; there seemed steel springs in his legs.

From Leysin, too breathless to interfere, came a cry of warning. "Stop him! Take his hand!" his tired voice instantly smothered by the roaring skies. He turned to catch Hendricks by the cloak. "You see *that!*" he shouted in alarm. "For the love of God, don't lose sight of him! He must see, but not take part—remember—!"

And Hendricks yelled after the vanishing figure, "Bindy, go slow, go slow! Keep in touch with us." But he quickened his pace instantly, as though to overtake the boy. He passed his companion the same minute, and was out of sight. "I'll wait for you," came back the boy's shrill answer through the thinning trees. And a flare of light fell with it from the sky, for the final climb of a steep five hundred feet had now begun, and overhead the naked ridge ran east and west with its line of blazing fires. Boulders and rocky ground replaced the pines and spruces.

"But you'll never find the way," shouted Leysin, while a deep trumpeting roar of the storm beyond muffled the remainder of the sentence.

Hendricks heard the next words close beside him from a clump of shadows. He was in touching distance of the excited boy.

"The fires and the singing guide me. Only a fool could miss the way."

"But you *are* a—"

He swallowed the unuttered word. A new, extraordinary respect was suddenly in him. That tall, virile figure, instinct with life, springing so cleverly through the choking darkness, guiding with decision and intelligence, almost infallible—it was no fool that led them thus. He hurried after till his very sinews ached. His eyes, troubled and confused, strained through the trees to find him. But these same trees now fled past him in a torrent.

"Bindy, Bindy!" he cried, at the top of his voice, yet not with the imperious tone the situation called for. The sentence dropped into a lull of wind. Instead of command there was entreaty, almost supplication, in it. "Wait for me, I'm coming. We'll see the glorious thing together!"

And then suddenly the forest lay behind him, with a belt of open pasture-land in front below the actual ridge. He felt the first great draught of heat, as a line of furnaces burst their doors with a mighty roar and turned the sky into a blaze of golden daylight. There was a crackling as of musketry. The flare shot up and burned the air about him, and the voices of a multitude, as yet invisible, drove through it like projectiles on the wind. This was the first impression, wholesale and terrific, that met him as he paused an instant on the edge of the sheltering forest and looked forward. Leysin and Lord Ernie seemed to leave his mind, forgotten in this first attack of splendour, but forgotten, as it were, the first with contempt, the latter with an overwhelming regret. For the Pasteur's mistake in that instant seemed obvious. In half measures lay the fatal error, and in compromise the danger. Bindy all along had known the better way and followed it. The lukewarm was the worthless.

"Bindy, boy, where are you? I'm coming . . ." and stepping on to the grassy strip of ground, soft to his feet, he met a wind that fell upon his body with a shower of blows from all directions at once and beat him to his knees. He dropped, it seemed, into the cover of a sheltering rock, for there followed then a moment of sudden and delicious stillness in which the weary muscles recovered themselves and thought grew slightly steadier. Crouched thus close to the earth he no longer offered a target to the hurricane's attack. He peered upwards, making a screen of his hands.

The ridge, some fifty feet above him, he saw, ran in a generous platform along the mountain crest; it was wide and flat; between the enormous fires of piled-up wood that stretched for half a mile coiled a medley of dense smoke and tearing sparks. No human beings were visible, and yet he was aware of crowding life quite near. On hands and knees, crawling painfully, he then slowly retreated again into the shelter of the forest he had sought to leave. He stood up. The awful blaze was veiled by the roof of branches once more. But, as he rose, seizing a sapling to steady himself by, two hands caught him with violence from behind, and a familiar voice came shouting against his ear. Leysin, panting, dishevelled, and half broken with the speed, stood beside him.

"The boy! Where is he? We're just in time!" He roared the words to make them carry above the din. "Hurry, hurry! I'll follow. . . . My older legs . . . See, for the love of God, that he is not taken. . . . I warned you!"

And for a second, as he heard, Hendricks caught at the vanished sense of responsibility again. He saw the face of the old Marquess watching him among the tree trunks. He heard his voice, amazed, reproachful, furious: "It was criminal of you, criminal—!"

"Where is the boy—*your* boy?" again broke in the shout of the Pasteur with a slap of hurricane, as he staggered against the tutor, half collapsing, and trying to point the direction. "Watch him, find him for the love of heaven before it is too late—before they see him . . . !"

The tutor's normal and responsible self dived out of sight again as he heard the cry of weakness and alarm. It seemed the wind got under him, lifting him bodily from his feet. He did not pause to think. Like a man midway in a whirling prize-fight, he felt dazed but confident, only conscious of one thing—that he must hold out to the end, take part in all the splendid fighting—*win.* The lust of the arena, the pride of youth and battle, the impetuous recklessness of the charge in primitive war caught at his heart, brimming it with headlong courage. To play the game for all it might be worth seemed shouted everywhere about him, as the abandon of wind and fire rushed through him like a storm. He felt lifted above all possibility of little failure. The Marquess with his conventional traditions, the Pasteur with his considerations of half-way safety, both vanished utterly; safety, indeed, both for himself and for the boy in his charge lay in unconditional surrender. This was no time for little thought-out actions. It was all or nothing!

"God bless the whirlwind and the fire!" he shouted, opening wide his arms.

But his voice was inaudible amid the uproar, and the forward movement of his body remained at first only in the brain. He turned to push the old man aside, even to strike him down if necessary. "Lukewarm yourself and a coward!" rose in his throat, yet found no utterance, for in that moment a tall, slim figure, swift as a shadow, steady as a hawk, shot hard across the open space between the forest and the ridge. In the direction of the blazing platform it disappeared against a curtain of thick smoke, emerged for one second in a storm of light, then vanished finally behind a ruin of loose rocks. And Hendricks, his eyes wounded by heat and wind, his muscles paralysed, understood that the boy deliberately invited capture. The multitude that hid behind the smoke and fire, feeding the blazing heaps with eager hands, had become aware of him, and presently would appear to claim him. They would take him to themselves. Already answering flares ran east and west along the desolate ridge.

"I'll join you! I'm coming! Wait for me!" he tried to cry. The uproar smothered it.

VIII

And this uproar, he now perceived, was composed entirely of wind and fire. Here, on the roof of the hills beneath a starry sky, these two great elements expressed their nature with unhampered freedom, for there was neither rain to modify the one, nor solid obstacle to check the other. Their voices merged in a single sound—the hollow boom of wind and the deep, resounding clap of flame. The splitting crackle of burning branches imitated the high, shrill whistle of the tearing gusts that, javelin-like, flew to and fro in darts of swifter sound. But one shout rose from the summit, no human cry distinguishable in it, nor amid the thousand lines of skeleton wood that pierced the golden background was any human outline visible. Fire and wind encouraged one another to madness, manifesting in prodigious splendour by themselves.

Then, suddenly, before a gigantic canter of the wind, the driving smoke rolled upwards like a curtain, and the flames, ceasing their wild flapping, soared steadily in gothic windows of living gold towards the stars. In towering rows between columns of black night they transformed the empty space between them into a colossal temple aisle. They tapered aloft symmetrically into vanishing crests. And Hendricks stood upright. Rising so that his shoulders topped the edge of the boulder, and utterly contemptuous of Leysin's hand that sought with violence to drag him into shelter, he gazed as one who sees a vision. For at first he could only stand and stare, aware of sensation but not of thought. An enormous, overpowering conviction blew his whole being to white heat. Here was a supply of elemental power that human beings—empty, needy, starved, deficient human beings—could use. His love for the boy leaped headlong at the skirts of this terrific salvation. A majestic possibility stormed through him.

Yet it was no nightmare wonder that met his staring and half-shielded eyes, although some touch of awful dream seemed in it, set, moreover, to a scale that scantier minds might deem distortion. The heat from some thirty fires, placed at regular intervals, made midnight quiver with immense vibrations. Of varying, yet calculated size, these towering heaps emitted notes of measured and alternating depth, until the roar along the entire line produced a definite scale almost of melody, the near ones shrilly singing, those more distant booming with mountainous pedal notes. The consonance was monstrous, yet conformed to some magnificent diapason. This chord of fire-music paced the starlit sky, directed, but never overmastered, by the wind that measured it somehow into meaning. Repeated in quick succession, the notes now crashing in a mass, now singing alone in solitary beauty, the effect suggested an idea of ordered sequence, of gigantic rhythm. It seemed, indeed, as though some controlling agency, mastering excess, coerced both raging elements to express through this stupendous dance some definite idea. Here, as it were, was the alphabet of some natural, undifferentiated language, a language of sight and sound, predating speech, symbolical in the ultimate, deific sense. Some Lord of Fire and some Lord of Air were in command. Harnessed and regulated, these formless cohorts of energy that men call stupidly mere flame and wind, obeyed a higher power that had invoked them, yet a power that, by understanding their laws of being, held him most admirably in control.

This, at least, seems a hint of the explanation that flashed into Hendricks as he stared in amazed bewilderment from the shelter of the nearest boulder. He read a sentence in some natural, forgotten script. He watched a primitive ritual that once invoked the gods. He was aware of rhythm, and he was aware of system, though as yet he did not see the hand that wrote this marvellous sentence on the night. For still the human element remained invisible. He only realised—in dim, blundering fashion—that he witnessed a revelation of those two powers which, in large, lie at the foundations of the Universe, and, in little, are the basic essentials of human existence—the powers behind heat and air. Fragments of that talk with Leysin stammered back across his mind, like letters in some stupendous word he dared not reconstruct entire. He shuddered and grew wise. Realms of forgotten being opened their doors before his dazzled sight. Vision fluttered into far, piercing vistas of ancient wonder, haunting and half-remembered, then lost its way in blindness that was pain. For a moment, it seemed, he was aware of majestic Presences behind the turmoil, shadowy but mighty, charged with a vague potentiality as of immense algebraical formulæ, symbolical and beyond full comprehension, yet willing and able to be used for practical results. He *felt* the elements as nerves of a living Universe. . . . Yet thinking was not really in him anywhere; feeling was all he knew. The world he moved in, as the script he read, belonged to conditions too utterly remote for reason to recover a single clue to their intelligible reconstruction. Glory, clean and strong as of primitive star-worship, passed between what he saw and all that he had ever known before. The curtain of conventional belief was rent in twain. The terrific thing was true. . . .

For an unmeasured interval the tutor, oblivious of time and actual place, stood on the brink of this majestic pageant, staring with breathless awe, while the swaying of the entire scenery increased like the sway of an ocean lifted to the sky by many winds. Then, suddenly, in one of those temporary lulls that passed between the beat of the great notes, his searching eyes discovered a new thing. The focus of his sight was altered, and he realised at last the source of the directing and the controlling power. Behind the fires and beyond the smoke he recognised the disc-like, shining ovals that upon this little earth stand in the image of the one, eternal Likeness. He saw the human faces, symbols of spiritual dominion over all lesser orders, each one possessed of belief, intelligence, and will. Singly so feeble, together so invincible, this assemblage, unscorched by the fire and by the wind unmoved, seemed to him impressive beyond all possible words. And a further inkling of the truth flashed on him as he stared: that a group of humans, a crowd, combining upon a given object with concentrated purpose, possessed of that terrific power, certain faith, may know in themselves the energy to move great mountains, and therefore that lesser energy to guide the fluid forces of the elements. And a sense of cosmic exultation leaped into his being. For a moment he knew a touch of almost frenzy. Proud joy rose in him like a splendour of omnipotence. Humanity, it seemed to him, here came into a grand but long neglected corner of its kingdom as originally planned by heaven. Into the hands of a weakling and deficient boy the guidance had been given.

Motionless beneath the stars, lit by the glare till they shone like idols of yellow stone, and magnified by the sheets of flying, intolerable light the wind chased to and fro, these rows of faces appeared at first as a single line of undifferentiated fire against the background of the night. The eyes were all cast down in prayer, each mind focussed steadily upon one clear idea—the control and assimilation of two elemental powers. The crowd was one; feeling was one; desire, command, and certain faith were one. The controlling power that resulted was irresistible.

Then came a remarkable, concerted movement. With one accord the eyes all opened, blazing with reflected fire. A hundred human countenances rose in a single shining line. The men stood upright. Swarthy faces, tanned by sun and wind, heads uncovered, hair and beards tossing in the air, turned all one way. Mouths opened too. There came a roar that even the hurricane could not drown—a word of command, it seemed, that sprang into the pulses of the dancing elements and reduced their turmoil to a wave of steadier movement. And at the same moment a hundred bodies, naked above the waist, arms outstretched and hands with the palms held upwards, swayed forwards through the smoke and fire. They came towards the spot, where, half concealed from view, the tutor crouched and watched.

And Hendricks, thinking himself discovered, first quailed, then rose to meet them. No power to resist was in him. It was, rather, willing response that he experienced. He stepped out from the shelter of the boulder and entered the brilliant glare. Hatless himself, shoulders squared, cloak flying in the wind, he took three strides towards the advancing battalion—then, undecided, paused. For the line, he saw, disregarded him as though he were not there at all. It was not *him* the worshippers sought. The entire troop swept past to a point some fifty feet below where the end of the ridge broke out of the thinning trees.

Beautiful as a curving wave of flame, the figures streamed across the narrow, open space with a drilled precision as of some battle line, and Hendricks, with a sense of wild, secret triumph, saw them pause at the brink of the platformed ridge, form up their serried ranks yet closer, then open two hundred arms to welcome some one whom the darkness should immediately deliver. Simultaneously, from the covering trees, the tall, slim shadow of Lord Ernie darted out into the light.

"Magnificent!" cried Hendricks, but his voice was smothered instantly in a mightier sound, and his movement forward seemed ineffective stumbling. The hundred voices thundered out a single note. Like a deer the boy leaped; like a tongue of flame he flew to join his own; and instantly was surrounded, borne shoulder high upon those upturned palms, swept back in triumph towards the procession of enormous fires. Wrapped by smoke and sparks, lifted by wind, he became part of the monstrous rhythm that turned that mountain ridge alive. He stood upright upon the platform of interlacing arms; he swayed with their movements as a thing of wind and fire that flew. The shining faces vanished then, turned all towards the blazing piles so that the boy had the appearance of standing on a wall of living black. His outline was visible a moment against the sky, firelight between his wide-stretched legs, streaming from his hair and horizontal arms, issuing almost, as it seemed, from his very body. The next second he leaped to the ground, ran forward—appallingly close—between two heaped-up fires, flung both hands heavenwards, and—knelt.

And Hendricks, sympathetically following the boy's performance as though his own mind and body took part in it, experienced then a singular result: it seemed the heart in him began to roar. This was no rustle of excited blood that the little cavern of his skull increased, but a deeper sound that proclaimed the kinship of his entire being with the ritual. His own nature had begun to answer. From that moment he perceived the spectacle, not with the senses of sight and hearing, separately, but with his entire body—synthetically. He became a part of this assembly that was itself one single instrument: a cosmic sounding-board for the rhythmical expression of impersonal Nature Powers. Leysin, he dimly realised, fixed in his churchy tenets, remained outside, apart, and compromising; Hendricks accepted and went with. All little customary feelings dipped utterly away, lost, false, denied, even as a unit in a crowd loses its normal characteristics in the greater mood that sways the whole. The fire no longer burned him, for he was the fire; nor did he stagger against the furious wind, because the wind was in his heart. He moved all over, alive in every point and corner. With his skin he breathed, his bones and tissue ran with glorious heat. He cried aloud. He praised. "I am the whirlwind and I am the fire! Fire that lights but does not burn, and wind that blows the hearts to flame!" His body sang it, or rather the elements sang it through his body; for the sound of his voice was not audible, and it was wind and fire that thundered forth his feeling in their crashing rhythm.

IX

And so it was that he no longer saw this thing pictorially, nor in the little detached reports the individual senses brought, but knew it in himself complete, as a man knows love and passion. Memory afterwards translated these vast central feelings into pictures, but the pictures touched reality without containing it. Like a vision it happened all at once, as a room or landscape happens, and what happens all at once, coming through a synthesis of the senses, is not properly describable later. To instantaneous knowledge mere sequence is a falsehood. The sequence first comes in with the telling afterwards. That kneeling form, he understood, was the empty vessel to which conventional life had hitherto denied the heat and air it craved. The breath of life now poured at full tide into it, the fire of deity lit its heart of touchwood, wind blew into desire; and later flame would burst forth in action, consuming opposition. He must let it fill to the brim. It was not salvation, but creation. Then thought went out, extinguished by a puff of something greater. . . .

For beyond the smoke and sparks, beyond the space the men had occupied, a new and gentler movement, lyrical with bird-like beauty, ran suddenly along the ridge. What Hendricks had taken for branches heaped in rows for the burning, stirred marvellously throughout their whole collective mass, stirred sweetly, too, and with an exquisite loveliness. The entire line rose gracefully into the air with a whirr as of sweeping birds. There was a soft and undulating motion as though a draught of flowing wind turned faintly visible, yet with an increasing brilliance, like shining lilies of flame that now flocked forward in a troop, bending deliciously all one way. And in the same second these tall lilies of fire revealed themselves as figures, naked above the waist, hair streaming on the wind, eyes alight and bare arms waving. Above the men's deep pedal bass their voices rose with clear, shrill sweetness on the storm. The band swept forwards swift as wind towards the kneeling boy. The long line curved about him foldingly. The women took him as the south wind takes a bird.

There may have been—indeed, there was—an interval, for Hendricks caught, again and again repeated, the boy's great cry of passionate delight above the tumult. Ringing and virile it rose to heaven, clear as a fine-wrought bell. And instantaneously the knitted figures of flame disentangled themselves again, the mass unfolded like an opening flower, and, as by a military word of command, dissolved itself once more into a long thin line of running fire. The women advanced, and the waiting men flowed forward in a stream to meet them. This interweaving of the figures was as easily accomplished as the mingling of light and heavy threads upon some living loom. Hands joining hands, all singing, these naked worshippers of fire and wind passed in and out among the blazing piles with a headlong precision that was torrential and yet orderly. The speed increased; the faces flashed and vanished, then flashed and passed again; each woman between two men, each man between two women, and Lord Ernie, radiantly alive, between two girls of rich, o'erflowing beauty. Their movements were undulating, like the undulations of fire, yet with sudden, unexpected upward leaps as when fire is partnered abruptly by a cantering wind. For the women were fire, and the men were wind. The imitative dance was in full swing. The marvellous wind and fire ritual unrolled its old-world magic.

It was awe-inspiring certainly, but for Hendricks, as he watched, the terror of big conflagrations was wholly absent: rather, he felt the sense of deep security that rhythmic movement causes. Bathed in a sea of elemental power, he burned to share the pagan splendour and the rush of primitive delight. It seemed he had a cosmic body in which new centres stirred to life, linking him on to this source of natural forces. Through these centres he drew the chaotic energy into nerves and blood and muscle, into the very substance of his thought, indeed, transmuting them into the magic of the will. Abundant and inexhaustible vigour filled the air, pouring freely into whatever empty receptacle lay at hand. Sheets of flame, whole separate fragments of it, torn at the edges, raced, loudly, hungrily flapping on vehement gusts of wind; curved as they flew; leaped, twisted, flashed, and vanished. And the figures closely copied them. The women tossed their bodies aloft, then dipped suddenly to the earth, invisible, till the rushing men urged them into view again with wild impetuous swing, so that the entire line stretched and contracted like an immense elastic band of life, now knotted, now dissolved.

Yet, while of raging and terrific beauty, there was never that mad abandon which is disorder; but rather a kind of sacred natural revel that prohibited mere licence. There was even a singular austerity in it that betrayed a definite ritual and not mere reckless pageantry. No walls could possibly have contained it. In cathedral, temple, or measured space, however grand, it could only have seemed exaggerated and apostate; here, beneath the open sky, it was beautiful and true. For overhead the stars burned clear and steady, the constellations watching it from their immovable towers—a representation of their own leisured and hierarchic dance in swifter miniature. And indeed this relationship it bore to a universal rhythm was the key, it seemed, to its deep significance; for the close imitation of natural movements seduced the colossal powers of fire and wind to swell human emotions till they became mould and vessel for this elemental manifestation in men and women. Golden yellow in the blaze, the limbs of the women flashed and passed; their hair flew dark a moment across gleaming breasts; and their waving arms tossed in ever-shifting patterns through the driving smoke. The fires boiled and roared, scattering torrents of showering sparks like stars; and amid it all the slim, white shoulders of the boy, his clothes torn from him, his eyes ablaze, and his lips opened to the singing as though he had known it always, drove to and fro on the crest of the ritual like some flying figure of wind and fire incarnate.

All of which, instantaneously yet in sequence, Hendricks witnessed, painted upon the wild night sky. A volcanic energy poured through him too. He knew a golden enthusiasm of immeasurable strength, of unconquerable hope, of irresistible delight. Wind set his feet to dancing, and fire swept across his face without a trace of burning.

Nature was part of him. He had stepped inside. No obstacle existed that could withstand for a single second the torrential energy that fired his heart and blood. There was lightning in his veins. He could sweep aside life's difficult barriers with the ease of a tornado, and shake the rubbish of doubt and care from the years with earthquake shocks. Empires he could mould, and play with nations, drive men and women before him like a flock of sheep, shatter convention, and dislocate the machinery time has foisted upon natural energies. He knew in himself the omnipotence of the lesser elemental deities. Yet, as sympathetic observer, he can but have felt a tithe of what Lord Ernie felt.

"We are the whirlwind and we are the fire!" he cried aloud with the rushing worshippers. "We are unconquerable and immense! We destroy the lukewarm and absorb the weak! For we can make evil into good by bending it all one way! . . ."

The roar swept thunderingly past him, catching at his voice and body. He felt himself snatched forward by the wind. The fire licked sweetly at him. It was the final abandonment. He plunged recklessly towards the surge of dancers. . . .

X

What stopped him he did not know. Some hard and steely thing pricked sharply into him. An opposing power, fierce as a sword, stabbed at his heart—and he heard a little sound quite close beside him, a sound that pierced the babel, reaching his consciousness as from far away.

"Keep still! Cling tight to this old rock! Hold yourself in, or else they'll have you too!"

It was as if some insect scratched within his ear. His arm, that same instant, was violently seized. He came down with a crash. He had been half in the air. He had been dancing.

"Turn your eyes away, away! Take hold of this big tree!" The voice cried furiously, but with a petty human passion in it that marred the world. There was an intolerable revulsion in him as he heard it. He felt himself dragged forcibly backwards. He lost his balance, stumbling among loose stones.

"Loose me! Let me go!" he shouted, struggling like a wild animal, yet vainly, against the inflexible grip that held him. "I am one with the fire that lights but does not burn. I am the wind that blows the worlds along. Damnation take you. . . . Let me free! . . ."

Confusion caught him, smothering speech and blinding sight. He fell backwards, away from the heat and wind. He was furious, but furious with he knew not whom or what. The interference had destroyed the rhythm, broken it into fragments. Violent impulses clashed through him without the will to choose or guide them. For power had deserted him and flowed elsewhere. He stood no longer in the stream of energy. He was emptied. And at first he could not tell whether his instinct was to return himself, to rescue his precious boy, or—to crush the interfering object out of existence with what was left to him of raging anger. He turned, stood up, and flung the Pasteur aside with violence. He raised his feet to stamp and kill . . . when a phrase with meaning darted suddenly across his wild confusion and recalled him to some fragment of truer responsibility and life.

". . . There'll be only violence in him—reckless violence instead of strength—destructive. Save him before it is too late!"

"It *is* too late," he roared in answer. "What devil hinders me?"

But his roar was feeble, and his ironed boots refused the stamping. Power slipped wholly out of him. The rhythm poured past, instead of through him. Interference had destroyed the circuit. More glimmerings of responsibility came back. He stooped like a drunken man and helped the other to his feet. The rapidity of the change was curious, proving that the spell had been put upon him from without. It was not, as with the boy, mere development of pre-existing tendencies.

"Help me," he implored suddenly instead, "help me! There has been madness in me. For God's sake, help me to get him out!" It seemed the face of the old Marquess, stern and terrible, broke an instant through the smoky air, black with reproach and anger. And, with a violent effort of the will, Hendricks turned round to face the elemental orgy, bent on rescue. But this time the heat was intolerable and drove him back. The hair, hitherto untouched, now singed upon his head. Fire licked his very breath away. He bent double, covering his face with arms and cloak.

"Pray!" shouted Leysin, dropping to his knees. "It is the only way. My God is higher than this. Pray, pray!"

And, automatically, Hendricks fell upon his knees beside him, though to pray he knew not how. For no real faith was in him as in the other, and his eye was far from single. The fast fading grandeur of what he had experienced still left its pagan tumult in his blood. The pretence of prayer could only have been blasphemy. He watched instead, letting the other invoke his mighty Deity alone, that Deity he had served, unflinchingly all his life with faith and fasting, and with belief beyond assault.

It was an impressive picture, fraught with passionate drama. On his knees behind a sheltering boulder, a blackened pine-tree tossing scorched branches above his head, this righteous man prayed to his God, sure of his triumphant answer. Hendricks watched with an admiration that made him realise his own insignificance. The eyes were closed, the leonine big head set firm upon the diminutive body, the face now lit by flame, now veiled by smoke, the strong hands clasped together and upraised. He envied him. He recognised, too, that the elements themselves, with all their chaos of might and terror, were after all but servants of the Vastness which dips the butterflies in colour and puts down upon the breasts of little robins. And, because the Pasteur's life had been always prayer in action, his little human will invoked the Will of Greatness, merged with it, used it, and directed it steadily against the commotion of these unleashed elements. Certain of himself and of his God, the Pasteur never doubted. His prayer set instantly in action those forces which balance suns and keep the stars afloat.

Thus, trembling with terror that made him wholly ineffective, Hendricks watched, and, as he watched, became aware of the amazing change. For it seemed as if a stream of power, steady and in opposition to the tumult, now poured audaciously against the elemental rhythm, altering its direction, modifying gradually its stupendous impetus. There were pauses in the huge vibrations: they wavered, broke, and fled. They knew confusion, as when the prow of a steel-nosed vessel drives against the tide. The tide is vaster, but the steel is—different. The whole sky shivered, as this new entering force, so small, so soft, yet of such incalculable energy, began at once its overmastering effect. Signs of violence or rout, or of anything disordered, had no part in it; excess before it slipped into willing harness; there was light that sponged away all glare, as when morning sunshine cleans a forest of its shadows. Some little whispering power sang marvellously as of old across the desolate big mountains, "Peace! Be still!" turning the monstrous turbulence into obedient sweetness. And upon his face and hands Hendricks felt faint, delicate touches of some refreshing softness that he could not understand.

Yet not instantly was this harmony restored; at first there was the stress of vehement opposition. The night of wind and fire drove roaring through the sky. There were bursts of triumphant tumult, but convulsion in them and no true steadiness as before. The human figures hitherto had danced with that fluid appearance which belongs to fire, and with that instantaneous rush which is of wind, the men increasing the women, and the women answering with joy; limbs and faces had melted into each other till the circular ritual looked like a glowing wheel of flame rotating audibly. But slowly now the speed of the wheel decreased; the single utterance was marred by the crying of many voices, all at different pitch, discordant, inharmonious, dismayed. The fires somehow dwindled; there came pauses in the wind; and Hendricks became aware of a curious hissing noise, as more and more of these odd soft touches found his face and hands. Here and there, he saw, a figure stumbled, fell, then gathered itself clumsily together again with a frightened shout, breaking violently out of the circle. More and more these figures blundered and dropped out; and although they returned again, so that the dance apparently increased, these were but moments in the final violence of the dispersing hurricane. The rejected ones dashed back wildly into the wrong places; men and women no longer stood alternate, but in groups together, falsely related. The entire movement was dislocated; the ceremony grew rapidly incoherent; meaning forsook it. The composite instrument that had transmuted the elemental forces into human, emotional storage was imperfect, broken, out of tune. The disarray turned rout.

And then it was, while Leysin continued without ceasing his burning and successful prayer, that his companion, conscious of returning harmony, rose to his feet, aware suddenly that he could also help. A portion of the powers he had absorbed still worked in him, but in a new direction. He felt confident and unafraid. He did not stumble. With unerring tread he advanced towards the lessening fires, feeling as he did so the cold soft touches multiply with a rush upon his skin. From all sides they came by hundreds, like messengers of help.

"Ernest!" he cried aloud, and his voice, though little raised, carried resonantly above the dying turmoil; "Ernest! Come back to us. Your father calls you!"

And from threescore faces hurrying in confusion through the smoke, one paused and turned. It stood apart, hovering as though in air, while the mob of disordered figures rushed in a body along the ridge. Plunging like frightened cattle below the farther edge, then vanishing into thick darkness, they left behind them this one solitary face. A final dying flame licked out at it; a rush of smoke drove past to hide it; there was a high, wild scream—and the figure shot forward with a headlong leap and fell with a crash at Hendricks' feet. Lord Ernie, blackened by smoke and scorched by fire, lay safe outside the danger zone.

And Hendricks knelt beside him. Remorse and shame made him powerless to do more as he pulled the torn clothing over the neck and chest and heard his own heart begging for forgiveness. He realised his own weakness and faithlessness. A great temptation had found him wanting. . . .

It was owing to Leysin that the rescue was complete. The Pasteur was instantly by his side.

"Saved as by water," he cried, as he folded his cloak about the prostrate body, and then raised the head and shoulders; "saved by His ministers of rain. For His miracles are love, and work through natural laws."

He made a sign to Hendricks. Carrying the boy between them, they scrambled down the slope into the shelter of the trees below. The cold, soft touches were then explained. The *joran* had dropped as suddenly as it rose, and the torrential rain that invariably follows now poured in rivers from the sky. Water, drenching the fires and padding the savage wind, had stopped the dancers midway in their frenzied ritual. It was the element they dreaded, for it was hostile. Rain soused the mountain ridge, extinguishing the last embers of the numerous fires. It rushed in rivulets between their feet. The heated earth gave out a hissing steam, and the only sound in the spaces where wind and fire had boomed and thundered a little while before was now the splash of water and the drip of quenching drops.

In the cover of the sheltering trees the body stirred, lifted its head, and sat up slowly. The eyes opened.

"I'm cold. I'm frightened," whispered a shivering voice. "Where am I?"

Only the pelt and thud of the rain sounded behind the quavering words.

"Where are the others? Have I been away? Hendricks—Mr. Hendricks—is that you—?"

He stared about him, his face now a mere luminous disc in the thick darkness. No breath of wind was loose. They spoke to him till he answered with assurance, groping to find their hands with his own, his words confused and strange with hidden meaning for a time. "I'm all right now," he kept repeating. "I know exactly. It was one of my big dreams. . . . I suppose I fell asleep . . . and the rain woke me. Great heavens! What a night to be out." And then he clambered vigorously to his feet with a sudden movement of great energy again, saying that hunger was in him and he must eat. There was no complaint of heat or cold, of burning or of bruises. The boy recovered marvellously. In ten minutes, breaking away from all support, he led, as they descended through the dripping forest in the gloom and chill of very early morning. It was the others who called to him for guidance in the tangled woods. Lord Ernie was in the lead. Throughout the difficult woods he was ever in front, and singing:

"Fire that lights but does not burn! And wind that blows the heart to flame! They both are in me now for ever and ever! Oh, praise the Lord of Fire and the Lord of Wind . . . !"

And this voice, now near, now distant, sounding through the dripping forest on their homeward journey, was an experience weird and unforgettable for those other two. Leysin, it seemed, had one sentence only which he kept repeating to himself—"Heaven grant he may direct it all for good. For they have filled him to the brim, and he is become an instrument of power."

But Hendricks, though he understood the risk, felt only confidence. Lord Ernie's regeneration had begun.

Soaked and bedraggled, all three, they reached the village about two o'clock. The boy, utterly unmanageable, said an emphatic No to spirits, soup, or medical appliances. His skin, indeed, showed no signs of burning, nor was there the smallest symptom of cold or fever in him. "I'm a perfect furnace," he laughed; "I feel health and strength personified." And the brightness of his eyes, his radiant colour, the vigour of his voice and manner—both in some way astonishing—made all pretence of assistance unnecessary and absurd. "It's like a new birth," he cried to Hendricks, as he almost cantered beside him down the road to their house, "and, by Jove, I'll wake 'em up at home and make the world go round. I know a hundred schemes. I tell you, sir, I'm simply bursting! For the first time I'm alive!"

And an hour later, when the tutor peeped in upon him, the boy was calmly sleeping. The candlelight, shaded carefully with one hand, fell upon the face. There were new lines and a new expression in it. Will and purpose showed in the stern set of the lips and jaw. It was the face of a man, and of a man one would not lightly trifle with. Purpose, will, and power were established on their thrones. To such a man the entire world might one day bow the head.

"If only it will last," thought Hendricks, as, shaken, bewildered, and more than a little awed, he tiptoed out of the room again and went to bed. But through his dreams, sheeted in flame and veiled in angry smoke, the face of the old Marquess glowered upon him from a heavy sky above ancestral towers.

XI

From the obituary notices of the 9th Marquess of Oakham the following selections have their interest: He succeeded to his father, then in the Cabinet as Minister for Foreign Affairs, at the age of twenty-one. His career was brief but singular, the early magnificence of the younger Pitt offering a standard of comparison, though by no means a parallel, to his short record of astonishing achievement. His effect upon the world, first as Chief of the Government Labour Department and subsequently as Home Secretary, and Minister of War, is described as shattering, even cataclysmic. His public life lasted five years. He died at the age of twenty-nine. His personality was revolutionary and overwhelming.

For, judging by these extracts, he was a "Napoleonic figure whose personal influence combined the impetus of Mirabeau and the dominance of Alexander. His authority held an incalculable element, precisely described as uncanny. His spirit was puissant, elemental, his activity irresistible." Yet, according to another journal, "he was, properly speaking, neither intellectual, astute, nor diplomatic, and possessed as little subtlety as might be expected of a miner whose psychology was called upon to explain the Trinity. In no sense was he Statesman, and even less strategist, yet his name swept Europe, changed the map of the Nearer East, its mere whisper among the Chancelleries convulsing men's counsels with an influence almost menacing."

His enthusiasm appears to have been amazing. "Some stupendous and untiring energy drove through him, paralysing attack, and rendering the bitterest and most skilful opposition nugatory. His hand was imperious, upsetting with a touch the chessboards set by the most able statecraft, and his voice was heard with a kind of reverence in every capital."

The brevity of his astonishing career called for universal comment, as did the hypnotising effect of his singular ascendancy. "In five short years of power he achieved his sway. He rushed upon the world, he shook it, he retired," as one journal picturesquely phrased it. "The manner of his ending, moreover—a stroke of lightning,—seemed in keeping with his life. There was neither lingering, delay, nor warning. Of distinguished stock, noble, yet ordinary enough in all but name, his power is unexplained by heredity; his family furnished no approach to greatness, as history supplied no parallel to his dynamic intensity. Nor, we are informed, among his near of kin, does any inherit his volcanic energy."

The world, however, was apparently well relieved of his tumultuous presence, for his influence was generally surveyed as "destructive rather than constructive." He was unmarried, and the title went to a nephew.

The cheaper journals abounded, of course, in details of his personal and private life that were freely copied into the foreign press, and supply curious material for the student of human nature and the psychologist. The amazing revelations no doubt were picturesquely exaggerated, yet the substratum of truth in them all was generally admitted. No contradictions, at any rate, appeared. They read like the story of some primitive, wild giant let loose upon the world—primitive, because his specific brain power was admittedly of no high order; wild, because he was in favour of fierce, spontaneous action, and his mere presence, on occasions, could stir a nation, not alone a crowd, to vehement, terrific methods. His energy seemed inexhaustible, his fire inextinguishable.

Legends were rife, even before he died, among the peasantry of his Scotch estates, that he was in league with the devil. His habit of keeping enormous fires in his private rooms, fires that burned day and night from January to December, and in open hearths widened to thrice their natural size, stimulated the growth of this particular myth among those of his personal environment. All manner of stories raged. But it was his strange custom out-of-doors that provided the diabolical suggestion. For, "behind a specially walled-in space on an open ridge, denuded of pines, in a distant part of the estate, a series of gigantic heaps of wood, all ready to ignite, were—it was said—kept in a state of constant preparedness. And on stormy nights, especially when winds were high, and invariably at the period of the equinoctial tempests, his lordship would himself light these tremendous bonfires, and spend the nocturnal hours in their blazing presence, communing, the stories variously relate, with the witches at their Sabbath, or with hordes of fire-spirits, who emerged from the Bottomless Pit in order to feed his soul with their unquenchable supplies. From these nightly orgies, it seems clear, at any rate, he returned at dawn with a splendour of energy that no one could resist, and with a mien whose grandeur invited worship rather than inspired alarm."

His biography, it was further stated, would be written by Sir John Hendricks, Bt., who began life as Private Secretary to his father, the 8th Marquess, but whose rapid rise to position was due to his intimate association as trusted friend and adviser to the subject of these obituary notices. The biography, however, had not appeared, within five years of Lord Oakham's sudden death, and curiosity is only further stimulated by the suggestive whisper that it never will, and never can appear.

The Damned

I

I'm over forty, Frances, and rather sot in my ways," I said good-naturedly, ready to yield if she insisted that our going together on the visit involved her happiness. "My work is rather heavy just now too, as you know. The question is, *could* I work there—with a lot of unassorted people in the house?"

"Mabel doesn't mention any other people, Bill," was my sister's rejoinder. "I gather she's alone—as well as lonely."

By the way she looked sideways out of the window at nothing, it was obvious she was disappointed, but to my surprise she did not urge the point; and as I glanced at Mrs. Franklyn's invitation lying upon her sloping lap the neat, childish handwriting conjured up a mental picture of the banker's widow, with her timid, insignificant personality, her pale grey eyes and her expression as of a backward child. I thought, too, of the roomy country mansion her late husband had altered to suit his particular needs, and of my visit to it a few years ago when its barren spaciousness suggested a wing of Kensington Museum fitted up temporarily as a place to eat and sleep in. Comparing it mentally with the poky Chelsea flat where I and my sister kept impecunious house, I realised other points as well. Unworthy details flashed across me to entice: the fine library, the organ, the quiet work-room I should have, perfect service, the delicious cup of early tea, and hot baths at any moment of the day—without a geyser!

"It's a longish visit, a month—isn't it?" I hedged, smiling at the details that seduced me, and ashamed of my man's selfishness, yet knowing that Frances expected it of me. "There *are* points about it, I admit. If you're set on my going with you, I could manage it all right."

I spoke at length in this way because my sister made no answer. I saw her tired eyes gazing into the dreariness of Oakley Street and felt a pang strike through me. After a pause, in which again she said no word, I added: "So, when you write the letter, you might hint, perhaps, that I usually work all the morning, and—er—am not a very lively visitor! Then she'll understand, you see." And I half-rose to return to my diminutive study, where I was slaving, just then, at an absorbing article on Comparative Æsthetic Values in the Blind and Deaf.

But Frances did not move. She kept her grey eyes upon Oakley Street where the evening mist from the river drew mournful perspectives into view. It was late October. We heard the omnibuses thundering across the bridge. The monotony of that broad, characterless street seemed more than usually depressing. Even in June sunshine it was dead, but with autumn its melancholy soaked into every house between King's Road and the Embankment. It washed thought into the past, instead of inviting it hopefully towards the future. For me, its easy width was an avenue through which nameless slums across the river sent creeping messages of depression, and I always regarded it as Winter's main entrance into London—fog, slush, gloom trooped down it every November, waving their forbidding banners till March came to rout them. Its one claim upon my love was that the south wind swept sometimes unobstructed up it, soft with suggestions of the sea. These lugubrious thoughts I naturally kept to myself, though I never ceased to regret the little flat whose cheapness had seduced us. Now, as I watched my sister's impassive face, I realised that perhaps she, too, felt as I felt, yet, brave woman, without betraying it.

"And, look here, Fanny," I said, putting a hand upon her shoulder as I crossed the room, "it would be the very thing for you. You're worn out with catering and housekeeping. Mabel is your oldest friend, besides, and you've hardly seen her since *he* died—"

"She's been abroad for a year, Bill, and only just came back," my sister interposed. "She came back rather unexpectedly, though I never thought she would go *there* to live—" She stopped abruptly. Clearly, she was only speaking half her mind. "Probably," she went on, "Mabel wants to pick up old links again."

"Naturally," I put in, "yourself chief among them." The veiled reference to the house I let pass. It involved discussing the dead man for one thing.

"I feel *I* ought to go anyhow," she resumed, "and of course it would be jollier if you came too. You'd get in such a muddle here by yourself, and eat wrong things, and forget to air the rooms, and—oh, everything!" She looked up laughing. "Only," she added, "there's the British Museum—?"

"But there's a big library there," I answered, "and all the books of reference I could possibly want. It was of you I was thinking. You could take up your painting again; you always sell half of what you paint. It would be a splendid rest too, and Sussex is a jolly country to walk in. By all means, Fanny, I advise—"

Our eyes met, as I stammered in my attempts to avoid expressing the thought that hid in both our minds. My sister had a weakness for dabbling in the various "new" theories of the day, and Mabel, who before her marriage had belonged to foolish societies for investigating the future life to the neglect of the present one, had fostered this undesirable tendency. Her amiable, impressionable temperament was open to every psychic wind that blew. I deplored, detested the whole business. But even more than this I abhorred the later influence that Mr. Franklyn had steeped his wife in, capturing her body and soul in his sombre doctrines. I had dreaded lest my sister also might be caught.

"Now that she is alone again—"

I stopped short. Our eyes now made pretence impossible, for the truth had slipped out inevitably, stupidly, although unexpressed in definite language. We laughed, turning our faces a moment to look at other things in the room. Frances picked up a book and examined its cover as though she had made an important discovery, while I took my case out and lit a cigarette I did not want to smoke. We left the matter there. I went out of the room before further explanation could cause tension. Disagreements grow into discord from such tiny things—wrong adjectives, or a chance inflection of the voice. Frances had a right to her views of life as much as I had. At least, I reflected comfortably, we had separated upon an agreement this time, recognised mutually, though not actually stated.

And this point of meeting was, oddly enough, our way of regarding some one who was dead. For we had both disliked the husband with a great dislike, and during his three years' married life had only been to the house once—for a week-end visit; arriving late on Saturday, we had left after an early breakfast on Monday morning. Ascribing my sister's dislike to a natural jealousy at losing her old friend, I said merely that he displeased me. Yet we both knew that the real emotion lay much deeper. Frances, loyal, honourable creature, had kept silence; and beyond saying that house and grounds—he altered one and laid out the other—distressed her as an expression of his personality somehow ("distressed" was the word she used), no further explanation had passed her lips.

Our dislike of his personality was easily accounted for—up to a point, since both of us shared the artist's point of view that a creed, cut to measure and carefully dried, was an ugly thing, and that a dogma to which believers must subscribe or perish everlastingly was a barbarism resting upon cruelty. But while my own dislike was purely due to an abstract worship of Beauty, my sister's had another twist in it, for with her "new" tendencies, she believed that all religions were an aspect of truth and that no one, even the lowest wretch, could escape "heaven" in the long run.

Samuel Franklyn, the rich banker, was a man universally respected and admired, and the marriage, though Mabel was fifteen years his junior, won general applause; his bride was an heiress in her own right—breweries—and the story of her conversion at a revivalist meeting where Samuel Franklyn had spoken fervidly of heaven, and terrifyingly of sin, hell, and damnation, even contained a touch of genuine romance. She was a brand snatched from the burning; his detailed eloquence had frightened her into heaven; salvation came in the nick of time; his words had plucked her from the edge of that lake of fire and brimstone where their worm dieth not and the fire is not quenched. She regarded him as a hero, sighed her relief upon his saintly shoulder, and accepted the peace he offered her with a grateful resignation.

For her husband was a "religious man" who successfully combined great riches with the glamour of winning souls. He was a portly figure, though tall, with masterful, big hands, his fingers rather thick and red; and his dignity, that just escaped being pompous, held in it something that was implacable. A convinced assurance, almost remorseless, gleamed in his eyes when he preached especially, and his threats of hell fire must have scared souls stronger than the timid, receptive Mabel whom he married. He clad himself in long frock-coats that buttoned unevenly, big square boots, and trousers that invariably bagged at the knee and were a little short; he wore low collars, spats occasionally, and a tall black hat that was not of silk. His voice was alternately hard and unctuous; and he regarded theatres, ball-rooms, and race-courses as the vestibule of that brimstone lake of whose geography he was as positive as of his great banking offices in the City. A philanthropist up to the hilt, however, no one ever doubted his complete sincerity; his convictions were ingrained, his faith borne out by his life—as witness his name upon so many admirable Societies, as treasurer, patron, or heading the donation list. He bulked large in the world of doing good, a broad and stately stone in the rampart against evil. And his heart was genuinely kind and soft for others—who believed as he did.

Yet in spite of this true sympathy with suffering and his desire to help, he was narrow as a telegraph wire and unbending as a church pillar; he was intensely selfish; intolerant as an officer of the Inquisition, his bourgeois soul constructed a revolting scheme of heaven that was reproduced in miniature in all he did and planned. Faith was the *sine qua non* of salvation, and by "faith" he meant belief in his own particular view of things—"which faith, except every one do keep whole and undefiled, without doubt he shall perish everlastingly." All the world but his own small, exclusive sect must be damned eternally—a pity, but alas, inevitable. *He* was right.

Yet he prayed without ceasing, and gave heavily to the poor—the only thing he could not give being big ideas to his provincial and suburban deity. Pettier than an insect, and more obstinate than a mule, he had also the superior, sleek humility of a "chosen one." He was churchwarden, too. He read the Lessons in a "place of worship," either chilly or overheated, where neither organ, vestments, nor lighted candles were permitted, but where the odour of hairwash on the boys' heads in the back rows pervaded the entire building.

This portrait of the banker, who accumulated riches both on earth and in heaven, may possibly be overdrawn, however, because Frances and I were "artistic temperaments" that viewed the type with a dislike and distrust amounting to contempt. The majority considered Samuel Franklyn a worthy man and a good citizen. The majority, doubtless, held the saner view. A few years more, and he certainly would have been made a baronet. He relieved much suffering in the world, as assuredly as he caused many souls the agonies of torturing fear by his emphasis upon damnation. Had there been one point of beauty in him, we might have been more lenient; only we found it not, and, I admit, took little pains to search. I shall never forget the look of dour forgiveness with which he heard our excuses for missing Morning Prayers that Sunday morning of our single visit to The Towers. My sister learned that a change was made soon afterwards, prayers being "conducted" after breakfast instead of before.

The Towers stood solemnly upon a Sussex hill amid park-like modern grounds, but the house cannot better be described—it would be so wearisome for one thing—than by saying that it was a cross between an overgrown, pretentious Norwood villa and one of those saturnine Institutes for cripples the train passes as it slinks ashamed through South London into Surrey. It was "wealthily" furnished and at first sight imposing, but on closer acquaintance revealed a meagre personality, barren and austere. One looked for Rules and Regulations on the walls, all signed By Order. The place was a prison that shut out "the world." There was, of course, no billiard-room, no smoking-room, no room for play of any kind, and the great hall at the back, once a chapel which might have been used for dancing, theatricals, or other innocent amusements, was consecrated in his day to meetings of various kinds, chiefly brigades, temperance or missionary societies. There was a harmonium at one end—on the level floor—a raised dais or platform at the other, and a gallery above for the servants, gardeners, and coachmen. It was heated with hot-water pipes, and hung with Doré's pictures, though these latter were soon removed and stored out of sight in the attics as being too unspiritual. In polished, shiny wood, it was a representation in miniature of that poky exclusive Heaven he took about with him, externalising it in all he did and planned, even in the grounds about the house.

Changes in The Towers, Frances told me, had been made during Mabel's year of widowhood abroad—an organ put into the big hall, the library made liveable and recatalogued—when it was permissible to suppose she had found her soul again and returned to her normal, healthy views of life, which included enjoyment and play, literature, music, and the arts, without, however, a touch of that trivial thoughtlessness usually termed worldliness. Mrs. Franklyn, as I remembered her, was a quiet little woman, shallow, perhaps, and easily influenced, but sincere as a dog and thorough in her faithful friendship. Her tastes at heart were catholic, and that heart was simple and unimaginative. That she took up with the various movements of the day was a sign merely that she was searching in her limited way for a belief that should bring her peace. She was, in fact, a very ordinary woman, her calibre a little less than that of Frances. I knew they used to discuss all kinds of theories together, but as these discussions never resulted in action, I had come to regard her as harmless. Still, I was not sorry when she married, and I did not welcome now a renewal of the former intimacy. The philanthropist had given her no children, or she would have made a good and sensible mother. No doubt she would marry again.

"Mabel mentions that she's been alone at The Towers since the end of August," Frances told me at tea-time; "and I'm sure she feels out of it and lonely. It would be a kindness to go. Besides, I always liked her."

I agreed. I had recovered from my attack of selfishness. I expressed my pleasure.

"You've written to accept," I said, half statement and half question.

Frances nodded. "I thanked for you," she added quietly, "explaining that you were not free at the moment, but that later, if not inconvenient, you might come down for a bit and join me."

I stared. Frances sometimes had this independent way of deciding things. I was convicted, and punished into the bargain.

Of course there followed argument and explanation, as between brother and sister who were affectionate, but the recording of our talk could be of little interest. It was arranged thus, Frances and I both satisfied. Two days later she departed for The Towers, leaving me alone in the flat with everything planned for my comfort and good behaviour—she was rather a tyrant in her quiet way—and her last words as I saw her off from Charing Cross rang in my head for a long time after she was gone:

"I'll write and let you know, Bill. Eat properly, mind, and let me know if anything goes wrong."

She waved her small gloved hand, nodded her head till the feather brushed the window, and was gone.

II

After the note announcing her safe arrival a week of silence passed, and then a letter came; there were various suggestions for my welfare, and the rest was the usual rambling information and description Frances loved, generously italicised.

". . . and we are quite alone," she went on in her enormous handwriting that seemed such a waste of space and labour, "though some others are coming presently, I believe. You could work here to your heart's content. Mabel *quite* understands, and says she would love to have you when you feel free to come. She has changed a bit—back to her old natural self: she never mentions *him*. The place has changed too in certain ways: it has more cheerfulness, I think. *She* has put it in, this cheerfulness, spaded it in, if you know what I mean; but it lies about uneasily and is not natural—quite. The organ is a beauty. She must be very rich now, but she's as gentle and sweet as ever. Do you know, Bill, I think he must have *frightened* her into marrying him. I get the impression she was afraid of him." This last sentence was inked out, but I read it through the scratching; the letters being too big to hide. "He had an inflexible will beneath all that oily kindness which passed for spiritual. He was a real personality, I mean. I'm sure he'd have sent you and me cheerfully to the stake in another century—*for our own good.* Isn't it odd she never speaks of him, even to me?" This, again, was stroked through, though without the intention to obliterate—merely because it was repetition, probably. "The only reminder of him in the house now is a big copy of the presentation portrait that stands on the stairs of the Multitechnic Institute at Peckham—you know—that life-size one with his fat hand sprinkled with rings resting on a thick Bible and the other slipped between the buttons of a tight frock-coat. It hangs in the dining-room and rather dominates our meals. I wish Mabel would take it down. I think she'd like to, if she *dared.* There's not a single photograph of him anywhere, even in her own room. Mrs. Marsh is here—you remember her, *his* housekeeper, the wife of the man who got penal servitude for killing a baby or something,—*you* said she robbed him and justified her stealing because the story of the unjust steward was in the Bible! How we laughed over that! *She's* just the same, too, gliding about all over the house and turning up when least expected."

Other reminiscences filled the next two sides of the letter, and ran, without a trace of punctuation, into instructions about a Salamander stove for heating my work-room in the flat; these were followed by things I was to tell the cook, and by requests for several articles she had forgotten and would like sent after her, two of them blouses, with descriptions so lengthy and contradictory that I sighed as I read them—"unless you come down soon, in which case perhaps you wouldn't mind bringing them; *not* the mauve one I wear in the evening sometimes, but the pale blue one with lace round the collar and the crinkly front. They're in the cupboard—or the drawer, I'm not sure which—of my bedroom. *Ask Annie* if you're in doubt. Thanks most *awfully*. Send a telegram, remember, and we'll meet you in the motor any time. I don't quite know if I shall stay the whole month—*alone*. It all depends. . . ." And she closed the letter, the italicised words increasing recklessly towards the end, with a repetition that Mabel would love to have me "for myself," as also to have a "man in the house," and that I only had to telegraph the day and the train. . . . This letter, coming by the second post, interrupted me in a moment of absorbing work, and, having read it through to make sure there was nothing requiring instant attention, I threw it aside and went on with my notes and reading. Within five minutes, however, it was back at me again. That restless thing called "between the lines" fluttered about my mind. My interest in the Balkan States—political article that had been "ordered" —faded. Somewhere, somehow I felt disquieted, disturbed. At first I persisted in my work, forcing myself to concentrate, but soon found that a layer of new impressions floated between the article and my attention. It was like a shadow, though a shadow that dissolved upon inspection. Once or twice I glanced up, expecting to find some one in the room, that the door had opened unobserved and Annie was waiting for instructions. I heard the 'buses thundering across the bridge. I was aware of Oakley Street. Montenegro and the blue Adriatic melted into the October haze along that depressing Embankment that aped a river bank, and sentences from the letter flashed before my eyes and stung me. Picking it up and reading it through more carefully, I rang the bell and told Annie to find the blouses and pack them for the post, showing her finally the written description, and resenting the superior smile with which she at once interrupted, "*I* know them, sir," and disappeared.

But it was not the blouses: it was that exasperating thing "between the lines" that put an end to my work with its elusive teasing nuisance. The first sharp impression is alone of value in such a case, for once analysis begins the imagination constructs all kinds of false interpretation. The more I thought, the more I grew fuddled. The letter, it seemed to me, wanted to say another thing; instead the eight sheets *conveyed* it merely. It came to the edge of disclosure, then halted. There was something on the writer's mind, and I felt uneasy. Studying the sentences brought, however, no revelation, but increased confusion only; for while the uneasiness remained, the first clear hint had vanished. In the end I closed my books and went out to look up another matter at the British Museum Library. Perhaps I should discover it that way—by turning the mind in a totally new direction. I lunched at the Express Dairy in Oxford Street close by, and telephoned to Annie that I would be home to tea at five.

And at tea, tired physically and mentally after breathing the exhausted air of the Rotunda for five hours, my mind suddenly delivered up its original impression, vivid and clear-cut; no proof accompanied the revelation; it was mere presentiment, but convincing. Frances was disturbed in her mind, her orderly, sensible, housekeeping mind; she was uneasy, even perhaps afraid; something in the house distressed her, and she had need of me. Unless I went down, her time of rest and change, her quite necessary holiday, in fact, would be spoilt. She was too unselfish to say this, but it ran everywhere between the lines. I saw it clearly now. Mrs. Franklyn, moreover—and that meant Frances, too—would like a "man in the house." It was a disagreeable phrase, a suggestive way of hinting something she dared not state definitely. The two women in that great, lonely barrack of a house were afraid.

My sense of duty, affection, unselfishness, whatever the composite emotion may be termed, was stirred; also my vanity. I acted quickly, lest reflection should warp clear, decent judgment. "Annie," I said, when she answered the bell, "you need not send those blouses by the post. I'll take them down to-morrow when I go. I shall be away a week or two, possibly longer." And, having looked up a train, I hastened out to telegraph before I could change my fickle mind.

But no desire came that night to change my mind. I was doing the right, the necessary thing. I was even in something of a hurry to get down to The Towers as soon as possible. I chose an early afternoon train.

III

A telegram had told me to come to a town ten miles from the house, so I was saved the crawling train to the local station, and travelled down by an express. As soon as we left London the fog cleared off, and an autumn sun, though without heat in it, painted the landscape with golden browns and yellows. My spirits rose as I lay back in the luxurious motor and sped between the woods and hedges. Oddly enough, my anxiety of overnight had disappeared. It was due, no doubt, to that exaggeration of detail which reflection in loneliness brings. Frances and I had not been separated for over a year, and her letters from The Towers told so little. It had seemed unnatural to be deprived of those intimate particulars of mood and feeling I was accustomed to. We had such confidence in one another, and our affection was so deep. Though she was but five years younger than myself, I regarded her as a child. My attitude was fatherly. In return, she certainly mothered me with a solicitude that never cloyed. I felt no desire to marry while she was still alive. She painted in water-colours with a reasonable success, and kept house for me; I wrote, reviewed books, and lectured on æsthetics; we were a humdrum couple of quasi-artists, well satisfied with life, and all I feared for her was that she might become a suffragette or be taken captive by one of these wild theories that caught her imagination sometimes, and that Mabel, for one, had fostered. As for myself, no doubt she deemed me a trifle solid or stolid—I forget which word she preferred—but on the whole there was just sufficient difference of opinion to make intercourse suggestive without monotony, and certainly without quarrelling. Drawing in deep draughts of the stinging autumn air, I felt happy and exhilarated. It was like going for a holiday, with comfort at the end of the journey instead of bargaining for centimes.

But my heart sank noticeably the moment the house came into view. The long drive, lined with hostile monkey trees and formal wellingtonias that were solemn and sedate, was mere extension of the miniature approach to a thousand semi-detached suburban "residences"; and the appearance of The Towers, as we turned the corner with a rush, suggested a commonplace climax to a story that had begun interestingly, almost thrillingly. A villa had escaped from the shadow of the Crystal Palace, thumped its way down by night, grown suddenly monstrous in a shower of rich rain, and settled itself insolently to stay. Ivy climbed about the opulent red-brick walls, but climbed neatly and with disfiguring effect, sham as on a prison or—the simile made me smile—an orphan asylum. There was no hint of the comely roughness of untidy ivy on a ruin. Clipped, trained, and precise it was, as on a brand-new protestant church. I swear there was not a bird's nest nor a single earwig in it anywhere. About the porch it was particularly thick, smothering a seventeenth-century lamp with a contrast that was quite horrible. Extensive glass-houses spread away on the farther side of the house; the numerous towers to which the building owed its name seemed made to hold school bells; and the window-sills, thick with potted flowers, made me think of the desolate suburbs of Brighton or Bexhill. In a commanding position upon the crest of a hill, it overlooked miles of undulating, wooded country southwards to the Downs, but behind it, to the north, thick banks of ilex, holly, and privet protected it from the cleaner and more stimulating winds. Hence, though highly placed, it was shut in. Three years had passed since I last set eyes upon, it, but the unsightly memory I had retained was justified by the reality. The place was deplorable.

It is my habit to express my opinions audibly sometimes, when impressions are strong enough to warrant it; but now I only sighed "Oh, dear," as I extricated my legs from many rugs and went into the house. A tall parlour-maid, with the bearing of a grenadier, received me, and standing behind her was Mrs. Marsh, the housekeeper, whom I remembered because her untidy back hair had suggested to me that it had been burnt. I went at once to my room, my hostess already dressing for dinner, but Frances came in to see me just as I was struggling with my black tie that had got tangled like a bootlace. She fastened it for me in a neat, effective bow, and while I held my chin up for the operation, staring blankly at the ceiling, the impression came—I wondered, was it her touch that caused it?—that something in her trembled. Shrinking perhaps is the truer word. Nothing in her face or manner betrayed it, nor in her pleasant, easy talk while she tidied my things and scolded my slovenly packing, as her habit was, questioning me about the servants at the flat. The blouses, though right, were crumpled, and my scolding was deserved. There was no impatience even. Yet somehow or other the suggestion of a shrinking reserve and holding back reached my mind. She had been lonely, of course, but it was more than that; she was glad that I had come, yet for some reason unstated she could have wished that I had stayed away. We discussed the news that had accumulated during our brief separation, and in doing so the impression, at best exceedingly slight, was forgotten. My chamber was large and beautifully furnished; the hall and dining-room of our flat would have gone into it with a good remainder; yet it was not a place I could settle down in for work. It conveyed the idea of impermanence, making me feel transient as in a hotel bedroom. This, of course, was the fact. But some rooms convey a settled, lasting hospitality even in a hotel; this one did not; and as I was accustomed to work in the room I slept in, at least when visiting, a slight frown must have crept between my eyes.

"Mabel has fitted a work-room for you just out of the library," said the clairvoyant Frances. "No one will disturb you there, and you'll have fifteen thousand books all catalogued within easy reach. There's a private staircase, too. You can breakfast in your room and slip down in your dressing-gown if you want to." She laughed. My spirits took a turn upwards as absurdly as they had gone down.

"And how are *you?*" I asked, giving her a belated kiss. "It's jolly to be together again. I did feel rather lost without you, I'll admit."

"That's natural," she laughed. "I'm so glad!"

She looked well and had country colour in her cheeks. She informed me that she was eating and sleeping well, going out for little walks with Mabel, painting bits of scenery again, and enjoying a complete change and rest; and yet, for all her brave description, the words somehow did not quite ring true. Those last words in particular did not ring true. There lay in her manner, just out of sight, I felt, this suggestion of the exact reverse—of unrest, shrinking, almost of anxiety. Certain small strings in her seemed overtight. "Keyed-up" was the slang expression that crossed my mind. I looked rather searchingly into her face as she was telling me this.

"Only—the evenings," she added, noticing my query, yet rather avoiding my eyes, "the evenings are—well, rather heavy sometimes, and I find it difficult to keep awake."

"The strong air after London makes you drowsy," I suggested, "and you like to get early to bed."

Frances turned and looked at me for a moment steadily. "On the contrary, Bill, I dislike going to bed—here. And Mabel goes so early." She said it lightly enough, fingering the disorder upon my dressing-table in such a stupid way that I saw her mind was working in another direction altogether. She looked up suddenly with a kind of nervousness from the brush and scissors. "Billy," she said abruptly, lowering her voice, "isn't it odd, but I *hate* sleeping alone here? I can't make it out quite; I've never felt such a thing before in my life. Do you—think it's all nonsense?" And she laughed, with her lips but not with her eyes; there was a note of defiance in her I failed to understand.

"Nothing a nature like yours feels strongly is nonsense, Frances," I replied soothingly.

But I, too, answered with my lips only, for another part of my mind was working elsewhere, and among uncomfortable things. A touch of bewilderment passed over me. I was not certain how best to continue. If I laughed she would tell me no more, yet if I took her too seriously the strings would tighten further. Instinctively, then, this flashed rapidly across me: that something of what she felt, I had also felt, though interpreting it differently. Vague it was, as the coming of rain or storm that announce themselves hours in advance with their hint of faint, unsettling excitement in the air. I had been but a short hour in the house—big, comfortable, luxurious house,—but had experienced this sense of being unsettled, unfixed, fluctuating—a kind of impermanence that transient lodgers in hotels must feel, but that a guest in a friend's home ought not to feel, be the visit short or long. To Frances, an impressionable woman, the feeling had come in the terms of alarm. She disliked sleeping alone, while yet she longed to sleep. The precise idea in my mind evaded capture, merely brushing through me, three-quarters out of sight; I realised only that we both felt the same thing, and that neither of us could get at it clearly. Degrees of unrest we felt, but the actual thing did not disclose itself. It did not happen.

I felt strangely at sea for a moment. Frances would interpret hesitation as endorsement, and encouragement might be the last thing that could help her.

"Sleeping in a strange house," I answered at length, "is often difficult at first, and one feels lonely. After fifteen months in our tiny flat one feels lost and uncared for in a big house. It's an uncomfortable feeling—I know it well. And this *is* a barrack, isn't it? The masses of furniture only make it worse. One feels in storage somewhere underground—the furniture doesn't furnish. One must never yield to fancies, though—"

Frances looked away towards the windows; she seemed disappointed a little.

"After our thickly-populated Chelsea," I went on quickly, "it seems isolated here."

But she did not turn back, and clearly I was saying the wrong thing. A wave of pity rushed suddenly over me. Was she really frightened, perhaps? She was imaginative, I knew, but never moody; common sense was strong in her, though she had her times of hypersensitiveness. I caught the echo of some unreasoning, big alarm in her. She stood there, gazing across my balcony towards the sea of wooded country that spread dim and vague in the obscurity of the dusk. The deepening shadows entered the room, I fancied, from the grounds below. Following her abstracted gaze a moment, I experienced a curious sharp desire to leave, to escape. Out yonder was wind and space and freedom. This enormous building was oppressive, silent, still. Great catacombs occurred to me, things beneath the ground, imprisonment and capture. I believe I even shuddered a little.

I touched her shoulder. She turned round slowly, and we looked with a certain deliberation into each other's eyes.

"Fanny," I asked, more gravely than I intended, "you are not frightened, are you? Nothing has happened, has it?"

She replied with emphasis, "Of course not! How could it—I mean, why should I?" She stammered, as though the wrong sentence flustered her a second. "It's simply—that I have this ter—this dislike of sleeping alone."

Naturally, my first thought was how easy it would be to cut our visit short. But I did not say this. Had it been a true solution, Frances would have said it for me long ago.

"Wouldn't Mabel double-up with you?" I said instead, "or give you an adjoining room, so that you could leave the door between you open? There's space enough, heaven knows."

And then, as the gong sounded in the hall below for dinner, she said, as with an effort, this thing:

"Mabel did ask me—on the third night—after I had told her. But I declined."

"You'd rather be alone than with her?" I asked, with a certain relief.

Her reply was so gravely given, a child would have known there was more behind it: "Not that; but that she did not really want it."

I had a moment's intuition and acted on it impulsively. "She feels it too, perhaps, but wishes to face it by herself—and get over it?"

My sister bowed her head, and the gesture made me realise of a sudden how grave and solemn our talk had grown, as though some portentous thing were under discussion. It had come of itself—indefinite as a gradual change of temperature. Yet neither of us knew its nature, for apparently neither of us could state it plainly. Nothing happened, even in our words.

"That *was* my impression," she said, "—that if she yields to it she encourages it. And a habit forms so easily. Just think," she added, with a faint smile that was the first sign of lightness she had yet betrayed, "what a nuisance it would be—everywhere—if everybody was afraid of being alone—like that."

I snatched readily at the chance. We laughed a little, though it was a quiet kind of laughter that seemed wrong. I took her arm and led her towards the door.

"Disastrous, in fact," I agreed.

She raised her voice to its normal pitch again, as I had done. "No doubt it will pass," she said, "now that you have come. Of course, it's chiefly my imagination." Her tone was lighter, though nothing could convince me that the matter itself was light—just then. "And in any case," tightening her grip on my arm as we passed into the bright enormous corridor and caught sight of Mrs. Franklyn waiting in the cheerless hall below, "I'm *very* glad you're here, Bill, and Mabel, I know, is too."

"If it doesn't pass," I just had time to whisper with a feeble attempt at jollity, "I'll come at night and snore outside your door. After that you'll be so glad to get rid of me that you won't mind being alone."

"That's a bargain," said Frances.

I shook my hostess by the hand, made a banal remark about the long interval since last we met, and walked behind them into the great dining-room, dimly lit by candles, wondering in my heart how long my sister and I should stay, and why in the world we had ever left our cosy little flat to enter this desolation of riches and false luxury at all. The unsightly picture of the late Samuel Franklyn, Esq., stared down upon me from the further end of the room above the mighty mantelpiece. He looked, I thought, like some pompous Heavenly Butler who denied to all the world, and to us in particular, the right of entry without presentation cards signed by his hand as proof that we belonged to his own exclusive set. The majority, to his deep grief, and in spite of all his prayers on their behalf, must burn and "perish everlastingly."

IV

With the instinct of the healthy bachelor I always try to make myself a nest in the place I live in, be it for long or short. Whether visiting, in lodging-house, or in hotel, the first essential is this nest—one's own things built into the walls as a bird builds in its feathers. It may look desolate and uncomfortable enough to others, because the central detail is neither bed nor wardrobe, sofa nor arm-chair, but a good solid writing-table that does not wriggle, and that has wide elbow-room. And The Towers is vividly described for me by the single fact that I could not "nest" there. I took several days to discover this, but the first impression of impermanence was truer than I knew. The feathers of the mind refused here to lie one way. They ruffled, pointed, and grew wild.

Luxurious furniture does not mean comfort; I might as well have tried to settle down in the sofa and arm-chair department of a big shop. My bedroom was easily managed; it was the private work-room, prepared especially for my reception, that made me feel alien and outcast. Externally, it was all one could desire: an ante-chamber to the great library, with not one, but two generous oak tables, to say nothing of smaller ones against the walls with capacious drawers. There were reading-desks, mechanical devices for holding books, perfect light, quiet as in a church, and no approach but across the huge adjoining room. Yet it did not invite.

"I hope you'll be able to work here," said my little hostess the next morning, as she took me in—her only visit to it while I stayed in the house—and showed me the ten-volume Catalogue. "It's absolutely quiet and no one will disturb you."

"If you can't, Bill, you're not much good," laughed Frances, who was on her arm. "Even I could write in a study like this!"

I glanced with pleasure at the ample tables, the sheets of thick blotting-paper, the rulers, sealing-wax, paper-knives, and all the other immaculate paraphernalia. "It's perfect," I answered with a secret thrill, yet feeling a little foolish. This was for Gibbon or Carlyle, rather than for my pot-boiling insignificancies. "If I can't write masterpieces here, it's certainly not *your* fault," and I turned with gratitude to Mrs. Franklyn. She was looking straight at me, and there was a question in her small pale eyes I did not understand. Was she noting the effect upon me, I wondered?

"You'll write here—perhaps a story about the house," she said; "Thompson will bring you anything you want; you only have to ring." She pointed to the electric bell on the central table, the wire running neatly down the leg. "No one has ever worked here before, and the library has been hardly used since it was put in. So there's no previous atmosphere to affect your imagination—er—adversely."

We laughed. "Bill isn't that sort," said my sister; while I wished they would go out and leave me to arrange my little nest and set to work.

I thought, of course, it was the huge listening library that made me feel so inconsiderable—the fifteen thousand silent, staring books, the solemn aisles, the deep, eloquent shelves. But when the women had gone and I was alone, the beginning of the truth crept over me, and I felt that first hint of disconsolateness which later became an imperative No. The mind shut down, images ceased to rise and flow. I read, made copious notes, but I wrote no single line at The Towers. Nothing completed itself there. Nothing happened.

The morning sunshine poured into the library through ten long narrow windows; birds were singing; the autumn air, rich with a faint aroma of November melancholy that stung the imagination pleasantly, filled my ante-chamber. I looked out upon the undulating wooded landscape, hemmed in by the sweep of distant Downs, and I tasted a whiff of the sea. Rooks cawed as they floated above the elms, and there were lazy cows in the nearer meadows. A dozen times I tried to make my nest and settle down to work, and a dozen times, like a turning fastidious dog upon a hearth-rug, I rearranged my chair and books and papers. The temptation of the Catalogue and shelves, of course, was accountable for much, yet not, I felt, for all. That was a manageable seduction. My work, moreover, was not of the creative kind that requires absolute absorption; it was the mere readable presentation of data I had accumulated. My note-books were charged with facts ready to tabulate—facts, too, that interested me keenly. A mere effort of the will was necessary, and concentration of no difficult kind. Yet, somehow, it seemed beyond me: something for ever pushed the facts into disorder . . . and in the end I sat in the sunshine, dipping into a dozen books selected from the shelves outside, vexed with myself and only half-enjoying it. I felt restless. I wanted to be elsewhere.

And even while I read, attention wandered. Frances, Mabel, her late husband, the house and grounds, each in turn and sometimes all together, rose uninvited into the stream of thought, hindering any consecutive flow of work. In disconnected fashion came these pictures that interrupted concentration, yet presenting themselves as broken fragments of a bigger thing my mind already groped for unconsciously. They fluttered round this hidden thing of which they were aspects, fugitive interpretations, no one of them bringing complete revelation. There was no adjective, such as pleasant or unpleasant, that I could attach to what I felt, beyond that the result was unsettling. Vague as the atmosphere of a dream, it yet persisted, and I could not dissipate it. Isolated words or phrases in the lines I read sent questions scouring across my mind, sure sign that the deeper part of me was restless and ill at ease.

Rather trivial questions too—half-foolish interrogations, as of a puzzled or curious child: Why was my sister afraid to sleep alone, and why did her friend feel a similar repugnance, yet seek to conquer it? Why was the solid luxury of the house without comfort, its shelter without the sense of permanence? Why had Mrs. Franklyn asked *us* to come, artists, unbelieving vagabonds, types at the furthest possible remove from the saved sheep of her husband's household? Had a reaction set in against the hysteria of her conversion? I had seen no signs of religious fervour in her; her atmosphere was that of an ordinary, high-minded woman, yet a woman of the world. Lifeless, though, a little, perhaps, now that I came to think about it: she had made no definite impression upon me of any kind. And my thoughts ran vaguely after this fragile clue.

Closing my book, I let them run. For, with this chance reflection came the discovery that I could not see her clearly—could not feel her soul, her personality. Her face, her small pale eyes, her dress and body and walk, all these stood before me like a photograph; but her Self evaded me. She seemed not there, lifeless, empty, a shadow—nothing. The picture was disagreeable, and I put it by. Instantly she melted out, as though light thought had conjured up a phantom that had no real existence. And at that very moment, singularly enough, my eye caught sight of her moving past the window, going silently along the gravel path. I watched her, a sudden new sensation gripping me. "There goes a prisoner," my thought instantly ran, "one who wishes to escape, but cannot."

What brought the outlandish notion, heaven only knows. The house was of her own choice, she was twice an heiress, and the world lay open at her feet. Yet she stayed—unhappy, frightened, caught. All this flashed over me, and made a sharp impression even before I had time to dismiss it as absurd. But a moment later explanation offered itself, though it seemed as far-fetched as the original impression. My mind, being logical, was obliged to provide something, apparently. For Mrs. Franklyn, while dressed to go out, with thick walking-boots, a pointed stick, and a motor-cap tied on with a veil as for the windy lanes, was obviously content to go no further than the little garden paths. The costume was a sham and a pretence. It was this, and her lithe, quick movements that suggested a caged creature—a creature tamed by fear and cruelty that cloaked themselves in kindness—pacing up and down, unable to realise why it got no further, but always met the same bars in exactly the same place. The mind in her was barred.

I watched her go along the paths and down the steps from one terrace to another, until the laurels hid her altogether; and into this mere imagining of a moment came a hint of something slightly disagreeable, for which my mind, search as it would, found no explanation at all. I remembered then certain other little things. They dropped into the picture of their own accord. In a mind not deliberately hunting for clues, pieces of a puzzle sometimes come together in this way, bringing revelation, so that for a second there flashed across me, vanishing instantly again before I could consider it, a large, distressing thought that I can only describe vaguely as a Shadow. Dark and ugly, oppressive certainly it might be described, with something torn and dreadful about the edges that suggested pain and strife and terror. The interior of a prison with two rows of occupied condemned cells, seen years ago in New York, sprang to memory after it—the connection between the two impossible to surmise even. But the "certain other little things" mentioned above were these: that Mrs. Franklyn, in last night's dinner talk, had always referred to "this house," but never called it "home"; and had emphasised unnecessarily, for a well-bred woman, our "great kindness" in coming down to stay so long with her. Another time, in answer to my futile compliment about the "stately rooms," she said quietly, "It is an enormous house for so small a party; but I stay here very little, and only till I get it straight again." The three of us were going up the great staircase to bed as this was said, and, not knowing quite her meaning, I dropped the subject. It edged delicate ground, I felt. Frances added no word of her own. It now occurred to me abruptly that "stay" was the word made use of, when "live" would have been more natural. How insignificant to recall! Yet why did they suggest themselves just at this moment? . . . And, on going to Frances's room to make sure she was not nervous or lonely, I realised abruptly, that Mrs. Franklyn, of course, had talked with *her* in a confidential sense that I, as a mere visiting brother, could not share. Frances had told me nothing. I might easily have wormed it out of her, had I not felt that for us to discuss further our hostess and her house merely because we were under the roof together, was not quite nice or loyal.

"I'll call you, Bill, if I'm scared," she had laughed as we parted, my room being just across the big corridor from her own. I had fallen asleep, thinking what in the world was meant by "getting it straight again."

And now in my ante-chamber to the library, on the second morning, sitting among piles of foolscap and sheets of spotless blotting-paper, all useless to me, these slight hints came back and helped to frame the big, vague Shadow I have mentioned. Up to the neck in this Shadow, almost drowned, yet just treading water, stood the figure of my hostess in her walking costume. Frances and I seemed swimming to her aid. The Shadow was large enough to include both house and grounds, but further than that I could not see. . . . Dismissing it, I fell to reading my purloined book again. Before I turned another page, however, another startling detail leaped out at me: the figure of Mrs. Franklyn in the Shadow was not living. It floated helplessly, like a doll or puppet that has no life in it. It was both pathetic and dreadful.

Any one who sits in reverie thus, of course, may see similar ridiculous pictures when the will no longer guides construction. The incongruities of dreams are thus explained. I merely record the picture as it came. That it remained by me for several days, just as vivid dreams do, is neither here nor there. I did not allow myself to dwell upon it. The curious thing, perhaps, is that from this moment I date my inclination, though not yet my desire, to leave. I purposely say "to leave." I cannot quite remember when the word changed to that aggressive, frantic thing which is escape.

V

We were left delightfully to ourselves in this pretentious country mansion with the soul of a villa. Frances took up her painting again, and, the weather being propitious, spent hours out of doors, sketching flowers, trees, and nooks of woodland, garden, even the house itself where bits of it peered suggestively across the orchards. Mrs. Franklyn seemed always busy about something or other, and never interfered with us except to propose motoring, tea in another part of the lawn, and so forth. She flitted everywhere, preoccupied, yet apparently doing nothing. The house engulfed her rather. No visitors called. For one thing, she was not supposed to be back from abroad yet; and for another, I think, the neighbourhood—her husband's neighbourhood—was puzzled by her sudden cessation from good works. Brigades and temperance societies did not ask to hold their meetings in the big hall, and the vicar arranged the school-treats in another's field without explanation. The full-length portrait in the dining-room, and the presence of the housekeeper with the "burnt" back-hair, indeed, were the only reminders of the man who once had lived here. Mrs. Marsh retained her place in silence, well-paid sinecure as it doubtless was, yet with no hint of that suppressed disapproval one might have expected from her. Indeed, there was nothing positive to disapprove, since nothing "worldly" entered grounds or building. In her master's lifetime she had been another "brand snatched from the burning," and it had then been her custom to give vociferous "testimony" at the revival meetings where he adorned the platform and led in streams of prayer. I saw her sometimes on the stairs, hovering, wandering, half-watching and half-listening, and the idea came to me once that this woman somehow formed a link with the departed influence of her bigoted employer. She, alone among us, *belonged* to the house, and looked at home there. When I saw her talking—oh, with such correct and respectful mien—to Mrs. Franklyn, I had the feeling that for all her unaggressive attitude, she yet exerted some influence that sought to make her mistress stay in the building for ever—live there. She would prevent her escape, prevent "getting it straight again," thwart somehow her will to freedom, if she could. The idea in me was of the most fleeting kind. But another time, when I came down late at night to get a book from the library ante-chamber, and found her sitting in the hall—alone—the impression left upon me was the reverse of fleeting. I can never forget the vivid, disagreeable effect it produced upon me. What was she doing there at half-past eleven at night, all alone in the darkness? She was sitting upright, stiff, in a big chair below the clock. It gave me a turn. It was so incongruous and odd. She rose quietly as I turned the corner of the stairs, and asked me respectfully, her eyes cast down as usual, whether I had finished with the library, so that she might lock up. There was no more to it than that; but the picture stayed with me—unpleasantly.

These various impressions came to me at odd moments, of course, and not in a single sequence as I now relate them. I was hard at work before three days were past, not writing, as explained, but reading, making notes, and gathering material from the library for future use. It was in chance moments that these curious flashes came, catching me unawares with a touch of surprise that sometimes made me start. For they proved that my under-mind was still conscious of the Shadow, and that far away out of sight lay the cause of it that left me with a vague unrest, unsettled, seeking to "nest" in a place that did not want me. Only when this deeper part knows harmony, perhaps, can good brain work result, and my inability to write was thus explained. Certainly, I was always seeking for something here I could not find—an explanation that continually evaded me. Nothing but these trivial hints offered themselves. Lumped together, however, they had the effect of defining the Shadow a little. I became more and more aware of its very real existence. And, if I have made little mention of Frances and my hostess in this connection, it is because they contributed at first little or nothing towards the discovery of what this story tries to tell. Our life was wholly external, normal, quiet, and uneventful; conversation banal—Mrs. Franklyn's conversation in particular. They said nothing that suggested revelation. Both were in this Shadow, and both knew that they were in it, but neither betrayed by word or act a hint of interpretation. They talked privately, no doubt, but of that I can report no details.

And so it was that, after ten days of a very commonplace visit, I found myself looking straight into the face of a Strangeness that defied capture at close quarters. "There's something here that never happens," were the words that rose in my mind, "and that's why none of us can speak of it." And as I looked out of the window and watched the vulgar blackbirds, with toes turned in, boring out their worms, I realised sharply that even they, as indeed everything large and small in the house and grounds, shared this strangeness, and were twisted out of normal appearance because of it. Life, as expressed in the entire place, was crumpled, dwarfed, emasculated. God's meanings here were crippled, His love of joy was stunted. Nothing in the garden danced or sang. There was hate in it. "The Shadow," my thought hurried on to completion, "is a manifestation of hate; and hate is the Devil." And then I sat back frightened in my chair, for I knew that I had partly found the truth.

Leaving my books I went out into the open. The sky was overcast, yet the day by no means gloomy, for a soft, diffused light oozed through the clouds and turned all things warm and almost summery. But I saw the grounds now in their nakedness because I understood. Hate means strife, and the two together weave the robe that terror wears. Having no so-called religious beliefs myself, nor belonging to any set of dogmas called a creed, I could stand outside these feelings and observe. Yet they soaked into me sufficiently for me to grasp sympathetically what others, with more cabined souls (I flattered myself), might feel. That picture in the dining-room stalked everywhere, hid behind every tree, peered down upon me from the peaked ugliness of the bourgeois towers, and left the impress of its powerful hand upon every bed of flowers. "You must not do this, you must not do that," went past me through the air. "You must not leave these narrow paths," said the rigid iron railings of black. "You shall not walk here," was written on the lawns. "Keep to the steps," "Don't pick the flowers; make no noise of laughter, singing, dancing," was placarded all over the rose-garden, and "Trespassers will be—not prosecuted but—*destroyed*" hung from the crest of monkey-tree and holly. Guarding the ends of each artificial terrace stood gaunt, implacable policemen, warders, gaolers. "Come with us," they chanted, "or be damned eternally."

I remember feeling quite pleased with myself that I had discovered this obvious explanation of the prison-feeling the place breathed out. That the posthumous influence of heavy old Samuel Franklyn might be an inadequate solution did not occur to me. By "getting the place straight again," his widow, of course, meant forgetting the glamour of fear and foreboding his depressing creed had temporarily forced upon her; and Frances, delicately-minded being, did not speak of it because it was the influence of the man her friend had loved. I felt lighter; a load was lifted from me. "To trace the unfamiliar to the familiar," came back a sentence I had read somewhere, "is to understand." It was a real relief. I could talk with Frances now, even with my hostess, no danger of treading clumsily. For the key was in my hands. I might even help to dissipate the Shadow, "to get it straight again." It seemed, perhaps, our long invitation was explained!

I went into the house laughing—at myself a little. "Perhaps after all the artist's outlook, with no hard and fast dogmas, is as narrow as the others! How small humanity is! And why is there no possible and true combination of *all* outlooks?"

The feeling of "unsettling" was very strong in me just then, in spite of my big discovery which was to clear everything up. And at the moment I ran into Frances on the stairs, with a portfolio of sketches under her arm.

It came across me then abruptly that, although she had worked a great deal since we came, she had shown me nothing. It struck me suddenly as odd, unnatural. The way she tried to pass me now confirmed my new-born suspicion that—well, that her results were hardly what they ought to be.

"Stand and deliver!" I laughed, stepping in front of her. "I've seen nothing you've done since you've been here, and as a rule you show me all your things. I believe they are atrocious and degrading!" Then my laughter froze.

She made a sly gesture to slip past me, and I almost decided to let her go, for the expression that flashed across her face shocked me. She looked uncomfortable and ashamed; the colour came and went a moment in her cheeks, making me think of a child detected in some secret naughtiness. It was almost fear.

"It's because they're not finished then?" I said, dropping the tone of banter, "or because they're too good for me to understand?" For my criticism of painting, she told me, was crude and ignorant sometimes. "But you'll let me see them later, won't you?"

Frances, however, did not take the way of escape I offered. She changed her mind. She drew the portfolio from beneath her arm instead. "You can see them if you *really* want to, Bill," she said quietly, and her tone reminded me of a nurse who says to a boy just grown out of childhood, "you are old enough now to look upon horror and ugliness—only I don't advise it."

"I do want to," I said, and made to go downstairs with her. But, instead, she said in the same low voice as before, "Come up to my room, we shall be undisturbed there." So I guessed that she had been on her way to show the paintings to our hostess, but did not care for us all three to see them together. My mind worked furiously.

"Mabel asked me to do them," she explained in a tone of submissive horror, once the door was shut, "in fact, she begged it of me. You know how persistent she is in her quiet way. I—er—had to."

She flushed and opened the portfolio on the little table by the window, standing behind me as I turned the sketches over—sketches of the grounds and trees and garden. In the first moment of inspection, however, I did not take in clearly why my sister's sense of modesty had been offended. For my attention flashed a second elsewhere. Another bit of the puzzle had dropped into place, defining still further the nature of what I called "the Shadow." Mrs. Franklyn, I now remembered, had suggested to me in the library that I might perhaps write something about the place, and I had taken it for one of her banal sentences and paid no further attention. I realised now that it was said in earnest. She wanted our interpretations, as expressed in our respective "talents," painting and writing. Her invitation was explained. She left us to ourselves on purpose.

"I should like to tear them up," Frances was whispering behind me with a shudder, "only I promised—" She hesitated a moment.

"Promised not to?" I asked with a queer feeling of distress, my eyes glued to the papers.

"Promised always to show them to her first," she finished so low I barely caught it.

I have no intuitive, immediate grasp of the value of paintings; results come to me slowly, and though every one believes his own judgment to be good, I dare not claim that mine is worth more than that of any other layman. Frances had too often convicted me of gross ignorance and error. I can only say that I examined these sketches with a feeling of amazement that contained revulsion, if not actual horror and disgust. They were outrageous. I felt hot for my sister, and it was a relief to know she had moved across the room on some pretence or other, and did not examine them with me. Her talent, of course, is mediocre, yet she has her moments of inspiration—moments, that is to say, when a view of Beauty not normally her own flames divinely through her. And these interpretations struck me forcibly as being thus "inspired,"—not her own. They were uncommonly well done; they were also atrocious. The meaning in them, however, was never more than hinted. There the unholy skill and power came in; they suggested so abominably, leaving most to the imagination. To find such significance in a bourgeois villa garden, and to interpret it with such delicate yet legible certainty, was a kind of symbolism that was sinister, even diabolical. The delicacy was her own, but the point of view was another's. And the word that rose in my mind was not the gross description of "impure," but the more fundamental qualification—"un-pure."

In silence I turned the sketches over one by one, as a boy hurries through the pages of an evil book lest he be caught.

"What does Mabel do with them?" I asked presently in a low tone, as I neared the end. "Does she keep them?"

"She makes notes about them in a book and then destroys them," was the reply from the end of the room. I heard a sigh of relief. "I'm glad you've seen them, Bill. I wanted you to—but was afraid to show them. You understand?"

"I understand," was my reply, though it was not a question intended to be answered. All I understood really was that Mabel's mind was as sweet and pure as my sister's, and that she had some good reason for what she did. She destroyed the sketches, but first made notes! It was an interpretation of the place she sought. Brother-like, I felt resentment, though, that Frances should waste her time and talent, when she might be doing work that she could sell. Naturally, I felt other things as well. . . .

"Mabel pays me five guineas for each one," I heard. "Absolutely insists."

I stared at her stupidly a moment, bereft of speech or wit.

"I must either accept, or go away," she went on calmly, but a little white. "I've tried everything. There was a scene the third day I was here—when I showed her my first result. I wanted to write to you, but hesitated—"

"It's unintentional, then, on your part—forgive my asking it, Frances, dear?" I blundered, hardly knowing what to think or say. "Between the lines" of her letter came back to me. "I mean, you make the sketches in your ordinary way and—the result comes out of itself, so to speak?"

She nodded, throwing her hands out like a Frenchman. "We needn't keep the money for ourselves, Bill. We can give it away, but—I must either accept or leave," and she repeated the shrugging gesture. She sat down on the chair facing me, staring helplessly at the carpet.

"You say there was a scene?" I went on presently. "She insisted?"

"She begged me to continue," my sister replied very quietly. "She thinks—that is, she has an idea or theory that there's something about the place—something she can't get at quite." Frances stammered badly. She knew I did not encourage her wild theories.

"Something she feels, yes," I helped her, more than curious.

"Oh, you know what I mean, Bill," she said desperately. "That the place is saturated with some influence that she is herself too positive or too stupid to interpret. She's trying to make herself negative and receptive, as she calls it, but can't, of course, succeed. Haven't you noticed how dull and impersonal and insipid she seems, as though she had no personality? She thinks impressions will come to her that way. But they don't—"

"Naturally."

"So she's trying me—us—what she calls the sensitive and impressionable artistic temperament. She says that until she is sure exactly what this influence is, she can't fight it, turn it out, 'get the house straight,' as she phrases it."

Remembering my own singular impressions, I felt more lenient than I might otherwise have done. I tried to keep impatience out of my voice.

"And this influence, what—whose is it?"

We used the pronoun that followed in the same breath, for I answered my own question at the same moment as she did:

"His." Our heads nodded involuntarily towards the floor, the dining-room being directly underneath.

And my heart sank, my curiosity died away on the instant, I felt bored. A commonplace haunted house was the last thing in the world to amuse or interest me. The mere thought exasperated, with its suggestions of imagination, overwrought nerves, hysteria, and the rest. Mingled with my other feelings was certainly disappointment. To see a figure or feel a "presence," and report from day to day strange incidents to each other would be a form of weariness I could never tolerate.

"But really, Frances," I said firmly, after a moment's pause, "it's too far-fetched, this explanation. A curse, you know, belongs to the ghost stories of early Victorian days." And only my positive conviction that there *was* something after all worth discovering, and that it most certainly was *not* this, prevented my suggesting that we terminate our visit forthwith, or as soon as we decently could. "This is not a haunted house, whatever it is," I concluded somewhat vehemently, bringing my hand down upon her odious portfolio.

My sister's reply revived my curiosity sharply.

"I was waiting for you to say that. Mabel says exactly the same. *He* is in it—but it's something more than that alone, something far bigger and more complicated." Her sentence seemed to indicate the sketches, and though I caught the inference I did not take it up, having no desire to discuss them with her just then, indeed, if ever.

I merely stared at her and listened. Questions, I felt sure, would be of little use. It was better she should say her thought in her own way.

"He is one influence, the most recent," she went on slowly, and always very calmly, "but there are others—deeper layers, as it were—underneath. If his were the only one, something would happen. But nothing ever does happen. The others hinder and prevent—as though each were struggling to predominate."

I had felt it already myself. The idea was rather horrible. I shivered.

"That's what is so ugly about it—that nothing ever happens," she said. "There is this endless anticipation—always on the dry edge of a result that never materialises. It is torture. Mabel is at her wits' end, you see. And when she begged me—what I felt about my sketches—I mean—" She stammered badly as before.

I stopped her. I had judged too hastily. That queer symbolism in her paintings, pagan and yet not innocent, was, I understood, the result of mixture. I did not pretend to understand, but at least I could be patient. I consequently held my peace. We did talk on a little longer, but it was more general talk that avoided successfully our hostess, the paintings, wild theories, and *him*—until at length the emotion Frances had hitherto so successfully kept under burst vehemently forth again. It had hidden between her calm sentences, as it had hidden between the lines of her letter. It swept her now from head to foot, packed tight in the thing she then said.

"Then, Bill, if it is not an ordinary haunted house," she asked, *"what is it?"*

The words were commonplace enough. The emotion was in the tone of her voice that trembled; in the gesture she made, leaning forward and clasping both hands upon her knees, and in the slight blanching of her cheeks as her brave eyes asked the question and searched my own with anxiety that bordered upon panic. In that moment she put herself under my protection. I winced.

"And why," she added, lowering her voice to a still and furtive whisper, "does nothing ever happen? If only,"—this with great emphasis—"something *would* happen—break this awful tension—bring relief. It's the waiting I cannot stand." And she shivered all over as she said it, a touch of wildness in her eyes.

I would have given much to have made a true and satisfactory answer. My mind searched frantically for a moment, but in vain. There lay no sufficient answer in me. I felt what she felt, though with differences. No conclusive explanation lay within reach. Nothing happened. Eager as I was to shoot the entire business into the rubbish heap where ignorance and superstition discharge their poisonous weeds, I could not honestly accomplish this. To treat Frances as a child, and merely "explain away" would be to strain her confidence in my protection, so affectionately claimed. It would further be dishonest to myself—weak, besides—to deny that I had also felt the strain and tension even as she did. While my mind continued searching, I returned her stare in silence; and Frances then, with more honesty and insight than my own, gave suddenly the answer herself—an answer whose truth and adequacy, so far as they went, I could not readily gainsay:

"I think, Bill, because it is too big to happen here—to happen anywhere, indeed, all at once—and too awful!"

To have tossed the sentence aside as nonsense, argued it away, proved that it was really meaningless, would have been easy—at any other time or in any other place; and, had the past week brought me none of the vivid impressions it had brought me, this is doubtless what I should have done. My narrowness again was proved. We understand in others only what we have in ourselves. But her explanation, in a measure, I knew was true. It hinted at the strife and struggle that my notion of a Shadow had seemed to cover thinly.

"Perhaps," I murmured lamely, waiting in vain for her to say more. "But you said just now that you felt the thing was 'in layers,' as it were. Do you mean each one—each influence—fighting for the upper hand?"

I used her phraseology to conceal my own poverty. Terminology, after all, was nothing, provided we could reach the idea itself.

Her eyes said yes. She had her clear conception, arrived at independently, as was her way. And, unlike her sex, she kept it clear, unsmothered by too many words.

"One set of influences gets at me, another gets at you. It's according to our temperaments, I think." She glanced significantly at the vile portfolio. "Sometimes they are mixed—and therefore false. There has always been in me, more than in you, the pagan thing, perhaps, though never, thank God, like *that*."

The frank confession of course invited my own, as it was meant to do. Yet it was difficult to find the words.

"What I have felt in this place, Frances, I honestly can hardly tell you, because—er—my impressions have not arranged themselves in any definite form I can describe. The strife, the agony of vainly-sought escape, and the unrest—a sort of prison atmosphere—this I have felt at different times and with varying degrees of strength. But I find, as yet, no final label to attach. I couldn't say pagan, Christian, or anything like that, I mean, as you do. As with the blind and deaf, you may have an intensification of certain senses denied to me, or even another sense altogether in embryo—"

"Perhaps," she stopped me, anxious to keep to the point, "you feel it as Mabel does. She feels the whole thing *complete*."

"That also is possible," I said very slowly. I was thinking behind my words. Her odd remark that it was "big and awful" came back upon me as true. A vast sensation of distress and discomfort swept me suddenly. Pity was in it, and a fierce contempt, a savage, bitter anger as well. Fury against some sham authority was part of it.

"Frances," I said, caught unawares, and dropping all pretence, "what in the world can it be?" I looked hard at her. For some minutes neither of us spoke.

"Have *you* felt no desire to interpret it?" she asked presently.

"Mabel did suggest my writing something about the house," was my reply, "but I've felt nothing imperative. That sort of writing is not my line, you know. My only feeling," I added, noticing that she waited for more, "is the impulse to explain, discover, get it out of me somehow, and so get rid of it. Not by writing, though—as yet." And again I repeated my former question: "What in the world do you think it is?" My voice had become involuntarily hushed. There was awe in it.

Her answer, given with slow emphasis, brought back all my reserve: the phraseology provoked me rather:—

"Whatever it is, Bill, it is not of God."

I got up to go downstairs. I believe I shrugged my shoulders. "Would you like to leave, Frances? Shall we go back to town?" I suggested this at the door, and hearing no immediate reply, I turned back to look. Frances was sitting with her head bowed over and buried in her hands. The attitude horribly suggested tears. No woman, I realised, can keep back the pressure of strong emotion as long as Frances had done, without ending in a fluid collapse. I waited a moment uneasily, longing to comfort, yet afraid to act—and in this way discovered the existence of the appalling emotion in myself, hitherto but half guessed. At all costs a scene must be prevented: it would involve such exaggeration and over-statement. Brutally, such is the weakness of the ordinary man, I turned the handle to go out, but my sister then raised her head. The sunlight caught her face, framed untidily in its auburn hair, and I saw her wonderful expression with a start. Pity, tenderness, and sympathy shone in it like a flame. It was undeniable. There shone through all her features the imperishable love and yearning to sacrifice self for others which I have seen in only one type of human being. It was the great mother look.

"We must stay by Mabel and help her get it straight," she whispered, making the decision for us both.

I murmured agreement. Abashed and half ashamed, I stole softly from the room and went out into the grounds. And the first thing clearly realised when alone was this: that the long scene between us was without definite result. The exchange of confidence was really nothing but hints and vague suggestion. We had decided to stay, but it was a negative decision not to leave rather than a positive action. All our words and questions, our guesses, inferences, explanations, our most subtle allusions and insinuations, even the odious paintings themselves, were without definite result. Nothing had happened.

VI

And instinctively, once alone, I made for the places where she had painted her extraordinary pictures; I tried to see what she had seen. Perhaps, now that she had opened my mind to another view, I should be sensitive to some similar interpretation—and possibly by way of literary expression. If I were to write about the place, I asked myself, how should I treat it? I deliberately invited an interpretation in the way that came easiest to me—writing.

But in this case there came no such revelation. Looking closely at the trees and flowers, the bits of lawn and terrace, the rose-garden and corner of the house where the flaming creeper hung so thickly, I discovered nothing of the odious, unpure thing her colour and grouping had unconsciously revealed. At first, that is, I discovered nothing. The reality stood there, commonplace and ugly, side by side with her distorted version of it that lay in my mind. It seemed incredible. I tried to force it, but in vain. My imagination, ploughed less deeply than hers, or to another pattern, grew different seed. Where I saw the gross soul of an overgrown suburban garden, inspired by the spirit of a vulgar, rich revivalist who loved to preach damnation, she saw this rush of pagan liberty and joy, this strange licence of primitive flesh which, tainted by the other, produced the adulterated, vile result.

Certain things, however, gradually then became apparent, forcing themselves upon me, willy nilly. They came slowly, but overwhelmingly. Not that facts had changed, or natural details altered in the grounds—this was impossible—but that I noticed for the first time various aspects I had not noticed before—trivial enough, yet for me, just then, significant. Some I remembered from previous days; others I saw now as I wandered to and fro, uneasy, uncomfortable,—almost, it seemed, watched by some one who took note of my impressions. The details were so foolish, the total result so formidable. I was half aware that others tried hard to make me see. It was deliberate. My sister's phrase, "one layer got at me, another gets at you," flashed, undesired, upon me.

For I saw, as with the eyes of a child, what I can only call a goblin garden—house, grounds, trees, and flowers belonged to a goblin world that children enter through the pages of their fairy tales. And what made me first aware of it was the whisper of the wind behind me, so that I turned with a sudden start, feeling that something had moved closer. An old ash tree, ugly and ungainly, had been artificially trained to form an arbor at one end of the terrace that was a tennis lawn, and the leaves of it now went rustling together, swishing as they rose and fell. I looked at the ash tree, and felt as though I had passed that moment between doors into this goblin garden that crouched behind the real one. Below, at a deeper layer perhaps, lay hidden the one my sister had entered.

To deal with my own, however, I call it goblin, because an odd aspect of the quaint in it yet never quite achieved the picturesque. Grotesque, probably, is the truer word, for everywhere I noticed, and for the first time, this slight alteration of the natural due either to the exaggeration of some detail, or to its suppression, generally, I think, to the latter. Life everywhere appeared to me as blocked from the full delivery of its sweet and lovely message. Some counter influence stopped it—suppression; or sent it awry—exaggeration. The house itself, mere expression, of course, of a narrow, limited mind, was sheer ugliness; it required no further explanation. With the grounds and garden, so far as shape and general plan were concerned, this was also true; but that trees and flowers and other natural details should share the same deficiency perplexed my logical soul, and even dismayed it. I stood and stared, then moved about, and stood and stared again. Everywhere was this mockery of a sinister, unfinished aspect. I sought in vain to recover my normal point of view. My mind had found this goblin garden and wandered to and fro in it, unable to escape.

The change was in myself, of course, and so trivial were the details which illustrated it, that they sound absurd, thus mentioned one by one. For me, they proved it, is all I can affirm. The goblin touch lay plainly everywhere: in the forms of the trees, planted at neat intervals along the lawns; in this twisted ash that rustled just behind me; in the shadow of the gloomy wellingtonias, whose sweeping skirts obscured the grass; but especially, I noticed, in the tops and crests of them. For here, the delicate, graceful curves of last year's growth seemed to shrink back into themselves. None of them pointed upwards. Their life had failed and turned aside just when it should have become triumphant. The character of a tree reveals itself chiefly at the extremities, and it was precisely here that they all drooped and achieved this hint of goblin distortion—in the growth, that is, of the last few years. What ought to have been fairy, joyful, natural, was instead uncomely to the verge of the grotesque. Spontaneous expression was arrested. My mind perceived a goblin garden, and was caught in it. The place grimaced at me.

With the flowers it was similar, though far more difficult to detect in detail for description. I saw the smaller vegetable growth as impish, half-malicious. Even the terraces sloped ill, as though their ends had sagged since they had been so lavishly constructed; their varying angles gave a queerly bewildering aspect to their sequence that was unpleasant to the eye. One might wander among their deceptive lengths and get lost—lost among open terraces!—with the house quite close at hand. Unhomely seemed the entire garden, unable to give repose, restlessness in it everywhere, almost strife, and discord certainly.

Moreover, the garden grew into the house, the house into the garden, and in both was this idea of resistance to the natural—the spirit that says No to joy. All over it I was aware of the effort to achieve another end, the struggle to burst forth and escape into free, spontaneous expression that should be happy and natural, yet the effort for ever frustrated by the weight of this dark shadow that rendered it abortive. Life crawled aside into a channel that was a cul-de-sac, then turned horribly upon itself. Instead of blossom and fruit, there were weeds. This approach of life I was conscious of—then dismal failure. There was no fulfilment. Nothing happened.

And so, through this singular mood, I came a little nearer to understand the unpure thing that had stammered out into expression through my sister's talent. For the unpure is merely negative; it has no existence; it is but the cramped expression of what is true, stammering its way brokenly over false boundaries that seek to limit and confine. Great, full expression of anything is pure, whereas here was only the incomplete, unfinished, and therefore ugly. There was a strife and pain and desire to escape. I found myself shrinking from house and grounds as one shrinks from the touch of the mentally arrested, those in whom life has turned awry. There was almost mutilation in it.

Past items, too, now flocked to confirm this feeling that I walked, liberty captured and half-maimed, in a monstrous garden. I remembered days of rain that refreshed the countryside, but left these grounds, cracked with the summer heat, unsatisfied and thirsty; and how the big winds, that cleaned the woods and fields elsewhere, crawled here with difficulty through the dense foliage that protected The Towers from the North and West and East. They were ineffective, sluggish currents. There was no real wind. Nothing happened. I began to realise—far more clearly than in my sister's fanciful explanation about "layers" —that here were many contrary influences at work, mutually destructive of one another. House and grounds were not haunted merely; they were the arena of past thinking and feeling, perhaps of terrible, impure beliefs, each striving to suppress the others, yet no one of them achieving supremacy because no one of them was strong enough, no one of them was true. Each, moreover, tried to win me over, though only one was able to reach my mind at all. For some obscure reason—possibly because my temperament had a natural bias towards the grotesque—it was the goblin layer. With me, it was the line of least resistance. . . .

In my own thoughts this "goblin garden" revealed, of course, merely my personal interpretation. I felt now objectively what long ago my mind had felt subjectively. My work, essential sign of spontaneous life with me, had stopped dead; production had become impossible. I stood now considerably closer to the cause of this sterility. The Cause, rather, turned bolder, had stepped insolently nearer. Nothing happened anywhere; house, garden, mind alike were barren, abortive, torn by the strife of frustrate impulse, ugly, hateful, sinful. Yet behind it all was still the desire of life—desire to escape—accomplish. Hope—an intolerable hope—I became startlingly aware—crowned torture.

And, realising this, though in some part of me where Reason lost her hold, there rose upon me then another and a darker thing that caught me by the throat and made me shrink with a sense of revulsion that touched actual loathing. I knew instantly whence it came, this wave of abhorrence and disgust, for even while I saw red and felt revolt rise in me, it seemed that I grew partially aware of the layer next below the goblin. I perceived the existence of this deeper stratum. One opened the way for the other, as it were. There were so many, yet all inter-related; to admit one was to clear the way for all. If I lingered I should be caught—horribly. They struggled with such violence for supremacy among themselves, however, that this latest uprising was instantly smothered and crushed back, though not before a glimpse had been revealed to me, and the redness in my thoughts transferred itself to colour my surroundings thickly and appallingly—with blood. This lurid aspect drenched the garden, smeared the terraces, lent to the very soil a tinge as of sacrificial rites, that choked the breath in me, while it seemed to fix me to the earth my feet so longed to leave. It was so revolting that at the same time I felt a dreadful curiosity as of fascination—I wished to stay. Between these contrary impulses I think I actually reeled a moment, transfixed by a fascination of the Awful.

Through the lighter goblin veil I felt myself sinking down, down, down into this turgid layer that was so much more violent and so much more ancient. The upper layer, indeed, seemed fairy by comparison with this terror born of the lust for blood, thick with the anguish of human sacrificial victims.

Upper! Then I was already sinking; my feet were caught; I was actually in it! What atavistic strain, hidden deep within me, had been touched into vile response, giving this flash of intuitive comprehension, I cannot say. The coatings laid on by civilisation are probably thin enough in all of us. I made a supreme effort. The sun and wind came back. I could almost swear I opened my eyes. Something very atrocious surged back into the depths, carrying with it a thought of tangled woods, of big stones standing in a circle, motionless, white figures, the one form bound with ropes, and the ghastly gleam of the knife. Like smoke upon a battlefield, it rolled away. . . .

I was standing on the gravel path below the second terrace when the familiar goblin garden danced back again, doubly grotesque now, doubly mocking, yet, by way of contrast, almost welcome. My glimpse into the depths was momentary, it seems, and had passed utterly away. The common world rushed back with a sense of glad relief, yet ominous now for ever, I felt, for the knowledge of what its past had built upon. In street, in theatre, in the festivities of friends, in music-room or playing-field, even indeed in church—how could the memory of what I had seen and felt not leave its hideous trace? The very structure of my Thought, it seemed to me, was stained. What has been thought by others can never be obliterated until . . .

With a start my reverie broke and fled, scattered by a violent sound that I recognised for the first time in my life as wholly desirable. The returning motor meant that my hostess was back. Yet, so urgent had been my temporary obsession, that my first presentation of her was—well, not as I knew her now. Floating along with a face of anguished torture I saw Mabel, a mere effigy captured by others' thinking, pass down into those depths of fire and blood that only just had closed beneath my feet. She dipped away. She vanished, her fading eyes turned to the last towards some saviour who had failed her. And that strange intolerable hope was in her face.

The mystery of the place was pretty thick about me just then. It was the fall of dusk, and the ghost of slanting sunshine was as unreal as though badly painted. The garden stood at attention all about me. I cannot explain it, but I can tell it, I think, exactly as it happened, for it remains vivid in me for ever—that, for the first time, something *almost happened,* myself apparently the combining link through which it pressed towards delivery:

I had already turned towards the house. In my mind were pictures—not actual thoughts—of the motor, tea on the verandah, my sister, Mabel—when there came behind me this tumultuous, awful rush—as I left the garden. The ugliness, the pain, the striving to escape, the whole negative and suppressed agony that *was* the Place, focussed that second into a concentrated effort to produce a result. It was a blinding tempest of long-frustrate desire that heaved at me, surging appallingly behind me like an anguished mob. I was in the act of crossing the frontier into my normal self again, when it came, catching fearfully at my skirts. I might use an entire dictionary of descriptive adjectives yet come no nearer to it than this—the conception of a huge assemblage determined to escape with me, or to snatch me back among themselves. My legs trembled for an instant, and I caught my breath—then turned and ran as fast as possible up the ugly terraces.

At the same instant, as though the clanging of an iron gate cut short the unfinished phrase, I *thought* the beginning of an awful thing:

"The Damned . . ."

Like this it rushed after me from that goblin garden that had sought to keep me:

"The Damned!"

For there was sound in it. I know full well it was subjective, not actually heard at all; yet somehow sound was in it—a great volume, roaring and booming thunderously, far away, and below me. The sentence dipped back into the depths that gave it birth, unfinished. Its completion was prevented. As usual, nothing happened. But it drove behind me like a hurricane as I ran towards the house, and the sound of it I can only liken to those terrible undertones you may hear standing beside Niagara. They lie behind the mere crash of the falling flood, within it somehow, not audible to all—felt rather than definitely heard.

It seemed to echo back from the surface of those sagging terraces as I flew across their sloping ends, for it was somehow underneath them. It was in the rustle of the wind that stirred the skirts of the drooping wellingtonias. The beds of formal flowers passed it on to the creepers, red as blood, that crept over the unsightly building. Into the structure of the vulgar and forbidding house it sank away; The Towers took it home. The uncomely doors and windows seemed almost like mouths that had uttered the words themselves, and on the upper floors at that very moment I saw two maids in the act of closing them again.

And on the verandah, as I arrived breathless, and shaken in my soul, Frances and Mabel, standing by the tea-table, looked up to greet me. In the faces of both were clearly legible the signs of shock. They watched me coming, yet so full of their own distress that they hardly noticed the state in which I came. In the face of my hostess, however, I read another and a bigger thing than in the face of Frances. Mabel *knew.* She had experienced what I had experienced. She had heard that awful sentence I had heard, but heard it not for the first time; heard it, moreover, I verily believe, complete and to its dreadful end.

"Bill, did you hear that curious noise just now?" Frances asked it sharply before I could say a word. Her manner was confused; she looked straight at me; and there was a tremor in her voice she could not hide.

"There's wind about," I said, "wind in the trees and sweeping round the walls. It's risen rather suddenly." My voice faltered rather.

"No. It wasn't wind," she insisted, with a significance meant for me alone, but badly hidden. "It was more like distant thunder, we thought. How you ran too!" she added. "What a pace you came across the terraces!"

I knew instantly from the way she said it that they both had already heard the sound before and were anxious to know if I had heard it, and how. My interpretation was what they sought.

"It was a curiously deep sound, I admit. It may have been big guns at sea," I suggested, "forts or cruisers practising. The coast isn't so very far, and with the wind in the right direction—"

The expression on Mabel's face stopped me dead.

"Like huge doors closing," she said softly in her colourless voice, "enormous metal doors shutting against a mass of people clamouring to get out." The gravity, the note of hopelessness in her tones, was shocking.

Frances had gone into the house the instant Mabel began to speak. "I'm cold," she had said; "I think I'll get a shawl." Mabel and I were alone. I believe it was the first time we had been really alone since I arrived. She looked up from the teacups, fixing her pallid eyes on mine. She had made a question of the sentence.

"You hear it like that?" I asked innocently. I purposely used the present tense.

She changed her stare from one eye to the other; it was absolutely expressionless. My sister's step sounded on the floor of the room behind us.

"If only—" Mabel began, then stopped, and my own feelings leaping out instinctively completed the sentence I felt was in her mind:

"—something would happen."

She instantly corrected me. I had caught her thought, yet somehow phrased it wrongly.

"We could escape!" She lowered her tone a little, saying it hurriedly. The "we" amazed and horrified me; but something in her voice and manner struck me utterly dumb. There was ice and terror in it. It was a dying woman speaking—a lost and hopeless soul.

In that atrocious moment I hardly noticed what was said exactly, but I remember that my sister returned with a grey shawl about her shoulders, and that Mabel said, in her ordinary voice again, "It *is* chilly, yes; let's have tea inside," and that two maids, one of them the grenadier, speedily carried the loaded trays into the morning-room and put a match to the logs in the great open fireplace. It was, after all, foolish to risk the sharp evening air, for dusk was falling steadily, and even the sunshine of the day just fading could not turn autumn into summer. I was the last to come in. Just as I left the verandah a large black bird swooped down in front of me past the pillars; it dropped from overhead, swerved abruptly to one side as it caught sight of me, and flapped heavily towards the shrubberies on the left of the terraces, where it disappeared into the gloom. It flew very low, very close. And it startled me, I think because in some way it seemed like my Shadow materialised—as though the dark horror that was rising everywhere from house and garden, then settling back so thickly yet so imperceptibly upon us all, were incarnated in that whirring creature that passed between the daylight and the coming night.

I stood a moment, wondering if it would appear again, before I followed the others indoors, and as I was in the act of closing the windows after me, I caught a glimpse of a figure on the lawn. It was some distance away, on the other side of the shrubberies, in fact where the bird had vanished. But, in spite of the twilight that half magnified, half obscured it, the identity was unmistakable. I knew the housekeeper's stiff walk too well to be deceived. "Mrs. Marsh taking the air," I said to myself. I felt the necessity of saying it, and I wondered why she was doing so at this particular hour. If I had other thoughts they were so vague, and so quickly and utterly suppressed, that I cannot recall them sufficiently to relate them here.

And, once indoors, it was to be expected that there would come explanation, discussion, conversation, at any rate, regarding the singular noise and its cause, some uttered evidence of the mood that had been strong enough to drive us all inside. Yet there was none. Each of us purposely, and with various skill, ignored it. We talked little, and when we did it was of anything in the world but that. Personally, I experienced a touch of that same bewilderment which had come over me during my first talk with Frances on the evening of my arrival, for I recall now the acute tension, and the hope, yet dread, that one or other of us must sooner or later introduce the subject. It did not happen, however; no reference was made to it even remotely. It was the presence of Mabel, I felt positive, that prohibited. As soon might we have discussed Death in the bedroom of a dying woman.

The only scrap of conversation I remember, where all was ordinary and commonplace, was when Mabel spoke casually to the grenadier asking why Mrs. Marsh had omitted to do something or other—what it was I forget—and that the maid replied respectfully that "Mrs. Marsh was very sorry, but her 'and still pained her." I enquired, though so casually that I scarcely know what prompted the words, whether she had injured herself severely, and the reply, "She upset a lamp and burnt herself," was said in a tone that made me feel my curiosity was indiscreet, "but she always has an excuse for not doing things she ought to do." The little bit of conversation remained with me, and I remember particularly the quick way Frances interrupted and turned the talk upon the delinquencies of servants in general, telling incidents of her own at our flat with a volubility that perhaps seemed forced, and that certainly did not encourage general talk as it may have been intended to do. We lapsed into silence immediately she finished.

But for all our care and all our calculated silence, each knew that something had, in these last moments, come very close; it had brushed us in passing; it had retired; and I am inclined to think now that the large dark thing I saw, riding the dusk, probably bird of prey, was in some sense a symbol of it in my mind—that actually there had been no bird at all, I mean, but that my mood of apprehension and dismay had formed the vivid picture in my thoughts. It had swept past us, it had retreated, but it was now, at this moment, in hiding very close. And it was watching us.

Perhaps, too, it was mere coincidence that I encountered Mrs. Marsh, *his* housekeeper, several times that evening in the short interval between tea and dinner, and that on each occasion the sight of this gaunt, half-saturnine woman fed my prejudice against her. Once, on my way to the telephone, I ran into her just where the passage is somewhat jammed by a square table carrying the Chinese gong, a grandfather's clock, and a box of croquet mallets. We both gave way, then both advanced, then again gave way—simultaneously. It seemed impossible to pass. We stepped with decision to the same side, finally colliding in the middle, while saying those futile little things, half apology, half excuse, that are inevitable at such times. In the end she stood upright against the wall for me to pass, taking her place against the very door I wished to open. It was ludicrous.

"Excuse me—I was just going in—to telephone," I explained. And she sidled off, murmuring apologies, but opening the door for me while she did so. Our hands met a moment on the handle. There was a second's awkwardness—it was too stupid. I remembered her injury, and by way of something to say, I enquired after it. She thanked me; it was entirely healed now, but it might have been much worse; and there was something about the "mercy of the Lord" that I didn't quite catch. While telephoning, however—a London call, and my attention focussed on it—I realised sharply that this was the first time I had spoken with her; also, that I had—touched her.

It happened to be a Sunday, and the lines were clear. I got my connection quickly, and the incident was forgotten while my thoughts went up to London. On my way upstairs, then, the woman came back into my mind, so that I recalled other things about her—how she seemed all over the house, in unlikely places often; how I had caught her sitting in the hall alone that night; how she was for ever coming and going with her lugubrious visage and that untidy hair at the back that had made me laugh three years ago with the idea that it looked singed or burnt; and how the impression on my first arrival at The Towers was that this woman somehow kept alive, though its evidence was outwardly suppressed, the influence of her late employer and of his sombre teachings. Somewhere with her was associated the idea of punishment, vindictiveness, revenge. I remembered again suddenly my odd notion that she sought to keep her present mistress here, a prisoner in this bleak and comfortless house, and that really, in spite of her obsequious silence, she was intensely opposed to the change of thought that had reclaimed Mabel to a happier view of life.

All this in a passing second flashed in review before me, and I discovered, or at any rate reconstructed, the real Mrs. Marsh. She was decidedly in the Shadow. More, she stood in the forefront of it, stealthily leading an assault, as it were, against The Towers and its occupants, as though, consciously or unconsciously, she laboured incessantly to this hateful end.

I can only judge that some state of nervousness in me permitted the series of insignificant thoughts to assume this dramatic shape, and that what had gone before prepared the way and led her up at the head of so formidable a procession. I relate it exactly as it came to me. My nerves were doubtless somewhat on edge by now. Otherwise I should hardly have been a prey to the exaggeration at all. I seemed open to so many strange impressions.

Nothing else, perhaps, can explain my ridiculous conversation with her, when, for the third time that evening, I came suddenly upon the woman half-way down the stairs, standing by an open window as if in the act of listening. She was dressed in black, a black shawl over her square shoulders and black gloves on her big, broad hands. Two black objects, prayer-books apparently, she clasped, and on her head she wore a bonnet with shaking beads of jet. At first I did not know her, as I came running down upon her from the landing; it was only when she stood aside to let me pass that I saw her profile against the tapestry and recognised Mrs. Marsh. And to catch her on the front stairs, dressed like this, struck me as incongruous—impertinent. I paused in my dangerous descent. Through the opened window came the sound of bells—church bells—a sound more depressing to me than superstition, and as nauseating. Though the action was ill-judged, I obeyed the sudden prompting—was it a secret desire to attack, perhaps?—and spoke to her.

"Been to church, I suppose, Mrs. Marsh?" I said. "Or just going, perhaps?"

Her face, as she looked up a second to reply, was like an iron doll that moved its lips and turned its eyes, but made no other imitation of life at all.

"Some of us still goes, sir," she said unctuously.

It was respectful enough, yet the implied judgment of the rest of the world made me almost angry. A deferential insolence lay behind the affected meekness.

"For those who believe no doubt it *is* helpful," I smiled. "True religion brings peace and happiness, I'm sure—joy, Mrs. Marsh, JOY!" I found keen satisfaction in the emphasis.

She looked at me like a knife. I cannot describe the implacable thing that shone in her fixed, stern eyes, nor the shadow of felt darkness that stole across her face. She glittered. I felt hate in her. I knew—she knew too—who was in the thoughts of us both at that moment.

She replied softly, never forgetting her place for an instant:

"There is joy, sir—in 'eaven —over one sinner that repenteth, and in church there goes up prayer to Gawd for those 'oo—well, for the others, sir, 'oo—"

She cut short her sentence thus. The gloom about her as she said it was like the gloom about a hearse, a tomb, a darkness of great hopeless dungeons. My tongue ran on of itself with a kind of bitter satisfaction:

"We must believe there are *no* others, Mrs. Marsh. Salvation, you know, would be such a failure if there were. No merciful, all-foreseeing God could ever have devised such a fearful plan—"

Her voice, interrupting me, seemed to rise out of the bowels of the earth:

"They rejected the salvation when it was offered to them, sir, on earth."

"But you wouldn't have them tortured for ever because of one mistake in ignorance," I said, fixing her with my eye. "Come now, would you, Mrs. Marsh? No God worth worshipping could permit such cruelty. Think a moment what it means."

She stared at me, a curious expression in her stupid eyes. It seemed to me as though the "woman" in her revolted, while yet she dared not suffer her grim belief to trip. That is, she would willingly have had it otherwise but for a terror that prevented.

"We may pray for them, sir, and we do—we *may* 'ope." She dropped her eyes to the carpet.

"Good, good!" I put in cheerfully, sorry now that I had spoken at all. "That's more hopeful, at any rate isn't it?"

She murmured something about Abraham's bosom, and the "time of salvation not being for ever," as I tried to pass her. Then a half gesture that she made stopped me. There was something more she wished to say—to ask. She looked up furtively. In her eyes I saw the "woman" peering out through fear.

"Per'aps, sir," she faltered, as though lightning must strike her dead, "per'aps, would you think, a drop of cold water, given in His name, might moisten—?"

But I stopped her, for the foolish talk had lasted long enough.

"Of course," I exclaimed, "of course. For God is love, remember, and love means charity, tolerance, sympathy, and sparing others pain," and I hurried past her, determined to end the outrageous conversation for which yet I knew myself entirely to blame. Behind me, she stood stock-still for several minutes, half bewildered, half alarmed, as I suspected. I caught the fragment of another sentence, one word of it, rather—"punishment"—but the rest escaped me. Her arrogance and condescending tolerance exasperated me, while I was at the same time secretly pleased that I might have touched some string of remorse or sympathy in her after all. Her belief was iron; she dared not let it go; yet somewhere underneath there lurked the germ of a wholesome revulsion. She would help "them"—if she dared. Her question proved it.

Half-ashamed of myself, I turned and crossed the hall quickly lest I should be tempted to say more, and in me was a disagreeable sensation as though I had just left the Incurable Ward of some great hospital. A reaction caught me as of nausea. Ugh! I wanted such people cleansed by fire. They seemed to me as centres of contamination whose vicious thoughts flowed out to stain God's glorious world. I saw myself, Frances, Mabel too especially, on the rack, while that odious figure of cruelty and darkness stood over us and ordered the awful handles turned in order that we might be "saved"—forced, that is, to think and believe exactly as *she* thought and believed.

I found relief for my somewhat childish indignation by letting myself loose upon the organ then. The flood of Bach and Beethoven brought back the sense of proportion. It proved, however, at the same time that there *had* been this growth of distortion in me, and that it had been provided apparently by my closer contact—for the first time—with that funereal personality, the woman who, like her master, believed that all holding views of God that differed from her own, must be damned eternally. It gave me, moreover, some faint clue perhaps, though a clue I was unequal to following up, to the nature of the strife and terror and frustrate influence in the house. That housekeeper had to do with it. She kept it alive. Her thought was like a spell she waved above her mistress's head.

VII

That night I was wakened by a hurried tapping at my door, and before I could answer, Frances stood beside my bed. She had switched on the light as she came in. Her hair fell straggling over her dressing-gown. Her face was deathly pale, its expression so distraught it was almost haggard. The eyes were very wide. She looked almost like another woman.

She was whispering at a great pace: "Bill, Bill, wake up, quick!"

"I *am* awake. What is it?" I whispered too. I was startled.

"Listen!" was all she said. Her eyes stared into vacancy.

There was not a sound in the great house. The wind had dropped, and all was still. Only the tapping seemed to continue endlessly in my brain. The clock on the mantelpiece pointed to half-past two.

"I heard nothing, Frances. What is it?" I rubbed my eyes; I had been very deeply asleep.

"Listen!" she repeated very softly, holding up one finger and turning her eyes towards the door she had left ajar. Her usual calmness had deserted her. She was in the grip of some distressing terror.

For a full minute we held our breath and listened. Then her eyes rolled round again and met my own, and her skin went even whiter than before.

"It woke me," she said beneath her breath, and moving a step nearer to my bed. "It was the Noise." Even her whisper trembled.

"The Noise!" The word repeated itself dully of its own accord. I would rather it had been anything in the world but that—earthquake, foreign cannon, collapse of the house above our heads! "The noise, Frances! Are you *sure?*" I was playing really for a little time.

"It was like thunder. At first I thought it *was* thunder. But a minute later it came again—from underground. It's appalling." She muttered the words, her voice not properly under control.

There was a pause of perhaps a minute, and then we both spoke at once. We said foolish, obvious things that neither of us believed in for a second. The roof had fallen in, there were burglars downstairs, the safes had been blown open. It was to comfort each other as children do that we said these things; also it was to gain further time.

"There's some one in the house, of course," I heard my voice say finally, as I sprang out of bed and hurried into dressing-gown and slippers. "Don't be alarmed. I'll go down and see," and from the drawer I took a pistol it was my habit to carry everywhere with me. I loaded it carefully while Frances stood stock-still beside the bed and watched. I moved towards the open door.

"You stay here, Frances," I whispered, the beating of my heart making the words uneven, "while I go down and make a search. Lock yourself in, girl. Nothing can happen to you. It was downstairs, you said?"

"Underneath," she answered faintly, pointing through the floor.

She moved suddenly between me and the door.

"Listen! Hark!" she said, the eyes in her face quite fixed; "it's coming again," and she turned her head to catch the slightest sound. I stood there watching her, and while I watched her, shook. But nothing stirred. From the halls below rose only the whirr and quiet ticking of the numerous clocks. The blind by the open window behind us flapped out a little into the room as the draught caught it.

"I'll come with you, Bill—to the next floor," she broke the silence.

"Then I'll stay with Mabel—till you come up again." The blind sank down with a long sigh as she said it.

The question jumped to my lips before I could repress it:

"Mabel is awake. She heard it too?"

I hardly know why horror caught me at her answer. All was so vague and terrible as we stood there playing the great game of this sinister house where nothing ever happened.

"We met in the passage. She was on her way to me."

What shook in me, shook inwardly. Frances, I mean, did not see it. I had the feeling just then that the Noise was upon us, that any second it would boom and roar about our ears. But the deep silence held. I only heard my sister's little whisper coming across the room in answer to my question:

"Then what is Mabel doing now?"

And her reply proved that she was yielding at last beneath the dreadful tension, for she spoke at once, unable longer to keep up the pretence. With a kind of relief, as it were, she said it out, looking helplessly at me like a child:

"She is weeping and gna——"

My expression must have stopped her. I believe I clapped both hands upon her mouth, though when I realised things clearly again, I found they were covering my own ears instead. It was a moment of unutterable horror. The revulsion I felt was actually physical. It would have given me pleasure to fire off all the five chambers of my pistol into the air above my head; the sound—a definite, wholesome sound that explained itself—would have been a positive relief. Other feelings, though, were in me too, all over me, rushing to and fro. It was vain to seek their disentanglement; it was impossible. I confess that I experienced, among them, a touch of paralysing fear—though for a moment only; it passed as sharply as it came, leaving me with a violent flush of blood to the face such as bursts of anger bring, followed abruptly by an icy perspiration over the entire body. Yet I may honestly avow that it was not ordinary personal fear I felt, nor any common dread of physical injury. It was, rather, a vast, impersonal shrinking—a sympathetic shrinking—from the agony and terror that countless others, somewhere, somehow, felt for themselves. The first sensation of a prison overwhelmed me in that instant, of bitter strife and frenzied suffering, and the fiery torture of the yearning to escape that was yet hopelessly uttered. . . . It was of incredible power. It was real. The vain, intolerable hope swept over me.

I mastered myself, though hardly knowing how, and took my sister's hand. It was as cold as ice, as I led her firmly to the door and out into the passage. Apparently she noticed nothing of my so near collapse, for I caught her whisper as we went. "You *are* brave, Bill; splendidly brave."

The upper corridors of the great sleeping house were brightly lit; on her way to me she had turned on every electric switch her hand could reach; and as we passed the final flight of stairs to the floor below, I heard a door shut softly and knew that Mabel had been listening—waiting for us. I led my sister up to it. She knocked, and the door was opened cautiously an inch or so. The room was pitch black. I caught no glimpse of Mabel standing there. Frances turned to me with a hurried whisper, "Billy, you *will* be careful, won't you?" and went in. I just had time to answer that I would not be long, and Frances to reply, "You'll find us here—" when the door closed and cut her sentence short before its end.

But it was not alone the closing door that took the final words. Frances—by the way she disappeared I knew it—had made a swift and violent movement into the darkness that was as though she sprang. She leaped upon that other woman who stood back among the shadows, for, simultaneously with the clipping of the sentence, another sound was also stopped—stifled, smothered, choked back lest I should also hear it. Yet not in time. I heard it—a hard and horrible sound that explained both the leap and the abrupt cessation of the whispered words.

I stood irresolute a moment. It was as though all the bones had been withdrawn from my body, so that I must sink and fall. That sound plucked them out, and plucked out my self-possession with them. I am not sure that it was a sound I had ever heard before, though children, I half remembered, made it sometimes in blind rages when they knew not what they did. In a grown-up person certainly I had never known it. I associated it with animals rather—horribly. In the history of the world, no doubt, it has been common enough, alas, but fortunately to-day there can be but few who know it, or would recognise it even when heard. The bones shot back into my body the same instant, but red-hot and burning; the brief instant of irresolution passed; I was torn between the desire to break down the door and enter, and to run—run for my life from a thing I dared not face.

Out of the horrid tumult, then, I adopted neither course. Without reflection, certainly without analysis of what was best to do for my sister, myself, or Mabel, I took up my action where it had been interrupted. I turned from the awful door and moved slowly towards the head of the stairs. But that dreadful little sound came with me. I believe my own teeth chattered. It seemed all over the house—in the empty halls that opened into the long passages towards the music-room, and even in the grounds outside the building. From the lawns and barren garden, from the ugly terraces themselves, it rose into the night, and behind it came a curious driving sound, incomplete, unfinished, as of wailing for deliverance, the wailing of desperate souls in anguish, the dull and dry beseeching of hopeless spirits in prison.

That I could have taken the little sound from the bedroom where I actually heard it, and spread it thus over the entire house and grounds, is evidence, perhaps, of the state my nerves were in. The wailing assuredly was in my mind alone. But the longer I hesitated, the more difficult became my task, and, gathering up my dressing-gown, lest I should trip in the darkness, I passed slowly down the staircase into the hall below. I carried neither candle nor matches; every switch in room and corridor was known to me. The covering of darkness was indeed rather comforting than otherwise, for if it prevented seeing, it also prevented being seen. The heavy pistol, knocking against my thigh as I moved, made me feel I was carrying a child's toy, foolishly. I experienced in every nerve that primitive vast dread which is the Thrill of darkness. Merely the child in me was comforted by that pistol.

The night was not entirely black; the iron bars across the glass front door were visible, and, equally, I discerned the big, stiff wooden chairs in the hall, the gaping fireplace, the upright pillars supporting the staircase, the round table in the centre with its books and flower-vases, and the basket that held visitors' cards. There, too, was the stick and umbrella-stand and the shelf with railway guides, directory, and telegraph forms. Clocks ticked everywhere with sounds like quiet footfalls. Light fell here and there in patches from the floor above. I stood a moment in the hall, letting my eyes grow more accustomed to the gloom, while deciding on a plan of search. I made out the ivy trailing outside over one of the big windows . . . and then the tall clock by the front door made a grating noise deep down inside its body—it was the Presentation clock, large and hideous, given by the congregation of his church—and, dreading the booming strike it seemed to threaten, I made a quick decision. If others beside myself were about in the night, the sound of that striking might cover their approach.

So I tiptoed to the right, where the passage led towards the dining-room. In the other direction were the morning- and drawing-room, both little used, and various other rooms beyond that had been *his,* generally now kept locked. I thought of my sister, waiting upstairs with that frightened woman for my return. I went quickly, yet stealthily.

And, to my surprise, the door of the dining-room was open. It had been opened. I paused on the threshold, staring about me. I think I fully expected to see a figure blocked in the shadows against the heavy sideboard, or looming on the other side beneath his portrait. But the room was empty; I *felt* it empty. Through the wide bow-windows that gave onto the verandah came an uncertain glimmer that even shone reflected in the polished surface of the dinner-table, and again I perceived the stiff outline of chairs, waiting tenantless all round it, two larger ones with high carved backs at either end. The monkey-trees on the upper terrace, too, were visible outside against the sky, and the solemn crests of the wellingtonias on the terraces below. The enormous clock on the mantelpiece ticked very slowly, as though its machinery were running down, and I made out the pale round patch that was its face. Resisting my first inclination to turn the lights up—my hand had gone so far as to finger the friendly knob—I crossed the room so carefully that no single board creaked, nor a single chair, as I rested a hand upon its back, moved on the parquet flooring. I turned neither to the right nor left, nor did I once look back.

I went towards the long corridor filled with priceless *objets d'art,* that led through various ante-chambers into the spacious music-room, and only at the mouth of this corridor did I next halt a moment in uncertainty. For this long corridor, lit faintly by high windows on the left from the verandah, was very narrow, owing to the mass of shelves and fancy tables it contained. It was not that I feared to knock over precious things as I went, but that, because of its ungenerous width, there would be no room to pass another person—if I met one. And the certainty had suddenly come upon me that somewhere in this corridor another person at this actual moment stood. Here, somehow, amid all this dead atmosphere of furniture and impersonal emptiness, lay the hint of a living human presence; and with such conviction did it come upon me, that my hand instinctively gripped the pistol in my pocket before I could even think. Either some one had passed along this corridor just before me, or some one lay waiting at its farther end—withdrawn or flattened into one of the little recesses, to let me pass. It was the person who had opened the door. And the blood ran from my heart as I realised it.

It was not courage that sent me on, but rather a strong impulsion from behind that made it impossible to retreat: the feeling that a throng pressed at my back, drawing nearer and nearer; that I was already half surrounded, swept, dragged, coaxed into a vast prison-house where there was wailing and gnashing of teeth, where their worm dieth not and their fire is not quenched. I can neither explain nor justify the storm of irrational emotion that swept me as I stood in that moment, staring down the length of the silent corridor towards the music-room at the far end, I can only repeat that no personal bravery sent me down it, but that the negative emotion of fear was swamped in this vast sea of pity and commiseration for others that surged upon me.

My senses, at least, were no whit confused; if anything, my brain registered impressions with keener accuracy than usual. I noticed, for instance, that the two swinging doors of baize that cut the corridor into definite lengths, making little rooms of the spaces between them, were both wide open—in the dim light no mean achievement. Also that the fronds of a palm plant, some ten feet in front of me, still stirred gently from the air of some one who had recently gone past them. The long green leaves waved to and fro like hands. Then I went stealthily forward down the narrow space, proud even that I had this command of myself, and so carefully that my feet made no sound upon the Japanese matting on the floor.

It was a journey that seemed timeless. I have no idea how fast or slow I went, but I remember that I deliberately examined articles on each side of me, peering with particular closeness into the recesses of wall and window. I passed the first baize doors, and the passage beyond them widened out to hold shelves of books; there were sofas and small reading-tables against the wall. It narrowed again presently, as I entered the second stretch. The windows here were higher and smaller, and marble statuettes of classical subjects lined the walls, watching me like figures of the dead. Their white and shining faces saw me, yet made no sign. I passed next between the second baize doors. They, too, had been fastened back with hooks against the wall. Thus all doors were open—had been recently opened.

And so, at length, I found myself in the final widening of the corridor which formed an ante-chamber to the music-room itself. It had been used formerly to hold the overflow of meetings. No door separated it from the great hall beyond, but heavy curtains hung usually to close it off, and these curtains were invariably drawn. They now stood wide. And here—I can merely state the impression that came upon me—I knew myself at last surrounded. The throng that pressed behind me, also surged in front: facing me in the big room, and waiting for my entry, stood a multitude; on either side of me, in the very air above my head, the vast assemblage paused upon my coming. The pause, however, was momentary, for instantly the deep, tumultuous movement was resumed that yet was silent as a cavern underground. I felt the agony that was in it, the passionate striving, the awful struggle to escape. The semi-darkness held beseeching faces that fought to press themselves upon my vision, yearning yet hopeless eyes, lips scorched and dry, mouths that opened to implore but found no craved delivery in actual words, and a fury of misery and hate that made the life in me stop dead, frozen by the horror of vain pity. That intolerable, vain Hope was everywhere.

And the multitude, it came to me, was not a single multitude, but many; for, as soon as one huge division pressed too close upon the edge of escape, it was dragged back by another and prevented. The wild host was divided against itself. Here dwelt the Shadow I had "imagined" weeks ago, and in it struggled armies of lost souls as in the depths of some bottomless pit whence there is no escape. The layers mingled, fighting against themselves in endless torture. It was in this great Shadow I had clairvoyantly seen Mabel, but about its fearful mouth, I now was certain, hovered another figure of darkness, a figure who sought to keep it in existence, since to her thought were due those lampless depths of woe without escape. . . . Towards me the multitudes now surged.

It was a sound and a movement that brought me back into myself. The great clock at the further end of the room just then struck the hour of three. That was the sound. And the movement—? I was aware that a figure was passing across the distant centre of the floor. Instantly I dropped back into the arena of my little human terror. My hand again clutched stupidly at the pistol butt. I drew back into the folds of the heavy curtain. And the figure advanced.

I remember every detail. At first it seemed to me enormous—this advancing shadow—far beyond human scale; but as it came nearer, I measured it, though not consciously, by the organ pipes that gleamed in faint colours, just above its gradual soft approach. It passed them, already half-way across the great room. I saw then that its stature was that of ordinary men. The prolonged booming of the clock died away. I heard the footfall, shuffling upon the polished boards. I heard another sound—a voice, low and monotonous, droning as in prayer. The figure was speaking. It was a woman. And she carried in both hands before her a small object that faintly shimmered—a glass of water. And then I recognised her.

There was still an instant's time before she reached me, and I made use of it. I shrank back, flattening myself against the wall. Her voice ceased a moment, as she turned and carefully drew the curtains together behind her, closing them with one hand. Oblivious of my presence, though she actually touched my dressing-gown with the hand that pulled the cords, she resumed her dreadful, solemn march, disappearing at length down the long vista of the corridor like a shadow. But as she passed me, her voice began again, so that I heard each word distinctly as she uttered it, her head aloft, her figure upright, as though she moved at the head of a procession:

"A drop of cold water, given in His name, shall moisten their burning tongues."

It was repeated monotonously over and over again, droning down into the distance as she went, until at length both voice and figure faded into the shadows at the farther end.

For a time, I have no means of measuring precisely, I stood in that dark corner, pressing my back against the wall, and would have drawn the curtains down to hide me had I dared to stretch an arm out. The dread that presently the woman would return passed gradually away. I realised that the air had emptied, the crowd her presence had stirred into activity had retreated; I was alone in the gloomy under-spaces of the odious building. . . . Then I remembered suddenly again the terrified women waiting for me on that upper landing; and realised that my skin was wet and freezing cold after a profuse perspiration. I prepared to retrace my steps. I remember the effort it cost me to leave the support of the wall and covering darkness of my corner, and step out into the grey light of the corridor. At first I sidled, then, finding this mode of walking impossible, turned my face boldly and walked quickly, regardless that my dressing-gown set the precious objects shaking as I passed. A wind that sighed mournfully against the high, small windows seemed to have got inside the corridor as well; it felt so cold; and every moment I dreaded to see the outline of the woman's figure as she waited in recess or angle against the wall for me to pass.

Was there another thing I dreaded even more? I cannot say. I only know that the first baize doors had swung-to behind me, and the second ones were close at hand, when the great dim thunder caught me, pouring up with prodigious volume so that it seemed to roll out from another world. It shook the very bowels of the building. I was closer to it than that other time, when it had followed me from the goblin garden. There was strength and hardness in it, as of metal reverberation. Some touch of numbness, almost of paralysis, must surely have been upon me that I felt no actual terror, for I remember even turning and standing still to hear it better.

"That is the Noise," my thought ran stupidly, and I think I whispered it aloud; *"the Doors are closing."*

The wind outside against the windows was audible, so it cannot have been really loud, yet to me it was the biggest, deepest sound I have ever heard, but so far away, with such awful remoteness in it, that I had to doubt my own ears at the same time. It seemed underground—the rumbling of earthquake gates that shut remorselessly within the rocky Earth—stupendous ultimate thunder. *They* were shut off from help again. The doors had closed.

I felt a storm of pity, an agony of bitter, futile hate sweep through me. My memory of the figure changed then. The Woman with the glass of cooling water had stepped down from Heaven; but the Man—or was it Men?—who smeared this terrible layer of belief and Thought upon the world! . . .

I crossed the dining-room—it was fancy, of course, that held my eyes from glancing at the portrait for fear I should see it smiling approval—and so finally reached the hall, where the light from the floor above seemed now quite bright in comparison. All the doors I closed carefully behind me; but first I had to open them. The woman had closed every one. Up the stairs, then, I actually ran, two steps at a time. My sister was standing outside Mabel's door. By her face I knew that she had also heard. There was no need to ask. I quickly made my mind up.

"There's nothing," I said, and detailed briefly my tour of search. "All is quiet and undisturbed downstairs." May God forgive me!

She beckoned to me, closing the door softly behind her. My heart beat violently a moment, then stood still.

"Mabel," she said aloud.

It was like the sentence of a judge, that one short word.

I tried to push past her and go in, but she stopped me with her arm. She was wholly mistress of herself, I saw.

"Hush!" she said in a lower voice. "I've got her round again with brandy. She's sleeping quietly now. We won't disturb her."

She drew me farther out into the landing, and as she did so, the clock in the hall below struck half-past three. I had stood, then, thirty minutes in the corridor below. "You've been such a long time," she said simply. "I feared for you," and she took my hand in her own that was cold and clammy.

VIII

And then, while that dreadful house stood listening about us in the early hours of this chill morning upon the edge of winter, she told me, with laconic brevity, things about Mabel that I heard as from a distance. There was nothing so unusual or tremendous in the short recital, nothing indeed I might not have already guessed for myself. It was the time and scene, the inference, too, that made it so afflicting: the idea that Mabel believed herself so utterly and hopelessly lost—beyond recovery—*damned.*

That she had loved him with so passionate a devotion that she had given her soul into his keeping, this certainly I had not divined—probably because I had never thought about it one way or the other. He had "converted" her, I knew, but that she had subscribed whole-heartedly to that most cruel and ugly of his dogmas—this was new to me, and came with a certain shock as I heard it. In love, of course, the weaker nature is receptive to all manner of suggestion. This man had "suggested" his pet brimstone lake so vividly that she had listened and believed. He had frightened her into heaven; and his heaven, a definite locality in the skies, had its foretaste here on earth in miniature—The Towers, house, and garden. Into his dolorous scheme of a handful saved and millions damned, his enclosure, as it were, of sheep and goats, he had swept her before she was aware of it. Her mind no longer was her own. And it was Mrs. Marsh who kept the thought-stream open, though tempered, as she deemed, with that touch of craven, superstitious mercy.

But what I found it difficult to understand, and still more difficult to accept, was that, during her year abroad, she had been so haunted with a secret dread of that hideous after-death that she had finally revolted and tried to recover that clearer state of mind she had enjoyed before the religious bully had stunned her—yet had tried in vain. She had returned to The Towers to find her soul again, only to realise that it was lost eternally. The cleaner state of mind lay then beyond recovery. In the reaction that followed the removal of his terrible "suggestion," she felt the crumbling of all that he had taught her, but searched in vain for the peace and beauty his teachings had destroyed. Nothing came to replace these. She was empty, desolate, hopeless; craving her former joy and carelessness, she found only hate and diabolical calculation. This man, whom she had loved to the point of losing her soul for him, had bequeathed to her one black and fiery thing—the terror of the damned. His thinking wrapped her in this iron garment that held her fast.

All this Frances told me, far more briefly than I have here repeated it. In her eyes and gestures and laconic sentences lay the conviction of great beating issues and of menacing drama my own description fails to recapture. It was all so incongruous and remote from the world I lived in that more than once a smile, though a smile of pity, fluttered to my lips; but a glimpse of my face in the mirror showed rather the leer of a grimace. There was no real laughter anywhere that night. The entire adventure seemed so incredible, here, in this twentieth century—but yet delusion, that feeble word, did not occur once in the comments my mind suggested though did not utter. I remembered that forbidding Shadow too; my sister's water-colours; the vanished personality of our hostess; the inexplicable, thundering Noise, and the figure of Mrs. Marsh in her midnight ritual that was so childish yet so horrible. I shivered in spite of my own "emancipated" cast of mind.

"There *is* no Mabel," were the words with which my sister sent another shower of ice down my spine. "He has killed her in his lake of fire and brimstone."

I stared at her blankly, as in a nightmare where nothing true or possible ever happened.

"He killed her in his lake of fire and brimstone," she repeated more faintly.

A desperate effort was in me to say the strong, sensible thing which should destroy the oppressive horror that grew so stiflingly about us both, but again the mirror drew the attempted smile into the merest grin, betraying the distortion that was everywhere in the place.

"You mean," I stammered beneath my breath, "that her faith has gone, but that the terror has remained?" I asked it, dully groping. I moved out of the line of the reflection in the glass.

She bowed her head as though beneath a weight; her skin was the pallor of grey ashes.

"You mean," I said louder, "that she has lost her—mind?"

"She is terror incarnate," was the whispered answer. "Mabel has lost her soul. Her soul is—there!" She pointed horribly below. "She is seeking it . . . ?"

The word "soul" stung me into something of my normal self again.

"But her terror, poor thing, is not—cannot be—transferable to *us!*" I exclaimed more vehemently. "It certainly is not convertible into feelings, sights, and—even sounds!"

She interrupted me quickly, almost impatiently, speaking with that conviction by which she conquered me so easily that night.

"It is her terror that revived 'the Others.' It has brought her into touch with them. They are loose and driving after her. Her efforts at resistance have given them also hope—that escape, after all, is possible. Day and night they strive."

"Escape! Others!" The anger fast rising in me dropped of its own accord at the moment of birth. It shrank into a shuddering beyond my control. In that moment, I think, I would have believed in the possibility of anything and everything she might tell me. To argue or contradict seemed equally futile.

"His strong belief, as also the beliefs of others who have preceded him," she replied, so sure of herself that I actually turned to look over my shoulder, "have left their shadow like a thick deposit over the house and grounds. To them, poor souls imprisoned by thought, it was hopeless as granite walls—until her resistance, her effort to dissipate it—let in light. Now, in their thousands, they are flocking to this little light, seeking escape. Her own escape, don't you see, may release them all!"

It took my breath away. Had his predecessors, former occupants of this house, also preached damnation of all the world but their own exclusive sect? Was this the explanation of her obscure talk of "layers," each striving against the other for domination? And if men are spirits, and these spirits survive, could strong Thought thus determine their condition even afterwards?

So many questions flooded into me that I selected no one of them, but stared in uncomfortable silence, bewildered, out of my depth, and acutely, painfully distressed. There was so odd a mixture of possible truth and incredible, unacceptable explanation in it all; so much confirmed, yet so much left darker than before. What she said did, indeed, offer a quasi-interpretation of my own series of abominable sensations—strife, agony, pity, hate, escape—but so far-fetched that only the deep conviction in her voice and attitude made it tolerable for a second even. I found myself in a curious state of mind. I could neither think clearly nor say a word to refute her amazing statements, whispered there beside me in the shivering hours of the early morning with only a wall between ourselves and—Mabel. Close behind her words I remember this singular thing, however—that an atmosphere as of the Inquisition seemed to rise and stir about the room, beating awful wings of black above my head.

Abruptly, then, a moment's common sense returned to me. I faced her.

"And the Noise?" I said aloud, more firmly, "the roar of the closing doors? We have *all* heard that! Is that subjective too?"

Frances looked sideways about her in a queer fashion that made my flesh creep again. I spoke brusquely, almost angrily. I repeated the question, and waited with anxiety for her reply.

"What noise?" she asked, with the frank expression of an innocent child. "What closing doors?"

But her face turned from grey to white, and I saw that drops of perspiration glistened on her forehead. She caught at the back of a chair to steady herself, then glanced about her again with that sidelong look that made my blood run cold. I understood suddenly then. She did not take in what I said. I knew now. She was listening—for something else.

And the discovery revived in me a far stronger emotion than any mere desire for immediate explanation. Not only did I not insist upon an answer, but I was actually terrified lest she *would* answer. More, I felt in me a terror lest I should be moved to describe my own experiences below-stairs, thus increasing their reality and so the reality of all. She might even explain them too!

Still listening intently, she raised her head and looked me in the eyes. Her lips opened to speak. The words came to me from a great distance, it seemed, and her voice had a sound like a stone that drops into a deep well, its fate though hidden, known.

"We are in it with her, too, Bill. We are in it with her. Our interpretations vary—because we are—in parts of it only. Mabel is in it—*all*."

The desire for violence came over me. If only she would say a definite thing in plain King's English! If only I could find it in me to give utterance to what shouted so loud within me! If only—the same old cry—something would happen! For all this elliptic talk that dazed my mind left obscurity everywhere. Her atrocious meaning, nonetheless, flashed through me, though vanishing before it wholly divulged itself.

It brought a certain reaction with it. I found my tongue. Whether I actually believed what I said is more than I can swear to; that it seemed to me wise at the moment is all I remember. My mind was in a state of obscure perception less than that of normal consciousness.

"Yes, Frances, I believe that what you say is the truth, and that we are in it with her" —I meant to say it with loud, hostile emphasis, but instead I whispered it lest she should hear the trembling of my voice—

"and for that reason, my dear sister, we leave to-morrow, you and I—to-day, rather, since it is long past midnight—we leave this house of the damned. We go back to London."

Frances looked up, her face distraught almost beyond recognition. But it was not my words that caused the tumult in her heart. It was a sound—the sound she had been listening for—so faint I barely caught it myself, and had she not pointed I could never have known the direction whence it came. Small and terrible it rose again in the stillness of the night, the sound of gnashing teeth. And behind it came another—the tread of stealthy footsteps. Both were just outside the door.

The room swung round me for a second. My first instinct to prevent my sister going out—she had dashed past me frantically to the door—gave place to another when I saw the expression in her eyes. I followed her lead instead; it was surer than my own. The pistol in my pocket swung uselessly against my thigh. I was flustered beyond belief and ashamed that I was so.

"Keep close to me, Frances," I said huskily, as the door swung wide and a shaft of light fell upon a figure moving rapidly. Mabel was going down the corridor. Beyond her, in the shadows on the staircase, a second figure stood beckoning, scarcely visible.

"Before they get her! Quick!" was screamed into my ears, and our arms were about her in the same moment. It was a horrible scene. Not that Mabel struggled in the least, but that she collapsed as we caught her and fell with her dead weight, as of a corpse, limp, against us. And her teeth began again. They continued, even beneath the hand that Frances clapped upon her lips. . . .

We carried her back into her own bedroom, where she lay down peacefully enough. It was so soon over. . . . The rapidity of the whole thing robbed it of reality almost. It had the swiftness of something remembered rather than of something witnessed. She slept again so quickly that it was almost as if we had caught her sleep-walking. I cannot say. I asked no questions at the time; I have asked none since; and my help was needed as little as the protection of my pistol. Frances was strangely competent and collected. . . . I lingered for some time uselessly by the door, till at length, looking up with a sigh, she made a sign for me to go.

"I shall wait in your room next door," I whispered, "till you come." But, though going out, I waited in the corridor instead, so as to hear the faintest call for help. In that dark corridor upstairs I waited, but not long. It may have been fifteen minutes when Frances reappeared, locking the door softly behind her. Leaning over the banisters, I saw her.

"I'll go in again about six o'clock," she whispered, "as soon as it gets light. She is sound asleep now. Please don't wait. If anything happens I'll call—you might leave your door ajar, perhaps." And she came up, looking like a ghost.

But I saw her first safely into bed, and the rest of the night I spent in an arm-chair close to my opened door, listening for the slightest sound. Soon after five o'clock I heard Frances fumbling with the key, and, peering over the railing again, I waited till she reappeared and went back into her own room. She closed her door. Evidently she was satisfied that all was well.

Then, and then only, did I go to bed myself, but not to sleep. I could not get the scene out of my mind, especially that odious detail of it which I hoped and believed my sister had not seen—the still, dark figure of the housekeeper waiting on the stairs below—waiting, of course, for Mabel.

IX

It seems I became a mere spectator after that; my sister's lead was so assured for one thing, and, for another, the responsibility of leaving Mabel alone—Frances laid it bodily upon my shoulders—was a little more than I cared about. Moreover, when we all three met later in the day, things went on so exactly as before, so absolutely without friction or distress, that to present a sudden, obvious excuse for cutting our visit short seemed ill-judged. And on the lowest grounds it would have been desertion. At any rate, it was beyond my powers, and Frances was quite firm that *she* must stay. We therefore did stay. Things that happen in the night always seem exaggerated and distorted when the sun shines brightly next morning; no one can reconstruct the terror of a nightmare afterwards, nor comprehend why it seemed so overwhelming at the time.

I slept till ten o'clock, and when I rang for breakfast, a note from my sister lay upon the tray, its message of counsel couched in a calm and comforting strain. Mabel, she assured me, was herself again and remembered nothing of what had happened; there was no need of any violent measures; I was to treat her exactly as if I knew nothing. "And, if you don't mind, Bill, let us leave the matter unmentioned between ourselves as well. Discussion exaggerates; such things are best not talked about. I'm sorry I disturbed you so unnecessarily; I was stupidly excited. Please forget all the things I said at the moment." She had written "nonsense" first instead of "things," then scratched it out. She wished to convey that hysteria had been abroad in the night, and I readily gulped the explanation down, though it could not satisfy me in the smallest degree.

There was another week of our visit still, and we stayed it out to the end without disaster. My desire to leave at times became that frantic thing, desire to escape; but I controlled it, kept silent, watched and wondered. Nothing happened. As before, and everywhere, there was no sequence of development, no connection between cause and effect; and climax, none whatever. The thing swayed up and down, backwards and forwards like a great loose curtain in the wind, and I could only vaguely surmise what caused the draught or why there was a curtain at all. A novelist might mould the queer material into coherent sequence that would be interesting but could not be true. It remains, therefore, not a story but a history. Nothing happened.

Perhaps my intense dislike of the fall of darkness was due wholly to my stirred imagination, and perhaps my anger when I learned that Frances now occupied a bed in our hostess's room was unreasonable. Nerves were unquestionably on edge. I was for ever on the look-out for some event that should make escape imperative, but yet that never presented itself. I slept lightly, left my door ajar to catch the slightest sound, even made stealthy tours of the house below-stairs while everybody dreamed in their beds. But I discovered nothing; the doors were always locked; I neither saw the housekeeper again in unreasonable times and places, nor heard a footstep in the passages and halls. The Noise was never once repeated. That horrible, ultimate thunder, my intensest dread of all, lay withdrawn into the abyss whence it had twice arisen. And though in my thoughts it was sternly denied existence, the great black reason for the fact afflicted me unbelievably. Since Mabel's fruitless effort to escape, the Doors kept closed remorselessly. She had failed; *they* gave up hope. For this was the explanation that haunted the region of my mind where feelings stir and hint before they clothe themselves in actual language. Only I firmly kept it there; it never knew expression.

But, if my ears were open, my eyes were opened too, and it were idle to pretend that I did not notice a hundred details that were capable of sinister interpretation had I been weak enough to yield. Some protective barrier had fallen into ruins round me, so that Terror stalked behind the general collapse, feeling for me through all the gaping fissures. Much of this, I admit, must have been merely the elaboration of those sensations I had first vaguely felt, before subsequent events and my talks with Frances had dramatised them into living thoughts. I therefore leave them unmentioned in this history, just as my mind left them unmentioned in that interminable final week.

Our life went on precisely as before—Mabel unreal and outwardly so still; Frances, secretive, anxious, tactful to the point of slyness, and keen to save to the point of self-forgetfulness. There were the same stupid meals, the same wearisome long evenings, the stifling ugliness of house and grounds, the Shadow settling in so thickly that it seemed almost a visible, tangible thing. I came to feel the only friendly things in all this hostile, cruel place were the robins that hopped boldly over the monstrous terraces and even up to the windows of the unsightly house itself. The robins alone knew joy; they danced, believing no evil thing was possible in all God's radiant world. They believed in everybody; *their* god's plan of life had no room in it for hell, damnation, and lakes of brimstone. I came to love the little birds. Had Samuel Franklyn known them, he might have preached a different sermon, bequeathing love in place of terror! . . .

Most of my time I spent writing; but it was a pretence at best, and rather a dangerous one besides. For it stirred the mind to production, with the result that other things came pouring in as well. With reading it was the same. In the end I found an aggressive, deliberate resistance to be the only way of feasible defence. To walk far afield was out of the question, for it meant leaving my sister too long alone, so that my exercise was confined to nearer home. My saunters in the grounds, however, never surprised the goblin garden again. It was close at hand, but I seemed unable to get wholly into it. Too many things assailed my mind for any one to hold exclusive possession, perhaps.

Indeed, all the interpretations, all the "layers," to use my sister's phrase, slipped in by turns and lodged there for a time. They came day and night, and though my reason denied them entrance they held their own as by a kind of squatters' right. They stirred moods already in me, that is, and did not introduce entirely new ones; for every mind conceals ancestral deposits that have been cultivated in turn along the whole line of its descent. Any day a chance shower may cause this one or that to blossom. Thus it came to me, at any rate. After darkness the Inquisition paced the empty corridors and set up ghastly apparatus in the dismal halls; and once, in the library, there swept over me that easy and delicious conviction that by confessing my wickedness I could resume it later, since Confession is expression, and expression brings relief and leaves one ready to accumulate again. And in such mood I felt bitter and unforgiving towards all others who thought differently. Another time it was a Pagan thing that assaulted me—so trivial yet oh, so significant at the time—when I dreamed that a herd of centaurs rolled up with a great stamping of hoofs round the house to destroy it, and then woke to hear the horses tramping across the field below the lawns; they neighed ominously and their noisy panting was audible as if it were just outside my windows.

But the tree episode, I think, was the most curious of all—except, perhaps, the incident with the children which I shall mention in a moment—for its closeness to reality was so unforgettable. Outside the east window of my room stood a giant wellingtonia on the lawn, its head rising level with the upper sash. It grew some twenty feet away, planted on the highest terrace, and I often saw it when closing my curtains for the night, noticing how it drew its heavy skirts about it, and how the light from other windows threw glimmering streaks and patches that turned it into the semblance of a towering, solemn image. It stood there then so strikingly, somehow like a great old-world idol, that it claimed attention. Its appearance was curiously formidable. Its branches rustled without visibly moving and it had a certain portentous, forbidding air, so grand and dark and monstrous in the night that I was always glad when my curtains shut it out. Yet, once in bed, I had never thought about it one way or the other, and by day had certainly never sought it out.

One night, then, as I went to bed and closed this window against a cutting easterly wind, I saw—that there were two of these trees. A brother wellingtonia rose mysteriously beside it, equally huge, equally towering, equally monstrous. The menacing pair of them faced me there upon the lawn. But in this new arrival lay a strange suggestion that frightened me before I could argue it away. Exact counterpart of its giant companion, it revealed also that gross, odious quality that all my sister's paintings held. I got the odd impression that the rest of these trees, stretching away dimly in a troop over the further lawns, were similar, and that, led by this enormous pair, they had all moved boldly closer to my windows. At the same moment a blind was drawn down over an upper room; the second tree disappeared into the surrounding darkness. It was, of course, this chance light that had brought it into the field of vision, but when the black shutter dropped over it, hiding it from view, the manner of its vanishing produced the queer effect that it had slipped into its companion—almost that it had been an emanation of the one I so disliked, and not really a tree at all! In this way the garden turned vehicle for expressing what lay behind it all! . . .

The behaviour of the doors, the little, ordinary doors, seems scarcely worth mention at all, their queer way of opening and shutting of their own accord; for this was accountable in a hundred natural ways, and to tell the truth, I never caught one in the act of moving. Indeed, only after frequent repetitions did the detail force itself upon me, when, having noticed one, I noticed all. It produced, however, the unpleasant impression of a continual coming and going in the house, as though, screened cleverly and purposely from actual sight, some one in the building held constant invisible intercourse with—others.

Upon detailed descriptions of these uncertain incidents I do not venture, individually so trivial, but taken all together so impressive and so insolent. But the episode of the children, mentioned above, was different. And I give it because it showed how vividly the intuitive child-mind received the impression—one impression, at any rate—of what was in the air. It may be told in a very few words. I believe they were the coachman's children, and that the man had been in Mr. Franklyn's service; but of neither point am I quite positive. I heard screaming in the rose-garden that runs along the stable walls—it was one afternoon not far from the tea-hour—and on hurrying up I found a little girl of nine or ten fastened with ropes to a rustic seat, and two other children—boys, one about twelve and one much younger—gathering sticks beneath the climbing rose-trees. The girl was white and frightened, but the others were laughing and talking among themselves so busily while they picked that they did not notice my abrupt arrival. Some game, I understood, was in progress, but a game that had become too serious for the happiness of the prisoner, for there was a fear in the girl's eyes that was a very genuine fear indeed. I unfastened her at once; the ropes were so loosely and clumsily knotted that they had not hurt her skin; it was not that which made her pale. She collapsed a moment upon the bench, then picked up her tiny skirts and dived away at full speed into the safety of the stable-yard. There was no response to my brief comforting, but she ran as though for her life, and I divined that some horrid boys' cruelty had been afoot. It was probably mere thoughtlessness, as cruelty with children usually is, but something in me decided to discover exactly what it was.

And the boys, not one whit alarmed at my intervention, merely laughed shyly when I explained that their prisoner had escaped, and told me frankly what their "gime" had been. There was no vestige of shame in them, nor any idea, of course, that they aped a monstrous reality. That it was mere pretence was neither here nor there. To them, though make-believe, it was a make-believe of something that was right and natural and in no sense cruel. Grown-ups did it too. It was necessary for her good.

"We was going to burn her up, sir," the older one informed me, answering my "Why?" with the explanation, "Because she wouldn't believe what we wanted 'er to believe."

And, game though it was, the feeling of reality about the little episode was so arresting, so terrific in some way, that only with difficulty did I confine my admonitions on this occasion to mere words. The boys slunk off, frightened in their turn, yet not, I felt, convinced that they had erred in principle. It was their inheritance. They had breathed it in with the atmosphere of their bringing-up. They would renew the salutary torture when they could—till she "believed" as they did.

I went back into the house, afflicted with a passion of mingled pity and distress impossible to describe, yet on my short way across the garden was attacked by other moods in turn, each more real and bitter than its predecessor. I received the whole series, as it were, at once. I felt like a diver rising to the surface through layers of water at different temperatures, though here the natural order was reversed, and the cooler strata were uppermost, the heated ones below. Thus, I was caught by the goblin touch of the willows that fringed the field; by the sensuous curving of the twisted ash that formed a gateway to the little grove of sapling oaks where fauns and satyrs lurked to play in the moonlight before Pagan altars; and by the cloaking darkness, next, of the copse of stunted pines, close gathered each to each, where hooded figures stalked behind an awful cross. The episode with the children seemed to have opened me like a knife. The whole Place rushed at me.

I suspect this synthesis of many moods produced in me that climax of loathing and disgust which made me feel the limit of bearable emotion had been reached, so that I made straight to find Frances in order to convince her that at any rate *I* must leave. For, although this was our last day in the house, and we had arranged to go next day, the dread was in me that she would still find some persuasive reason for staying on. And an unexpected incident then made my dread unnecessary. The front door was open and a cab stood in the drive; a tall, elderly man was gravely talking in the hall with the parlour-maid we called the Grenadier. He held a piece of paper in his hand. "I have called to see the house," I heard him say, as I ran up the stairs to Frances, who was peering like an inquisitive child over the banisters. . . .

"Yes," she told me with a sigh, I know not whether of resignation or relief, "the house *is* to be let or sold. Mabel has decided. Some Society or other, I believe—"

I was overjoyed: this made our leaving right and possible. "You never told me, Frances!"

"Mabel only heard of it a few days ago. She told me herself this morning. It is a chance, she says. Alone she cannot get it 'straight.'"

"Defeat?" I asked, watching her closely.

"She thinks she has found a way out. It's not a family, you see, it's a Society, a sort of Community—they go in for thought—"

"A Community!" I gasped. "You mean religious?"

She shook her head. "Not exactly," she said smiling, "but some kind of association of men and women who want a headquarters in the country—a place where they can write and meditate—*think*—mature their plans and all the rest—I don't know exactly what."

"Utopian dreamers?" I asked, yet feeling an immense relief come over me as I heard. But I asked in ignorance, not cynically. Frances would know. She knew all this kind of thing.

"No, not that exactly," she smiled. "Their teachings are grand and simple—old as the world too, really—the basis of every religion before men's minds perverted them with their manufactured creeds—"

Footsteps on the stairs, and the sound of voices, interrupted our odd impromptu conversation, as the Grenadier came up, followed by the tall, grave gentleman who was being shown over the house. My sister drew me along the corridor towards her room, where she went in and closed the door behind me, yet not before I had stolen a good look at the caller—long enough, at least, for his face and general appearance to have made a definite impression on me. For something strong and peaceful emanated from his presence; he moved with such quiet dignity; the glance of his eyes was so steady and reassuring, that my mind labelled him instantly as a type of man one would turn to in an emergency and not be disappointed. I had seen him but for a passing moment, but I had seen him twice, and the way he walked down the passage, looking competently about him, conveyed the same impression as when I saw him standing at the door—fearless, tolerant, wise. "A sincere and kindly character," I judged instantly, "a man whom some big kind of love has trained in sweetness towards the world; no hate in him anywhere." A great deal, no doubt, to read in so brief a glance! Yet his voice confirmed my intuition, a deep and very gentle voice, great firmness in it too.

"Have I become suddenly sensitive to people's atmospheres in this extraordinary fashion?" I asked myself, smiling, as I stood in the room and heard the door close behind me. "Have I developed some clairvoyant faculty here?" At any other time I should have mocked.

And I sat down and faced my sister, feeling strangely comforted and at peace for the first time since I had stepped beneath The Towers' roof a month ago. Frances, I then saw, was smiling a little as she watched me.

"You know him?" I asked.

"You felt it too?" was her question in reply. "No," she added, "I don't know him—beyond the fact that he is a leader in the Movement and has devoted years and money to its objects. Mabel felt the same thing in him that you have felt—and jumped at it."

"But you've seen him before?" I urged, for the certainty was in me that he was no stranger to her.

She shook her head. "He called one day early this week, when you were out. Mabel saw him. I believe"—she hesitated a moment, as though expecting me to stop her with my usual impatience of such subjects—"I believe he has explained everything to her—the beliefs he embodies, she declares, are her salvation—might be, rather, if she could adopt them."

"Conversion again!" For I remembered her riches, and how gladly a Society would gobble them.

"The layers I told you about," she continued calmly, shrugging her shoulders slightly—"the deposits that are left behind by strong thinking and *real* belief—but especially by ugly, hateful belief, because, you see—unfortunately there's more vital passion in that sort—"

"Frances, I don't understand a bit," I said out loud, but said it a little humbly, for the impression the man had left was still strong upon me and I was grateful for the steady sense of peace and comfort he had somehow introduced. The horrors had been so dreadful. My nerves, doubtless, were more than a little overstrained. Absurd as it must sound, I classed him in my mind with the robins, the happy, confiding robins who believed in everybody and thought no evil! I laughed a moment at my ridiculous idea, and my sister, encouraged by this sign of patience in me, continued more fluently.

"Of course you don't understand, Bill. Why should you? You've never thought about such things. Needing no creed yourself, you think all creeds are rubbish."

"I'm open to conviction—I'm tolerant," I interrupted.

"You're as narrow as Sam Franklyn, and as crammed with prejudice," she answered, knowing that she had me at her mercy.

"Then, pray, what may be his, or his Society's beliefs?" I asked, feeling no desire to argue, "and how are they going to prove your Mabel's salvation? Can they bring beauty into all this aggressive hate and ugliness?"

"Certain hope and peace," she said, "that peace which is understanding, and that understanding which explains *all* creeds and therefore tolerates them."

"Toleration! The one word a religious man loathes above all others! His pet word is damnation—"

"Tolerates them," she repeated patiently, unperturbed by my explosion, "because it includes them all."

"Fine, if true," I admitted, "very fine. But how, pray, does it include them all?"

"Because the key-word, the motto, of their Society is, 'There is no religion higher than Truth,' and it has no single dogma of any kind. Above all," she went on, "because it claims that no individual can be 'lost.' It teaches universal salvation. To damn outsiders is uncivilised, childish, impure. Some take longer than others—it's according to the way they think and live—but all find peace, through development, in the end. What the creeds call a hopeless soul, it regards as a soul having further to go. There is no damnation—"

"Well, well," I exclaimed, feeling that she rode her hobby-horse too wildly, too roughly over me, "but what is the bearing of all this upon this dreadful place, and upon Mabel? I'll admit that there is this atmosphere—this—er—inexplicable horror in the house and grounds, and that if not of damnation exactly, it is certainly damnable. I'm not too prejudiced to deny *that,* for I've felt it myself."

To my relief she was brief. She made her statement, leaving me to take it or reject it as I would.

"The thought and belief its former occupants—have left behind. For there has been coincidence here, a coincidence that must be rare. The site on which this modern house now stands was Roman, before that early Britain, with burial mounds, before that again, Druid—the Druid stones still lie in that copse below the field, the Tumuli among the ilexes behind the drive. The older building Sam Franklyn altered and practically pulled down was a monastery; he changed the chapel into a meeting hall, which is now the music-room; but, before he came here, the house was occupied by Manetti, a violent Catholic without tolerance or vision; and in the interval between these two, Julius Weinbaum had it, Hebrew of most rigid orthodox type imaginable—so they all have left their—"

"Even so," I repeated, yet interested to hear the rest, "what of it?"

"Simply this," said Frances with conviction, "that each in turn has left his layer of concentrated thinking and belief behind him; because each believed intensely, absolutely, beyond the least weakening of any doubt—the kind of strong belief and thinking that is rare anywhere to-day, the kind that wills, impregnates objects, saturates the atmosphere, haunts, in a word. And each, believing he was utterly and finally right, damned with equally positive conviction the rest of the world. One and all preached that implicitly if not explicitly. It's the root of every creed. Last of the bigoted, grim series came Samuel Franklyn."

I listened in amazement that increased as she went on. Up to this point her explanation was so admirable. It was, indeed, a pretty study in psychology if it were true.

"Then why does nothing ever happen?" I enquired mildly. "A place so thickly haunted ought to produce a crop of no ordinary results!"

"There lies the proof," she went on in a lowered voice, "the proof of the horror and the ugly reality. The thought and belief of each occupant in turn kept all the others under. They gave no sign of life at the time. But the results of thinking never die. They crop out again the moment there's an opening. And, with the return of Mabel in her negative state, believing nothing positive herself, the place for the first time found itself free to reproduce its buried stores. Damnation, hell-fire, and the rest—the most permanent and vital thought of all those creeds, since it was applied to the majority of the world—broke loose again, for there was no restraint to hold it back. Each sought to obtain its former supremacy. None conquered. There results a pandemonium of hate and fear, of striving to escape, of agonised, bitter warring to find safety, peace—salvation. The place is saturated by that appalling stream of thinking—the terror of the damned. It concentrated upon Mabel, whose negative attitude furnished the channel of deliverance. You and I, according to our sympathy with her, were similarly involved. Nothing happened, because no one layer could ever gain the supremacy."

I was so interested—I dare not say amused—that I stared in silence while she paused a moment, afraid that she would draw rein and end the fairy tale too soon.

"The beliefs of this man, of his Society rather, vigorously thought and therefore vigorously given out here, will put the whole place straight. It will act as a solvent. These vitriolic layers actively denied, will fuse and disappear in the stream of gentle, tolerant sympathy which is love. For each member, worthy of the name, loves the world, and all creeds go into the melting pot; Mabel, too, if she joins them out of real conviction, will find salvation—"

"Thinking, I know, is of the first importance," I objected, "but don't you, perhaps, exaggerate the power of feeling and emotion which in religion are *au fond* always hysterical?"

"What *is* the world," she told me, "but thinking and feeling? An individual's world is entirely what that individual thinks and believes—interpretation. There is no other. And unless he really thinks and really believes, he has no permanent world at all. I grant that few people think, and still fewer believe, and that most take ready-made suits and make them do. Only the strong make their own things; the lesser fry, Mabel among them, are merely swept up into what has been manufactured for them. They get along somehow. You and I have made for ourselves, Mabel has not. She is a nonentity, and when her belief is taken from her, she goes with it."

It was not in me just then to criticise the evasion, or pick out the sophistry from the truth. I merely waited for her to continue.

"None of us have Truth, my dear Frances," I ventured presently, seeing that she kept silent.

"Precisely," she answered, "but most of us have beliefs. And what one believes and thinks affects the world at large. Consider the legacy of hatred and cruelty involved in the doctrines men have built into their creeds where the *sine quâ non* of salvation is absolute acceptance of one particular set of views or else perishing everlastingly—for only by repudiating history can they disavow it—"

"You're not quite accurate," I put in. "Not all the creeds teach damnation, do they? Franklyn did, of course, but the others are a bit modernised now surely?"

"Trying to get out of it," she admitted, "perhaps they are, but damnation of unbelievers—of most of the world, that is—is their rather favourite idea if you talk with them."

"I never have."

She smiled. "But I have," she said significantly, "so, if you consider what the various occupants of this house have so strongly held and thought and believed, you need not be surprised that the influence they have left behind them should be a dark and dreadful legacy. For thought, you know, does leave—"

The opening of the door, to my great relief, interrupted her, as the Grenadier led in the visitor to see the room. He bowed to both of us with a brief word of apology, looked round him, and withdrew, and with his departure the conversation between us came naturally to an end. I followed him out. Neither of us in any case, I think, cared to argue further.

And, so far as I am aware, the curious history of The Towers ends here too. There was no climax in the story sense. Nothing ever really happened. We left next morning for London. I only know that the Society in question took the house and have since occupied it to their entire satisfaction, and that Mabel, who became a member shortly afterwards, now stays there frequently when in need of repose from the arduous and unselfish labours she took upon herself under its ægis. She dined with us only the other night, here in our tiny Chelsea flat, and a jollier, saner, more interesting and happy guest I could hardly wish for. She was vital—in the best sense; the lay-figure had come to life. I found it difficult to believe she was the same woman whose fearful effigy had floated down those dreary corridors and almost disappeared in the depths of that atrocious Shadow.

What her beliefs were now I was wise enough to leave unquestioned, and Frances, to my great relief, kept the conversation well away from such inappropriate topics. It was clear, however, that the woman had in herself some secret source of joy, that she was now an aggressive, positive force, sure of herself, and apparently afraid of nothing in heaven or hell. She radiated something very like hope and courage about her, and talked as though the world were a glorious place and everybody in it kind and beautiful. Her optimism was certainly infectious.

The Towers were mentioned only in passing. The name of Marsh came up—not *the* Marsh, it so happened, but a name in some book that was being discussed—and I was unable to restrain myself. Curiosity was too strong. I threw out a casual enquiry Mabel could leave unanswered if she wished. But there was no desire to avoid it. Her reply was frank and smiling.

"Would you believe it? She married," Mabel told me, though obviously surprised that I remembered the housekeeper at all; "and is happy as the day is long. She's found her right niche in life. A sergeant—"

"The army!" I ejaculated.

"Salvation Army," she explained merrily.

Frances exchanged a glance with me. I laughed too, for the information took me by surprise. I cannot say why exactly, but I expected at least to hear that the woman had met some dreadful end, not impossibly by burning.

"And The Towers, now called the Rest House," Mabel chattered on, "seems to me the most peaceful and delightful spot in England—"

"Really," I said politely.

"When I lived there in the old days—while you were there, perhaps, though I won't be sure." Mabel went on, "the story got abroad that it was haunted. Wasn't it odd? A less likely place for a ghost I've never seen. Why, it had no atmosphere at all." She said this to Frances, glancing up at me with a smile that apparently had no hidden meaning. "Did *you* notice anything queer about it when you were there?"

This was plainly addressed to me.

"I found it—er—difficult to settle down to anything," I said, after an instant's hesitation. "I couldn't work there—"

"But I thought you wrote that wonderful book on the Deaf and Blind while you stayed with me," she asked innocently.

I stammered a little. "Oh, no, not then. I only made a few notes—er—at The Towers. My mind, oddly enough, refused to produce at all down there. But—why do you ask? Did anything—was anything *supposed* to happen there?"

She looked searchingly into my eyes a moment before she answered:

"Not that I know of," she said simply.

A Descent into Egypt

I

He was an accomplished, versatile man whom some called brilliant. Behind his talents lay a wealth of material that right selection could have lifted into genuine distinction. He did too many things, however, to excel in one, for a restless curiosity kept him ever on the move. George Isley was an able man. His short career in diplomacy proved it; yet, when he abandoned this for travel and exploration, no one thought it a pity. He would do big things in any line. He was merely finding himself.

Among the rolling stones of humanity a few acquire moss of considerable value. They are not necessarily shiftless; they travel light; the comfortable pockets in the game of life that attract the majority are too small to retain them; they are in and out again in a moment. The world says, "What a pity! They stick to nothing!" but the fact is that, like questing wild birds, they seek the nest they need. It is a question of values. They judge swiftly, change their line of flight, are gone, not even hearing the comment that they might have "retired with a pension."

And to this homeless, questing type George Isley certainly belonged. He was by no means shiftless. He merely sought with insatiable yearning that soft particular nest in which he could settle down permanently. And to an accompaniment of sighs and regrets from his friends he found it; he found it, however, not in the present, but by retiring from the world "without a pension," unclothed with honours and distinctions. He withdrew from the present and slipped softly back into a mighty Past where he belonged. Why; how; obeying what strange instincts—this remains unknown, deep secret of an inner life that found no resting place in modern things. Such instincts are not disclosable in twentieth-century language, nor are the details of such a journey properly describable at all. Except by the few—poets, prophets, psychiatrists, and the like—such experiences are dismissed with the neat museum label—"queer."

So, equally, must the recorder of this experience share the honour of that little label—he who by chance witnessed certain external and visible signs of this inner and spiritual journey. There remains, nevertheless, the amazing reality of the experience; and to the recorder alone was some clue of interpretation possible, perhaps, because in himself also lay the lure, though less imperative, of a similar journey. At any rate the interpretation may be offered, to the handful who realise that trains and motors are not the only means of travel left to our progressive race.

In his younger days I knew George Isley intimately. I know him now. But the George Isley I knew of old, the arresting personality with whom I travelled, climbed, explored, is no longer with us. He is not here. He disappeared—gradually—into the past. There is no George Isley. And that such an individuality could vanish, while still his outer semblance walks the familiar streets, normal apparently, and not yet fifty in the number of his years, seems a tale, though difficult, well worth the telling. For I witnessed the slow submergence. It was very gradual. I cannot pretend to understand the entire significance of it. There was something questionable and sinister in the business that offered hints of astonishing possibilities. Were there a corps of spiritual police, the matter might be partially cleared up, but since none of the churches have yet organised anything effective of this sort, one can only fall back upon variants of the blessed "Mesopotamia," and whisper of derangement, and the like. Such labels, of course, explain as little as most other *clichés* in life. That well-groomed, soldierly figure strolling down Piccadilly, watching the Races, dining out—there is no derangement there. The face is not melancholy, the eye not wild; the gestures are quiet and the speech controlled. Yet the eye is empty, the face expressionless. Vacancy reigns there, provocative and significant. If not unduly noticeable, it is because the majority in life neither expect, nor offer, more.

At closer quarters you may think questioning things, or you may think—nothing; probably the latter. You may wonder why something continually expected does not make its appearance; and you may watch for the evidence of "personality" the general presentment of the man has led you to expect. Disappointed, therefore, you may certainly be; but I defy you to discover the smallest hint of mental disorder, and of derangement or nervous affliction, absolutely nothing. Before long, perhaps, you may feel you are talking with a dummy, some well-trained automaton, a nonentity devoid of spontaneous life; and afterwards you may find that memory fades rapidly away, as though no impression of any kind has really been made at all. All this, yes; but nothing pathological. A few may be stimulated by this startling discrepancy between promise and performance, but most, accustomed to accept face values, would say, "a pleasant fellow, but nothing in him much . . ." and an hour later forget him altogether.

For the truth is as you, perhaps, divined. You have been sitting beside no one, you have been talking to, looking at, listening to—no one. The intercourse has conveyed nothing that can waken human response in you, good, bad, or indifferent. There is no George Isley. And the discovery, if you make it, will not even cause you to creep with the uncanniness of the experience, because the exterior is so wholly pleasing. George Isley to-day is a picture with no meaning in it that charms merely by the harmonious colouring of an inoffensive subject. He moves undiscovered in the little world of society to which he was born, secure in the groove first habit has made comfortably automatic for him. No one guesses; none, that is, but the few who knew him intimately in early life. And his wandering existence has scattered these; they have forgotten what he was. So perfect, indeed, is he in the manners of the commonplace fashionable man, that no woman in his "set" is aware that he differs from the type she is accustomed to. He turns a compliment with the accepted language of her text-book, motors, golfs, and gambles in the regulation manner of his particular world. He is an admirable, perfect automaton. He is nothing. He is a human shell.

II

The name of George Isley had been before the public for some years when, after a considerable interval, we met again in a hotel in Egypt, I for my health, he for I knew not what—at first. But I soon discovered: archæology and excavation had taken hold of him, though he had gone so quietly about it that no one seemed to have heard. I was not sure that he was glad to see me, for he had first withdrawn, annoyed, it seemed, at being discovered, but later, as though after consideration, had made tentative advances. He welcomed me with a curious gesture of the entire body that seemed to shake himself free from something that had made him forget my identity. There was pathos somewhere in his attitude, almost as though he asked for sympathy. "I've been out here, off and on, for the last three years," he told me, after describing something of what he had been doing. "I find it the most repaying hobby in the world. It leads to a reconstruction—an imaginative reconstruction, of course, I mean—of an enormous thing the world had entirely lost. A very gorgeous, stimulating hobby, believe me, and a very entic—" he quickly changed the word—"exacting one indeed."

I remember looking him up and down with astonishment. There was a change in him, a lack; a note was missing in his enthusiasm, a colour in the voice, a quality in his manner. The ingredients were not mixed quite as of old. I did not bother him with questions, but I noted thus at the very first a subtle alteration. Another facet of the man presented itself. Something that had been independent and aggressive was replaced by a certain emptiness that invited sympathy. Even in his physical appearance the change was manifested—this odd suggestion of lessening. I looked again more closely. Lessening *was* the word. He had somehow dwindled. It was startling, vaguely unpleasant too.

The entire subject, as usual, was at his fingertips; he knew all the important men; and had spent money freely on his hobby. I laughed, reminding him of his remark that Egypt had no attractions for him, owing to the organised advertisement of its somewhat theatrical charms. Admitting his error with a gesture, he brushed the objection easily aside. His manner, and a certain glow that rose about his atmosphere as he answered, increased my first astonishment. His voice was significant and suggestive. "Come out with me," he said in a low tone, "and see how little the tourists matter, how inappreciable the excavation is compared to what remains to be done, how gigantic"—he emphasised the word impressively—"the scope for discovery remains." He made a movement with his head and shoulders that conveyed a sense of the prodigious, for he was of massive build, his cast of features stern, and his eyes, set deep into the face, shone past me with a sombre gleam in them I did not quite account for. It was the voice, however, that brought the mystery in. It vibrated somewhere below the actual sound of it. "Egypt," he continued—and so gravely that at first I made the mistake of thinking he chose the curious words on purpose to produce a theatrical effect—"that has enriched her blood with the pageant of so many civilisations, that has devoured Persians, Greeks and Romans, Saracens and Mamelukes, a dozen conquests and invasions besides,—what can mere tourists or explorers matter to her? The excavators scratch their skin and dig up mummies; and as for tourists!" —he laughed contemptuously—"flies that settle for a moment on her covered face, to vanish at the first signs of heat! Egypt is not even aware of them. The real Egypt lies underground in darkness. Tourists must have light, to be seen as well as to see. And the diggers—!"

He paused, smiling with something between pity and contempt I did not quite appreciate, for, personally, I felt a great respect for the tireless excavators. And then he added, with a touch of feeling in his tone as though he had a grievance against them, and had not also "dug" himself, "Men who uncover the dead, restore the temples, and reconstruct a skeleton, thinking they have read its beating heart . . ." He shrugged his great shoulders, and the rest of the sentence may have been but the protest of a man in defence of his own hobby, but there seemed an undue earnestness and gravity about it that made me wonder more than ever. He went on to speak of the strangeness of the land as a mere ribbon of vegetation along the ancient river, the rest all ruins, desert, sun-drenched wilderness of death, yet so breakingly alive with wonder, power, and a certain disquieting sense of deathlessness. There seemed, for him, a revelation of unusual spiritual kind in this land where the Past survived so potently. He spoke almost as though it obliterated the Present.

Indeed, the hint of something solemn behind his words made it difficult for me to keep up the conversation, and the pause that presently came I filled in with some word of questioning surprise, which yet, I think, was chiefly in concurrence. I was aware of some big belief in him, some enveloping emotion that escaped my grasp. Yet, though I did not understand, his great mood swept me. . . . His voice lowered, then, as he went on to mention temples, tombs, and deities, details of his own discoveries and of their effect upon him, but to this I listened with half an ear, because in the unusual language he had first made use of I detected this other thing that stirred my curiosity more—stirred it uncomfortably.

"Then the spell," I asked, remembering the effect of Egypt upon myself two years before, "has worked upon you as upon most others, only with greater power?"

He looked hard at me a moment, signs of trouble showing themselves faintly in his rugged, interesting face. I think he wanted to say more than he could bring himself to confess. He hesitated.

"I'm only glad," he replied after a pause, "it didn't get hold of me earlier in life. It would have absorbed me. I should have lost all other interests. Now,"—that curious look of helplessness, of asking sympathy, flitted like a shadow through his eyes—"now that I'm on the decline . . . it matters less."

On the decline! I cannot imagine by what blundering I missed this chance he never offered again; somehow or other the singular phrase passed unnoticed at the moment, and only came upon me with its full significance later when it was too awkward to refer to it. He tested my readiness to help, to sympathise, to share his inner life. I missed the clue. For, at the moment, a more practical consideration interested me in his language. Being of those who regretted that he had not excelled by devoting his powers to a single object, I shrugged my shoulders. He caught my meaning instantly. Oh, he was glad to talk. He felt the possibility of my sympathy underneath, I think.

"No, no, you take me wrongly there," he said with gravity. "What I mean—and I ought to know if any one does!—is that while most countries give, others take away. Egypt changes you. No one can live here and remain exactly what he was before."

This puzzled me. It startled, too, again. His manner was so earnest. "And Egypt, you mean, is one of the countries that take away?" I asked. The strange idea unsettled my thoughts a little.

"First takes away from you," he replied, "but in the end takes *you* away. Some lands enrich you," he went on, seeing that I listened, "while others impoverish. From India, Greece, Italy, all ancient lands, you return with memories you can use. From Egypt you return with—nothing. Its splendour stupefies; it's useless. There is a change in your inmost being, an emptiness, an unaccountable yearning, but you find nothing that can fill the lack you're conscious of. Nothing comes to replace what has gone. You have been drained."

I stared; but I nodded a general acquiescence. Of a sensitive, artistic temperament this was certainly true, though by no means the superficial and generally accepted verdict. The majority imagine that Egypt has filled them to the brim. I took his deeper reading of the facts. I was aware of an odd fascination in his idea.

"Modern Egypt," he continued, "is, after all, but a trick of civilisation," and there was a kind of breathlessness in his measured tone, "but ancient Egypt lies waiting, hiding, underneath. Though dead, she is amazingly alive. And you feel her touching you. She takes from you. She enriches herself. You return from Egypt—less than you were before."

What came over my mind is hard to say. Some touch of visionary imagination burned its flaming path across my mind. I thought of some old Grecian hero speaking of his delicious battle with the gods—battle in which he knew he must be worsted, but yet in which he delighted because at death his spirit would join their glorious company beyond this world. I was aware, that is to say, of resignation as well as resistance in him. He already felt the effortless peace which follows upon long, unequal battling, as of a man who has fought the rapids with a strain beyond his strength, then sinks back and goes with the awful mass of water smoothly and indifferently—over the quiet fall.

Yet, it was not so much his words which clothed picturesquely an undeniable truth, as the force of conviction that drove behind them, shrouding my mind with mystery and darkness. His eyes, so steadily holding mine, were lit, I admit, yet they were calm and sane as those of a doctor discussing the symptoms of that daily battle to which we all finally succumb. This analogy occurred to me.

"There *is*"—I stammered a little, faltering in my speech—"an incalculable element in the country . . . somewhere, I confess. You put it—rather strongly, though, don't you?"

He answered quietly, moving his eyes from my face towards the window that framed the serene and exquisite sky towards the Nile.

"The real, invisible Egypt," he murmured, "I do find rather—strong. I find it difficult to deal with. You see," and he turned towards me, smiling like a tired child, "I think the truth is that Egypt deals with me."

"It draws—" I began, then started as he interrupted me at once.

"Into the Past." He uttered the little word in a way beyond me to describe. There came a flood of glory with it, a sense of peace and beauty, of battles over and of rest attained. No saint could have brimmed "Heaven" with as much passionately enticing meaning. He went willingly, prolonging the struggle merely to enjoy the greater relief and joy of the consummation.

For again he spoke as though a struggle were in progress in his being. I got the impression that he somewhere wanted help. I understood the pathetic quality I had vaguely discerned already. His character naturally was so strong and independent. It now seemed weaker, as though certain fibres had been drawn out. And I understood then that the spell of Egypt, so lightly chattered about in its sensational aspect, so rarely known in its naked power, the nameless, creeping influence that begins deep below the surface and thence sends delicate tendrils outwards, was in his blood. I, in my untaught ignorance, had felt it too; it is undeniable; one is aware of unaccountable, queer things in Egypt; even the utterly prosaic feel them. Dead Egypt is marvellously alive. . . .

I glanced past him out of the big windows where the desert glimmered in its featureless expanse of yellow leagues, two monstrous pyramids signalling from across the Nile, and for a moment—inexplicably, it seemed to me afterwards—I lost sight of my companion's stalwart figure that was yet so close before my eyes. He had risen from his chair; he was standing near me; yet my sight missed him altogether. Something, dim as a shadow, faint as a breath of air, rose up and bore my thoughts away, obliterating vision too. I forgot for a moment who I was; identity slipped from me. Thought, sight, feeling, all sank away into the emptiness of those sun-baked sands; sank, as it were, into nothingness, caught away from the Present, enticed, absorbed. . . . And when I looked back again to answer him, or rather to ask what his curious words could mean—he was no longer there. More than surprised—for there was something of shock in the disappearance—I turned to search. I had not seen him go. He had stolen from my side so softly, slipped away silently, mysteriously, and—so easily. I remember that a faint shiver ran down my back as I realised that I was alone.

Was it that, momentarily, I had caught a reflex of his state of mind? Had my sympathy induced in myself an echo of what he experienced in full—a going backwards, a loss of present vigour, the enticing, subtle draw of those immeasurable sands that hide the living dead from the interruptions of the careless living . . . ?

I sat down to reflect and, incidentally, to watch the magnificence of the sunset; and the thing he had said returned upon me with insistent power, ringing like distant bells within my mind. His talk of the tombs and temples passed, but this remained. It stimulated oddly. His talk, I remembered, had always excited curiosity in this way. Some countries give, while others take away. What did he mean precisely? What had Egypt taken away from him? And I realised more definitely that something in him *was* missing, something he possessed in former years that was no longer there. He had grown shadowy already in my thoughts. The mind searched keenly, but in vain . . . and after some time I left my chair and moved over to another window, aware that a vague discomfort stirred within me that involved uneasiness—for him. I felt pity. But behind the pity was an eager, absorbing curiosity as well. He seemed receding curiously into misty distance, and the strong desire leaped in me to overtake, to travel with him into some vanished splendour that he had re-discovered. The feeling was a most remarkable one, for it included yearning—the yearning for some nameless, forgotten loveliness the world has lost. It was in me too.

At the approach of twilight the mind loves to harbour shadows. The room, empty of guests, was dark behind me; darkness, too, was creeping across the desert like a veil, deepening the serenity of its grim, unfeatured face. It turned pale with distance; the whole great sheet of it went rustling into night. The first stars peeped and twinkled, hanging loosely in the air as though they could be plucked like golden berries; and the sun was already below the Libyan horizon, where gold and crimson faded through violet into blue. I stood watching this mysterious Egyptian dusk, while an eerie glamour seemed to bring the incredible within uneasy reach of the half-faltering senses. . . . And suddenly the truth dropped into me. Over George Isley, over his mind and energies, over his thoughts and over his emotions too, a kind of darkness was also slowly creeping. Something in him had dimmed, yet not with age; it had gone out. Some inner night, stealing over the Present, obliterated it. And yet he looked towards the dawn. Like the Egyptian monuments his eyes turned—eastwards.

And so it came to me that what he had lost was personal ambition. He was glad, he said, that these Egyptian studies had not caught him earlier in life; the language he made use of was peculiar: "Now I am on the decline it matters less." A slight foundation, no doubt, to build conviction on, and yet I felt sure that I was partly right. He was fascinated, but fascinated against his will. The Present in him battled against the Past. Still fighting, he had yet lost hope. The desire *not* to change was now no longer in him. . . .

I turned away from the window so as not to see that grey, encroaching desert, for the discovery produced a certain agitation in me. Egypt seemed suddenly a living entity of enormous power. She stirred about me. She was stirring now. This flat and motionless land pretending it had no movement, was actually busy with a million gestures that came creeping round the heart. She was reducing him. Already from the complex texture of his personality she had drawn one vital thread that in its relation to the general woof was of central importance—ambition. The mind chose the simile; but in my heart where thought fluttered in singular distress, another suggested itself as truer. "Thread" changed to "artery." I turned quickly and went up to my room where I could be alone. The idea was somewhere ghastly.

III

Yet, while dressing for dinner, the idea exfoliated as only a living thing exfoliates. I saw in George Isley this great question mark that had not been there formerly. All have, of course, some question mark, and carry it about, though with most it rarely becomes visible until the end. With him it was plainly visible in his atmosphere at the hey-day of his life. He wore it like a fine curved scimitar above his head. So full of life, he yet seemed willingly dead. For, though imagination sought every possible explanation, I got no further than the somewhat negative result—that a certain energy, wholly unconnected with mere physical health, had been withdrawn. It was more than ambition, I think, for it included intention, desire, self-confidence as well. It was life itself. He was no longer in the Present. He was no longer *here.*

"Some countries give while others take away. . . . I find Egypt difficult to deal with, I find it . . ." and then that simple, uncomplex adjective—"strong." In memory and experience the entire globe was mapped for him; it remained for Egypt, then, to teach him this marvellous new thing. But not Egypt of to-day; it was vanished Egypt that had robbed him of his strength. He had described it as underground, hidden, waiting. . . . I was again aware of a faint shuddering—as though something crept secretly from my inmost heart to share the experience with him, and as though my sympathy involved a willing consent that this should be so. With sympathy there must always be a shedding of the personal self; each time I felt this sympathy, it seemed that something left me. I thought in circles, arriving at no definite point where I could rest and say "that's it; I understand." The giving attitude of a country was easily comprehensible; but this idea of robbery, of deprivation baffled me. An obscure alarm took hold of me—for myself as well as for him.

At dinner, where he invited me to his table, the impression passed off a good deal, however, and I convicted myself of a woman's exaggeration; yet, as we talked of many a day's adventure together in other lands, it struck me that we oddly left the present out. We ignored to-day. His thoughts, as it were, went most easily backwards. And each adventure led, as by its own natural weight and impetus, towards one thing—the enormous glory of a vanished age. Ancient Egypt was "home" in this mysterious game life played with death. The specific gravity of his being, to say nothing for the moment of my own, had shifted lower, farther off, backwards and below, or as he put it—underground. The sinking sensation I experienced was of a literal kind. . . .

And so I found myself wondering what had led him to this particular hotel. I had come out with an affected organ the specialist promised me would heal in the marvellous air of Helouan, but it was queer that my companion also should have chosen it. Its clientèle was mostly invalid, German and Russian invalid at that. The Management set its face against the lighter, gayer side of life that hotels in Egypt usually encourage eagerly. It was a true rest-house, a place of repose and leisure, a place where one could remain undiscovered and unknown. No English patronised it. One might easily—the idea came unbidden, suddenly—hide in it.

"Then you're doing nothing just now," I asked, "in the way of digging? No big expeditions or excavating at the moment?"

"I'm recuperating," he answered carelessly. "I've had two years up at the Valley of the Kings, and overdid it rather. But I'm by way of working at a little thing near here across the Nile." And he pointed in the direction of Sakkhâra, where the huge Memphian cemetery stretches underground from the Dachûr pyramids to the Gizeh monsters, four miles lower down. "There's a matter of a hundred years in that alone!"

"You must have accumulated a mass of interesting material. I suppose later you'll make use of it—a book or—"

His expression stopped me—that strange look in the eyes that had stirred my first uneasiness. It was as if something struggled up a moment, looked bleakly out upon the present, then sank away again.

"More," he answered listlessly, "than I can ever use. It's much more likely to use me." He said it hurriedly, looking over his shoulder as though some one might be listening, then smiled significantly, bringing his eyes back upon my own again. I told him that he was far too modest. "If all the excavators thought like that," I added, "we ignorant ones should suffer." I laughed, but the laughter was only on my lips.

He shook his head indifferently. "They do their best; they do wonders," he replied, making an indescribable gesture as though he withdrew willingly from the topic altogether, yet could not quite achieve it. "I know their books; I know the writers too—of various nationalities." He paused a moment, and his eyes turned grave. "I cannot understand quite—how they do it," he added half below his breath.

"The labour, you mean? The strain of the climate, and so forth?" I said this purposely, for I knew quite well he meant another thing. The way he looked into my face, however, disturbed me so that I believe I visibly started. Something very deep in me sat up alertly listening, almost on guard.

"I mean," he replied, "that they must have uncommon powers of resistance."

There! He had used the very word that had been hiding in me! "It puzzles me," he went on, "for, with one exception, they are not unusual men. In the way of gifts—oh yes. It's in the way of resistance and protection that I mean. Self-protection," he added with emphasis.

It was the way he said "resistance" and "self-protection" that sent a touch of cold through me: I learned later that he himself had made surprising discoveries in these two years, penetrating closer to the secret life of ancient sacerdotal Egypt than any of his predecessors or co-labourers—then, inexplicably, had ceased. But this was told to me afterwards and by others. At the moment I was only conscious of this odd embarrassment. I did not understand, yet felt that he touched upon something intimately personal to himself. He paused, expecting me to speak.

"Egypt, perhaps, merely pours through them," I ventured. "They give out mechanically, hardly realising how much they give. They report facts devoid of interpretation. Whereas with you it's the actual spirit of the past that is discovered and laid bare. You live it. You feel old Egypt and disclose her. That divining faculty was always yours—uncannily, I used to think."

The flash of his sombre eyes betrayed that my aim was singularly good. It seemed a third had silently joined our little table in the corner. Something intruded, evoked by the power of what our conversation skirted but ever left unmentioned. It was huge and shadowy; it was also watchful. Egypt came gliding, floating up beside us. I saw her reflected in his face and gaze. The desert slipped in through walls and ceiling, rising from beneath our feet, settling about us, listening, peering, waiting. The strange obsession was sudden and complete. The gigantic scale of her swam in among the very pillars, arches, and windows of that modern dining-room. I felt against my skin the touch of chilly air that sunlight never reaches, stealing from beneath the granite monoliths. Behind it came the stifling breath of the heated tombs, of the Serapeum, of the chambers and corridors in the pyramids. There was a rustling as of myriad footsteps far away, and as of sand the busy winds go shifting through the ages. And in startling contrast to this impression of prodigious size, Isley himself wore suddenly an air of strangely dwindling. For a second he shrank visibly before my very eyes. He was receding. His outline seemed to retreat and lessen, as though he stood to the waist in what appeared like flowing mist, only his head and shoulders still above the ground. Far, far away I saw him.

It was a vivid inner picture that I somehow transferred objectively. It was a dramatised sensation, of course. His former phrase "now that I am declining" flashed back upon me with sharp discomfort. Again, perhaps, his state of mind was reflected into me by some emotional telepathy. I waited, conscious of an almost sensible oppression that would not lift. It seemed an age before he spoke, and when he did there was the tremor of feeling in his voice he sought nevertheless to repress. I kept my eyes on the table for some reason. But I listened intently.

"It's you that have the divining faculty, not I," he said, an odd note of distance even in his tone, yet a resonance as though it rose up between reverberating walls. "There *is,* I believe, something here that resents too close enquiry, or rather that resists discovery—almost—takes offence."

I looked up quickly, then looked down again. It was such a startling thing to hear on the lips of a modern Englishman. He spoke lightly, but the expression of his face belied the careless tone. There was no mockery in those earnest eyes, and in the hushed voice was a little creeping sound that gave me once again the touch of goose-flesh. The only word I can find is subterranean: all that was mental in him had sunk, so that he seemed speaking underground, head and shoulders alone visible. The effect was almost ghastly.

"Such extraordinary obstacles are put in one's way," he went on, "when the prying gets too close to the—reality; physical, external obstacles, I mean. Either that, or—the mind loses its assimilative faculties. One or other happens—" his voice died down into a whisper—"and discovery ceases of its own accord."

The same minute, then, he suddenly raised himself like a man emerging from a tomb; he leaned across the table; he made an effort of some violent internal kind, on the verge, I fully believe, of a pregnant personal statement. There was confession in his attitude; I think he was about to speak of his work at Thebes and the reason for its abrupt cessation. For I had the feeling of one about to hear a weighty secret, the responsibility unwelcome. This uncomfortable emotion rose in me, as I raised my eyes to his somewhat unwillingly, only to find that I was wholly at fault. It was not me he was looking at. He was staring past me in the direction of the wide, unshuttered windows. The expression of yearning was visible in his eyes again. Something had stopped his utterance.

And instinctively I turned and saw what he saw. So far as external details were concerned, at least, I saw it.

Across the glare and glitter of the uncompromising modern dining-room, past crowded tables, and over the heads of Germans feeding unpicturesquely, I saw—the moon. Her reddish disc, hanging unreal and enormous, lifted the spread sheet of desert till it floated off the surface of the world. The great window faced the east, where the Arabian desert breaks into a ruin of gorges, cliffs, and flat-topped ridges; it looked unfriendly, ominous, with danger in it; unlike the serener sand-dunes of the Libyan desert, there lay both menace and seduction behind its flood of shadows. And the moonlight emphasised this aspect: its ghostly desolation, its cruelty, its bleak hostility, turning it murderous. For no river sweetens this Arabian desert; instead of sandy softness, it has fangs of limestone rock, sharp and aggressive. Across it, just visible in the moonlight as a thread of paler grey, the old camel-trail to Suez beckoned faintly. And it was this that he was looking at so intently.

It was, I know, a theatrical stage-like glimpse, yet in it a seductiveness most potent. "Come out," it seemed to whisper, "and taste my awful beauty. Come out and lose yourself, and die. Come out and follow my moonlit trail into the Past . . . where there is peace and immobility and silence. My kingdom is unchanging underground. Come down, come softly, come through sandy corridors below this tinsel of your modern world. Come back, come down into my golden past. . . ."

A poignant desire stole through my heart on moonlit feet; I was personally conscious of a keen yearning to slip away in unresisting obedience. For it was uncommonly impressive, this sudden, haunting glimpse of the world outside. The hairy foreigners, uncouthly garbed, all busily eating in full electric light, provided a sensational contrast of emphatically distressing kind. A touch of what is called unearthly hovered about that distance through the window. There was weirdness in it. Egypt looked in upon us. Egypt watched and listened, beckoning through the moonlit windows of the heart to come and find her. Mind and imagination might flounder as they pleased, but something of this kind happened undeniably, whether expression in language fails to hold the truth or not. And George Isley, aware of being seen, looked straight into the awful visage—fascinated.

Over the bronze of his skin there stole a shade of grey. My own feeling of enticement grew—the desire to go out into the moonlight, to leave my kind and wander blindly through the desert, to see the gorges in their shining silver, and taste the keenness of the cool, sharp air. Further than this with me it did not go, but that my companion felt the bigger, deeper draw behind this surface glamour, I have no reasonable doubt. For a moment, indeed, I thought he meant to leave the table; he had half risen in his chair; it seemed he struggled and resisted—and then his big frame subsided again; he sat back; he looked, in the attitude his body took, less impressive, smaller, actually shrunken into the proportions of some minuter scale. It was as though something in that second had been drawn out of him, decreasing even his physical appearance. The voice, when he spoke presently with a touch of resignation, held a lifeless quality as though deprived of virile timbre.

"It's always there," he whispered, half collapsing back into his chair, "it's always watching, waiting, listening. Almost like a monster of the fables, isn't it? It makes no movement of its own, you see. It's far too strong for that. It just hangs there, half in the air and half upon the earth—a gigantic web. Its prey flies into it. That's Egypt all over. D'you feel like that too, or does it seem to you just imaginative rubbish? To me it seems that she just waits her time; she gets you quicker that way; in the end you're bound to go."

"There's power certainly," I said after a moment's pause to collect my wits, my distress increased by the morbidness of his simile. "For some minds there may be a kind of terror too—for weak temperaments that are all imagination." My thoughts were scattered, and I could not readily find good words. "There is startling grandeur in a sight like that, for instance," and I pointed to the window. "You feel drawn—as if you simply *had* to go." My mind still buzzed with his curious words, "In the end you're bound to go." It betrayed his heart and soul. "I suppose a fly does feel drawn," I added, "or a moth to the destroying flame. Or is it just unconscious on their part?"

He jerked his big head significantly. "Well, well," he answered, "but the fly isn't necessarily weak, or the moth misguided. Over-adventurous, perhaps, yet both obedient to the laws of their respective beings. They get warnings too—only, when the moth wants to know too much, the fire stops it. Both flame and spider enrich themselves by understanding the natures of their prey; and fly and moth return again and again until this is accomplished."

Yet George Isley was as sane as the head waiter who, noticing our interest in the window, came up just then and enquired whether we felt a draught and would prefer it closed. Isley, I realised, was struggling to express a passionate state of soul for which, owing to its rarity, no adequate expression lies at hand. There is a language of the mind, but there is none as yet of the spirit. I felt ill at ease. All this was so foreign to the wholesome, strenuous personality of the man as I remembered it.

"But, my dear fellow," I stammered, "aren't you giving poor old Egypt a bad name she hardly deserves? I feel only the amazing strength and beauty of it; awe, if you like, but none of this resentment you so mysteriously hint at."

"You understand, for all that," he answered quietly; and again he seemed on the verge of some significant confession that might ease his soul. My uncomfortable emotion grew. Certainly he was at high pressure somewhere. "And, if necessary, you could help. Your sympathy, I mean, *is* a help already." He said it half to himself and in a suddenly lowered tone again.

"A help!" I gasped. "My sympathy! Of course, if—"

"A witness," he murmured, not looking at me, "some one who understands, yet does not think me mad."

There was such appeal in his voice that I felt ready and eager to do anything to help him. Our eyes met, and my own tried to express this willingness in me; but what I said I hardly know, for a cloud of confusion was on my mind, and my speech went fumbling like a schoolboy's. I was more than disconcerted. Through this bewilderment, then, I just caught the tail-end of another sentence in which the words "relief it is to have . . . some one to hold to . . . when the disappearance comes . . ." sounded like voices heard in dream. But I missed the complete phrase and shrank from asking him to repeat it.

Some sympathetic answer struggled to my lips, though what it was I know not. The thing I murmured, however, seemed apparently well chosen. He leaned across and laid his big hand a moment on my own with eloquent pressure. It was cold as ice. A look of gratitude passed over his sunburned features. He sighed. And we left the table then and passed into the inner smoking-room for coffee—a room whose windows gave upon columned terraces that allowed no view of the encircling desert. He led the conversation into channels less personal and, thank heaven, less intensely emotional and mysterious. What we talked about I now forget; it was interesting but in another key altogether. His old charm and power worked; the respect I had always felt for his character and gifts returned in force, but it was the pity I now experienced that remained chiefly in my mind. For this change in him became more and more noticeable. He was less impressive, less convincing, less suggestive. His talk, though so knowledgeable, lacked that spiritual quality that drives home. He was uncannily less *real.* And I went up to bed, uneasy and disturbed. "It is not age," I said to myself, "and assuredly it is not death he fears, although he spoke of disappearance. It is mental—in the deepest sense. It is what religious people would call soul. Something is happening to his soul."

IV

And this word "soul" remained with me to the end. Egypt was taking his soul away into the Past. What was of value in him went willingly; the rest, some lesser aspect of his mind and character, resisted, holding to the present. A struggle, therefore, was involved. But this was being gradually obliterated too.

How I arrived gaily at this monstrous conclusion seems to me now a mystery; but the truth is that from a conversation one brings away a general idea that is larger than the words actually heard and spoken. I have reported, naturally, but a fragment of what passed between us in language, and of what was suggested—by gesture, expression, silence—merely perhaps a hint. I can only assert that this troubling verdict remained a conviction in my mind. It came upstairs with me; it watched and listened by my side. That mysterious Third evoked in our conversation was bigger than either of us separately; it might be called the spirit of ancient Egypt, or it might be called, with equal generalisation, the Past. This Third, at any rate, stood by me, whispering this astounding thing. I went out on to my little balcony to smoke a pipe and enjoy the comforting presence of the stars before turning in. It came out with me. It was everywhere. I heard the barking of dogs, the monotonous beating of a distant drum towards Bedraschien, the sing-song voices of the natives in their booths and down the dim-lit streets. I was aware of this invisible Third behind all these familiar sounds. The enormous night-sky, drowned in stars, conveyed it too. It was in the breath of chilly wind that whispered round the walls, and it brooded everywhere above the sleepless desert. I was alone as little as though George Isley stood beside me in person—and at that moment a moving figure caught my eye below. My window was on the sixth storey, but there was no mistaking the tall and soldierly bearing of the man who was strolling past the hotel. George Isley was going slowly out into the desert.

There was actually nothing unusual in the sight. It was only ten o'clock; but for doctor's orders I might have been doing the same myself. Yet, as I leaned over the dizzy ledge and watched him, a chill struck through me, and a feeling nothing could justify, nor pages of writing describe, rose up and mastered me. His words at dinner came back with curious force. Egypt lay round him, motionless, a vast grey web. His feet were caught in it. It quivered. The silvery meshes in the moonlight announced the fact from Memphis up to Thebes, across the Nile, from underground Sakkhâra to the Valley of the Kings. A tremor ran over the entire desert, and again, as in the dining-room, the leagues of sand went rustling. It seemed to me that I caught him in the act of disappearing.

I realised in that moment the haunting power of this mysterious still atmosphere which is Egypt, and some magical emanation of its mighty past broke over me suddenly like a wave. Perhaps in that moment I felt what he himself felt; the withdrawing suction of the huge spent wave swept something out of me into the past with it. An indescribable yearning drew something living from my heart, something that longed with a kind of burning, searching sweetness for a glory of spiritual passion that was gone. The pain and happiness of it were more poignant than may be told, and my present personality—some vital portion of it, at any rate—wilted before the power of its enticement.

I stood there, motionless as stone, and stared. Erect and steady, knowing resistance vain, eager to go yet striving to remain, and half with an air of floating off the ground, he went towards the pale grey thread which was the track to Suez and the far Red Sea. There came upon me this strange, deep sense of pity, pathos, sympathy that was beyond all explanation, and mysterious as a pain in dreams. For a sense of his awful loneliness stole into me, a loneliness nothing on this earth could possibly relieve. Robbed of the Present, he sought this chimera of his soul, an unreal Past. Not even the calm majesty of this exquisite Egyptian night could soothe the dream away; the peace and silence were marvellous, the sweet perfume of the desert air intoxicating; but all these intensified it only.

And though at a loss to explain my own emotion, its poignancy was so real that a sigh escaped me and I felt that tears lay not too far away. I watched him, yet felt I had no right to watch. Softly I drew back from the window with the sensation of eavesdropping upon his privacy; but before I did so I had seen his outline melt away into the dim world of sand that began at the very walls of the hotel. He wore a cloak of green that reached down almost to his heels, and its colour blended with the silvery surface of the desert's dark sea-tint. This sheen first draped and then concealed him. It covered him with a fold of its mysterious garment that, without seam or binding, veiled Egypt for a thousand leagues. The desert took him. Egypt caught him in her web. He was gone.

Sleep for me just then seemed out of the question. The change in *him* made me feel less sure of myself. To see him thus invertebrate shocked me. I was aware that I had nerves.

For a long time I sat smoking by the window, my body weary, but my imagination irritatingly stimulated. The big sign-lights of the hotel went out; window after window closed below me; the electric standards in the streets were already extinguished; and Helouan looked like a child's white blocks scattered in ruin upon the nursery carpet. It seemed so wee upon the vast expanse. It lay in a twinkling pattern, like a cluster of glow-worms dropped into a negligible crease of the tremendous desert. It peeped up at the stars, a little frightened.

The night was very still. There hung an enormous brooding beauty everywhere, a hint of the sinister in it that only the brilliance of the blazing stars relieved. Nothing really slept. Grouped here and there at intervals about this dune-coloured world stood the everlasting watchers in solemn, tireless guardianship—the soaring Pyramids, the Sphinx, the grim Colossi, the empty temples, the long-deserted tombs. The mind was aware of them, stationed like sentries through the night. "This is Egypt; you are actually in Egypt," whispered the silence. "Eight thousand years of history lie fluttering outside your window. *She* lies there underground, sleepless, mighty, deathless, not to be trifled with. Beware! Or she will change you too!"

My imagination offered this hint: Egypt *is* difficult to realise. It remains outside the mind, a fabulous, half-legendary idea. So many enormous elements together refuse to be assimilated; the heart pauses, asking for time and breath; the senses reel a little, and in the end a mental torpor akin to stupefaction creeps upon the brain. With a sigh the struggle is abandoned and the mind surrenders to Egypt on her own terms. Alone the diggers and archæologists, confined to definite facts, offer successful resistance. My friend's use of the words "resistance" and "protection" became clearer to me. While logic halted, intuition fluttered round this clue to the solution of the influences at work. George Isley realised Egypt more than most—but as she had been.

And I recalled its first effect upon myself, and how my mind had been unable to cope with the memory of it afterwards. There had come to its summons a colossal medley, a gigantic, coloured blur that merely bewildered. Only lesser points lodged comfortably in the heart. I saw a chaotic vision: sands drenched in dazzling light, vast granite aisles, stupendous figures that stared unblinking at the sun, a shining river and a shadowy desert, both endless as the sky, mountainous pyramids and gigantic monoliths, armies of heads, of paws, of faces—all set to a scale of size that was prodigious. The items stunned; the composite effect was too unwieldy to be grasped. Something that blazed with splendour rolled before the eyes, too close to be seen distinctly—at the same time very distant—unrealised.

Then, with the passing of the weeks, it slowly stirred to life. It had attacked unseen; its grip was quite tremendous; yet it could be neither told, nor painted, nor described. It flamed up unexpectedly—in the foggy London streets, at the Club, in the theatre. A sound recalled the street-cries of the Arabs, a breath of scented air brought back the heated sand beyond the palm groves. Up rose the huge Egyptian glamour, transforming common things; it had lain buried all this time in deep recesses of the heart that are inaccessible to ordinary daily life. And there hid in it something of uneasiness that was inexplicable; awe, a hint of cold eternity, a touch of something unchanging and terrific, something sublime made lovely yet unearthly with shadowy time and distance. The melancholy of the Nile and the grandeur of a hundred battered temples dropped some unutterable beauty upon the heart. Up swept the desert air, the luminous pale shadows, the naked desolation that yet brims with sharp vitality. An Arab on his donkey tripped in colour across the mind, melting off into tiny perspective, strangely vivid. A string of camels stood in silhouette against the crimson sky. Great winds, great blazing spaces, great solemn nights, great days of golden splendour rose from the pavement or the theatre-stall, and London, dim-lit England, the whole of modern life, indeed, seemed suddenly reduced to a paltry insignificance that produced an aching longing for the pageantry of those millions of vanished souls. Egypt rolled through the heart for a moment—and was gone.

I remembered that some such fantastic experience had been mine. Put it as one may, the fact remains that for certain temperaments Egypt can rob the Present of some thread of interest that was formerly there. The memory became for me an integral part of personality; something in me yearned for its curious and awful beauty. He who has drunk of the Nile shall return to drink of it again. . . . And if for myself this was possible, what might not happen to a character of George Isley's type? Some glimmer of comprehension came to me. The ancient, buried, hidden Egypt had cast her net about his soul. Grown shadowy in the Present, his life was being transferred into some golden, reconstructed Past, where it was real. Some countries give, while others take away. And George Isley was worth robbing. . . .

Disturbed by these singular reflections, I moved away from the open window, closing it. But the closing did not exclude the presence of the Third. The biting night air followed me in. I drew the mosquito curtains round the bed, but the light I left still burning; and, lying there, I jotted down upon a scrap of paper this curious impression as best I could, only to find that it escaped easily between the words. Such visionary and spiritual perceptions are too elusive to be trapped in language. Reading it over after an interval of years, it is difficult to recall with what intense meaning, what uncanny emotion, I wrote those faded lines in pencil. Their rhetoric seems cheap, their content much exaggerated; yet at the time truth burned in every syllable. Egypt, which since time began has suffered robbery with violence at the hands of all the world, now takes her vengeance, choosing her individual prey. Her time has come. Behind a modern mask she lies in wait, intensely active, sure of her hidden power. Prostitute of dead empires, she lies now at peace beneath the same old stars, her loveliness unimpaired, bejewelled with the beaten gold of ages, her breasts uncovered, and her grand limbs flashing in the sun. Her shoulders of alabaster are lifted above the sand-drifts; she surveys the little figures of to-day. She takes her choice. . . .

That night I did not dream, but neither did the whole of me lie down in sleep. During the long dark hours I was aware of that picture endlessly repeating itself, the picture of George Isley stealing out into the moonlight desert. The night so swiftly dropped her hood about him; so mysteriously he merged into the unchanging thing which cloaks the past. It lifted. Some huge shadowy hand, gloved softly yet of granite, stretched over the leagues to take him. He disappeared.

They say the desert is motionless and has no gestures! That night I saw it moving, hurrying. It went tearing after him. You understand my meaning? No! Well, when excited it produces this strange impression, and the terrible moment is—when you surrender helplessly—you desire it shall swallow you. You let it come. George Isley spoke of a web. It is, at any rate, some central power that conceals itself behind the surface glamour folk call the spell of Egypt. Its home is not apparent. It dwells with ancient Egypt—underground. Behind the stillness of hot windless days, behind the peace of calm, gigantic nights, it lurks unrealised, monstrous and irresistible. My mind grasped it as little as the fact that our solar system with all its retinue of satellites and planets rushes annually many million miles towards a star in Hercules, while yet that constellation appears no closer than it did six thousand years ago. But the clue dropped into me. George Isley, with his entire retinue of thought and life and feeling, was being similarly drawn. And I, a minor satellite, had become aware of the horrifying pull. It was magnificent. . . . And I fell asleep on the crest of this enormous wave.

V

The next few days passed idly; weeks passed too, I think; hidden away in this cosmopolitan hotel we lived apart, unnoticed. There was the feeling that time went what pace it pleased, now fast, now slow, now standing still. The similarity of the brilliant days, set between wondrous dawns and sunsets, left the impression that it was really one long, endless day without divisions. The mind's machinery of measurement suffered dislocation. Time went backwards; dates were forgotten; the month, the time of year, the century itself went down into undifferentiated life.

The Present certainly slipped away curiously. Newspapers and politics became unimportant, news uninteresting, English life so remote as to be unreal, European affairs shadowy. The stream of life ran in another direction altogether—backwards. The names and faces of friends appeared through mist. People arrived as though dropped from the skies. They suddenly were there; one saw them in the dining-room, as though they had just slipped in from an outer world that once was real—somewhere. Of course, a steamer sailed four times a week, and the journey took five days, but these things were merely known, not realised. The fact that here it was summer, whereas over there winter reigned, helped to make the distance not quite thinkable. We looked at the desert and made plans. "We will do this, we will do that; we must go there, we'll visit such and such a place . . ." yet nothing happened. It always was to-morrow or yesterday, and we shared the discovery of Alice that there was no real "to-day." For our thinking made everything happen. That was enough. It *had* happened. It was the reality of dreams. Egypt was a dream-world that made the heart live backwards.

It came about, thus, that for the next few weeks I watched a fading life, myself alert and sympathetic, yet unable somehow to intrude and help. Noticing various little things by which George Isley betrayed the progress of the unequal struggle, I found my assistance negatived by the fact that I was in similar case myself. What he experienced in large and finally, I, too, experienced in little and for the moment. For I seemed also caught upon the fringe of the invisible web. My feelings were entangled sufficiently for me to understand. . . . And the decline of his being was terrible to watch. His character went with it; I saw his talents fade, his personality dwindle, his very soul dissolve before the insidious and invading influence. He hardly struggled. I thought of those abominable insects that paralyse the motor systems of their victims and then devour them at their leisure—alive. The incredible adventure was literally true, but, being spiritual, may not be told in the terms of a detective story. This version must remain an individual rendering—an aspect of *one* possible version. All who know the real Egypt, that Egypt which has nothing to do with dams and Nationalists and the external welfare of the felaheen, will understand. The pilfering of her ancient dead she suffers still; she, in revenge, preys at her leisure on the living.

The occasions when he betrayed himself were ordinary enough; it was the glimpse they afforded of what was in progress beneath his calm exterior that made them interesting. Once, I remember, we had lunched together, at Mena, and, after visiting certain excavations beyond the Gizeh pyramids, we made our way homewards by way of the Sphinx. It was dusk, and the main army of tourists had retired, though some few dozen sight-seers still moved about to the cries of donkey-boys and baksheesh. The vast head and shoulders suddenly emerged, riding undrowned above the sea of sand. Dark and monstrous in the fading light, it loomed, as ever, a being of non-human lineage; no amount of familiarity could depreciate its grandeur, its impressive setting, the lost expression of the countenance that is too huge to focus as a face. A thousand visits leave its power undiminished. It has intruded upon our earth from some uncommon world. George Isley and myself both turned aside to acknowledge the presence of this alien, uncomfortable thing. We did not linger, but we slackened pace. It was the obvious, inevitable thing to do. He pointed then, with a suddenness that made me start. He indicated the tourists standing round.

"See," he said, in a lowered tone, "day and night you'll always find a crowd obedient to that thing. But notice their behaviour. People don't do that before any other ruin in the world I've ever seen." He referred to the attempts of individuals to creep away alone and stare into the stupendous visage by themselves. At different points in the deep sandy basin were men and women, standing solitary, lying, crouching, apart from the main company where the dragomen mouthed their exposition with impertinent glibness.

"The desire to be alone," he went on, half to himself, as we paused a moment, "the sense of worship which insists on privacy."

It *was* significant, for no amount of advertising could dwarf the impressiveness of the inscrutable visage into whose eyes of stone the silent humans gazed. Not even the red-coat, standing inside one gigantic ear, could introduce the commonplace. But my companion's words let another thing into the spectacle, a less exalted thing, dropping a hint of horror about that sandy cup: It became easy, for a moment, to imagine these tourists worshipping—against their will; to picture the monster noticing that they were there; that it might slowly turn its awful head; that the sand might visibly trickle from a stirring paw; that, in a word, they might be taken—changed.

"Come," he whispered in a dropping tone, interrupting my fancies as though he half divined them, "it is getting late, and to be alone with the thing is intolerable to me just now. But you notice, don't you," he added, as he took my arm to hurry me away, "how little the tourists matter? Instead of injuring the effect, they increase it. It uses *them*."

And again a slight sensation of chill, communicated possibly by his nervous touch, or possibly by his earnest way of saying these curious words, passed through me. Some part of me remained behind in that hollow trough of sand, prostrate before an immensity that symbolised the past. A curious, wild yearning caught me momentarily, an intense desire to understand exactly why that terror stood there, its actual meaning long ago to the hearts that set it waiting for the sun, what definite rôle it played, what souls it stirred and why, in that system of towering belief and faith whose indestructible emblem it still remained. The past stood grouped so solemnly about its menacing presentment. I was distinctly aware of this spiritual suction backwards that my companion yielded to so gladly, yet against his normal, modern self. For it made the past appear magnificently desirable, and loosened all the rivets of the present. It bodied forth three main ingredients of this deep Egyptian spell—size, mystery, and immobility.

Yet, to my relief, the cheaper aspect of this Egyptian glamour left him cold. He remained unmoved by the commonplace mysterious; he told no mummy stories, nor ever hinted at the supernatural quality that leaps to the mind of the majority. There was no play in him. The influence was grave and vital. And, although I knew he held strong views with regard to the impiety of disturbing the dead, he never in my hearing attached any possible revengeful character to the energy of an outraged past. The current tales of this description he ignored; they were for superstitious minds or children; the deities that claimed his soul were of a grander order altogether. He lived, if it may be so expressed, already in a world his heart had reconstructed or remembered; it drew him in another direction altogether; with the modern, sensational view of life his spirit held no traffic any longer; he was living backwards. I saw his figure receding mournfully, yet never sentimentally, into the spacious, golden atmosphere of recaptured days. The enormous soul of buried Egypt drew him down. The dwindling of his physical appearance was, of course, a mental interpretation of my own; but another, stranger interpretation of a spiritual kind moved parallel with it—marvellous and horrible. For, as he diminished outwardly and in his modern, present aspect, he grew within—gigantic. The size of Egypt entered into him. Huge proportions now began to accompany any presentment of his personality to my inner vision. He towered. These two qualities of the land already obsessed him—magnitude and immobility.

And that awe which modern life ignores contemptuously woke in my heart. I almost feared his presence at certain times. For one aspect of the Egyptian spell is explained by sheer size and bulk. Disdainful of mere speed to-day, the heart is still uncomfortable with magnitude; and in Egypt there is size that may easily appal, for every detail shunts it laboriously upon the mind. It elbows out the present. The desert's vastness is not made comprehensible by mileage, and the sources of the Nile are so distant that they exist less on the map than in the imagination. The effort to realise suffers paralysis; they might equally be in the moon or Saturn. The undecorated magnificence of the desert remains unknown, just as the proportions of pyramid and temple, of pylons and Colossi approach the edge of the mind yet never enter in. All stand outside, clothed in this prodigious measurement of the past. And the old beliefs not only share this titanic effect upon the consciousness, but carry it stages further. The entire scale haunts with uncomfortable immensity, so that the majority run back with relief to the measurable details of a more manageable scale. Express trains, flying machines, Atlantic liners—these produce no unpleasant stretching of the faculties compared to the influence of the Karnak pylons, the pyramids, or the interior of the Serapeum.

Close behind this magnitude, moreover, steps the monstrous. It is revealed not in sand and stone alone, in queer effects of light and shadow, of glittering sunsets and of magical dusks, but in the very aspect of the bird and animal life. The heavy-headed buffaloes betray it equally with the vultures, the myriad kites, the grotesqueness of the mouthing camels. The rude, enormous scenery has it everywhere. There is nothing lyrical in this land of passionate mirages. Uncouth immensity notes the little human flittings. The days roll by in a tide of golden splendour; one goes helplessly with the flood; but it is an irresistible flood that sweeps backwards and below. The silent-footed natives in their coloured robes move before a curtain, and behind that curtain dwells the soul of ancient Egypt—the Reality, as George Isley called it—watching, with sleepless eyes of grey infinity. Then, sometimes the curtain stirs and lifts an edge; an invisible hand creeps forth; the soul is touched. And some one disappears.

VI

The process of disintegration must have been at work a long time before I appeared upon the scene; the changes went forward with such rapidity.

It was his third year in Egypt, two of which had been spent without interruption in company with an Egyptologist named Moleson, in the neighbourhood of Thebes. I soon discovered that this region was for him the centre of attraction, or as he put it, of the web. Not Luxor, of course, nor the images of reconstructed Karnak; but that stretch of grim, forbidding mountains where royalty, earthly and spiritual, sought eternal peace for the physical remains. There, amid surroundings of superb desolation, great priests and mighty kings had thought themselves secure from sacrilegious touch. In caverns underground they kept their faithful tryst with centuries, guarded by the silence of magnificent gloom. There they waited, communing with passing ages in their sleep, till Ra, their glad divinity, should summon them to the fulfilment of their ancient dream. And there, in the Valley of the Tombs of the Kings, their dream was shattered, their lovely prophecies derided, and their glory dimmed by the impious desecration of the curious.

That George Isley and his companion had spent their time, not merely digging and deciphering like their practical confrères, but engaged in some strange experiments of recovery and reconstruction, was matter for open comment among the fraternity. That incredible things had happened there was the big story of two Egyptian seasons at least. I heard this later only—tales of an utterly incredible kind, that the desolate vale of rock was seen repeopled on moonlit nights, that the smoke of unaccustomed fires rose to cap the flat-topped peaks, that the pageantry of some forgotten worship had been seen to issue from the openings of these hills, and that sounds of chanting, sonorous and marvellously sweet, had been heard to echo from those bleak, repellent precipices. The tales apparently were grossly exaggerated; wandering Bedouins brought them in; the guides and dragomen repeated them with mysterious additions; till they filtered down through the native servants in the hotels and reached the tourists with highly picturesque embroidery. They reached the authorities too. The only accurate fact I gathered at the time, however, was that they had abruptly ceased. George Isley and Moleson, moreover, had parted company. And Moleson, I heard, was the originator of the business. He was, at this time, unknown to me; his arresting book on "A Modern Reconstruction of Sun-worship in Ancient Egypt" being my only link with his unusual mind. Apparently he regarded the sun as the deity of the scientific religion of the future which would replace the various anthropomorphic gods of childish creeds. He discussed the possibility of the zodiacal signs being some kind of Celestial Intelligences. Belief blazed on every page. Men's life is heat, derived solely from the sun, and men were, therefore, part of the sun in the sense that a Christian is part of his personal deity. And absorption was the end. His description of "sun-worship ceremonials" conveyed an amazing reality and beauty. This singular book, however, was all I knew of him until he came to visit us in Helouan, though I easily discerned that his influence somehow was the original cause of the change in my companion.

At Thebes, then, was the active centre of the influence that drew my friend away from modern things. It was there, I easily guessed, that "obstacles" had been placed in the way of these men's too close enquiry. In that haunted and oppressive valley, where profane and reverent come to actual grips, where modern curiosity is most busily organised, and even tourists are aware of a masked hostility that dogs the prying of the least imaginative mind—there, in the neighbourhood of the hundred-gated city, had Egypt set the headquarters of her irreconcilable enmity. And it was there, amid the ruins of her loveliest past, that George Isley had spent his years of magical reconstruction and met the influence that now dominated his entire life.

And though no definite avowal of the struggle betrayed itself in speech between us, I remember fragments of conversation, even at this stage, that proved his willing surrender of the present. We spoke of fear once, though with the indirectness of connection I have mentioned. I urged that the mind, once it is forewarned, can remain master of itself and prevent a thing from happening.

"But that does not make the thing unreal," he objected.

"The mind can deny it," I said. "It then becomes unreal."

He shook his head. "One does not deny an unreality. Denial is a childish act of self-protection against something you expect to happen." He caught my eye a moment. "You deny what you are afraid of," he said. "Fear invites." And he smiled uneasily. "You know it must get you in the end." And, both of us being aware secretly to what our talk referred, it seemed bold-blooded and improper; for actually we discussed the psychology of his disappearance. Yet, while I disliked it, there was a fascination about the subject that compelled attraction. . . . "Once fear gets in," he added presently, "confidence is undermined, the structure of life is threatened, and you—go gladly. The foundation of everything is belief. A man is what he believes about himself; and in Egypt you can believe things that elsewhere you would not even think about. It attacks the essentials." He sighed, yet with a curious pleasure; and a smile of resignation and relief passed over his rugged features and was gone again. The luxury of abandonment lay already in him.

"But even belief," I protested, "must be founded on some experience or other." It seemed ghastly to speak of his spiritual malady behind the mask of indirect allusion. My excuse was that he so obviously talked willingly.

He agreed instantly. "Experience of one kind or another," he said darkly, "there always is. Talk with the men who live out here; ask any one who thinks, or who has the imagination which divines. You'll get only one reply, phrase it how they may. Even the tourists and the little commonplace officials feel it. And it's not the climate, it's not nerves, it's not any definite tendency that they can name or lay their finger on. Nor is it mere orientalising of the mind. It's something that first takes you from your common life, and that later takes common life from you. You willingly resign an unremunerative Present. There are no half-measures either—once the gates are open."

There was so much undeniable truth in this that I found no corrective by way of strong rejoinder. All my attempts, indeed, were futile in this way. He meant to go; my words could not stop him. He wanted a witness—he dreaded the loneliness of going—but he brooked no interference. The contradictory position involved a perplexing state of heart and mind in both of us. The atmosphere of this majestic land, today so trifling, yesterday so immense, most certainly induced a lifting of the spiritual horizon that revealed amazing possibilities.

VII

It was in the windless days of a perfect December that Moleson, the Egyptologist, found us out and paid a flying visit to Helouan. His duties took him up and down the land, but his time seemed largely at his own disposal. He lingered on. His coming introduced a new element I was not quite able to estimate; though, speaking generally, the effect of his presence upon my companion was to emphasise the latter's alteration. It underlined the change, and drew attention to it. The new arrival, I gathered, was not altogether welcome. "I should never have expected to find you *here,*" laughed Moleson when they met, and whether he referred to Helouan or to the hotel was not quite clear. I got the impression he meant both; I remembered my fancy that it was a good hotel to hide in. George Isley had betrayed a slight involuntary start when the visiting card was brought to him at tea-time. I think he had wished to escape from his former co-worker. Moleson had found him out. "I heard you had a friend with you and were contemplating further exper—work," he added. He changed the word "experiment" quickly to the other.

"The former, as you see, is true, but not the latter," replied my companion dryly, and in his manner was a touch of opposition that might have been hostility. Their intimacy, I saw, was close and of old standing. In all they said and did and looked, there was an undercurrent of other meaning that just escaped me. They were up to something—they *had* been up to something; but Isley would have withdrawn if he could!

Moleson was an ambitious and energetic personality, absorbed in his profession, alive to the poetical as well as to the practical value of archæology, and he made at first a wholly delightful impression upon me. An instinctive flair for his subject had early in life brought him success and a measure of fame as well. His knowledge was accurate and scholarly, his mind saturated in the lore of a vanished civilisation.

Behind an exterior that was quietly careless, I divined a passionate and complex nature, and I watched him with interest as the man for whom the olden sun-worship of unscientific days held some beauty of reality and truth. Much in his strange book that had bewildered me now seemed intelligible when I saw the author. I cannot explain this more closely. Something about him somehow made it possible. Though modern to the finger-tips and thoroughly equipped with all the tendencies of the day, there seemed to hide in him another self that held aloof with a dignified detachment from the interests in which his "educated" mind was centred. He read living secrets beneath museum labels, I might put it. He stepped out of the days of the Pharaohs if ever man did, and I realised early in our acquaintance that this was the man who had exceptional powers of "resistance and self-protection," and was, in his particular branch of work, "unusual." In manner he was light and gay, his sense of humour strong, with a way of treating everything as though laughter was the sanest attitude towards life. There is, however, the laughter that hides—other things. Moleson, as I gathered from many clues of talk and manner and silence, was a deep and singular being. His experiences in Egypt, if any, he had survived admirably. There were at least two Molesons. I felt him more than double—multiple.

In appearance tall, thin, and fleshless, with a dried-up skin and features withered as a mummy's, he said laughingly that Nature had picked him physically for his "job"; and, indeed, one could see him worming his way down narrow tunnels into the sandy tombs, and writhing along sunless passages of suffocating heat without too much personal inconvenience. Something sinuous, almost fluid in his mind, expressed itself in his body too. He might go in any direction without causing surprise. He might go backwards or forwards. He might go in two directions at once.

And my first impression of the man deepened before many days were past. There was irresponsibility in him, insincerity somewhere, almost want of heart. His morality was certainly not to-day's, and the mind in him was slippery. I think the modern world, to which he was unattached, confused and irritated him. A sense of insecurity came with him. His interest in George Isley was the interest in a psychological "specimen." I remembered how in his book he described the selection of individuals for certain functions of that marvellous worship, and the odd idea flashed through me—well, that Isley exactly suited some purpose of his re-creating energies. The man was keenly observant from top to toe, but not with his sight alone; he seemed to be aware of motives and emotions before he noticed the acts or gestures that these caused. I felt that he took me in as well. Certainly he eyed me up and down by means of this inner observation that seemed automatic with him.

Moleson was not staying in our hotel; he had chosen one where social life was more abundant; but he came up frequently to lunch and dine, and sometimes spent the evening in Isley's rooms, amusing us with his skill upon the piano, singing Arab songs, and chanting phrases from the ancient Egyptian rituals to rhythms of his own invention. The old Egyptian music, both in harmony and melody, was far more developed than I had realised, the use of sound having been of radical importance in their ceremonies. The chanting in particular he did with extraordinary effect, though whether its success lay in his sonorous voice, his peculiar increasing of the vowel sounds, or to anything deeper, I cannot pretend to say. The result at any rate was of a unique description. It brought buried Egypt to the surface; the gigantic Presence entered sensibly into the room. It came, huge and gorgeous, rolling upon the mind the instant he began, and something in it was both terrible and oppressive. The repose of eternity lay in the sound. Invariably, after a few moments of that transforming music, I saw the Valley of the Kings, the deserted temples, titanic faces of stone, great effigies coiffed with zodiacal signs, but above all—the twin Colossi.

I mentioned this last detail.

"Curious *you* should feel that too—curious you should say it, I mean," Moleson replied, not looking at me, yet with an air as if I had said something he expected. "To me the Memnon figures express Egypt better than all the other monuments put together. Like the desert, they are featureless. They sum her up, as it were, yet leave the message unuttered. For, you see, they cannot." He laughed a little in his throat. "They have neither eyes nor lips nor nose; their features are gone."

"Yet they tell the secret—to those who care to listen," put in Isley in a scarcely noticeable voice. "Just because they have no words. They still sing at dawn," he added in a louder, almost a challenging tone. It startled me.

Moleson turned round at him, opened his lips to speak, hesitated, stopped. He said nothing for a moment. I cannot describe what it was in the lightning glance they exchanged that put me on the alert for something other than was obvious. My nerves quivered suddenly, and a breath of colder air stole in among us. Moleson swung round to me again. "I almost think," he said, laughing when I complimented him upon the music, "that I must have been a priest of Aton-Ra in an earlier existence, for all this comes to my finger-tips as if it were instinctive knowledge. Plotinus, remember, lived a few miles away at Alexandria with his great idea that knowledge is recollection," he said, with a kind of cynical amusement. "In those days, at any rate," he added more significantly, "worship was real and ceremonials actually expressed great ideas and teaching. There was power in them." Two of the Molesons spoke in that contradictory utterance.

I saw that Isley was fidgeting where he sat, betraying by certain gestures that uneasiness was in him. He hid his face a moment in his hands; he sighed; he made a movement—as though to prevent something coming. But Moleson resisted his attempt to change the conversation, though the key shifted a little of its own accord. There were numerous occasions like this when I was aware that both men skirted something that had happened, something that Moleson wished to resume, but that Isley seemed anxious to postpone.

I found myself studying Moleson's personality, yet never getting beyond a certain point. Shrewd, subtle, with an acute rather than a large intelligence, he was cynical as well as insincere, and yet I cannot describe by what means I arrived at two other conclusions as well about him: first, that this insincerity and want of heart had not been so always; and, secondly, that he sought social diversion with deliberate and un-ordinary purpose. I could well believe that the first was Egypt's mark upon him, and the second an effort at resistance and self-protection.

"If it wasn't for the gaiety," he remarked once in a flippant way that thinly hid significance, "a man out here would go under in a year. Social life gets rather reckless—exaggerated—people do things they would never dream of doing at home. Perhaps you've noticed it," he added, looking suddenly at me; "Cairo and the rest—they plunge at it as though driven—a sort of excess about it somewhere." I nodded agreement. The way he said it was unpleasant rather. "It's an antidote," he said, a sub-acid flavour in his tone. "I used to loathe society myself. But now I find gaiety—a certain irresponsible excitement—of importance. Egypt gets on the nerves after a bit. The moral fibre fails. The will grows weak." And he glanced covertly at Isley as with a desire to point his meaning, "It's the clash between the ugly present and the majestic past, perhaps." He smiled.

Isley shrugged his shoulders, making no reply; and the other went on to tell stories of friends and acquaintances whom Egypt had adversely affected: Barton, the Oxford man, school teacher, who had insisted in living in a tent until the Government relieved him of his job. He took to his tent, roamed the desert, drawn irresistibly, practical considerations of the present of no avail. This yearning took him, though he could never define the exact attraction. In the end his mental balance was disturbed. "But now he's all right again; I saw him in London only this year; he can't say what he felt or why he did it. Only—he's different." Of John Lattin, too, he spoke, whom agoraphobia caught so terribly in Upper Egypt; of Malahide, upon whom some fascination of the Nile induced suicidal mania and attempts at drowning; of Jim Moleson, a cousin (who had camped at Thebes with himself and Isley), whom megalomania of a most singular type attacked suddenly in a sandy waste—all radically cured as soon as they left Egypt, yet, one and all, changed and made otherwise in their very souls.

He talked in a loose, disjointed way, and though much he said was fantastic, as if meant to challenge opposition, there was impressiveness about it somewhere, due, I think, to a kind of cumulative emotion he produced.

"The monuments do not impress merely by their bulk, but by their majestic symmetry," I remember him saying. "Look at the choice of form alone—the pyramids, for instance. No other shape was possible: dome, square, spires, all would have been hideously inadequate. The wedge-shaped mass, immense foundations, and pointed apex were the *mot juste* in outline. Do you think people without greatness in themselves chose that form? There was no unbalance in the minds that conceived the harmonious and magnificent structures of the temples. There was stately grandeur in their consciousness that could only be born of truth and knowledge. The power in their images is a direct expression of eternal and essential things they knew."

We listened in silence. He was off upon his hobby. But behind the careless tone and laughing questions, there was this lurking passionateness that made me feel uncomfortable. He was edging up, I felt, towards some climax that meant life and death to himself and Isley. I could not fathom it. My sympathy let me in a little, yet not enough to understand completely. Isley, I saw, was also uneasy, though for reasons that equally evaded me.

"One can almost believe," he continued, "that something still hangs about in the atmosphere from those olden times." He half closed his eyes, but I caught the gleam in them. "It affects the mind through the imagination. With some it changes the point of view. It takes the soul back with it to former, quite different, conditions, that must have been almost another kind of consciousness."

He paused an instant and looked up at us. "The *intensity* of belief in those days," he resumed, since neither of us accepted the challenge, "was amazing—something quite unknown anywhere in the world today. It was so sure, so positive; no mere speculative theories, I mean;—as though something in the climate, the exact position beneath the stars, the 'attitude' of this particular stretch of earth in relation to the sun—thinned the veil between humanity—and other things. Their hierarchies of gods, you know, were not mere idols; animals, birds, monsters, and what-not, all typified spiritual forces and powers that influenced their daily life. But the strong thing is—they *knew.* People who were scientific as they were did not swallow foolish superstitions. They made colours that could last six thousand years, even in the open air; and without instruments they measured accurately—an enormously difficult and involved calculation—the precession of the equinoxes. You've been to Denderah?"—he suddenly glanced again at me. "No! Well, the minds that realised the zodiacal signs could hardly believe, you know, that Hathor was a cow!"

Isley coughed. He was about to interrupt, but before he could find words, Moleson was off again, some new quality in his tone and manner that was almost aggressive. The hints he offered seemed more than hints. There was a strange conviction in his heart. I think he was skirting a bigger thing that he and his companion knew, yet that his real object was to see how far I was open to attack—how far my sympathy might be with them. I became aware that he and George Isley shared this bigger thing. It was based, I felt, on some certain knowledge that experiment had brought them.

"Think of the grand teaching of Aknahton, that young Pharaoh who regenerated the entire land and brought it to its immense prosperity. He taught the worship of the sun, but not of the visible sun. The deity had neither form nor shape. The great disc of glory was but the manifestation, each beneficent ray ending in a hand that blessed the world. It was a god of everlasting energy, love, and power, yet men could know it at first hand in their daily lives, worshipping it at dawn and sunset with passionate devotion. No anthropomorphic idol masqueraded in *that!*"

An extraordinary glow was about him as he said it. The same minute he lowered his voice, shifting the key perceptibly. He kept looking up at me through half-closed eyelids.

"And another thing they wonderfully knew," he almost whispered, "was that, with the precession of their deity across the equinoctial changes, there came new powers down into the world of men. Each cycle—each zodiacal sign—brought its special powers which they quickly typified in the monstrous effigies we label to-day in our dull museums. Each sign took some two thousand years to traverse. Each sign, moreover, involved a change in human consciousness. There was this relation between the heavens and the human heart. All that they knew. While the sun crawled through the sign of Taurus, it was the Bull they worshipped; with Aries, it was the ram that coiffed their granite symbols. Then came, as you remember, with Pisces the great New Arrival, when already they sank from their grand zenith, and the Fish was taken as the emblem of the changing powers which the Christ embodied. For the human soul, they held, echoed the changes in the immense journey of the original deity, who is its source, across the Zodiac, and the truth of 'As above, so Below,' remains the key to all manifested life. And to-day the sun, just entering Aquarius, new powers are close upon the world. The old—that which has been for two thousand years—again is crumbling, passing, dying. New powers and a new consciousness are knocking at our doors. It is a time of change. It is also"—he leaned forward so that his eyes came close before me—"the time to make the change. The soul can choose its own conditions. It can—"

A sudden crash smothered the rest of the sentence. A chair had fallen with a clatter upon the wooden floor where the carpet left it bare. Whether Isley in rising had stumbled against it, or whether he had purposely knocked it over, I could not say. I only knew that he had abruptly risen and as abruptly sat down again. A curious feeling came to me that the sign was somehow prearranged. It was so sudden. His voice, too, was forced, I thought.

"Yes, but we can do without all that, Moleson," he interrupted with acute abruptness. "Suppose we have a tune instead."

VIII

It was after dinner in his private room, and he had sat very silent in his corner until this sudden outburst. Moleson got up quietly without a word and moved over to the piano. I saw—or was it imagination merely?—a new expression slide upon his withered face. He meant mischief somewhere.

From that instant—from the moment he rose and walked over the thick carpet—he fascinated me. The atmosphere his talk and stories had brought remained. His lean fingers ran over the keys, and at first he played fragments from popular musical comedies that were pleasant enough, but made no demand upon the attention. I heard them without listening. I was thinking of another thing—his walk. For the way he moved across those few feet of carpet had power in it. He looked different; he seemed another man; he was changed. I saw him curiously—as I sometimes now saw Isley too—bigger. In some manner that was both enchanting and oppressive, his presence from that moment drew my imagination as by an air of authority it held.

I left my seat in the far corner and dropped into a chair beside the window, nearer to the piano. Isley, I then noticed, had also turned to watch him. But it was George Isley not quite as he was now. I felt rather than saw the change. Both men had subtly altered. They seemed extended, their outlines shadowy.

Isley, alert and anxious, glanced up at the player, his mind of earlier years—for the expression of his face was plain—following the light music, yet with difficulty that involved effort, almost struggle. "Play that again, will you?" I heard him say from time to time. He was trying to take hold of it, to climb back to a condition where that music had linked him to the present, to seize a mental structure that was gone, to grip hold tightly of it—only to find that it was too far forgotten and too fragile. It would not bear him. I am sure of it, and I can swear I divined his mood. He fought to realise himself as he had been, but in vain. In his dim corner opposite I watched him closely. The big black Blüthner blocked itself between us. Above it swayed the outline, lean and half shadowy, of Moleson as he played. A faint whisper floated through the room. "You are in Egypt." Nowhere else could this queer feeling of presentiment, of anticipation, have gained a footing so easily. I was aware of intense emotion in all three of us. The least reminder of to-day seemed ugly. I longed for some ancient forgotten splendour that was lost.

The scene fixed my attention very steadily, for I was aware of something deliberate and calculated on Moleson's part. The thing was well considered in his mind, intention only half concealed. It was Egypt he interpreted by sound, expressing what in him was true, then observing its effect, as he led us cleverly towards—the past. Beginning with the present, he played persuasively, with penetration, with insistent meaning too. He had that touch which conjured up real atmosphere, and, at first, that atmosphere termed modern. He rendered vividly the note of London, passing from the jingles of musical comedy, nervous rag-times, and sensuous Tango dances, into the higher strains of concert rooms and "cultured" circles. Yet not too abruptly. Most dexterously he shifted the level, and with it our emotion. I recognised, as in a parody, various ultra-modern thrills: the tumult of Strauss, the pagan sweetness of primitive Debussy, the weirdness and ecstasy of metaphysical Scriabin. The composite note of To-day in both extremes, he brought into this private sitting-room of the desert hotel, while George Isley, listening keenly, fidgeted in his chair.

"'Après-midi d'un Faune,'" said Moleson dreamily, answering the question as to what he played. "Debussy's, you know. And the thing before it was from 'Til Eulenspiegel'—Strauss, of course."

He drawled, swaying slowly with the rhythm, and leaving pauses between the words. His attention was not wholly on his listener, and in the voice was a quality that increased my uneasy apprehension. I felt distress for Isley somewhere. Something, it seemed, was coming; Moleson brought it. Unconsciously in his walk, it now appeared consciously in his music; and it came from what was underground in him. A charm, a subtle change, stole oddly over the room. It stole over my heart as well. Some power of estimating left me, as though my mind were slipping backwards and losing familiar, common standards.

"The true modern note in it, isn't there?" he drawled; "cleverness, I think—intellectual—surface ingenuity—no depth or permanence—just the sensational brilliance of To-day." He turned and stared at me fixedly an instant. "Nothing *everlasting*," he added impressively. "It tells everything it knows—because it's small enough—"

And the room turned pettier as he said it; another, bigger shadow draped its little walls. Through the open windows came a stealthy gesture of eternity. The atmosphere stretched visibly. Moleson was playing a marvellous fragment from Scriabin's "Prometheus." It sounded thin and shallow. This modern music, all of it, was out of place and trivial. It was almost ridiculous. The scale of our emotion changed insensibly into a deeper thing that has no name in dictionaries, being of another age. And I glanced at the windows where stone columns framed dim sections of great Egypt listening outside. There was no moon; only deep draughts of stars blazed, hanging in the sky. I thought with awe of the mysterious knowledge that vanished people had of these stars, and of the Sun's huge journey through the Zodiac. . . .

And, with astonishing suddenness as of dream, there rose a pictured image against that starlit sky. Lifted into the air, between heaven and earth, I saw float swiftly past a panorama of the stately temples, led by Denderah, Edfu, Abou Simbel. It paused, it hovered, it disappeared. Leaving incalculable solemnity behind it in the air, it vanished, and to see so vast a thing move at that easy yet unhasting speed unhinged some sense of measurement in me. It was, of course, I assured myself, mere memory objectified owing to something that the music summoned, yet the apprehension rose in me that the whole of Egypt presently would stream past in similar fashion—Egypt as she was in the zenith of her unrecoverable past. Behind the tinkling of the modern piano passed the rustling of a multitude, the tramping of countless feet on sand. . . . It was singularly vivid. It arrested in me something that normally went flowing. . . . And when I turned my head towards the room to call attention to my strange experience, the eyes of Moleson, I saw, were laid upon my own. He stared at me. The light in them transfixed me, and I understood that the illusion was due in some manner to his evocation. Isley rose at the same moment from his chair. The thing I had vaguely been expecting had shifted closer. And the same moment the musician abruptly changed his key.

"You may like this better," he murmured, half to himself, but in tones he somehow made echoing. "It's more suited to the place." There was a resonance in the voice as though it emerged from hollows underground. "The other seems almost sacrilegious—here." And his voice drawled off in the rhythm of slower modulations that he played. It had grown muffled. There was an impression, too, that he did not strike the piano, but that the music issued from himself.

"Place! What place?" asked Isley quickly. His head turned sharply as he spoke. His tone, in its remoteness, made me tremble.

The musician laughed to himself. "I meant that this hotel seems really an impertinence," he murmured, leaning down upon the notes he played upon so softly and so well; "and that it's but the thinnest kind of pretence—when you come to think of it. We are in the desert really. The Colossi are outside, and all the emptied temples. Or ought to be," he added, raising his tone abruptly with a glance at me.

He straightened up and stared out into the starry sky past George Isley's shoulders.

"That," he exclaimed with betraying vehemence, "is where we are and what we play to!" His voice suddenly increased; there was a roar in it. "That," he repeated, "is the thing that takes our hearts away." The volume of intonation was astonishing.

For the way he uttered the monosyllable suddenly revealed the man beneath the outer sheath of cynicism and laughter, explained his heartlessness, his secret stream of life. He, too, was soul and body in the past. "That" revealed more than pages of descriptive phrases. His heart lived in the temple aisles, his mind unearthed forgotten knowledge; his soul had clothed itself anew in the seductive glory of antiquity: he dwelt with a quickening magic of existence in the reconstructed splendour of what most term only ruins. He and George Isley together had revivified a power that enticed them backwards; but whereas the latter struggled still, the former had already made his permanent home there. The faculty in me that saw the vision of streaming temples saw also this—remorselessly definite. Moleson himself sat naked at that piano. I saw him clearly then. He no longer masqueraded behind his sneers and laughter. He, too, had long ago surrendered, lost himself, gone out, and from the place his soul now dwelt in he watched George Isley sinking down to join him. He lived in ancient, subterranean Egypt. This great hotel stood precariously on the merest upper crust of desert. A thousand tombs, a hundred temples lay outside, within reach almost of our very voices. Moleson was merged with "that."

This intuition flashed upon me like the picture in the sky; and both were true.

And, meanwhile, this other thing he played had a surge of power in it impossible to describe. It was sombre, huge, and solemn. It conveyed the power that his walk conveyed. There was distance in it, but a distance not of space alone. A remoteness of time breathed through it with that strange sadness and melancholy yearning that enormous interval brings. It marched, but very far away; it held refrains that assumed the rhythms of a multitude the centuries muted; it sang, but the singing was underground in passages that fine sand muffled. Lost, wandering winds sighed through it, booming. The contrast, after the modern, cheaper music, was dislocating. Yet the change had been quite naturally effected.

"It would sound empty and monotonous elsewhere—in London, for instance," I heard Moleson drawling, as he swayed to and fro, "but here it is big and splendid—true. You hear what I mean," he added gravely. "You understand?"

"What is it?" asked Isley thickly, before I could say a word. "I forget exactly. It has tears in it—more than I can bear." The end of his sentence died away in his throat.

Moleson did not look at him as he answered. He looked at me.

"You surely ought to know," he replied, the voice rising and falling as though the rhythm forced it. "You have heard it all before—that chant from the ritual we—"

Isley sprang up and stopped him. I did not hear the sentence complete. An extraordinary thought blazed into me that the voices of both men were not quite their own. I fancied—wild, impossible as it sounds—that I heard the twin Colossi singing to each other in the dawn. Stupendous ideas sprang past me, leaping. It seemed as though eternal symbols of the cosmos, discovered and worshipped in this ancient land, leaped into awful life. My consciousness became enveloping. I had the distressing feeling that ages slipped out of place and took me with them; they dominated me; they rushed me off my feet like water. I was drawn backwards. I, too, was changing—being changed.

"I remember," said Isley softly, a reverence of worship in his voice. But there was anguish in it too, and pity; he let the present go completely from him; the last strands severed with a wrench of pain. I imagined I heard his soul pass weeping far away—below.

"I'll sing it," murmured Moleson, "for the voice is necessary. The sound and rhythm are utterly divine!"

IX

And forthwith his voice began a series of long-drawn cadences that seemed somehow the root-sounds of every tongue that ever was. A spell came over me I could touch and feel. A web encompassed me; my arms and feet became entangled; a veil of fine threads wove across my eyes. The enthralling power of the rhythm produced some magical movement in the soul. I was aware of life everywhere about me, far and near, in the dwellings of the dead, as also in the corridors of the iron hills. Thebes stood erect, and Memphis teemed upon the river banks. For the modern world fell, swaying, at this sound that restored the past, and in this past both men before me lived and had their being. The storm of present life passed o'er their heads, while they dwelt underground, obliterated, gone. Upon the wave of sound they went down into their recovered kingdom.

I shivered, moved vigorously, half rose up, then instantly sank back again, resigned and helpless. For I entered by their side, it seemed, the conditions of their strange captivity. My thoughts, my feelings, my point of view were transplanted to another centre. Consciousness shifted in me. I saw things from another's point of view—antiquity's.

The present forgotten but the past supreme, I lost Reality. Our room became a pin-point picture seen in a drop of water, while this subterranean world, replacing it, turned immense. My heart took on the gigantic, leisured stride of what had been. Proportions grew; size captured me; and magnitude, turned monstrous, swept mere measurement away. Some hand of golden sunshine picked me up and set me in the quivering web beside those other two. I heard the rustle of the settling threads; I heard the shuffling of the feet in sand; I heard the whispers in the dwellings of the dead. Behind the monotony of this sacerdotal music I heard them in their dim carved chambers. The ancient galleries were awake. The Life of unremembered ages stirred in multitudes about me.

The reality of so incredible an experience evaporates through the stream of language. I can only affirm this singular proof—that the deepest, most satisfying knowledge the Present could offer seemed insignificant beside some stalwart majesty of the Past that utterly usurped it. This modern room, holding a piano and two figures of To-day, appeared as a paltry miniature pinned against a vast transparent curtain, whose foreground was thick with symbols of temple, sphinx, and pyramid, but whose background of stupendous hanging grey slid off towards a splendour where the cities of the Dead shook off their sand and thronged space to its ultimate horizons. . . . The stars, the entire universe, vibrating and alive, became involved in it. Long periods of time slipped past me. I seemed living ages ago. . . . I was living backwards. . . .

The size and eternity of Egypt took me easily. There was an overwhelming grandeur in it that elbowed out all present standards. The whole place towered and stood up. The desert reared, the very horizons lifted; majestic figures of granite rose above the hotel, great faces hovered and drove past; huge arms reached up to pluck the stars and set them in the ceilings of the labyrinthine tombs. The colossal meaning of the ancient land emerged through all its ruined details . . . reconstructed—burningly alive. . . .

It became at length unbearable. I longed for the droning sounds to cease, for the rhythm to lessen its prodigious sweep. My heart cried out for the gold of the sunlight on the desert, for the sweet air by the river's banks, for the violet lights upon the hills at dawn. And I resisted, I made an effort to return.

"Your chant is horrible. For God's sake, let's have an Arab song—or the music of To-day!"

The effort was intense, the result was—nothing. I swear I used these words. I heard the actual sound of my voice, if no one else did, for I remember that it was pitiful in the way great space devoured it, making of its appreciable volume the merest whisper as of some bird or insect cry. But the figure that I took for Moleson, instead of answer or acknowledgment, merely grew and grew as things grow in a fairy tale. I hardly know; I certainly cannot say. That dwindling part of me which offered comments on the entire occurrence noted this extraordinary effect as though it happened naturally—that Moleson himself was marvellously increasing.

The entire spell became operative all at once. I experienced both the delight of complete abandonment and the terror of letting go what *had* seemed real. I understood Moleson's sham laughter, and the subtle resignation of George Isley. And an amazing thought flashed bird-like across my changing consciousness—that this resurrection into the Past, this rebirth of the spirit which they sought, involved taking upon themselves the guise of these ancient symbols each in turn. As the embryo assumes each evolutionary stage below it before the human semblance is attained, so the souls of those two adventurers took upon themselves the various emblems of that intense belief. The devout worshipper takes on the qualities of his deity. They wore the entire series of the old-world gods so potently that I perceived them, and even objectified them by my senses. The present was their pre-natal stage; to enter the past they were being born again.

But it was not Moleson's semblance alone that took on this awful change. Both faces, scaled to the measure of Egypt's outstanding quality of size, became in this little modern room distressingly immense. Distorting mirrors can suggest no simile, for the symmetry of proportion was not injured. I lost their human physiognomies. I saw their thoughts, their feelings, their augmented, altered hearts, the thing that Egypt put there while she stole their love from modern life. There grew an awful stateliness upon them that was huge, mysterious, and motionless as stone.

For Moleson's narrow face at first turned hawk-like in the semblance of the sinister deity, Horus, only stretched to tower above the toy-scaled piano; it was keen and sly and monstrous after prey, while a swiftness of the sunrise leaped from both the brilliant eyes. George Isley, equally immense of outline, was in general presentment more magnificent, a breadth of the Sphinx about his spreading shoulders, and in his countenance an inscrutable power of calm temple images. These were the first signs of obsession; but others followed. In rapid series, like lantern-slides upon a screen, the ancient symbols flashed one after another across these two extended human faces and were gone. Disentanglement became impossible. The successive signatures seemed almost superimposed as in a composite photograph, each appearing and vanishing before recognition was even possible, while I interpreted the inner alchemy by means of outer tokens familiar to my senses. Egypt, possessing them, expressed herself thus marvellously in their physical aspect, using the symbols of her intense, regenerative power. . . .

The changes merged with such swiftness into one another that I did not seize the half of them—till, finally, the procession culminated in a single one that remained fixed awfully upon them both. The entire series merged. I was aware of this single masterful image which summed up all the others in sublime repose. The gigantic thing rose up in this incredible statue form. The spirit of Egypt synthesised in this monstrous symbol, obliterated them both. I saw the seated figures of the grim Colossi, dipped in sand, night over them, waiting for the dawn. . . .

X

I made a violent effort, then, at self-assertion—an effort to focus my mind upon the present. And, searching for Moleson and George Isley, its nearest details, I was aware that I could not find them. The familiar figures of my two companions were not discoverable.

I saw it as plainly as I also saw that ludicrous, wee piano—for a moment. But the moment remained; the Eternity of Egypt stayed. For that lonely and terrific pair had stooped their shoulders and bowed their awful heads. They were in the room. They imaged forth the power of the everlasting Past through the little structures of two human worshippers. Room, walls, and ceiling fled away. Sand and the open sky replaced them.

The two of them rose side by side before my bursting eyes. I knew not where to look. Like some child who confronts its giants upon the nursery floor, I turned to stone, unable to think or move. I stared. Sight wrenched itself to find the men familiar to it, but found instead this symbolising vision. I could not see them properly. Their faces were spread with hugeness, their features lost in some uncommon magnitude, their shoulders, necks, and arms grown vast upon the air. As with the desert, there was physiognomy yet no personal expression, the human thing all drowned within the mass of battered stone. I discovered neither cheeks nor mouth nor jaw, but ruined eyes and lips of broken granite. Huge, motionless, mysterious, Egypt informed them and took them to herself. And between us, curiously presented in some false perspective, I saw the little symbol of To-day—the Blüthner piano. It was appalling. I knew a second of majestic horror. I blenched. Hot and cold gushed through me. Strength left me, power of speech and movement, too, as in a moment of complete paralysis.

The spell, moreover, was not within the room alone; it was outside and everywhere. The Past stood massed about the very walls of the hotel. Distance, as well as time, stepped nearer. That chanting summoned the gigantic items in all their ancient splendour. The shadowy concourse grouped itself upon the sand about us, and I was aware that the great army shifted noiselessly into place; that pyramids soared and towered; that deities of stone stood by; that temples ranged themselves in reconstructed beauty, grave as the night of time whence they emerged; and that the outline of the Sphinx, motionless but aggressive, piled its dim bulk upon the atmosphere. Immensity answered to immensity. . . . There were vast intervals of time and there were reaches of enormous distance, yet all happened in a moment, and all happened within a little space. It was now and here. Eternity whispered in every second as in every grain of sand. Yet, while aware of so many stupendous details all at once, I was really aware of one thing only—that the spirit of ancient Egypt faced me in these two terrific figures, and that my consciousness, stretched painfully yet gloriously, included all, as She also unquestionably included them—and me.

For it seemed I shared the likeness of my two companions. Some lesser symbol, though of similar kind, obsessed me too. I tried to move, but my feet were set in stone; my arms lay fixed; my body was embedded in the rock. Sand beat sharply upon my outer surface, urged upwards in little flurries by a chilly wind. There was nothing felt: I *heard* the rattle of the scattering grains against my hardened body. . . .

And we waited for the dawn; for the resurrection of that unchanging deity who was the source and inspiration of all our glorious life. . . . The air grew keen and fresh. In the distance a line of sky turned from pink to violet and gold; a delicate rose next flushed the desert; a few pale stars hung fainting overhead; and the wind that brought the sunrise was already stirring. The whole land paused upon the coming of its mighty God. . . .

Into the pause there rose a curious sound for which we had been waiting. For it came familiarly, as though expected. I could have sworn at first that it was George Isley who sang, answering his companion. There beat behind its great volume the same note and rhythm, only so prodigiously increased that, while Moleson's chant had waked it, it now was independent and apart. The resonant vibrations of what he sang had reached down into the places where it slept. *They* uttered synchronously. Egypt spoke. There was in it the deep muttering as of a thousand drums, as though the desert uttered in prodigious syllables. I listened while my heart of stone stood still. There were two voices in the sky. *They* spoke tremendously with each other in the dawn:

"So easily we still remain possessors of the land . . . while the centuries roar past us and are gone."

Soft with power the syllables rolled forth, yet with a booming depth as though caverns underground produced them.

"Our silence is disturbed. Pass on with the multitude towards the East. . . . Still in the dawn we sing the old-world wisdom. . . . They shall hear our speech, yet shall not hear it with their ears of flesh. At dawn our words go forth, searching the distances of sand and time across the sunlight. . . . At dusk they return, as upon eagles' wings, entering again our lips of stone. . . . Each century one syllable, yet no sentence yet complete. While our lips are broken with the utterance. . . ."

It seemed that hours and months and years went past me while I listened in my sandy bed. The fragments died far away, then sounded very close again. It was as though mountain peaks sang to one another above clouds. Wind caught the muffled roar away. Wind brought it back. . . . Then, in a hollow pause that lasted years, conveying marvellously the passage of long periods, I heard the utterance more clearly. The leisured roll of the great voice swept through me like a flood:

"We wait and watch and listen in our loneliness. We do not close our eyes. The moon and stars sail past us, and our river finds the sea.

We bring Eternity upon your broken lives. . . . We see you build your little lines of steel across our territory behind the thin white smoke. We hear the whistle of your messengers of iron through the air. . . . The nations rise and pass. The empires flutter westwards and are gone. . . . The sun grows older and the stars turn pale. . . . Winds shift the line of the horizons, and our River moves its bed. But we, everlasting and unchangeable, remain. Of water, sand, and fire is our essential being, yet built within the universal air. . . . There is no pause in life, there is no break in death. The changes bring no end. The sun returns. . . . There is eternal resurrection. . . . But our kingdom is underground in shadow, unrealised of your little day. . . . Come, come! The temples still are crowded, and our Desert blesses you. Our River takes your feet. Our sand shall purify, and the fire of our God shall burn you sweetly into wisdom. . . . Come, then, and worship, for the time draws near. It is the dawn. . . ."

The voices died down into depths that the sand of ages muffled, while the flaming dawn of the East rushed up the sky. Sunrise, the great symbol of life's endless resurrection, was at hand. About me, in immense but shadowy array, stood the whole of ancient Egypt, hanging breathlessly upon the moment of adoration. No longer stern and terrible in the splendour of their long neglect, the effigies rose erect with passionate glory, a forest of stately stone. Their granite lips were parted and their ancient eyes were wide. All faced the east. And the sun drew nearer to the rim of the attentive Desert.

XI

Emotion there seemed none, in the sense that *I* knew feeling. I knew, if anything, the ultimate secrets of two primitive sensations—joy and awe. . . . The dawn grew swiftly brighter. There was gold, as though the sands of Nubia split their brilliance on each shining detail; there was glory, as though the retreating tide of stars spilt their light foam upon the world; and there was passion, as though the beliefs of all the ages floated back with abandonment into the—Sun. Ruined Egypt merged into a single temple of elemental vastness whose floor was the empty desert, but whose walls rose to the stars.

Abruptly, then, chanting and rhythm ceased; they dipped below. Sand muffled them. And the Sun looked down upon its ancient world. . . .

A radiant warmth poured through me. I found that I could move my limbs again. A sense of triumphant life ran through my stony frame. For one passing second I heard the shower of gritty particles upon my surface like sand blown upwards by a gust of wind, but this time I could *feel* the sting of it upon my skin. It passed. The drenching heat bathed me from head to foot, while stony insensibility gave place with returning consciousness to flesh and blood. The sun had risen. . . . I was alive, but I was—changed.

It seemed I opened my eyes. An immense relief was in me. I turned; I drew a deep, refreshing breath; I stretched one leg upon a thick, green carpet. Something had left me; another thing had returned. I sat up, conscious of welcome release, of freedom, of escape.

There was some violent, disorganising break. I found myself; I found Moleson; I found George Isley too. He had got shifted in that room without my being aware of it. Isley had risen. He came upon me like a blow, I saw him move his arms. Fire flashed from below his hands; and I realised then that he was turning on the electric lights. They emerged from different points along the walls, in the alcove, beneath the ceiling, by the writing-table; and one had just that minute blazed into my eyes from a bracket close above me. I was back again in the Present among modern things.

But, while most of the details presented themselves gradually to my recovered senses, Isley returned with this curious effect of speed and distance—like a blow upon the mind. From great height and from prodigious size—he dropped. I seemed to find him rushing at me. Moleson was simply "there"; there was no speed or sudden change in him as with the other. Motionless at the piano, his long thin hands lay down upon the keys yet did not strike them. But Isley came back like lightning into the little room, signs of the monstrous obsession still about his altering features. There was battle and worship mingled in his deep-set eyes. His mouth, though set, was smiling. With a shudder I positively saw the vastness slipping from his face as shadows from a stretch of broken cliff. There was this awful mingling of proportions. The colossal power that had resumed his being drew slowly inwards.

There was collapse in him. And upon the sun-burned cheek of his rugged face I saw a tear.

Poignant revulsion caught me then for a moment. The present showed itself in rags. The reduction of scale was painful. I yearned for the splendour that was gone, yet still seemed so hauntingly almost within reach. The cheapness of the hotel room, the glaring ugliness of its tinsel decoration, the baseness of ideals where utility instead of beauty, gain instead of worship, governed life—this, with the dwindled aspect of my companions to the insignificance of marionettes, brought a hungry pain that was at first intolerable. In the glare of light I noticed the small round face of the portable clock upon the mantelpiece, showing half-past eleven. Moleson had been two hours at the piano. And this measuring faculty of my mind completed the disillusionment. I was, indeed, back among present things. The mechanical spirit of To-day imprisoned me again.

For a considerable interval we neither moved nor spoke; the sudden change left the emotions in confusion; we had leaped from a height, from the top of the pyramid, from a star—and the crash of landing scattered thought. I stole a glance at Isley, wondering vaguely why he was there at all; the look of resignation had replaced the power in his face; the tear was brushed away. There was no struggle in him now, no sign of resistance; there was abandonment only; he seemed insignificant. The real George Isley was elsewhere; he himself had not returned.

By jerks, as it were, and by awkward stages, then, we all three came back to common things again. I found that we were talking ordinarily, asking each other questions, answering, lighting cigarettes, and all the rest. Moleson played some commonplace chords upon the piano, while he leaned back listlessly in his chair, putting in sentences now and again and chatting idly to whichever of us would listen. And Isley came slowly across the room towards me, holding out cigarettes. His dark brown face had shadows on it. He looked exhausted, worn, like some soldier broken in the wars.

"You liked it?" I heard his thin voice asking. There was no interest, no expression; it was not the real Isley who spoke; it was the little part of him that had come back. He smiled like a marvellous automaton.

Mechanically I took the cigarette he offered me, thinking confusedly what answer I could make.

"It's irresistible," I murmured; "I understand that it's easier to go."

"Sweeter as well," he whispered with a sigh, "and very wonderful!"

XII

The hand that lit my cigarette, I saw, was trembling. A desire to do something violent woke in me suddenly—to move energetically, to push or drive something away.

"What was it?" I asked abruptly, in a louder, half-challenging voice, intended for the man at the piano. "Such a performance—upon others—without first asking their permission—seems to me unpermissible—it's—"

And it was Moleson who replied. He ignored the end of my sentence as though he had not heard it. He strolled over to our side, taking a cigarette and pressing it carefully into shape between his long thin fingers.

"You may well ask," he answered quietly; "but it's not so easy to tell. We discovered it" —he nodded towards Isley—"two years ago in the 'Valley.' It lay beside a Priest, a very important personage, apparently, and was part of the Ritual he used in the worship of the sun. In the Museum now—you can see it any day at the Boulak—it is simply labeled 'Hymn to Ra.' The period was Aknahton's."

"The words, yes," put in Isley, who was listening closely.

"The words?" repeated Moleson in a curious tone. "There *are* no words. It's all really a manipulation of the vowel sounds. And the rhythm, or chanting, or whatever you like to call it, I—I invented myself. The Egyptians did not write their music, you see." He suddenly searched my face a moment with questioning eyes. "Any words you heard," he said, "or thought you heard, were merely your own interpretation."

I stared at him, making no rejoinder.

"They made use of what they called a 'root-language' in their rituals," he went on, "and it consisted entirely of vowel sounds. There were no consonants. For vowel sounds, you see, run on for ever without end or beginning, whereas consonants interrupt their flow and break it up and limit it. A consonant has no sound of its own at all. Real language is continuous."

We stood a moment, smoking in silence. I understood then that this thing Moleson had done was based on definite knowledge. He had rendered some fragment of an ancient Ritual he and Isley had unearthed together, and while he knew its effect upon the latter, he chanced it on myself. Not otherwise, I feel, could it have influenced me in the extraordinary way it did. In the faith and poetry of a nation lies its soul-life, and the gigantic faith of Egypt blazed behind the rhythm of that long, monotonous chant. There were blood and heart and nerves in it. Millions had heard it sung; millions had wept and prayed and yearned; it was ensouled by the passion of that marvellous civilisation that loved the godhead of the Sun, and that now hid, waiting but still alive, below the ground. The majestic faith of ancient Egypt poured up with it—that tremendous, burning elaboration of the after-life and of Eternity that was the pivot of those spacious days. For centuries vast multitudes, led by their royal priests, had uttered this very form and ritual—believed it, lived it, felt it. The rising of the sun remained its climax. Its spiritual power still clung to the great ruined symbols. The faith of a buried civilisation had burned back into the present and into our hearts as well.

And a curious respect for the man who was able to produce this effect upon two modern minds crept over me, and mingled with the repulsion that I felt. I looked furtively at his withered, dried-up features. He wore some vague and shadowy impress still of what had just been in him. There was a stony appearance in his shrunken cheeks. He looked smaller. I saw him lessened. I thought of him as he had been so short a time before, imprisoned in his great stone captors that had obsessed him. . . .

"There's tremendous power in it,—an awful power," I stammered, more to break the oppressive pause than for any desire in me to speak with him. "It brings back Egypt in some extraordinary way—ancient Egypt, I mean—brings it close—into the heart." My words ran on of their own accord almost. I spoke with a hush, unwittingly. There was awe in me. Isley had moved away towards the window, leaving me face to face with this strange incarnation of another age.

"It must," he replied, deep light still glowing in his eyes, "for the soul of the old days is in it. No one, I think, can hear it and remain the same. It expresses, you see, the essential passion and beauty of that gorgeous worship, that splendid faith, that reasonable and intelligent worship of the sun, the only scientific belief the world has ever known. Its popular form, of course, was largely superstitious, but the sacerdotal form—the form used by the priests, that is—who understood the relationship between colour, sound, and symbol, was—"

He broke off suddenly, as though he had been speaking to himself. We sat down. George Isley leaned out of the window with his back to us, watching the desert in the moonless night.

"You have tried its effect before upon—others?" I asked point-blank.

"Upon myself," he answered shortly.

"Upon others?" I insisted.

He hesitated an instant.

"Upon one other—yes," he admitted.

"Intentionally?" And something quivered in me as I asked it.

He shrugged his shoulders slightly. "I'm merely a speculative archæologist," he smiled, "and—and an imaginative Egyptologist. My bounden duty is to reconstruct the past so that it lives for others."

An impulse rose in me to take him by the throat.

"You know perfectly well, of course, the magical effect it's sure—likely at least—to have?"

He stared steadily at me through the cigarette smoke. To this day I cannot think exactly what it was in this man that made me shudder.

"I'm sure of nothing," he replied smoothly, "but I consider it quite legitimate to try. Magical—the word you used—has no meaning for me. If such a thing exists, it is merely scientific—undiscovered or forgotten knowledge." An insolent, aggressive light shone in his eyes as he spoke; his manner was almost truculent. "You refer, I take it, to—our friend—rather than to yourself?"

And with difficulty I met his singular stare. From his whole person something still emanated that was forbidding, yet overmasteringly persuasive. It brought back the notion of that invisible Web, that dim gauze curtain, that motionless Influence lying waiting at the centre for its prey, those monstrous and mysterious Items standing, alert and watchful, through the centuries. "You mean," he added lower, "his altered attitude to life—his going?"

To hear him use the words, the very phrase, struck me with sudden chill. Before I could answer, however, and certainly before I could master the touch of horror that rushed over me, I heard him continuing in a whisper. It seemed again that he spoke to himself as much as he spoke to me.

"The soul, I suppose, has the right to choose its own conditions and surroundings. To pass elsewhere involves translation, not extinction." He smoked a moment in silence, then said another curious thing, looking up into my face with an expression of intense earnestness. Something genuine in him again replaced the pose of cynicism. "The soul is eternal and can take its place anywhere, regardless of mere duration. What is there in the vulgar and superficial Present that should hold it so exclusively; and where can it find to-day the belief, the faith, the beauty that are the very essence of its life—where in the rush and scatter of this tawdry age can it make its home? Shall it flutter for ever in a valley of dry bones, when a living Past lies ready and waiting with loveliness, strength, and glory?" He moved closer; he touched my arm; I felt his breath upon my face. "Come with us," he whispered awfully; "come back with us! Withdraw your life from the rubbish of this futile ugliness! Come back and worship with us in the spirit of the Past. Take up the old, old splendour, the glory, the immense conceptions, the wondrous certainty, the ineffable knowledge of essentials. It all lies about you still; it's calling, ever calling; it's very close; it draws you day and night—calling, calling, calling. . . ."

His voice died off curiously into distance on the word; I can hear it to this day, and the soft, droning quality in the intense yet fading tone: "Calling, calling, calling." But his eyes turned wicked. I felt the sinister power of the man. I was aware of madness in his thought and mind. The Past he sought to glorify I saw black, as with the forbidding Egyptian darkness of a plague. It was not beauty but Death that I heard calling, calling, calling.

"It's real," he went on, hardly aware that I shrank, "and not a dream. These ruined symbols still remain in touch with that which was. They are potent to-day as they were six thousand years ago. The amazing life of those days brims behind them. They are not mere masses of oppressive stone; they express in visible form great powers that still are—*knowable*." He lowered his head, peered up into my face, and whispered. Something secret passed into his eyes.

"I saw you change," came the words below his breath, "as you saw the change in us. But only worship can produce that change. The soul assumes the qualities of the deity it worships. The powers of its deity possess it and transform it into its own likeness. You also felt it. *You* also were possessed. I saw the stone-faced deity upon your own."

I seemed to shake myself as a dog shakes water from its body. I stood up. I remember that I stretched my hands out as though to push him from me and expel some creeping influence from my mind. I remember another thing as well. But for the reality of the sequel, and but for the matter-of-fact result still facing me to-day in the disappearance of George Isley—the loss to the present time of all George Isley *was*—I might have found subject for laughter in what I saw. Comedy was in it certainly. Yet it was both ghastly and terrific. Deep horror crept below the aspect of the ludicrous, for the apparent mimicry cloaked truth. It was appalling because it was real.

In the large mirror that reflected the room behind me I saw myself and Moleson; I saw Isley too in the background by the open window. And the attitude of all three was the attitude of hieroglyphics come to life. My arms indeed were stretched, but not stretched, as I had thought, in mere self-defence. They were stretched—unnaturally. The forearms made those strange obtuse angles that the old carved granite wears, the palms of the hands held upwards, the heads thrown back, the legs advanced, the bodies stiffened into postures that expressed forgotten, ancient minds. The physical conformation of all three was monstrous; and yet reverence and truth dictated even the uncouthness of the gestures. Something in all three of us inspired the forms our bodies had assumed. Our attitudes expressed buried yearnings, emotions, tendencies—whatever they may be termed—that the spirit of the Past evoked.

I saw the reflected picture but for a moment. I dropped my arms, aware of foolishness in my way of standing. Moleson moved forward with his long, significant stride, and at the same instant Isley came up quickly and joined us from his place by the open window. We looked into each other's faces without a word. There was this little pause that lasted perhaps ten seconds. But in that pause I felt the entire world slide past me. I heard the centuries rush by at headlong speed. The present dipped away. Existence was no longer in a line that stretched two ways; it was a circle in which ourselves, together with Past and Future, stood motionless at the centre, all details equally accessible at once. The three of us were falling, falling backwards. . . .

"Come!" said the voice of Moleson solemnly, but with the sweetness as of a child anticipating joy. "Come! Let us go together, for the boat of Ra has crossed the Underworld. The darkness has been conquered. Let us go out together and find the dawn. Listen! It is calling, calling, calling. . . ."

XIII

I was aware of rushing, but it was the soul in me that rushed. It experienced dizzy, unutterable alterations. Thousands of emotions, intense and varied, poured through me at lightning speed, each satisfyingly known, yet gone before its name appeared. The life of many centuries tore headlong back with me, and, as in drowning, this epitome of existence shot in a few seconds the steep slopes the Past had so laboriously built up. The changes flashed and passed. I wept and prayed and worshipped; I loved and suffered; I battled, lost, and won. Down the gigantic scale of ages that telescoped thus into a few brief moments, the soul in me went sliding backwards towards a motionless, reposeful Past.

I remember foolish details that interrupted the immense descent—I put on coat and hat; I remember some one's words, strangely sounding as when some bird wakes up and sings at midnight—"We'll take the little door; the front one's locked by now"; and I have a vague recollection of the outline of the great hotel, with its colonnades and terraces, fading behind me through the air. But these details merely flickered and disappeared, as though I fell earthwards from a star and passed feathers or blown leaves upon the way. There was no friction as my soul dropped backwards into time; the flight was easy and silent as a dream. I felt myself sucked down into gulfs whose emptiness offered no resistance . . . until at last the appalling speed decreased of its own accord, and the dizzy flight became a kind of gentle floating. It changed imperceptibly into a gliding motion, as though the angle altered. My feet, quite naturally, were on the ground, moving through something soft that clung to them and rustled while it clung.

I looked up and saw the bright armies of the stars. In front of me I recognised the flat-topped, shadowy ridges; on both sides lay the open expanses of familiar wilderness; and beside me, one on either hand, moved two figures who were my companions. We were in the desert, but it was the desert of thousands of years ago. My companions, moreover, though familiar to some part of me, seemed strangers or half known. Their names I strove in vain to capture; Mosely, Ilson, sounded in my head, mingled together falsely. And when I stole a glance at them, I saw dark lines of mannikins unfilled with substance, and was aware of the grotesque gestures of living hieroglyphics. It seemed for an instant that their arms were bound behind their backs impossibly, and that their heads turned sharply across their lineal shoulders.

But for a moment only; for at a second glance I saw them solid and compact; their names came back to me; our arms were linked together as we walked. We had already covered a great distance, for my limbs were aching and my breath was short. The air was cold, the silence absolute. It seemed, in this faint light, that the desert flowed beneath our feet, rather than that we advanced by taking steps. Cliffs with hooded tops moved past us, boulders glided, mounds of sand slid by. And then I heard a voice upon my left that was surely Moleson speaking:

"Towards Enet our feet are set," he half sang, half murmured, "towards Enet-te-ntōrē. There, in the House of Birth, we shall dedicate our hearts and lives anew."

And the language, no less than the musical intonation of his voice, enraptured me. For I understood he spoke of Denderah, in whose majestic temple recent hands had painted with deathless colours the symbols of our cosmic relationships with the zodiacal signs. And Denderah was our great seat of worship of the goddess Hathor, the Egyptian Aphrodite, bringer of love and joy. The falcon-headed Horus was her husband, from whom, in his home at Edfu, we imbibed swift kinds of power. And—it was the time of the New Year, the great feast when the forces of the living earth turn upwards into happy growth.

We were on foot across the desert towards Denderah, and this sand we trod was the sand of thousands of years ago.

The paralysis of time and distance involved some amazing lightness of the spirit that, I suppose, touched ecstasy. There was intoxication in the soul. I was not divided from the stars, nor separate from this desert that rushed with us. The unhampered wind blew freshly from my nerves and skin, and the Nile, glimmering faintly on our right, lay with its lapping waves in both my hands. I knew the life of Egypt, for it was in me, over me, round me. I was a part of it. We went happily, like birds to meet the sunrise. There were no pits of measured time and interval that could detain us. We flowed, yet were at rest; we were endlessly alive; present and future alike were inconceivable; we were in the Kingdom of the Past.

The Pyramids were just a-building, and the army of Obelisks looked about them, proud of their first balance; Thebes swung her hundred gates upon the world. New, shining Memphis glittered with myriad reflections into waters that the tears of Isis sweetened, and the cliffs of Abou Simbel were still innocent of their gigantic progeny. Alone, the Sphinx, linking timelessness with time, brooded unguessed and underived upon an alien world. We marched within antiquity towards Denderah. . . .

How long we marched, how fast, how far we went, I can remember as little as the marvellous speech that passed across me while my two companions spoke together. I only remember that suddenly a wave of pain disturbed my wondrous happiness and caused my calm, which had seemed beyond all reach of break, to fall away. I heard their voices abruptly with a kind of terror. A sensation of fear, of loss, of nightmare bewilderment came over me like cold wind. What *they* lived naturally, true to their inmost hearts, *I* lived merely by means of a temperamental sympathy. And the stage had come at which my powers failed. Exhaustion overtook me. I wilted. The strain—the abnormal backwards stretch of consciousness that was put upon me by another—gave way and broke. I heard their voices faint and horrible. My joy was extinguished. A glare of horror fell upon the desert and the stars seemed evil. An anguishing desire for the safe and wholesome Present usurped all this mad yearning to obtain the Past. My feet fell out of step. The rushing of the desert paused. I unlinked my arms. We stopped all three.

The actual spot is to this day well known to me. I found it afterwards; I even photographed it. It lies actually not far from Helouan—a few miles at most beyond the Solitary Palm, where slopes of undulating sand mark the opening of a strange, enticing valley called the Wadi

Gerraui. And it is enticing because it beckons and leads on. Here, amid torn gorges of a limestone wilderness, there is suddenly soft yellow sand that flows and draws the feet onward. It slips away with one too easily; always the next ridge and basin must be seen, each time a little farther. It has the quality of decoying. The cliffs say, No; but this streaming sand invites. In its flowing curves of gold there is enchantment.

And it was here upon its very lips we stopped, the rhythm of our steps broken, our hearts no longer one. My temporary rapture vanished. I was aware of fear. For the Present rushed upon me with attack in it, and I felt that my mind was arrested close upon the edge of madness. Something cleared and lifted in my brain.

The soul, indeed, could "choose its dwelling-place"; but to live elsewhere completely was the choice of madness, and to live divorced from all the sweet wholesome business of To-day involved an exile that was worse than madness. It was death. My heart burned for George Isley. I remembered the tear upon his cheek. The agony of his struggle I shared suddenly with him. Yet with him was the reality, with me a sympathetic reflection merely. *He* was already too far gone to fight. . . .

I shall never forget the desolation of that strange scene beneath the morning stars. The desert lay down and watched us. We stood upon the brink of a little broken ridge, looking into the valley of golden sand. This sand gleamed soft and wonderful in the starlight some twenty feet below. The descent was easy—but I would not move. I refused to advance another step. I saw my companions in the mysterious half-light beside me peering over the edge, Moleson in front a little.

And I turned to him, sure of the part I meant to play, yet conscious painfully of my helplessness. My personality seemed a straw in mid-stream that spun in a futile effort to arrest the flood that bore it. There was vivid human conflict in the moment's silence. It was an eddy that paused in the great body of the tide. And then I spoke. Oh, I was ashamed of the insignificance of my voice and the weakness of my little personality.

"Moleson, we go no farther with you. We have already come too far. We now turn back."

Behind my words were a paltry thirty years. His answer drove sixty centuries against me. For his voice was like the wind that passed whispering down the stream of yellow sand below us. He smiled.

"Our feet are set towards Enet-te-ntōrē. There is no turning back. Listen! It is calling, calling, calling!"

"We will go home," I cried, in a tone I vainly strove to make imperative.

"Our home is there," he sang, pointing with one long thin arm towards the brightening east, "for the Temple calls us and the River takes our feet. We shall be in the House of Birth to meet the sunrise—"

"You lie," I cried again, "you speak the lies of madness, and this Past you seek is the House of Death. It is the kingdom of the underworld."

The words tore wildly, impotently out of me. I seized George Isley's arm.

"Come back with me," I pleaded vehemently, my heart aching with a nameless pain for him. "We'll retrace our steps. Come home with me! Come back! Listen! The Present calls you sweetly!"

His arm slipped horribly out of my grasp that had seemed to hold it so tightly. Moleson, already below us in the yellow sand, looked small with distance. He was gliding rapidly further with uncanny swiftness. The diminution of his form was ghastly. It was like a doll's. And his voice rose up, faint as with the distance of great gulfs of space.

"Calling . . . calling. . . . You hear it for ever calling. . . ."

It died away with the wind along that sandy valley, and the Past swept in a flood across the brightening sky. I swayed as though a storm was at my back. I reeled. Almost I went too—over the crumbling edge into the sand.

"Come back with me! Come home!" I cried more faintly. "The Present alone is real. There is work, ambition, duty. There is beauty too—the beauty of good living! And there is love! There is—a woman . . . calling, calling . . . !"

That other voice took up the word below me. I heard the faint refrain sing down the sandy walls. The wild, sweet pang in it was marvellous.

"Our feet are set for Enet-te-ntōrē. It is calling, calling . . . !"

My voice fell into nothingness. George Isley was below me now, his outline tiny against the sheet of yellow sand. And the sand was moving. The desert rushed again. The human figures receded swiftly into the

Past they had reconstructed with the creative yearning of their souls.

I stood alone upon the edge of crumbling limestone, helplessly watching them. It was amazing what I witnessed, while the shafts of crimson dawn rose up the sky. The enormous desert turned alive to the horizon with gold and blue and silver. The purple shadows melted into grey. The flat-topped ridges shone. Huge messengers of light flashed everywhere at once. The radiance of sunrise dazzled my outer sight.

But if my eyes were blinded, my inner sight was focussed the more clearly upon what followed. I witnessed the disappearance of George Isley. There was a dreadful magic in the picture. The pair of them, small and distant below me in that little sandy hollow, stood out sharply defined as in a miniature. I saw their outlines neat and terrible like some ghastly inset against the enormous scenery. Though so close to me in actual space, they were centuries away in time. And a dim, vast shadow was about them that was not mere shadow of the ridges. It encompassed them; it moved, crawling over the sand, obliterating them. Within it, like insects lost in amber, they became visibly imprisoned, dwindled in size, borne deep away, absorbed.

And then I recognised the outline. Once more, but this time recumbent and spread flat upon the desert's face, I knew the monstrous shapes of the twin obsessing symbols. The spirit of ancient Egypt lay over all the land, tremendous in the dawn. The sunrise summoned her. She lay prostrate before the deity. The shadows of the towering Colossi lay prostrate too. The little humans, with their worshipping and conquered hearts, lay deep within them.

George Isley I saw clearest. The distinctness, the reality were appalling. He was naked, robbed, undressed. I saw him a skeleton, picked clean to the very bones as by an acid. His life lay hid in the being of that mighty Past. Egypt had absorbed him. He was gone. . . .

I closed my eyes, but I could not keep them closed. They opened of their own accord. The three of us were nearing the great hotel that rose yellow, with shuttered windows, in the early sunshine. A wind blew briskly from the north across the Mokattam Hills. There were soft cannon-ball clouds dotted about the sky, and across the Nile, where the mist lay in a line of white, I saw the tops of the Pyramids gleaming like mountain peaks of gold. A string of camels, laden with white stone, went past us, I heard the crying of the natives in the streets of Helouan, and as we went up the steps the donkeys arrived and camped in the sandy road beside their *bersim* till the tourists claimed them.

"Good morning," cried Abdullah, the man who owned them. "You all go Sakkhâra to-day, or Memphis? Beat'ful day to-day, and vair good donkeys!"

Moleson went up to his room without a word, and Isley did the same. I thought he staggered a moment as he turned the passage corner from my sight. His face wore a look of vacancy that some call peace. There was radiance in it. It made me shudder. Aching in mind and body, and no word spoken, I followed their example. I went upstairs to bed, and slept a dreamless sleep till after sunset. . . .

XIV

And I woke with a lost, unhappy feeling that a withdrawing tide had left me on the shore, alone and desolate. My first instinct was for my friend, George Isley. And I noticed a square, white envelope with my name upon it in his writing.

Before I opened it I knew quite well what words would be inside:

"We are going up to Thebes," the note informed me simply. "We leave by the night train. If you care to—" But the last four words were scratched out again, though not so thickly that I could not read them. Then came the address of the Egyptologist's house and the signature, very firmly traced, "Yours ever, GEORGE ISLEY." I glanced at my watch and saw that it was after seven o'clock. The night train left at half-past six. They had already started. . . .

The pain of feeling forsaken, left behind, was deep and bitter, for myself; but what I felt for him, old friend and comrade, was even more intense, since it was hopeless. Fear and conventional emotion had stopped me at the very gates of an amazing possibility—some state of consciousness that, *realising* the Past, might doff the Present, and by slipping out of Time, experience Eternity. That was the seduction I had escaped by the uninspired resistance of my pettier soul. Yet he, my friend, yielding in order to conquer, had obtained an awful prize—ah, I understood the picture's other side as well, with an unutterable poignancy of pity—the prize of immobility which is sheer stagnation, the imagined bliss which is a false escape, the dream of finding beauty away from present things. From that dream the awakening must be rude indeed. Clutching at vanished stars, he had clutched the oldest illusion in the world. To me it seemed the negation of life that had betrayed him. The pity of it burned me like a flame.

But I did not "care to follow" him and his companion. I waited at Helouan for his return, filling the empty days with yet emptier explanations. I felt as a man who sees what he loves sinking down into clear, deep water, still within visible reach, yet gone beyond recovery. Moleson had taken him back to Thebes; and Egypt, monstrous effigy of the Past, had caught her prey.

The rest, moreover, is easily told. Moleson I never saw again. To this day I have never seen him, though his subsequent books are known to me, with the banal fact that he is numbered with those energetic and deluded enthusiasts who start a new religion, obtain notoriety, a few hysterical followers and—oblivion.

George Isley, however, returned to Helouan after a fortnight's absence. I saw him, knew him, talked and had my meals with him. We even did slight expeditions together. He was gentle and delightful as a woman who has loved a wonderful ideal and attained to it—in memory. All roughness was gone out of him; he was smooth and polished as a crystal surface that reflects whatever is near enough to ask a picture. Yet his appearance shocked me inexpressibly: there was nothing in him—*nothing*. It was the representation of George Isley that came back from Thebes; the outer simulacra; the shell that walks the London streets to-day. I met no vestige of the man I used to know. George Isley had disappeared.

With this marvellous automaton I lived another month. The horror of him kept me company in the hotel where he moved among the cosmopolitan humanity as a ghost that visits the sunlight yet has its home elsewhere.

This empty image of George Isley lived with me in our Helouan hotel until the winds of early March informed his physical frame that discomfort was in the air, and that he might as well move elsewhere—elsewhere happening to be northwards.

And he left just as he stayed—automatically. His brain obeyed the conventional stimuli to which his nerves, and consequently his muscles, were accustomed. It sounds so foolish. But he took his ticket automatically; he gave the natural and adequate reasons automatically, he chose his ship and landing-place in the same way that ordinary people chose these things; he said good-bye like any other man who leaves casual acquaintances and "hopes" to meet them again; he lived, that is to say, entirely in his brain. His heart, his emotions, his temperament and personality, that nameless sum-total for which the great sympathetic nervous system is accountable—all this, his soul, had gone elsewhere. This once vigorous, gifted being had become a normal, comfortable man that everybody could understand—a commonplace nonentity. He was precisely what the majority expected him to be—ordinary; a good fellow; a man of the world; he was "delightful." He merely reflected daily life without partaking of it. To the majority it was hardly noticeable; "very pleasant" was a general verdict. His ambition, his restlessness, his zeal had gone; that tireless zest whose driving power is yearning had taken flight, leaving behind it physical energy without spiritual desire. His soul had found its nest and flown to it. He lived in the chimera of the Past, serene, indifferent, detached. I saw him immense, a shadowy, majestic figure, standing—ah, not moving! —in a repose that was satisfying because it *could* not change. The size, the mystery, the immobility that caged him in seemed to me—terrible. For I dared not intrude upon his awful privacy, and intimacy between us there was none. Of his experiences at Thebes I asked no single question—it was somehow not possible or legitimate; he, equally, vouchsafed no word of explanation—it was uncommunicable to a dweller in the Present. Between us was this barrier we both respected. He peered at modern life, incurious, listless, apathetic, through a dim, gauze curtain. He was behind it.

People round us were going to Sakkhâra and the Pyramids, to see the Sphinx by moonlight, to dream at Edfu and at Denderah. Others described their journeys to Assouan, Khartoum, and Abou Simbel, and gave details of their encampments in the desert. Wind, wind, wind! The winds of Egypt blew and sang and sighed. From the White Nile came the travellers, and from the Blue Nile, from the Fayum, and from nameless excavations without end. They talked and wrote their books. They had the magpie knowledge of the present. The Egyptologists, big and little, read the writing on the wall and put the hieroglyphs and papyri into modern language. Alone George Isley *knew* the secret. He lived it.

And the high passionate calm, the lofty beauty, the glamour and enchantment that are the spell of this thrice-haunted land, were in *my* soul as well—sufficiently for me to interpret his condition. I could not leave, yet having left I could not stay away. I yearned for the Egypt that he knew. No word I uttered; speech could not approach it. We wandered by the Nile together, and through the groves of palms that once were Memphis. The sandy wastes beyond the Pyramids knew our footsteps; the Mokattam Ridges, purple at evening and golden in the dawn, held our passing shadows as we silently went by. At no single dawn or sunset was he to be found indoors, and it became my habit to accompany him—the joy of worship in his soul was marvellous. The great, still skies of Egypt watched us, the hanging stars, the gigantic dome of blue; we felt together that burning southern wind; the golden sweetness of the sun lay in our blood as we saw the great boats take the northern breeze upstream. Immensity was everywhere and this golden magic of the sun. . . .

But it was in the Desert especially, where only sun and wind observe the faint signalling of Time, where space is nothing because it is not divided, and where no detail reminds the heart that the world is called To-day—it was in the desert this curtain hung most visibly between us, he on that side, I on this. It was transparent. He was with a multitude no man can number. Towering to the moon, yet spreading backwards towards his burning source of life, drawn out by the sun and by the crystal air into some vast interior magnitude, the spirit of George Isley hung beside me, close yet far away, in the haze of olden days.

And, sometimes, he moved. I was aware of gestures. His head was raised to listen. One arm swung shadowy across the sea of broken ridges. From leagues away a line of sand rose slowly. There was a rustling. Another—an enormous—arm emerged to meet his own, and two stupendous figures drew together. Poised above Time, yet throned upon the centuries, They knew eternity. So easily they remained possessors of the land. Facing the east, they waited for the dawn. And their marvellously forgotten singing poured across the world. . . .

Non-Human

I like old Kelly," said Jones, showing me the invitation; "we used to shoot big game together years ago—"

"Then I should accept. It's only for one night." I knew his dislike of visits.

But he still hesitated. "The fact is," he whispered, not wishing to appear disloyal, "I'm afraid of being bored. He's too imaginative for me. He showed the beginning of it long ago—used to object to camps for the most extraordinary reasons—and it's grown on him. The latest fad is that he thinks he's sensitive to what he calls 'atmospheres'—rooms or places. Gets on my nerves a bit. It's become a mania with him."

"A night can't hurt you. It might be even amusing." For I saw he wanted to go really.

"You don't understand," insisted Jones. "He's just settled into a new bungalow. He'll show me round. He'll expect me to feel what he feels—or pretends to feel."

In the end, however, Jones accepted and journeyed down to Essex, giving me the account of his visit in due course. Kelly showed him all over the new bungalow in the expected manner, and the pair cemented friendship again while gazing at heads and horns upon the wall, poring over old-time maps of distant lands and examining their favourite rifles with affectionate pride. They were a couple of good sporting cronies with much in common, and the bungalow was a bungalow only in the rich man's meaning of the word. There was comfort, not to say luxury, in all its appointments, and Kelly "did" his guest uncommonly well. A visit that turns out better than expected provides a kind of false joy that sends the spirits up. Jones felt quite glad he had come. Nothing had been said so far about "atmospheres," nor had he once been asked: "Now, what do you think of *this* room? Feel anything queer or odd about it?" Until Jones, aware of high spirits and relief caused by this false joy, ventured a risky observation on his own account. The trap is old as time; he fell headlong into it. "I quite envy you," he remarked, by way of the compliment expected of him; "you couldn't feel anything here but peace and cosiness—eh?"

And it was then—at dusk just before dinner on the lawn—that Kelly turned upon him with the sinister suggestion: "Oh, the bungalow itself is all right enough. It's that wood over there—" He stopped suggestively, and pointed to a small, dense copse of oaks and beeches that blocked itself darkly against the fading sky. It covered perhaps five acres and looked impenetrable, a thick undergrowth of brambles round the outer edge. "I'd like your opinion very much on *that!*"

"That wood over there?" said the good-natured Jones weakly, hoping to tide over the threatening danger, then caught the expression in the other's eyes, and the laugh inside him died away. "We'll go in there after dinner, if you don't mind," said Kelly with decision. "I'd like to know if you feel anything"—and then he added "too." Jones murmured something about "to-morrow after breakfast when it's light enough to see a bit," but Kelly was enthusiastic and the grip of his pet mania had him by the throat. To-morrow after breakfast wouldn't do, because in the dark, when the eye was not confused by a succession of pictures, "impressions" were more likely to be true. Kelly had set his heart upon it; there was no withstanding him; Jones yielded as pleasantly as he could, hoping the comfortable after-dinner mood would lessen the attractiveness of the proposal. And there was the dreaded boredom in his heart.

They dismissed the subject until the meal was over, when, instead of smoking comfortably in two easy chairs, they put on boots, chose stout walking sticks, and duly sallied forth to inspect what Jones called beneath his breath "the blasted wood." It was the only hope of peace—to get over and done with. They crossed the lawn, climbed a fence, scrambled over a ditch, and found then lees on the outskirts quickly. The wood, Jones learned in the brief interval, was part of the "common" land which stretched for miles. On one side some gipsies were encamped; on the other a travelling circus had settled down for Christmas week; whistles and shouting clashed with the din of merry-go-rounds; there was evidently a miniature shooting gallery as well, and the lights flared up into the sky where faint moonlight struggled fitfully through hurrying clouds. Besides these customary attractions for the country folk, there was also an assortment of first-class freaks who had formed a rare bait for the villagers because they were exhibited in cages. Kelly mentioned these particularly, suggesting a visit later. The grotesque apparently amused him.

On the edge of the wood they paused a moment—then Kelly led the way. It was too dark to see anything clearly. A shower of heavy rain during dinner brought out scents of earth and decaying leaves that hung in the air. The wood, Jones realised, was too near London to be really fresh and sweet. The black trunks glistened when the moonlight touched them, as in a genuine forest; but he felt sure there was rubbish deposited somewhere near, or at least a notice forbidding such deposit. The peculiar odour of a rubbish heap was noticeable, with the acrid flavour belonging to tin cans and rusted iron. The odour thickened with the darkness as they stumbled deeper in. They talked in lowered voices. "Do you expect me to feel—er—anything in particular?" enquired the exasperated Jones, thinking of his London chambers with keen regret, "or—just any old thing?" Kelly shrugged his shoulders; he seemed very much in earnest; the tiresome journey was a ritual to him. "It's an extraordinary wood," he whispered over his shoulder, "crammed full of every sort of thing. Personally, I always feel something non-human in it." Jones gasped. "Non-human," he exclaimed, "what in the world d'you mean by that?" He didn't quite like to add "rubbish," but it was in his mind. "I don't want to suggest to you," mumbled Kelly, darkly. "Just make a note of anything you feel, and let me know. We'll compare notes. There's a ring of Druid stones in the centre," he added, significantly. "That's where you'll feel it strongest probably. We'll get there presently." And with that he floundered forward between big, round bramble bushes, while Jones followed him, cursing inwardly, among the clustering oaks and beeches. "Keep close to me," he heard, as they tapped the ground cautiously with their heavy sticks.

The darkness and the density of the underbrush made advance difficult and uncomfortable. The copse had evidently been untouched for years. Everybody's business was nobody's business. It had become a pathless tangle where anything might hide with small risk of discovery. The moonlight slipped in here and there, and the glare from the circus tossed odd splashes from the sky into unexpected places, but otherwise the gloom was impenetrable. To the constant enquiry, "Feel anything yet?" Jones, being honest, replied that he felt discomfort, thorns, heat, wet feet, and an increasing desire to return to the bungalow smoking-room. "Wait till we get to the centre," was the invariable rejoinder. "The stones stand in a clearing. You'll see better." And they stumbled deeper and deeper into the enveloping blackness. Ten minutes, perhaps longer, passed. Judging by the music and shouting—rifles firing at a halfpenny a shot, and so forth—their direction was towards the western edge, though it seemed to Jones that they moved merely in a circle. Kelly grumbled under his breath from time to time at the "infernal din," saying that it disturbed impressions and prevented accurate receptivity, but otherwise nothing happened until suddenly Jones became aware that there was something he actually did feel. In spite of his hostile and incredulous temperament, he had got a vivid and distinct "impression."

And it brought him up sharply with an unpleasant start that was something of a shock. A living being had moved past him in the gloom: so close, so actual that the conviction of reality was beyond all question. Something alive and stirring had gone past him. Until now he had merely felt what anybody might have felt—that the trees moved sometimes of their own accord, that they, closed up behind him, shifted their ranks, that figures were secreted among the underbrush, or that footsteps followed stealthily. Collectively, these vague impressions might conceivably have worked upon his nerves; yet, if so, he had merely acknowledged, explained, and so dismissed them. This other thing, however, was *real.* And he did not like it. He had distinctly caught a stealthy tread, a movement of air displaced, a hushed snapping of a twig, and the sound of moving foliage. Something had gone past him close enough to touch. Moreover, there was a certain peculiar odour that brought the tang of danger in—a sudden faint suggestion of a foreign country—he couldn't remember quite—only that it was unpleasant, dangerous, and somewhere—terrible.

"Feel anything?" asked Kelly sharply, under his breath, noticing that his companion halted dead in his, tracks. "We're just upon the stones. Look out!" Jones made his confession, wondering why he trembled and clutched his stick so tightly. "We're being watched," he whispered thickly. But Kelly was delighted. "I knew you'd feel it," he chuckled. "It's not a human feel exactly, is it? Come on," he added louder, to overcome the increasing noise of the shouting, rifles, and merry-go-rounds. "This wood *has* an extraordinary atmosphere. I told you." And he led the way into a little clearing where the pale moonlight revealed a circle of tall monoliths overgrown with ivy—but revealed them dimly. "The Druid stones," he whispered with a touch of awe. He pointed to where the alternate shadow and moonlight mingled with the yellowish glare reflected from the clouds. "Now," he added with satisfaction, "tell me exactly what it was you felt." But Jones did not answer. His eyes, fixed upon the clearing, had seen a long, low form, as of a being on all fours, glide swiftly behind the further stones and lose itself in the thick darkness that lay beyond. In the yellowish glare from the sky it, too, seemed yellow. And his heart leaped into his mouth; his teeth began to chatter; he had seen that form before, though not in foggy England.

"You *saw* something?" asked Kelly, startled by the expression in his face. "By George! I've *felt* things, but I've never seen a thing. What was it? Tell me, man, tell me quickly!" He was delighted, thrilled, excited.

But Jones knew his man too well to tell the truth. There was battle and confusion in his mind, and a moment's horrible bewilderment. He glanced swiftly about him. There was no hiding-place; the smooth, bare stems were impossible to climb. His courage was not great, and he felt collapse upon him. He had the sensations of a man in a jungle with a little walking stick. "What was it? What the devil did you see?" cried Kelly above the din of voices that seemed coming nearer every minute. But, instead of answering the question, Jones clutched him savagely by the arm. He put his mouth against his ear. "I'll tell you later," he hissed. "You're right—it's not a human thing. Do what I tell you. Follow me!" And, instinctively, he did the wisest thing—turned and ran full pelt towards the advancing voices. Kelly, bewildered and scared as well, ran after him, calling out foolish instructions. "Don't run that way! We don't want the circus crowd! They'll spoil it all. What was it you saw?" But Jones made only one reply, bawling it as he fled: "Follow me if you want to save your life. Can't you guess?" Torn by brambles, and banged by stems and low-hanging branches, they met at length a line of excited, yelling men all carrying lanterns, torches, heavy sticks, and—rifles.

"Have you seen him? He ran in here. The cage turned over!" cried the men. They shouted in an unintelligible chorus. There was wild confusion. Kelly, his mind full of wonder and alarm that an escaped freak could cause such tumult, had no useful information to impart, but Jones yelled, "Yes, yes! He's hiding among the stones a hundred yards behind us. I saw him—not two minutes ago," and rushed headlong on towards the edge of the wood from where the bungalow was visible. "Get your rifles and come and help us," shouted the men as they reached the open. And then Kelly got an inkling of the truth.

He led the way by a short cut that he knew, his psychical leanings overwhelmed by instincts of a still more primitive kind. They reached the bungalow at top speed, Jones following, now. They dashed into the gun-room. While standing to load by the open window they saw in the fitful moonlight upon the lawn the long, low form come gliding from another angle of the wood—the yellow form that Jones had already seen slinking behind the Druid stones. It was somewhat indeterminate, yet unmistakable. Frightened on one side by the army of beaters, and on the other by the fires of the gipsy camp, it had run out into the open space before the bungalow. "Aim carefully," whispered Jones, "it's pretty close." They fired simultaneously. There was a magnificent, tremendous leap towards them. "Again," said Kelly, and a second volley rang out like a single crack. They waited a moment; then, as it did not move, they went forward cautiously to examine, rifles in hand. "I told you it wasn't human," said Jones, as they looked down upon the body of a huge Bengal tiger, stretched along the grass.

An Egyptian Hornet

The word has an angry, malignant sound that brings the idea of attack vividly into the mind. There is a vicious sting about it somewhere—even a foreigner, ignorant of the meaning, must feel it. A hornet is wicked; it darts and stabs; it pierces, aiming without provocation for the face and eyes. The name suggests a metallic droning of evil wings, fierce flight, and poisonous assault. Though black and yellow, it sounds scarlet. There is blood in it. A striped tiger of the air in concentrated form! There is no escape—if it attacks.

In Egypt an ordinary bee is the size of an English hornet, but the Egyptian hornet is enormous. It is truly monstrous—an ominous, dying terror. It shares that universal quality of the land of the Sphinx and Pyramids—great size. It is a formidable insect, worse than scorpion or tarantula. The Rev. James Milligan, meeting one for the first time, realised the meaning of another word as well, a word he used prolifically in his eloquent sermons—devil.

One morning in April, when the heat began to bring the insects out, he rose as usual betimes and went across the wide stone corridor to his bath. The desert already glared in through the open windows. The heat would be afflicting later in the day, but at this early hour the cool north wind blew pleasantly down the hotel passages. It was Sunday, and at half-past eight o'clock he would appear to conduct the morning service for the English visitors. The floor of the passage-way was cold beneath his feet in their thin native slippers of bright yellow. He was neither young nor old; his salary was comfortable; he had a competency of his own, without wife or children to absorb it; the dry climate had been recommended to him; and—the big hotel took him in for next to nothing. And he was thoroughly pleased with himself, for he was a sleek, vain, pompous, well-advertised personality, but mean as a rat. No worries of any kind were on his mind as, carrying sponge and towel, scented soap, and a bottle of Scrubb's ammonia, he travelled amiably across the deserted, shining corridor to the bathroom. And nothing went wrong with the Rev. James Milligan until he opened the door, and his eye fell upon a dark, suspicious-looking object clinging to the window-pane in front of him.

And even then, at first, he felt no anxiety or alarm, but merely a natural curiosity to know exactly what it was—this little clot of an odd-shaped, elongated thing that stuck there on the wooden framework six feet before his aquiline nose. He went straight up to it to see—then stopped dead. His heart gave a distinct, unclerical leap. His lips formed themselves into unregenerate shape. He gasped: "Good God! What is it?" For something unholy, something wicked as a secret sin, stuck there before his eyes in the patch of blazing sunshine. He caught his breath.

For a moment he was unable to move, as though the sight half fascinated him. Then, cautiously and very slowly—stealthily, in fact—he withdrew towards the door he had just entered. Fearful of making the smallest sound, he retraced his steps on tiptoe. His yellow slippers shuffled. His dry sponge fell, and bounded till it settled, rolling close beneath the horribly attractive object facing him. From the safety of the open door, with ample space for retreat behind him, he paused and stared. His entire being focused itself in his eyes. It was a hornet that he saw. It hung there, motionless and threatening, between him and the bathroom door. And at first he merely exclaimed—below his breath—"Good God! It's an Egyptian hornet!"

Being a man with a reputation for decided action, however, he soon recovered himself. He was well schooled in self-control. When people left his church at the beginning of the sermon, no muscle of his face betrayed the wounded vanity and annoyance that burned deep in his heart. But a hornet sitting directly in his path was a very different matter. He realised in a flash that he was poorly clothed—in a word, that he was practically half naked.

From a distance he examined this intrusion of the devil. It was calm and very still. It was wonderfully made, both before and behind. Its wings were folded upon its terrible body. Long, sinuous things, pointed like temptation, barbed as well, stuck out of it. There was poison, and yet grace, in its exquisite presentment. Its shiny black was beautiful, and the yellow stripes upon its sleek, curved abdomen were like the gleaming ornaments upon some feminine body of the seductive world he preached against. Almost, he saw an abandoned dancer on the stage. And then, swiftly in his impressionable soul, the simile changed, and he saw instead more blunt and aggressive forms of destruction. The well-filled body, tapering to a horrid point, reminded him of those perfect engines of death that reduce hundreds to annihilation unawares—torpedoes, shells, projectiles, crammed with secret, desolating powers. Its wings, its awful, quiet head, its delicate, slim waist, its stripes of brilliant saffron—all these seemed the concentrated prototype of abominations made cleverly by the brain of man, and beautifully painted to disguise their invisible freight of cruel death.

"Bah!" he exclaimed, ashamed of his prolific imagination. "It's only a hornet after all—an insect!" And he contrived a hurried, careful plan. He aimed a towel at it, rolled up into a ball—but did not throw it. He might miss. He remembered that his ankles were unprotected. Instead, he paused again, examining the black and yellow object in safe retirement near the door, as one day he hoped to watch the world in leisurely retirement in the country. It did not move. It was fixed and terrible. It made no sound. Its wings were folded. Not even the black antennæ, blunt at the tips like clubs, showed the least stir or tremble. It breathed, however. He watched the rise and fall of the evil body; it breathed air in and out as he himself did. The creature, he realised, had lungs and heart and organs. It had a brain! Its mind was active all this time. It knew it was being watched. It merely waited. Any second, with a whiz of fury, and with perfect accuracy of aim, it might dart at him and strike. If he threw the towel and missed—it certainly would.

There were other occupants of the corridor, however, and a sound of steps approaching gave him the decision to act. He would lose his bath if he hesitated much longer. He felt ashamed of his timidity, though "pusillanimity" was the word thought selected owing to the pulpit vocabulary it was his habit to prefer. He went with extreme caution towards the bathroom door, passing the point of danger so close that his skin turned hot and cold. With one foot gingerly extended, he recovered his sponge. The hornet did not move a muscle. But—it had seen him pass. It merely waited. All dangerous insects had that trick. It knew quite well he was inside; it knew quite well he must come out a few minutes later; it also knew quite well that he was—naked.

Once inside the little room, he closed the door with exceeding gentleness, lest the vibration might stir the fearful insect to attack. The bath was already filled, and he plunged to his neck with a feeling of comparative security. A window into the outside passage he also closed, so that nothing could possibly come in. And steam soon charged the air and left its blurred deposit on the glass. For ten minutes he could enjoy himself and pretend that he was safe. For ten minutes he did so. He behaved carelessly, as though nothing mattered, and as though all the courage in the world were his. He splashed and soaped and sponged, making a lot of reckless noise. He got out and dried himself. Slowly the steam subsided, the air grew clearer, he put on dressing-gown and slippers. It was time to go out.

Unable to devise any further reason for delay, he opened the door softly half an inch—peeped out—and instantly closed it again with a resounding bang. He had heard a drone of wings. The insect had left its perch and now buzzed upon the floor directly in his path. The air seemed full of stings; he felt stabs all over him; his unprotected portions winced with the expectancy of pain. The beast knew he was coming out, and was waiting for him. In that brief instant he had felt its sting all over him, on his unprotected ankles, on his back, his neck, his cheeks, in his eyes, and on the bald clearing that adorned his Anglican head. Through the closed door he heard the ominous, dull murmur of his striped adversary as it beat its angry wings. Its oiled and wicked sting shot in and out with fury. Its deft legs worked. He saw its tiny waist already writhing with the lust of battle. Ugh! That tiny waist! A moment's steady nerve and he could have severed that cunning body from the directing brain with one swift, well-directed thrust. But his nerve had utterly deserted him.

Human motives, even in the professedly holy, are an involved affair at any time. Just now, in the Rev. James Milligan, they were quite inextricably mixed. He claims this explanation, at any rate, in excuse of his abominable subsequent behaviour. For, exactly at this moment, when he had decided to admit cowardice by ringing for the Arab servant, a step was audible in the corridor outside, and courage came with it into his disreputable heart. It was the step of the man he cordially "disapproved of," using the pulpit version of "hated and despised." He had overstayed his time, and the bath was in demand by Mr. Mullins. Mr. Mullins invariably followed him at seven-thirty; it was now a quarter to eight. And Mr. Mullins was a wretched drinking man—"a sot."

In a flash the plan was conceived and put into execution. The temptation, of course, was of the devil. Mr. Milligan hid the motive from himself, pretending he hardly recognised it. The plan was what men call a dirty trick; it was also irresistibly seductive. He opened the door, stepped boldly, nose in the air, right over the hideous insect on the floor, and fairly pranced into the outer passage. The brief transit brought a hundred horrible sensations—that the hornet would rise and sting his leg, that it would cling to his dressing-gown and stab his spine, that he would step upon it and die, like Achilles, of a heel exposed. But with these, and conquering them, was one other stronger emotion that robbed the lesser terrors of their potency—that Mr. Mullins would run precisely the same risks five seconds later, unprepared. He heard the gloating insect buzz and scratch the oilcloth. But it was behind him. *He* was safe!

"Good morning to you, Mr. Mullins," he observed with a gracious smile. "I trust I have not kept you waiting."

"Mornin'!" grunted Mullins sourly in reply, as he passed him with a distinctly hostile and contemptuous air. For Mullins, though depraved, perhaps, was an honest man, abhorring parsons and making no secret of his opinions—whence the bitter feeling.

All men, except those very big ones who are supermen, have something astonishingly despicable in them. The despicable thing in Milligan came uppermost now. He fairly chuckled. He met the snub with a calm, forgiving smile, and continued his shambling gait with what dignity he could towards his bedroom opposite. Then he turned his head to see. His enemy would meet an infuriated hornet—an Egyptian hornet!—and might not notice it. He might step on it. He might not. But he was bound to disturb it, and rouse it to attack. The chances were enormously on the clerical side. And its sting meant death.

"May God forgive me!" ran subconsciously through his mind. And side by side with the repentant prayer ran also a recognition of the tempter's eternal skill: "I hope the devil it will sting him!"

It happened very quickly. The Rev. James Milligan lingered a moment by his door to watch. He saw Mullins, the disgusting Mullins, step blithely into the bathroom passage; he saw him pause, shrink back, and raise his arm to protect his face. He heard him swear out aloud: "What's the d——d thing doing here? Have I really got 'em again—?" And then he heard him laugh—a hearty, guffawing laugh of genuine relief—"It's *real!*"

The moment of revulsion was overwhelming. It filled the churchly heart with anguish and bitter disappointment. For a space he hated the whole race of men.

For the instant Mr. Mullins realised that the insect was not a fiery illusion of his disordered nerves, he went forward without the smallest hesitation. With his towel he knocked down the flying terror. Then he stooped. He gathered up the venomous thing his well-aimed blow had stricken so easily to the floor. He advanced with it, held at arm's length, to the window. He tossed it out carelessly. The Egyptian hornet flew away uninjured, and Mr. Mullins—the Mr. Mullins who drank, gave nothing to the church, attended no services, hated parsons, and proclaimed the fact with enthusiasm—this same detestable Mr. Mullins went to his unearned bath without a scratch. But first he saw his enemy standing in the doorway across the passage, watching him—and understood. That was the awful part of it. Mullins would make a story of it, and the story would go the round of the hotel.

The Rev. James Milligan, however, proved that his reputation for self-control was not undeserved. He conducted morning service half an hour later with an expression of peace upon his handsome face. He conquered all outward sign of inward spiritual vexation; the wicked, he consoled himself, ever flourish like green bay trees. It was notorious that the righteous never have any luck at all! That was bad enough. But what was worse—and the Rev. James Milligan remembered for very long—was the superior ease with which Mullins had relegated both himself and hornet to the same level of comparative insignificance. Mullins ignored them both—which proved that he felt himself superior. Infinitely worse than the sting of any hornet in the world: he really *was* superior.

The God

Jones looked at his secretary sharply. It was the fourth mistake. The youth sat before his typewriter, all eagerness as usual, but turned his head a moment while his employer repeated: "I wish you would listen. Or perhaps I'm not speaking quite distinctly. Is that it?"

"I'm sorry, sir. I heard all right. You're speaking quite clearly."

Jones continued to walk up and down the room, where the morning sunlight fell in patches on the carpet; and, while he walked, the sentences of his uncompleted novel issued fluently from his lips. It was a tale of love and woe in ancient Greece. The hero was distraught; his maiden had been captured by a God. . . . Jones dictated the story admirably; the action was full of life, the emotion vivid, the scenery divine. His phrases issued from a brain that visualised the drama from a heart that shared the feeling of the actors. The story lived and pulsed. Reality was in it. His ten thousand readers would find comfort and relaxation from the strain of the European war. It would do them good, relieve and strengthen them. Jones was what the publishers called "a big seller." He helped in the afternoons "with the Belgians," but in the mornings he put all his heart and soul into the completion of his novel. He regarded it as "doing his bit." The public—his public—couldn't "think war" all the time. Business as usual, for those who could not fight, had its meaning after all. Besides, he had his wife and children. He had subscribed to the War Loan. What more could he possibly do—at forty-six?

He felt in great vein this morning, full of his story, especially stimulated by his newspaper's account of the fabulous Russian resistance, that seemed to him full of a Marathonic glory, sublime, heroic, marvellous. It charged him with emotion to the brim. There was a superhuman sacrifice in it, something of deity too. The emotion in him poured forth in his sentences, touched with pathos, polished with classical allusion—and Robinson, his secretary, then made his fifth mistake.

"It runs along well, doesn't it?" Jones asked, wondering if anything was wrong, and glancing at the youth impatiently. "I mean, it flows? It doesn't stick anywhere—eh?" He used his secretary as a preliminary chorus too, a sort of foretaste of success, half critic and half public. Robinson, though alert as a typist, was useful also as a standard. This morning, however, he seemed stupid, absent-minded, un-forthcoming somehow. There was something wrong with him, something different. Jones couldn't make it out. "D'you think it's too highly coloured—too fanciful?" he asked.

The young man with the round shoulders turned his anæmic face.

"No, sir," he said. "It sounds as usual—quite all right. I thought you said 'in the trenches.' I'm sorry, sir."

"'Entrenched' was what I said," repeated Jones, but not too impatiently, for it was a pardonable mistake. "Entrenched upon Olympus, was the phrase. Have you got it *now?*"

Robinson said he had, but the way he said it, the tone, the attitude, made Jones look hard at him. There was something different in the youth. A curious, subtle shock ran down the spine of Reginald Jones, popular novelist and "big seller." He caught his breath an instant.

"'Robinson," he said, recovering himself quickly, "is anything wrong with you this morning?"

"No, sir; I feel very well, thank you. Quite well."

"Good," said Jones shortly. "I thought your face seemed a little flushed."

"Not that I know of," was the reply. "I feel splendid." And the way he said "splendid" sent another faint shiver down the novelist's back. There stole an atmosphere of ancient Greece into the modern flat, almost of the breezy, sunny glory of Olympus. What, in the name of heaven, caused it? Was it Hymettus honey he had eaten for breakfast? . . . Jones felt bewildered, slightly frightened. He forgot his novel, his public, his publisher even! He entirely forgot his sense of humour, what the critics called his "rare and saving sense of humour." Something about his secretary, his anæmic, round-shouldered typist, whom he employed partly because he was cheap, but partly also because he had others to support—something about Robinson introduced another standard. It was as though he suddenly judged his novel by another test, another level of value. What did it mean? For interest in his "characters" faded a little, they seemed unreal, mere puppets, whereas hitherto—yesterday only—they had seemed heroic, moulded upon the heroic scale of sublime antiquity. He had been proud of them; he now felt shamed a little. He looked a second time at his round-shouldered secretary.

"Feel splendid, do you?" repeated Jones in an uneven voice whose trembling he could not in the least explain. What d'you mean by 'splendid'?"

Robinson looked up respectfully, yet with deep earnestness in his eyes. "I mean true, useful, self-forgetful," he replied, this time without the "sir."

"Patriotic—eh?" enquired Jones, wondering why he said it.

"True," said the typist gravely, but with a smile, rising from his stool before the desk. His shoulders squared visibly, no longer round from stooping. "I feel—I'm wanted," he added the same moment. Jones started in sheer amazement.

"Of course," he said in a voice that hardly seemed his own, "of course you're wanted. *I* want you. Your mother and sister want you. I understand that perfectly. In the same way I'm wanted too; my work, my books, my cheerful and absorbing stories are wanted. My family want my novels and the money they produce; your mother and sister want your work and the salary you earn—"

"I'm wanted," repeated Robinson. with emphasis. There seemed a glow of sun and wind about his standing figure.

"Stories like mine are wanted," Jones continued, aware for the first time that he spoke from his brain rather than from his heart. "Stories that help people to forget the pain, the misery, the loss, that bring a breath of something nobler than the cruelty of war, stories that tell of love and hope, that bring back the Gods, by Jove! Artists are necessary folk in a time like this—creative artists who can help to build against the—"

"I'm wanted," Robinson interrupted softly, and his eyes were shining sternly.

Jones stood and stared, while something lifted in his heart. Vicarious emotion paled and fled. He felt reality. His "characters" sneered and disappeared through some trap-door just opened in his mind. They sniffed at him across the sun-flecked carpet before they vanished.

He realised suddenly that his "gods" were bunkum, and his ancient Greece a sham. There was God—but the gods were a false creation of poetic licence. An abrupt reversal of his faith took place—there, in the modern study where his "masterpieces" had been dictated to a typist in order to obtain £100 paid down "in advance of royalties" to come. Whence came the strange upheaval, the rude dislocation of his normal self, he knew not. But it seemed to come from little, round-shouldered Robinson, standing there before him with something sublime, heroic, magical in his pale, anæmic face. A touch of the terrific shone like fire in the eye, resolution emanated from the thin, spare figure, there was courage, nobility in his very attitude. The whole atmosphere of ancient and heroic Greece, which Jones believed he had captured for his story, breathed animate before his eyes—in Robinsen. And he caught his breath a second time and stared.

"What could be more fitting at a time like this," he faltered, "more suitable, more necessary, more helpful—than to reproduce—to re-create for the anxious public—the spirit of old Greece. That grand ideal of the older gods—"

He stopped, or rather, the breath stopped in his throat. His empty words died down before a reality he perceived for the first time—with a touch of awe and reverence. And little Robinson, his typist who worked to keep his "family" alive, was the cause of the deep revelation. It was amazing, it was genuinely transforming. For Robinson seemed suddenly heroic, masterful, symbolic. Jones saw him grow before his very eyes. He smelt the honey blown from far Hymettus through the dingy room. He heard the tramp of many feet. He heard distant singing of men's voices. He saw, it seemed, a god . . .

And through the open window of the Chelsea flat came then the sound of many voices singing a rag-time melody somewhat out of tune. He heard a rumble of a dozen drums. There was a roaring, booming thunder that had a note of menace in it. And through his bewildered mind ran words he had forgotten in his pursuit of love and passion. He saw them flash and vanish: Empire—Liberty—Justice—Truth—and Honour—terrific, godlike words that clanged upon the air and seemed to shake the world.

He turned. The figure of the typist beside him seemed to fill the room. His voice, as he spoke, was like a god's. "No wonder," thought

Jones, a sense of worship marvellously in him, "no wonder he felt 'splendid'!" There was power, devotion, beauty in his heart—the spirit of ancient Greece and all its deities . . . Robinson, it seemed, was saying something: Jones heard the words like music rising from Marathon and Salamis:

". . . if you'll forgive me, sir, and waive the month's notice. I feel I'm wanted. I'm going to enlist to-morrow. . . ."

The Soldier's Visitor

I sit in my room and dream. . . . Autumn steals across the slanting sunlight on the lawn, for the year stands at the keen, and the smells of childhood float beneath the thinning branches. In my long chair by the open window I sit and dream. . . . I played upon that lawn, I took the hawks' eggs from the dizzy, topmost branches; it was on turf like that I won the hundred yards. Sure of myself, I moved swiftly, easily, a few weeks, a few months—or was it years?—ago. . . . I have forgotten. It is past. I sit and dream. . . .

The little room is narrow, but autumn, entering softly, brings in distance as of the open sky, with misty places that are immense. Once they seemed endless. The whole world enters; there are two magnificent horizons, where the sun sets and where it rises: both I could reach easily, without toil or pain, without the help of any one. Birds pass from one horizon to the other, singing, high above all obstacles; I toyed free space as they do; the sails are flashing white on blue, blue seas; there is the plash of mountain streams, the rustle of foliage . . . and the autumn wind goes past my window, picking the crisp, dying leaves from every bough.

"He will recover. At least, he will not lose the other," are the words I remember dimly, each syllable a century, each word an age. It was so long ago. And I try to rise and see the folded daisies as they take the sunset by the grey thatched summer-house. But my body stops—I cannot move without assistance. . . . I remember how it happened. I remember a pause, then saying aloud as quietly as if I were playing tennis, "Now, old chap, it's your turn! Go it!" There was a blank, but no terror, and no pain. I heard no noise, the explosion was quite soundless; my last cartridge was gone, my bayonet was in . . . then came the stretcher. . . . God bless those fellows, those brave and tireless bearers. . . . A dirty job! He'll bless them for me. I can't even go across the field to find them.

The sunlight dies; the leaves are down; the chill air cloaks the laurel shrubberies in white and gauze; the soaking dew begins to fall. I am in England. England! She was in danger, so they said. That's why I'm here, I suppose. She's taking care of me. I did my bit, my best. Nine months of weary training, three days of glorious fighting. Then this . . .

I am carried back into the bed, the lamp is lit, the figures, speaking low and with marvellous tenderness, are gone. I am alone, my pals are out there . . . where there is singing, stories, action. There is no singing here, no stories. I am in a hothouse—damn . . . !

I glance at my little table by the pillow, at the small white jug of liquid food, at the little silver bell, the glass with the sleeping draught . . . and I turn the lamp out and watch through the open window the faces of the peeping stars. A bat flies past; I hear a moth's big wings; a corncrake whirrs and rattles far away—I used to chase all three. . . . No other sound is in the world. The hours are asleep. Autumn sits in her lonely wood, weaving her red and yellow leaves into a net to hold me lest I fall! When I wake in the morning, I shall see her tears upon the crimson leaves, upon the grass, upon the iron railing, big, big drops as clear as crystal, holding all the sky. I shall see the few lost stitches that she dropped, floating on cobwebs in the yellow sunlight. I shall hear her cloak sweep trailing through the beech-wood on the hill. And that is the cloak I ask to cover me—below the knees. I shall also smell the perfume of her lustrous hair—but that hair, that perfume I shall take to wrap my thoughts in, and my dreams, through years to come. . . .

For I shall recover. But I shall not—no, I shall never again in this world—I cannot say it—below both knees—I know it—I am nothing.

There came a knock quite suddenly at the door . . . and I shut my eyes, because I had no liking for my night-nurse. I left my hand outside upon the coverlet, that she might take my pulse, then leave me without that meeting of the eye, that intimate gesture, that exchange of little words that were distasteful to me. It was, no doubt, a sick man's whim, and yet to me just then it was intolerable. To meet the eye is an intimacy that draws the other person near, too near, unless she be desired and desirable. I feel the soul in contact. It is only one degree more intimate than to hear the mention of my name, my little name. . . . And yet, before my mind could question—it works slowly, thickly in this pain—who it was for certain my voice had answered, I had said, "Come in. . . ."

I closed my eyes, however, none the less. But, through my lids, I felt the searching glance that saw me—more—that met my own. And I heard my name, my little name. A strange and marvellous thrill went through me. The very intimacies I had dreaded I now claimed eagerly. I opened my eyes and looked.

No especial revelation of beauty have I ever claimed in life, but I have known ideals, I have had my dreams like other men. The figure I now saw before me was surely not of this earth. The stars, the moon, sunlight, and wild flowers had made her, perhaps. . . . I was speechless.

"I have come like this," said the woman in the soft brown garment, "because there are things that I can give you now. Before—when you could seek them—you could not find them. Now that you cannot go to them they may come to you. They are all within your reach."

And then I saw that, while more beautiful and desirable than any one I had ever known, she was yet strangely familiar to me. Where, how, under what conditions, I could not recall. She was some Grandeur, surely. Queens and the like, I knew, were visiting chaps like me, and yet she was not dressed as such folks dress, and her robe of russet-brown spread in some kind of imperial way behind her. It trailed, I fancied, through the open window, joining the mist above the lawn. The stars shone in it very faintly. But it was her incomparable beauty that made it difficult to speak, for my heart became suddenly so large it choked me.

"I must have dreamed of you," I murmured at length. A feeling of endless life rose in me—the life people so glibly call eternal. It was beyond description.

"Dreamed!" she echoed gently, shaking her head and smiling. "Oh no; not dreamed! I called you and you came." There was a touch of sternness in her smile that stirred the blood in me. But I did not understand.

"You *called* me?" I asked faintly, for such beauty put confusion in me.

"And you came," she answered. "It was no dream. You gave me all you had to give." She paused an instant; there was moisture in her eyes. "It is now my turn to give all you desire, all you ask or dream."

The feeling of familiarity was afflicting; but still I could not understand. As she spoke I saw burning love in the great clear eyes. But there was more than love; there was sympathy, understanding—a woman who could understand everything in the world—there was admiration, gratitude, and more than these—I swear it—there was worship.

"I have asked for nothing," I faltered, an unbelievable happiness rising. "I did not call—I had no thought—at least I only—"

"It is yours—all, all," she answered, "because of that. You did not ask, you did not think of self."

My face, of course, betrayed me hopelessly. The strange joy found utterance in a somewhat trembling voice, humbly, perhaps a little awed.

"I meant your Beauty . . . !" I whispered it in my inmost heart. For there was a shyness in me I could not understand.

And then a strange thing happened, for, as she stood between me and the open window, a light air stirred her dress, and I caught the gleam of something bright beneath, almost as though she wore a breastplate of some kind—like shining armour.

"Who are you, then?" I murmured, trying to raise myself, but sinking back again before the painful effort. I had the feeling that for such love as hers, such beauty, splendour, strength, no loss, no pain was of the least account. I forgot my conditions, almost my identity. I was just—a man like other men.

"I am rich," she answered, "I am true, and I am faithful unto death and after it. All that you ask is mine to give. And I am here to give it you."

"Me—?" I could not believe my ears. Something broke within me, bathing my soul in light. I repeated my astonished questions. I mentioned my name. I thought swiftly. Everything, by heaven, was worth it, if this were true.

She looked down at me for a long time without speaking. Then her lips moved a little; the wonderful eyes brimmed over; she said two perfect words as she gazed at me: "Thank you. . . ." It was followed by my name, my little name.

What happened exactly I cannot tell. I remember thinking it must be somewhere a miserable mistake, that it was too impossible for truth, when in the midst of my anguish she again repeated my name with such pride and gratitude in her voice, such love and admiration in her eyes, that my doubts were gone and I felt re-made in joy. "It is written here," she said, pointing to where her heart lay beating behind the gleaming metal.

She then bent over me and kissed me . . . she took me in her comforting arms . . . I fell asleep. And in my sleep I dreamed of a new and glorious movement, light as air, and easy, swift as wind. Everything in the world was mine, for everything came to me of its own accord. All space lay within my reach. I was no longer walking, running, climbing. I had wings. . . . But also I remembered where it was that I had seen her, and consequently why I loved her so. I understood at last, God bless her, and I loved her all the more.

Hitherto, indeed, I had asked nothing of her knowingly, yet I had taken all she had to give. I suppose, unconsciously as it were, I knew this well enough. That, apparently, was why I fought. . . . At any rate, I remembered clearly where I had seen her, and why she seemed so curiously familiar, yet unrealised; for her face, now stamped upon my soul, is also stamped upon every copper penny of the Realm.

The Paper Man

Dimble was not too proud to fight, but he was too old, too stiff, too blind; he could not drill properly, because he really had to think a moment before he knew which was his left and which his right. There are some men who can positively do nothing; he was one of them. With the best intentions in the world, burning, zealous intentions too, he was yet useless. Unable to help, he lost that comfort which comes the moment one's smaller burden is merged in the collective burden of the nation. That peace being denied him, his interest in the war on the other hand being intense, he merely—*read.* Morning, noon, and night, he read. He read all the papers, but on Sunday he read only four, not counting "extras." Sunday was his day off.

He plunged with the ease of a bird from the heights of optimism to the depths of pessimism. It wore him out. He believed everything he read. Every move made on the great chess-board was a clever trap into which either the enemy or the Allies would march blind-eyed. He yearned to warn the latter. In time, however, the "trap" idea collapsed; it never came off; the lure was non-existent. A certain paper declared that the enemy would never be caught without its glasses . . . he gave up buying it for a week, then surreptitiously went back to it because it *proved* that the Germans were using their last reserves. A bad communiqué could keep him awake at night, so could a very good one. . . .

From the Eastern and Western fronts, at length, he switched off upon the Balkans, till he became so entangled that he—well, though his walls were covered with maps, he never could remember even whether Roumania was north of Bulgaria, or vice versa; nor which country claimed Bucharest or Sofia as its capital. Invariably he had to inspect his maps. Bucharest, since it began with B, ought to belong to Bulgaria; sometimes, judging by the telegrams, it did, sometimes, judging by the articles, it didn't. The Balkans became a gigantic jig-saw puzzle, all corners and curves and points and angles that would not fit.

The coloured flags pricked his fingers, the maps got stained, the strip of carpet below them grew threadbare.

For a time he confined himself to picture-papers, till he read that most of the scenes were made somewhere in Surrey, or taken from manœuvres of five years ago. He flung himself next upon strategy and diagrams of positions, till the chintzes on his chairs expressed surprise and peril, and the very blood in his strained eye-balls mapped the empty air with danger. Reality faded from the world. He himself "advanced" up the street or "retired" to his bedroom. On the way to his bath he muttered left, right, left, left, left—halt, then had to "retreat in perfect order" for his forgotten sponge and towel. He confined himself in the last resort to "official news." . . .

This called for grim restraint, but the truth was he was getting a little frightened. His speech showed signs of trouble, and sounds became audible in his head occasionally—z . . . sz . . . scz . . . czs . . . and pmj or mjp . . . and the like. He became aware of showers of them sprinkling almost visibly through the air—in the darkness, explosive, spitting sparks. They even pricked him. His tongue and throat grew sore. And there were other symptoms that alarmed him. The worst, perhaps, was the mute j's. He had somehow got full of them without knowing—it either swallowed them or breathed them in, he knew not which; but in any case he was interiorly somewhat crowded with soft heaps of these mute j's. They were akin to microbes of a suppressed illness; for any moment—it was horrible to think of—they might emerge, appear, express themselves, become not mute!

"And what are you doing, Dimble? " asked Spriggins at the Club one day, good-naturedly. Spriggins, though bald and crooked, wore "G. R." and a big red armlet every Sunday on route marches that nearly killed him. Dimble looked up helplessly into his face. He answered. Speech of a kind, at least, came twanging, buzzing from his lips:

"Czskz . . . kivitch . . . ski . . . kzs . . . z . z . z . jjjjijj!" he replied. His voice cracked oddly; tiny explosions, were audible inside his chest; his throat held soda-water.

He did not notice how Spriggins got away; he "retreated," apparently in good order. It was certainly a rapid movement. Spriggins was not surrounded, at all events. And he left Dimble standing there as though he had been burned, destroyed, utterly devastated till nothing of any value remained inside his outer physical frame.

Matters had grown so serious by this time that he made a prodigious effort, and renounced all papers whatsoever—for an entire day. For twenty-four hours he read no news, no expert articles, no forecasts, no résumés, no analyses of the Balkan soul, nor one single report from a neutral traveller just returned from everywhere. He did not even look at a line from an official or diplomatic source whose authority it is impossible to doubt. He moved no single pin upon his many maps. He lay in darkness—he also lay in bed. He starved. A strange hunger woke in him. He knew an intolerable emptiness. He slept a little, however, and murmured in his sleep—for it was troubled—"Official news, official news . . . csz . . ksz . . j.j.j. . . . !"

Dimble recovered a bit and lived his life as best he could. He was careful now, not to say cautious. He reconnoitred before every single act; also he deployed. But things went rather quickly after that. He slept by day in a darkened room, and went out only in the night. He could not see the posters thus; the paper man at the corner, who now cut him dead instead of smiling cheerfully, could be avoided. This was the serious stage for Dimble. By the candlelight in his bedroom he noticed curious marks upon his arm; the skin seemed mottled. He said, "Bites, by Nicholas!" and thought of queer, invisible insects. Yet the marks apparently traced a pattern; they had design, meaning, almost rhythm. They were horribly familiar. And then he knew—they were j's. The mute j's were coming out! "Spies!" he cried in terror. "I'm betrayed! I've harboured spies! All this time they've been in my very midst!" He knew he was done for then, but he did not fully realise his ghastly position until, the following night, he detected further marks. They were quite distinct. He easily made them out in the dark. He saw "Official . . ."

It was a dreadful business. He could not tell a soul, because his communications were all cut. He faced the worst with courage; no one should say he was a coward or a slacker. He ordered *all* the papers again, and sat reading them by daylight in his room. He went boldly to the Club and read them openly, brazenly, with true defiance. He agreed with everything he read, he understood it all, but he had no feelings now, he was neither optimistic nor the reverse. He simply read. . . . It was odd, but no one noticed him. In his room one day the landlady came in to brush and sweep—she ignored his presence, tidying the papers up all round him as though he were not there at all. The same thing happened at the Club. A waiter even tried to smooth him out and hang him on the file, and once he was nearly—oh, it was wicked—nearly picked up and offered to another member, Spriggins. Only luckily, Spriggins had the decency to refuse him. He did it so nicely too: "No, thanks," he said with a little smile, "I've read it. There's nothing in it, anyhow!"

It was that very night when Dimble woke towards the early hours, and heard a crackling as he turned in bed. Terror gripped him. He lay quite still and listened. It was at the end of the bed apparently—a faint swishing, crackling noise with tiny reports accompanying it. He moved his foot; the sound was repeated. Something glimmered dimly. He moved the other foot, his arm as well, he sat up briskly. There was a leaping rush of the vague white form across the air; with a tap and slither it fell upon the floor beside him. He stooped over to pick it up, and his hand came into contact with something smooth and warm that was in the act of settling upon the floor. He felt the little wind it made. It was, of course, a newspaper. But the same instant, and before he removed his hand, he knew by the warmth of it that it was something more besides. It was not different from himself. What in the world had happened to him? It *was* himself. His hand was on the skin of his bare chest. He was crackling all over . . . but very nicely, very crisply. He settled back into bed with a kind of rush and slither. His terror passed. He felt well pleased with himself. "It's all right," he murmured, as he fell asleep. "For a moment I thought I was a halfpenny one! I must be more careful. Near shave, that I must mention it to Spriggins . . . when I'm out!" There was an odd smell of printers' ink in the air.

Next morning he came out duly, and Spriggins bought him for a penny, right enough, and took him in his pocket on a long route march. While resting for lunch with his company, out by the Welsh Harp, which is 'Endon Wy,' he lit his pipe with him. Dimble tried to utter protest, but he stammered horribly. He could not get his words at all. He made a fizzy, crackling noise instead—of which Spriggins, puffing the smoke at him, took no slightest notice.

Then Dimble curled up, turned slowly black, and passed away into the wind, and fell into a stubble-field near by, and lay there quite happily until the dew that night came softly down and dissolved him into nothing—nothing visible or of value, at any rate.

The Other Wing

I

It used to puzzle him that, after dark, some one *would* look in round the edge of the bedroom door, and withdraw again too rapidly for him to see the face. When the nurse had gone away with the candle this happened: "Good-night, Master Tim," she said usually, shading the light with one hand to protect his eyes; "dream of me and I'll dream of you." She went out slowly. The sharp-edged shadow of the door ran across the ceiling like a train. There came a whispered colloquy in the corridor outside, about himself, of course, and—he was alone. He heard her steps going deeper and deeper into the bosom of the old country house; they were audible for a moment on the stone flooring of the hall; and sometimes the dull thump of the baize door into the servants' quarters just reached him, too—then silence. But it was only when the last sound, as well as the last sign of her had vanished, that the face emerged from its hiding-place and flashed in upon him round the corner. As a rule, too, it came just as he was saying, "Now I'll go to sleep. I won't think any longer. Good-night, Master Tim, and happy dreams." He loved to say this to himself; it brought a sense of companionship, as though there were two persons speaking.

The room was on the top of the old house, a big, high-ceilinged room, and his bed against the wall had an iron railing round it; he felt very safe and protected in it. The curtains at the other end of the room were drawn. He lay watching the firelight dancing on the heavy folds, and their pattern, showing a spaniel chasing a long-tailed bird towards a bushy tree, interested and amused him. It was repeated over and over again. He counted the number of dogs, and the number of birds, and the number of trees, but could never make them agree. There was a plan somewhere in that pattern; if only he could discover it, the dogs and birds and trees would "come out right." Hundreds and hundreds of times he had played this game, for the plan in the pattern made it possible to take sides, and the bird and dog were against him. They always won, however; Tim usually fell asleep just when the advantage was on his own side. The curtains hung steadily enough most of the time, but it seemed to him once or twice that they stirred—hiding a dog or bird on purpose to prevent his winning. For instance, he had eleven birds and eleven trees, and, fixing them in his mind by saying, "that's eleven birds and eleven trees, but only ten dogs," his eyes darted back to find the eleventh dog, when—the curtain moved and threw all his calculations into confusion again. The eleventh dog was hidden. He did not quite like the movement; it gave him questionable feelings, rather, for the curtain did not move of itself. Yet, usually, he was too intent upon counting the dogs to feel positive alarm.

Opposite to him was the fireplace, full of red and yellow coals; and, lying with his head sideways on the pillow, he could see directly in between the bars. When the coals settled with a soft and powdery crash, he turned his eyes from the curtains to the grate, trying to discover exactly which bits had fallen. So long as the glow was there the sound seemed pleasant enough, but sometimes he awoke later in the night, the room huge with darkness, the fire almost out—and the sound was not so pleasant then. It startled him. The coals did not fall of themselves. It seemed that some one poked them cautiously. The shadows were very thick before the bars. As with the curtains, moreover, the morning aspect of the extinguished fire, the ice-cold cinders that made a clinking sound like tin, caused no emotion whatever in his soul.

And it was usually while he lay waiting for sleep, tired both of the curtain and the coal games, on the point, indeed, of saying, "I'll go to sleep now," that the puzzling thing took place. He would be staring drowsily at the dying fire, perhaps counting the stockings and flannel garments that hung along the high fender-rail when, suddenly, a person looked in with lightning swiftness through the door and vanished again before he could possibly turn his head to see. The appearance and disappearance were accomplished with amazing rapidity always.

It was a head and shoulders that looked in, and the movement combined the speed, the lightness, and the silence of a shadow. Only it was not a shadow. A hand held the edge of the door. The face shot round, saw him, and withdrew like lightning. It was utterly beyond him to imagine anything more quick and clever. It darted. He heard no sound. It went. But—it had seen him, looked him all over, examined him, noted what he was doing with that lightning glance. It wanted to know if he were awake still, or asleep. And though it went off, it still watched him from a distance; it waited somewhere; it knew all about him. *Where* it waited no one could ever guess. It came probably, he felt, from beyond the house, possibly from the roof, but most likely from the garden or the sky. Yet, though strange, it was not terrible. It was a kindly and protective figure, he felt. And when it happened he never called for help, because the occurrence simply took his voice away.

"It comes from the Nightmare Passage," he decided; "but it's *not* a nightmare." It puzzled him.

Sometimes, moreover, it came more than once in a single night. He was pretty sure—not *quite* positive—that it occupied his room as soon as he was properly asleep. It took possession, sitting perhaps before the dying fire, standing upright behind the heavy curtains, or even lying down in the empty bed his brother used when he was home from school. Perhaps it played the curtain game, perhaps it poked the coals; it knew, at any rate, where the eleventh dog had lain concealed. It certainly came in and out; certainly, too, it did not wish to be seen. For, more than once, on waking suddenly in the midnight blackness, Tim knew it was standing close beside his bed and bending over him. He felt, rather than heard, its presence. It glided quietly away. It moved with marvellous softness, yet he was positive it moved. He felt the difference, so to speak. It had been near him, now it was gone. It came back, too—just as he was falling into sleep again. Its midnight coming and going, however, stood out sharply different from its first shy, tentative approach. For in the firelight it came alone; whereas in the black and silent hours, it had with it—others.

And it was then he made up his mind that its swift and quiet movements were due to the fact that it had wings. It flew. And the others that came with it in the darkness were "its little ones." He also made up his mind that all were friendly, comforting, protective, and that while positively *not* a Nightmare, it yet came somehow along the Nightmare Passage before it reached him. "You see, it's like this," he explained to the nurse: "The big one comes to visit me alone, but it only brings its little ones when I'm *quite* asleep."

"Then the quicker you get to sleep the better, isn't it, Master Tim?"

He replied: "Rather! I always do. Only I wonder where they come *from!*" He spoke, however, as though he had an inkling.

But the nurse was so dull about it that he gave her up and tried his father. "Of course," replied this busy but affectionate parent, "it's either nobody at all, or else it's Sleep coming to carry you away to the land of dreams." He made the statement kindly but somewhat briskly, for he was worried just then about the extra taxes on his land, and the effort to fix his mind on Tim's fanciful world was beyond him at the moment. He lifted the boy on to his knee, kissed and patted him as though he were a favourite dog, and planted him on the rug again with a flying sweep. "Run and ask your mother," he added; "she knows all that kind of thing. Then come back and tell me all about it—another time."

Tim found his mother in an arm-chair before the fire of another room; she was knitting and reading at the same time—a wonderful thing the boy could never understand. She raised her head as he came in, pushed her glasses on to her forehead, and held her arms out. He told her everything, ending up with what his father said.

"You see, it's *not* Jackman, or Thompson, or any one like that," he exclaimed. "It's some one real."

"But nice," she assured him, "some one who comes to take care of you and see that you're all safe and cosy."

"Oh, yes, I know that. But—"

"I think your father's right," she added quickly. "It's Sleep, I'm sure, who pops in round the door like that. Sleep *has* got wings, I've always heard."

"Then the other thing—the little ones?" he asked. "Are they just sorts of dozes, you think?"

Mother did not answer for a moment. She turned down the page of her book, closed it slowly, put it on the table beside her. More slowly still she put her knitting away, arranging the wool and needles with some deliberation.

"Perhaps," she said, drawing the boy closer to her and looking into his big eyes of wonder, "they're dreams!"

Tim felt a thrill run through him as she said it. He stepped back a foot or so and clapped his hands softly. "Dreams!" he whispered with enthusiasm and belief; "of course! I never thought of that."

His mother, having proved her sagacity, then made a mistake. She noted her success, but instead of leaving it there, she elaborated and explained. As Tim expressed it she "went on about it." Therefore he did not listen. He followed his train of thought alone. And presently, he interrupted her long sentences with a conclusion of his own:

"Then I know where She hides," he announced with a touch of awe. "Where She lives, I mean." And without waiting to be asked, he imparted the information: "It's in the Other Wing."

"Ah!" said his mother, taken by surprise. "How clever of you, Tim!"—and thus confirmed it.

Thenceforward this was established in his life—that Sleep and her attendant Dreams hid during the daytime in that unused portion of the great Elizabethan mansion called the Other Wing. This other wing was unoccupied, its corridors untrodden, its windows shuttered, and its rooms all closed. At various places green baize doors led into it, but no one ever opened them. For many years this part had been shut up; and for the children, properly speaking, it was out of bounds. They never mentioned it as a possible place, at any rate; in hide-and-seek it was not considered, even; there was a hint of the inaccessible about the Other Wing. Shadows, dust, and silence had it to themselves.

But Tim, having ideas of his own about everything, possessed special information about the Other Wing. He believed it *was* inhabited. Who occupied the immense series of empty rooms, who trod the spacious corridors, who passed to and fro behind the shuttered windows, he had not known exactly. He had called these occupants "they," and the most important among them was "The Ruler." The Ruler of the Other Wing was a kind of deity, powerful, far away, ever present yet never seen.

And about this Ruler he had a wonderful conception for a little boy; he connected her, somehow, with deep thoughts of his own, the deepest of all. When he made up adventures to the moon, to the stars, or to the bottom of the sea, adventures that he lived inside himself, as it were—to reach them he must invariably pass through the chambers of the Other Wing. Those corridors and halls, the Nightmare Passage among them, lay along the route; they were the first stage of the journey. Once the green baize doors swung to behind him and the long dim passage stretched ahead, he was well on his way into the adventure of the moment; the Nightmare Passage once passed, he was safe from capture; but once the shutters of a window had been flung open, he was free of the gigantic world that lay beyond. For then light poured in and he could see his way.

The conception, for a child, was curious. It established a correspondence between the mysterious chambers of the Other Wing and the occupied, but unguessed chambers of his Inner Being. Through these chambers, through these darkened corridors, along a passage, sometimes dangerous, or at least of questionable repute, he must pass to find all adventures that were *real*. The light—when he pierced far enough to take the shutters down—was discovery. Tim did not actually think, much less say, all this. He was aware of it, however. He felt it. The Other Wing was inside himself as well as through the green baize doors. His inner map of wonder included both of them.

But now, for the first time in his life, he knew who lived there and who the Ruler was. A shutter had fallen of its own accord; light poured in; he made a guess, and Mother had confirmed it. Sleep and her Little Ones, the host of dreams, were the daylight occupants. They stole out when the darkness fell. All adventures in life began and ended by a dream—discoverable by first passing through the Other Wing.

II

And, having settled this, his one desire now was to travel over the map upon journeys of exploration and discovery. The map inside himself he knew already, but the map of the Other Wing he had not seen. His mind knew it, he had a clear mental picture of rooms and halls and passages, but his feet had never trod the silent floors where dust and shadows hid the flock of dreams by day. The mighty chambers where Sleep ruled he longed to stand in, to see the Ruler face to face. He made up his mind to get into the Other Wing.

To accomplish this was difficult; but Tim was a determined youngster, and he meant to try; he meant, also, to succeed. He deliberated. At night he could not possibly manage it; in any case, the Ruler and her host all left it after dark, to fly about the world; the Wing would be empty, and the emptiness would frighten him. Therefore he must make a daylight visit; and it was a daylight visit he decided on. He deliberated more. There were rules and risks involved: it meant going out of bounds, the danger of being seen, the certainty of being questioned by some idle and inquisitive grown-up: "Where in the world have you been all this time"—and so forth. These things he thought out carefully, and though he arrived at no solution, he felt satisfied that it would be all right. That is, he recognised the risks. To be prepared was half the battle, for nothing then could take him by surprise.

The notion that he might slip in from the garden was soon abandoned; the red bricks showed no openings; there was no door; from the courtyard, also, entrance was impracticable; even on tiptoe he could barely reach the broad window-sills of stone. When playing alone, or walking with the French governess, he examined every outside possibility. None offered. The shutters, supposing he could reach them, were thick and solid.

Meanwhile, when opportunity offered, he stood against the outside walls and listened, his ear pressed against the tight red bricks; the towers and gables of the Wing rose overhead; he heard the wind go whispering along the eaves; he imagined tiptoe movements and a sound of wings inside. Sleep and her Little Ones were busily preparing for their journeys after dark; they hid, but they did not sleep; in this unused Wing, vaster alone than any other country house he had ever seen, Sleep taught and trained her flock of feathered Dreams. It was very wonderful. They probably supplied the entire county. But more wonderful still was the thought that the Ruler herself should take the trouble to come to his particular room and personally watch over him all night long. That was amazing. And it flashed across his imaginative, enquiring mind: "Perhaps they take me with them! The moment I'm asleep! That's why she comes to see me!"

Yet his chief preoccupation was, how Sleep got out. Through the green baize doors, of course! By a process of elimination he arrived at a conclusion: he, too, must enter through a green baize door and risk detection.

Of late, the lightning visits had ceased. The silent, darting figure had not peeped in and vanished as it used to do. He fell asleep too quickly now, almost before Jackman reached the hall, and long before the fire began to die. Also, the dogs and birds upon the curtains always matched the trees exactly, and he won the curtain game quite easily; there was never a dog or bird too many; the curtain never stirred. It had been thus ever since his talk with Mother and Father. And so he came to make a second discovery: his parents did not really believe in his Figure. She kept away on that account. They doubted her; she hid. Here was still another incentive to go and find her out. He ached for her, she was so kind, she gave herself so much trouble—just for his little self in the big and lonely bedroom. Yet his parents spoke of her as though she were of no account. He longed to see her, face to face, and tell her that *he* believed in her and loved her. For he was positive she would like to hear it. She cared. Though he had fallen asleep of late too quickly for him to see her flash in at the door, he had known nicer dreams than ever in his life before—travelling dreams. And it was she who sent them. More—he was sure she took him out with her.

One evening, in the dusk of a March day, his opportunity came; and only just in time, for his brother Jack was expected home from school on the morrow, and with Jack in the other bed, no Figure would ever care to show itself. Also it was Easter, and after Easter, though Tim was not aware of at the time, he was to say good-bye finally to governesses and become a day-boarder at a preparatory school for Wellington. The opportunity offered itself so naturally, moreover, that Tim took it without hesitation. It never occurred to him to question, much less to refuse it. The thing was obviously meant to be. For he found himself unexpectedly in front of a green baize door; and the green baize door was—swinging! Somebody, therefore, had just passed through it.

It had come about in this wise. Father, away in Scotland, at Inglemuir, the shooting place, was expected back next morning; Mother had driven over to the church upon some Easter business or other; and the governess had been allowed her holiday at home in France. Tim, therefore, had the run of the house, and in the hour between tea and bedtime he made good use of it. Fully able to defy such second-rate obstacles as nurses and butlers, he explored all manner of forbidden places with ardent thoroughness, arriving finally in the sacred precincts of his father's study. This wonderful room was the very heart and centre of the whole big house; he had been birched here long ago; here, too, his father had told him with a grave yet smiling face: "You've got a new companion, Tim, a little sister; you must be very kind to her." Also, it was the place where all the money was kept. What he called "father's jolly smell" was strong in it—papers, tobacco, books, flavoured by hunting crops and gunpowder.

At first he felt awed, standing motionless just inside the door; but presently, recovering equilibrium, he moved cautiously on tiptoe towards the gigantic desk where important papers were piled in untidy patches. These he did not touch; but beside them his quick eye noted the jagged piece of iron shell his father brought home from his Crimean campaign and now used as a letter-weight. It was difficult to lift, however. He climbed into the comfortable chair and swung round and round. It was a swivel-chair, and he sank down among the cushions in it, staring at the strange things on the great desk before him, as if fascinated. Next he turned away and saw the stick-rack in the corner—this, he knew, he was allowed to touch. He had played with these sticks before. There were twenty, perhaps, all told, with curious carved handles, brought from every corner of the world; many of them cut by his father's own hand in queer and distant places. And, among them, Tim fixed his eye upon a cane with an ivory handle, a slender, polished cane that he had always coveted tremendously. It was the kind he meant to use when he was a man. It bent, it quivered, and when he swished it through the air it trembled like a riding-whip, and made a whistling noise. Yet it was very strong in spite of its elastic qualities. A family treasure, it was also an old-fashioned relic; it had been his grandfather's walking stick. Something of another century clung visibly about it still. It had dignity and grace and leisure in its very aspect. And it suddenly occurred to him: "How grandpapa must miss it! Wouldn't he just love to have it back again!"

How it happened exactly, Tim did not know, but a few minutes later he found himself walking about the deserted halls and passages of the house with the air of an elderly gentleman of a hundred years ago, proud as a courtier, flourishing the stick like an eighteenth century dandy in the Mall. That the cane reached to his shoulder made no difference; he held it accordingly, swaggering on his way. He was off upon an adventure. He dived down through the byways of the Other Wing, inside himself, as though the stick transported him to the days of the old gentleman who had used it in another century.

It may seem strange to those who dwell in smaller houses, but in this rambling Elizabethan mansion there were whole sections that, even to Tim, were strange and unfamiliar. In his mind the map of the Other Wing was clearer by far than the geography of the part he travelled daily. He came to passages and dim-lit halls, long corridors of stone beyond the Picture Gallery; narrow, wainscoted connecting-channels with four steps down and a little later two steps up; deserted chambers with arches guarding them—all hung with the soft March twilight and all bewilderingly unrecognised. With a sense of adventure born of naughtiness he went carelessly along, farther and farther into the heart of this unfamiliar country, swinging the cane, one thumb stuck into the armpit of his blue serge suit, whistling softly to himself, excited yet keenly on the alert—and suddenly found himself opposite a door that checked all further advance. It was a green baize door. And it was swinging.

He stopped abruptly, facing it. He stared, he gripped his cane more tightly, he held his breath. "The Other Wing!" he gasped in a swallowed whisper. It was an entrance, but an entrance he had never seen before. He thought he knew every door by heart; but this one was new. He stood motionless for several minutes, watching it; the door had two halves, but one half only was swinging, each swing shorter than the one before; he heard the little puffs of air it made; it settled finally, the last movements very short and rapid; it stopped. And the boy's heart, after similar rapid strokes, stopped also—for a moment.

"Some one's just gone through," he gulped. And even as he said it he knew who the some one was. The conviction just dropped into him. "It's Grandfather; he knows I've got his stick. He wants it!" On the heels of this flashed instantly another amazing certainty. "He sleeps in there. He's having dreams. That's what being dead means."

His first impulse, then, took the form of, "I must let Father know; it'll make him burst for joy"; but his second was for himself—to finish his adventure. And it was this, naturally enough, that gained the day. He could tell his father later. His first duty was plainly to go through the door into the Other Wing. He must give the stick back to its owner. He must *hand* it back.

The test of will and character came now. Tim had imagination, and so knew the meaning of fear; but there was nothing craven in him. He could howl and scream and stamp like any other person of his age when the occasion called for such behaviour, but such occasions were due to temper roused by a thwarted will, and the histrionics were half "pretended" to produce a calculated effect. There was no one to thwart his will at present. He also knew how to be afraid of Nothing, to be afraid without ostensible cause, that is—which was merely "nerves." He could have "the shudders" with the best of them.

But, when a real thing faced him, Tim's character emerged to meet it. He would clench his hands, brace his muscles, set his teeth—and wish to heaven he was bigger. But he would not flinch. Being imaginative, he lived the worst a dozen times before it happened, yet in the final crash he stood up like a man. He had that highest pluck—the courage of a sensitive temperament. And at this particular juncture, somewhat ticklish for a boy of eight or nine, it did not fail him. He lifted the cane and pushed the swinging door wide open. Then he walked through it—into the Other Wing.

III

The green baize door swung to behind him; he was even sufficiently master of himself to turn and close it with a steady hand, because he did not care to hear the series of muffled thuds its lessening swings would cause. But he realised clearly his position, knew he was doing a tremendous thing.

Holding the cane between fingers very tightly clenched, he advanced bravely along the corridor that stretched before him. And all fear left him from that moment, replaced, it seemed, by a mild and exquisite surprise. His footsteps made no sound, he walked on air; instead of darkness, or the twilight he expected, a diffused and gentle light that seemed like the silver on the lawn when a half-moon sails a cloudless sky, lay everywhere. He knew his way, moreover, knew exactly where he was and whither he was going. The corridor was as familiar to him as the floor of his own bedroom; he recognised the shape and length of it; it agreed exactly with the map he had constructed long ago. Though he had never, to the best of his knowledge, entered it before, he knew with intimacy its every detail.

And thus the surprise he felt was mild and far from disconcerting.

"I'm here again!" was the kind of thought he had. It was *how* he got here that caused the faint surprise, apparently. He no longer swaggered, however, but walked carefully, and half on tiptoe, holding the ivory handle of the cane with a kind of affectionate respect. And as he advanced, the light closed softly up behind him, obliterating the way by which he had come. But this he did not know, because he did not look behind him. He only looked in front, where the corridor stretched its silvery length towards the great chamber where he knew the cane must be surrendered. The person who had preceded down this ancient corridor, passing through the green baize door just before he reached it, this person, his father's father, now stood in that great chamber, waiting to receive his own. Tim knew it as surely as he knew he breathed. At the far end he even made out the larger patch of silvery light which marked its gaping doorway.

There was another thing he knew as well—that this corridor he moved along between rooms with fast-closed doors, was the Nightmare Corridor; often and often he had traversed it; each room was occupied. "This is the Nightmare Passage," he whispered to himself, "but I know the Ruler—it doesn't matter. None of them can get out or do anything." He heard them, none the less, inside, as he passed by; he heard them scratching to get out. The feeling of security made him reckless; he took unnecessary risks; he brushed the panels as he passed. And the love of keen sensation for its own sake, the desire to feel "an awful thrill," tempted him once so sharply that he raised his stick and poked a fast-shut door with it!

He was not prepared for the result, but he gained the sensation and the thrill. For the door opened with instant swiftness half an inch, a hand emerged, caught the stick, and tried to draw it in. Tim sprang back as if he had been struck. He pulled at the ivory handle with all his strength, but his strength was less than nothing. He tried to shout, but his voice had gone. A terror of the moon came over him, for he was unable to loosen his hold of the handle; his fingers had become a part of it. An appalling weakness turned him helpless. He was dragged inch by inch towards the fearful door. The end of the stick was already through the narrow crack. He could not see the hand that pulled, but he knew it was terrific. He understood now why the world was strange, why horses galloped furiously, and why trains whistled as they raced through stations. All the comedy and terror of nightmare gripped his heart with pincers made of ice. The disproportion was abominable. The final collapse rushed over him when, without a sign of warning, the door slammed silently, and between the jamb and the wall the cane was crushed as flat as it were a bulrush. So irresistible was the force behind the door that the solid stick just went flat as a stalk of a bulrush.

He looked at it. It *was* a bulrush.

He did not laugh; the absurdity was so distressingly unnatural. The horror of finding a bulrush where he had expected a polished cane—this hideous and appalling detail held the nameless horror of the nightmare. It betrayed him utterly. Why had he not always known really that the stick was not a stick, but a thin and hollow reed . . . ?

Then the cane was safely in his hand, unbroken. He stood looking at it. The Nightmare was in full swing. He heard another door opening behind his back, a door he had not touched. There was just time to see a hand thrusting and waving dreadfully, familiarly, at him through the narrow crack—just time to realise that this was another Nightmare acting in atrocious concert with the first, when he saw closely beside him, towering to the ceiling, the protective, kindly Figure that visited his bedroom. In the turning movement he made to meet the attack he became aware of her. And his terror passed. It was a nightmare terror merely. The infinite horror vanished. Only the comedy remained. He smiled.

He saw her dimly only, she was so vast, but he saw her, the Ruler of the Other Wing at last, and knew that he was safe again. He gazed with a tremendous love and wonder, trying to see her clearly; but the face was hidden far aloft and seemed to melt into the sky beyond the roof. He discerned that she was larger than the Night, only far, far softer, with wings that folded above him more tenderly even than his mother's arms; that there were points of light like stars among the feathers, and that she was vast enough to cover millions and millions of people all at once. Moreover, she did not fade or go, so far as he could see, but spread herself in such a way that he lost sight of her. She spread over the entire Wing . . .

And Tim remembered that this was all quite natural really. He had often and often been down this corridor before; the Nightmare Corridor was no new experience; it had to be faced as usual. Once knowing what hid inside the rooms, he was bound to tempt them out. They drew, enticed, attracted him; this was their power. It was their special strength that they could suck him helplessly towards them, and that he was obliged to go. He understood exactly why he was tempted to tap with the cane upon their awful doors, but, having done so, he had accepted the challenge and could now continue his journey quietly and safely. The Ruler of the Other Wing had taken him in charge.

A delicious sense of carelessness came on him. There was softness as of water in the solid things about him, nothing that could hurt or bruise. Holding the cane firmly by its ivory handle, he went forward along the corridor, walking as on air.

The end was quickly reached: he stood upon the threshold of the mighty chamber where he knew the owner of the cane was waiting; the long corridor lay behind him, in front he saw the spacious dimensions of a lofty hall that gave him the feeling of being in the Crystal Palace, Euston Station, or St. Paul's. High, narrow windows, cut deeply into the wall, stood in a row upon the other side; an enormous open fireplace of burning logs was on his right; thick tapestries hung from the ceiling to the floor of stone; and in the centre of the chamber was a massive table of dark, shining wood, great chairs with carved stiff backs set here and there beside it. And in the biggest of these thronelike chairs there sat a figure looking at him gravely—the figure of an old, old man.

Yet there was no surprise in the boy's fast-beating heart; there was a thrill of pleasure and excitement only, a feeling of satisfaction. He had known quite well the figure would be there, known also it would look like this exactly. He stepped forward on to the floor of stone without a trace of fear or trembling, holding the precious cane in two hands now before him, as though to present it to its owner. He felt proud and pleased. He had run risks for this.

And the figure rose quietly to meet him, advancing in a stately manner over the hard stone floor. The eyes looked gravely, sweetly down at him, the aquiline nose stood out. Tim knew him perfectly: the knee-breeches of shining satin, the gleaming buckles on the shoes, the neat dark stockings, the lace and ruffles about neck and wrists, the coloured waistcoat opening so widely—all the details of the picture over father's mantelpiece, where it hung between two Crimean bayonets, were reproduced in life before his eyes at last. Only the polished cane with the ivory handle was not there.

Tim went three steps nearer to the advancing figure and held out both his hands with the cane laid crosswise on them.

"I've brought it, Grandfather," he said, in a faint but clear and steady tone; "here it is."

And the other stooped a little, put out three fingers half concealed by falling lace, and took it by the ivory handle. He made a courtly bow to Tim. He smiled, but though there was pleasure, it was a grave, sad smile. He spoke then: the voice was slow and very deep. There was a delicate softness in it, the suave politeness of an older day.

"Thank you," he said; "I value it. It was given to me by my grandfather. I forgot it when I—" His voice grew indistinct a little.

"Yes?" said Tim.

"When I—left," the old gentleman repeated.

"Oh," said Tim, thinking how beautiful and kind the gracious figure was.

The old man ran his slender fingers carefully along the cane, feeling the polished surface with satisfaction. He lingered specially over the smoothness of the ivory handle. He was evidently very pleased.

"I was not quite myself—er—at the moment," he went on gently; "my memory failed me somewhat." He sighed, as though an immense relief was in him.

"*I* forget things, too—sometimes," Tim mentioned sympathetically. He simply loved his grandfather. He hoped—for a moment—he would be lifted up and kissed. "I'm *awfully* glad I brought it," he faltered—"that you've got it again."

The other turned his kind grey eyes upon him; the smile on his face was full of gratitude as he looked down.

"Thank you, my boy. I am truly and deeply indebted to you. You courted danger for my sake. Others have tried before, but the Nightmare Passage—er—" He broke off. He tapped the stick firmly on the stone flooring, as though to test it. Bending a trifle, he put his weight upon it. "Ah!" he exclaimed with a short sigh of relief, "I can now—"

His voice again grew indistinct; Tim did not catch the words.

"Yes?" he asked again, aware for the first time that a touch of awe was in his heart.

"—get about again," the other continued very low. "Without my cane," he added, the voice failing with each word the old lips uttered, "I could not . . . possibly . . . allow myself . . . to be seen. It was indeed . . . deplorable . . . unpardonable of me . . . to forget in such a way. Zounds, sir . . . ! I—I . . ."

His voice sank away suddenly into a sound of wind. He straightened up, tapping the iron ferrule of his cane on the stones in a series of loud knocks. Tim felt a strange sensation creep into his legs. The queer words frightened him a little.

The old man took a step towards him. He still smiled, but there was a new meaning in the smile. A sudden earnestness had replaced the courtly, leisurely manner. The next words seemed to blow down upon the boy from above, as though a cold wind brought them from the sky outside.

Yet the words, he knew, were kindly meant, and very sensible. It was only the abrupt change that startled him. Grandfather, after all, was but a man! The distant sound recalled something in him to that outside world from which the cold wind blew.

"My eternal thanks to you," he heard, while the voice and face and figure seemed to withdraw deeper and deeper into the heart of the mighty chamber. "I shall not forget your kindness and your courage. It is a debt I can, fortunately, one day repay. . . . But now you had best return and with dispatch. For your head and arm lie heavily on the table, the documents are scattered, there is a cushion fallen . . . and my son is in the house. . . . Farewell! You had best leave me quickly. See! *She* stands behind you, waiting. Go with her! Go now . . . !"

The entire scene had vanished even before the final words were uttered. Tim felt empty space about him. A vast, shadowy Figure bore him through it as with mighty wings. He flew, he rushed, he remembered nothing more—until he heard another voice and felt a heavy hand upon his shoulder.

"Tim, you rascal! What are you doing in my study? And in the dark, like this!"

He looked up into his father's face without a word. He felt dazed. The next minute his father had caught him up and kissed him.

"Ragamuffin! How did you guess I was coming back to-night?" He shook him playfully and kissed his tumbling hair. "And you've been asleep, too, into the bargain. Well—how's everything at home—eh? Jack's coming back from school to-morrow, you know, and . . ."

IV

Jack came home, indeed, the following day, and when the Easter holidays were over, the governess stayed abroad and Tim went off to adventures of another kind in the preparatory school for Wellington. Life slipped rapidly along with him; he grew into a man; his mother and his father died; Jack followed them within a little space; Tim inherited, married, settled down into his great possessions—and opened up the Other Wing. The dreams of imaginative boyhood all had faded; perhaps he had merely put them away, or perhaps he had forgotten them. At any rate, he never spoke of such things now, and when his Irish wife mentioned her belief that the old country house possessed a family ghost, even declaring that she had met an eighteenth century figure of a man in the corridors, "an old, old man who bends down upon a stick"—Tim only laughed and said:

"That's as it ought to be! And if these awful land taxes force us to sell some day, a respectable ghost will increase the market value."

But one night he woke and heard a tapping on the floor. He sat up in bed and listened. There was a chilly feeling down his back. Belief had long since gone out of him; he felt uncannily afraid. The sound came nearer and nearer; there were light footsteps with it. The door opened—it opened a little wider, that is, for it already stood ajar—and there upon the threshold stood a figure that it seemed he knew. He saw the face as with all the vivid sharpness of reality. There was a smile upon it, but a smile of warning and alarm. The arm was raised. Tim saw the slender hand, lace falling down upon the long, thin fingers, and in them, tightly gripped, a polished cane. Shaking the cane twice to and fro in the air, the face thrust forward, spoke certain words, and—vanished. But the words were inaudible; for, though the lips distinctly moved, no sound, apparently, came from them.

And Tim sprang out of bed. The room was full of darkness. He turned the light on. The door, he saw, was shut as usual. He had, of course, been dreaming. But he noticed a curious odour in the air. He sniffed it once or twice—then grasped the truth. It was a smell of burning!

Fortunately, he awoke just in time. . . .

He was acclaimed a hero for his promptitude. After many days, when the damage was repaired, and nerves had settled down once more into the calm routine of country life, he told the story to his wife—the entire story. He told the adventure of his imaginative boyhood with it. She asked to see the old family cane. And it was this request of hers that brought back to memory a detail Tim had entirely forgotten all these years. He remembered it suddenly again—the loss of the cane, the hubbub his father kicked up about it, the endless, futile search. For the stick had never been found, and Tim, who was questioned very closely concerning it, swore with all his might that he had not the smallest notion where it was. Which was, of course, the truth.

Cain's Atonement

So many thousands to-day have deliberately put Self aside, and are ready to yield their lives for an ideal, that it is not surprising a few of them should have registered experiences of a novel order. For to step aside from Self is to enter a larger world, to be open to new impressions. If Powers of Good exist in the universe at all, they can hardly be inactive at the present time. . . .

The case of two men, who may be called Jones and Smith, occurs to the mind in this connection. Whether a veil actually was lifted for a moment, or whether the tension of long and terrible months resulted in an exaltation of emotion, the experience claims significance. Smith, to whom the experience came, holds the firm belief that it was real. Jones, though it involved him too, remained unaware.

It is a somewhat personal story, their peculiar relationship dating from early youth: a kind of unwilling antipathy was born between them, yet an antipathy that had no touch of hate or even of dislike. It was rather in the nature of an instinctive rivalry. Some tie operated that flung them ever into the same arena with strange persistence, and ever as opponents. An inevitable fate delighted to throw them together in a sense that made them rivals; small as well as large affairs betrayed this malicious tendency of the gods. It showed itself in earliest days, at school, at Cambridge, in travel, even in house-parties and the lighter social intercourse. Though distant cousins, their families were not intimate, and there was no obvious reason why their paths should fall so persistently together. Yet their paths did so, crossing and recrossing in the way described. Sooner or later, in all his undertakings, Smith would note the shadow of Jones darkening the ground in front of him; and later, when called to the Bar in his chosen profession, he found most frequently that the learned counsel in opposition to him was the owner of this shadow, Jones. In another matter, too, they became rivals, for the same girl, oddly enough, attracted both, and though she accepted neither offer of marriage (during Smith's lifetime!), the attitude between them was that of unwilling rivals. For they were friends as well.

Jones, it appears, was hardly aware that any rivalry existed; he did not think of Smith as an opponent, and as an adversary, never. He did notice, however, the constantly recurring meetings, for more than once he commented on them with good-humoured amusement. Smith, on the other hand, was conscious of a depth and strength in the tie that certainly intrigued him; being of a thoughtful, introspective nature, he was keenly sensible of the strange competition in their lives, and sought in various ways for its explanation, though without success. The desire to find out was very strong in him. And this was natural enough, owing to the singular fact that in all their battles he was the one to lose. Invariably Jones got the best of every conflict. Smith always paid; sometimes he paid with interest.

Occasionally, too, he seemed forced to injure himself while contributing to his cousin's success. It was very curious. He reflected much upon it; he wondered what the origin of their tie and rivalry might be, but especially why it was that he invariably lost, and why he was so often obliged to help his rival to the point even of his own detriment. Tempted to bitterness sometimes, he did not yield to it, however; the relationship remained frank and pleasant; if anything, it deepened.

He remembered once, for instance, giving his cousin a chance introduction which yet led, a little later, to the third party offering certain evidence which lost him an important case—Jones, of course, winning it. The third party, too, angry at being dragged into the case, turned hostile to him, thwarting various subsequent projects. In no other way could Jones have procured this particular evidence; he did not know of its existence even. That chance introduction did it all. There was nothing the least dishonourable on the part of Jones—it was just the chance of the dice. The dice were always loaded against Smith—and there were other instances of similar kind.

About this time, moreover, a singular feeling that had lain vaguely in his mind for some years past, took more definite form. It suddenly assumed the character of a conviction, that yet had no evidence to support it. A voice, long whispering in the depths of him, became much louder, grew into a statement that he accepted without further ado: "I'm paying off a debt," he phrased it, "an old, old debt is being discharged. I owe him this—my help and so forth." He accepted it, that is, as just; and this certainty of justice kept sweet his heart and mind, shutting the door on bitterness or envy. The thought, however, though it recurred persistently with each encounter, brought no explanation.

When the war broke out both offered their services; as members of the O.T.C., they got commissions quickly; but it was a chance remark of Smith's that made his friend join the very regiment he himself was in. They trained together, were in the same retreats and the same advances together. Their friendship deepened. Under the stress of circumstances the tie did not dissolve, but strengthened. It was indubitably real, therefore. Then, oddly enough, they were both wounded in the same engagement.

And it was here the remarkable fate that jointly haunted them betrayed itself more clearly than in any previous incident of their long relationship—Smith was wounded in the act of protecting his cousin. How it happened is confusing to a layman, but each apparently was leading a bombing-party, and the two parties came together. They found themselves shoulder to shoulder, both brimmed with that pluck which is complete indifference to Self; they exchanged a word of excited greeting; and the same second one of those rare opportunities of advantage presented itself which only the highest courage could make use of. Neither, certainly, was thinking of personal reward; it was merely that each saw the chance by which instant heroism might gain a surprise advantage for their side. The risk was heavy, but there *was* a chance; and success would mean a decisive result, to say nothing of high distinction for the man who obtained it—if he survived. Smith, being a few yards ahead of his cousin, had the moment in his grasp. He was in the act of dashing forward when something made him pause. A bomb in mid-air, flung from the opposing trench, was falling; it seemed immediately above him; he saw that it would just miss himself, but land full upon his cousin—whose head was turned the other way. By stretching out his hand, Smith knew he could field it like a cricket ball. There was an interval of a second and a half, he judged. He hesitated—perhaps a quarter of a second—then he acted. He caught it. It was the obvious thing to do. He flung it back into the opposing trench.

The rapidity of thought is hard to realise. In that second and a half Smith was aware of many things: He saved his cousin's life unquestionably; unquestionably also Jones seized the opportunity that otherwise was his cousin's. But it was neither of these reflections that filled Smith's mind. The dominant impression was another. It flashed into actual words inside his excited brain: "I must risk it. I owe it to him—and more besides!" He was, further, aware of another impulse than the obvious one. In the first fraction of a second it was overwhelmingly established. And it was this: that the entire episode was familiar to him. A subtle familiarity was present. All this had happened before. He had already—somewhere, somehow—seen death descending upon his cousin from the air. Yet with a difference. The "difference" escaped him; the familiarity was vivid. That he missed the deadly detonators in making the catch, or that the fuse delayed, he called good luck. He only remembers that he flung the gruesome weapon back whence it had come, and that its explosion in the opposite trench materially helped his cousin to find glory in the place of death. The slight delay, however, resulted in his receiving a bullet through the chest—a bullet he would not otherwise have received, presumably.

It was some days later, gravely wounded, that he discovered his cousin in another bed across the darkened floor. They exchanged remarks. Jones was already "decorated," it seemed, having snatched success from his cousin's hands, while little aware whose help had made it easier. . . . And once again there stole across the inmost mind of Smith that strange, insistent whisper: "I owed it to him . . . but, by God, I owe more than that . . . I mean to pay it too . . . !"

There was not a trace of bitterness or envy now; only this profound conviction, of obscurest origin, that it was right and absolutely just—full, honest repayment of a debt incurred. Some ancient balance of account was being settled; there was no "chance"; injustice and caprice played no role at all. . . . And a deeper understanding of life's ironies crept into him; for if everything was *just,* there was no room for whimpering.

And the voice persisted above the sound of busy footsteps in the ward: "I owe it . . . I'll pay it gladly . . . !"

Through the pain and weakness the whisper died away. He was exhausted. There were periods of unconsciousness, but there were periods of half-consciousness as well; then flashes of another kind of consciousness altogether, when, bathed in high, soft light, he was aware of things he could not quite account for. He *saw.* It was absolutely real. Only, the critical faculty was gone. He did not question what he saw, as he stared across at his cousin's bed. He knew. Perhaps the beaten, worn-out body let something through at last. The nerves, over-strained to numbness, lay very still. The physical system, battered and depleted, made no cry. The clamour of the flesh was hushed. He was aware, however, of an undeniable exaltation of the spirit in him, as he lay and gazed towards his cousin's bed. . . .

Across the night of time, it seemed to him, the picture stole before his inner eye with a certainty that left no room for doubt. It was not the cells of memory in his brain of To-day that gave up their dead, it was the eternal Self in him that remembered and understood—the soul. . . .

With that satisfaction which is born of full comprehension, he watched the light glow and spread about the little bed. Thick matting deadened the footsteps of nurses, orderlies, doctors. New cases were brought in, "old" cases were carried out; he ignored them; he saw only the light above his cousin's bed grow stronger. He lay still and stared. It came neither from the ceiling nor the floor; it unfolded like a cloud of shining smoke. And the little lamp, the sheets, the figure framed between them—all these slid cleverly away and vanished utterly. He stood in another place that had lain behind all these appearances—a landscape with wooded hills, a foaming river, the sun just sinking below the forest, and dusk creeping from a gorge along the lonely banks. In the warm air there was a perfume of great flowers and heavy-scented trees; there were fire-flies, and the taste of spray from the tumbling river was on his lips. Across the water a large bird flapped its heavy wings, as it moved down-stream to find another fishing place. For he and his companion had disturbed it as they broke out of the thick foliage and reached the river-bank. The companion, moreover, was his brother; they ever hunted together; there was a passionate link between them born of blood and of affection—they were twins. . . .

It all was as clear as though of Yesterday. In his heart was the lust of the hunt; in his blood was the lust of woman; and thick behind these lurked the jealousy and fierce desire of a primitive day. But, though clear as of Yesterday, he knew that it was of long, long ago. . . . And his brother came up close beside him, resting his bloody spear with a clattering sound against the boulders on the shore. He saw the gleaming of the metal in the sunset, he saw the shining glitter of the spray upon the boulders, he saw his brother's eyes look straight into his own. And in them shone a light that was neither the reflection of the sunset, nor the excitement of the hunt just over.

"It escaped us," said his brother. "Yet I know my first spear struck."

"It followed the fawn that crossed," was the reply. "Besides, we came down wind, thus giving it warning. Our flocks, at any rate, are safer—"

The other laughed significantly.

"It is not the safety of our flocks that troubles me just now, brother," he interrupted eagerly, while the light burned more deeply in his eyes. "It is, rather, that *she* waits for me by the fire across the river, and that I would get to her. With your help added to my love," he went on in a trusting voice, "the gods have shown me the favour of true happiness!" He pointed with his spear to a camp-fire on the farther bank, turning his head as he strode to plunge into the stream and swim across.

For an instant, then, the other felt his natural love turn into bitter hate. His own fierce passion, unconfessed, concealed, burst into instant flame. That the girl should become his brother's wife sent the blood surging through his veins in fury. He felt his life and all that he desired go down in ashes. . . . He watched his brother stride towards the water, the deer-skin cast across one naked shoulder—when another object caught his practised eye. In mid-air it passed suddenly, like a shining gleam; it seemed to hang a second; then it swept swiftly forward past his head—and downward. It had leaped with a blazing fury from the overhanging bank behind; he saw the blood still streaming from its wounded flank. It must land—he saw it with a secret, awful pleasure—full upon the striding figure, whose head was turned away!

The swiftness of that leap, however, was not so swift but that he could easily have used his spear. Indeed, he gripped it strongly. His skill, his strength, his aim—he knew them well enough. But hate and love, fastening upon his heart, held all his muscles still. He hesitated. He was no murderer, yet he paused. He heard the roar, the ugly thud, the crash, the cry for help—too late . . . and when, an instant afterwards, his steel plunged into the great beast's heart, the human heart and life he might have saved lay still for ever. . . . He heard the water rushing past, an icy wind came down the gorge against his naked back, he saw the fire shine upon the farther bank . . . and the figure of a girl in skins was wading across, seeking out the shallow places in the dusk, and calling wildly as she came. . . . Then darkness hid the entire landscape, yet a darkness that was deeper, bluer than the velvet of the night alone. . . .

And he shrieked aloud in his remorseful anguish: "May the gods forgive me, for I did not mean it! Oh, that I might undo . . . that I might repay. . . . !"

That his cries disturbed the weary occupants in more than one bed is certain, but he remembers chiefly that a nurse was quickly by his side, and that something she gave him soothed his violent pain and helped him into deeper sleep again. There was, he noticed, anyhow, no longer the soft, clear, blazing light about his cousin's bed. He saw only the faint glitter of the oil-lamps down the length of the great room. . . .

And some weeks later he went back to fight. The picture, however, never left his memory. It stayed with him as an actual reality that was neither delusion nor hallucination. He believed that he understood at last the meaning of the tie that had fettered him and puzzled him so long. The memory of those far-off days of shepherding beneath the stars of long ago remained vividly beside him. He kept his secret, however. In many a talk with his cousin beneath the nearer stars of Flanders no word of it ever passed his lips.

The friendship between them, meanwhile, experienced a curious deepening, though unacknowledged in any spoken words. Smith, at any rate, on his side, put into it an affection that was a brave man's love. He watched over his cousin. In the fighting especially, when possible, he sought to protect and shield him, regardless of his own personal safety. He delighted secretly in the honours his cousin had already won. He himself was not yet even mentioned in dispatches, and no public distinction of any kind had come his way.

His V.C. eventually—well, he was no longer occupying his body when it was bestowed. He had already "left." . . . He was now conscious, possibly, of other experiences besides that one of ancient, primitive days when he and his brother were shepherding beneath other stars. But the reckless heroism which saved his cousin under fire may later enshrine another memory which, at some far future time, shall reawaken as a "hallucination" from a Past that to-day is called the Present. . . . The notion, at any rate, flashed across his mind before he "left."

The Celestial Motor-'bus

The title, of course, belongs to another—almost. For the inspired vehicle that started from Surbiton, according to E. M. Forster's brilliant report, was an omnibus. The Company, perhaps, has extended its operations as well as introduced electricity since those days. This motor-'bus, at any rate, crawls now across the wintry flats of Essex. Six or seven miles an hour, for an electric vehicle, is crawling, yet many of the passengers considered it unnecessarily rapid. They were sorry to get out. At the corner of the village where the three roads meet under the leafless elms, it came lumbering up to take us to the early morning rain at Chelmsford. Long before it was visible we heard it, then saw its ungainly outline heaving along above a hedge. "Makes noise enough, don't it, like a Zep?" remarked the soldier who was waiting with me. It was bitterly cold, the dull sky almost foggy over the gloomy Essex landscape. "It's going to snow," he said a few minutes later, and shivered. The motor-'bus took as long as that to come round the bend of the lane. Then, abruptly, it was there and we got in. He smiled. I smiled. It seemed the sun was shining. How was it? Certainly the inside of the 'bus that icy morning was warm and radiant.

The change, though bewildering at first, was quite natural. It began as we pushed past the conductor to clamber in. "Yes," she said in a silvery voice and with a happy smile, "you're quite right for Chelmsford," and pulled the cord with energy, as though she played a game, and the entire 'bus was her latest toy. But the voice, the smile, the gesture! Surely her hand was on my arm, and I was taking her in to dinner down the stairs of some great London mansion; there were flowers and brilliant dresses; there would be music and dancing afterwards; her father was late—there had been a Cabinet meeting or something . . . ! I took my seat in the far corner, and watched her surreptitiously. No, it was not The Lady Violet or Ethel. It was a 'bus conductor. She had not mentioned a Cabinet meeting or her father; she had merely mentioned respectfully that we were "all right for Chelmsford." Two and two, I remembered, still made four. Yet the flowers, the brilliant dresses, the atmosphere of culture and refinement still remained. And outside the sun was shining as in May. But the delightful thing was here: that this cold, cheerless morning in November at eight o'clock all the passengers in a country motor-'bus were—happy.

I watched her with an increasing admiration. We all watched her. To what distinguished county family she belonged we were not told, of course. She attended to her business strictly, and most efficiently. Who was the man, we wondered, she had replaced? Was he in Flanders or Gallipoli? Was he somewhere north of Salonica, fighting with his back to the unfriendly sea? And was he doing his bit with extra pluck and spirit, knowing that a fair young girl was pulling his cord and taking fares for him at home with a pluck and spirit equal to his own? The questions flew on wireless all through that motor-'bus blundering along the Essex lanes into Chelmsford.

We have all read of the women who release our fighting men by taking on their jobs; we have seen them photographed; we know them personally. But there was about this young conductor just that extra touch that made the incident somehow beautiful and poignant. If there was any one among the passengers who was not doing his or her bit shame must have whispered it. The slim and graceful conductor, born obviously to luxury and comfort, accustomed to motors and first-class carriages, surrounded with soft fur rugs, to late breakfast, if not to breakfast in bed, to days of music, concerts, theatres, merry visits, and all the rest . . . rising now at five these dark winter mornings, hurrying to the 'bus offices and starting-place, and spending her entire day taking coppers, making change, pulling the bell-cord . . . giving up all her time and energy . . . up and down the steps incessantly to collect fares on the top, and the rest . . . and all day long, the weather wet or fine. The picture, with its vivid contrast, rose before the mind with every word she spoke, with every gesture, with every smile . . . and it was the cheerful, happy spirit in which she did her job that made that comfortless and cold interior of the vehicle shine. She played with that old motor-'bus as with a toy—but she played in splendid earnest.

She came down to my far corner in such a way that I felt ashamed to be sitting while she stood. She waited politely while my cold fingers fumbled in various pockets for the money. I wanted to hear her voice again. I asked the fare. "Oh, it's fourpence, please," said the silvery voice. "Thanks very much," as I gave her the disgraceful—coppers! The hand that took them, the hand that punched my ticket and held it out to me, was slender and beautifully shaped. A pretty ring or two, I noticed, and a silver bangle on the wrist. Those fingers, quite obviously, knew the touch of ivory keys, and the transparent, delicate skin, the almond nails—by rights I should have risen, bowed, and raised them reverently to my lips, instead of grunting "Thank you" inside my heavy overcoat. The other hand—it was a relief to notice it—wore a warm fur-lined glove. The long green coat that reached below the knees, in neatly at the waist, and fitting her slim figure in a way that told of a skilled cutter, the sou'-wester on her dark bronze hair, the high waterproof boots (we saw them when she went skipping cheerfully up the awkward steps to the top), the two straps that crossed over the shoulders, holding the ticket-clips and leather bag of change, the cord with its gleaming whistle—it all was certainly becoming. She was eighteen or twenty years of age at a guess, she may have known that she looked neat and charming; but there was nothing in her manner to betray self-consciousness, at any rate. She was a most competent conductor; she meant to do her job, and did it, to the very best of her ability. It was the cheerful, jolly spirit, mixture of play and deep earnestness, that touched the heart into respect and admiration. A fine, plucky English girl doing her bit of war-work simply! The fine, grand touch; the simple courage that our women now show everywhere, shaming even the men. There were three soldiers in that motor-'bus. I noticed that they never took their eyes off her. . . .

We lumbered along the ugly roads. By the door were some children on their way to early school. The conductor made friends with them, talking and laughing when her work allowed. She read over their lessons with them, holding the book to hear them say their bits of poetry, their dates, their other scraps—but ever with one eye on the road for passengers. An old man got in; she helped him by the arm, tenderly almost, and led him to a seat. The 'bus was getting somewhat crowded. "Oh, I say, would you mind moving up—just a tiny bit? Ah, thank you; now there's room!" And it was within an ace of being "a teeny weeny bit," instead of "tiny." Friends and acquaintances got in too; she chatted with them a moment about the weather, books, music; several she knew by their first names; then, with a nod and a smile, she was up the stairs again collecting pennies and giving change out of her leather bag. And once or twice—"as a great treat"—she allowed one of the children to pull the bell that stopped or started this celestial motor-'bus. "It's your turn next," she whispered to a mite with red hair and more books than she could manage quite. "But that's the last, mind. You've each had your turn." But never for one single instant did she neglect her work; she missed no passenger; she stopped and started the 'bus in perfect time. And her gleaming whistle—how she loved blowing it! A short, sharp, business-like blast each time, and off we went again. There was nothing careless or slipshod about her from head to foot; she was ever the prompt, efficient, polite, and very alert conductor.

We were getting into the outskirts of Chelmsford by now. No one was calling to get in. There was a pause in her labours. I watched her standing on the step, leaning for a moment's rest against the door, her back to us. I saw her adding up the tickets, entering figures with a neat pencil on the time-card, or whatever it was. Then she turned. With a smile and a word of apology she put her hand behind the passenger next to the door, feeling for something in the cushioned seat. I expected to see her take out a new package of coloured tickets. But, instead, I saw a mysterious sort of object that no conductor of my acquaintance had ever taken out before from between the cushions. It was a bag, a little bag of shining material that I think was silk. It was what the feuilleton writers call a *reticule.* Off came a glove. I watched the slender fingers open the neat gold clasp, and take out a handkerchief—one of those tiny handkerchiefs that are scarcely bigger than a postage stamp or, say, a luggage label. She opened it; she turned away; she blew her nose . . . . There was just time to slip the small lace object back into the silken bag, snap the clasp, and tuck it all away with a smile behind the passenger again, when the bus slowed up and stopped. "Chelmsford! Last stop!" cried the silvery voice—and I left the celestial vehicle and climbed the stairs to get into a very earthly train for London.

The Snake

The Monday morning train from X-on-Sea stood waiting to start, when two elderly men got in and took the corner-seats reserved for them by a guard who evidently knew their habits. They continued a conversation begun on the platform; they discussed the war with such intensity that I lost interest in my new paper. I found myself reading the same lines over and over. Then I listened. They said the obvious things; there was no subtlety in them; they were typical Men in the Street, but their outspoken language had such honest conviction behind it that I caught myself wishing they were addressing an audience of millions instead of one.

Evidently they expected other companions on the journey to London. These others presently arrived and took their seats. The carriage was now full. Pipes were lit and windows closed. But, with the new arrival, the war was forgotten as though it was of no importance. It passed from their minds as from their talk. A change came over the group. They had found something of greater interest than Armageddon. This "something" was a snake.

"When I came down on Saturday," said No. 3, "what d'you think happened? You'd never guess, not one of you." He looked round with challenge. "I'll tell you: a snake crawled out from underneath the seat. Out it came, wriggling—just as we slowed up. It hadn't moved till that moment. Out it came—on the floor of the carriage. And a soldier picked it tip and put it in his pocket. He said it was a grass-snake—'armless!" He stopped and looked round again, but this time without challenge. He was believed. He had touched the personal interest of each one of his companions.

At first they discussed the actual incident itself—till there was nothing more to be said about it by any one. They established the fact beyond all doubt. A snake, a grass-snake, a harmless grass-snake, a snake two feet long, a snake that had escaped from the pocket of a boy, a soldier, or a crank, had unquestionably travelled down last Saturday in the smoking-compartment of a second-class railway carriage—and had shown itself as described just when the train was stopping.

"It was the heat, of course," explained one. "It found the warm pipes."

"That's it," agreed the originator; "it liked the warmth, you see." This point of safety he never left. He repeated it a hundred and sixteen times. He insisted upon it. "Snakes always make for warmth, don't they?"

"My earliest recollection—" began No. 4, remembering a snake story of his own. But he was interrupted.

"They love the sun," resumed the originator. "Makes them feel 'appy, I suppose, heat and warmth—"

"I shall never forget once when I was shooting over dogs in Scotland, and one of the dogs pointed at something—" Again No. 4 was baulked of his undelivered epic. The originator desired a little more interest in his own story before he was prepared to listen to the stories of others.

"You see, the soldier knew it, luckily, knew it was 'armless. But, think of it—a snake on the floor like that. Might have got up your trousers or anything. Suppose there'd been an old woman in the carriage, for instance—or a dawg!"

"Extraordinary," resumed No. 4, *obliquely* this time and in a superior tone, "extraordinary the terror some folk have of snakes. Even keepers and gillies. In Scotland that time, I remember—" and he enlisted the attention of his companions and told his story at last without a break. It had to do with the difficulty of killing a snake "really dead." This particular snake he had struck some thirty times with the butt of his gun. Yet it revived—at sunset, of course.

"Switch is the best way," declared another member of the group, who plainly had a story of his own en route. "A sharp cut with a switch does it. There's a particular spot just behind the 'ead."

"Funny thing, though, wasn't it?" said the originator. "In a railway carriage, of all places. And it's not the season, anyway. It was the warm pipes—"

"Lucky it wasn't a adder," put in No. 5, speaking for the first time.

"D'you know the difference between a adder and a viper, now?" asked No. 3. "There *is* a difference."

No. 3 had struck out a new line, and the discussion lasted for some dozen stations, three long tunnels, and probably at least forty miles of track. At the end the group found itself so far as accurate knowledge was concerned, about where they started. "They like warm places, any-how," observed the originator at the finish, "adders or vipers. *That's* clear." It was. But this new line having been broached, the conversa-tion began to travel quickly. And the remarkable thing about it was that it was never for one minute dull. The usual things about snakes were said, but said in such a way that interest was kept alive spontane-ously for ninety minutes without a single break. An apprentice journal-ist might have had an admirable lesson gratis on how to write an "informing and chatty article on nothing." The snake was sometimes called a reptile, sometimes a serpent, but it never once lost its hold on the mind of those five elderly men and their enthralled listener behind his newspaper.

"Pretty little creatures—really," the originator added, in a kindly tone, peaking of adders still. "They eat insects, I believe. But poison-ous—oh, my!"

And the nature of the poison, method of treatment by alcohol, in-cluding a poetical description of the fangs and poison-glands, attitude of the snake when striking, and so forth, followed with encyclopædic detail. The poison might be sucked out—that was one way. "Shouldn't care to do it," said the approved judgment on *that*. "*I* wouldn't either," said the originator with obstinate decision.

This led to a side-issue: what snake-charmers did to make their pets obedient, it being fairly well agreed that the charmers were com-mon swindlers who first extracted the poison-glands, then humbugged their audience with "utter flummox." Ten minutes' friendly chat, led by No. 5, was then enjoyed with regard to a serpent's method of at-tack, but it was finally decided that no snake will strike unless it is first stepped upon—"an' oo wouldn't, I ask you?" from No. 5 indignantly. "They look jest like bits of dry stick, I'm told, so as you can't distin-guish them—not easily," he added, the irrelevant observation univer-sally approved.

This being too conclusive to enlarge upon usefully, a boa constrictor was next introduced, with the verdict that "it's an awful death, that squeezing"; and then followed an elaborate entertainment upon the feeding of large reptiles at the Zoological Gardens.

"How they swallow a goat 'ole beats me—" began No. 5, but was not allowed to continue, as he had been heard a good deal lately. It was another's turn. No. 2 saw his chance, and seized it. A friend of his had a wife who knew a Keeper. "Ah! but, you see, it's only once in six months they're fed. And it takes a few days to get the thing down inside them. Once in six months they get a young goat and swallow it by inches—a few inches every day—and it lasts for weeks, of course, digesting it. But they swell something awful. You can see the outline of the goat through their skin—the skin's that extended."

Earlswood was passed by now, the train approaching Clapham Junction. No. 4 mentioned something about a "serum they've discovered for neutralising: the poison," but no one took him up. Somebody looked out of the window. Another opened half an inch at the top, with the remark, "Bit stuffy, ain't it? Don't you think?"—then closed it with a snap fifteen seconds later. But the spell was weakened, if not broken. The snake had had its day. London was creeping into the mind again, London and the war. Stray shots were made, however.

"Simplifies cooking, anyway!" observed No. 2, still dwelling upon the feeding of the big reptiles. "And that's somethin' in these 'ard times."

There was a general silence, broken at length by the originator. He felt his main point perhaps had not been clearly made after all. "Curious experience, wasn't it?" he appealed to the group generally. "It must have escaped from some one's luggage or something, and made a bee line for the hot pipes. It's heat and warmth they—"

The audience of one lost the remainder of the sentence in the bustle of getting down from the rack various articles that were never intended to be placed there. When he sat down again, he noticed that two of the men had opened their newspapers. Battersea Bridge was passed. He felt sorry the snake-anthology was over. There was wholesomeness and sanity in the entire performance.

"Good majority at the Labour Congress—eh?" said one, as they left the train. "Now the Govunment knows the country's be'ind them, I hope they'll take a stronger line. . . ."

Initiation

A few years ago, on a Black Sea steamer heading for the Caucasus, I fell into conversation with an American. He mentioned that he was on his way to the Baku oil-fields, and I replied that I was going up into the mountains. He looked at me questioningly a moment. "Your first trip?" he asked with interest. I said it was. A conversation followed; it was continued the next day, and renewed the following day, until we parted company at Batoum. I don't know why he talked so freely to me in particular. Normally, he was a taciturn, silent man. We had been fellow travellers from Marseilles, but after Constantinople we had the boat pretty much to ourselves. What struck me about him was his vehement, almost passionate, love of natural beauty—in seas and woods and sky, but above all in mountains. It was like a religion in him. His taciturn manner hid deep poetic feeling.

And he told me it had not always been so with him. A kind of friendship sprang up between us. He was a New York business man—buying and selling exchange between banks—but was English born. He had gone out thirty years before, and become naturalised. His talk was exceedingly "American," slangy, and almost Western. He said he had roughed it in the West for a year or two first. But what he chiefly talked about was mountains. He said it was in the mountains an unusual experience had come to him that had opened his eyes to many things, but principally to the beauty that was now everything to him, and to the—insignificance of death.

He knew the Caucasus well where I was going. I think that was why he was interested in me and my journey. "Up there," he said, "you'll feel things—and maybe find out things you never knew before."

"What kind of things?" I asked.

"Why, for one," he replied with emotion and enthusiasm in his voice, "that living and dying ain't either of them of much account.

That if you know Beauty, I mean, and Beauty is in your life, you live on in it and with it for others—even when you're dead."

The conversation that followed is too long to give here, but it led to his telling me the experience in his own life that had opened his eyes to the truth of what he said. "Beauty is imperishable," he declared, "and you live with it, why, you're imperishable too!"

The story, as he told it verbally in his curious language, remains vividly in my memory. But he had written it down, too, he said. And he gave me the written account, with the remark that I was free to hand it on to others if I "felt that way." He called it "Initiation." It runs as follows.

I

In my own family this happened, for Arthur was my nephew. And a remote Alpine valley was the place. It didn't seem to me in the least suitable for such occurrences, except that it was Catholic, and the "Church," I understand—at least, scholars who ought to know have told me so—has subtle Pagan origins incorporated unwittingly in its observations of certain Saints' Days, as well as in certain ceremonials. All this kind of thing is Dutch to me, a form of poetry or superstition, for I am interested chiefly in the buying and selling of exchange, with an office in New York City, just off Wall Street, and only come to Europe now occasionally for a holiday. I like to see the dear old musty cities, and go to the Opera, and take a motor run through Shakespeare's country or round the Lakes, get in touch again with London and Paris at the Ritz Hotels—and then back again to the greatest city on earth, where for years now I've been making a good thing out of it. Repton and Cambridge, long since forgotten, had their uses. They were all right enough at the time. But I'm now "on the make," with a good fat partnership, and have left all that truck behind me.

My half-brother, however—he was my senior and got the cream of the family wholesale chemical works—has stuck to the trade in the Old Country, and is making probably as much as I am. He approved my taking the chance that offered, and is only sore now because his son, Arthur, is on the stupid side. He agreed that finance suited my temperament far better than drugs and chemicals, though he warned me that all American finance was speculative and therefore dangerous. "Arthur is getting on," he said in his last letter, "and will some day take the director's place you would be in now had you cared to stay. But he's a plodder, rather." That meant, I knew, that Arthur was a fool. Business, at any rate, was not suited to his temperament. Five years ago, when I came home with a month's holiday to be used in working up connections in English banking circles, I saw the boy. He was fifteen years of age at the time, a delicate youth, with an artist's dreams in his big blue eyes, if my memory goes for anything, but with a tangle of yellow hair and features of classical beauty that would have made half the young girls of my New York set in love with him, and a choice of heiresses at his disposal when he wanted them.

I have a clear recollection of my nephew then. He struck me as having grit and character, but as being wrongly placed. He had his grandfather's tastes. He ought to have been, like him, a great scholar, a poet, an editor of marvellous old writings in new editions. I couldn't get much out of the boy, except that he "liked the chemical business fairly," and meant to please his father by "knowing it thoroughly" so as to qualify later for his directorship. But I have never forgotten the evening when I caught him in the hall, staring up at his grandfather's picture, with a kind of light about his face, and the big blue eyes all rapt and tender (almost as if he had been crying) and replying, when I asked him what was up: "*That* was worth living for. He brought Beauty back into the world!"

"Yes," I said, "I guess that's right enough. He did. But there was no money in it to speak of."

The boy looked at me and smiled. He twigged somehow or other that deep down in me, somewhere below the money-making instinct, a poet, but a dumb poet, lay in hiding. "You know what I mean," he said. "It's in you too."

The picture was a copy—my father had it made—of the presentation portrait given to Baliol, and "the grandfather" was celebrated in his day for the translations he made of Anacreon and Sappho, of Homer, too, I remember rightly, as well as for a number of classical studies and essays that he wrote. A lot of stuff like that he did, and made a name at it too. His *Lives of the Gods* went into six editions. They said—the big critics of his day—that he was "a poet who wrote no poetry, yet lived it passionately in the spirit of old-world, classical Beauty," and I know he was a wonderful fellow in his way and made the dons and schoolmasters all sit up. We're proud of him all right. After twenty-five years of successful "exchange" in New York City, I confess I am unable to appreciate all that, feeling more in touch with the commercial and financial spirit of the age, progress, development, and the rest. But, still, I'm not ashamed of the classical old boy, who seems to have been a good deal of a Pagan, judging by the records we have kept. However, Arthur peering up at that picture in the dusk, his eyes half moist with emotion, and his voice gone positively shaky, is a thing I never have forgotten. He stimulated my curiosity uncommonly. It stirred something deep down in me that I hardly cared to acknowledge on Wall Street—something burning.

And the next time I saw him was in the summer of 1910, when I came to Europe for a two months' look around—my wife at Newport with the children—and hearing that he was in Switzerland, learning a bit of French to help him in the business, I made a point of dropping in upon him just to see how he was shaping generally and what new kinks his mind had taken on. There was something in Arthur I never could quite forget. Whenever his face came into my mind I began to think. A kind of longing came over me—a desire for Beauty, I guess, it was. It made me dream.

I found him at an English tutor's—a lively old dog, with a fondness for the cheap native wines, and a financial interest in the tourist development of the village. The boys learnt French in the mornings, possibly, but for the rest of the day were free to amuse themselves exactly as they pleased and without a trace of supervision—provided the parents footed the bills without demur.

This suited everybody all round; and as long as the boys came home with an accent and a vocabulary, all was well. For myself, having learned in New York to attend strictly to my own business—exchange between different countries with a profit—I did not deem it necessary to exchange letters and opinions with my brother—with no chance of profit anywhere. But I got to know Arthur, and had a queer experience of my own into the bargain. Oh, there was profit in it for me. I'm drawing big dividends to this day on the investment.

I put up at the best hotel in the village, a one-horse show, differing from the other inns only in the prices charged for a lot of cheap decoration in the dining-room, and went up to surprise my nephew with a call the first thing after dinner. The tutor's house stood some way back from the narrow street, among fields where there were more flowers than grass, and backed by a forest of fine old timber that stretched up several thousand feet to the snow. The snow at least was visible, peeping out far overhead just where the dark line of forest stopped; but in reality, I suppose, that was an effect of foreshortening, and whole valleys and pastures intervened between the trees and the snow-fields. The sunset, long since out of the valley, still shone on those white ridges, where the peaks stuck up like the teeth of a gigantic saw. I guess it meant five or six hours' good climbing to get up to them—and nothing to do when you got there. Switzerland, anyway, seemed a poor country, with its little bit of watch-making, sour wines, and every square yard hanging upstairs at an angle of 60 degrees used for hay. Picture postcards, chocolate, and cheap tourists kept it going apparently, but I dare say it was all right enough to learn French in—and cheap as Hoboken to live in!

Arthur was out; I just left a card and wrote on it that I would be very pleased he cared to step down to take luncheon with me at my hotel next day. Having nothing better to do, I strolled homewards by way of the forest.

Now what came over me in that bit of dark pine forest is more than I can quite explain, but I think it must have been due to the height—the village was 4,000 feet above sea-level—and the effect of the rarefied air upon my circulation. The nearest thing to it in my experience is rye whisky, the queer touch of wildness, of self-confidence, a kind of whooping rapture and the reckless sensation of being a tin god of sorts that comes from a lot of alcohol—a memory, please understand, of years before, when I thought it a grand thing to own the earth and paint the old town red. I seemed to walk on air, and there was a smell about those trees that made me suddenly—well, that took my mind clean out of its accustomed rut. It was just too lovely and wonderful for me to describe it. I had got well into the forest and lost my way a bit. The smell of an old-world garden wasn't in it. It smelt to me as if some one had just that minute turned out the earth all fresh and new. There was moss and tannin, a hint of burning, something between smoke and incense, say, and a fine clean odour of pitch-pine bark when the sun gets on it after rain—and a flavour of the sea thrown in for luck. That was the first I noticed, for I had never smelt anything half so good since my camping days on the coast of Maine. And I stood still to enjoy it. I threw away my cigar for fear of mixing things and spoiling it. "If that could be bottled," I said to myself , "it'd sell for two dollars a pint in every city in the Union!"

And it was just then, while standing and breathing it in, that I got the queer feeling of some one watching me. I kept quite still. Some one was moving near me. The sweat went trickling down my back. A kind of childhood thrill got hold of me.

It was very dark. I was not afraid exactly, but I was a stranger in these parts and knew nothing about the habits of the mountain peasants. There might be tough customers lurking around after dark on the chance of striking some guy of a tourist with money in his pockets. Yet, somehow, that wasn't the kind of feeling that came to me at all, for, though I had a pocket Browning at my hip, the notion of getting at it did not even occur to me. The sensation was new—a kind of lifting, exciting sensation that made my heart swell out with exhilaration. There was happiness in it. A cloud that *weighed* seemed to roll off my mind, same as that light-hearted mood when the office door is locked and I'm off on a two months' holiday—with gaiety and irresponsibility at the back of it. It was invigorating. I felt youth sweep over me.

I stood there, wondering what on earth was coming on me, and half expecting that any moment some one would come out of the darkness and show himself; and as I held my breath and made no movement at all the queer sensation grew stronger. I believe I even resisted a temptation to kick up my heels and dance, to let out a flying shout as a man with liquor in him does. Instead of this, however, I just kept dead still. The wood was black as ink all round me, too black to see the tree-trunks separately, except far below where the village lights came up twinkling between them, and the only way I kept the path was by the soft feel of the pine-needles that were thicker than a Brussels carpet. But nothing happened, and no one stirred. The idea that I was being watched remained, only there was no sound anywhere except the roar of falling water that filled the entire valley. Yet some one was very close to me in the darkness.

I can't say how long I might have stood there, but I guess it was the best part of ten minutes, and I remember it struck me that I had run up against a pocket of extra-rarefied air that had a lot of oxygen in it—oxygen or something similar—and that was the cause of my elation. The idea was nonsense, I have no doubt; but for the moment it half explained the thing to me. I realised it was all *natural* enough, at any rate—and so moved on. It took a longish time to reach the edge of the wood, and a footpath led me—oh, it was quite a walk, I tell you—into the village street again. I was both glad and sorry to get there. I kept myself busy thinking the whole thing over again. What caught me all of a heap was that million-dollar sense of beauty, youth, and happiness. Never in my born days had I felt anything to touch it. And it hadn't cost a cent!

Well, I was sitting there enjoying my smoke and trying to puzzle it all out, and the hall was pretty full of people smoking and talking and reading papers, and so forth, when all of a sudden I looked up and caught my breath with such a jerk that I actually bit my tongue. There was grandfather in front of my chair! I looked into his eyes. I saw him as clear and solid as the porter standing behind his desk across the lounge, and it gave me a touch of cold all down the back that I needn't forget unless I want to. He was looking into my face, and he had a cap in his hand, and he was speaking to me. It was my grandfather's picture come to life, only much thinner and younger and a kind of light in his eyes like fire.

"I beg your pardon, but you *are*—Uncle Jim, aren't you?"

And then, with another jump of my nerves, I understood.

"You, Arthur! Well, I'm jiggered. So it is. Take a chair, boy. I'm right glad you found me. Shake! Sit down." And I shook his hand and pushed a chair up for him. I was never so surprised in my life. The last time I set eyes on him he was a boy. Now he was a young man, and the very image of his ancestor.

He sat down, fingering his cap. He wouldn't have a drink and he wouldn't smoke. "All right," I said, "let's talk then. I've lots to tell you and I've lots to hear. How are you, boy?"

He didn't answer at first. He eyed me up and down. He hesitated. He was as handsome as a young Greek god.

"I say, Uncle Jim," he began presently, "it *was* you—just now—in the wood—wasn't it?" It made me start, that question put so quietly.

"I *have* just come through that wood up there," I answered, pointing in the direction as well as I could remember, "if that's what you mean. But why? *You* weren't there, were you?" It gave me a queer sort of feeling to hear him say it. What in the name of heaven did he mean?

He sat back in his chair with a sigh of relief.

"Oh, that's all right then," he said, "if it *was* you. Did you see," he asked suddenly; "did you see—anything?"

"Not a thing," I told him honestly. "It was far too dark." I laughed. I fancied I twigged his meaning. But I was not the sort of uncle to come prying on him. Life must be dull enough, I remembered, in this mountain village.

But he didn't understand my laugh. He didn't mean what I meant.

And there came a pause between us. I discovered that we were talking different lingoes. I leaned over towards him.

"Look here, Arthur," I said in a lower voice, "what is it, and what do you mean? I'm all right, you know, and you needn't be afraid of telling me. What d'you mean by—did I see anything?"

We looked each other squarely in the eye. He saw he could trust me, and I saw—well, a whole lot of things, perhaps, but I felt chiefly that he liked me and would tell me things later, all in his own good time. I liked him all the better for that too.

"I only meant," he answered slowly, "whether you really *saw*—anything?"

"No," I said straight, "I didn't see a thing, but, by the gods, I *felt* something."

He started. I started too. An astonishing big look came swimming over his fair, handsome face. His eyes seemed all lit up. He looked as if he'd just made a cool million in wheat or cotton.

"I knew—you were that sort," he whispered. "Though I hardly remembered what you looked like."

"Then what on earth was it?" I asked.

His reply staggered me a bit. "It was just that," he said—"the Earth!"

And then, just when things were getting interesting and promising a dividend, he shut up like a clam. He wouldn't say another word. He asked after my family and business, my health, what kind of crossing I'd had, and all the rest of the common stock. It fairly bowled me over. And I couldn't change him either.

I suppose in America we get pretty free and easy, and don't quite understand reserve. But this young man of half my age kept me in my place as easily as I might have kept a nervous customer quiet in my own office. He just refused to take me on. He was polite and cool and distant as you please, and when I got pressing sometimes he simply pretended he didn't understand. I could no more get him back again to the subject of the wood than a customer could have gotten me to tell him about the prospects of exchange being cheap or dear—when I didn't know myself but wouldn't let him see I didn't know. He was charming, he was delightful, enthusiastic, and even affectionate; downright glad to see me, too, and to chin with me—but I couldn't draw him worth a cent. And in the end I gave up trying.

And the moment I gave up trying he let down a little—but only a very little.

"You'll stay here some time, Uncle Jim, won't you?"

"That's my idea," I said, "if I can see you, and you can show me round some."

He laughed with pleasure. "Oh, rather. I've got lots of time. After three in the afternoon I'm free till—any time you like. There's a lot to see," he added.

"Come along to-morrow then," I said. "If you can't take lunch, perhaps you can come just afterwards. You'll find me waiting for you—right here."

"I'll come at three," he replied, and we said good-night.

II

He turned up sharp at three, and I liked his punctuality. I saw him come swinging down the dusty road; tall, deep-chested, his broad shoulders a trifle high, and his head set proudly. He looked like a young chap in training, a thoroughbred, every inch of him. At the same time there was a touch of something a little too refined and delicate for a man, I thought. That was the poetic, scholarly vein in him, I guess—grandfather cropping out. This time he wore no cap. His thick light hair, not brushed back like the London shop-boys, but parted on the side, yet untidy for all that, suited him exactly and gave him a touch of wildness.

"Well," he asked, "what would you like to do, Uncle Jim? I'm at your service, and I've got the whole afternoon till supper at seven-thirty." I told him I'd like to go through that wood. "All right," he said, "come along. I'll show you." He gave me one quick glance, but said no more. "I'd like to see if I feel anything this time," I explained. "We'll locate the very spot, maybe." He nodded.

"You know where I mean, don't you?" I asked, "because you saw me there?" He just said yes, and then we started.

It was hot, and air was scarce. I remember that we went uphill, and that I realised there was considerable difference in our ages. We crossed some fields first—smothered in flowers so thick that I wondered how much grass the cows got out of it!—and then came to a sprinkling of fine young larches that looked as soft as velvet. There was no path, just a wild mountain side. I had very little breath on the steep zigzags, but Arthur talked easily—and talked mighty well, too: the light and shade, the colouring, and the effect of all this wilderness of lonely beauty on the mind. He kept all this suppressed at home in business. It was safety valves. I twigged *that.* It was the artist in him talking. He seemed to think there was nothing in the world but Beauty—with a big B all the time. And the odd thing was he took for granted that I felt the same. It was cute of him to flatter me that way. "Daulis and the lone Cephissian vale," I heard; and a few moments later—with a sort of reverence in his voice like worship—he called out a great singing name: *"Astarte!"*

"Day is her face, and midnight is her hair,
And morning hours are but the golden stair
By which she climbs to Night."

It was here first that a queer change began to grow upon me too.

"Steady on, boy! I've forgotten all my classics ages ago," I cried.

He turned and gazed down on me, his big eyes glowing, and not a sign of perspiration on his skin.

"That's nothing," he exclaimed in his musical, deep voice. "You know it, or you'd never have felt things in this wood last night; and you wouldn't have wanted to come out with me *now!*"

"How?" I gasped. "How's that?"

"You've come," he continued quietly, "to the only valley in this artificial country that has atmosphere. This valley is *alive*—especially this end of it. There's superstition here, thank God! Even the peasants know things."

I stared at him. "See here, Arthur," I objected. "I'm not a Cath. And I don't know a thing—at least it's all dead in me and forgotten—about poetry or classics or your gods and pan—pantheism—in spite of grandfather—"

His face turned like a dream face.

"Hush!" he said quickly. "Don't mention *him*. There's a bit of him in you as well as in me, and it was here, you know, he wrote—"

I didn't hear the rest of what he said. A creep came over me. I remembered that this ancestor of ours lived for years in the isolation of some Swiss forest where he claimed—he used that setting for his writing—he had found the exiled gods, their ghosts, their beauty, their eternal essences—or something astonishing of that sort. I had clean forgotten it till this moment. It all rushed back upon me, a memory of my boyhood.

And, as I say, a creep came over me—something as near to awe as ever could be. The sunshine on that field of yellow daisies and blue forget-me-nots turned pale. That warm valley wind had a touch of snow in it. And, ashamed and frightened of my baby mood, I looked at Arthur, meaning to choke him off with all this rubbish—and then saw something in his eyes that scared me stiff.

I admit it. What's the use? There was an expression on his fine big face that made my blood go curdled. I got cold feet right there. It mastered me. In him, behind him, near him—blest I know which, *through* him probably—came an enormous thing that turned me insignificant. It downed me utterly.

It was over in a second, the flash of a wing. I recovered instantly. No mere boy should come these muzzy tricks on me, scholar or no scholar. For the change in me was on the increase, and I shrank.

"See here, Arthur," I said plainly once again, "I don't know what your game is, but—there's something queer up here I don't quite get at. I'm only a business man, with classics and poetry all gone dry in me twenty years ago and more—"

He looked at me so strangely that I stopped, confused.

"But, Uncle Jim," he said as quietly as though we talked tobacco brands, "you needn't be alarmed. It's natural you should feel the place. You and I belong to it. We've both got *him* in us. You're just as proud of him as I am, only in a different way." And then he added, with a touch of disappointment: "I thought you'd like it. You weren't afraid last night. You felt the beauty *then*."

Flattery is a darned subtle thing at any time. To see him standing over me in that superior way and talking down at my poor business mind—well, it just came over me that I was laying my cards on the table a bit too early. After so many years of city life—!

Anyway, I pulled myself together. "I was only kidding you, boy," I laughed. "I feel this beauty just as much as you do. Only, I guess, you're more accustomed to it than I am. Come on now," I added with energy, getting upon my feet, "let's push on and see the wood. I want to find that place again."

He pulled me with a hand of iron, laughing as he did so. Gee! I wished I had his teeth, as well as the muscles in his arm. Yet I felt younger, somehow, too—youth flowed more and more into my veins. I had forgotten how sweet the winds and woods and flowers could be Something melted in me. For it was spring, and the whole world was singing like a dream. Beauty was creeping over me. I don't know. I began to feel all big and tender and open to a thousand wonderful sensations. The thought of streets and houses seemed like death. . . .

We went on again, not talking much; my breath got shorter and shorter, and he kept looking about him as though he expected something. But we passed no living soul, not even a peasant; there were no châlets, no cattle, no cattle shelters even. And then I realised that the valley lay at our feet in haze and that we had been climbing at least a couple of hours. "Why, last night I got home in twenty minutes at the outside," I said. He shook his head, smiling. "It seemed like that," he replied, "but you really took much longer. It was long after ten when I found you in the hall." I reflected a moment. "Now I come to think of it, you're right, Arthur. Seems curious, though, somehow." He looked closely at me. "I followed you all the way," he said.

"You followed me!"

"And you went at a good pace too. It was your feelings that made it seem so short—you were singing to yourself and happy as a dancing faun. We kept close behind you for a long way."

I think it was "we" he said, but for some reason or other I didn't care to ask.

"Maybe," I answered shortly, trying uncomfortably to recall what particular capers I had cut. "I guess that's right." And then I added something about the loneliness, and how deserted all this slope of mountain was. And he explained that the peasants were afraid of it and called it No Man's Land. From one year's end to another no human foot went up or down it; the hay was never cut; no cattle grazed along the splendid pastures; no châlet had even been built within a mile of the wood we slowly made for. "They're superstitious," he told me. "It was just the same a hundred years ago when *he* discovered it—there was a little natural cave on the edge of the forest where he used to sleep sometimes—I'll show it to you presently—but for generations this entire mountain-side has been undisturbed. You'll never meet a living soul in any part of it." He stopped and pointed above us to where the pine wood hung in mid-air, like a dim blue carpet. "It's just the place for Them, you see."

And a thrill of power went smashing through me. I can't describe it. It drenched me like a waterfall. I thought of Greece—Mount Ida and a thousand songs! Something in me—it was like the click of a shutter—announced that the "change" was suddenly complete. I was another man; or rather a deeper part of me took command. My very language showed it.

The calm of halcyon weather lay over all. Overhead the peaks rose clear as crystal; below us the village lay in a bluish smudge of smoke and haze, as though a great finger had rubbed them softly into the earth. Absolute loneliness fell upon me like a clap. From the world of human beings we seemed quite shut off. And there began to steal over me again the strange elation of the night before. . . . We found ourselves almost at once against the edge of the wood.

It rose in front of us, a big wall of splendid trees, motionless as if cut out of dark green metal, the branches hanging stiff, and the crowd of trunks lost in the blue dimness underneath. I shaded my eyes with one hand, trying to peer into the solemn gloom. The contrast between the brilliant sunshine on the pastures and this region of heavy shadows blurred my sight.

"It's like the entrance to another world," I whispered.

"It is," said Arthur, watching me. "We will go in. You shall pluck asphodel. . . ."

And, before I knew it, he had me by the hand. We were advancing. We left the light behind us. The cool air dropped upon me like a sheet. There was a temple silence. The sun ran down behind the sky, leaving a marvellous blue radiance everywhere. Nothing stirred. But through the stillness there rose power, power that has no name, power that hides at the foundations somewhere—foundations that are changeless, invisible, everlasting. What do I mean? My mind grew to the dimensions of a planet. We were among the roots of life—whence issues that *one thing* in infinite guise that seeks so many temporary names from the protean minds of men.

"You shall pluck asphodel in the meadows this side of Erebus," Arthur was chanting. "Hermes himself, the Psychopomp, shall lead, and Malahide shall welcome us."

Malahide . . . !

To hear him use that name, the name of our scholar-ancestor, now dead and buried close upon a century—the way he half chanted it—gave me the goose-flesh. I stopped against a tree-stem, thinking of escape. No words came to me at the moment, for I didn't know what to say; but, on turning to find the bright green slopes just left behind, I saw only a crowd of trees and shadows hanging thick as a curtain—as though we had walked a mile. And it was a shock. The way out was lost. The trees closed up behind us like a tide.

"It's all right," said Arthur; "just keep an open mind and a heart alive with love. It has a shattering effect at first, but that will pass." He saw I was afraid, for I shrank visibly enough. He stood beside me in his grey flannel suit, with his brilliant eyes and his great shock of hair, looking more like a column of light than a human being. "It's all quite right and natural," he repeated; "we have passed the gateway, and Hecate, who presides over gateways, will let us out again. Do not make discord by feeling fear. This is a pine wood, and pines are the oldest, simplest trees; they are true primitives. They are an open channel; and in a pine wood where no human life has ever been you shall often find gateways where Hecate is kind to such as us."

He took my hand—he must have felt mine trembling, but his own was cool and strong and felt like silver—and led me forward into the depths of a wood that seemed to me quite endless. It felt endless, that is to say. I don't know what came over me. Fear slipped away, and elation took its place. . . . As we advanced over ground that seemed level, or slightly undulating, I saw bright pools of sunshine here and there upon the forest floor. Great shafts of light dropped in slantingly between the trunks. There was movement everywhere, though I never could see what moved. A delicious, scented air stirred through the lower branches. Running water sang not very far away. Figures I did not actually see; yet there were limbs and flowing draperies and flying hair from time to time, ever just beyond the pools of sunlight. . . . Surprise went from me too. I was on air. The atmosphere of dream came round me, but a dream of something just hovering outside the world I knew—a dream wrought in gold and silver, with shining eyes, with graceful beckoning hands, and with voices that rang like bells of music. . . . And the pools of light grew larger, merging one into another, until a delicate soft light shone equably throughout the entire forest. Into this zone of light we passed together. Then something fell abruptly at our feet, as though thrown down . . . two marvellous, shining sprays of blossom such as I had never seen in all my days before!

"Asphodel!" cried my companion, stooping to pick them up and handing one to me. I took it from him with a delight I could not understand. "Keep it," he murmured; "it is the sign that we are welcome. For Malahide has dropped these on our path."

And at the use of that ancestral name it seemed that a spirit passed before my face and the hair of my head stood up. There was a sense of violent, unhappy contrast. A composite picture presented itself, then rushed away. What was it? My youth in England, music and poetry at Cambridge, and my passionate love of Greek that lasted two terms at most, when Malahide's great books formed part of the curriculum. Over against this, then, the drag and smother of solid worldly business, the sordid weight of modern ugliness, the bitterness of an ambitious, over-striving life. And abruptly—beyond both pictures—a shining, marvellous Beauty that scattered stars beneath my feet and scarved the universe with gold. All this flashed before me with the utterance of that old family name. An alternative sprang up. There seemed some radical, elemental choice presented to me—to what I used to call my soul. My soul could take or leave it as it pleased. . . .

I looked at Arthur moving beside me like a shaft of light. What had come over me? How had our walk and talk and mood, our quite recent everyday and ordinary view, our normal relationship with the things of the world—how had it all slipped into this? So insensibly, so easily, so naturally!

"Was it worth while?"

The question—*I* didn't ask it—jumped up in me of its own accord. Was "what" worth while? Why, my present life of commonplace and grubbing toil, of course; my city existence, with its meagre, unremunerative ambitions. Ah, it was this new Beauty calling me, this shining dream that lay beyond the two pictures I have mentioned. . . . I did not argue it, even to myself. But I understood. There was a radical change in me. The buried poet, too long hidden, rushed into the air like some great singing bird.

I glanced again at Arthur moving along lightly by my side, half dancing almost in his brimming happiness. "Wait till you see Them," I heard him singing. "Wait till you hear the call of Artemis and the footsteps of her flying nymphs. Wait till Orion thunders overhead and Selene, crowned with the crescent moon, drives up the zenith in her white-horsed chariot. The choice will be beyond all question then. . . . !"

A great silent bird, with soft brown plumage, whirred across our path, pausing an instant as though to peep, then disappearing with a muted sound into an eddy of the wind it made. The big trees hid it. It was an owl. The same moment I heard a rush of liquid song come pouring through the forest with a gush of almost human notes, and a pair of glossy wings flashed past us, swerving upwards to find the open sky—blue-black, pointed wings.

"His favourites!" exclaimed my companion with clear joy in his voice. "They all are here! Athene's bird, Procne and Philomela too! The owl—the swallow—and the nightingale! Tereus and Itys are not far away." And the entire forest, as he said it, stirred with movement, as though that great bird's quiet wings had waked the sea of ancient shadows. There were voices too—ringing, laughing voices, as though his words woke echoes that had been listening for it. For I heard sweet singing in the distance. The names he had used perplexed me. Yet even I, stranger as I was to such refined delights, could not mistake the passion of the nightingale and the dart of the eager swallow. That wild burst of music, that curve of swift escape, were unmistakable.

And I struck a stalwart tree-stem with my open hand, feeling the need of hearing, touching, sensing it. My link with known, remembered things was breaking. I craved the satisfaction of the commonplace. I got that satisfaction; but I got something more as well. For the trunk was round and smooth and comely. It was no dead thing I struck. Somehow it brushed me into intercourse with inanimate Nature. And next the desire came to hear my voice—my own familiar, high-pitched voice with the twang and accent the New World climate brings, so-called American:

"Exchange Place, Noo York City. I'm in that business, buying and selling of exchange between the banks of two civilised countries, one of them stoopid and old-fashioned, the other leading all creation . . . !"

It was an effort, but I made it firmly. It sounded odd, remote, unreal.

"Sunlit woods and a wind among the branches," followed close and sweet upon my words. But who, in the name of Wall Street, said it?

"England's buying gold," I tried again. "We've had a private wire. Cut in quick. First National is selling!"

Great-faced Hephæstus, how ridiculous! It was like saying, "I'll take your scalp unless you give me meat." It was barbaric, savage, centuries ago. Again there came another voice that caught up my own and turned it into common syntax. Some heady beauty of the Earth rose about me like a cloud.

"Hark! Night comes, with the dusk upon her eyelids. She brings those dreams that every dew-drop holds at dawn. Daughter of Thanatos and Hypnos . . . !"

But again—who said the words? It surely was not Arthur, my nephew Arthur, of To-day, learning French in a Swiss mountain village! I felt—well, what did I feel? In the name of the Stock Exchange and Wall Street, what was the cash surrender of amazing feelings?

III

And, turning to look at him, I made a discovery. I don't know how to tell it quite; such shadowy marvels have never been my line of goods. He looked several things at once—taller, slighter, sweeter, but chiefly—it sounds so crazy when I write it down—grander is the word, I think. And all spread out with some power that flowed like spring when it pours upon a landscape. Eternally young and glorious—young, I mean, in the sense of a field of flowers in the spring looks young; and glorious in the sense the sky looks glorious at dawn or sunset. Something big shone through him like a storm, something that would go on for ever just as the Earth goes on, always renewing itself, something of gigantic life that in the human sense could never age at all—something the old gods had. But the figure, so far as there was any figure at all, was that old family picture come to life. Our great ancestor and Arthur were one being, and that one being was vaster than a million people. Yet it was Malahide I saw. . . .

"They laid me in the earth I loved," he said in a strange, thrilling voice like running wind and water, "and I found eternal life. I live now for ever in Their divine existence. I share the life that changes yet can never pass away."

I felt myself rising like a cloud as he said it. A roaring beauty captured me completely. I could tell it in honest newspaper language—the common language used in flats and offices—why, I guess I could patent a new meaning in ordinary words, a new power of expression, the thing that all the churches and poets and thinkers have been trying to say since the world began. I caught on to a fact so fine and simple that it knocked me silly to think I'd never realised it before. I had read it, yes; but now I *knew* it. The Earth, the whole bustling universe, was nothing after all but a visible production of eternal, living Powers—spiritual powers, mind you—that just happened to include the particular little type of strutting creature we called mankind. And these Powers, as seen in Nature, were the gods. It was our refusal of their grand appeal, so wild and sweet and beautiful, that caused "evil." It was this barrier between ourselves and the rest of . . .

My thoughts and feelings swept away upon the rising flood as the "figure" came upon me like a shaft of moonlight, melting the last remnant of opposition that was in me. I took my brain, my reason, chucking them aside for the futile little mechanism I suddenly saw them to be. In place of them came—oh, God, I hate to say it, for only nursery talk can get within a mile of it, and yet what I need is something simpler even than the words that children use. Under one arm I carried a whole forest breathing in the wind, and beneath the other a hundred meadows full of singing streams with golden marigolds and blue forget-me-nots along their banks. Upon my back and shoulders lay the clouded hills with dew and moonlight in their brimmed, capacious hollows. Thick in my hair hung the unaging powers that are stars and sunlight; though the sun was far away, it sweetened the currents of my blood with liquid gold. Breast and throat and face, as I advanced, met all the rivers of the world and all the winds of heaven, their strength and swiftness melting into me as light melts into everything it touches. And into my eyes passed all the radiant colours that weave the cloth of Nature as she takes the sun.

And this "figure," pouring upon me like a burst of moonlight, spoke:

"They all are in you—air, and fire, and water. . . ."

"And I—my feet stand—on the *Earth,*" my own voice interrupted, deep power lifting through the sound of it.

"The Earth!" He laughed gigantically. He spread. He seemed everywhere about me. He seemed a race of men. My life swam forth in waves of some immense sensation that issued from the mountain and the forest, then returned to them again. I reeled. I clutched at something in me that was slipping beyond control, slipping down a bank towards a deep, dark river flowing at my feet. A shadowy boat appeared, a still more shadowy outline at the helm. I was in the act of stepping into it. For the tree I caught at was only air. I couldn't stop myself. I tried to scream.

"You have plucked asphodel," sang the voice beside me, "and you shall pluck more. . . ."

I slipped and slipped, the speed increasing horribly. Then something caught, as though a cog held fast and stopped me. I remembered my business in New York City.

"Arthur!" I yelled. "Arthur!" I shouted again as hard as I could shout. There was frantic terror in me. I felt as though I should never get back to myself again. Death!

The answer came in his normal voice: "Keep close to me. I know the way. . . ."

The scenery dwindled suddenly; the trees came back. I was walking in the forest beside my nephew, and the moonlight lay in patches and little shafts of silver. The crests of the pines just murmured in a wind that scarcely stirred, and through an opening on our right I saw the deep valley clasped about the twinkling village lights. Towering in splendour the spectral snowfields hung upon the sky, huge summits guarding them. And Arthur took my arm—oh, solidly enough this time. Thank heaven, he asked no questions of me.

"There's a smell of myrrh," he whispered, "and we are very near the undying, ancient things."

I said something about the resin from the trees, but he took no notice.

"It enclosed its body in an egg of myrrh," he went on, smiling down at me; "then, setting it on fire, rose from the ashes with its life renewed. Once every five hundred years, you see—"

"What did?" I cried, feeling that loss of self stealing over me again. And his answer came like a blow between the eyes:

"The Phœnix. They called it a bird, but, of course, the true . . ."

"But my life's insured in that," I cried, for he had named the company that took large yearly premiums from me; "and I pay . . ."

"Your life's insured in *this,*" he said quietly, waving his arms to indicate the Earth. "Your love of Nature and your sympathy with it make you safe." He gazed at me. There was a marvellous expression in his eyes. I understood why poets talked of stars and flowers in a human face. But behind the face crept back another look as well. There grew about his figure an indeterminate extension. The outline of Malahide again stirred through his own. A pale, delicate hand reached out to take my own. And something broke in me.

I was conscious of two things—a burst of joy that meant losing myself entirely, and a rush of terror that meant staying as I was, a small, painful, struggling item of individual life. Another spray of that awful asphodel fell fluttering through the air in front of my face. It rested on the earth against my feet. And Arthur—this weirdly changing Arthur—stooped to pick it for me. I kicked it with my foot beyond his reach . . . then turned and ran as though the Furies of that ancient world were after me. I ran for my very life. How I escaped from that thick wood without banging my body to bits against the trees I can't explain. I ran from something I desired and yet feared. I leaped along in a succession of flying bounds. Each tree I passed turned of its own accord and flung after me until the entire forest followed. But I got out. I reached the open. Upon the sloping field in the full, clear light of the moon I collapsed in a panting heap. The Earth drew back with a great shuddering sigh behind me. There was this strange, tumultuous sound upon the night. I lay beneath the open heavens that were full of moonlight. I was myself—but there were tears in me. Beauty too high for understanding had slipped between my fingers. I had lost Malahide. I had lost the gods of Earth. . . . Yet I had seen . . . and felt. I had not lost all. Something remained that I could never lose again. . . .

I don't know how it happened exactly, but presently I heard Arthur saying: "You'll catch your death of cold you lie on that soaking grass," and felt his hand seize mine to pull me to my feet.

"I feel safer on earth," believe I answered. And then he said: "Yes, but it's such a stupid way to die—a chill!"

IV

I got up then, and we went downhill together towards the village lights. I danced—oh, I admit it—I sang as well. There was a flood of joy and power about me that beat anything I'd ever felt before. I didn't think or hesitate; there was no self-consciousness; I just let it rip for all there was, and if there had been ten thousand people there in front of me, I could have made them feel it too. That was the kind of feeling—power and confidence and a sort of raging happiness. I think I know what it was too. I say this soberly, with reverence . . . all wool and no fading. There was a bit of God in me, God's power that drives the Earth and pours through Nature—the imperishable Beauty expressed in those old-world nature-deities!

And the fear I'd felt was nothing but the little tickling point of losing my ordinary two-cent self, the dread of letting go, the shrinking before the plunge—what a fellow feels when he's falling in love, and hesitates, and tries to think it out and hold back, and is afraid to let the enormous tide flow in and drown him.

Oh, yes, I began to think it over a bit as we raced down the mountain-side that glorious night. I've read some in my day; my brain's all right; I've heard of dual personality and subliminal uprush and conversion—no new line of goods, all that. But somehow these stunts of the psychologists and philosophers didn't cut any ice with me just then, because I'd *experienced* what they merely *explained*. And explanation was just a bargain sale. The best things can't be explained at all. There's no real value in a bargain sale.

Arthur had trouble to keep up with me. We were running due east, and the Earth was turning, therefore, with us. We all three ran together at *her* pace—terrific! The moonlight danced along the summits, and the snow-fields flew like spreading robes, and the forests everywhere, far and near, hung watching us and booming like a thousand organs. There were uncaged winds about; you could hear them whistling among the precipices. But the great thing that I knew was—Beauty, a beauty of the common old familiar Earth, and a beauty that's stayed with me ever since, and given me joy and strength and a source of power and delight I'd never guessed existed before.

As we dropped lower into the thicker air of the valley I sobered down. Gradually the ecstasy passed from me. We slowed up a bit. The lights and the houses and the sight of the hotel where people were dancing in a stuffy ballroom, all this put blotting-paper on something that had been flowing.

Now you'll think this an odd thing too—but when we reached the village street, I just took Arthur's hand and shook it and said good-night and went up to bed and slept like a two-year-old till morning. And from that day to this I've never set eyes on the boy again.

Perhaps it's difficult to explain, and perhaps it isn't. I can explain it to myself in two lines—I was afraid to see him. I was afraid he might "explain." I was afraid he might explain "away." I just left a note—he never replied to it—and went off by a morning train. Can you understand that? Because if you can't you haven't understood this account I've tried to give of the experience Arthur gave me. Well—anyway—I'll just let it go at that.

Arthur's a director now in his father's wholesale chemical business, and I—well, I'm doing better than ever in the buying and selling of exchange between banks in New York City as before.

But when I said I was still drawing dividends on my Swiss investment, I meant it. And it's not "scenery." Everybody gets a thrill from "scenery." It's a darned sight more than that. It's those little wayward patches of blue on a cloudy day; those blue pools in the sky just above Trinity Church steeple when I pass out of Wall Street into Lower Broadway; it's the rustle of the sea-wind among the Battery trees; the wash of the waves when the Ferry's starting for Staten Island, and the glint of the sun far down the Bay, or dropping a bit of pearl into the old East River. And sometimes it's the strip of cloud in the west above the Jersey shore of the Hudson, the first star, the sickle of the new moon behind the masts and shipping. But usually it's something nearer, bigger, simpler than all or any of these. It's just the certainty that, when I hurry along the hard stone pavements from bank to bank, I'm walking on the—Earth. It's just that—*the Earth!*

Proportion

> I have been looking at the stars and thinking what an immense distance they are away. What an insignificant thing the loss of, say, forty years of life is compared with them! It seems scarcely worth talking about. . . .

(*From letter written home by a young officer on June 30. He was killed on July 1.*)

Tired out with business by day and special-constabling by night, Heber contrived a day or two at the sea—what people called before the war a week-end. The town was full of soldiers, nurses, countless figures in blue with crutches, bandages, arm-slings, eye-shades, and the rest. An extraordinarily cheerful lot; he watched them with deep admiration. "If I were younger," he thought, "I should be doing their job, and if they were older they would be doing mine." Self seemed eliminated before two mighty symbols—England and the Empire.

He pictured the little island on the map, so insignificant in size, so unconquerable in spirit. He saw in his mind huge India and the distant Colonies flocking in to help. His thoughts, inspired by the khaki and blue on all sides, ran in this groove, and his mind was crammed with detail he wanted to discuss. But he had no companion, so had to keep his thoughts to himself.

He strolled out after the early hotel dinner, and walked idly along the front. A few convalescents were about. Not a light was visible anywhere. The big stone houses stood in rows with sightless windows—a desolate, deserted town, empty and shuttered. No gleam, no single ray escaped; the blinds were down, the curtains closely drawn, even the hotel front-doors were thickly shaded. The inhabitants, it seemed, had fled. From a mile at sea no one could have known there was anything but a lonely strip of undulating shore.

It was warm. A moon, somewhere between the half and quarter, sank on her side into the quiet sea beyond a headland. Heber sat down in one of the shelters, and began to smoke; and just as he neared the end of his cigarette a figure came shuffling in and sat down a few feet away—a convalescent soldier; even in the dimness the outline was unmistakable, and the broad band of white where the long trousers turned up above the boots gleamed faintly. It was a Tommy, but the voice was cultivated. A Tommy in these days may be anybody. Heber wondered. "Pretty dark, isn't it?" he ventured. "Oh, you get used to that," was the reply. "It's right. In these sheltered coves the submarines are apt to slip up for a breather, and to get their bearings. And the smallest light may help them."

There was something in the voice that made Heber interested. It stirred imagination in him. He thought of the stealthy, prowling underwater life, sneaking to and fro past wrecks and deep-sea fish, striking swift blows that seemed treacherous compared to fighting in the open. He wondered about the psychology of the men who did it. But these thoughts he did not utter. He offered a cigarette instead.

"Oh, that's kind of you. I'd like one. No—better not strike matches here. I'll take a light from yours, if I may." The man, he saw, had one arm in a sling. The face he could not see, beyond that the eyes were shaded with dark glasses.

"Flanders or the East?" he allowed himself to ask sympathetically.

"Gallipoli. A bit of shrapnel," was the brief reply.

"Bad luck."

"Might have been much worse. The eyes are nearly well now. I'd rather lose two legs than one eye." And he laughed lightly. "Sight means a lot to me."

The moon went down, the stars shone thickly, making little tremulous golden pathways on the sea. Heber fell to wondering who the man was, and what he did. He seemed about thirty or thereabouts. Somehow he did not make the impression of a soldier only. "You joined for this war, I suppose?" Heber ventured presently.

"That's right. And then he added, "New Zealand. My father's in sheep." Yet the man himself did not quite sound like "sheep." They smoked in silence for some minutes. Then came: "First time I'd seen these stars." And he began to talk about them. They were familiar to him as though he had lived beneath them all his life. He pointed out

Jupiter and Venus, described the position of Sirius, mentioned Orion, just rising, and referred to the great nebula in his Belt; he knew their various magnitudes, indicated coloured Vega, and another brilliant star that he said was two stars actually, revolving round each other. Stranger still, he spoke of Jupiter's eight moons as though he knew accurately how many would be visible from the earth just now. While he did not say very much, his words were suggestive in some way that made Heber forget the details of the war he had wanted to discuss, and respond involuntarily to this less personal note. "You know quite a lot about the stars," he remarked. "It's fascinating. I'd like to be an astronomer."

"Never tried it, have you?" said the other.

Heber laughed. "Costs too much for one thing—telescopes and so on."

"Telescopes, yes; they do cost a bit. I had one." He mentioned the power, and Heber knew it was not procurable under many thousand pounds. "It was up at my father's place in the hills. Hobby of mine. In fact I did nothing else. I gave it up, though—after a bit." He paused. There was a note of longing in his voice. "The strain was too much, I found." "Health?" enquired his companion. The soldier laughed. "Never had a day's illness in my life till Gallipoli knocked me out." A note of passion crept in somehow. "It was another kind of strain," he went on quietly. He seemed to hesitate. "A kid of strain—on the soul," he finished abruptly.

Heber was not a stupid man; he had an inkling of what the other meant.

"Distance and that kind of thing?" he said understandingly. "Immensity, eh?"

"That's right. I had to give it up. Went back to sheep instead."

"But how did it affect you exactly?" Hebel asked presently, with real interest.

"It's no easy to explain, perhaps," said the soldier who had once been an amateur astronomer by choice, "but—well, once you get into it as deep as I did, you—forget the earth a bit, that's all. It's all right, no doubt, if it's your regular job, paid by Government, I mean, and for a useful purpose. Because then imagination hardly comes into it, does it? But for a hobby—as I did it—imaginatively—trying to *realise*—well, it was too much. Distance, space, number, they're all too vast to mean anything. You're always on the edge of infinity—the mind's always trying to conceive something far beyond its powers. The unit of measurement, you see, is a bit staggering to start with—the distance light travels in a second. And then so many stars whose light takes four or five thousand years to reach us even at that rate—may have gone out when the Sphinx was being carved—yet we still see them—" He stopped abruptly and puffed his cigarette a moment. "It's a bit unsettling," he went on. "Yet that's only a beginning—"

"No words for it are there?" put in Heber.

"That's where the strain comes in," continued the Tommy from New Zealand damaged by Turkish shrapnel. "You get dizzy—unfit for daily life. You get the feeling that nothing matters. You move and think all day against that stupendous background." He turned in the gloom and peered at Heber. "It gets terrifying," he said in a lower voice with conviction. "And I'll tell you why: the intellect knows it can't bridge that gulf, but the soul knows it can. And the soul goes on trying."

"The touch of the infinite, I suppose."

"That's why I went back to sheep."

"Sanity!"

"Why—think of it!—even the biggest telescope can't bring one star near enough to show it as a disc. It is still nothing but a point in space. D'you know how they measure distance, too? Take a triangle with the star you want at the apex. Then measure the two base angles. Only most of the stars are so distant that the earth isn't broad enough to give a base-line. So they take the position of the earth in June, then again in December—the length it's travelled in those six months provides a base-line *just* long enough, perhaps, for the angles to be measurable. Whew! It's appalling, eh? With *that* scale in your mind for six weeks, you're apt to forget that you can't drop out of a second-floor window without breaking something."

"Proportion;" said Heber, feeling that the earth beneath his feet was not of the importance he had always believed.

"Yes, everything's proportion. But that's just where the mind gets unhappy—with such a scale. There's. horror in magnitude of that kind. You feel scared, and think of a paternal deity—it comforts. Not a sparrow falleth, you see, and all that. But that's if you've got belief. If you haven't, you just—shiver. The mind shrinks. You feel so insignificant, it doesn't seem to matter if you live or die, or what you do. You lose proportion, as you said just now—get out of relation with the rest of life. Why, there's not one man in a hundred who knows what you mean when you tell him that our sun is actually in the Milky Way, and if you mention that our own System travels thirty-five million miles every year nearer to a certain star in Hercules, yet Hercules looks the same to-day as it did to Rameses—look no nearer—well, he just says 'Oh,' or 'Really,' and wonders what you mean—luckily for him!"

"And of course, there are dozen of other suns and other solar systems," put in Heber, knowing himself classed with the men who would say "oh," or "really."

"Scores upon scores, enormous, endless, prodigious! It's an awful word—e*ndless!* A big telescope simply frightens you. The Coal-Sack, for instance, where you peep through in to outer space, so called, the only spot in the heavens where it's empty of any stars at all—! Why, our solar system's nothing but a few marbles placed at intervals round a football on some endless prairie compared to—"

"And our earth we think so important," broke in Heber, "one of the smallest planets in it—"

"Covered with a few million two-legged creatures who—are squabbling—and killing each other—"

A man came in at that moment and sat down to smoke on the same bench. A band shone faintly on his sleeve. He was a special constable. The *War*—!

"—having a rough-and-tumble fight on a comparatively small section of it—" the soldier finished his sentence, then hesitated.

For the arrival of the stranger made it difficult to continue talking freely. Heber felt as though he had just dropped from some gigantic height—upon the front of the little English sea-coast town. They got up to go. Heber gave his arm to the wounded soldier. They walked along together beside the quiet sea, beneath the brilliant stars. "It's a good thing," remarked the latter presently, "men's senses are so nicely limited. Still, with bigger powers—say with sight of a million miles or so—the mind would be different too, I suppose. Better as it is, though isn't it?"

They talked a little about the war.

"I almost wonder," ventured Heber, before they parted, "that a fellow with thoughts like yours—enlisted."

"That's just it. That's where proportion comes in. I wouldn't fight for anything less than—*this!*" He turned his shaded eyes towards the sky. "What I'm fighting for, personally, is to keep all this beautiful and fit to live in—" And he added "Good-night," and shuffled off past the Pier towards his Convalescent Home.

Camping Out

I

It was the afternoon of the Longest Day, and on the lawn of the old country house sat Billy, Jill, and Tim—doing nothing.

Billy, aged twelve, was a Boy Scout; he could light a fire with a single match! Jill, aged ten, had chestnut hair and dark-brown eyes, and was so plucky that Billy said she was as plucky as a boy. (Miss Mullins, the jolly governess, and Gooch, the grumpy head gardener, said she was as mischievous as a boy!) Tim, aged eight, was small and gentle. His name suited him rather well, for, though mischievous enough, he was also a little tim-id.

And now, tired of doing nothing, Billy, who was always leader, suddenly sat up and said in a voice of excitement: "Look here, you kids, I tell you what. It's the Longest Day, and we're going to sleep out! We'll *camp!*"

"Billy—but how splendid!" exclaimed Jill.

"Oh, I *say!*" echoed Tim. "Me too?"

"Of course," replied their leader. "Follow me and I'll tell you what to do. Come on!" They went to a quiet corner behind the laurel bushes, where no one would see them plotting mischief. Miss Mullins was reading in the hammock; Gooch was gone to market; Daddy and Mother were out driving. The garden seemed deserted.

"Now, listen," began Billy with authority. "First, we choose a place and make a fire. Then we cook supper, roll up in our blankets, set a watch, and—"

"But we haven't got one," interrupted Jill.

"Oh, not *that* kind," he explained. "We know the time by the stars. Set a watch about the camp, *I* mean. You're best for that," he added, looking down at Tim.

"Rather," cried Tim eagerly, "if I can keep awake."

"You'll have to," said Billy. "Otherwise you'll be shot at dawn for neglect of duty."

"I don't mind," cried Tim; "I'm so small they'd never hit me."

"Now, *do* be serious a minute," continued Billy. "Jill makes the beds and washes up. That's always the woman's job. She's cook too, of course."

Jill didn't care much about the washing up. But cooking she liked. Shepherd's pie, she decided, was the proper dish for a camp.

"*We* catch the supper," Billy went on, interrupting her reflections. "Tim and I do that. We're the hunters."

"What shall we catch?" enquired Tim. "Something with a tail's best, I suppose."

"Why, a fish, or rabbit, or something," said Billy sharply. "Only you ask so many questions! It all depends—" He hesitated.

"I might catch a chicken in the yard with my butterfly-net," suggested Tim.

"Chickens have to be plucked," put in Jill; "it's rather a business. And a rabbit has to be skinned!"

"All right," declared Billy. "Don't make a fuss about nothing. We'll take our grub out with us. That's just as good!"

He made a list at once. Jill was to get them, because she was the cook's favourite and was allowed in the kitchen.

1 loaf.
1 pot of jam, strawberry preferred.
1 jug of milk—full.
2 bottles home-made ginger-beer.
6 eggs, hard-boiled.
1 cake, large plum.
3 apples.
Potatoes to cook in the ashes—a lot.

A second list was also made, Tim to see to everything in it.

1 candle lantern—the stable one would do.
1 newspaper to start the fire.

3 piles of dry bracken for the beds.
3 blankets, one from each bed upstairs.
1 big pile of wood, to be collected before dark.
1 match.

"I'll bring the match," Billy mentioned; "you've got enough to look after with the other things."

"Where's the camp to be?" asked Jill.

"Big cedar," was the prompt reply. "And everything must be there before sunset—hidden carefully, mind—on the north side of the trunk."

"But which *is* the north side?" Jill asked.

"Quite simple," said Billy. "You know the south side, don't you? Well, the north side is just opposite to it, of course." Then, as Jill still looked rather doubtful, he added: "In case you get muddled, there's moss on the north side—moss always grows on the north side of a trunk."

"Shall I bring an umbrella?" Tim wanted to know. "It may rain."

"It mayn't," he replied shortly. "Besides—it won't." He looked at the sky, then held up a wet finger to feel which way the wind was blowing. "It'll be a fine night," he informed them, "and very warm."

"What about dew?" Jill asked finally.

"Under a tree there's *never* any dew," explained Billy. "And the place is simply perfect for a camp. It's got shelter, wood, and water. Now, hide everything so that old Gooch won't notice them. And, remember, I'll come for you both at eleven o'clock when everybody's gone to sleep, and the password is *Look out!*"

Jill repeated the password, then glanced at her little brother. She really mothered both the boys without their knowing it. "Tim won't freeze, will he? Or be frightened?" she asked anxiously.

"Freeze, indeed!" cried Tim indignantly. "Why, I'm always boiling. And I've never been frightened in my life!"

But Billy settled the difficulty at once with his usual confidence. "Look here, you two," he said, as he got up to go, "we shan't be cold, because we shall have a baking fire all night. And you won't be frightened, because—" he finished with an impressive air, "*I* shall be there. *I* know how to take charge of camp, my dear! So look out!"

He made them repeat the password once again, and the next minute was off across the lawn like an arrow from a bow.

II

There was much to be done, and time was rather short. For the next hour or two, figures carrying strange bundles flitted down the passages and went scurrying across the lawn. They whispered, they went on tiptoe, they were very quiet. Each time they met, the password was exchanged: "Look out!" Tim worked hard, collecting bracken and wood; while Jill was in and out of the kitchen so often that the Cook at last remarked: "You're up to something wicked, I'll be bound!" But Jill knew how to manage *that.* "It's very nice of you to let me come," she said with a smile. "I think you're the best cook in the whole world, you know!" At which Mrs. Horton was so pleased that she said no more—*at the moment!*

By tea-time everything was safely "in camp" beneath the cedar; the beds all made, the fire laid, the food hidden under a pile of bracken. Billy examined it all to make sure nothing was forgotten. Some of the things he rejected, however. Tim had brought a tooth-brush, for instance. "Rubbish!" he exclaimed. "Teeth don't matter when you're camping. You might as well bring a concertina!" Jill's little hand-glass he thought might stay. "We can flash signals with it," he explained. "You never know."

There were narrow escapes before the dusk came down and helped to hide their preparations. Gooch went past the cedar once or twice—rather too close to please them. Miss Mullins, too, looked out of the window at tea-time and exclaimed: "But what *have* they been doing to the cedar, children? Look!" Only, luckily, the kitten upset the milk-jug just then, and there was such a fuss that the cedar was forgotten.

"Well done, Smuts!" whispered. Jill in its furry ear, as she stroked and kissed it. "You're on *our* side, aren't you?"

The dusk began to deepen, the shadows fell across the lawn, everything was prepared, and bed-time near. Daddy was saying good-night to Jill and Tim, who went to bed an hour before their older brother. He looked rather searchingly at Tim. Had he guessed anything, they wondered?

"What mischief have you been up to, I'd like to know?" he asked. Tim looked sleepy and made no reply, while Billy whispered the password softly in his brother's ear: "Look out!"

"We *have* got a secret, Daddy," observed Jill discreetly. "But you can't be in it *this* time. P'raps to-morrow you can be, though," she added mysteriously. But Daddy looked so unhappy at being left out that she went on quickly: "You'd be so awfully uncomfortable, we thought—at your age!"

"All right," he said, kissing them both good-night. "Of course I—I don't want to be *too* uncomfortable—at my age." His eyes were rather twinkly, Tim thought. Still, no more was said, and half an hour later Jill and Tim were lying snugly in bed. The room was dark. Through the open window they could see the stars. They lay as still as mice. They whispered together very softly. They waited. They kept a good "look out."

The time passed very slowly. It was only half-past eight, and Billy was to come for them at eleven. There was still light in the western sky, but the first stars were peeping. The bats were out. The owls called softly. The two children whispered to one another across the darkening room.

"I got all *my* list," Jill said in a low voice, and went over them all under her breath. "We'll take the blankets off the beds, of course. I'm so afraid you may be cold, Tim."

"I shall lie close to the fire," her brother murmured. "You can have my blanket—half of it, anyhow. Girls are always cold out of doors."

They went on whispering and thinking. More stars slipped out. The night came slowly; slowly. Tim grew quiet, mumbling his list over to himself to make quite sure he had remembered everything. "I do hope Billy won't forget to come for us," he said, as he lay back on the pillow. Jill replied that of course he wouldn't. "It's after nine now. They've finished dinner, I expect. I'll just pop out to the head of the stairs and see what's up." Tim told her to come back soon, and watched her tiptoe out in her white night-gown.

And when she was gone, he sat up in bed and listened. A sound of distant voices rose from the lower part of the house. That meant that Daddy and Mother and Aunt Eliza were going across the hall into the drawing-room. How far away it seemed! The daylight seemed far away too. He heard the night-wind sighing past the window. He got out of bed, flattened his nose against the glass, and stared out into the garden. And a little shiver ran down his back. The lawn and cedar—how dim and mysterious they looked! He wondered how it would feel to be out there, away from the friendly walls and cosy bed. A thrill ran through him. And then, suddenly, he saw a figure moving too. He was sure of it. He watched a moment. It came swiftly over the lawn, and vanished beneath the blackness under the cedar. It looked like Gooch. It seemed to him a little light—like a lantern—accompanied it. He ran back into bed, and dived beneath the sheets. He lay very still.

And when Jill came back softly on tiptoe, whispering that everybody was safely in the drawing-room, and that she had met Billy going to his room, Tim poked his nose out to ask a question: "I say, Jill, it's awfully dark out there. I saw some one moving by the cedar; I believe it was old Gooch."

She ran to the window and looked out. "There's no one there now," she reported. "It must have been a shadow, Tim. There are lots of shadows about. It's nothing." She tucked him up tightly, and watched him cuddle down into bed again. "Look here, Tim," she whispered, "you go to sleep, and I'll wake you just before eleven when we dress for Billy."

Tim turned over, curled up, and a few minutes later was as quiet as a turnip lying in a field. Jill watched him for some time, then got into bed herself, and waited—and waited—and waited. She heard the clock strike ten. She heard the quarter. She also heard the half-hour, but only *just*, for other noises were murmuring inside her head and she felt drowsy. "I hope Tim won't be frightened," she said to herself; and then she, too, lay very still in her warm and cosy bed. And, while she lay thus, the soft fingers of the Night, tipped with starshine, pressed gently on her eyelids. The room was very quiet. The world lay asleep.

Down in the hall the gilt clock struck eleven; and as the sound died away a figure came quietly along the passage, and peeped round the door. First the head came in, then the shoulders, next the legs and body. It was Billy. He was half undressed; in one hand he held a matchbox. He moved softly to each bed in turn.

"Asleep!" he whispered. "I thought they would be!" He shrugged his shoulders. But, strange to say, he didn't seem annoyed!

Then he crossed to the window and looked out. The garden lay in shadow. It was a lovely night; but—it was awfully dark!

He thought a moment, hesitating; then glanced at his little brother. "It's a bit late for him," he reflected doubtfully. He went to the other bed, and at that moment he heard a door bang down below. Some one was about! He stood a moment, listening and wondering, then stooped down and looked at his sister's tight-closed eyes. He straightened up. He came to a decision.

"Better not wake them now," he thought. "We'll camp out when there's a moon. It's stupid of 'em to go to sleep like this and spoil it all! But still, it *is* awfully dark."

And he tiptoed out again, and hurried down the long dark passage to his own bedroom. Another door banged softly as he went. It sounded like the outside door—the door on to the lawn! Half an hour later, when the gilt clock sounded across the deserted hall, he too lay very quiet, asleep and dreaming.

Next day, of course, there were explanations! The children discussed their preparations all over again. They meant to camp out the moment there was a moon. They said so *most* distinctly.

But—it was *very* odd—everything had gone from under the cedar! Miss Mullins said nothing; Gooch knew nothing; the cook was silent—and, naturally, the children couldn't ask questions! Daddy, however, said a mysterious thing as he left to catch the train. He said it in rhyme, so of course it wasn't serious:

"Beneath the cedar, in the dark,
They lay and caught their death of cold;
They said they did it for a lark,
And thought that nobody would scold!
But in the night somebody came
And carted all the things away,
Because, you see, the Camping Game
Was really better played—by *day!*"

The Tryst

"Je suis la première au rendez-vous. Je vous attends."

As he got out of the train at the little wayside station he remembered the conversation as if it had been yesterday, instead of fifteen years ago—and his heart went thumping against his ribs so violently that he almost heard it. The original thrill came over him again with all its infinite yearning. He felt it as he had felt it *then*—not with that tragic lessening the interval had brought to each repetition of its memory. Here, in the familiar scenery of its birth, he realised with mingled pain and wonder that the subsequent years had not destroyed, but only dimmed it. The forgotten rapture flamed back with all the fierce beauty of its genesis, desire at white heat. And the shock of the abrupt discovery shattered time. Fifteen years became a negligible moment; the crowded experiences that had intervened seemed but a dream. The farewell scene, the conversation on the steamer's deck, were clear as of the day before. He saw the hand holding her big hat that fluttered in the wind, saw the flowers on the dress where the long coat was blown open a moment, recalled the face of a hurrying steward who had jostled them; he even heard the voices—his own and hers:

"Yes," she said simply, "I promise you. You have my word. I'll wait—"

"Till I come back to find you," he interrupted.

Steadfastly she repeated his actual words, then added: "Here; at home—that is."

"I'll come to the garden gate as usual," he told her, trying to smile. "I'll knock. You'll open the gate—as usual—and come out to me."

These words, too, she attempted to repeat, but her voice failed, her eyes filled suddenly with tears; she looked into his face and nodded. It was just then that her little hand went up to hold the hat on—he saw the very gesture still. He remembered that he was vehemently tempted to tear his ticket up there and then, to go ashore with her, to stay in England, to brave all opposition—when the siren roared its third horrible warning . . . and the ship put out to sea.

Fifteen years, thick with various incident, had passed between them since that moment. His life had risen, fallen, crashed, then risen again. He had come back at last, fortune won by a lucky coup—at thirty-five; had come back to find her, come back, above all, to keep his word. Once every three months they had exchanged the brief letter agreed upon: "I am well; I am waiting; I am happy; I am unmarried. Yours—." For his youthful wisdom had insisted that no "man" had the right to keep "any woman" too long waiting; and she, thinking that letter brave and splendid, had insisted likewise that he was free—if freedom called him. They had laughed over this last phrase in their agreement. They put five years as the possible limit of separation. By then he would have won success, and obstinate parents would have nothing more to say.

But when the five years ended he was "on his uppers" in a western mining town, and with the end of ten in sight those uppers, though changed, were little better, apparently, than patched and mended. And it was just then, too, that the change which had been stealing over him betrayed itself. He realised it abruptly, a sense of shame and horror in him. The discovery was made unconsciously—it disclosed itself. He was reading her letter as a labourer on a Californian fruit farm: "Funny she doesn't marry—some one else!" he heard himself say. The words were out before he knew it, and certainly before he could suppress them. They just slipped out, startling him into the truth; and he knew instantly that the thought was fathered in him by a hidden wish. . . . He was older. He had lived. It was a memory he loved.

Despising himself in a contradictory fashion—both vaguely and fiercely—he yet held true to his boyhood's promise. He did not write and offer to release her, as he knew they did in stories. He persuaded himself that he meant to keep his word. There was this fine, stupid, selfish obstinacy in his character. In any case, she would misunderstand and think he wanted to set free—himself. "Besides—I'm still—awfully fond of her," he asserted. And it was true; only the love, it seemed, had gone its way. Not that another woman took it; he kept himself clean, held firm as steel. The love, apparently, just faded of its own accord; her image dimmed, her letters ceased to thrill, then ceased to interest him.

Subsequent reflection made him realise other details about himself. In the interval he had suffered hardships, had learned the uncertainty of life that depends for its continuance on a little food, but that food often hard to come by, and had seen so many others go under that he held it more cheaply than of old. The wandering instinct, too, had caught him, slowly killing the domestic impulse; he lost his desire for a settled place of abode, the desire for children of his own, lost the desire to marry at all. Also—he reminded himself with a smile—he had lost other things: the expression of youth *she* was accustomed to and held always in her thoughts of him, two fingers of one hand, his hair! He wore glasses, too. The gentlemen-adventurers of life get scarred in those wild places where he lived. He saw himself a rather battered specimen well on the way to middle age.

There was confusion in his mind, however, *and* in his heart: a struggling complex of emotions that made it difficult to know exactly what he did feel. The dominant clue concealed itself. Feelings shifted. A single, clear determinant did not offer. He was an honest fellow. "I can't quite make it out," he said. "What is it I really feel? And why?" His motive seemed confused. To keep the flame alight for ten long buffeting years was no small achievement; better men had succumbed in half the time. Yet something in him still held fast to the girl as with a band of steel that *would* not let her go entirely. Occasionally there came strong reversions, when he ached with longing, yearning, hope; when he loved her again; remembered passionately each detail of the far-off courtship days in the forbidden rectory garden beyond the small, white garden gate. Or was it merely the image and the memory he loved "again"? He hardly knew himself. He could not tell. That "again" puzzled him. It was the wrong word surely. . . . He still wrote the promised letter, however; it was so easy; those short sentences could not betray the dead or dying fires. One day, besides, he would return and claim her. He meant to keep his word.

And he had kept it. Here he was, this calm September afternoon, within three miles of the village where he first had kissed her, where the marvel of first love had come to both; three short miles between him and the little white garden gate of which at this very moment she was intently thinking, and behind which some fifty minutes later she would be standing, waiting for him. . . .

He had purposely left the train at an earlier station; he would walk over in the dusk, climb the familiar steps, knock at the white gate in the wall as of old, utter the promised words, "I have come back to find you," enter, and—keep his word. He had written from Mexico a week before he sailed; he had made careful, even accurate calculations: "In the dusk, on the sixteenth of September, I shall come and knock," he added to the usual sentences. The knowledge of his coming, therefore, had been in her possession seven days. Just before sailing, moreover, he had heard from her—though not in answer, naturally. She was well; she was happy; she was unmarried; she was waiting.

And now, as by some magical process of restoration—possible to deep hearts only, perhaps, though even by them quite inexplicable—the state of first love had blazed up again in him. In all its radiant beauty it lit his heart, burned unextinguished in his soul, set body and mind on fire. The years had merely veiled it. It burst upon him, captured, overwhelmed him with the suddenness of a dream. He stepped from the train. He met it in the face. It took him prisoner. The familiar trees and hedges, the unchanged countryside, the "field-smells known in infancy," all these, with something subtly added to them, rolled back the passion of his youth upon him in a flood. No longer was he bound upon what he deemed, perhaps, an act of honourable duty; it was love that drove him, as it drove him fifteen years before. And it drove him with the accumulated passion of desire long forcibly repressed; almost as if, out of some fancied notion of fairness to the girl, he had deliberately, yet still unconsciously, said "No" to it; that *she* had not faded, but that he had decided, "*I* must forget her." That sentence: "Why doesn't she marry—some one else?" had not betrayed change in himself. It surprised another motive: "It's not fair to—her!"

His mind worked with a curious rapidity, but worked within one circle only. The stress of sudden emotion was extraordinary. He remembered a thousand things—yet, chief among them, those occasional reversions when he had felt he "loved her again." Had he not, after all, deceived himself? Had she ever really "faded" at all? Had he not felt he ought to let her fade—release her that way? And the change in himself?—that sentence on the Californian fruit-farm—what did they mean? Which had been true, the fading or the love?

The confusion in his mind was hopeless, but, as a matter of fact, he did not think at all: he only *felt.* The momentum, besides, was irresistible, and before the shattering onset of the sweet revival he did not stop to analyse the strange result. He knew certain things, and cared to know no others: that his heart was leaping, his blood running with the heat of twenty, that joy recaptured him, that he must see, hear, touch her, hold her in his arms—and marry her. For the fifteen years had crumbled to a little thing, and at thirty-five he felt himself but twenty, rapturously, deliciously in love.

He went quickly, eagerly down the little street to the inn, still feeling only, not thinking anything. The vehement uprush of the old emotion made reflection of any kind impossible. He gave no further thought to those long years "out there," when her name, her letters, the very image of her in his mind, had found him, if not cold, at least without keen response. All that was forgotten as though it had not been. The steadfast thing in him, this strong holding to a promise which had never wilted, ousted the recollection of fading and decay that, whatever caused them, certainly *had* existed. And this steadfast thing now took command. This enduring quality in his character led him. It was only towards the end of the hurried tea he first received the singular impression—vague, indeed, but undeniably persistent—the strange impression that he was *being* led.

Yet, though aware of this, he did not pause to argue or reflect. The emotional displacement in him, of course, had been more than considerable: there had been upheaval, a change whose abruptness was even dislocating, fundamental in a sense he could not estimate—shock. Yet he took no count of anything but the one mastering desire to get to her as soon as possible, knock at the small, white garden gate, hear her answering voice, see the low wooden door swing open—take her. There was joy and glory in his heart, and a yearning sweet delight. At this very moment she was expecting him. And he—had come.

Behind these positive emotions, however, there lay concealed all the time others that were of a negative character. Consciously, he was not aware of them, but they were there; they revealed their presence in various little ways that puzzled him. He recognised them absentmindedly, as it were; did not analyse or investigate them. For, through the confusion upon his faculties, rose also a certain hint of insecurity that betrayed itself by a slight hesitancy or miscalculation in one or two unimportant actions. There was a touch of melancholy, too, a sense of something lost. It lay, perhaps, in that tinge of sadness which accompanies the twilight of an autumn day, when a gentler, mournful beauty veils a greater beauty that is past. Some trick of memory connected it with a scene of early boyhood, when, meaning to see the sunrise, he overslept, and, by a brief half-hour, was just—too late. He noted it merely, then passed on; he did not understand it; he hurried all the more, this hurry the only sign that it *was* noted. "I must be quick," flashed up across his strongly positive emotions.

And, due to this hurry, possibly, were the slight miscalculations that he made. They were very trivial. He rang for sugar, though the bowl stood just before his eyes, yet when the girl came in he forgot completely what he rang for—and enquired instead about the evening trains to London. And, when the time-table was laid before him, he examined it without intelligence, then looked up suddenly into the maid's face with a question about flowers. Were there flowers to be had in the village anywhere? What kind of flowers? "Oh, a bouquet or a"—he hesitated, searching for a word that tried to present itself, yet was not the word *he* wanted to make use of—"or a wreath—of some sort?" he finished. He took the very word he did not want to take. In several things he did and said, this hesitancy and miscalculation betrayed themselves—such trivial things, yet significant in an elusive way that he disliked. There was sadness, insecurity somewhere in them. And he resented them, aware of their existence only because they qualified his joy. There was a whispered "No" floating somewhere in the dusk. Almost he felt disquiet. He hurried, more and more eager to be off upon his journey—the final part of it.

Moreover, there were other signs of an odd miscalculation—dislocation, perhaps, properly speaking—in him. Though the inn was familiar from his boyhood days, kept by the same old couple, too, he volunteered no information about himself, nor asked a single question about the village he was bound for. He did not even enquire if the rector—her father—still were living. And when he left he entirely neglected the gilt-framed mirror above the mantelpiece of plush, dusty pampas-grass in waterless vases on either side. It did not matter, apparently, whether he looked well or ill, tidy or untidy. He forgot that when his cap was off the absence of thick, accustomed hair must alter him considerably, forgot also that two fingers were missing from one hand, the right hand, the hand that she would presently clasp. Nor did it occur to him that he wore glasses, which must change his expression and add to the appearance of the years he bore. None of these obvious and natural things seemed to come into his thoughts at all. He was in a hurry to be off. He did not think. But, though his mind may not have noted these slight betrayals with actual sentences, his attitude, nevertheless, expressed them. This was, it seemed, the *feeling* in him: "What could such details matter to her *now?* Why, indeed, should he give to them a single thought? It was himself she loved and waited for, not separate items of his external, physical image." As well think of the fact that she, too, must have altered—outwardly. It never once occurred to him. Such details were of To-day. . . . He was only impatient to come to her quickly, very quickly, instantly, if possible. He hurried.

There was a flood of boyhood's joy in him. He paid for his tea, giving a tip that was twice the price of the meal, and set out gaily and impetuously along the winding lane. Charged to the brim with a sweet picture of a small, white garden gate, the loved face close behind it, he went forward at a headlong pace, singing "Nancy Lee" as he used to sing it fifteen years before.

With action, then, the negative sensations hid themselves, obliterated by the positive ones that took command. The former, however, merely lay concealed; they waited. Thus, perhaps, does vital emotion, overlong restrained, denied, indeed, of its blossoming altogether, take revenge. Repressed elements in his psychic life asserted themselves, selecting, as though naturally, a dramatic form.

The dusk fell rapidly, mist rose in floating strips along the meadows by the stream; the old, familiar details beckoned him forwards, then drove him from behind as he went swiftly past them. He recognised others rising through the thickening air beyond; they nodded, peered, and whispered; sometimes they almost sang. And each added to his inner happiness; each brought its sweet and precious contribution, and built it into the reconstructed picture of the earlier, long-forgotten rapture. It was an enticing and enchanted journey that he made, something impossibly blissful in it, something, too, that seemed curiously—inevitable.

For the scenery had not altered all these years, the details of the country were unchanged, everything he saw was rich with dear and precious association, increasing the momentum of the tide that carried him along. Yonder was the stile over whose broken step he had helped her yesterday, and there the slippery plank across the stream where she looked above her shoulder to ask for his support; he saw the very bramble bushes where she scratched her hand, a-blackberrying, the day before . . . and, finally, the weather-stained signpost, "To the Rectory." It pointed to the path through the dangerous field where Farmer Sparrow's bull provided such a sweet excuse for holding, leading—protecting her. From the entire landscape rose a steam of recent memory, each incident alive, each little detail brimmed with its cargo of fond association.

He read the rough black lettering on the crooked arm—it was rather faded, but he knew it too well to miss a single letter—and hurried forward along the muddy track; he looked about him for a sign of Farmer Sparrow's bull; he even felt in the misty air for the little hand that he might take and lead her into safety. The thought of her drew him on with such irresistible anticipation that it seemed as if the cumulative drive of vanished and unsated years evoked the tangible phantom almost. He actually felt it, soft and warm and clinging in his own, that was no longer incomplete and mutilated.

Yet it was not he who led and guided now, but, more and more, he who was being led. The hint had first betrayed its presence at the inn; it now openly declared itself. It had crossed the frontier into a positive sensation. Its growth, swiftly increasing all this time, had accomplished itself; he had ignored, somehow, both its genesis and quick development; the result he plainly recognised. She was expecting him, indeed, but it was more than expectation; there was calling in it—she summoned him. Her thought and longing reached him along that old, invisible track love builds so easily between true, faithful hearts. All the forces of her being, her very voice, came towards him through the deepening autumn twilight. He had not noticed the curious physical restoration in his hand, but he was vividly aware of this more magical alteration—that *she* led and guided him, drawing him ever more swiftly towards the little, white garden gate where she stood at this very moment, waiting. Her sweet strength compelled him; there was this new touch of something irresistible about the familiar journey, where formerly had been delicious yielding only, shy, tentative advance. He realised it—inevitable.

His footsteps hurried, faster and ever faster; so deep was the allurement in his blood, he almost ran. He reached the narrow, winding lane, and raced along it. He knew each bend, each angle of the holly hedge, each separate incident of ditch and stone. He could have plunged blindfold down it at top speed. The familiar perfumes rushed at him—dead leaves and mossy earth and ferns and dock leaves, bringing the bewildering currents of strong emotion in him all together as in a rising wave. He saw, then, the crumbling wall, the cedars topping it with spreading branches, the chimneys of the rectory. On his right bulked the outline of the old, grey church; the twisted, ancient yews, the company of gravestones, upright and leaning, dotting the ground like listening figures. But he looked at none of these. For, on his left, he already saw the five rough steps of stone that led from the lane towards a small, white garden gate. That gate at last shone before him, rising through the misty air. He reached it.

He stopped dead a moment. His heart, it seemed, stopped too, then took to violent hammering in his brain. There was a roaring in his mind, and yet a marvellous silence—just behind it. Then the roar of emotion died away. There was utter stillness. This stillness, silence, was all about him. The world seemed preternaturally quiet.

But the pause was too brief to measure. For the tide of emotion had receded only to come on again with redoubled power. He turned, leaped forward, clambered impetuously up the rough stone steps, and flung himself, breathless and exhausted, against the trivial barrier that stood between his eyes and—hers. In his wild, half violent impatience, however, he stumbled. That roaring, too, confused him. He fell forward, it seemed, for twilight had merged in darkness, and he misjudged the steps, the distances he yet knew so well. For a moment, certainly, he lay at full length upon the uneven ground against the wall; the steps had tripped him. And then he raised himself and knocked. His right hand struck upon the small, white garden gate. Upon the two lost fingers he felt the impact. "I am here," he cried, with a deep sound in his throat as though utterance was choked and difficult. "I have come back—to find you."

For a fraction of a second he waited, while the world stood still and waited with him. But there was no delay. Her answer came at once: "I am well. . . . I am happy. . . . I am waiting."

And the voice was dear and marvellous as of old. Though the words were strange, reminding him of something dreamed, forgotten, lost, it seemed, he did not take special note of them. He only wondered that she did not open instantly that he might see her. Speech could follow, but sight came surely first! There was this lightning-flash of disappointment in him. Ah, she was lengthening out the marvellous moment, as often and often she had done before. It was to tease him that she made him wait. He knocked again; he pushed against the unyielding surface. For he noticed that it was unyielding; and there was a depth in the tender voice that he could not understand.

"Open!" he cried again, but louder than before. "I have come back to find you!" And as he said it the mist struck cold and thick against his face.

But her answer froze his blood.

"I cannot open."

And a sudden anguish of despair rose over him; the sound of her voice was strange; in it was faintness, distance—as well as depth. It seemed to echo. Something frantic seized him then—the panic sense.

"Open, open! Come out to me!" he tried to shout. His voice failed oddly; there was no power in it. Something appalling struck him between the eyes. "For God's sake, open. I'm waiting here! Open, and come out to me!"

The reply was muffled by distance that already seemed increasing; he was conscious of freezing cold about him—in his heart.

"I cannot open. You must come in to me. I'm here and—waiting—always."

He knew not exactly then what happened, for the cold grew deeper and the icy mist was in his throat. No words would come. He rose to his knees, and from his knees to his feet. He stooped. With all his force he knocked again; in a blind frenzy of despair he hammered and beat against the unyielding barrier of the small, white garden gate. He battered it till the skin of his knuckles was torn and bleeding—the first two fingers of a hand already mutilated. He remembers the torn and broken skin, for he noticed in the gloom that stains upon the gate bore witness to his violence; it was not till afterwards that he remembered the other fact—that the hand had already suffered mutilation, long, long years ago. The power of sound was feebly in him; he called aloud; there was no answer. He tried to scream, but the scream was muffled in his throat before it issued properly; it was a nightmare scream. As a last resort he flung himself bodily upon the unyielding gate, with such precipitate violence, moreover, that his face struck against its surface.

From the friction, then, along the whole length of his cheek he knew that the surface was not smooth. Cold and rough that surface was; but also—it was not of wood. Moreover, there was writing on it he had not seen before. How he deciphered it in the gloom, he never knew. The lettering was deeply cut. Perhaps he traced it with his fingers; his right hand certainly lay stretched upon it. He made out a name, a date, a broken verse from the Bible, and the words, "died peacefully." The lettering was sharply cut with edges that were new. For the date was of a week ago; the broken verse ran, "When the shadows flee away . . ." and the small, white garden gate was unyielding because it was of—stone.

At the inn he found himself staring at a table from which the tea things had not been cleared away. There was a railway time-table in his hands, and his head was bent forwards over it, trying to decipher the lettering in the growing twilight. Beside him, still fingering a shilling, stood the serving-girl; her other hand held a brown tray with a running dog painted upon its dented surface. It swung to and fro a little as she spoke, evidently continuing a conversation her customer had begun. For she was giving information—in the colourless, disinterested voice such persons use:

"We all went to the funeral, sir, all the country people went. The grave was her father's—the family grave. . . ." Then, seeing that her customer was too absorbed in the time-table to listen further, she said no more but began to pile the tea things on to the tray with noisy clatter.

Ten minutes later, in the road, he stood hesitating. The signal at the station just opposite was already down. The autumn mist was rising. He looked along the winding road that melted away into the distance, then slowly turned and reached the platform just as the London train came in. He felt very old—too old to walk six miles. . . .

The Touch of Pan

I

An idiot, Heber understood, was a person in whom intelligence had been arrested—instinct acted, but not reason. A lunatic, on the other hand, was some one whose reason had gone awry—the mechanism of the brain was injured. The lunatic was out of relation with his environment; the idiot had merely been delayed *en route.*

Be that as it might, he knew at any rate that a lunatic was not to be listened to, whereas an idiot—well, the one he fell in love with certainly had the secret of some instinctual knowledge that was not only joy, but a kind of sheer natural joy. Probably it was that sheer natural joy of living that reason argues to be untaught, degraded. In any case—at thirty—he married her instead of the daughter of a duchess he was engaged to. They lead to-day that happy, natural, vagabond life called idiotic, unmindful of that world the majority of reasonable people live only to remember.

Though born into an artificial social clique that made it difficult, Heber had always loved the simple things. Nature, especially, meant much to him. He would rather see a woodland misty with bluebells than all the châteaux on the Loire; the thought of a mountain valley in the dawn made his feet lonely in the grandest houses. Yet in these very houses was his home established. Not that he under-estimated worldly things—their value was too obvious—but that it was another thing he wanted. Only he did not know precisely *what* he wanted until this particular idiot made it plain.

Her case was a mild one, possibly; the title bestowed by implication rather than by specific mention. Her family did not say that she was imbecile or half-witted, but that she "was not all there" they probably did say. Perhaps she saw men as trees walking, perhaps she saw through a glass darkly. Heber, who had met her once or twice, though never yet to speak to, did not analyse her degree of sight, for in him, personally, she woke a secret joy and wonder that almost involved a touch of awe. The part of her that was not "all there" dwelt in an "elsewhere" that he longed to know about. He wanted to share it with her. She seemed aware of certain happy and desirable things that reason and too much thinking hide.

He just felt this instinctively without analysis. The values they set upon the prizes of life were similar. Money to her was just stamped metal, fame a loud noise of sorts, position nothing. Of people she was aware as a dog or bird might be aware—they were kind or unkind. Her parents, having collected much metal and achieved position, proceeded to make a loud noise of sorts with some success; and since she did not contribute, either by her appearance or her tastes, to their ambitions, they neglected her and made excuses. They were ashamed of her existence. Her father in particular justified Nietzsche's shrewd remark that no one with a loud voice can listen to subtle thoughts.

She was, perhaps, sixteen—for, though she looked it, eighteen or nineteen was probably more in accord with her birth certificate. Her mother was content, however, that she should dress the lesser age, preferring to tell strangers that she was childish, rather than admit that she was backward.

"You'll never marry at all, child, much less marry as you might," she said, "if you go about with that rabbit expression on your face. That's not the way to catch a nice young man of the sort we get down to stay with us now. Many a chorus-girl with less than you've got has caught them easily enough. Your sister's done well. Why not do the same? There's nothing to be shy or frightened about."

"But I'm not shy or frightened, mother. I'm bored. I mean *they* bore me."

It made no difference to the girl; she was herself. The bored expression in the eyes—the rabbit, not-all-there expression—gave place sometimes to another look. Yet not often, nor with anybody. It was this other look that stirred the strange joy in the man who fell in love with her. It is not to be easily described. It was very wonderful. Whether sixteen or nineteen, she then looked—a thousand.

* * *

The house-party was of that up-to-date kind prevalent in Heber's world. Husbands and wives were not asked together. There was a cynical disregard of the decent (not the stupid) conventions that savoured of abandon, perhaps of decadence. He only went himself in the hope of seeing the backward daughter once again. Her millionaire parents afflicted him, the smart folk tired him. Their peculiar affectation of a special language, their strange belief that they were of importance, their treatment of the servants, their calculated self-indulgence, all jarred upon him more than usual. At bottom he heartily despised the whole vapid set. He felt uncomfortable and out of place. Though not a prig, he abhorred the way these folk believed themselves the climax of fine living. Their open immorality disgusted him, their indiscriminate love-making was merely rather nasty; he watched the very girl he was at last to settle down with behaving as the tone of the clique expected over her final fling—and, bored by the strain of so much "modernity," he tried to get away. Tea was long over, the sunset interval invited, he felt hungry for trees and fields that were not self-conscious—and he escaped. The flaming June day was turning chill. Dusk hovered over the ancient house, veiling the pretentious new wing that had been added. And he came across the idiot girl at the bend of the drive, where the birch trees shivered in the evening wind. His heart gave a leap.

She was leaning against one of the dreadful statues—it was a satyr—that sprinkled the lawn. Her back was to him; she gazed at a group of broken pine trees in the park beyond. He paused an instant, then went on quickly, while his mind scurried to recall her name. They were within easy speaking range.

"Miss Elizabeth!" he cried, yet not too loudly lest she might vanish as suddenly as she had appeared. She turned at once. Her eyes and lips were smiling welcome at him without pretence. She showed no surprise.

"You're the first one of the lot who's said it properly," she exclaimed, as he came up. "Everybody calls me Elizabeth instead of Elspeth. It's idiotic. They don't even take the trouble to get a name right."

"It is," he agreed. "Quite idiotic." He did not correct her. Possibly he had said Elspeth after all—the names were similar. Her perfectly natural voice was grateful to his ear, and soothing. He looked at her all over with an open admiration that she noticed and, without concealment, liked. She was very untidy, the grey stockings on her vigorous legs were torn, her short skirt was spattered with mud. Her nut-brown hair, glossy and plentiful, flew loose about neck and shoulders. In place of the usual belt she had tied a coloured handkerchief round her waist. She wore no hat. What she had been doing to get in such a state, while her parents entertained a "distinguished" party, he did not know, but it was not difficult to guess. Climbing trees or riding bareback and astride was probably the truth. Yet her dishevelled state became her well, and the welcome in her face delighted him. She remembered him, she was glad. He, too, was glad, and a sense both happy and reckless stirred in his heart. "Like a wild animal," he said, "you come out in the dusk—"

"To play with my kind," she answered in a flash, throwing him a glance of invitation that made his blood go dancing.

He leaned against the statue a moment, asking himself why this young Cinderella of a parvenu family delighted him when all the London beauties left him cold. There was a lift through his whole being as he watched her, slim and supple, grace shining through the untidy modern garb—almost as though she wore no clothes. He thought of a panther standing upright. Her poise was so alert—one arm upon the marble ledge, one leg bent across the other, the hip-line showing like a bird's curved wing. Wild animal or bird, flashed across his mind: something untamed and natural. Another second, and she might leap away—or spring into his arms.

It was a deep, stirring sensation in him that produced the mental picture. "Pure and natural," a voice whispered with it in his heart, "as surely as *they* are just the other thing!" And the thrill struck with unerring aim at the very root of that unrest he had always known in the state of life to which he was called. She made it natural, clean, and pure. This girl and himself were somehow kin. The primitive thing broke loose in him.

In two seconds, while he stood with her beside the vulgar statue, these thoughts passed through his mind. But he did not at first give utterance to any of them. He spoke more formally, although laughter, due to his happiness, lay behind:

"They haven't asked you to the party, then? Or you don't care about it? Which is it?"

"Both," she said, looking fearlessly into his face. "But I've been here ten minutes already. Why were you so long?"

This outspoken honesty was hardly what he expected, yet in another sense he was not surprised. Her eyes were very penetrating, very innocent, very frank. He felt her as clean and sweet as some young fawn that asks plainly to be stroked and fondled. He told the truth: "I couldn't get away before. I had to play about and—" when she interrupted with impatience:

"*They* don't really want you," she exclaimed scornfully. "I do."

And, before he could choose one out of the several answers that rushed into his mind, she nudged him with her foot, holding it out a little so that he saw the shoelace was unfastened. She nodded her head towards it, and pulled her skirt up half an inch as he at once stooped down.

"And, anyhow," she went on as he fumbled with the lace, touching her ankle with his hand, "you're going to marry one of them. I read it in the paper. It's idiotic. You'll be miserable."

The blood rushed to his head, but whether owing to his stooping or to something else, he could not say.

"I only came—I only accepted," he said quickly, "because I wanted to see *you* again."

"Of course. I made mother ask you."

He did an impulsive thing. Kneeling as he was, he bent his head a little lower and suddenly kissed the soft grey stocking—then stood up and looked her in the face. She was laughing happily, no sign of embarrassment in her anywhere, no trace of outraged modesty. She just looked very pleased.

"I've tied a knot that won't come undone in a hurry—" he began, then stopped dead. For as he said it, gazing into her smiling face, another expression looked forth at him from the two big eyes of hazel. Something rushed from his heart to meet it. It may have been that playful kiss, it may have been the way she took it; but, at any rate, there was a strength in the new emotion that made him unsure of who he was and of whom he looked at. He forgot the place, the time, his own identity and hers. The lawn swept from beneath his feet, the English sunset with it. He forgot his host and hostess, his fellow guests, even his father's name and his own into the bargain. He was carried away upon a great tide, the girl always beside him. He left the shore-line in the distance, already half forgotten, the shore-line of his education, learning, manners, social point of view—everything to which his father had most carefully brought him up as the scion of an old-established English family. This girl had torn up the anchor. Only the anchor had previously been loosened a little by his own unconscious and restless efforts. . . .

Where was she taking him to? Upon what island would they land?

"I'm younger than you—a good deal," she broke in upon his rushing mood. "But that doesn't matter a bit, does it? We're about the same age really."

With the happy sound of her voice the extraordinary sensation passed—or, rather, it became normal. But that it had lasted an appreciable time was proved by the fact that they had left the statue on the lawn, the house was no longer visible behind them, and they were walking side by side between the massive rhododendron clumps. They brought up against a five-barred gate into the park. They leaned upon the topmost bar, and he felt her shoulder touching his—edging into it—as they looked across to the grove of pines.

"I feel absurdly young," he said without a sign of affectation, "and yet I've been looking for you a thousand years and more."

The afterglow lit up her face; it fell on her loose hair and tumbled blouse, turning them amber red. She looked not only soft and comely, but extraordinarily beautiful. The strange expression haunted the deep eyes again, the lips were a little parted, the young breast heaving slightly, joy and excitement in her whole presentment. And as he watched her he knew that all he had just felt was due to her close presence, to her atmosphere, her perfume, her physical warmth and vigour. It had emanated directly from her being.

"Of course," she said, and laughed so that he felt her breath upon his face. He bent lower to bring his own on a level, gazing straight into her eyes that were fixed upon the field beyond. They were clear and luminous as pools of water, and in their centre, sharp as a photograph, he saw the reflection of the pine grove, perhaps a hundred yards away. With detailed accuracy he saw it, empty and motionless in the glimmering June dusk.

Then something caught his eye. He examined the picture more

closely. He drew slightly nearer. He almost touched her face with his own, forgetting for a moment whose were the eyes that served him for a mirror. For, looking intently thus, it seemed to him that there was a movement, a passing to and fro, a stirring as of figures among the trees. . . . Then suddenly the entire picture was obliterated. She had dropped her lids. He heard her speaking—the warm breath was again upon his face:

"In the heart of that wood dwell I."

His heart gave another leap—more violent than the first—for the wonder and beauty of the sentence caught him like a spell. There was a lilt and rhythm in the words that made it poetry. She laid emphasis upon the pronoun and the nouns. It seemed the last line of some delicious runic verse:

"In the *heart* of the *wood*—dwell *I*. . . ."

And it flashed across him: That living, moving, inhabited pine wood was her thought. It was thus she saw it. Her nature flung back to a life she understood, a life that needed, claimed her. The ostentatious and artificial values that surrounded her, she denied, even as the distinguished house-party of her ambitious, masquerading family neglected her. Of course she was unnoticed by them, just as a swallow or a wild-rose were unnoticed.

He knew her secret then, for she had told it to him. It was his own secret too. They were akin, as the birds and animals were akin. They belonged together in some free and open life, natural, wild, untamed. That unhampered life was flowing about them now, rising, beating with delicious tumult in her veins and his, yet innocent as the sunlight and the wind—because it was as freely recognised.

"Elspeth!" he cried, "come, take me with you! We'll go at once. Come—hurry—before we forget to be happy, or remember to be wise again—!"

His words stopped half-way towards completion, for a perfume floated past him, born of the summer dusk, perhaps, yet sweet with a penetrating magic that made his senses reel with some remembered joy. No flower, no scented garden bush delivered it. It was the perfume of young, spendthrift life, sweet with the purity that reason had not yet stained. The girl moved closer. Gathering her loose hair between her fingers, she brushed his cheeks and eyes with it, her slim, warm body pressing against him as she leaned over laughingly.

"In the darkness," she whispered in his ear; "when the moon puts the house upon the statue!"

And he understood. Her world lay behind the vulgar, staring day. He turned. He heard the flutter of skirts—just caught the grey stockings, swift and light, as they flew behind the rhododendron masses. And she was gone.

He stood a long time, leaning upon that five-barred gate. . . . It was the dressing-gong that recalled him at length to what seemed the present. By the conservatory door, as he went slowly in, he met his distinguished cousin—who was helping the girl he himself was to marry to enjoy her "final fling." He looked at his cousin. He realised suddenly that he was merely vicious. There was no sun and wind, no flowers—there was depravity only, lust instead of laughter, excitement in place of happiness. It was calculated, not spontaneous. His mind was in it. Without joy it was. He was not natural.

"Not a girl in the whole lot fit to look at," he exclaimed with peevish boredom, excusing himself stupidly for his illicit conduct. "I'm off in the morning." He shrugged his blue-blooded shoulders. "These millionaires! Their shooting's all right, but their mixum-gatherum weekends—bah!" His gesture completed all he had to say about this one in particular. He glanced sharply, nastily, at his companion. "*You* look as if you'd found something!" he added, with a suggestive grin. "Or have you seen the ghost that was paid for with the house?" And he guffawed and let his eyeglass drop. "Lady Hermione will be asking for an explanation—eh?"

"Idiot!" replied Heber, and ran upstairs to dress for dinner.

But the word was wrong, he remembered, as he closed his door. It was lunatic he had meant to say, yet something more as well. He saw the smart, modern philanderer somehow as a beast.

II

It was nearly midnight when he went up to bed, after an evening of intolerable amusement. The abandoned moral attitude, the common rudeness, the contempt of all others but themselves, the ugly jests, the horseplay of tasteless minds that passed for gaiety, above all the shamelessness of the women that behind the cover of fine breeding aped emancipation, afflicted him to a boredom that touched desperation.

He understood now with a clarity unknown before. As with his cousin, so with these. They took life, he saw, with a brazen effrontery they thought was freedom, while yet it was life that they denied. He felt vampired and degraded; spontaneity went out of him. The fact that the geography of bedrooms was studied openly seemed an affirmation of vice that sickened him. Their ways were nauseous merely. He escaped—unnoticed.

He locked his door, went to the open window, and looked out into the night—then started. For silver dressed the lawn and park, the shadow of the building lay dark across the elaborate garden, and the moon, he noticed, was just high enough to put the house upon the statue. The chimney-stacks edged the pedestal precisely.

"Odd!" he exclaimed. "Odd that I should come at the very moment—!" then smiled as he realised how his proposed adventure would be misinterpreted, its natural innocence and spirit ruined—if he were seen. "And some one would be sure to see me on a night like this. There are couples still hanging about in the garden." And he glanced at the shrubberies and secret paths that seemed to float upon the warm June air like islands.

He stood for a moment framed in the glare of the electric light, then turned back into the room; and at that instant a low sound like a bird-call rose from the lawn below. It was soft and flutey, as though some one played two notes upon a reed, a piping sound. He had been seen, and she was waiting for him. Before he knew it, he had made an answering call, of oddly similar kind, then switched the light out. Three minutes later, dressed in simpler clothes, with a cap pulled over his eyes, he reached the back lawn by means of the conservatory and the billiard-room. He paused a moment to look about him. There was no one, although the lights were still ablaze. "I am an idiot," he chuckled to himself. "I'm acting on instinct!" He ran.

The sweet night air bathed him from head to foot; there was strength and cleansing in it. The lawn shone wet with dew. He could almost smell the perfume of the stars. The fumes of wine, cigars, and artificial scent were left behind, the atmosphere exhaled by civilisation, by heavy thoughts, by bodies overdressed, unwisely stimulated—all, all forgotten. He passed into a world of magical enchantment. The hush of the open sky came down. In black and white the garden lay, brimmed full with beauty, shot by the ancient silver of the moon, spangled with the stars' old-gold. And the night wind rustled in the rhododendron masses as he flew between them.

In a moment he was beside the statue, engulfed now by the shadow of the building, and the girl detached herself silently from the blur of darkness. Two arms were flung about his neck, a shower of soft hair fell on his cheek with a heady scent of earth and leaves and grass, and the same instant they were away together at full speed—towards the pine wood. Their feet were soundless on the soaking grass. They went so swiftly that they made a whir of following wind that blew her hair across his eyes.

And the sudden contrast caused a shock that put a blank, perhaps, upon his mind, so that he lost the standard of remembered things. For it was no longer merely a particular adventure; it seemed a habit and a natural joy resumed. It was not new. He knew the momentum of an accustomed happiness, mislaid, it may be, but certainly familiar. They sped across the gravel paths that intersected the well-groomed lawn, they leaped the flower-beds, so laboriously shaped in mockery, they clambered over the ornamental iron railings, scorning the easier five-barred gate into the park. The longer grass then shook the dew in soaking showers against his knees. He stooped, as though in some foolish effort to turn up something, then realised that his legs, of course, were bare. *Her* garment was already high and free, for she, too, was barelegged like himself. He saw her little ankles, wet and shining in the moonlight, and flinging himself down, he kissed them happily, plunging his face into the dripping, perfumed grass. Her ringing laughter mingled with his own, as she stooped beside him the same instant; her hair hung in a silver cloud; her eyes gleamed through its curtain into his; then, suddenly, she soaked her hands in the heavy dew and passed them over his face with a softness that was like the touch of some scented southern wind.

"Now you are anointed with the Night," she cried. "No one will know you. You are forgotten of the world. Kiss me!"

"We'll play for ever and ever," he cried, "the eternal game that was old when the world was yet young," and lifting her in his arms he kissed her eyes and lips. There was some natural bliss of song and dance and laughter in his heart, an elemental bliss that caught them together as wind and sunlight catch the branches of a tree. She leaped from the ground to meet his swinging arms. He ran with her, then tossed her off and caught her neatly as she fell. Evading a second capture, she danced ahead, holding out one shining arm that he might follow. Hand in hand they raced on together through the clean summer moonlight. Yet there remained a smooth softness as of fur against his neck and shoulders, and he saw then that she wore skins of tawny colour that clung to her body closely, that he wore them too, and that her skin, like his own, was of a sweet dusky brown.

Then, pulling her towards him, he stared into her face. She suffered the close gaze a second, but no longer, for with a burst of sparkling laughter again she leaped into his arms, and before he shook her free she had pulled and tweaked the two small horns that hid in the thick curly hair behind, and just above, the ears.

And that wilful tweaking turned him wild and reckless. That touch ran down him deep into the mothering earth. He leaped and ran and sang with a great laughing sound. The wine of eternal youth flushed all his veins with joy, and the old, old world was young again with every impulse of natural happiness intensified with the Earth's own foaming tide of life.

From head to foot he tingled with the delight of spring, prodigal with creative power. Of course he could fly the bushes and fling wild across the open! Of course the wind and moonlight fitted close and soft about him like a skin! Of course he had youth and beauty for playmates, with dancing, laughter, singing, and a thousand kisses! For he and she were natural once again. They were free together of those long-forgotten days when "Pan leaped through the roses in the month of June . . . !"

With the girl swaying this way and that upon his shoulders, tweaking his horns with mischief and desire, hanging her flying hair before his eyes, then bending swiftly over again to lift it, he danced to join the rest of their companions in the little moonlit grove of pines beyond. . . .

III

They rose somewhat pointed, perhaps, against the moonlight, those English pines—more with the shape of cypresses, some might have thought. A stream gushed down between their roots, there were mossy ferns, and rough grey boulders with lichen on them. But there was no dimness, for the silver of the moon sprinkled freely through the branches like the faint sunlight that it really was, and the air ran out to meet them with a heady fragrance that was wiser far than wine.

The girl, in an instant, was whirled from her perch on his shoulders and caught by a dozen arms that bore her into the heart of the jolly, careless throng. Whisht! Whew! Whir! She was gone, but another, fairer still, was in her place, with skins as soft and knees that clung as tightly. Her eyes were liquid amber, grapes hung between her little breasts, her arms entwined about him, smoother than marble, and as cool. She had a crystal laugh.

But he flung her off, so that she fell plump among a group of bigger figures lolling against a twisted root and roaring with a jollity that boomed like wind through the chorus of a song. They seized her, kissed her, then sent her flying. They were happier with their glad singing. They held stone goblets, red and foaming, in their broad-palmed hands.

"The mountains lie behind us!" cried a figure dancing past. "We are come at last into our valley of delight. Grapes, breasts, and rich red lips! Ho! Ho! It is time to press them that the juice of life may run!" He waved a cluster of ferns across the air and vanished amid a cloud of song and laughter.

"It is ours. Use it!" answered a deep, ringing voice. "The valleys are our own. No climbing now!" And a wind of echoing cries gave answer from all sides. "Life! Life! Life! Abundant, flowing over—use it, use it!"

A troop of nymphs rushed forth, escaped from clustering arms and lips they yet openly desired. He chased them in and out among the waving branches, while she who had brought him ever followed, and sped past him and away again. He caught three gleaming soft brown bodies, then fell beneath them, smothered, bubbling with joyous laughter—next freed himself and, while they sought to drag him captive again, escaped and raced with a leap upon a slimmer, sweeter outline that swung up—only just in time—upon a lower bough, whence she leaned down above him with hanging net of hair and merry eyes. A few feet beyond his reach, she laughed and teased him—the one who had brought him in, the one he ever sought, and who for ever sought him too. . . .

It became a riotous glory of wild children who romped and played with an impassioned glee beneath the moon. For the world was young and they, her happy offspring, glowed with the life she poured so freely into them. All intermingled, the laughing voices rose into a foam of song that broke against the stars. The difficult mountains had been climbed and were forgotten. Good! Then, enjoy the luxuriant, fruitful valley and be glad! And glad they were, brimful with spontaneous energy, natural as birds and animals that obeyed the big, deep rhythm of a simpler age—natural as wind and innocent as sunshine.

Yet, for all the untamed riot, there was a lift of beauty pulsing underneath. Even when the wildest abandon approached the heat of orgy, when the recklessness appeared excess—there hid that marvellous touch of loveliness which makes the natural sacred. There was coherence, purpose, the fulfilling of an exquisite law: there was worship. The form it took, haply, was strange as well as riotous, yet in its strangeness dreamed innocence and purity, and in its very riot flamed that spirit which is divine.

For he found himself at length beside her once again; breathless and panting, her sweet brown limbs aglow from the excitement of escape denied; eyes shining like a blaze of stars, and pulses beating with tumultuous life—helpless and yielding against the strength that pinned her down between the roots. His eyes put mastery on her own. She looked up into his face, obedient, happy, soft with love, surrendered with the same delicious abandon that had swept her for a moment into other arms. "You caught me in the end," she sighed. "I only played awhile."

"I hold you for ever," he replied, half wondering at the rough power in his voice.

It was here the hush of worship stole upon her little face, into her obedient eyes, about her parted lips. She ceased her wilful struggling.

"Listen!" she whispered. "I hear a step upon the glades beyond.

The iris and the lily open; the earth is ready, waiting; we must be ready too! *He* is coming!"

He released her and sprang up; the entire company rose too. All stood, all bowed the head. There was an instant's subtle panic, but it was the panic of reverent awe that preludes a descent of deity. For a wind passed through the branches with a sound that is the oldest in the world and so the youngest. Above it there rose the shrill, faint piping of a little reed. Only the first, true sounds were audible—wind and water—the tinkling of the dewdrops as they fell, the murmur of the trees against the air. This was the piping that they heard. And in the hush the stars bent down to hear, the riot paused, the orgy passed and died. The figures waited, kneeling then with one accord. They listened with—the Earth.

"He comes. . . . He comes . . ." the valley breathed about them.

There was a footfall from far away, treading across a world unruined and unstained. It fell with the wind and water, sweetening the valley into life as it approached. Across the rivers and forests it came gently, tenderly, but swiftly and with a power that knew majesty.

"He comes. . . . He comes . . . !" rose with the murmur of the wind and water from the host of lowered heads.

The footfall came nearer, treading a world grown soft with worship. It reached the grove. It entered. There was a sense of intolerable loveliness, of brimming life, of rapture. The thousand faces lifted like a cloud. They heard the piping close. And so He came.

But He came with blessing. With the stupendous Presence there was joy, the joy of abundant, natural life, pure as the sunlight and the wind. He passed among them. There was great movement—as of a forest shaking, as of deep water falling, as of a cornfield swaying to the wind, yet gentle as of a harebell shedding its burden of dew that it has held too long because of love. He passed among them, touching every head. The great hand swept with tenderness each face, lingered a moment on each beating heart. There was sweetness, peace, and loveliness; but above all, there was—life. He sanctioned every natural joy in them and blessed each passion with his power of creation. . . . Yet each one saw him differently: some as a wife or maiden desired with fire, some as a youth or stalwart husband, others as a figure veiled with stars or cloaked in luminous mist, hardly attainable; others, again—the fewest these, not more than two or three—as that mysterious wonder which tempts the heart away from known familiar sweetness into a wilderness of undecipherable magic without flesh and blood. . . .

To two, in particular, He came so near that they could feel his breath of hills and fields upon their eyes. He touched them with both mighty hands. He stroked the marble breasts, He felt the little hidden horns . . . and, as they bent lower so that their lips met together for an instant, He took her arms and twined them about the curved, brown neck that she might hold him closer still. . . .

Again a footfall sounded far away upon an unruined world . . . and He was gone—back into the wind and water whence He came. The thousand faces lifted; all stood up; the hush of worship still among them. There was a quiet as of the dawn. The piping floated over woods and fields, fading into silence. All looked at one another. . . . And then once more the laughter and the play broke loose.

IV

"We'll go," she cried, "and peep upon that other world where life hangs like a prison on their eyes!" And, in a moment, they were across the soaking grass, the lawn and flower-beds, and close to the walls of the heavy mansion. He peered in through a window, lifting her up to peer in with him. He recognised the world to which outwardly he belonged; he understood; a little gasp escaped him; and a slight shiver ran down the girl's body into his own. She turned her eyes away. "See," she murmured in his ear, "it's ugly, it's not natural. They feel guilty and ashamed. There is no innocence!" She saw the men; it was the women that he saw chiefly.

Lolling ungracefully, with a kind of boldness that asserted independence, the women smoked their cigarettes with an air of invitation they sought to conceal and yet showed plainly. He saw his familiar world in nakedness. Their backs were bare, for all the elaborate clothes they wore; they hung their breasts uncleanly; in their eyes shone light that had never known the open sun. Hoping they were alluring and desirable, they feigned a guilty ignorance of that hope. They all pretended. Instead of wind and dew upon their hair, he saw flowers grown artificially to ape wild beauty, tresses without lustre borrowed from the slums of city factories. He watched them manœuvring with the men; heard dark sentences; caught gestures half delivered whose meaning should just convey that glimpse of guilt they deemed to increase pleasure. The women were calculating, but nowhere glad; the men experienced, but nowhere joyous. Pretended innocence lay cloaked with a veil of something that whispered secretly, clandestine, ashamed, yet with a brazen air that laid mockery instead of sunshine in their smiles. Vice masqueraded in the ugly shape of pleasure; beauty was degraded into calculated tricks. They were not natural. They knew not joy.

"The forward ones, the civilised!" she laughed in his ear, tweaking his horns with energy. "*We* are the backward!"

"Unclean," he muttered, recalling a catchword of the world he gazed upon.

They were the civilised! They were refined and educated—advanced. Generations of careful breeding, mate cautiously selecting mate, laid the polish of caste upon their hands and faces where gleamed ridiculous, untaught jewels—rings, bracelets, necklaces hanging absurdly from every possible angle.

"But—they are dressed up—for fun," he exclaimed, more to himself than to the girl in skins who clung to his shoulders with her naked arms.

"*Un*dressed!" she answered, putting her brown hand in play across his eyes. "Only they have forgotten even that!" And another shiver passed through her into him. He turned and hid his face against the soft skins that touched his cheek. He kissed her body. Seizing his horns, she pressed him to her, laughing happily.

"Look!" she whispered, raising her head again; "they're coming out." And he saw that two of them, a man and a girl, with an interchange of secret glances, had stolen from the room and were already by the door of the conservatory that led into the garden. It was his wife to be—and his distinguished cousin.

"Oh, Pan!" she cried in mischief. The girl sprang from his arms and pointed. "We will follow them. We will put natural life into their little veins!"

"Or panic terror," he answered, catching the yellow panther skin and following her swiftly round the building. He kept in the shadow, though she ran full into the blaze of moonlight. "But they can't see us," she called, looking over her shoulder a moment. "They can only feel our presence, perhaps." And, as she danced across the lawn, it seemed a moonbeam slipped from a sapling birch tree that the wind curved earthwards, then tossed back against the sky.

Keeping just ahead, they led the pair, by methods known instinctively to elemental blood yet not translatable—led them towards the little grove of waiting pines. The night wind murmured in the branches; a bird woke into a sudden burst of song. These sounds were plainly audible. But four little pointed ears caught other, wilder notes behind the wind and music of the bird—the cries and ringing laughter, the leaping footsteps and the happy singing of their merry kin within the wood.

And the throng paused then amid the revels to watch the "civilised" draw near. They presently reached the trees, halted, looked about them, hesitated a moment—then, with a hurried movement as of shame and fear lest they be caught, entered the zone of shadow.

"Let's go in here," said the man, without music in his voice. "It's dry on the pine needles, and we can't be seen." He led the way; she picked up her skirts and followed over the strip of long wet grass. "Here's a log all ready for us," he added, sat down, and drew her into his arms with a sigh of satisfaction. "Sit on my knee; it's warmer for your pretty figure." He chuckled; evidently they were on familiar terms, for though she hesitated, pretending to be coy, there was no real resistance in her, and she allowed the ungraceful roughness. "But are we *quite* safe? Are you sure?" she asked between his kisses.

"What does it matter, even if we're not?" he replied, establishing her more securely on his knees. "But, as a matter of fact, we're safer here than in my own house." He kissed her hungrily. "By Jove, Hermione, but you're divine," he cried passionately, "divinely beautiful. I love you with every atom of my being—with my soul."

"Yes, dear, I know—I mean, I know you do, but—"

"But what?" he asked impatiently.

"Those detectives—"

He laughed. Yet it seemed to annoy him. "My wife is a beast, isn't she?—to have me watched like that," he said quickly.

"They're everywhere," she replied, a sudden hush in her tone. She looked at the encircling trees a moment, then added bitterly: "I hate her, simply *hate* her."

"I love you," he cried, crushing her to him, "that's all that matters now. Don't let's waste time talking about the rest." She contrived to shudder, and hid her face against his coat, while he showered kisses on her neck and hair.

And the solemn pine trees watched them, the silvery moonlight fell on their faces, the scent of new-mown hay went floating past.

"I love you with my very soul," he repeated with intense conviction. "I'd do anything, give up anything, bear anything—just to give you a moment's happiness. I swear it—before God!"

There was a faint sound among the trees behind them, and the girl sat up, alert. She would have scrambled to her feet, but that he held her tight.

"What the devil's the matter with you to-night?" he asked in a different tone, his vexation plainly audible. "You're as nervy as if *you* were being watched, instead of me."

She paused before she answered, her finger on her lip. Then she said slowly, hushing her voice a little:

"Watched! That's exactly what I did feel. I've felt it ever since we came into the wood."

"Nonsense, Hermione. It's too many cigarettes." He drew her back into his arms, forcing her head up so that he could kiss her better.

"I suppose it is nonsense," she said, smiling. "It's gone now, anyhow."

He began admiring her hair, her dress, her shoes, her pretty ankles, while she resisted in a way that proved her practice. "It's not *me* you love," she pouted, yet drinking in his praise. She listened to his repeated assurances that he loved her with his "soul" and was prepared for any sacrifice.

"I feel so safe with you," she murmured, knowing the moves in the game as well as he did. She looked up guiltily into his face, and he looked down with a passion that he thought perhaps was joy.

"You'll be married before the summer's out," he said, "and all the thrill and excitement will be over. Poor Hermione!" She lay back in his arms, drawing his face down with both hands, and kissing him on the lips. "You'll have more of him than you can do with—eh? As much as you care about, anyhow."

"I shall be much more free," she whispered. "Things will be easier.

And I've got to marry some one—"

She broke off with another start. There was a sound again behind them. The man heard nothing. The blood in his temples pulsed too loudly, doubtless.

"Well, what is it this time?" he asked sharply.

She was peering into the wood, where the patches of dark shadow and moonlit spaces made odd, irregular patterns in the air. A low branch waved slightly in the wind.

"Did you hear that?" she asked nervously.

"Wind," he replied, annoyed that her change of mood disturbed his pleasure.

"But something moved—"

"Only a branch. We're quite alone, quite safe, I tell you," and there was a rasping sound in his voice as he said it. "Don't be so imaginative. I can take care of you."

She sprang up. The moonlight caught her figure, revealing its exquisite young curves beneath the smother of the costly clothing. Her hair had dropped a little in the struggle. The man eyed her eagerly, making a quick, impatient gesture towards her, then stopped abruptly. He saw the terror in her eyes.

"Oh, hark! What's that?" she whispered in a startled voice. She put her finger up. "Oh, let's go back. I don't like this wood. I'm frightened."

"Rubbish," he said, and tried to catch her by the waist.

"It's safer in the house—my room—or yours—" She broke off again. "There it is—don't you hear? It's a footstep!" Her face was whiter than the moon.

"I tell you it's the wind in the branches," he repeated gruffly. "Oh, come on, *do*. We were just getting jolly together. There's nothing to be afraid of. Can't you believe me?" He tried to pull her down upon his knee again with force. His face wore an unpleasant expression that was half leer, half grin.

But the girl stood away from him. She continued to peer nervously about her. She listened.

"You give me the creeps," he exclaimed crossly, clawing at her waist again with passionate eagerness that now betrayed exasperation. His disappointment turned him coarse.

The girl made a quick movement of escape, turning so as to look in every direction. She gave a little scream.

"That *was* a step. Oh, oh, it's close beside us. I heard it. We're being watched!" she cried in terror. She darted towards him, then shrank back. He did not try to touch her this time.

"Moonshine!" he growled. "You've spoilt my—spoilt our chance with your silly nerves."

But she did not hear him apparently. She stood there shivering as with sudden cold.

"There! I saw it again. I'm sure of it. Something went past me through the air."

And the man, still thinking only of his own pleasure frustrated, got up heavily, something like anger in his eyes. "All right," he said testily; "if you're going to make a fuss, we'd better go. The house *is* safer, possibly, as you say. You know my room. Come along!" Even that risk he would not take. He loved her with his "soul."

They crept stealthily out of the wood, the girl slightly in front of him, casting frightened backward glances. Afraid, guilty, ashamed, with an air as though they had been detected, they stole back towards the garden and the house, and disappeared from view.

And a wind rose suddenly with a rushing sound, poured through the wood as though to cleanse it, swept out the artificial scent and trace of shame, and brought back again the song, the laughter, and the happy revels. It roared across the park, it shook the windows of the house, then sank away as quickly as it came. The trees stood motionless again, guarding their secret in the clean, sweet moonlight that held the world in dream until the dawn stole up and sunshine took the earth with joy.

The Laughter of Courage

It was at a big cinema house. The lights were turned down and the general audience was a blur, faces at a few feet distance not clearly discernible. On the screen a comic story was being shown, some scenes very comic, and amusement was audible all over the crowded building. There was tittering, sniggering, gasps of surprise, and occasionally an exclamation. Everybody seemed sufficiently tickled to make a noise of one kind or another, when suddenly a new sound was heard, a sound that presently dominated the entire house. A man was—laughing.

At first, so concentrated was attention on the screen, that his laughter did not attract attention. It merged in the general murmur of the crowd. But gradually it differentiated itself from this general murmur, and rose above it. It became a sound apart. More than mere amusement, more than a pleasant sense of the ludicrous made audible, it drew attention to itself. It was a genuine, hearty laughter.

And people turned their heads. First one, then another, looked away from the screen to see who was so unadulteratedly happy, enjoying himself with such spontaneous hilarity. One must be a child to laugh like that, felt many, with a touch of envy, perhaps, at the thought. No grown-up could forget himself for so slight a cause. It certainly was unaffected laughter, the man was unselfconscious. He did not know he was making such a noise. And everybody looked at the rows behind them, peering eagerly to see his face; they made remarks to their neighbours; they waited, listening for the next outburst, then nudged each other again—and finally began laughing themselves.

They laughed with the man, not at him, for it was such infectious laughter that bubbled from him in a ceaseless stream. Actors on the stage must have been seriously disconcerted, but the pictures, of course, showed no signs of injured vanity; for the fact was that, while the comic story lasted, the entire audience laughed with the man instead of with the moving photographs. The screen was neglected shamefully; its changes merely supplied the question from one moment to another:—"Listen! That will set him off again! You see if it doesn't!" And off he went—the stream of delicious, unselfconscious, heart-felt laughter that it did one good to hear.

There was no marked peculiarity about it, the voice was not unusual in any way, there was nothing about it that made one inclined to laugh at instead of with him. It was the genuine, happy joy in the sound that caught so many hearts along. The desire to see the man became, apparently, universal; what was he like, what sort of fellow to look at, what age, what size, what type of man—that he could laugh like this? People leaned forward, backwards, sideways, to discover him; but the semi-darkness screened him from their view; they could not see the shaking sides, the merry eyes, the jolly mouth and cheeks. He was audible only, not visible. The few in the back rows who sat near him had him to themselves.

But all listened with keen delight. Every few seconds the spontaneous laughter broke forth with what seemed new freshness. It cheered, it made the day seem brighter, there was more happiness in the world than one knew, evidently; life itself took on a gayer, and more careless aspect with such a proof of brave enjoyment in one's ears. The screen amused, but this man's laughter heartened. It was very good to hear. He must, indeed, be a jolly, reckless, light-hearted fellow, without a care or worry in the world. If only that laughter could be bottled up and delivered by cartloads in the unhappy houses of the world! There was such hope and courage in it. The man must be an optimist with confident outlook.

And every one who heard it shared one longing—for the story to end and the lights to be turned up that the laugher might be visible. For it seemed that no one cared any longer what happened on the screen; all wanted to see the jovial face of the jolly, happy man who had cheered them up without knowing that he did so. And at last the story ended, the lights began to rise. Hundreds of necks were craned.

I shall never forget him. He was still laughing, though not loudly now. He leaned over to a pal to talk about the pictures. He was utterly oblivious of the sensation that he caused—this happy, cheerful, jolly man who was a wounded soldier, holding two crutches lightly against his shoulder. I saw his grim, determined face; I saw his bright blue eyes, laughter still in them; and, when the performance ended, I also saw him carried out tenderly by his two pals. He was young, perhaps twenty-six at most, and his body ended at the knees. And a sigh went through the great silent audience as, without watching, they yet saw—a sigh of wonder and admiration, of gratitude, also, I think, of love. There was a feeling of reverence; there were certainly moistened eyes.

Appendix

Egypt: An Impression

A considerable amount of nonsense has been written about the spell of Egypt. Cheapened by exaggeration, vulgarised by familiarity, it has become for many a picture post-card spell, pinned against the mind like the posters at a railway terminus. The moment Alexandria is reached, this huge post-card hangs across the heavens, blazing in an over-coloured sunset, composed theatrically of temple, pyramid, palm trees by the shining Nile, and the inevitable Sphinx. And the monstrosity of it paralyses the mind. Its strident shout deafens the imagination. Memory escapes with difficulty from the insistent, gross advertisement. The post-card and the poster smother sight.

Behind this glare and glitter there hides, however, another delicate yet potent thing that is somehow nameless—not acknowledged by all, perhaps because so curiously elusive, yet surely felt by all because it is so true: intensely vital, certainly, since it thus survives the suffocation of its vile exaggeration. For the ordinary tourist yields to it, and not alone the excavator and archæologist; the latter, indeed, who live long in the country, cease to be aware of it as an outside influence, having changed insensibly in thought and feeling till they have become it: it is in their blood. An effect is wrought subtly upon the mind that does not pass away. Having once "gone down into Egypt," you are never quite the same again. Certain values have curiously changed, perspective has altered, emotions have shifted their specific gravity, some attitude to life, in a word, has been emphasised, and another, as it were, obliterated. The spell works underground, and, being not properly comprehensible, is nameless. Moreover, it is the casual visitor, unburdened by antiquarian and historical knowledge, who may best estimate its power—the tourist who knows merely what he has gleaned, for instance, from reading over Baedeker's general synopsis on the voyage. He is aware of this floating power everywhere, yet unable to fix it to a definite cause. It remains at large, evasive, singularly fascinating.

All countries, of course, colour thought and memory, and work a spell upon the imagination of any but the hopelessly inanimate. Greece, India, Japan, Ireland, or the Channel Islands leave their mark and imprint—whence the educational value of travel-psychology—but from these the traveller brings back feelings and memories he can evoke at will and label. He returns from Egypt with a marvellous blur. All, in differing terms, report a similar thing. From the first few months in Egypt, saturated maybe with overmuch, the mind recalls with definiteness—nothing. There comes to its summons a colossal medley that half stupefies: vast reaches of yellow sand drenched in a sunlight that stings; dim, solemn aisles of granite silence; stupendous monoliths that stare unblinking at the sun; the shining river, licking softly at the lips of a murderous desert; and an enormous night-sky literally drowned in stars. A score of temples melt down into a single monster; the Nile spreads everywhere; great pyramids float across the sky like clouds; palms rustle in mid-air; and from caverned leagues of subterranean gloom there issues a roar of voices, thunderous yet muffled, that seem to utter the hieroglyphics of a forgotten tongue. The entire mental horizon, oddly lifted, brims with this procession of gigantic things, then empties again without a word of explanation, leaving a litter of big adjectives chasing one another chaotically—chief among them "mysterious," "unchanging," "formidable," "terrific." But the single, bigger memory that should link all these together intelligibly hides from sight the emotion too deep for specific recognition, too vast, somehow, for articulate recovery. The Acropolis, the wonders of Japan and India, the mind can grasp—or thinks so; but this composite enormity of Ramesseum, Serapeum, Karnak, Cheops, Sphinx, with a hundred temples and a thousand miles of sand, it *knows* it cannot. The mind is a blank. Egypt, it seems, has faded. Memory certainly fails, and description wilts. There seems nothing precisely to report, no interesting, clear, intelligible thing. "What did you see in Egypt? What did you like best? What impression did Egypt make upon you?" seem questions impossible to answer. Imagination flickers, stammers, and goes out. Thought hesitates and stops. A little shudder, probably, makes itself felt. There is an impotent attempt to describe a temple or two, an expedition on donkey-back into the desert; but it sounds unreal, the language wrong, foolish, even affected. That dreadful Post-card rises like a wall. "Oh, I liked it all immensely. The delightful dry heat, you know—and one can always count upon the weather for picnics arranged ahead, and—" until the conversation can be changed to theatres or the crops at home. Yet, behind the words, behind the Post-card, one is aware all the time of some huge, alluring thing, alive with a pageantry of ages, strangely brilliant, dignified, magnificent, appealing almost to tears—something that drifts past like a ghostly full-rigged vessel with crowded decks and sails painted in an under-world, and yet the whole too close before the eyes for proper sight. The spell has become operative! Having been warned to expect this, I, personally, had yet remained sceptical—until I experienced its truth. . . . And it was undeniably disappointing. After time and money spent, one had apparently brought back so little.

I remember asking myself point blank, in solitude, what I had gained, and I remember the fruitless result. Nothing came but that abominable, shouting Post-card, endlessly extended. Its very endlessness, however, was a clue. Egypt *is* endless and inexhaustible; some hint of eternity lies there, an awareness of immortality almost. To-day, after a doze of four or five thousand years, subterranean Egypt peeps up again at the sun. The vast Memphian cemetery that stretches from Sakkhâra to the Mena House has begun to whisper in the daylight. The Theban worship of the sun is being reconstructed. There is a sense of deathlessness about the ancient Nile, about the grim Sphinx and Pyramids, in the very colonnades of Karnak, whose pylons now once more stand upright after a sleep of forty centuries on their backs; above all, in the appealing strength of the floating, rustling sand—something that defies time and repudiates change in death. Out of that flat, undifferentiated landscape which is Egypt, still stand the unconquerable finger-posts of stone, pointing, like symbols of eternity, to the equally unchanging skies. The spell is laid upon you once you have looked into the battered visages of those Memnon terrors, which reveal, yet hide, far better than the Sphinx. They have neither eyes nor lips nor nose; their features, as their message, inscrutable. Yet they tell this nameless thing plainly *because* they have no words. Out of the green fields of millet they stand like portions of the Theban Mountains that have slid down into the plain, then stopped for a few more centuries to stare across the Nile and watch the sunrise. From them, as partly from the opened tombs of priest and Pharaoh, comes some ingredient of this singular spell.

But the mind has to escape first from the picture post-card influence before the genuine effect emerges. For the mind has in reality suffered a bludgeoning that is partly stunning. Then, with the passing of the weeks amid surroundings of lesser scale, the glamour asserts its magical accomplishment. Slowly it stirred to life in me; and its grip may be, with some, tremendous. It has attacked unseen, and few escape it altogether, while yet it can neither be told nor painted, nor quite explained. Unguessed at first, because sought for in some crude, tangible form it never, never assumes, it flames up unexpectedly—perhaps in a London street when fog shrouds the chimneys; perhaps at a concert; perhaps in a tearoom among perfumed, gossiping women; in church, at the club, even in bed when falling asleep just after a commonplace evening at a commonplace play. A sound recalls the street cries of the Arabs, with its haunting sing-song melody, a breath of air brings back the heated sand, a rustle of the curtain whispers as palms and acacia whisper—and the truth is realised. Up steals the immense Egyptian glamour. It pours, it rushes up. It is over you in a moment. All this time it has lain coiled in deep recesses of the inner being—recesses where there is silence because they are inaccessible amid the clamour of daily life. There is awe in it, a hint of cold eternity, a glimpse of something unchanging and terrific, yet, at the same time, soft and very tender too. The pictures unroll and spread. You feel again the untold melancholy of the Nile. The grandeur of a hundred battered temples beats upon the heart. There is a sense of unutterable beauty. Something in you bows to the procession that includes great figures of non-human lineage. Up sweeps the electric desert air, the alive wind, the wild and delicate perfume of the sand; the luminous grey shadows brush you; you feel the enormous scale of naked desolation which yet brims with strange vitality. An Arab on his donkey flits in colour across the mind, melting off into tiny perspective. A string of camels stands against the sky, swaying forwards the same moment as though it never ceased. A dozen pyramids cleave the air with monstrous wedges, pointing holes in space. In peace and silence, belonging to a loneliness of ages, rise heads and shoulders of towering gods of stone, little jackals silhouetted, perhaps, an instant against thighs half buried in sand. Great winds, great blazing spaces, great days and nights of shining wonder float past from the pavement or the theatre stall, and London, dim-lit England, the whole of modern life indeed, are reduced sharply to a miniature of trifling ugliness that seems the unreality. Egypt rolls through the heart for a second, and is gone. You remember resignedly that you have an appointment to play golf tomorrow with Jones, or you are to lunch with Lady X., and that it may probably rain, and you must go in tubes and taxis, be crowded, jostled, pressed upon by ugly details of time and space. Conventions drive you; your top-hat has to be blocked before you can wear it. You have calls to pay. But out there the days swam past in a flood of golden light, and, caught in a procession of ancient splendors, changeless as the leisured Nile, majestic as the tameless desert, and fresh still with the wonder that first created them, you moved with the tide as of some unconditioned world. Egypt steals out and whispers to you in your dreams. Once more you float in an atmosphere of passionate mirages. The spell is upon you heavily. And this is not mere spinning of words in an attempt to conjure up an atmosphere. The thing is really there. You feel it always, and it always evades analysis. The mind is aware of something that is unmanageable. The idea suggests itself that, while some countries give, others may take away.

Egypt, with a power of seduction almost uncanny, has robbed the mind of a faculty best described perhaps as the faculty of measurement. Its scale has stupefied the ability to measure, appraise, estimate; and this balance once destroyed, wonder and awe capture the heart, going what pace they please. Size works half the miracle, for it is size including a quality of terror—monstrous; and, but for the glorious beauty that thunders through it, this sheer size might easily work a very different spell—dismay. The modern mind, no longer terrified by Speed, to which it has grown contemptuously accustomed, yet shrinks a little before this display of titanic and bewildering size. Egypt makes it realise that it has no handy standard of measurement. It listens to words that are meaningless. The vast proportions uplift, then stupefy. The girth of the Pyramids, the height of the Colossi, the cubic content of the granite columns and the visage of the Sphinx expressed in yards—these convey as little truth as the numbered leagues of the frightening desert or the length of that weary and interminable Nile.

You draw a deep breath of astonishment—then give up the vain attempt to grapple with a thing you cannot readily assimilate. A dizziness of star-distances steals over you; there is a breathlessness of astronomical scale in it that exhilarates while it stuns. What mind can gain by the information that our sun, with all its retinue of planets, sweeps annually thirty-five million miles nearer to a certain star in Hercules—yet that Hercules *looks* no closer than it did thousands of years ago? Such distance lies beyond comprehension. Similarly, in Egypt, there is something that continually evades capture in the monstrous details of sheer size, beautiful with majesty, that day and night tower above the shrinking reason. You believe because you see, but though you know you see, you are not sure what you quite believe. Herein lies one letter, at least, of the spell of Egypt. The mind is for ever aware of something that haunts from the further side of experience.

But assuredly it is only one letter in a sentence that no one hears complete, for there seems an other-worldly element in this strange land that is acknowledged by every type, its presence detected in the most ordinary remarks. At a Cairo dance or a Heliopolis gymkhana you may hear a thoughtless woman observe: "But, you know, there is something queer in Egypt, isn't there? One simply can't deny it!" while the man, half puzzled and half contemptuous, laughs it off, falling back for explanation upon historical associations, vanished civilisations, mummies, temples, and the rest. The "queer thing," however, is not so easily denied, for it is more than any of these. Just as in good conversation there is present among the talkers something that is greater than any one of them separately, so, when your mind meets Egypt and communes with it, there rises up this odd other-worldly presence, equally real, equally undecipherable. A party of us—to quote an instance of its effect upon an ordinary wholesome mind, called usually "level-headed"—were on our way one night to see the Sphinx by moonlight under the guidance of a distinguished Egyptologist. We were on donkey-back. The night was very still, the sky thick with stars, moonlight flooding everything. As we skirted the huge flanks of the Great Pyramid, half in silver, half in black, its soaring edges lit by stars as by stationary lanterns, the business man asked a question of our learned leader. And in daily life he was a man of acute intelligence, guided by logic and reason, successful, rich. "Did they build the pyramid from within outwards?" was his question, as he gazed up at the towering mystery of the colossal outline. The question seemed quite natural, its utter absurdity not at first apparent. A second afterwards one realised the nonsense of it, and longed to hear the grave reply: "No; they hung the apex in mid-air, and then built downwards from it." But, though the Egyptologist resisted the temptation to be funny at his questioner's expense, one somehow felt that, had he answered thus, the man would have accepted the explanation without demur. It would have caused him no surprise, for *credo quia incredibile* does actually represent one's attitude to things in this ancient and mysterious country. "Ah, I see," was all he said, with a sigh, when told that a pyramid was merely a king's mausoleum, and that a layer of stone was added for each year he lived; "a big job for a contractor, wasn't it?" He was no whit ashamed of his idiotic question. "A hundred thousand men working for twenty years built this one," added the other, as we turned its corner and saw the dark head of the monster guarding its approach through all the centuries.

So everywhere—one hears this kind of question, as though the mind grew childish before an incomprehensible thing. Some shadowy magic pervades the faculties; their natural alertness fails; talk is in whispers, almost as if some one were listening; unreality broods over mood and speech and action. The Impossible, dressed in colours of strange, unfading brilliance, stoops down from some tremendous height, steals close past the windows of the mind, halts a moment, peers in—and vanishes. But the mind has seen the outline, has felt the eerie fascination. What it would instantly reject in the Midlands, on a Scotch moor, on a Rhine steamer, or on Brighton Pier, it harbours here with semi-acceptance and belief. The land exhales a steam of enchantment that lulls the senses. You move through this almost visible glamour. All about you is a high, transparent screen, built by the centuries, and left standing; and here and there are gaps in it; modern life, cast like a cinema picture upon this screen, becomes the unreality; but, behind it, a vast audience gathered by the ages watches and looks on—at *us*. And occasionally, aware of being watched, the mind sees through a gap—and asks a wild question, as the business man at the pyramid asked one. Anything is possible, and anything may happen.

There are some who claim things *do* happen. Imagination constructs swiftly in Egypt, with small opposition from the reason. The creative instinct fairly strides. "I always expect something unusual to happen when I'm out here," is a sentence repeatedly heard. "Last time I came out there was disaster. Something unexpected will happen this year, too." As though in this coaxing heat of climate, in this rich glory of a past now being unearthed from day to day, and in this brilliant, vivid quality of its present personality, so oddly stimulating, there lies some quality that acts with the effect of a forcing-house upon the character, bringing out latent possibilities, hurrying on events, developing a rush of life too swift for comfort or full understanding. Certainly no one can see Egypt and remain quite what they were before, however much interpretation of its haunting effect may vary for individuals.

For some, a rather dominant impression is undoubtedly "the monstrous." A splendour of awful dream, yet never quite of nightmare, stalks everywhere, suggesting an atmosphere of Khubla Khan. There is nothing lyrical. Even the silvery river, the slender palms, the fields of clover and barley and the acres of flashing poppies convey no lyrical sweetness, as elsewhere they might. All moves to a statelier measure. Stern issues of life and death are in the air, and in the grandeur of the tombs and temples there is a solemnity of genuine awe that makes the blood run slow a little. Those Theban Hills, where the kings and queens lay buried, are forbidding to the point of discomfort almost. The listening silence in the grim Valley of the Tombs of the Kings, the intolerable glare of sunshine on the stones, the naked absence of any sign of animal or vegetable life, the slow approach to the secret hiding-place where the mummy of a once powerful monarch lies ghastly now beneath the glitter of an electric light, the implacable desert, deadly with heat and distance on every side—this picture, once seen, rather colours one's memory of the rest of Egypt with its sombre and funereal character. And with the great deific monoliths the effect is similar. Proportions and sheer size strike blow after blow upon the mind. Stupendous figures, shrouded to the eyes, shoulder their way slowly through the shifting sands, deathless themselves and half-appalling. Their attitudes and gestures express the hieroglyphic drawings come to life. Their towering heads, coiffed with zodiacal signs, or grotesque animal or bird, bend down to watch you everywhere. There is no hurry in them; they move with the leisure of the moon, with the stateliness of the sun, with the slow silence of the constellations. But they move. There *is,* between you and them, this effect of a screen, erected by the ages, yet that any moment may turn thin and let them through upon you. A hand of shadow, but with granite grip, may steal forth and draw you away into some region where they dwell among changeless symbols like themselves, a region vast, ancient, and undifferentiated as the desert that has produced them. Their effect in the end is weird, difficult to describe, but real. Talk with a mind that has been steeped for years in their atmosphere and presence, and you will appreciate this odd reality. The spell of Egypt is an other-worldly spell. Its vagueness, its elusiveness, its undeniable reality are ingredients, at any rate, in a total result whose detailed analysis lies hidden in mystery and silence—inscrutable.

Bibliography

I. Collections

Ten Minute Stories. London: John Murray, 1914. New York: Dutton, 1914. [*Contents:* Accessory Before the Fact; The Deferred Appointment; The Prayer; Strange Disappearance of a Baronet; The Secret; The Lease; Up and Down; Faith Cure on the Channel; The Goblin's Collection; Imagination; The Invitation; The Impulse; Her Birthday; Two in One; Ancient Lights; Dream Trespass; Let Not the Sun—; Entrance and Exit; You *May* Telephone from Here; The Whisperers; Violence; The House of the Past; Jimbo's Longest Day; If the Cap Fits—; News *v.* Nourishment; Wind; Pines; The Winter Alps; The Second Generation.]

Incredible Adventures. London: Macmillan, 1914. New York: Macmillan, 1914. [*Contents:* The Regeneration of Lord Ernie; The Sacrifice; The Damned; A Descent into Egypt; Wayfarers.]

Day and Night Stories. London: Cassell, 1917. New York: Dutton, 1917. [*Contents:* The Tryst; The Touch of Pan; The Wings of Horus; A Bit of Wood; Initiation; A Desert Episode; Transition; The Other Wing; The Occupant of the Room; Cain's Atonement; An Egyptian Hornet; By Water; H.S.H.; The Tradition; A Victim of Higher Space.]

The Wolves of God and Other Fey Stories (with Wilfred Wilson). London: Cassell, 1921. New York: Dutton, 1921. [*Contents:* The Wolves of God; Chinese Magic; Running Wolf; First Hate; The Tarn of Sacrifice; The Valley of the Beasts; The Call; Egyptian Sorcery; The Decoy; The Man Who Found Out; The Empty Sleeve; Wireless Confusion; Confession; The Lane That Ran East and West; "Vengeance Is Mine."]

Tongues of Fire and Other Sketches. London: Herbert Jenkins, 1924. New York: Dutton, 1925 (as *Tongues of Fire and Other Stories*). [*Contents:* Tongues of Fire; The Little Beggar; Malahide and Forden; Playing Catch; The Pikestaff Case; Alexander Alexander; Lost!; The Olive; A Continuous Performance; The World-Dream of McCallister; The Other Woman; Picking Fir-Cones; The Open Window; Petershin and Mr. Snide; The Man Who Was Milligan; The Falling Glass; A Man of Earth; The Laughter of Courage; S.O.S.; Nephelé.]

Ancient Sorceries and Other Tales. London: Collins, 1927. [*Contents:* Ancient Sorceries; The Willows; The Return; Running Wolf; The Man Whom the Trees Loved; The Man Who Played upon the Leaf.]

The Dance of Death and Other Tales. London: Herbert Jenkins, 1927. New York: Lincoln MacVeagh/Dial Press, 1928. [*Contents:* The Dance of Death; A Psychical Invasion; The Old Man of Visions; The South Wind; The Touch of Pan; The Valley of the Beasts.]

Strange Stories. London: Heinemann, 1929. [*Contents:* The Man Whom the Trees Loved; The Sea Fit; The Glamour of the Snow; The Tryst; Transition; The Occupant of the Room; The Wings of Horus; By Water; Malahide and Forden; Alexander Alexander; The Man Who Was Milligan; The Little Beggar; The Pikestaff Case; Accessory Before the Fact; The Deferred Appointment; Ancient Lights; You *May* Telephone from Here; the Goblin's Collection; Running Wolf; The Valley of the Beasts; The Decoy; Confession; A Descent into Egypt; The Damned; The Willows; Ancient Sorceries.]

[*Short Stories.*] (Short Stories of To-day and Yesterday.) London: George G. Harrap, 1930. [*Contents:* The Regeneration of Lord Ernie; The Sacrifice; Chinese Magic; The Land of Green Ginger; The Stranger; First Hate; The Olive; Two in One; Dream Trespass; Cain's Atonment.]

The Willows and Other Queer Tales. London: Collins, 1932. [*Contents:* The Willows; Ancient Sorceries; The Return; Running Wolf; The Man Whom the Trees Loved; The Man Who Played upon the Leaf; The Tryst; By Water; The Occupant of the Room; The Decoy; Dream Trespass.]

Tales of Algernon Blackwood. London: Martin Secker, 1938. New York: Dutton, 1939. [*Contents:* The Empty House; A Case of Eavesdropping; Strange Adventures of a Private Secretary; With Intent to Steal; Keeping His Promise; The Wood of the Dead; A Suspicious Gift; The Listener; Max Hensig; The Willows; The Insanity of Jones; The Dance of Death; May Day Eve; The Woman's Ghost Story; A Psychical Invasion; Ancient Sorceries; The Nemesis of Fire; Secret Worship; The Camp of the Dog; The Man from the "Gods"; The Wendigo.]

Tales of the Uncanny and Supernatural. London: Peter Nevill, 1949. [*Contents:* The Doll; Running Wolf; The Little Beggar; The Occupant of the Room; The Man Whom the Trees Loved; The Valley of the Beasts; The South Wind; The Man Who Was Milligan; The Trod; The Terror of the Twins; The Deferred Appointment; Accessory Before the Fact; The Glamour of the Snow; The House of the Past; The Decoy; The Tradition; The Touch of Pan; Entrance and Exit; The Pikestaffe Case; The Empty Sleeve; Violence; The Lost Valley.]

II. First Appearances of Individual Stories

"A Barmecide Feast." *Country Life* 34 (19 July 1913): 83–84.

"A Bit of Wood." *Morning Post* (London) (28 April 1914): 5. In *Day and Night Stories* (1917).

"Breakfast Honey." *Morning Post* (London) (9 June 1914): 5.

"By Water." *Westminster Gazette* (18 April 1914): 3. In *Day and Night Stories* (1917), *Strange Stories* (1929), *The Willows* (1932).

"Cain's Atonement." *Land and Water* 66 (20 November 1915): 19–20. In *Day and Night Stories* (1917), *Short Stories* (1930).

"Camping Out." *Blackie's Children's Annual* (Christmas 1916): 13–24.

"The Celestial Motor-'bus." *Saturday Westminster Gazette* (18 December 1915): 13–14.

"The Daisy World." *Quest* 5, No. 4 (July 1914): 738–58.

"The Damned." In *Incredible Adventures* (1914), *Strange Stories* (1929).

"A Descent into Egypt." In *Incredible Adventures* (1914), *Strange Stories* (1929).

"A Desert Episode." *Country Life* 35 (10 January 1914): 47–50. In *Day and Night Stories* (1917).

"An Egyptian Hornet." *Reedy's Mirror* (March 1915). In *Day and Night Stories* (1917).

"The Falling Glass." *Country Life* 35 (23 May 1914): 725–28. In *Tongues of Fire* (1924).

"The God." *Saturday Westminster Gazette* (7 August 1915): 13.

"H.S.H." *British Review* 6, No. 1 (October 1913): 122–38. In *Day and Night Stories* (1917).

"Her Birthday." *Westminster Gazette* (3 May 1913): 3. In *Ten Minute Stories* (1914).

"Initiation." *Quest* 7, No. 4 (July 1916): 730–53. In *Day and Night Stories* (1917).

"Jimbo's Longest Day." *Morning Post* (London) (24 June 1913): 5. In *Ten Minute Stories* (1914).

"The Kiss of a Psychologist." *Country Life* 34 (13 September 1913): 349–50.

"The Laughter of Courage." In *Tongues of Fire* (1924).

"Maria." *Morning Post* (London) (28 March 1914): 7.

"The Night Wind." *Country Life* 35 (9 May 1914): 659–61. *Outlook* 112 (26 April 1916): 984–89.

"Non-Human." *New Witness* 5, No. 110 (10 December 1914): 27–29.

"The Other Wing." *McBride's* 96 (November 1915): 83–95. In *Day and Night Stories* (1917).

"The Paper Man." *Saturday Westminster Gazette* (9 October 1915): 13–14.

"The Philosopher." *Westminster Gazette* (13 June 1914): 3.

"Proportion." *Saturday Westminster Gazette* (5 August 1916): 13–14.

"The Regeneration of Lord Ernie." In *Incredible Adventures* (1914), *Short Stories* (1930).

"The Sacrifice." *Quest* 4, No. 3 (April 1913): 540–63. In *Incredible Adventures* (1914).

"The Snake." *Saturday Westminster Gazette* (18 March 1916): 13–14.

"The Soldier's Visitor." *Land and Water* 65 (9 October 1915): 15–16.

"The Story Hour." *Morning Post* (London) (18 November 1913): 6.

"The Touch of Pan." In *Day and Night Stories* (1917), *The Dance of Death* (1927), *Tales of the Uncanny and Supernatural* (1949).

"The Tradition." *Westminster Gazette* (29 November 1913): 2. In *Day and Night Stories* (1917), *Tales of the Uncanny and Supernatural* (1949).

"Transition." *New Witness* 3, No. 38 (11 December 1913): 171–73. In *Day and Night Stories* (1917), *Strange Stories* (1929).

"The Tryst." In *Day and Night Stories* (1917), *Strange Stories* (1929), *The Willows* (1932).

"Violence." *New Witness* 2, No. 29 (22 May 1913): 77–79. In *Ten Minute Stories* (1914), *Tales of the Uncanny and Supernatural* (1949).

"Wayfarers." *English Review* 13, No. 1 (December 1912): 24–42. In *Incredible Adventures* (1914).

"What Nobody Understands." *Morning Post* (London) (17 February 1914): 5.

"Who Was She?" *New Witness* 2, No. 34 (26 June 1913): 237–39; 2, No. 37 (17 July 1913): 339–41; 2, No. 43 (28 August 1913): 531–34. *Lantern* 1, No. 10 (January 1916): 323–30 [Chapter 1 only].

"The Wings of Horus." *Century Magazine* 89, No. 1 (November 1914): 129–43. In *Day and Night Stories* (1917), *Strange Stories* (1929).

Appendix:

"Egypt: An Impression." *Country Life* No. 879 (8 November 1913): 625–28.

www.ingramcontent.com/pod-product-compliance
Lightning Source LLC
LaVergne TN
LVHW020515100826
845148LV00010B/1237

* 9 7 8 1 6 1 4 9 8 4 6 8 9 *